The Heir and the Spare

COMPLETE COLLECTION

FIONA MIERS

Sarah's Reluctant Duke

Chapter One

London 1812

Lord Oliver Lyre, the newly-inherited tenth Duke of Lincoln, let his eyes be drawn to a corner of the ballroom where the birthday girl stood. If the ball hadn't been in honour of Lady Charlotte Dunford—the little sister he'd never had—he would not have attended. Lady Charlotte was the younger sister of his best friend, Sir John Dunford, son of the Duke of Arrow.

Oliver smiled as he watched her moving about the room, a sense of pride and love warming his chest. She'd grown into a lovely young woman. He'd known Charlotte since she was in short skirts, running around the grounds showing off her ankles. She had always treated him like she had treated her brother—with unwaning, absolute hatred one day and intense affection the next. Oliver had only his elder brother Gerald for company, who had seen the younger Oliver as well beneath him.

Unfortunately, due to a tragic carriage accident, his absent father and his indifferent brother had passed together, leaving Oliver with a title he neither coveted nor felt worthy of.

He hated it, in fact. The attention of the ton, mothers trying to marry off their daughters to him, the huge amount of work involved in owning multiple estates, looking after so many tenants... It had only been a year since he'd inherited the title and he'd already sworn off most ton events.

Lady Charlotte, the little brat, had used every trick she possessed, including fake tears, pleading, and even threats, to get Oliver to attend her twenty-first birthday. He, of course, had succumbed. It would take a force of nature to stop Charlotte when she had her mind set on something.

"Excuse me." Oliver turned and bowed to the two gentlemen with whom he had been speaking moments earlier, before making his way across the room to where Charlotte stood, holding court.

The crowd parted in front of him like the Red Sea before Moses. Oliver's heart sank, and he couldn't stop the sigh that escaped. He missed being the second son, relatively unimportant and unnoticed by the haut ton. He'd have given absolutely anything to have Gerald back, even with his brother's indifference to Oliver's existence. Gerald had known how to behave; how to be the esteemed holder of a dukedom. He'd been raised for it——bred for it, even. How he would have laughed to see Oliver struggle with the responsibility.

A wry smile crept onto Oliver's face as he thought about his deceased elder brother, and he drew up next to the now-unoccupied Charlotte.

"My lady." Oliver leaned closer than was proper and spoke directly into her ear.

"My lord!" Charlotte spun to face him and greeted him with a smile that was both warm and genuine.

The icy discomfort he'd been feeling from the moment he entered the room melted away. Lady Charlotte was worth the pain. She would never be one to call him by his brother's title, and he would be forever grateful for that.

"May I claim my dance? I do believe this is ours." Oliver extended his arm and grinned at the woman he saw as his surrogate sister. An action he knew would cause the dimple in his right cheek to become pronounced.

"Of course." Charlotte took his arm.

Swinging her into the perfect waltz position that included at least six inches between their bodies and no hands below the waist, he looked down at her laughing blue eyes and mock-scowled at her.

"Having fun, are you?" He didn't even attempt a polite start to the conversation now that they were out of general earshot.

She giggled, and once again Oliver struggled with the frustration he felt at his position.

"Of course, I am. It's my birthday. How are you enjoying my night, Oliver? There are so many eligible young ladies in this room that I expected you to have run away screaming by now." Charlotte spoke with her characteristic bluntness.

"You mean to torture me, then?"

Charlotte smiled slowly, appearing to think deeply about her answer.

"I have been hoping you may find a wife, yes. You need to spend more time consorting with ladies rather than the type of women I hear you and my brother have been consorting with lately."

"That is none of your business, scamp," Oliver hissed at Charlotte through his teeth. What sort of lady would say that to a gentleman?

"Which part? The part where I said you should marry?" She emphasized the word with a cheeky smile. "Or the part where I mentioned the not-so-ladylike women you frequently visit?"

Oliver gasped and only just stopped himself from taking a step back. Girls of Charlotte's social rank were not meant to know about such women, let alone speak about them. Was this the same girl who had put worms under his pillow and cried on his lap when she'd scraped her knees running down a path? Impossible.

"Lady Charlotte! You shouldn't speak of it. I'm barely six and twenty, hardly old enough for you to be marrying me off to some title-adoring, bird-brained, barely-out-of-the-school-room debutante."

Oliver took a deep breath as he struggled to hold in his frustration. He knew he had to marry a woman who would be an appropriate duchess, but he wasn't ready, or willing. Not yet. After already being forced into a role he didn't want, husband was a role he could do without for a few more years.

Charlotte laughed with delight, obviously pleased at getting the reaction she'd anticipated.

Time for a change of subject, I think.

"What about you, scamp? Are you planning on finding a husband this season? You are getting a little long in the tooth compared to some of these pretty young faces I see tonight." He liked turning the tables on the quick-witted Lady Charlotte Dunford, even though his jibes were empty and they both knew it. With Charlotte's handsome face, pleasing figure, sharp wit and generous dowry, she'd still be good marriage material when she was one and thirty.

"Do not even think of turning it back on me, Lord Oliver," she said, addressing him by his former title and therefore pleasing him greatly. "We both know that I'll marry as soon as I find someone who is remotely interesting." Charlotte managed to laugh softly and shrugged one creamy shoulder.

Oliver cocked his head and tried to see Charlotte as a marriageable woman, rather than the younger sister he'd always wanted. She was beautiful in a dark-haired, pale-skinned, classic sort of way. Her curvaceous figure wasn't precisely in fashion but was certainly pleasing. Her rather ample breasts swelled up from her low neckline.

If Oliver hadn't known her for most of his life, then he would likely have found her desirable. She was intelligent, and not in any way flighty. A plus on both accounts. He couldn't stand a woman whose main goal in life was to be a lovely ornament on a shelf.

"It's a pity I can't marry you, Charlotte. You would make me the perfect duchess."

Charlotte laughed without humour and Oliver could understand why. Unlike him, she'd never had a reprieve from the bevy of suitors at her doorstep. She had been courted since her coming out by men who wanted her for breeding, as well as her dowry.

"I know, Lord Oliver, if only I could stand the idea of marrying you."

Oliver laughed wholeheartedly, ignoring the glances that swung their way. He did love this girl.

They finished their waltz and he walked her over to the edge of the ballroom with almost every eye in the room following them. Oliver tried his best to ignore the attention.

He turned his head and spotted a rather large matron towing not one, but two daughters in her wake. It was time to remove himself from the reach of this possible matchmaker. He had no intention of being anyone's target this evening.

"Kindly allow me to take my leave, Lady Charlotte. Would you forgive me for taking a walk around the gardens?" Oliver started bowing before he had even finished his sentence.

Charlotte glanced over his shoulder at the woman making a direct line through the crowd for them and chuckled.

"Go, go," she urged discreetly. "Just don't get caught compromising anyone."

Oliver didn't even break stride as he simultaneously scowled over his shoulder at Charlotte and made his escape from the room. He could still hear her tinkling laughter as he exited into the gardens.

"ARE these not the most beautiful gardens you have ever seen, Mr. Millington?" Sarah Collins turned to her handsome escort for the night, enchanted by her unfamiliar surroundings.

It had been such a lovely suggestion of Mr. Millington's for her to get some fresh air. London truly was a wonder and she had not expected such a delightful garden space in the middle of such a large city.

"No one in Somerset has gardens such as these. Imagine the time and care it must have taken the gardeners."

Mr. Patrick Millington had spent the previous two weeks courting Sarah and she rather liked him. He was untitled but wealthy enough for her family's needs due to an inheritance he had recently acquired. Millington came from a good family—and if the gossip was to be believed — was well-educated and loved horses. As did Sarah.

Although he did talk about himself and his horses a little too often for her liking, Sarah didn't perceive that to be an insurmountable problem. After all, how often would she be conversing with her husband once they were married? Surely not much, except for over the dinner table? She could handle that.

"They are handsome gardens indeed, Miss Collins," he agreed, glancing over his shoulder toward the ballroom. Sarah noticed where Millington's gaze landed and she stopped short, her stomach jumping. They were much further away from the safety of the crowded ballroom than she had at first realized. Her mother would be wondering where she was.

"Oh." Sarah turned, one hand landing on her throat as she smiled up at the large man next to her. "I didn't realize we were so far from the house, Mr. Millington. Shall we return?" She could smell the sweet stench of liquor on his breath as he bent his head in her direction. She would have gagged if she had not taken a quick step sideways.

"In a moment." Mr. Millington's cold hands came up to grip the tops of her bare arms and Sarah winced as his touch gripped tight and turned painful. He twisted her arms, forcing her back up against a tree. The bark scratched against her bare skin.

"Ow." She blinked back sudden hot tears. "You're hurting me. Let go this instant, Mr. Millington!"

Instead of complying, he crashed his mouth down onto hers.

Sarah's heart, instead of jumping for joy at a sign of affection, leapt in fear. She struggled, squirming her head from side to side and trying to wriggle out of his hold. But he had such a firm grip on her, she couldn't break free. Horror sprung up. When he forced his slimy tongue into her mouth, she could taste the acidic alcohol and gagged.

Enough!

As her supposed suitor moved one hand to her breast and squeezed roughly, causing pain to shoot through her tender flesh, Sarah bit down on the offensive tongue invading her mouth.

When Millington drew back in shock she managed to turn her head away. Her chest heaved as she drew air into her starving lungs.

"Stop," she cried, pushing at his heavy form. "You must let me go."

Why was he doing this? Things had been going well up until this point. What had changed?

"I think I deserve a taste of this body before I decide if we are getting leg-shackled, don't you?" He spoke gruffly, his hot breath putrid against her turned cheek and ear.

Undeterred by her obvious distress, he began pulling down her bodice with one hand and feeling under her skirt with his other. Cold air froze her nipples and panic forced her heart into a gallop.

"No!" Sarah began struggling again, bashing against his solid chest with her clenched fists and simultaneously trying to drag her dress back up to cover her exposed breasts.

Her head flew back against the tree as Millington shoved her. The force was enough for black spots to form at the edges of her vision.

Oh Lord! She couldn't faint. Not now. He might have his way with her and if she wasn't conscious, she couldn't fight back.

Pain splintered across the back of her head as she fought to stay awake. Fabric ripped and cool air brushed her ribs.

I refuse to let this happen, she thought, desperate to stop him any way she could.

She let herself go limp against him, closing her eyes against the dulling pain in her head and quietly gathering her remaining strength. When he moved away to fumble with his trousers, she raised her hands and leapt forward. She forced her pointed fingers into his eye sockets, scratching at his eyes with as much force as she could manage. She could feel wet skin and blood beneath her nails, but she didn't stop.

Millington stumbled backwards, letting out a yell, and Sarah picked up her skirts, heedless of the state of her bodice, and ran as fast as she could. Thanking the years she had spent chasing her brothers up and down cobblestone steps, she made a mad dash for her life.

She found a small, dark alcove created by a cluster of dense trees and crouched beneath it, her heaving chest aching in her attempts not to breathe too loudly.

"You little... bitch," came Millington's voice from the darkness.

He walked past the spot where she was hiding, and she held her breath so as not to be heard. Her lungs burned and she bit her bruised lip, tears stinging her eyes.

Her heart hammered in her ears and her body trembled. What would she do if he found her? Could she fight him off again? Cold air shocked her bare skin, but she didn't dare move. Not yet.

After the longest minutes of her life, Millington let out a crude word and stalked back toward the house, mumbling to himself. His footsteps became less audible until finally, Sarah couldn't hear any movement around her at all.

It was only then, when she was sure he was gone, that she let the tears fall, hot and wet against her cheeks. She pulled the remains of her dress together, feelings of disgust and betrayal foremost in her mind. How could a gentleman do such a thing?

Clearly, he was no gentleman after all.

Then came the terrifying realization of what would happen if she were seen now. She would be ruined forever. The weight of her family's future still rested on her shoulders, and within weeks of their arrival in London, she had destroyed everything with her naive trust in the wrong man.

Sarah wrapped her arms around her knees and bent her head, muffling her cries with her skirts, fearful of being heard and unsure how she would ever be able to get herself home.

～

ONCE HIS IRRITATION HAD RECEDED, Oliver quite enjoyed wandering slowly through the gardens, delaying the inevitable return to the ballroom. Something Charlotte had said had touched a raw nerve inside him.

Back when he was just the second son and not the heir, he had happily conversed with gently-bred females, knowing their mamas would soon steer their attention to someone older or of a higher rank.

He'd pursued a lot of physical ventures also that he no longer had time for. His shoulders, that his tailor had once called too large to be fashionable, were shrinking in size at the lack of activity.

His days as an amateur pugilist and horse rider were behind him, and he wanted nothing more than to have those pastimes back.

He'd missed the chance to find a woman who didn't want him for his rank. Too late to playfully flirt and get to know someone properly. He knew why those women yearned for him now and thanks to a painful twist of fate, he would never know who wanted him for more than his title. Like a prize goose at Christmastime, he could not get away from the hunt fast enough.

Oliver stopped, noticing a strange noise coming from the pathway up ahead of him. Something, or someone, was hiding under or behind a cluster of trees.

"Hello, who's there?" he called out.

There was a loud gasp and then nothing. Lamps were hanging throughout the garden and from where he stood, he could make out a figure in the shadows. He assumed it was a woman hiding there, judging by the little piece of material peeking out from the bush. She seemed to be holding her breath, for now there was no noise coming from behind the trees.

Oliver laughed softly to himself. Maybe an assignation had been organised for this spot? It was certainly far enough away from the house for her and her partner not to be seen.

"Come out, whoever you are," Oliver called again, feeling slightly mischievous.

He would bet that some bored married lady had seen him and jumped behind the bush to preserve her reputation. Maybe he should speak to her. It was probably time he joined the ranks of the 'titled men with a mistress'. He grinned slightly at the cynical thought. What was a duke without a mistress?

A woman crawled out from beneath the trees and slowly stood, holding together the remains of her torn bodice.

"Please, don't hurt me," she whispered, her face hidden, eyes on the ground.

Chapter Two

Struck speechless, his heart lodged in his throat. It seemed no merry wife was hiding in the brush, but a fallen angel. Golden ringlets pulled askew and what was once a pale, virginal ball gown was now dirty and ripped. Too much of her creamy skin had been bared to his gaze for decency, but what caught his eye was the way her cheeks glistened from recently shed tears from her beautiful pale eyes. The young woman had clearly been crying.

He removed his coat immediately to help her cover herself.

Her head lifted a touch and her mouth fell open. As he stepped forward, she took a step back.

"Please, no." She looked positively stricken and began pulling her ruined gown closer around her small body. He couldn't help but notice she had rather full breasts though he tried hard not to look.

Oliver stopped moving and instead just held his jacket out to her like one would to a wounded animal.

It was evident the poor girl had been brutalised. The sick churning in his stomach that had begun at the initial sight of her, intensified as anger set in.

Who would dare touch a creature this beautiful and angelic? She would be lucky to be half the weight of an average man. What chance would she have of defending herself?

"Please, take my jacket." Oliver's voice cracked like a green boy, and he didn't care. "You must be freezing."

New tears welled up in the angel's violet eyes as she reached for his jacket with trembling fingers. Taking it from him, she turned her back to shield herself as she slipped her arms into it.

Oliver gaped at the unsightly red scratches marring the perfect skin of her upper back. Either she had been pushed against a tree or the ground, and in quite a violent manner. Bloody bastard!

"What happened to you?"

The woman turned around. Tears began to slide down her cheeks. Her face crumpled as she sank to her knees.

Oliver rushed forward and dropped to his knees, reaching out and wrapping his arms around her small frame and holding her against his body. She gripped his lapels like a child and cried.

Oliver stroked his angel's soft hair and made soft crooning noises into her ear. She continued to sob against his evening suit. He rarely felt needed by anyone, and it gave him a satisfaction to be able to help someone in such a small, but significant way. Though he would give anything for her not to have endured the violence against her in the first place.

"It's all right, you're safe," he reassured her. Although he had no idea if it was all right, or if it ever could be again. If she'd been molested, he could not imagine a worse fate for a gently-bred woman.

Wiping at her eyes, the woman finally straightened and clamoured to her feet before stepping back from him. He stood too. Despite her red nose and puffy cheeks, he'd never seen anyone more beautiful.

His heart clenched tighter the longer he stared at her. As he handed her his white handkerchief, she rewarded him with a smile. The angel dabbed at her face and wiped her nose before taking a few deep breaths to steady herself.

"Thank you so much, sir. I need to leave before anyone sees me. Can you help me, please?"

"Of course, I can."

Oliver's mind raced with the logistics of how to get her out of the grounds unseen. Why hadn't he thought about that before she mentioned it? He should have been the one to offer practical aid.

"I can't be seen like this." Her voice broke on the words and two fresh, shimmering tears slipped down her cheeks. "No one would ever marry me."

Oliver's heart all but broke at the pitiful look on her face, for it was indeed true. Her beauty and virginity were the two things that would be her greatest assets on the marriage market. If society regarded her as damaged goods, no one of any consequence would marry her, no matter how beautiful she was.

He wasn't having that. Although he'd known the girl only a few minutes, something about her smile, her gentle voice, told him that she was indeed a prize. Sweet, honest, and a rare find. A diamond of the finest quality.

"I'll get you out of here. Let's walk toward the front of the house and you can stay back in the shadows while I arrange a carriage." Oliver offered his arm to the angel, and she took it. He ushered her toward the house.

"I'm Sarah, by the way." She sniffed as she wiped her face again with his now-soaked handkerchief.

"Oh, well…" Oliver stammered, his brain temporarily locking out the ability to speak. How did this rare beauty keep flabbergasting him? He'd never been so verbally incompetent in his life.

"I think we're past polite names, do you not? After all, you have probably seen more of me tonight than anyone should before marriage."

Oliver's mouth dropped open, the trees closing in around him. What had he done?

Her honest, and far too accurate, assessment of the situation was unsettling. If someone saw them in her current state of 'dress', it would be his head on the chopping block, or in the parson's trap as the case may be.

"I'm not interested in getting married," he blurted out. He spoke louder than he should have, grabbing her arm and planting his feet, stopping her in their race to the front entrance.

Sarah chuckled and turned to look up at him, her violet eyes sparkling with the reflected lights from the nearby ballroom.

My God, she's beautiful.

"I didn't mean I wanted to marry you, sir. Just that considering the state you found me in, and after all you have done for me tonight, the least I could do was introduce myself as Sarah and not Miss such and such, daughter of such and such." She sighed loudly and waved her hand in a dismissive way. "I hate all that."

Oliver smiled despite himself. Incredible. Was there a marriageable female in London who didn't care about connections? He frowned as his cynical voice crowded his thoughts. He didn't think she'd feel the same way when they were properly introduced, and that was such a shame. Why couldn't he just be who he'd always been?

"I'm Oliver." He smiled at her, a strange swirling feeling blossoming deep inside him.

He'd never been introduced as just "Oliver" in his entire six and twenty years of life. Even as the spare son he was a lord. What an odd, exhilarating feeling it was. "Oliver" could be anyone, do anything.

"Oliver." She repeated his name. The tone of her voice had a huskiness that sent a bolt of desire to his groin.

"Please wait here, Sarah." He forced himself to let go of her arm and stepped away, needing to put some distance between them.

The last thing he wanted to feel for an almost-ravished woman was desire. The thought disgusted him. She needed his compassion. She need sympathy, not more lust.

Oliver left her near a garden gate and went in search of his cloak and servants, arranging for his carriage to take Sarah home and then come back to retrieve him.

It wasn't the first time Oliver was grateful to have so many people at his disposal, but tonight he'd used his power to help someone other than himself.

Her situation made him want to protect her, go out of his way to help her, and he liked this new side of himself. Somehow, helping Sarah in this way gave him a deep satisfaction, as if his life suddenly had a meaningful purpose.

He stepped back into the crowded, loud ballroom and found his hostess as quickly as possible. He pulled Charlotte aside again, ignoring the look of annoyance the lady she was speaking to shot in his direction.

"Where have you been? And where is your jacket? There has been such a commotion." Charlotte beamed at him, her blue eyes sparkling in the candlelight.

Lady Charlotte knew as any good hostess does, that gossip——either good or bad——was the only real thing that made any ball memorable.

"Patrick Millington came back to the ballroom half an hour ago with blood dripping down his face. He said he was escorting Miss Collins and made a remark to which she took exception and attacked him. I applaud her, really. The man is disgusting, but she shouldn't have gone quite that far." Charlotte started to laugh but stopped short. "What's the matter, Oliver?"

Oliver ground his teeth together, the crunch inside his skull doing nothing to halt the rage from building. He forced the words out. "I found Sarah in the back garden." His hands were clenched into fists at his sides as he realised the attempted seduction of an innocent was going to go completely unreported.

Lady Charlotte gasped and took a small step back, her eyes opening wide as she took in his rage.

"He didn't just say something that offended her. Her bodice was torn apart and her back was scratched." Oliver's chest rapidly rose and fell as he struggled to control his breathing. "Where is that bastard? I'll show him what happens to a man who attacks someone half his size." Turning on his heel, he took a step in the direction of the card room. Millington would pay for this.

"You can't." Lady Charlotte grabbed at his forearm and pulled him back to face her, her grip tight and unforgiving.

"He's already gone home, and you know it would ruin Miss Collins if people found out he stole even a kiss, let alone... more."

Oliver forced himself to think clearly through the red haze engulfing his common sense. Breathing was hard, but he inhaled and exhaled slowly, until relative calm descended. Charlotte was right. She always was. If he made a scene, then his angel would be ruined, and he could not save her from that.

He observed somewhere in his brain that he kept calling her 'his angel'. The pet name seemed too intimate for so short an acquaintance, but with her ethereal glow, golden hair and violet eyes, angelic was the perfect description for her. She was, by far, the most beautiful woman he had ever laid eyes on.

"Fine. You need to tell her mother that she had a sudden headache attack from the cold night air, and she needs to be taken home immediately. I've had my carriage drive around to the side entrance to pick her up, and her mother needs to go to her. Have her wait at the front entrance. I will instruct the carriage to pick up Sarah's mother on the way through to the exit. You need to help her, Charlotte."

"I'll do everything I can, Oliver," she reassured him, giving his forearm a squeeze before releasing him. "Go join my brother in the card room for some time, then go home, please. It sounds like you've had an exhausting night."

"I'm going to check on Sarah first, and then I will. Thank you, Lady Charlotte."

He bowed to his friend and kissed her extended hand.

She curtseyed and moved off to where he assumed Sarah's mother must be mingling among the ladies.

Oliver stepped out into the garden again.

Sarah was waiting for him exactly where he had left her. She was pacing up and down, still wrapped in his jacket and wringing her hands in front of her ruined dress. Her face lit up as he approached, her huge smile hitting him low in the belly, forcing the air from his lungs. She accepted his cloak and wrapped it around herself with easy, elegant movements.

As soon as she was covered, she handed him back his jacket, and he slipped it back on. He was once again presentable, yet the heat from her body that had transferred into the jacket almost made him groan. He would be smelling her subtle perfume all night now, and it would torment his dreams, he was sure.

Sarah gestured helplessly to herself and looked up at him with wide, beautiful eyes.

"Oliver, what am I going to do about my mother? She's still inside, and I can't go in."

"I've just discreetly spoken with Lady Charlotte who will fetch your mother, and she will meet you at the side entrance where my carriage awaits you. She will tell them that you have come down with a sudden headache, and no one will be the wiser." Oliver paused. How did one ask about the virtue of a maiden? Did he have the right? Would she even understand what he wanted to know? "Sarah, I have to ask, did he... ah..."

She stared at him a moment, then dipped her head to avoid his gaze.

"He didn't force me, if that is what you want to know," Sarah told him in a quiet voice. "I scratched his eyes and ran, before..."

"Oh, thank God."

Her head shot up at his words, and she beamed at him. Her eyes shone, and her whole face seemed to grin, not just her lips. Oliver's heart melted. He'd never seen a smile so wondrous.

"Oliver, I know I shouldn't ask you this, considering the encounter we've had, but... I suppose it's the only time I'd ever have the courage." She bit her lip again, and although it was as seductive a move as anything Oliver had ever seen, he was cautious of what she was about to ask.

"Of course, my lady. What is it you wish to know?" Oliver added a formal bow to his question.

She fluttered her hands and bit her lip.

"I want... oh, bother." Sarah looked from side to side and twisted her hands in front of her.

Oliver attempted a reassuring smile, trying not to imagine what she would ask of him. Did she need money? Help in society? Had she worked out who he was and wanted to enjoy the privileges his rank may afford her?

"It's all right, ask me."

She was wringing his white handkerchief in her hands now.

"It's not a question, more... a request."

Oliver frowned. The problems she may be facing piled up inside his head. Did she need somewhere to stay, perhaps?

"Would you kiss me?" Sarah's words came out in a rush.

His mouth dropped open. Surely, he'd misheard her. There was no possible way someone who had gone through what she had obviously been through tonight, would ask for such a thing. Was there?

"I'm not sure I heard you correctly, Sarah." His tone was light, but his heart thumped against his ribcage in acknowledgment of the truth. A marriageable virgin was asking him for a kiss. As an unmarried gentleman of the ton—and a duke, to make matters worse—he should run for the safety of his estate.

She blushed at his words, pink flushing from the place the cloak met her neck, all the way up to the roots of her golden hair.

That blush affected Oliver more than the tears, and something inside him shifted. A blush could not be faked and showed a real depth of emotion that had been lacking in every woman Oliver had ever met. Genuine warmth, an ability to forge past her fears and ask for something she wanted. He admired that.

"I know I must look an absolute mess, but I cannot have tonight's experience be my only experience of intimacy between a man and a woman. Would you please help me to forget? Help me to make a new and more pleasant memory?" She all but whispered the last part of the sentence.

Oliver's tenuous grip on control slipped. Before he'd made the decision to move, he was already cupping her face with both hands and bringing his lips down onto hers.

He wanted to moan at the delicious feel of her soft lips beneath his, but he swallowed the sound down. She was like touching the finest silk and drinking the most expensive port. Soft, warm, intoxicating. It was a heady feeling indeed.

Feather light.

Sarah may have asked for a kiss, but he could tell she was an innocent. He was not, and his mind was already conjuring up images of kissing her in places much less decent than her lips. His body tightened in response to his thoughts as his loins pulsed with need.

Using every last drop of control in his body, Oliver stepped back from the sweetest lips he had ever kissed, and Sarah almost toppled forward.

He dropped his hands down to his sides, his lips and hands tingling from the contact with her skin.

"Thank you," Sarah whispered, lifting her hand and running her fingertips over her swollen mouth. A look of awe and wonder washed over her face.

He cleared his throat, his mind still abuzz with sensation.

Ducking her head shyly she added, "That was what my first kiss should have been."

His eyebrows rose high on his forehead. First kiss? He'd never kissed a virgin before; had never understood the allure some men found in them. But looking at Sarah's beautiful face, knowing he was the first person she had happily been touched by, pleased him more than he expected.

"My carriage will be here any moment, and it will take you around to the front of the house where your mother will be waiting. It will take you both home from there."

It was a relief to give her the instructions, his overwhelming thoughts confusing him. He didn't want to leave her and couldn't understand why. He knew it was better to sever their ties sooner rather than later, and yet knowing something and wanting to do it were two different things.

His carriage pulled up outside the gate, bearing the crest of the Lincolns.

"Oh, is that a ducal crest?" Sarah's voice sounded stunned.

"Yes, my brother." The unintentional lie left Oliver's mouth and he grimaced.

He often still forgot that he was now the Lincoln heir and his father and brother were both gone. Easy to do, considering he had spent five and twenty years in one situation and only twelve months in the other.

Before he could correct his mistake, she was dancing happily on the spot in front of him.

"Thank you so much, Oliver, for everything you have done for me. I have no idea how I could have managed without you."

She held out her hand to him, and he automatically picked it up. Instead of allowing him to kiss her fingers as was proper, Sarah bowed down, turned his hand over and pressed her soft, warm lips to his palm instead.

Shocked into immovability, the beat of his heart was the only thing he could hear. Last week he had lain with an experienced woman, and yet the feel of Sarah's lips on his gloved hand seemed more intimate, and oddly more arousing, than anything he had experienced before.

"Go." His throat tightened on the word.

With one more backwards glance at him, Sarah tucked Oliver's cloak around her body and slipped into the carriage.

He took a deep breath of cold night air and exhaled slowly. His body hurt as though he'd been in a fight and come out the loser. His arms and legs ached, and although he would have loved to head straight home, he had to wait for his carriage to come back.

He headed back into the ballroom, inclined his head at Charlotte, who was watching him carefully, turned on his heel and headed toward the male-only den. While he waited for his carriage, he could mentally plot all the different ways he would love to destroy Patrick Millington.

Chapter Three

Sarah waited with bated breath in the carriage outside the Dunford's front entrance. When her mother finally climbed into the carriage, she took one look at Sarah and her brows dipped down in a frown. She quickly pulled Sarah onto the seat next to her.

"Lay your head on my shoulder, Sarah, and we will discuss this when we get home."

Sarah nodded with gratitude and let her head fall onto her mother's shoulder, the night's events racing through her mind as the carriage drove through the London streets.

When they finally arrived at their rented townhouse, her mother helped Sarah inside and upstairs to her bedchamber, then excused herself to call for their servants and arrange a hot bath for Sarah.

"I will change into my nightgown, dear, and then I will return to help you."

"A bath sounds very... sensible. Thank you, Mama."

IF THE SERVANTS minded the timing of the request, then no one said anything as they filled the copper tub to brimming with hot water.

Sarah dismissed them soon after, and as soon as they left, she removed the concealing cloak and stripped herself of her gown. She almost cried as she looked at herself properly in the light. Her body was bruised and cut, and her ruined gown unsalvageable.

She slipped into the steaming bath, the horrors of the night slowly washing away.

Her mother stepped into her room not ten minutes later and stood next to the tub. Her chin lifted and worry lines marred her forehead. She appeared to prepare herself for the worst. "Sarah, now tell me. What happened to you tonight?"

Well, quite simply... "I was attacked."

Her mother's eyebrows rose so high on her forehead it made her look quite silly. She sank onto the bed with one hand at her throat as she stared at Sarah's ruined gown.

An evening gown, Sarah knew, that they had saved for years to pay for. Sarah was only getting one season. It was all her family could afford and destroying her prettiest ball gown wasn't a good beginning.

"Tell me what happened," her mother demanded, as the colour drained from her face.

Sarah related what had befallen her, right up to the point that Oliver had put her in his carriage. She left out Oliver's kiss at the end of the night. Her mother didn't need to know everything, and that was a secret she wished to hold close to her heart.

"And you have no idea who this 'Oliver' is? Are you sure he can be trusted not to talk about what happened tonight?"

Her mother was wringing her hands as she often did when she was nervous. Sarah sighed, knowing her mother could fret until she had a headache, but what was done was done.

"I don't know who he was, Mama, but he seemed to be a gentleman. Unlike the other one." She scowled. "Oliver helped me find you and lent us his carriage to take us home. Surely, he wouldn't do that unless he had a kind heart. He was the brother of a duke, I think." She couldn't remember all the details. Everything around the time of Oliver's kiss seemed to be a little fuzzy.

"You think?" Her mother all but screeched.

Sarah grimaced. Whether or not her rescuer was a brother to a duke was hardly a detail that one should forget.

"Mama, I'm sorry, I'm still a little shaken up."

"Of course!" Her mother jumped up and reached out to her, concern written in her blue eyes. Sarah took her mother's hand and squeezed. "Don't be sorry, Sarah. I'm sorry. I shouldn't have reacted like that, but you know if someone finds out, you'll never make the match we were hoping for you." Her mother accompanied her words with a reluctant shrug. "You say Millington was trying to... ah... undo his breeches?" Her mother turned beet-red as she asked the question.

"Yes, Mama. That is how I managed to get away from him—because he had to let go of me for a minute." Sarah spoke in a matter-of-fact tone. She was trying not to be overly emotional about it, even though she was still in shock and could not believe that a man had tried to force her to couple with him.

"And... you know what he was trying to do?" Her mother looked down at the carpet on the floor. Was her mother wanting to talk about this *now*?

Now Sarah's cheeks heated.

"Yes, Mama." She had a few married friends at home in Somerset, and she had coaxed the bare facts from them. She knew he had wanted to put that male part of himself in her female parts.

Her mother's head lifted, a mixture of alarm and surprise showing on her once beautiful face. "How?"

Sarah shrugged, washing her breasts for the hundredth time that night. They still felt unclean. "I asked Mary for some of the details." Mary was one of her married friends and quite a gossip. "And Mama, I have to say, it sounds horrible. Do I have to do that when I marry?"

This time, her mother blushed so dark that Sarah was afraid she had finally rendered her mother mute.

Alas, no such luck.

"Time for our tête-à-tête, then." Her mother sat down on the bed again and Sarah sank lower into the still-warm water, giving her mother her full attention. "It does sound horrible when described, I suppose, but it is how God designed us to make children. Therefore, it should be a natural thing between a husband and his wife."

Really? She didn't think so.

"But doesn't it hurt, Mama?"

Sarah thought back to her conversation with her friend, Mary. She didn't say it had hurt, but the look on Mary's face had not inspired confidence.

Mrs. Collins blushed again, and Sarah smiled up at her. Goodness, her mother was almost forty. Sarah would have thought that she had outgrown blushes by now.

"It does to begin with, because your body will not be used to it. But if your husband is careful with you, and loves you, it can be quite... ah... enjoyable after a while." At this last revelation, her mother dropped her gaze to her hands.

Sarah's almost sputtered. *Enjoyable?* She reminded herself that her mother had more knowledge on the subject than she, so instead of stating his disbelief, she digested this new information carefully. Thinking of her future spouse, she could only picture one man. If Oliver were her husband, he would be careful, she knew. And if her mother was correct, then the experience's pleasure mostly depended on the man.

"Then we'll have to choose well, Mama," Sarah finally said with a smile. She wanted to finish the awkward conversation, more for her mother's sake than her own.

"I'll leave you then, Sarah. Take rest and sleep well. You are safe, and that is the main thing."

"Yes, Mama. Thank you, and goodnight."

The door shut with a soft click and she stood up carefully, shivering as the water ran down her body and the cold air hit her skin. She should have asked one of the servants to light the fire in her chambers.

She stepped out of the tub, dried herself with the towel left by the servants and put on her nightgown.

Despite worrying she would not be able to fall asleep, Sarah slept all night long and well into the following day, her head filled with the strangest dreams.

~

WHAT DID she want from her life and the person with whom she might share it? What sort of man did she want to marry? Which man did she have to marry to give her siblings a future?

Dressing for another ball the following evening caused excited butterflies to flutter around Sarah's belly. Her lady's maid coaxed her naturally curly hair into the ringlets that were loved by the fashionable ton and pulled her laces tight.

She had a decent bosom, neither too small nor too large. Looking down at herself, she thought they were quite pretty, as far as breasts went. Hopefully, her future husband would feel the same way.

Her gown for this evening lay on her bed, a pale pink that seemed to suit her skin tone. She knew that the lighter the skin, the better, as far as the ton was concerned. But living in Somerset meant they had many functions out of doors, and she never bothered to cover herself completely. She could only hope that her future husband wouldn't find her slightly tanned complexion a problem.

Would she see Oliver again tonight? She tried not to be too hopeful that he would attend, but she so wished to enjoy his company once more. He had said he had no desire to be married, so did that mean they would never cross paths again? Only those interested in matrimony attended balls. Once dressed, she donned a wrap to hide the scratches on her back, and pulled out her reticule. It was time to leave.

The ball was an even bigger crush than had been anticipated and within minutes of entering the heated room, Sarah found herself seeking the calm of the outdoors. Too many sweaty people in one place could not be good for the constitution, she was sure.

Her need for a wrap made her doubly warm. Her back was still visibly injured from Millington's foiled attack, so she dare not remove the wrap.

"Mama, I need some fresh air."

Her mother nodded and fluttered her fan. "Just stick to the balcony."

"Of course, Mama."

She definitely would not be venturing far this evening. Not after what had happened last time. She made her way out the open doors to breathe once again.

OLIVER SPENT two minutes in the crowded ballroom and could sense her. Sarah was here, somewhere. Walking toward the balcony, his pulse sped up, and when he stepped into the cold evening air, his breath caught in his throat at the sight of her.

All he could see was the back of her curled, blonde hair and lovely pink dress with a light wrap thrown across her shoulders. Yet his heart was hammering, and his belly swirled with unaccustomed feelings. He was excited and nervous at the same time.

Why did this beautiful young woman affect him so much? It was an uncomfortable feeling, and yet he couldn't stop himself wanting to be near her.

He swallowed and took a breath, forcing her name from his throat.

"Sarah?" Oliver called out and walked onto the balcony behind her.

She visibly jumped and whirled around to face him. Her hand came up to rest between her breasts, drawing his gaze to the plump flesh there. Arousal shot down his belly to his groin.

"Oh goodness, Oliver, you scared me." Her beautiful face transformed as she smiled up at him.

Oliver blinked. He felt as if he were in a dream. His brain was a bit sluggish in wonder, like he'd just consumed a bottle of port.

She was breath-taking. Why had he thought she was only pretty? Flawless skin, glorious golden hair and the most kissable lips he had ever had the good fortune to taste.

She didn't seem to notice his discomfort because she put her hand on his elbow and pulled him further away from the ballroom. It was the only place he wanted to be—away from everyone else, and closer to her.

"I wasn't sure if I'd see you tonight. You said you're not on the marriage mart." She laughed as though it were a joke, but Oliver heard the question behind the statement.

He had struggled with himself for hours over the issue of whether or not to seek her out tonight. He had chosen the lesser of two evils. He could deal with the torture of seeing her again, even though she was off-limits to him, as long as she was healthy and well. To worry that she wasn't all right was a torment he wasn't able to endure.

"I wasn't planning on it, to be honest, but I needed to make sure you were feeling a little better after your dreadful experience last night."

If only she weren't so beautiful. It would make this so much easier. Less personal.

Oliver only had a few more years of freedom until he would be forced to marry a lady to produce an heir to the dukedom. He shuddered at the thought. However, he had always planned to marry someone he wanted, someone he cared for.

But since he had inherited the title, his new responsibility as the duke and being the only one left of his father's line meant he was obliged to marry someone who would be a proper duchess. Someone who had the appropriate training and breeding for the position. Oliver's back teeth ground together at the thought. When had he started thinking about the fairer sex as though they were horses?

Sarah flushed prettily, the blood giving her cheeks a healthy tinge that made her glow all the more.

"Thank you, I really do appreciate your concern."

She lifted her gaze to his and Oliver had to fight the urge to pull her into his arms for a real kiss. That light touch of his mouth on hers from the night before had only whet his appetite for more of her. He had thought of little else and now that she was so close, he ached for another taste.

"It was no bother at all." He patted her hand lightly, striving for a paternal type of reassurance and removed her small hand from his arm. He turned his back on the gardens and leaned against the banister at the end of the balcony.

"Since we have already discussed my lack of interest in a marriage partner, tell me, is there any gentleman at whom you have been looking?" He gestured toward the ballroom and watched her carefully.

It had been a long time since he'd been so comfortable to be himself with another person. To be this comfortable with a woman to whom he was attracted, well, that had never happened before!

"After the other night, I'm not sure I trust my instincts."

She smiled sadly and Oliver clenched his hands into fists at his side.

Damn Patrick Millington.

"Well, tell me what you're looking for and perhaps I can recommend someone for you." The words were out of his mouth before he even thought to halt them. He was stupid and a glutton for punishment, it would seem.

She smiled at that, although the smile didn't quite reach her eyes.

"I need someone with, well..."

"Money," he sighed, finishing her sentence for her and feeling disappointed despite himself. For once, he wanted to be wrong about a woman.

"Yes, unfortunately." Sarah sighed just as heavily as he had and leaned back against the railing beside him.

Oliver looked up from where he'd been staring at the ground, confused by her words.

Sarah had just admitted to something to which most ladies would never openly admit, yet she sounded so sad about the fact.

"Why unfortunately?" He tried to keep his tone light, curious to hear her actual opinion. He knew that as soon as she found out who he was, her candour would disappear into thin air.

"Well, I very much would like to marry for love. My parents have a wonderful marriage, and I have always hoped for a similar pairing, myself. My parents want to give me, my brother and my sister, a better chance at marrying well, but they only have money for one season. As I'm the eldest, I need to marry someone who can help my family. If I marry a penniless wastrel, my sister will never get to have a season and my baby brother will never go to Eton." She sounded like she was about to cry again, and Oliver fought the urge to wrap his arms around her. That certainly wouldn't be appropriate.

He chuckled to break the tension. Hearing Sarah's voice so forlorn made his throat ache. "Well, the answer is simple. Make sure you fall in love with someone who can support your family."

Sarah broke into a huge grin.

"I'll try," she said and then she laughed too. Hers was loud, and she chortled with her whole body. A most unladylike display, indeed, yet truly charming, Oliver decided.

A smile stretched across his face. He'd never before heard a lady laugh like that, and he didn't think he'd ever get sick of hearing the sound.

Sarah clapped one hand over her mouth to stifle the noise and the other to her trim belly, obviously trying to hold back her laughter.

"I shouldn't be so loud. People will come over to find out what we're talking about and ruin our conversation." She sighed, looking back at the ballroom full of people.

Damn. He needed to know how she felt about titles before someone stupidly told her who he was.

Chapter Four

" A nd what about a title? Should I introduce you to a viscount? A second son? Do you have a preference?" He tried to sound as though her answer wasn't important, but he would be a fool not to acknowledge, to himself at least, how much her reply meant to him.

She was so sweet, so deliciously naïve in so many ways. It would pain him to discover she was after a gentleman who would give her a title. He'd grown up with women like that—his mother for one. His gut twisted.

Of course, there was also his sister-in-law. She had wanted nothing more than to be the Duchess of Lincoln. She had been promised since birth to his brother, and when he had died and left her childless, all her dreams had crashed down around her.

The woman had been abominable ever since. She hounded Oliver, as did his mother. They both wanted him to marry his brother's widow, and he adamantly refused. He knew she'd been bred to be a duchess, that she was thin and young and would likely produce a suitable heir for the line. His skin crawled at the very idea.

Crossing swords with his brother was not something he would ever do. He'd already spent his life being unfavourably compared to his perfect sibling. He wouldn't allow the comparison to extend to his marriage.

Sarah laughed again, pulling him out of his reverie, and it was like stepping into a patch of sunshine after a chill. Light after the dark. She was heaven. There was no other word for it.

"Goodness, Oliver, how mercenary we sound discussing husbands in such a way. I was thinking about titles, funnily enough, as I was getting dressed tonight. I really don't want a title."

Oliver's heart stopped in his chest, his ribs squeezing tight. That wasn't what he had expected her to say. He should have felt relief, knowing that she wasn't one of the ladies he loathed. But for some reason he didn't feel relieved in the slightest.

"I don't have the bloodline to attract a title," she continued, oblivious to his distress. "And I don't have a dowry for a second son to enjoy, so I suppose I was hoping for a man who would be able to look after my family, but also overlook my faults." Her eyes dropped, but before he could correct her about how few faults she had, she jumped in again.

"Oh, and I don't want him to be over forty. And I want him to be gentle."

Oliver coughed because he felt that laughing might be rude. She had the most amusing matrimonial list he had ever heard. She was the most beautiful thing he had ever seen, and she thought she should engage the attentions of a man—probably in trade from the sounds of it—who would be nice to her, but not be old. *Goodness, she was frank!*

"So? Do you know anyone who could be all those things?" she asked.

Her gaze slid over to him in a way that made his blood run first hot, then cold. Was she suggesting he put his hat in the ring? Or was she indeed asking if he knew someone good enough for her? Either way, he felt suddenly ill.

He cleared his throat and tore his eyes away from her to look out over the gardens.

She put her hand on his arm again. "I shouldn't have asked. I'm sorry, Oliver. I know you're only being kind, standing here with me."

She sounded so lost, and yet her words were clearly honest. Oliver was once again shocked into silence. She was hoping he would offer for her. Why did that make his heart lift and his chest puff with pride? She knew hardly anything about him—not his family connections, nor his occupation, nor even his last name. Certainly not his title.

But she wanted him.

He knew from the small amount of time they had spent together already, that they would suit each other well. She was kind and intelligent and as beautiful as the sun and moon combined. He'd have married her in an instant if he had met her two years earlier. If only he hadn't become the new Duke of Lincoln and it wasn't required that he should marry someone suitable for the title.

He slammed his hand into the banister, and she jumped a little. Why did this have to happen now? The unfairness of it all made him want to scream.

Sarah cleared her throat, then spoke into the awkward silence.

"Well, I don't know about you, but I shall never again venture into a garden at night." Her tone was teasing, but Oliver knew only too well how true her words were. It made him sick to his stomach that a supposed gentleman had taken advantage of her in such a way.

Just as Oliver was taking advantage of her kindness now. He had to tell her the truth about who he was.

"Sarah, I need to tell you—"

"Oh, here you are," came a familiar voice from behind them. Oliver closed his eyes briefly and said a little prayer. Hopefully, Sarah would forgive him.

Together they turned to the gentleman and lady who had interrupted their private moment. It was Lady Charlotte and her brother, Lord John Dunford.

"Miss Collins, so lovely to see you again, and looking so well," Charlotte said, curtseying politely.

Sarah swept into a low enough curtsey to pass for the king's arrival.

"Lady Charlotte, so nice to see you," Sarah returned quietly.

Oliver frowned at the change in his companion. He didn't like seeing Sarah so unnaturally timid. It didn't suit her. He wasn't sure if his familiarity with the Dunford siblings was giving her pause or if it was the fact they were one of the wealthiest and oldest families in London——next to his, of course.

John looked pointedly at Oliver.

"Oh, I'm sorry. Miss Sarah Collins, this is an old school friend of mine, Lord John Dunford." Again, Sarah swept into an embarrassingly low curtsey and gave John a small smile.

Although John was a second son, his father's title was usually enough to intimidate the debutantes. Sarah was no exception, obviously.

"It is, indeed, an honour to make your acquaintance, my lord."

"And I, yours, Miss Collins." John swept gallantly into a low bow to match her curtsey. The corners of his friend's mouth quirked up when he spoke, and Oliver stifled the desire to push him—and Charlotte—away.

"Are you enjoying the evening?" John tilted his head politely.

"Oh, yes." She nodded; her eyes as big as a doe's. "I have never been to a house so beautiful. Except perhaps your birthday celebration last night, Lady Charlotte. I would like to thank you again for the invitation." She smiled at Charlotte and then, in turn, at John.

John's eyes widened a fraction as if in surprise. Oliver didn't like him looking at Sarah in that way—as if he found her attractive.

"We were so pleased you could come, Miss Collins," Charlotte replied.

John dropped his voice to make sure that no other person on the balcony could hear him. "I heard that my friend managed to give you a small amount of assistance that night, Miss Collins. I hope you are feeling better this evening?"

Sarah blushed deeply, her beautiful face turning the colour of one of the red roses in the gardens surrounding them. Instead of avoiding the topic, however, her gaze held firmly to John's face, and her eyes flashed with a strange expression. Oliver thought she might be embarrassed, but trying to hide it.

She was doing a gallant job of it.

"He did indeed, sir," Sarah said at last. "Although, it was no small thing. Without Oliver there that night, I'm afraid I would have been packed and on my way back to Somerset today from the horror of it all."

Sarah lifted her chin in a defiant manner and Oliver could do nothing but stare at her. She wasn't afraid to thank him publicly for his rescue and she looked so incredible when she was defending him.

"Oliver?" John asked, one eyebrow rising. Oliver silently cursed.

He'd never told Sarah his surname, and she didn't know his title. Trust John to notice. Most people called Oliver 'His Grace' or 'Lincoln'. No one except his mother and a few select friends called him Oliver.

"Oh, I'm so sorry." Sarah gasped, as if realizing her error.

She turned to Oliver and laid a hand on his arm in an intimate gesture that neither Charlotte nor John missed.

Oliver grimaced, knowing they would have something to say afterward.

"I don't know what name or title to call you by." Sarah turned, innocent eyes on him.

Oliver wanted to kick himself for not speaking up and letting her know the truth earlier.

Oh, hell!

Lady Charlotte and Lord John both burst into amused chuckles.

Sarah looked back at them, obviously startled.

He glared at his friends. They must have thought it a fantastic joke. They had found the only woman in London society who didn't know every detail about him, down to his shoe size.

"May I present His Grace, the Duke of Lincoln, formerly Oliver Lyre," John announced to Sarah, with another bow and a great flourish of his right hand.

Sarah jerked her hand back from his jacket sleeve and took a step away from him with a wounded look in her huge, violet eyes.

"I thought... you said... oh my," Sarah stuttered. She stumbled back toward the ballroom. Then she picked up her skirts and ran from the balcony.

Oliver gaped after her. What would possess her to run from him like that? He hadn't told her his title when they met, but surely it wasn't something from which to run like a scared rabbit?

Her words floated back through his mind. "I do not have the bloodline to attract a title." And he possessed one of the highest titles in London, save for royalty. He could only conclude she must be severely embarrassed she'd made such a statement. Maybe she truly did want a title and was now shocked that she had missed the opportunity? He had no idea what she was thinking, but he had to find out.

Blindly, he moved to follow her, but a strong hand wrapped around his forearm and held him in place.

"Unless you intend to marry that girl, I suggest you don't go after her," warned the voice of reason. John's brown eyes burned into his own. His hands clenched into fists.

"I just want to see if she is all right." He shook off John's arm with an abrupt flick. "I think she was embarrassed that she didn't know I was a duke."

"Well, of course, she was embarrassed. It's obvious the girl likes you, you dolt," Charlotte hissed at him. She was one of the few who could get away with calling him such a thing. "I'll check the retiring room; I'm sure that is where she would have gone."

Charlotte swept away with her regal air, and John pulled Oliver back toward the edge of the balcony. There was a crowd gathering now, their narrowed gazes making him want to leave.

The sight of a debutante running from the balcony had naturally caused a stir. Ladies didn't run, ever.

Except, his angel did. She seemed to break almost every rule he knew.

"Well?" John asked, his eyes narrowing while he crossed his arms over his chest.

"Well, what, John?" Oliver turned away from his friend and faced the trees that moments ago had been his saving grace from other embarrassing questions.

"Why didn't you tell that poor girl who you were? She looked at you like you were the devil himself just now. People will be talking about this for weeks." He gestured ominously to the crowd behind them, which seemed to be growing bigger.

"I didn't get the chance the other night, between trying to avoid being seen and smuggling her out of the party before anyone saw her." What did John want from him?

"And tonight?"

Good question.

Tonight, he had been enjoying her honest answers and beautiful face too much to let her know that he should be on the very top of her list of 'good catches'.

"I was getting to it."

John looked at him strangely, then rested his back against the balustrade.

"She's quite beautiful," John said airily, waving one hand like a dandy.

Oliver bared his teeth. The whoremonger could keep his hands off his Sarah.

John grinned. "Did you see those eyes? And those breasts! If a man ever wanted to dream up a woman, that is what she would look like." He sighed grandly.

Oliver's gut tightened and his anger exploded. He grabbed his best friend by the lapels and almost pushed him off the edge of the balcony.

"Do not talk about her like that."

His heart was pumping hard, and his hands were clenching around the black material of John's collar.

John's smile seemed forced as he answered. "Why ever not? Are you planning on marrying her, after all?" His tone was serious, though they both knew Oliver had no marital plans for the near future.

Oliver looked down at his hands, clenched in his friend's evening jacket, and hastily stepped back, letting go as he did so. "I apologise."

John quirked one eyebrow again, asking him a silent question.

"I think I'm protective of her after what happened the other night. That is all."

Oliver reached for the easiest answer. That sounded like a plausible excuse for almost doing harm to a man he had known for over thirteen years. Simply because he'd dared to admire Sarah.

You're losing your mind.

John pulled Oliver further away from the door before quietly asking, "Do you know what happened to her last night?"

"Not exactly. I didn't ask her for specific details. Her dress was torn and her back was scratched, but Sarah said she fought him off before he could... you know." He ground his teeth together.

"Fight him off? How? She's so small, she'd fit in your pocket."

John had as little respect for Patrick Millington as Oliver had, even before that night. They both knew him to be a nasty drunk and a stupid gambler, but a rapist of an innocent? They didn't think he was that bad. Or, Oliver hadn't thought so.

"Charlotte told me later that Millington had come back to the ballroom with blood around his eyes, from where she scratched him." He heard the surprise and pride in his own voice, as he imagined his little angel turning into a hellcat.

Amazing.

John gave a low whistle and shook his head. "She's got some backbone then."

"Indeed."

"Let's go back inside and see what else my dear sister has discovered."

They both headed back to the ballroom, and a feeling of dread sank into Oliver's bones. Why, oh why, had he come to a marriage mart event? He wondered if his friend John felt the same way.

Chapter Five

Sarah's heart ached as much as her throat, a sob rising and falling in her chest as she strained to stop the tears that flowed. It was ridiculous to cry over such a thing. She would get herself together in just a moment.

"What has happened, Miss Collins?"

Lady Charlotte's voice made Sarah jump, but when she looked up relief flooded her.

Charlotte locked the door to the retiring room and took the seat next to Sarah on the chaise lounge.

"I didn't know... he was a... *duke*," Sarah admitted, as Charlotte reached out and held her hand.

Sarah was aware that Charlotte was a duke's daughter, and far above her station, but at this moment, she was grateful for the kindness shown to her.

Charlotte laughed softly; the sound musical.

"So?"

"I thought he liked me." Sarah was unable to explain why she was so upset, but at least she had managed to stop crying. She dabbed at her eyes with her handkerchief and determined to be strong about the situation.

She shouldn't be so disappointed, but as the pain flowed through her, she knew she'd put more hope in making a match with Oliver than she'd admitted to herself.

"So, what's wrong with that? Can't he like you *and* be a duke?" Charlotte asked gently.

"No, he cannot." Sarah pushed herself to her feet. "You don't understand, I wasn't taught to worship a title, I was taught to fear and respect one," she blurted out.

Then she remembered to whom she was speaking, and her cheeks filled with heat.

"People like Oliver don't marry little nobodies like me," Sarah added.

Charlotte gasped, her eyes wide and her mouth open.

"Did he give you a reason to think that an offer of marriage was forthcoming?"

"No, of course not," Sarah said, embarrassed all over again. Charlotte would likely believe she was a simpleton.

"I built it up in my head after his gallant rescue the other night. I need to marry this year, and he was the first person I thought might suit. Oh, what am I saying? He told me he wasn't interested in marrying in the foreseeable future, but we get along so well, and it's so easy to talk to him."

Charlotte nodded encouragingly. "How can I help you?"

"Oh, Lady Charlotte, you have already been of so much assistance, I do not know how to thank you. Goodness me, I have been such a trouble to you." Sarah sighed and slid back onto a chair.

She had never been in trouble in her life, and she had now found herself in tears twice in two nights. What had become of her?

"I meant to ask, are you feeling better after last night? I'm afraid Patrick Millington has gotten away almost scot-free whilst you now have a reputation for being quite, shall we say, violent." A wry smile touched Charlotte's lips.

Sarah's shoulders slumped. She felt utterly exhausted and suddenly weary of London altogether. "Thank you for being honest about that. I can only imagine what he told people."

Charlotte sat beside Sarah and patted her hand. "He just said you took offence at something he said and attacked him. Which, all in all, isn't too bad."

"Considering what he did, then yes, not too bad," Sarah agreed. Then she grinned fiercely. "I did get him squarely in the eyes, that's certain."

For a moment there was silence, and then the two women burst into a fit of giggles.

"Perhaps we ought to get you home, Miss Collins." Charlotte reached out and helped to pin up a curl that had fallen loose in Sarah's mad rush from the balcony.

"Please, call me Sarah," she said, ignoring the protocol that suggested that Lady Charlotte, being of higher rank, must offer her Christian name first.

"I would love to. And you may call me Charlotte."

"Oh, no, I could not, Lady Charlotte. I just thought, considering I have soaked your beautiful dress with my tears, the least I could do was offer you the option to address me by my Christian name."

Charlotte smiled a kind, bright smile that lifted Sarah's heart.

"Sarah, please call me Charlotte. Now let's see if I can get my carriage brought around, and you can get home before anyone sees you've been crying."

Sarah focused her gaze on a mirror and saw how red and blotchy her face was. She swallowed her pride and said, "I would greatly appreciate that."

Later that night, she lay in her bed, reliving each precious moment she'd had with Oliver. There would be no more. She was resigned to marrying someone suitable—someone who would be able to help her family. She had no other option.

She would plead a head cold for a few days, adjust her expectations and start her spouse hunt again the following week.

~

OLIVER GLANCED around another ballroom at yet another ton event, panic gripping his gut. *Where was she?*

"She's not here," came a voice to his right.

Bloody Charlotte. She stepped in front of him, looking poised and beautiful in her gown of pink silk.

"Do you know why?" He was too worried about Sarah to feign ignorance.

Lady Charlotte smiled smugly, pausing too long for Oliver's comfort. "Of course, I do."

"Well? Are you going to tell me or do I have to drag it out of you?" Oliver demanded in a raised voice.

"Sarah decided she needed a couple of days off the circuit, but she will be attending the opera tomorrow evening, as my guest."

Charlotte said this as though she had known Sarah for years. Oliver wanted to punch his fist through a wall. Charlotte barely knew Sarah and yet she knew more about her than he did.

"But is she not here? I thought she wanted to marry as soon as possible." Oliver dropped his voice when he noticed the curious looks from the ladies around them.

"You'll have to ask her, I'm afraid." Lady Charlotte smiled again and Oliver had an overwhelming urge to wrap his hands around her smug neck.

He knew he'd made a blunder with Sarah, but did Charlotte have to make him feel worse than he already did?

"Oh, bother." Charlotte's eyes widened, and she fluttered her fan in front of her face.

Oliver turned in the direction in which she was looking.

"What's wrong?" He looked for something to justify her present stricken look, but couldn't see anything.

"Here comes your sanctimonious friend."

Oliver had never seen that particular look on Charlotte's face before. A faint blush rose in her usually pale cheeks and her eyebrows were low and tight over angry, sparkling, blue eyes.

Finally he spiedArchibald Turner, one of his oldest friends.

"Archie? What's wrong with Archie?" Oliver asked, baffled.

Charlotte could not have such a strong reaction to his quiet friend. Could she?

"He always makes me feel like I'm a tease because I have refused more than one marriage proposal. How does he even know about them?"

"Everyone knows about the men you have turned down, Charlotte." Oliver grinned. How the tables had turned.

"Well, it shouldn't be common knowledge." Charlotte was indeed scowling now, and Oliver struggled to contain his laugh.

"Archie, old boy." Oliver greeted his friend, feeling better than he had in days.

"Your Grace, Lady Charlotte." Archie bowed politely to them both, low enough to indicate their rank but also to reflect his friendship with Oliver.

Oliver scowled at his lifelong friend. "If you call me Your Grace in company again, I'll give you the cut direct."

Archie smiled at that, the expression lighting up his rather solemn face.

"Oliver, what are you doing here? I thought you had decided one ball a month was enough? And didn't you already fill your quota with Lady Charlotte's ball?" Archie nodded politely toward Charlotte, who glared back.

"I didn't realise you had attended my birthday," came Lady Charlotte's prompt reply.

"Of course, you wouldn't. I was with your brother in the card room most of the night. Why would I need to circulate the ballroom?" Archie's eyebrows rose with his question, which was a longer response than Oliver had received in years.

"Oh, I don't know. Isn't it good manners to greet the person for whose birthday the function is being held?" Charlotte's eyes were firing, and Oliver noticed with interest that so were Archie's.

How strange.

"I hadn't realised you would care if I greeted you or not, Lady Charlotte," Archie returned politely, but his words had an edge of steel that Oliver had never heard from his friend before.

"I don't," Charlotte snapped back. "I just assumed that, as a gentleman, you would have wanted to wish me a happy birthday. Given you attended my birthday event." She lifted her chin. She was breathing rather quickly too. Did she dislike Archie so much?

Archie's brown eyes were still flickering with lightning, but his face was calm and his voice polite. Oliver had always wanted the type of control Archie had. It was impressive.

"Why would I wish you happy birthday last week when your birthday isn't until tomorrow?"

Archie raised one eyebrow and Oliver could not help chuckling softly. His friend remembered everything. His brilliant memory was one of the many reasons he did so well on the stock market.

Charlotte opened her mouth to reply, but no sound came out. Archie took advantage of the rare silence to continue.

"I assure you that you will receive your customary bouquet of flowers tomorrow, which will only add to the fifty or so that I'm sure already decorate your home." The tone, again, was polite, but Oliver noticed a tightening around Archie's mouth.

Charlotte blushed furiously in acknowledgment of the truth of Archie's words.

"I do not get... I do not expect..." At a loss for words, she stopped.

Oliver smothered his laugh with a cough and covered his mouth in an attempt to hide his smile. He had never seen Charlotte bested by anyone in a conversation. She was trained by her mother, a real dragon of the ton.

"Excuse me." Lady Charlotte bobbed a shallow curtsey and turned on her heel.

Oliver shook his head and turned to his friend. "What was that about? That is the first time I have ever seen Charlotte back down from a fight."

"She probably doesn't think I'm worth fighting with." Archie's eyes followed Charlotte's retreating figure.

What had Oliver just witnessed? If he didn't know better, he would have thought Archie was interested in Charlotte, but that couldn't be.

Could it? Their group of friends didn't think of her like that, having only brotherly feelings toward her.

"John tells me you have shown interest in someone. Is she here?" Archie carefully pitched his voice so that no one else could hear him.

"No, she's not. And I'm not interested in her."

He should have thought before opening his mouth.

Archie chuckled softly.

"Where is she, then?" Archie asked.

"Not here, that is for certain. Let's join John for a brandy in the card room. I'm in the mood for a night at the cards."

They retreated to the card room. Oliver didn't stop at one drink. He gambled too much and drank more than he had in years. His plans for meeting the demimondaines and staying out until the early hours of the morning were forgotten in the endless glasses of hard liquor.

John poured him into his carriage and it was the last thing Oliver remembered. He didn't remember getting home, nor his butler getting him into bed. All he remembered the next day was a pounding in his head that beat to the drum of: Where is Sarah?

Chapter Six

"Sarah, the duke's carriage has arrived." Her mother's shrill voice rang through the house.

Sarah resisted the urge to roll her eyes. Her mother was more nervous than she was, if that were possible.

"I'll be down in a moment," Sarah called out, smoothing her dress down her slim waist and noting the roundness of her full breasts, which her opera dress did nothing to disguise.

With a final check in the mirror, she descended the stairs and made her way to the front door.

"Good night, Mama." Sarah kissed her mother on the cheek, picked up her cloak and stepped outside their rented townhouse.

A coachman opened the carriage door for her, and she took a moment to admire the ducal crest before stepping inside.

"Good evening to you, Miss Collins." John nodded, as the carriage didn't allow him to stand and make his bow.

She slid into the seat next to her new friend, Charlotte.

"Good evening, Lord John, Charlotte." Sarah breathed deeply. Almost unable to get past the anxiety in her stomach, she grabbed her friend's hands.

"Oh, Charlotte, what if I do something wrong? What am I meant to do at the opera? I have never been and I'm so nervous. Please tell me everything."

Charlotte and John both laughed, making Sarah stop and bite her lip.

"You don't have to do anything other than be yourself. Walk in, watch the opera and go home again." Charlotte smiled confidently, and Sarah's stomach dropped nervously.

"But will I have to talk to anyone? Will people be able to see me?"

This time, only John laughed, but Charlotte smiled.

"Of course, people can see you. That is half the fun of the opera. Being able to see what everyone else is wearing and doing, but not having to talk to them."

"Oh."

"Is anyone else going to be there tonight, whom I know?" Sarah asked quietly, dropping her eyes so her new friends would not see the emotion in them.

"None of whom I am aware."

"Oh, that is good," Sarah said, putting on her sunniest smile.

John and Charlotte shared a glance but didn't say anything more, so Sarah rode the rest of the way happily, listening to the idle chatter and hoping that she would be noticed by her husband-to-be, whoever he may be.

. . .

WHEN THEY ARRIVED, they were personally escorted to their box by a footman and Sarah's heart fluttered in her ribcage the whole way. She had never seen anything so grand or beautiful. The velvet curtains, the view of the stage... Oh, that she had lived to see this day.

"Oh, my goodness," she cried, and rushed toward the edge of the box to take in the view.

John chuckled softly beside her.

"You shouldn't get so close to the edge, Miss Collins," he teased, putting one hand on her wrist and the other on her waist to draw her back to the safety of the first row of seats.

"Please, call me Sarah. I prefer it over Miss Collins," she told John, complimented by his attention. But she was safe in the knowledge that he wasn't pursuing her in any way.

John's hand on her waist fell away, but he held onto her hand and raised it to his lips.

"I would be delighted, Sarah." He bent at the waist and chastely kissed her gloved knuckles, making her smile.

What a lovely gentleman.

A strangled sound in the entrance of the opera box had them both turning.

Oliver stood at the entrance with a look on his face that made Sarah cower. He seemed furious. John held tightly onto her fingers when she tried to withdraw them. He drew her hand onto his arm.

"Good evening, Oliver, have you come to join our small party?" John was apparently ignoring Oliver's scowl and the tightening of his fists, but she certainly couldn't.

Sarah dug her fingers into John's arm as the flutters of panic rose inside her. He stroked her fingers reassuringly.

Oliver looked ready to murder someone. She wasn't sure why, but she knew that look was focused on John and her. He couldn't be jealous, could he?

When he didn't reply, Sarah gathered her courage and slipped her hand from John's arm and dropped into her lowest curtsey.

"Your Grace," she said, coming up so slowly that Oliver had time to walk over to her and impatiently tap his black leather boot against the carpet, before her eyes came up to his.

"You look well, considering you have been ill for a week."

Charlotte gasped, and Sarah's eyebrows rose.

Oliver continued to glower. "I apologise, Miss Collins, for my rudeness. I was just shocked to see you looking so healthy."

Sarah closed her gaping mouth and nodded slowly. Was she supposed to say something to that?

Oliver ground his teeth together. "Well?"

"Well?" she repeated, with a slight twitch in the corner of her mouth.

"Well, how are you here, looking so healthy?"

Oliver's eyes widened as though he were surprised by his own rudeness, then a muscle in his jaw jumped, indicating he was clenching his teeth again.

"I wasn't sick, Your Grace," Sarah whispered in a conspiratorial tone.

"No?" he whispered back, his face softening.

"No, I was just having a week away from the circuit. I can see why you and your counterparts rarely attend balls. They are just exhausting." Sarah let out an exaggerated sigh, and John chuckled.

"Well, it seems that the rest did you good. You are glowing tonight," said Oliver.

Sarah frowned. What was he doing now? He'd come into the box like a thundercloud, she'd chided him out of his bad mood, and now he was complimenting her?

The man appeared to be as changeable in moods as her capricious Aunt Eustacia. Her aunt was a character of extremes, and Sarah sincerely hoped that this would not be the case with Oliver, as this would make him less than pleasant company in the long term.

"Shall we sit down, Lord John? I believe the opera is about to start, and I would not want to miss any of it."

John smirked and held out his arm again.

"Shall we see you at the interval, Oliver?" John asked with a raised eyebrow.

"If you do not mind, I might stay here. My mother tends to snore through the second half."

A shiver danced along Sarah's spine. How could she relax with Oliver here in the box with them?

. . .

INTERMISSION ARRIVED and Lord John and Charlotte both made excuses to leave the box. Sarah watched Oliver carefully when they asked if she'd like to join them. He didn't move. So, right or wrong, she chose to stay.

She was a little surprised that her friends left them alone, unchaperoned, but it was an open box, people could clearly see them, and the lights were on.

The minute they were alone, Oliver moved into the empty seat beside her.

"So, tell me the real reason you stayed at home for the past week."

"Your Grace, I do not believe that topic is in the realm of polite conversation. Shall we discuss the opera or would you like to talk about the weather?" Sarah asked, with a deliberately false flutter of her eyelashes.

Sarah knew Oliver was a duke, but he was acting like one of her five-year-old cousins. He had the nerve to question her when she was the one who was owed an apology? Well, she wasn't standing for it.

Oliver's eyes narrowed at her tone.

"It's Oliver, do not 'Your Grace' me. I don't like it."

"Oh, are you sure you want to admit to the title?" A hint of anger crept into her voice, and she didn't care. Her belly tightened, and her hands clenched in her lap.

His face fell. "I should have told you when we first met. I'm sorry."

Her shoulders slumped, and the tightness receded. He seemed genuine, and it tugged at her heart.

"Why didn't you?"

"Because I only came into the title a year ago and I don't feel like a duke. It's not right. I'm not a duke. I'm a second son."

His words were soft, but she could feel the pain behind them. During her week away from the ton her mother had gossiped with the servants, who had told her of Oliver's recent rise to the position of duke.

"I'm sorry about your brother, Oliver, and your father too. How horrible for you." She placed her hand in his, the warmth of his skin passing through their gloves.

"Thank you," Oliver choked out.

"It must have been horrible to lose both of them in the same day," Sarah whispered again, looking into his eyes for the first time that evening and seeing the sorrow in the beautiful brown depths.

Oliver nodded slowly.

"My twenty-fifth birthday."

Sarah gasped and automatically lifted her arms to embrace him. What a terrible thing to have happened. Sorrow filled her heart.

She stopped herself before she touched him, noting the interested looks they were receiving from surrounding boxes.

"Come with me," she whispered, moving into the darkest corner of the booth. It was concealed from everyone and would allow her time to do what she wanted.

Oliver stood up, moving slowly up to her, a confused frown on his face.

Sarah waited until he was within the fold of darkness, then reached around his broad shoulders to embrace him.

She soon began to regret her instinctive action as Oliver held himself stiff. He needed comfort and this was how she was used to giving it. It was either too late in his life to learn how to be held, or too late in his grieving to be consoled.

Sarah pulled back and instead reached her hands up and placed them on either side of his jaw. Lifting his face to hers she whispered, "I am so sorry for your loss," and brought her lips down onto his.

As Oliver shivered beneath her touch, she knew she'd chosen the right way to let him know how she felt.

His lips were warm and soft, and she held there as long as she could. Pulling away reluctantly, she looked back into his eyes and saw a change. Something smoky and dangerous was emerging through the pain, and heat curled in her belly.

Oliver stood and pressed her up against the wall. The feeling was delicious. Her breasts pressed against his chest and her hips cradled him. Then he swooped and devoured her.

There was no other way of describing the kiss. He pressed his lips to hers in desperation, seeking not only reassurance, but a physical response. Having no resistance left, she gave everything to him.

She wrapped her arms around his neck and pressed her body closer to his until she heard him groan. His lips were coaxing and warm, and she soon felt his tongue licking her bottom lip. She pulled back, puzzled.

"Let me in," he whispered, using his right thumb to push her bottom lip softly apart from her top.

Before she could comprehend what he meant, Oliver swooped again, this time dipping his tongue into her mouth.

Sarah gasped at this intrusion, and he withdrew. She was soon drowning in his lips once again, and when she felt his tongue probing for entrance, she let him in.

Oliver abruptly pulled away from her after several moments' connection and took a step back.

"I'm sorry, I shouldn't have done that," he said, twitching at his breeches with his hand in a rather unusual way.

"Don't be sorry, I enjoyed it," Sarah admitted. "I'm sorry, I shouldn't have said that."

"No, you shouldn't have, because it makes me want to kiss you again." Oliver grinned, his eyes smouldering. "But that would be unwise. If we were caught..." He let his voice trail off.

Sarah nodded and her eyes drifted back to the stage.

"It looks like we have a few moments still. I wonder where the Dunfords are?" she mused, breathing slowly to try to bring her heart rate back to a reasonable pace.

"You mean Charlotte and Lord John?" Oliver asked a little tersely.

She smiled at him. He sounded jealous.

"It's funny, isn't it? I never expected to meet a duke's daughter, let alone be invited to attend the opera with one."

"Lady Charlotte is slightly unconventional for her class."

The pain hit her across the chest like a blow to her ribcage. "So, you don't approve of her associating with me either."

"Of course I do, and what do you mean 'either'?" Oliver asked sharply.

Sarah shrugged. She shouldn't be sharing her parents' opinions with him. However, she quite wanted to.

"My mother could not believe Lady Charlotte and I would have anything in common to speak about. She didn't think I would attract the attention of anyone of her station."

"And me?" he asked, his voice rising with an emotion she couldn't quite identify.

"What about you, Your Grace?" Sarah dropped her eyes, suddenly unable to look at him.

"Oliver," he growled. She looked up again and the heated look he was giving her sent another bolt of warmth to the spot between her legs.

"What about you, Oliver?" Sarah asked the question with the same bravery it took to step off a cliff. She hadn't a clue where she was going to land.

"What would your parents think about your association with me?" he repeated.

"They don't know. I thought I had been rescued the other night by a duke's brother. I haven't told them that he turned out to be the duke himself. I think my mother would have apoplexy."

"Why would she care?"

"She would worry that you would ruin my chances of a good marriage by telling people what happened. She's suspicious of the aristocracy. My father is the youngest son of the late Viscount Crimsbury, but my mother has never had much to do with his family. They never condescended to visit us, and my father, the Reverend James Collins, is so committed to his church that we rarely leave the area."

Oliver's face paled, then a moment later reddened, in complete contrast.

"Oh, my Lord, what am I doing?" He looked up at the ceiling and held his arms out wide.

"What do you mean, Oliver?" Sarah asked, failing to understand why he appeared to be in complete turmoil all of a sudden.

What had happened now?

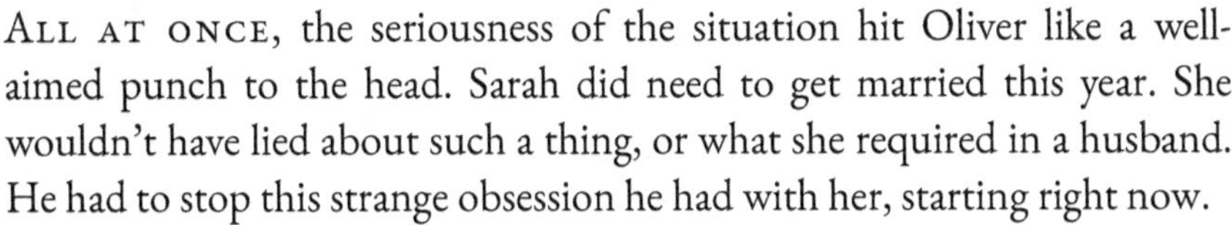

ALL AT ONCE, the seriousness of the situation hit Oliver like a well-aimed punch to the head. Sarah did need to get married this year. She wouldn't have lied about such a thing, or what she required in a husband. He had to stop this strange obsession he had with her, starting right now.

For her sake, not for his.

He opened his mouth to explain this newfound realization when John and Charlotte burst back into the box in a shower of laughter.

"Did we miss anything interesting?" Lady Charlotte asked, with an amused twinkle in her eye.

Sarah blushed faintly at the insinuation but answered readily enough.

"Not at all. Dull conversation. The weather, the opera..." There was a mischievous glint in her eye when she looked his way and despite his best intentions, he smiled back.

"Most definitely. Very dull. How was your intermission?" he asked benignly, but inside he was grinning like a loon.

The rest of the opera passed smoothly, and Oliver didn't attempt to interfere when John and Charlotte whisked Sarah home.

He had come to a tough conclusion tonight. He could not marry her, and therefore, had to stay away from her. It didn't matter that he craved her touch and her company. She deserved more than what he could offer someone of her standing.

Although there was nothing wrong with her bloodline and her gentility, despite what she believed, they were just not quality enough to be a duchess.

He had been told since birth that he was neither needed nor wanted by his parents or family. They had their heir to a dukedom. Sarah would never survive in that world of hateful alliances and looming responsibility.

He despised it and he couldn't throw her into that world after growing up the way she had. If leaving her alone was the only way to protect her, then that is what he would do.

Chapter Seven

The following week, Oliver found himself at yet another ball, this one hosted by Rupert's mother. He stood with the hostess's son, another of his oldest friends and a spare son of the aristocracy.

He'd seen Sarah dancing but had tried his best not to care. He had a night of carousing ahead of him. As soon as Rupert had done his duty to his family, they could take their leave and pursue other, more masculine activities.

Out of the corner of his eye, Oliver saw a gentleman moving to Sarah's side. He recognized Millington's large frame and wavy blond hair at once.

That cad again. Without a word to Rupert, he strode toward Sarah.

The terror in her eyes when she saw Millington made his hands clench into fists, and the way she clasped her fan and reticule in front of her body, as though such flimsy items could shield her from the man who had abused her, made his blood boil.

Oliver's heart was hammering in his chest as he bowed in a perfunctory manner to the other gentleman. Beside him, Millington invited Sarah to dance. Thinking of nothing except protecting her, Oliver moved to her side and held out his hand.

"Miss Collins has promised the next to me, Millington."

"Y...y...yes," Sarah stammered, placing her hand quickly in his. "Please excuse me, my lord."

She bobbed a quick curtsey to Millington without letting go of Oliver's hand, and moved with him to the dance floor.

Oliver swept her into the waltz with grace and poise. He may not have liked dancing very much, but he certainly knew how to do it.

"Oh, thank you, Oliver. I didn't know how I was going to escape him." Sarah's relief at being in his arms was evident by the way she was gripping him.

"I'll talk to him."

Alarm spread across Sarah's face.

"Please, no. I don't want any trouble for you."

Oliver chuckled softly, his heart melting even more for this woman. Was she worried about him?

"I'll be discreet," he promised, enjoying the feel of her hand in his far too much.

"Thank you." The look of adoration, so bright in her eyes, made him swallow and grip her more tightly.

When the music stopped, Oliver didn't want to leave her. He put his hand around her waist and steered her toward the music room. Two elderly ladies sat on chairs, chaperoning any couple wanting to be alone.

"I love our music room at home. I'm always there with my sister," Sarah said, walking slowly around the room, admiring the different instruments on display.

"Is your family very musical?"

Another odd thing about his feelings for Sarah—he was interested in what she had to say. He could not say that about any other female, except maybe Charlotte. And that was because she made him laugh.

"Oh, very. My mother plays the piano for the church choir and my sister and I both play the piano, flute, and harp."

"That is impressive," he said.

He imagined how good she would look playing the harp, the large piece of curved wood cradled between her thighs. Biting back a curse, he turned toward the wall, hoping she wouldn't notice how his body had responded to that intriguing idea. Form-fitting breeches were not made for being with a female one desired.

Sarah laughed, the sound healthy and vigorous.

"I didn't say we played well," she joked, making Oliver smile again. "I hope I can teach my children to love music as much as I do." She looked distracted as she absently ran her fingers over a child-sized violin.

Oliver stopped short. Ladies were not meant to mention children, even when they had them. Hearing Sarah speak of her future children so casually sent up so many red flags as to make his mind look festive.

"You want children?" Oliver choked out. Not many of his friends actually wanted children. An heir, yes, but that wasn't the same thing.

"Of course. Who doesn't?" Sarah answered with a smile.

They had reached the piano now, and Oliver's cravat felt as if it was tied too tightly around his neck. He cleared his throat and leaned against the nearest instrument.

"Will you play, Sarah?" He gestured toward the pianoforte, not even sure why he had asked, but desperate to change the subject.

"Of course." Sarah moved over to the piano stool, sat down and began tinkling on the keys.

She looked up and gave Oliver the most blinding smile yet, and he took a step toward her, his breath hitching. He couldn't be feeling this strongly now, for this woman. It was painful.

A small group entered the room.

"Lincoln." One of the gentlemen greeted him with a nod.

"Miss Collins was just about to play us a tune," Oliver announced, throwing her in the deep end to see if she could handle this small group.

Sarah blushed, but kept her head high.

"Anything particular you would like to hear?" she asked brightly, glaring at Oliver behind the others' backs.

Someone named a complicated piece, and Oliver waited to see her reaction. She only smiled and turned to the relevant page.

The next ten minutes was torture. Sarah played and sang like an angel. She had a naturally sweet singing voice and she could play very well. The level of technical skill required for the piece astounded Oliver. Whoever had suggested it had been testing Sarah's ability.

In a blinding flash, Oliver saw his life ahead of him if he married Sarah. She would be a wonderful wife. She would entertain in their home. Play for their guests, love their children.

Oliver swallowed the uncomfortable lump in his throat. She would be a horrible duchess. What duchess actually spoke to her children? Sarah didn't know a thing about society. She was awkward and shy. She was a vicar's daughter, for God's sake—she would never survive in his world. He left the room with a lame excuse and a bow.

Before he called for his carriage, he managed to coax Patrick Millington into the study, alone.

"Millington, I know what happened at Lady Charlotte's ball." He opened with the bald statement, not willing to beat around the proverbial bush.

Millington's handsome face coloured unhealthily.

"We went for a walk in the garden. She misunderstood my intentions, and attacked me," he blustered.

"*She* attacked *you*?" Oliver willed his clenched fists to relax. "Is that why her dress was ripped, and her back was bleeding?" he asked through his teeth.

Oliver's temper was slipping free of his control. He never lost his temper, never. But the memories of that night were coming in hard and fast, and he was wondering who would miss Patrick Millington if he never returned home. Oliver had enough money; he could make sure the vile man stayed gone.

Millington could obviously see the internal battle Oliver was waging. Oliver watched him mentally cataloguing his answers before he opened his mouth.

"As I said, she misunderstood my intentions," he said slowly, gauging Oliver's reaction.

He smiled grimly.

"We both know that's not what happened. Perhaps it would be wise for you to leave Miss Collins alone." Oliver gave Millington a stare imbued with all the power the Lincoln name had behind it.

Millington's eyes flashed rebelliously, and he opened his mouth to say something obstinate.

Instead of waiting for him to speak, Oliver ploughed his fist into Millington's stomach with as much force as he could muster at short range.

Patrick Millington gasped like a landed fish and fell backward onto his arse, clutching his belly.

"Leave her alone, or I will ruin you." Pleasure radiated through Oliver's body as he glared down at the man who would have raped Sarah. Millington lay on the floor, gasping for air.

With one more ducal glance at his fallen nemesis, he let himself out of the study, and out of Sarah's life.

~

OLIVER MANAGED to avoid all ton events for the next fortnight. He visited his club every day and met his friends at night. He did everything possible to make it appear as though nothing was wrong.

He had no interest in any of the high-priced brothels he had frequented in the past, and even less in finding a permanent mistress. Both situations repulsed him, and he was ignoring the reason why.

He was sitting at his club with a drink in hand when Rupert walked in.

"Lyre!" his old friend greeted him, blue eyes bright and shrewd, glowing beneath almost black brows.

Oliver smiled up at his friend, letting his usual facade of indifference wash away. He loved that Rupert never greeted him with his new title.

"Rupert, how are you doing this uninteresting Wednesday?" Oliver pushed out a chair in clear invitation.

Rupert grinned and called over a footman to order a port.

"I have been catching up on the latest gossip. It looks as though another of our school friends is doing the pretty. We can't keep our heads out of that noose it seems." Rupert shook his head in resignation of the fate that awaited them all.

Rupert, although also a second son, had been made his brother's heir. He'd have to marry and produce an heir of his own, but he was putting off the task as long as possible, instead bedding every married woman in sight.

"Oh, who?" Oliver asked, interested for once.

"Jamie McTavish, and he's set to marry one of our ladies."

Oliver sat up and moved forward in his chair. This was news, indeed.

"You jest, man? He's lowered himself to marry an Englishwoman? I'm shocked."

The footman set down a crystal decanter and Oliver poured a glass of port for himself and for Rupert.

Jamie McTavish was a good man, Scottish by blood and birth. His parents had sent him to London for schooling and the boys had teased him mercilessly for his accent. The Scot had put his fist through a few English faces and the teasing had stopped. He had a hot temper, but he loved his land and his family. Oliver admired him.

"He has a bit of a fortune too, from what I understand. So, who has he found? He didn't stoop to finding an heiress, I hope." That would definitely not fit with the picture he had of Jamie.

"No, he's about to offer for a lady of good, but lowborn family and no money," Rupert confided in hushed tones.

"Good on him, although I'm sure she makes up for it in beauty. Do you know her name?" Oliver asked the question, although it would be unlikely he knew the young lady.

"A Miss Sarah Collins." Rupert announced as Oliver was taking a sip of his port.

Oliver choked and spluttered his drink across the polished wood of the table. Air wasn't getting into his lungs properly. A moment of panic assailed him as he wheezed and slammed his hands down.

"Are you all right, man?" Rupert helpfully bashed Oliver on the back with his large fist, making his lungs seize even more.

It took several minutes for Oliver to recover his breath, and for the footmen to get the table cleaned and reset. He took several long breaths, concentrating on the flow of air into his aching lungs and attempting to calm his still-thundering heart.

"What happened? Are you sure you're all right now?"

"Yes. I'm fine. Sarah Collins, you say?"

"Yes, it seems she's quite a beauty and with more than half a brain as well."

"She has *far* more than half a brain. She has a whole brain." Oliver scowled at his friend.

Rupert's eyes flickered dangerously. "You know her?" he asked, flicking an imaginary piece of lint from his jacket sleeve in an obvious attempt to defuse the situation.

"Yes, I know her," Oliver snapped, unable to hold in the torrent of emotion pouring from him.

His heart was galloping in his chest and a hot sweat had broken out on his forehead. He took a long drink of his port—this time more carefully— and embraced the burn that slid down his throat, draining the glass before he could speak again, gasping against the alcohol's effect on his mouth.

How had she found someone so quickly? It had only been two weeks.

"I met Sarah Collins a month ago at Lady Charlotte's birthday ball. She was attacked by that animal, Millington, in the gardens. I found her and helped her to get home unnoticed." Oliver confided in his friend, his gaze darting around the room quickly to make sure no one nearby heard him.

"Are you serious? I hadn't heard anything about that." Rupert whistled low and his eyes widened.

"No, we kept it quiet for obvious reasons. She needs to marry this year."

"Well, she's found her husband, it seems. McTavish is working out a settlement before he talks to her father. Sounds like he'll have to travel to Somerset, though. The father never leaves."

"Yes, she told me," Oliver said absentmindedly.

So, the beautiful little vicar's daughter had found a decent husband all on her own. She could not have chosen better and pride fluttered in his chest.

Jamie had a small but profitable estate and enough money to look after her brother and sister if he so chose. He was also not even thirty and a nice man. Yes, she'd done well indeed. His stomach knotted at the thought, but he tried his best to ignore it.

Chapter Eight

"How well do you know her?" Rupert twirled his glass between his fingers and stared into the golden liquid as though it contained the secrets of life.

"Well enough to know she'll be a wonderful wife," Oliver admitted quietly. He couldn't say that about any other lady of his acquaintance.

"She won't care about being buried in Scotland for the rest of her life?" Rupert asked.

Oliver shook his head. No, she would not. She would be happy as long as her family was set up. She would watch over McTavish's tenants, give him children, share his bed.

A sudden vision of the big Scot covering Sarah's small but lush body with his own flashed before Oliver's eyes and he saw red. He clenched his teeth and let out a small groan as jealousy ripped through him. Before he could control his wayward emotions, the fragile crystal of the port glass shattered in his hand.

Gasping as pain sliced through his palm, he jumped up and away from the fragments of glass that splintered across the table. Rupert jumped up and they both looked down at the blood dripping from his hand.

Rupert whipped out his handkerchief and pressed it into Oliver's palm. Pain throbbed right up his arm.

Oliver's brain wasn't turning over; he couldn't drag his eyes away from the blood-soaked linen. All he could think about was Jamie and Sarah. He couldn't breathe properly.

"You are having no luck with your alcohol today," Rupert joked. "I think that may need a few stitches."

He motioned to the butler and in a few concise statements, Oliver's drinks were put on Rupert's account, and then he was being assisted into his carriage, on his way home, to be met there by the surgeon.

Oliver sat in his bedroom in his family's townhouse, alcohol dulling his senses as the surgeon stitched up his hand.

He marvelled over his response to Sarah's upcoming betrothal. He hadn't gone a day without thinking of her or a night without dreaming about her since the moment they'd met. But did that mean he had the right to interfere in her life, when he could never give her what she wanted?

When he awoke the next morning, he was in a hot sweat, amidst a nightmare. He'd dreamed of Sarah in her new life, happy and content, while he grew old and bitter with some faceless duchess by his side.

He had to do something.

~

SARAH STOOD at the entrance to the ballroom, waiting for her mother who was still handing her coat over to a footman. Tonight, she expected a proposal of marriage from Jamie McTavish, and after only two weeks of courting!

She should be elated, blissfully happy about the turn of events. After all, she had succeeded in finding a man who would not only look after her family but would hopefully be a good and kind husband to her as well.

Then why was she not waltzing around the room with happiness? She turned her face toward the wall and grimaced. She knew why. Because she missed Oliver. There was something missing in her interactions with Jamie. There wasn't any spark or excitement the way there was when she was with Oliver.

Her mother finally joined her and they were announced as they stepped into the large, opulent room. There was a quadrille in progress and the hum of conversation already surrounded the well-heated room.

"Good evening, Miss Collins."

Sarah turned to smile at the Scottish devil himself, who bowed low to her. She held her hand out to him.

"Please, call me Sarah. I told you that last night," she reminded him with a smile.

"True," he conceded with a grin.

Sarah looked into his kind blue eyes and knew that this man would be a good husband. He was handsome in an unusual way and looked as strong as an ox. She had no reason at all to deny him if he offered for her.

"But I was hoping to wait to use it at a special moment..." He let his voice trail off and her stomach lurched. "If that would be all right?"

Sarah was lightheaded all of a sudden, black spots swimming before her eyes.

"Of course," she forced out, breathless although she wasn't moving.

"You look a little pale, my dear. Would you like to sit down?"

Yes, I would love to. But first she needed a moment to compose herself.

"Thank you, Mr. McTavish, as usual you are so thoughtful. But perhaps you will excuse me as I need to find the ladies' retiring room." She smiled politely.

He seemed to like her smile and her mother had instructed her to use it as much as possible.

"Of course." He bowed again.

Sarah moved along the plush carpet of the hallway. How was she going to get through tonight feeling this unwell?

Someone came up behind her, so close she could feel the heat of the person's body. She moved to the left so the person could go around her, but instead a firm hand grabbed her under the elbow and she was steered into a room off the corridor.

What was this?

Sarah gulped and took a fast breath as panic rose in her chest.

The door closed behind her and she swung around to see if her abductor was the man of her nightmares, or her dreams.

"Oliver!" Sarah said, her hand fluttering at her throat. He had obviously startled her.

"I've heard that Jamie McTavish has been courting you."

He was unable to hold in his feelings any longer. He knew he should have opened the conversation with small talk or at least a greeting, but as usual he could not remain aloof when he was within touching distance of Sarah.

She blushed but didn't look away, her mouth thinning as though she was unhappy. The air around them crackled with tension and Oliver swallowed hard.

"He has."

Oliver waited for her to continue but she didn't. That was it?

"I have also heard you have entranced him so thoroughly that he is on the verge of offering you everything you want."

He sounded like a jealous idiot, but he couldn't stop the flow of venomous words falling from his mouth. He had seen her standing with the Scottish laird and had been blinded to anything except the need to pull her into him, behind him, anywhere she would be safe from all other men.

Sarah's eyes narrowed. "And pray tell, how did you come by that information when you haven't been into society since I last saw you two weeks ago?"

"I go to my gentlemen's club every day. Just because I don't go to balls designed to trap men into marriage, doesn't mean I have disappeared altogether."

Had she really forgotten about him that quickly?

Sarah's shoulders slumped a little and she sighed. "Oliver, why did you drag me in here? What is it you want?"

Oliver pulled her into his arms without another thought and claimed her mouth with his. She was soft and warm beneath him, and his hands trembled as he slid them around her back and pressed her closer. He had barely a taste of her before she was pulling away from him.

"What are you about, Your Grace?" Sarah stiffly pulled out of his arms.

"I'm sorry, I shouldn't have done that." Oliver was already breathing hard. Blood raced through his body, making his heart pound like a drum and his loins ache.

"No, you should not have," she agreed, eyeing him warily. "Oliver, I must go. If we're caught here, without a chaperone..."

She trailed off just as he had at the opera, repeating the same warning. At the time it had seemed sensible, but coming out of her mouth now it sounded like an accusation.

"Yes, I know. You wouldn't want to lose your husband before he's properly caught."

Sarah gasped and there was a sudden silence in the small room that was deafening.

Did I just say that?

"What exactly do you mean by that, Oliver?"

He took a deep breath in through his nose and stared at the blonde angel before him. She made him want to do unspeakable things to her. Starting with ripping that perfect, pale green gown from her delectable body. She couldn't become another man's wife.

"I mean exactly what I said. Getting caught in here with me would destroy your chances of marrying McTavish, and him saving your family. That is all you want, isn't it?" Oliver knew he was being vicious but couldn't control what was coming out of his mouth.

Sarah's breath caught and her eyes sparked with what appeared to be anger.

"I hadn't thought of you as cruel, Oliver. We need to leave this room.

You don't want to marry me. You've told me that fact over and over again. Or are you suggesting that I should have waited for you to propose marriage?"

Panic flooded Oliver and heat flushed his cheeks. "No, I didn't mean..."

"Well, what did you mean?" Sarah demanded, crossing her arms and tapping her foot impatiently against the carpeted floor.

Damn. I should have thought this through.

"I just want to make sure you're marrying the right person," Oliver amended.

"What's wrong with Mr. McTavish?" Sarah demanded, her voice rising in volume a couple of notches.

"Nothing, he's a good man," Oliver admitted, though he was reluctant to give the man praise.

"Then what's the problem, Oliver?"

He tugged at his cravat with his hands, loosening the knot. It was too tight. How was he going to get out of this now?

"I don't want you settling for less than you deserve," Oliver admitted quietly.

"And what is that?" Sarah asked just as quietly.

"Love, or at least passion."

Sarah bit her lip and appeared thoughtful for a moment.

"I don't believe you can fall in love in just two weeks. But passion, yes, I have found that."

Pure rage filled Oliver, clawing, hot, terrible anger. Red clouded his vision as sweat droplets popped out on his upper lip.

"Passion? You've found passion with him?" He advanced on Sarah like a predator would his prey. His shoulders ached as he flexed and stretched his muscles.

Sarah nodded and Oliver growled, pulling her into his arms. The need to stake his claim on her was undeniable as his fingers wrapped around her tiny waist.

"Like the passion you have found with me?" He ducked his head and ran his lips down her smooth throat.

Sarah gasped but leaned into him. "That's not fair to say such things to me. To do such things. You don't want to marry me."

Oliver groaned against her sweet, smooth skin. "I would if I could." He pressed his lips to the spot beneath her ear and inhaled the scent of rose petals.

"I beg your pardon?" Sarah shrieked, pushing hard against his chest.

His arms held tightly around her.

"Sarah, you have no idea how much I want you," Oliver admitted, rolling his hips against her which caused his prick to harden and throb.

"You want to seduce me. You don't wish to marry me." Sarah attempted to pull away again, struggling harder, but Oliver held her tighter.

He had to make her understand.

"I would never seduce you. I would marry you in a heartbeat if I wasn't a duke."

Sarah laughed again, with so much bitterness and anger that when she tried to pull away, he had to let her go.

"What do you call this, then?" She motioned angrily to their surroundings with flicking hands. "Is this the part where you offer to make me your mistress instead? Or do you already have one, like most men of rank do?"

The jealousy in her tone and disgust at the subject was obvious in her features.

"I would never insult you with such an offer."

Sarah's eyebrows rose high in silent question.

"And, no, I don't have one." He couldn't believe she'd asked him such a question.

"Well, my lord. I'm sorry, Your Grace, from what I have learned in the past few weeks, it would be very unusual for you not to have one, and it is insulting in the extreme for you to say that you would marry me if you could."

"I'm not lying, I have never had a permanent mistress, but I am aware that most men do. And I was speaking the truth, I would marry you in an instant if I had met you two years ago."

She had to believe him. He was telling the truth.

"What's different now?"

"Everything. I'm not who I once was, and everything I was never meant to be." Oliver turned away from her.

Memories bombarded him, ice sliding over his spine and skin.

"My father once told me that I was born because society expected him to have a second son, but he had no real reason to need one. He had actually wished for a daughter the night I was born. In ten generations the dukedom has always passed from first son to first son. I am the only second son to inherit in my family, and my mother has told me all my life that I wasn't needed... nor really wanted."

"Oh, Oliver." Sarah reached out her hand and touched his shoulder, the effect like throwing a small stone into a still pond. The ripples cascaded out in increasingly large waves.

With a frustrated roar, Oliver grabbed and spun her, pinning her up against the wall. His hands landed on either side of her and he stared down into the liquid violet eyes that haunted his dreams.

"You will never know how much I burn for you. Only you."

"Show me," she whispered, placing her small hands against his chest.

Oliver moaned and swooped down for a kiss, plundering her warm mouth with his tongue, all restraint gone. His hands curved around her slight body and he moved to her breasts, kneading and stroking the soft, abundant flesh through the silk of her dress.

She was like liquid heat in his arms, pressing against him and making soft, mewling noises that made his blood boil. He slid his other hand down to her rounded bottom and pulled her snugly into him. She fit so perfectly that he couldn't help imagining how easily she'd take him into her body.

Sarah threw her arms around his neck and Oliver groaned against her lips.

He pulled back and stared down at her. He had to get closer. Lifting his arms, he reached for the ribbons on her dress. He unfastened her bodice and soon he had a plump breast free. It was creamy in the candlelight, the erect little nipple a beautiful dusky pink.

"Oliver, you shouldn't... are you sure..."

Oliver chuckled happily in his throat. She was enjoying this, he could tell. He dipped his head and licked her tight pink nipple, which caused her to gasp and arch her back for him.

Oh, yes. You beautiful girl.

He bent her over his arm and sucked the hard tip of her breast deeply into his mouth, tasting the sweetness of her skin.

Sarah shrieked and Oliver glanced up to see her flushed face contorted in pleasure.

He told her gently, "Ssh," before resuming his pleasuring of her breast.

She tasted like heaven itself. Sweet, pure and perfect. How would her very centre taste?

He was reaching down to pull up her skirt when a loud voice said, "I think I saw them come through here."

The door swung open and light filled the small dark room. Oliver turned toward the doorway and squared his shoulders, blocking Sarah's body from view.

"What the bloody hell is going on here?"

He knew that Scottish accent.

Damn.

Chapter Nine

Oliver blinked a few times and stared at the entrance to the room. Once his eyes had adjusted to the light he saw his friend John Dunford, the Scottish gentleman who wanted to marry the woman in his arms, and his sister-in-law. Lady Honoria Lyre, the Countess of Sombury, the widow of his brother and the woman who believed herself the rightful Duchess of Lincoln.

"Oliver. How could you?" gasped Honoria, though the shock in her voice was clearly put on.

"If you would allow us a minute, we will be out momentarily."

He strode forward and soundly slammed the door, cursing in three different languages. If it had only been John and his sister-in-law, they could have brazened it out, but now there was no other way. Marriage or ruin for Sarah. Oliver only hoped McTavish wouldn't call him out for this.

He pivoted on the ball of his foot to find Sarah frantically doing up her bodice with trembling hands.

"They saw... he saw... oh my..." She was babbling as she sank into a chair, her shoulders slumping in defeat. "What am I going to do?"

"You will marry me." He was unable and unwilling to see any other solution.

"Oliver, I can't marry you. We just finished discussing it before... before..." She was clearly struggling to hold herself together.

"Sarah, I respect you, I desire you, I am a duke, yes, but you are from a good family." He heard himself trying to convince her and wondered when he had changed his mind.

"But I have had no training in this. How would I even know how to be a duchess?" She was trembling now.

Good question, I have no idea. Perhaps...

"You will ask my mother, or even Lady Charlotte," he answered with a smile as the solution occurred to him. Charlotte—she had been born to it. She would help.

This seemed to give Sarah pause. She got on well with his friend and if anyone could and would help her, it would be Lady Charlotte Dunford.

"But, Oliver, I'm not sure if I could be a wife who would look the other way when you go to other women, or not care that you never came home. And I want children, lots of children..."

Oliver took a steadying breath. It was understandable that she had fears, but it still rankled his pride. He would be a good husband, unlike his father before him. He never wanted to see Sarah go through the pain he'd seen on his own mother's face in the early years of his life.

"I will be faithful, Sarah. I have never wanted a woman as I want you. I don't think that will ever change."

Sarah bit her lip and then looked up at him again. "Children?"

He had to produce an heir, but that wasn't what she was asking. She wanted to know if he wanted children. Oliver could imagine that any child of Sarah's would be loved and cherished in a way that he never had been. That knowledge made the idea of progeny much more palatable. The mental picture of Sarah large with his child made him smile.

"I want children, Sarah, as many as you want. As many as you can give me." He smiled at the thought. He would enjoy giving them to her, that was certain.

"But I don't have any connections and I have no dowry…"

Oliver laughed, bubbles of happiness filling his belly. He had never thought of how his proposal of marriage would go, but he'd never have dreamed that he'd have to talk the lady into it.

"Sarah, I don't need a dowry and I don't need you to have any connections. I just want *you*." As soon as the words were out, he realised how true they were.

He already had too much money, why did he need to marry a woman with more?

Sarah stilled and appeared to be thinking over his words as she chewed on her lush bottom lip.

Her face cleared and she stood up, smiling at him as she moved toward him. "Then we will marry."

He held out his hands to her and watched as her eyes widened.

"Oh, I forgot to ask about Beatrix and John," Sarah cried, horrified hands flying up to cover her mouth.

Oliver grinned. He loved the fact she had discussed their marriage as though it was only the two of them, without any thought to the siblings that she obviously loved, and the main reasons her parents had paid for her to attend a London Season. To land a rich husband.

He could afford to give her family anything they wanted, not just education and a season or two. Perhaps he would permanently lease her family a home in London as a wedding present.

"Your siblings can have whatever you want, Sarah. Your brother can attend Eton, your sister can have whatever dowry you think would be suitable. You may have anything you want." Oliver stared at the woman opposite him and, ignoring the fact they had people waiting for them on the other side of the door, swept her into his arms.

Sarah would be a good wife to him and a great mother to their children. She would inspire him to be a better person, and he swore to himself that he would be the best husband to her that he could be.

"Just a season for Beatrix please, Oliver. I don't want you thinking that I would ask so much from you." Sarah averted her eyes in the most adorable way.

Oliver bent his head, taking his fiancée's mouth in a deep and fiery kiss that he felt all the way to his belly.

Just as they were breaking apart, the door swung open, lighting up the dark corners of their intimate little cubby.

"What is this I hear?"

Oliver flinched and turned very slowly. That was a voice he recognized only too well. He should have known his sister-in-law wouldn't have waited patiently for him to emerge. She had run straight for his mother.

"Mother." He pulled Sarah protectively into his side, laying her hand on his arm. "May I present Miss Sarah Collins. Miss Collins has just agreed to marry me."

"You can't marry her!" cried the Dowager Duchess of Lincoln. "You're meant to marry Honoria. She is the only person with the breeding to take my position when I am gone."

Oliver sighed and mentally girded his loins.

"Mother, I will be marrying Sarah. Her father is a vicar and I believe we could persuade him to perform the ceremony within the week."

He'd been caught compromising a virgin and now would pay the ultimate price. Yet, as he waited for the disappointment to register, that his life as a bachelor had ended, that he had failed in his acquisition of a proper duchess, the feelings of loss and anger didn't come.

"The Duke of Lincoln does not get married in such a way. You must not! What will people think?" The dowager gripped her cane and slammed it into the floor. The thump resonated around them and Sarah gripped his hand tighter.

"What did you do?" Oliver's mother hissed at Sarah, turning to glare at the beautiful young woman at his side.

Sarah tried to take a step back, but Oliver held her firmly against him. Now was not the time to show any weakness.

"Sarah did nothing but gain my regard, Mother. We will marry as soon as is feasible." He heard the authority in his tone and felt a moment of pride in standing up to the matriarch of his family.

"Yes, you bloody will," growled a Scottish voice behind his mother.

Oliver bowed deeply to Jamie McTavish, his heart rate picking up. "I owe you an apology, McTavish."

He turned his head and looked down at Sarah's beautiful face. She stared up at him, her eyes warm, her cheeks flushed with heat. He looked back at the gentleman he'd wronged. "It wasn't intentional."

"Yes, I can see that. I will see myself back to the ballroom, I think. My felicitations to you both." McTavish bowed himself out.

Oliver took one look at his mother's pinched, twisted face and decided a retreat was in order.

"We have all had an exciting night, but I believe we should retire. Mother, shall we? Miss Collins, I will call upon you at your residence in the morning." He took a step back and bowed over Sarah's arm, taking her gloved hand in his and pressing a brief kiss to her knuckles.

Sarah smiled shyly and nodded her head in thanks and agreement.

Oliver ushered his mother to their carriage and they sat in silence on the ride home.

As soon as they stepped inside their home, his mother turned on him.

"How dare you propose to that girl! You are meant to marry Honoria, as your father promised her father."

He removed his coat and allowed the footman to take his gloves and hat away.

"Mother, Honoria was promised to my brother. She married him. Father's promise and his honour are intact."

She furrowed her brow and frowned at him with all the weight and displeasure he'd felt as a child. "Honoria was promised that she would be the next Duchess of Lincoln. You must honour that. She is the only one fit to take my place. You must not marry a peasant girl."

Oliver turned toward his mother, holding onto his temper despite the burn in his gut. "Sarah is not a peasant girl." He sighed. "What do you suggest I do with Sarah then, Mother?"

"Pay her off, of course. Set her up in the cheap side of London as your mistress, if you are very fond of the girl."

"Stop, Mother, now. Sarah Collins will be my wife. I will not walk away from her, nor pay her off as though she did something wrong."

"Oliver, you cannot."

"I can. And I will. Goodnight, Mother."

For the first time in his entire life, Oliver turned and walked away. He made his way to the ducal bedchamber and undressed slowly, his hands shaking despite the heat of the room.

He could not let his mother determine his fate. Too much of his control had been taken away already. His freedom, his life as he knew it, was gone. All because of a ridiculous accident.

Sarah would be his, and together they would build a life of their own.

Chapter Ten

"Did you enjoy the wedding, my dear?"

Sarah was deep in her thoughts and jumped in her seat as her new husband spoke into the quiet of the carriage.

"I did. Thank you for letting my father conduct the service." Sarah smiled at Oliver, hoping that the contentment she was feeling showed on her face. She had never been so happy.

"I'm glad you were pleased, Sarah," he murmured, the huskiness in his voice making her belly quiver.

Only six days ago Oliver had proposed marriage, and now here she was, sitting in another ducal carriage, a gold ring on her finger and wearing the most beautiful lace gown she'd ever seen.

"I am excited to see your home."

"It is your home now too, Sarah. We have many properties, country estates, and townhouses. But this is by far my favourite. It's where I have the best childhood memories."

"Then I very much look forward to seeing it."

He gave her a gentle smile and lay his head back against the seat back. "It is six miles travel. I suggest you rest. We have an exciting few weeks ahead, with our honeymoon."

Sarah nodded and tried to do as Oliver suggested, but how could she relax with so many new things running though her mind?

Her belly tightened again, and she laid her hand against the uncomfortable feeling. She was so nervous about what was to happen next that she could barely keep her wedding breakfast down.

Oliver had the right to have her anywhere he wanted.

At any time.

Would he wait until tonight or would he want her sooner?

The glances he had been giving her since she walked into the church that morning had her body heating in embarrassing ways. Her breasts tingled and her thighs ached.

Her mother had sat her down the previous evening for the wedding night talk, and Sarah had taken the opportunity to tell her mother her greatest fear.

"Mother, I am worried that Oliver will go to other women if I do not keep him happy in the... err..." Sarah stumbled over the end of her embarrassing sentence.

"I understand." Her mother patted Sarah's knee. "I believe that the reason most men of rank have mistresses is that their wives do not enjoy their marital duties."

Sarah nodded. The idea made sense to her. Why would a man want to join his wife in her bed if she didn't want him there? She couldn't be sure if she would enjoy Oliver's bed, but if what he was doing to her when they had been interrupted was any indication, she probably would.

"So if I enjoy it, he will stay faithful?"

That seemed too simple an answer, but she was hopeful.

Her mother laughed softly. "This is such a hard conversation to have with one's daughter."

"Can you tell me what to do, Mother? What must I do to keep him faithful to me?"

Again, her mother had laughed, but at least she answered. "All men are different as all women are, but the best and the only advice I can give you is not to be detached."

"What do you mean by that?" Sarah focused on her mother's flushed face, determined not to misinterpret her advice.

"I mean," she began, turning an entirely unhealthy-looking shade of red, "that we aren't meant just to lie down and wait for them to leave once they're done. Everything they do to you, you can also do to them."

"Everything?" Sarah repeated sceptically. That didn't sound right.

"Well, not everything, obviously, but all of the touching that happens before the actual joining you can do to each other."

Sarah thought of the way Oliver had sucked at her breast. Could she do that to him? Of course, she could.

"Thank you, Mother," she had replied and got herself ready to be the best wife Oliver could have.

~

OLIVER PACED outside the adjoining door between their bedrooms. Had he waited long enough? Had she dismissed her maid yet?

The day had been wonderful so far. The wedding, simple and lovely. Her countenance while meeting the staff and over dinner, charming and happy. But what would happen now? Had her mother prepared her?

He huffed out a sigh and faced the door, his heart thumping against his ribs. He couldn't wait any longer. He took the three steps forward and knocked on the door. A faint giggle sounded behind the solid wood.

"Come in, Oliver." The siren call of his wife's voice made his groin ache, and he let out a low groan as he pushed open the door.

He stepped through and smiled as he surveyed the scene before him. His beautiful young wife sat in front of her dressing table. Her long, blonde hair was glistening in the firelight, a gentle smile playing on her happy face.

"What are you laughing at, darling?"

"You knocked." She giggled again.

Oliver didn't see what was funny about that.

"Well, this is your room."

"I know. Couldn't we just have one bedroom? My parents always did," Sarah asked, then blushed.

Oliver could not help staring at her. Did she want to share his bed every night? Even on nights that they couldn't make love?

"Well, let's start with two and see how we go."

It was very uncommon in his society not to have two bedchambers. In the extreme, he knew friends who only visited their wives when they needed to conceive.

Sarah stood and walked toward him. He swallowed hard. He had never seen anyone more beautiful than his wife. Her face was glowing with happiness, and her nightgown clung to her slim body, accentuating both her tiny waist and full breasts.

I'm a fortunate man.

"I want to make love to you, Sarah. Are you ready?"

He wanted her to be completely willing to make love to him, not just feel as though she needed to fulfil her 'duty'.

"Of course, I am. You're my husband, aren't you?" Sarah smiled shyly up at him, and his heart melted even more. This woman wasn't just beautiful, her heart shone like a beacon in the dark.

"Not yet," he answered throatily, barely able to recognize his own voice. She had come to him and was standing before him, brave and beautiful.

"Will you also let me make love to you?"

"What do you mean?" Oliver stared at his wife, unease fluttering in his chest.

Sarah's violet eyes were glowing in the light. Was that an indication of arousal?

"Will you teach me how to please you?" Sarah reached out and lay her hands on his chest, and tingles spread across his heart.

"Touching you and pleasing you will please me." He didn't understand what she was saying.

"Well, let's start with that, then." Sarah reached up and pressed her lips to his, tentatively moving closer to him.

Oliver's heart stuttered in his chest. His beautiful, virginal wife had just openly offered herself to him. He had to make this good for her.

He stepped closer, closing the distance between their two bodies so that her breasts pressed against his chest and her soft belly cradled his pelvis. He kissed Sarah gently, holding tight to the reins of his control as she moaned low in her throat.

One flick of her tongue across his lips and that tenuous control broke. He gathered his wife tightly against him and plundered her warm and willing mouth until his erection became painful, and adrenaline raced through his body.

Oliver pulled away from the kiss and looked down at his beautiful angel. She was glowing brightly tonight. There was no fear, no apprehension in her eyes. Only desire and excitement in her face. He grabbed the hem of her nightdress and pulled it up over her head in one motion.

Sarah lifted her arms for him and gasped as her body was unveiled, but she didn't move to cover her naked breasts when he dropped the silk to the floor.

Oliver stopped and stared, wanting just to enjoy the first time he ever saw Sarah half-naked. Her pearlescent skin was glowing like satin in the candlelight, her dusky pink nipples already erect and pointing towards him, begging for his touch.

"You are so beautiful," Oliver whispered, bringing his right hand up to weigh her full, pert breast in his hand. Plump and delicious, his mouth watered at the sight of them. He stroked the nipple with his thumb, the flesh pebbling tighter beneath his touch and Sarah moaned softly, causing an immediate response in his body. His manhood was hardening and tightening in readiness for their night together.

Oliver swept Sarah up into his arms and placed her in the centre of the bed. His skin itched. He needed to be naked as well. He pulled his linen shirt off in seconds, removed his stockings and his boots, but faltered there. He weighed his options, then nodded, choosing to keep his breeches on to make himself last as long as possible.

Sarah gasped from the bed, and he looked up to see her kneeling in front of him on the mattress.

"You're beautiful too." She brought her hands up tentatively to caress his bare skin and sensations like none he'd ever experienced fluttered through him.

Oliver kissed her softly, his eyes sliding shut as she pressed herself closer. He pulled back and gently maneuvered them so that he lay next to her. He looked into her eyes as her hands floated over his skin like a pair of butterfly wings. Who knew that the touch of a woman's hands could feel so good?

He lay still and closed his eyes to enjoy the sensation. In a world where the only person who ever touched you was your valet, the feel of Sarah's hands on his naked skin was heaven. Oliver was so sensitive to her touch that it was terrifying. He could get far too used to it.

Sarah moved, and wet suction was applied to his nipple as she sucked it into her mouth. Sensations zinged through Oliver at the unexpected movement, and his eyes flew open. He gasped as he looked down and saw her with her mouth to his chest. He pulled away from her, shocked. No woman had ever done that to him.

"Where did you learn that?"

"You showed me last week," she answered, frowning at his expression. "You don't like it?"

Of course, he liked it, but that wasn't the point. He was so shocked by her move that he had considered asking her if she was as virginal as she appeared. But he was glad he hadn't. The hurt look on her face showed such disappointment, he was worried he had put her off her explorations.

"Of course, I do. I just didn't realise you would want to touch me, too."

Sarah smiled a "cat who got the cream" smile and shuffled closer. "Of course, I do. You're my husband."

And with that statement, she pushed him gently, so he lay on his back, and touched his nipples with her fingertips until they tightened into little points. She then leaned over him and sucked on one until he gasped and bucked his hips. That went straight to his groin.

Then she looked up at him and moved back, so she was laying on her side.

"You'll have to show me something else, so I know what else I can do."

Oliver grinned; how could he not? He had envisioned their love-making as being a quiet affair, with her laying back and letting him do as he pleased with her body. He'd heard many a story from his friends, his brother, his father. They'd all told him that whores were much better bed companions. Ladies were cold, tiresome and hated the experience.

He had never had the opportunity to compare before. He would never consort with a marriageable young lady, and the widows didn't appeal to him. So, the whores it had always been for him.

However, it seemed the fates had granted him a much better marriage than those who had come before him.

"Definitely," he growled, rolling over the top of her and swooping down for a hot kiss.

Chapter Eleven

Oliver broke away to run his lips and tongue down the smooth skin of her throat all the way to the curve of her breast. Here he took his time, nipping and lapping at the flesh around the nipple until she began writhing and moving it to the position she wanted it, into his mouth.

Oliver smiled against her skin and enjoyed both the taste of sweet skin and her moans of pleasure. His hand toyed with the soft flesh of her other breast until he turned his attention to that one. The second was just as warm, sweet and delicious.

Sarah arched her back off the bed and brought her hands up to his hair to bind him to her.

Oliver chuckled against her skin, marvelling at her wantonness. He kissed his way down her flat belly, enjoying her navel, dipping his tongue into the crevice there in imitation of what he intended to do next. He had never performed this act on any woman as it wasn't something he had wished to try with any courtesan. But his wife was responsive and beautifully honest in her passion, and he couldn't wait to taste every inch of her body.

The knowledge that she had never known another man was a much stronger aphrodisiac than he imagined. He moved back so that he was kneeling next to her, pulling the pantalettes down her slightly rounded hips.

The curls at the apex of her thighs were only a few shades darker than the blonde curls on her head. She brought her hands up to cover herself, but he grabbed them and laced his fingers with hers.

"Trust me. I would never hurt you," he soothed, watching the beginnings of a tentative fear rising in her eyes.

At his words, the tightness in her shoulders relaxed, and she opened her legs in invitation. Oliver inhaled a sharp breath, releasing her hands and rolling back into his place between her thighs.

When he slid down to the thatch of hair between her legs, Sarah sat up and grabbed his head as though to stop him. He flicked out his tongue and touched the most sensitive place he knew of. Sarah's knees came together like a vice, locking his shoulders in place, then her whole body relaxed and she dropped back onto the bed with a moan.

Oliver pushed her legs apart and stared down at her, marvelling at how pink and perfect she was. The lips were soft and open for him like a rose. He dropped his head and kissed her flesh, loving the scent of her in his nose, the taste of her sweetness on his tongue. He licked and enjoyed her body, giving Sarah as much pleasure as he could. When he lowered his head and darted his tongue out to taste her core she screamed.

"Oliver, I can't... It feels so..."

Oliver watched Sarah's body tighten, and her legs start to quiver beneath his palms. So, at the same time as he lapped at the hidden button at the top of her folds, he thrust a finger slowly inside her wet entrance. She gasped and writhed, but made no attempt to stop him as he thrust a second finger in alongside it and began moving his fingers in the rhythm his body longed to mimic.

Sarah thrashed her head from side to side, then her body jerked, a breathy moan sounding as she began to orgasm. Oliver groaned as his fingers were coated in a thicker wetness and her sheath contracted around him over and over again. Amazing.

Her body went limp, and he removed his fingers, kissing the pink, wet flesh.

"Don't fall asleep on me yet, wife," Oliver teased, his voice strained. His balls ached, begging for release.

Sarah opened her eyes and groggily attempted to sit up, but he pushed her gently down again.

"But I want to touch you too, Oliver."

"Next time." Oliver captured her lips in a kiss before she could start to worry about what he would be doing next.

He lay down between her thighs and on her, skin to skin, groin to groin. They both moaned in unison. Oliver panted, enjoying the feeling for one moment before levering himself up onto his forearms and reaching down to position himself between her thighs.

"Goodness me, Oliver, you're so very... different to me."

She ran her hands down his chest and pressed her hand against his muscles as though she'd never seen a naked man before.

And of course, he realized, she hadn't.

Oliver clenched his teeth against the urge to impale her in one thrust. Why did she have to be so desirable?

"Your mother did tell you there would be some pain the first time?" he asked through clenched teeth. He needed to hold on for another couple of moments.

"Yes," Sarah whispered, looking down between their bodies to where his prick lay against the opening to her body.

"Are you sure you'll be able to fit? I know you have done this before, but I'm not so sure..."

Oliver tried to smile but didn't quite manage it.

"We'll go slowly, trust me," he reassured her, pushing in the first inch and pausing as her body gave easily to the resistance and wrapped tightly around him.

He relaxed against her and held onto his control by his fingernails. She was so wet and tight he almost shot his seed before he had even taken her virginity. He pulled completely out of her again, and when she arched her back, he gave her another inch. His cock was screaming at him to take her, but his head begged him to take it slow.

This time, he paused and looked down at her. She was staring at him with wide eyes and a trusting smile, but he knew the hard part was yet to come.

When Oliver came up against the barrier of her innocence, he thanked God she had been telling the truth about Millington. There was something so satisfying in knowing he was the only man to share this with her.

"Thank you for marrying me," he murmured, sharing the thought he had been chanting inside his head all day.

Sarah, caught off guard, smiled up at him and relaxed her tight grip around him.

Oliver took the opportunity and plunged deep, groaning loudly as tight heat engulfed his entire shaft. Breathing deeply to hold back his release, he kissed her softly, waiting for the tension to dissolve from her muscles.

"I'm sorry," he whispered. "But it will never hurt like that again."

Sarah lifted her legs and wound them around his waist.

"That's better." She smiled up at him, and as her pelvis tilted and pulled him in deeper, he moaned in appreciation.

He began to move and the pressure built in his head like a boiling pot, his balls tightening. He wouldn't last long enough to bring her to a second climax, but he couldn't stop. He thrust slowly in and out of her trying to hurt her as little as possible, but as she moved her hips in time with his, he felt the reins on his control slip from his grasp.

He thrust heavily into her, their skin slapping together and echoing around the room. The roaring in his head matched the aching in his groin, and he cried out. His body shook and shuddered as his cock jerked inside his new wife, his heart thundering against his ribs as bliss descended over his body.

Oliver's arms shook and he let his body sink onto Sarah, his brain so foggy he could barely think. His angel stroked his hair and held him to her breast, and a contentment he'd never known before flowed through him like a tide.

He forced his body to move, and gently rolled to the side, still maintaining contact with Sarah, but removing his weight from her smaller body.

"I can't believe how amazing that felt." Oliver pressed his lips to Sarah's bare shoulder, inhaling the sweaty scent of their lovemaking. Every nerve fibre in his body was singing in rapture, having been touched and stimulated by the incredible woman still in his arms.

Oliver settled onto his back, and Sarah rolled toward him, nestling into his side and laying a hand on his belly.

"Thank you, Oliver. That was beautiful."

He kissed the top of her head and reached down to pull the blankets up to cover them.

"It was wonderful," he agreed, laughing out loud as he settled in to sleep. He should be getting out of his wife's bed and going back to his room. But as her body pressed close and she sighed in contentment, he decided that he wanted to stay.

He had once heard his brother talk of his wedding night. The whimpers of pain and the unresponsive body of his cold, virgin wife. Oliver had feared he had been sentenced to the same life. Fate, fickle female that she was, had blessed him instead.

"I'm sorry I couldn't last longer at the end," Oliver murmured, feeling the heat of a slight blush despite himself.

Sarah laughed. "I'm glad you didn't, I would be much sorer if you kept going."

"I hurt you?" Oliver pulled back the coverlet, sitting up to examine the spot between her legs. He had tried so hard not to hurt her.

A faint stain of blood coloured her otherwise creamy thighs, and Oliver gulped at this physical evidence of what they had just done.

Sarah reached down to pull the blanket back over them both.

"Only a little, Oliver, but you said it would." She pushed him down so that he lay back again. "Thank you," she whispered once more, her eyes sliding closed and her breathing evening out.

Oliver was quick to follow her, sated to his bones in a way he had never been before. The feeling went so much deeper than the physical. There was a sense of being safe, warm and blissfully happy. They were such unusual feelings for him that he didn't stop to examine them, passing quickly into the land of dreams with the soft body of his wife pressed against him.

Chapter Twelve

For the next month, all of Sarah's dreams came true. She and her husband enjoyed each other in every way imaginable. They slept until noon, eating breakfast from trays left outside their bedroom door. They rode horseback beside each other, they walked together and shared intimacy all the time, in more interesting places than Sarah could have dreamed.

They made love in the stables at dusk, in the boat on the lake, and on his desk in his library. They spoke to each other all of the time as well.

Sarah made her husband talk about his family, and then she told him about hers. Despite her earlier fears about what sort of marriage they would have, Oliver was a kind, attentive, loving husband and her heart ached with happiness.

Oliver showed her his beautiful home, the trees he used to climb as a young boy, the places he would hide from his nanny when he didn't want to do his lessons. She was utterly enchanted with the estate she now called home. Oliver even took Sarah around to meet all of his tenants.

It was all going so well she could barely believe it.

Until the day the Dowager arrived.

The butler cursed under his breath and rushed to the front door. Sarah, passing through the entrance on her way to the parlour, frowned as he opened the ancient door and bowed deeply.

Who could it be? Obviously, not a well-liked person or the very stoic, traditional butler would never have cursed like that.

Sarah's stomach dropped when her mother-in-law stepped onto their rug.

Resisting the urge to run for cover as her legs trembled and her throat tightened, Sarah curtseyed to the Dowager Duchess of Lincoln, and her companion, the Countess of Sombury.

As she lifted her head and pushed her legs to stand once again, she tried not to flinch under the gaze of the women who were now her family. She didn't want to be unkind, but her new mother-in-law had not aged well. Her skin was very wrinkled and too pale. She had an enormous hooked nose and her hair was pulled tightly against her head.

However, she was dressed in the most beautiful of materials, and her posture was so rigid, she would pass for royalty. Good breeding was stamped all over her, and a shiver ran down Sarah's spine when her gaze connected with the cold, grey eyes of her husband's mother.

"Good morning." Despite the fact that her belly jumped with nerves, Sarah greeted the two women with a smile.

Neither of the ladies greeted her back or curtseyed in response. They looked Sarah up and down, taking in her simple morning gown, and grimaced in unison. Both of their upper lips lifted in sneers.

They then started barking orders to the servants, and within moments they were in their rooms being served.

Sarah looked at the butler, who gave her one of the most genuinely sorry looks she had ever received.

Hot tears tickled in Sarah's eyes as a myriad of feelings warred within her. Why had they arrived? She knew they didn't like her, and yet they'd left London in the middle of the Season to visit.

A strange darkness filled her tight chest, and she took a deep breath, hoping to remove some of the foreboding that settled there.

It would be fine. It had to be. She lifted her chin, nodded once to herself, and went to inform her husband that they had visitors.

THAT EVENING, Sarah put on her best dinner gown and made sure she was in the sitting room before everyone else. She didn't want to be accused of not being a proper hostess.

"Well, if it isn't the new Duchess of Lincoln," came the cold, nasty voice of Oliver's sister-in-law as she entered the room. Lady Honoria Lyre, Countess of Sombury.

"Lady Lyre." Sarah stood and curtseyed deeply.

The woman didn't curtsey in return, which as far as Sarah knew, was vulgar indeed. Sarah studied her, now that she was close enough to have a good look at her. Lady Lyre was twenty-one years old and quite handsome. Dark hair, green eyes, and perfect, alabaster skin. Her nose and features spoke of aristocratic breeding.

Her gown was one of the most beautiful Sarah had ever seen. Incredibly delicate and expensive lace adorned the entire bodice. Sarah's family would never have been able to afford such clothing. Looking down at her pale blue gown, Sarah felt inadequate, ugly. *Vanity is a sin*, she reminded herself and straightened her spine.

"I hope your carriage ride was pleasant."

The woman wrinkled her nose. "As entertaining as one expects ten miles in a carriage to be."

Well, at least that was the start of a conversation.

"Will you be staying with us for long on this visit?" Hopefully, they were merely stopping on their way to another destination.

There was something almost evil about these women. She hated even to think such a thing. Her father would be extremely upset with her, but there was no other word for the air around them.

"Visit?" Lady Lyre repeated, her eyes widening and her mouth pulling down on one side. "This is our home. We'll be staying as long as we wish. You aren't mistress here yet."

Sarah's mouth dropped open. Did she really say that?

Oliver walked into the room, accompanied by his mother. "Do close your mouth, girl. You look like a simpleton," the Dowager snapped.

"Mother!" Oliver admonished, but the woman barely broke stride.

"Shall we go in to dinner?" She grabbed Oliver's arm and steered him toward the door.

Oliver threw an apologetic look over his shoulder at her but did as his mother bade.

Sarah simply watched as her husband was dragged from the room by his mother, and she cringed. As the highest-ranking woman, and a guest, it was the correct thing for Oliver to escort his mother. However, it didn't sit well.

Dinner was a sombre affair. Any conversation that Sarah tried to make was quickly dismissed and a new, supposedly more interesting topic was introduced. Oliver did ask her questions and gave her smiles that lit up her heart, but the Dowager and Lady Honoria dominated.

They spent the night talking about society and people whom Oliver had obviously known all his life. Sarah didn't know any of them and therefore had little to add to the conversation. Which, she supposed, was the point.

That night in bed, Oliver came to her, silently, and she clung to him.

They had been so happy, cocooned at his estate. Now she had to deal with the censure of his family. They made love slowly and almost silently. Enjoying each other for every minute that they had together, they made their world exist in their bed.

~

THE NEXT DAY when she rose, Sarah barely saw her new relatives. They stayed all day abed and only came down when it was time for dinner.

"Would you mind organising for the housekeeper to speak to me after dinner please, Cosgrove?" She wanted to speak to the woman about her bedroom and the way they were cleaning her bed sheets.

Her mother-in-law stepped up next to her and took her roughly by the elbow, hauling Sarah into the sitting room like an errant child. Heat blossomed in her cheeks as she tugged her arm back.

"You do not ask Cosgrove anything, you demand he does what you want. What sort of duchess are you going to be, girl?"

"I'm sorry, Your Grace." Sarah had no idea what else to say; she didn't realise she'd been speaking to the butler so poorly.

"You should be. Haven't you learnt anything?"

"I didn't know..."

"Of course, you don't know how to talk to the servants, that is why I'm telling you. You are their mistress. You tell them what to do, and they do it. They are there to serve you."

Sarah stared at her husband's mother, her brain stumbling over the new definition of how she was meant to treat people in her employ. In their home, the servants were treated with respect and thanked for doing a good job. Her mother was proud to be a kind mistress.

"I apologise." Sarah curtseyed again, dipping her eyes away from the nasty face still grimacing at her.

"Humph."

The same routine as the night before ensued. Oliver's mother commandeered him for an escort into dinner, and then Honoria and the dowager occupied all of the conversation.

Oliver stared at her often and tried to get her attention, but the longer she sat there surrounded by their unpleasant voices, the more she wished they'd go back to London.

Halfway through the main meal of pheasant and vegetables the dowager said, "I think you should hold a dinner party, Oliver."

Sarah's head came up. Wasn't it her role to organise dinner parties and balls? Why was his mother suggesting a party now? They had barely been married five weeks. No one even knew her yet.

"It's the middle of the Season, Mother. Surely there will be no one around to attend." Oliver shot her a sideways glance, and Sarah let her eyebrows rise in surprise.

"An informal dinner for those local families who haven't travelled to

London would be a perfect way to introduce your new wife to the area." The dowager nodded toward Sarah.

Sarah smiled hesitantly in return, shocked by this new side to her mother-in-law.

Oliver turned to her. "What do you think, Sarah?"

A moment of panic ensued. Sarah's heart raced inside her chest, but she resolutely clenched her hands in her lap.

"I think that would be lovely, Oliver. And if your mother would help me with a list of guests, I'm sure I can handle the rest."

The Dowager nodded, and Sarah's whole body relaxed. Perhaps this would help her mother-in-law and sister-in-law see that she truly did belong by Oliver's side.

∼

OLIVER'S MOTHER presented Sarah with a guest list the following morning and then left her alone. Sarah had to assume the ages and status of the people on the list, as her mother-in-law disappeared and was not available to ask. Few had titles and due to them remaining in the country, Sarah assumed they were local gentry.

She sent out the invitations for a Saturday night dinner and planned the menu with the cook. The cook expressed concern over the simplicity of the fare, but Sarah was determined to have simple, good food and plenty of it. This English preference for small amounts of delicate, complicated French food sat badly in her stomach.

The night of the dinner arrived, and Sarah's nerves were stretched thin. Her in-laws had managed to avoid her most days in the past week. It was almost as though they were determined not to help her, although they said nothing untoward about her in front of Oliver.

Looking down at her pale blue evening gown, Sarah knew she should have ordered a new dress for the occasion. As the hostess, she was expected to be the most stunning woman in the room. She knew that both the dowager and Honoria had gowns more beautiful than the one she had on. There was no help for it, though. It was too late now.

Sarah's maid was just finishing pinning her curly hair up into a complicated arrangement on top of her head when a knock sounded at the door.

"Come in," Sarah called, before remembering herself and shutting her mouth with a clap. A duchess didn't shout.

The housekeeper herself walked in.

"The dowager sent you some jewellery, Your Grace. To wear tonight," she said, making it clear that it was only a loan.

Sarah sighed. The woman had no daughters, and Sarah was the wife to the dowager's only remaining son. To whom else would her jewels belong, after her demise? Unless, of course, Honoria did not re-marry.

She opened the case and gasped. Inside was a horrendously expensive set of emerald earrings and a matching chunky necklace. The style was antique, and the green clashed horribly with her gown, but they were charming.

Her maid clucked her tongue. "It won't look well w' yer gown, yer Grace."

"I know." Sarah handed the necklace up to her maid.

She had no choice. She was in trouble either way. She would look a fright in an ill-matching ensemble, or her mother-in-law would cut her for going against her wishes.

Sarah was tired of it all. She took a deep breath and stared at her reflection, her glistening gold wedding ring catching her eye. She was Oliver's wife, and no one could take that away from her.

Chapter Thirteen

Oliver paced the drawing room for the fifth time. Where was his wife? She had to be here before the first guests arrived and he could hear carriage wheels rolling along the cobblestones in the driveway. He lifted his hand to call for a footman when the butler announced her.

Sarah walked in, all beautiful golden skin and hair the colour of sunshine. She saw him and made her way over to him the way a compass needle points due north. A lump swelled in his throat, and he swallowed against the emotion stuck there.

She curtseyed before him and gave him a cheeky grin. "Your Grace."

"Your Grace." He bowed back, grinning at his beautiful wife. He was so lucky to have this lovely lady in his home, in his life.

He caught a green shimmer around her neck, and he narrowed his eyes on the horrible necklace around her throat. "Where did that necklace come from?"

"Your mother. She loaned it to me for the party."

Her hand came up self-consciously to rest upon the emeralds.

Oliver bit back a groan. Why hadn't he bought her something new to wear for the evening? It was her first-night hosting, and he hadn't even thought to recommend a new dress. Not that he would have ever thought of it until now; the ladies in his family bought anything they wanted. Perhaps he should have allocated her money to spend on herself every month?

Lifting his gaze from the fashion blunder, he looked into her cautious eyes and forced himself to smile.

"You look beautiful." He stepped forward and brought her knuckles to his lips, kissing her gloved hand.

"Well, that is what I like to see, Reverend. A man who knows how to treat his wife."

Oliver rolled his eyes and slowly straightened up, recognising the loud and rather obnoxious voice of the local countess.

"The Countess of Tremble and Reverend Holland," the butler announced.

Oliver stepped forward and introduced his wife to a dragon he had known his whole life.

"It is lovely to make your acquaintance." Sarah curtseyed prettily, and Oliver grimaced. Sarah needn't curtsey to anyone if she didn't want to, especially a woman beneath her in rank.

The countess smiled knowingly and gave Oliver a wink. "It is, my dear. I can see Oliver married you for your looks, but what are your connections like?"

Oh, dear God.

Sarah's chin rose valiantly. "My father is a vicar from Somerset."

The countess's humph was loud in the silent room. "Married a bit below you, didn't you?"

Oliver's spine straightened as he placed Sarah's shaking hand on his arm and drew her close.

"I don't believe so, my lady," he drawled.

The woman cackled with laughter.

Oliver's mother chose that moment to enter the room.

"Your Grace," the countess greeted the dowager with a short curtsey.

The dowager nodded back.

"You let Oliver marry someone with no connections?" the countess asked.

"My son chose his wife, not I."

Sarah flushed and Oliver bristled, pulling his wife closer to his side. He started walking toward the door before he spoke.

"If you don't like my choices, Mother, you are welcome to retire to the dowager house."

The room went silent, and he turned to his angel.

"Let us stand at the door to greet our guests, my dear."

Sarah nodded once and followed his lead. Oliver knew his mother could be very nasty indeed, but he'd seen little so far to indicate any real malice.

Even so, he was determined to protect Sarah if need be. He could only hope the rest of the night would go better.

~

THEY WERE ALL DRESSED EXQUISITELY. No simple country gentry, these people.

Some of their guests were downright rude, others just curious. There was one girl Sarah's age that she had hoped might become a friend, but she was soon informed that, "I was meant to marry His Grace; how dare he marry you?"

Sarah managed, "Oh? I thought he was supposed to marry Honoria," but at the shocked gasps around her, she was relieved that Oliver pulled her out of that conversation quickly. But the damage had been done.

They were escorted into dinner by the footmen. Sarah hadn't been told the hierarchy of her guests so had placed them evenly around the room, putting wives and husbands on opposite sides of the dinner table.

She knew that most dinner parties were seated gentleman, then lady, but she thought Oliver would enjoy it more to be seated with a man on either side of him, and Sarah placed a woman on either side of her.

When everyone was seated, there was silence for a good five minutes, and Sarah drank her glass of red wine with shaking hands.

Why wasn't anyone talking? What had she done wrong already?

The first course was served, and Sarah heard one of the male guests make an encouraging remark about the serving size. Happy with one thing, at least, Sarah tried to converse with the elderly woman to her right. Unfortunately, the woman was stone deaf, and Sarah could not bring herself to shout in her ear.

The woman to her left spent the whole dinner flirting atrociously with the man opposite her, who Sarah knew wasn't her husband.

By the end of the meal, the table was loudly conversing, and Sarah was proud in the knowledge that people finally appeared to be having a good time. After their chocolate pudding dessert, that few ladies touched, Oliver called the men to the library for cigars and port, and the dowager announced that the women would retire to the sitting room.

Despite feeling completely out of her depth, Sarah kept her chin up and made a resolution to keep smiling, even if things turned ugly. Being separated from Oliver was not a good thing. She would be vulnerable to attack now.

It didn't take long.

"I cannot believe what she served us for dinner," one of the ladies hissed at her friend as Sarah entered the room.

"Good enough for the servants," came the nasty reply.

Sarah saw her mother-in-law smirking in the corner, but she didn't waver in her stride as she walked around the room. Her stomach gripped hard, making her food churn.

"Weren't you taught how to seat a table for dinner?" a rather tight-lipped woman asked her, glaring through her black spectacles.

Sarah recognised her as the wife of the man whom the woman next to her had been flirting with throughout dinner. Blood flowed into her cheeks, making her want to run. She hated how obvious her blushes were, but as the hostess, hiding in a corner wasn't an option.

"I thought it would be more interesting this way," Sarah answered honestly.

Why was she being attacked for such a simple thing? Did she have to follow all the rules laid down by society, all the time?

"Pardon me?" came a familiar voice from behind her.

Sarah shivered as a cold hand danced along her spine, and she turned to her sister-in-law.

"How is it interesting to flout every rule, and insult the hierarchy upon which the civilization of England is proudly based?"

Sarah's heart jumped up into her throat. How did one even try to answer that question?

"Stop picking on the poor girl; she's a vicar's daughter," said the Countess of Tremble, and dismissed the issue with a wave of her large hand.

Sarah stared at Honoria a moment longer, wishing she had the strength to simply tell the woman she was not welcome here. But of course, she could not do that.

"I loved the food, myself," the countess declared, and went on happily talking about the meal, the chocolate pudding in particular.

At least one person enjoyed the dinner, she thought, absurdly grateful to the countess despite her obnoxious manner.

She sat down on a settee with a cup of tea and held her tongue for the rest of the evening, afraid she would either burst into tears or shout some unruly words at those of the guests ruder than others. Eventually, she stood to say goodnight. She struggled to maintain her smile, and there was a heavy weight sitting in her belly, unlike anything she'd ever known.

She had never felt so useless in her life.

~

"WHAT A HORRIBLE EVENING."

Sarah shared the remark with her husband in an attempt to lighten the weight gripping her, as Oliver pulled back the blankets and climbed into the bed next to her.

"Hardly. I had more fun than I've had in ages." Oliver chuckled, reaching out to pull her into his side.

"But I did everything wrong. The seating wasn't organised properly, the food was too plain, and your mother said I was dressed like a servant." Sarah shuddered as she relived the moment the dowager pulled her aside to tell her that her dress was little better than the housekeeper's. At least it hadn't been in front of their guests.

Her mother-in-law was, quite simply, a horrible woman, as was Oliver's sister-in-law.

Oliver sighed. "Sarah, I conversed with people I never get to speak to and the food was delicious. If you didn't feel pretty enough in that gown, then we will order some new ones. Get the seamstress in the village to come to the house."

Disappointment assailed her as Oliver dismissed her concerns by offering to buy her dresses, but as Sarah stared at him, she saw nothing to alarm her. He looked drowsy and happy, as though he had spent a pleasant evening with his friends, rather than the dreadful night she had experienced. She had hated every minute of it, but if Oliver was happy, then she was resolved not to let it upset her.

Time to shift the mood to something more appropriate.

"What sort of dresses do you want me in, Oliver?"

Sarah let a small moan escape her as she stretched her body under the sheet so that he could see the mounds of her breasts and the smooth slope of her belly.

"Anything that covers this delicious body up so that no one else gets to see it."

Oliver pulled the sheet down and her nightgown up so that cool air brushed her breasts. He set his lips to one sensitive nipple and suckled greedily. Sarah moaned loudly and held the man she loved to her. Their conversation was at an end.

THE NEXT DAY was another round of "who can make Sarah feel bad without Oliver hearing." Her mother-in-law criticised her for wearing a dress not fitting of her station and then told Sarah she needed lessons in deportment.

Honoria went to the housekeeper and changed all the menus for the week without telling Sarah, adding several seafood dishes to which Sarah was allergic.

It was only when the housekeeper mentioned it, that Sarah became aware. She explained her allergies and the menus were amended once more.

To deal with the stress, Sarah began dusting. She always did that at home. If she had something on her mind or needed to think, then an easy, yet constructive task was always best. She was dusting one of the sitting rooms when her mother-in-law came in, dragging one of the maids by the ear.

"Look, just look at what she is doing. If you did your job right then she would not be dusting the shelves!" The dowager screamed at the poor girl, who could not have been more than sixteen.

The maid turned bright pink and promptly burst into tears. Sarah's heart squeezed tight in her chest. She was obviously the worst mistress in the world.

"I should not have been cleaning, Your Grace," Sarah apologised, blinking rapidly and trying her best not to burst into tears herself.

"No, you should not. You obviously have problems with the cleanliness of the house. Therefore, I will dismiss this maid instantly."

The maid in question fell to her knees, sobbing into her white pinafore.

Don't you dare!

She could not be the reason this poor girl lost her job. Goodness knows what fate she would have without it.

"No, please do not do that, Your Grace. I was simply selfish and vain wanting to do it myself." She looked down at the maid on the floor. "You will not lose your job," she assured the girl.

Her mother-in-law eyed her critically, and then inhaled deeply and screamed for Oliver.

Sarah cringed at the sound, clenching her teeth as her anger rose.

"Yes, Mother," came a weary voice from the doorway.

"Your wife has been *dusting*."

Oliver's gaze swung to her and narrowed onto the feather duster in her hand.

"And what is the problem, Mother?"

Thank you!

"She is a *duchess*. What will people think when they find out that she takes chores away from the servants?"

Oliver stiffened. Embarrassment sliced through her and tears threatened. No. She would not cry. She was determined not to cry in front of this hideous woman.

"Sarah isn't used to having the servant numbers that we have, Mother. You can't expect her to know what to do in every situation."

Sarah's tears melted away as her anger grew. Was what she was doing so wrong? This was *their* home, not his mother's any longer. She belonged in the Dowager House. Yet the manners Sarah had been brought up with made her refrain from saying so out loud.

His mother continued. "This is my home, Oliver, and I will not have her undermining me. This maid is to be let go immediately."

"No," Sarah said stubbornly. "She is not to be let go."

Oliver groaned and motioned for the girl to leave the room. "Mother, this is not a subject for me. Sarah is the mistress here now, and I am sure you will find her very agreeable. I need to get back to the library. Can you and Sarah sort this out, please?"

His mother nodded, triumphant, obviously assuming she would now get her way. Sarah sagged, exhausted at dealing with this on a constant basis.

Plus, she was annoyed with Oliver, if she was honest with herself. How could her husband not stand up for her? She sent him a glare as he bowed himself out of the room. Sarah received another nasty look from her mother-in-law before she too, left Sarah alone.

Sarah immediately went to the housekeeper and asked for that particular maid to attend her in her rooms that evening. When the maid arrived that night, she was immensely relieved. At least she had won that round, and the guilt of the maid's unemployment wasn't hanging over Sarah's head. Having two ladies' maids came in quite handy, too.

Sarah put a hand to her chest to take a deep breath. She was constantly out of breath these days and often felt faint. She needed to sort things out with Oliver, and find a solution for the dowager—and Honoria too—as quickly as possible. Her health was beginning to suffer.

Chapter Fourteen

That night, Oliver joined Sarah in her bed as he always did, and yet there was something different about their encounter. They came together almost violently, each seeking reassurance that they were there for each other.

Sarah clung to her husband, revelling in the deep thrusts of his body. Knowing that in this, at least, she was a perfect wife and he a perfect husband. She was helpless not to respond and came apart loudly in his arms, calling forth his own release within moments. They lay beside each other panting and together they drifted into sleep, hands linked.

OVER THE NEXT week things got steadily worse. The dowager began to criticize Sarah's piano playing, so Sarah stopped playing the instrument that had given her great joy since she could walk.

Honoria told her that her embroidery was little better than a child's, so she stopped her needlework. She didn't know where to turn, and when she tried to speak to Oliver about it, he brushed it off with the cavalier statement, "That is just the way they are."

Sarah felt alone, and the constant berating caused her to begin doubting herself in everything. She started to believe that she was completely inadequate in all areas of her life, and she didn't know how to fix any of it. Never had she been so close to despair. She wanted her parents—her mother in particular. Who better to guide her out of this pit of blackness? But she was frightened to send her mother a letter that could be intercepted by Oliver's mother or sister-in-law. She couldn't bear to put her mother in danger of their hideous abuse.

Everywhere Sarah looked were reminders of the difference between herself and her husband's way of life. The house, the food, the servants, his family.

Sarah was close to breaking point with no way of turning back.

OLIVER WASN'T oblivious to Sarah's pain. He knew, or had a fair idea, how bad it was getting for her. He had heard his mother criticise Sarah for her piano playing through an open door and hadn't said anything.

He knew that Honoria went over Sarah's head when it came to the housekeeping. Never in public conversation, and never in front of him. But his valet kept him informed.

Initially he thought it would make things worse if he stepped in. He hoped things would naturally settle, or that the women would find a new rhythm with living together.

But then his mother began to ridicule him too—as she had done all his life, but she seemed to step up her taunts to an intolerable level. Telling him his coat wasn't the latest style or that his speech wasn't eloquent enough, or that his father would be ashamed of the state of the grounds and the way the tenants were not being looked after.

She stated bluntly one day that he was a dreadful duke and it was a shame his brother was the one who had died alongside their father.

He'd erected armour around his feelings for most of his life, but the implication that she'd have preferred him dead over his brother, stung.

Every day he sensed the holes in his armour getting larger as she chipped away at him.

The only solace in the whole day was when he climbed into Sarah's bed at night. There he found heaven. Sarah opened her arms and her heart and welcomed him. She never turned him away; she never said no to his needs.

Even one night when he didn't feel able to make love to her, he held her all night, and she clung tightly to him. She never reproached or criticised him.

The only thing she did was complain about how his mother and Honoria treated her. He didn't know what to do about that—either for her, or himself.

~

SARAH HAD HAD ENOUGH. She had been spoken down to, criticised and glared at every day for almost a month and she was at breaking point.

She loved her husband, but she couldn't keep living like this. It wasn't good for her, and it wasn't healthy for the baby she suspected was growing inside her. She hadn't had her monthly flux in the eight weeks since her wedding.

Sarah knew she needed to approach her husband and give him a chance to be the man she knew he could be.

She walked the lonely halls of his estate and found Oliver in his study, where he normally remained during the day.

"Oliver, I don't think I can stay in this house with your mother any longer."

The words came out in a rush. It had taken all day to find the courage to speak up and now that she had, she wondered why she hadn't done it a month before.

"It's her home. I can't ask her to leave." Oliver looked at her, his eyes rimmed with dark circles. He looked tired and out of sorts, but for once her heart did not soften when she saw him. Not when he refused to ask his mother to leave.

"And, Honoria…" Sarah began, unsure how she could describe her husband's sister-in-law without using a curse word. "She looks at me as though I were a rodent who had the audacity to find its way into her room."

"Surely Honoria's not that bad, Sarah. Are you not exaggerating a little? I know you didn't grow up with ladies like Honoria and my mother, but in my experience they are not unusual. Can you not find a way to cope better with their disagreeable natures?"

Cope better? Me?

Anger rose in her chest. "Why is she still living here?" She placed her hands on hips as she glared at her husband.

"Because I promised her she would always have a place to live within our family. I didn't have much choice. My brother didn't leave her enough money to afford her own home. Also, she's good company for my mother."

"But I'm your *wife*," Sarah argued. *She* was supposed to be the one his mother wanted to keep her company.

"Of course, you are."

"Then why do they both hate me so much? I knew they weren't happy that you had married so far beneath your station, but I never thought they would be so horrible to me." Sarah allowed every ounce of hurt to show in her face and voice, hoping to reach Oliver.

Instead, he seemed to shrink further into himself.

"Sarah, you're exaggerating, and it is unbecoming, especially in a duchess."

"I'm not exaggerating. They don't think I'm good enough for you."

Oliver remained silent.

"Oliver!" She yelled His name, furious that he was not automatically taking her side.

"Yes?"

"Tell me the truth. Do *you* think I'm good enough to be your wife?"

"Of course, you are. You are the only one I've ever wanted." The sadness in his voice just about broke her heart.

"Then why can't you see that your mother and your brother's wife are totally disrespectful toward me?"

"What can I say, Sarah? Nothing I am telling you is making you feel better. Tell me what you want me to say?"

"Tell me why they don't like me," She needed an answer to that question, but she was also desperate to reach Oliver on a level that wasn't just physical.

Oliver sighed, the sound long and tired.

"Because my mother was raised to believe only people who were born with titles have any value, and my sister-in-law not only feels the same way, but she's also jealous that I chose you over her."

"What? She wanted you to marry *her*?"

That is just ludicrous!

"It's not that uncommon. She was raised to be the Duchess of Lincoln. She was betrothed to my brother from birth."

Sarah inhaled sharply, fear suffocating her. "Did you *want* to marry her?"

"Of course not. If I had, the wedding would have taken place the week we were out of mourning." Oliver sounded angry that she had even asked.

"Oh. Good." Sarah exhaled, unable to keep her relief from showing.

"Not that she wouldn't have been a perfect duchess, but the idea of sharing a bed with her, in the same bed that my brother had... no."

Sarah didn't hear anything except that Oliver thought that his sister-in-law would be a better duchess than her.

"So, you believe it too!" She exploded, her heart hammering in her chest as every muscle in her body grew taut. "You don't think I'm good enough to be your duchess."

Oliver opened his mouth to answer, but nothing came out.

Pain similar to a knife sliding between her ribs hit her. "*What is wrong with you, Oliver?*" She screeched the words then turned and fled, running all the way back to her bedroom, and cried until she could barely draw breath. Her maid rushed in after she had cried herself hoarse.

"You must stop, yer Grace, it is not good fer the baby."

Her maid, Sophie, applied a cold cloth to her face, and Sarah choked on a fresh wave of tears.

"How did you…" Sarah started to ask, before realising who washed her underclothes every day.

"Please don't say anything to anyone. I haven't told my husband yet," Sarah begged her. Her mother-in-law's voice taunted her in the back of her head. *A duchess does not ask, she commands.*

"Of course not, yer Grace. It is sometimes good to wait to make sure it is safe."

Sarah pressed an anxious hand to her abdomen. She could not lose her baby. It was the one thing she had been able to do that her horrible sister-in-law hadn't. Provide the dukedom with an heir.

"I think I need to sleep. Will you inform the cook and the dowager duchess that I won't be down for dinner?" Sarah lay back and closed her eyes, wishing herself far away.

"Of course, yer Grace. Could I perhaps draw you a bath before you retire?" Sophie's concern coloured her voice.

Usually, this would have soothed Sarah, knowing there was one person in her life who cared how she felt, but she was too miserable to think about it today.

"No thank you, I just need to lie here." She was so emotionally exhausted that she fell straight into a dreamless sleep.

"Not even two months she's been here and already she's started thinking of herself as too important to meet with us for dinner."

Oliver heard his mother from his end of the table, and wished that the already huge table was even longer.

"Mother. Enough."

"Did you hear her directing the housekeeper to change the menus that I had already ordered for the week?" Honoria asked the dowager, disgust apparent in her voice.

Now they were both ignoring him.

"Have you heard the way she speaks to the servants? She treats them as though they are her equals!" the dowager said.

"That is because they are." The both laughed, and Oliver reached for the port decanter.

He tried once more. "You both need to give Sarah a chance. She is a beautiful lady."

The two ladies acted as though he hadn't spoken and dinner continued in this vein. Oliver drowned himself in a bottle of his best port, and his closest relations spent the evening saying horrible things about his new wife.

He spoke up several times against them, but again he was ignored.

He was so cup shot by dessert he had to have a footman help him to bed, where he slept off his intoxication alone.

Chapter Fifteen

Sarah woke partway through the night and listened, hoping to hear some movement in the room next door. For the first time since they had married, Oliver didn't join her in her bed. She was completely alone now, and it was her fault. She had destroyed the one good thing they had together by speaking her fears aloud, and now her husband wouldn't come to her.

Around dawn she fell asleep again, only to re-awaken when her maid came in to inform her that lunch would be served soon.

Sarah gasped and sat bolt upright. How could she have missed breakfast? She twisted and placed her feet on the floor, jumping out of bed. She swooned and would have fainted dead away if her quick thinking maid hadn't pushed her in the direction of the bed.

She landed with a thump on the soft mattress, black spots still swimming in her eyes. They slowly receded, and she took long, deep breaths.

"There now, yer Grace. Do not you be getting up so quickly. The last thing you need is a fall."

Sarah lay a hand to her spinning head and swallowed the bile that rose in her throat. The dizziness she usually felt had been multiplied this morning, and she was feeling very sick in the stomach, too.

"Thank you, Sophie. I am feeling quite ill. Do you think I could have some toast and tea in my room?" Sarah winced at the tone she was using to talk to her servant. Her mother-in-law would be disgusted.

Well, her mother-in-law could fall in the lake for all she cared. She had a new priority, her baby.

She wasn't willing to give up on her husband, but until her pregnancy was better established she would have to protect herself. That would mean not allowing her in-laws to cause her distress, and not upsetting herself over Oliver's withdrawal from everything.

Sophie brought in her tray of toast and tea, and Sarah sat up in her bed and nibbled on her very late breakfast. Drinking slowly and eating slower, she waited for her body to respond to the food. After eating, she had another nap.

The next time she awoke, Sarah felt more relaxed than she had in a month. The weight of the world had been lifted from her shoulders. She was pregnant. She had to get outside, get some fresh air, and avoid her toxic mother-in-law and sister-in-law at all costs.

Dressing in one of her old walking dresses, Sarah slipped out the servant's entrance with help from Sophie and the housekeeper and made her way to the stables. Walking slowly and enjoying the gentle breeze, she almost bumped into Oliver.

"Oh, Oliver, I'm sorry." Sarah stepped back from where her husband was talking to his horse. It looked like he had just gotten back from a ride. He was sweating, and his hair was windswept and unkempt. He looked so delicious Sarah's body heated, and her nipples peaked beneath her dress.

"Sarah." Oliver greeted her with a bow. "Are you all right? You look pale."

At least he still noticed what she looked like, even if it wasn't very complimentary.

"I think I stayed indoors for too long. I decided to go for a walk around the lake." Sarah gathered her courage and managed to smile invitingly at her husband. "Would you care to join me?"

Oliver hesitated. "I would love to, but I need to get back to the house to bathe in time for dinner. Perhaps tomorrow?"

Sarah nodded and glanced away, ignoring the sadness that threatened to overwhelm her.

Oliver headed back to the house, and Sarah continued on her journey. She meandered around the beautiful lake that was one of the many places Oliver had shown her in the first days they were here together.

Her cheeks heated when she passed a secluded grassy patch where he had made love to her. Pressing a hand to her belly, she wondered when they had conceived this child. Perhaps it had been that day? Perhaps it had even been their wedding night? Either way, this child had been conceived in love, and she would fight to keep it safe.

Sarah lost track of time, returning to the house when the sun was setting, and the family was assembling for dinner.

"What time do you call this?" The dowager boomed from the sitting room where they were taking pre-dinner drinks.

Sarah went to drop into an automatic curtsey but stopped herself. She was now of the same rank as her mother-in-law, and she needn't curtsey to anyone ever again. Straightening her spine, she stared into the older woman's cold, grey eyes.

"I lost track of time."

"Well, you'll never be ready in time for dinner, and you are not wearing that peasant dress in my dining room."

"Mother, stop. We'll wait for Sarah, as long as is necessary."

Sarah smiled and inclined her head. "I will wear what I wish in *my* dining room. But I've changed my mind. Please, don't wait for me. I will dine in my room."

Oliver's mouth dropped open, as did the dowager and Honoria's mouths beside him. Without a backward glance, she turned and walked up the grand staircase.

One footman was trying to suppress a smile as she walked past him and she started to giggle. What a relief it was to be able to ignore them now. She was sorry she would not be eating with Oliver, but it had to be done. For the sake of her baby, she would not subject herself to the stress of that dining room again.

∽

OLIVER COULD NOT BELIEVE what had just happened. He had been waiting anxiously for his wife to arrive, fearing the explosion from his mother that was sure to come because of Sarah's tardiness.

Instead, Sarah had refused to curtsey to his mother, a first for her, of which Oliver was intensely proud, but then she had made that comment about her dining room, and left him to have dinner alone. Well, not alone exactly, but without her, he may as well be.

"We will return to London on Friday, Oliver," his mother announced during the main course.

"Of course, Mother, I understand." He tried his best to look disappointed, but inside, he was relieved.

If they left, perhaps he and Sarah could go back to how they had been before his mother had arrived. He wanted to return to her bed, but how could he, whilst things were still so strained between them?

"All of us," his mother corrected.

"Pardon?" Oliver's eyebrows rose as he sat up straighter in his chair.

"You will join Honoria and me for the remainder of the Season." The dowager's tone brooked no argument.

"I'm not sure if Sarah wants to return for the Season, Mother."

Sarah loved being out of London, and he knew she wouldn't like having to share a house with his mother and sister-in-law in town.

"I do not care what that woman wants. You will return with us and do your duty to your family. Your father would be horrified to think that you let Honoria and me go to London without you. Who will be there to look after us?"

Oliver bit the inside of his cheek. He didn't care who looked after them, but she was right. It was his duty, his obligation, to make sure his mother and Honoria were safe. He could not do that from here.

"I will discuss it with my wife."

"You will do your duty for the first time in your life," his mother fairly yelled. "You have been nothing but a disappointment since the day you were born, and I will not have you failing us now."

Oliver cringed and reached for the port. How could he argue with her? He *was* a disappointment to her, and to his late father and his late brother. He was a disappointment to Sarah, too. He'd always known that he wasn't up to the task of a dukedom.

OLIVER PACED IN HIS BEDCHAMBER. Should he go into his wife? *Could* he go into his wife? After their horrible talk two days before, when he'd all but told her she wasn't good enough to be his wife, he hadn't felt free to touch her, let alone make love to her. Since his mother had arrived, the only moments of happiness they'd had were in Sarah's bed, and now he felt barred from that too.

He sat down on his own bed with a thump and called himself ten types of a coward. He hadn't even told Sarah that he would be returning to London with his mother. After being degraded and derided for the entire evening, not an unusual event, he had finally acquiesced and agreed to return with them, just to stop her picking on him.

Climbing into his vast, cold and lonely bed, Oliver had the urge to weep. Ultimately defeated on every front, he was a failure to the title of duke and all the responsibilities that came with it. He was a failure to his wife. She was miserable and alone. And most of all, he was a failure as a man, who could not even bring himself to apologise and seek comfort in his wife's body, as he knew she would offer.

That was probably the worst part. He was aware that she would never deny him, but did she still want him? After everything he had done and said, could she care for him the same way she had before? Did she still love him as she had? Because although the words had never been said, Oliver had seen her hurt and pain written ten feet high in her expression when she'd looked at him.

∼

THE NEXT MORNING, after a fitful night's sleep, Sarah awoke to her maid beside her bed with a tray of tea, buttered toast, and a note from Oliver.

Terrified of what this note would say, she sipped her tea without opening it, trying to keep her nausea at bay. Once she was satisfied that she would not be sick, Sarah picked up the expensive paper and unfolded it, her breath hitching in her throat.

My dear,

Once you have awoken, would you please meet me in my study?

I have something to discuss with you.

Oliver

Sarah's heart sank. Pressing a hand to cover her baby, she took a deep, steadying breath. Whatever he had to say, she would endure it. Perhaps he had decided to take her away from here? Or he wanted to discuss sharing her bed again? Although Sarah tried to be as positive as possible, optimism coming naturally to her, she could not stop herself from believing that something dreadful was afoot.

With those hideous women in the house, anything was possible.

Sarah deliberately dressed in another of her old walking dresses, feeling comfortable and like herself. She made her way to the duke's study, smiling her thanks to the butler as he opened the door for her.

"Good morning, my dear." Oliver's voice sounded hoarse.

"Good morning, Oliver. Did you sleep well?"

Oliver's eyebrows rose, but he didn't comment on her odd tone.

"I did, thank you. And you?"

"Not particularly," she answered honestly.

"Sarah, you're not happy at the moment, and I'm not sure what I can do to change that. On Friday, I will be escorting my mother and Honoria back to London for the rest of the Season."

A cool calm descended on Sarah, stilling her racing mind. She blinked slowly.

"Do you wish to stay here, or would you prefer to come with me to London?"

Sarah heard the softly pitched words and real terror struck at her heart. How could Oliver abandon her? And worse yet, how could she go with him? She knew that his townhouse was half the size of this house, and she would never be able to escape the two other women there.

Gathering her courage, Sarah informed him of her decision. "Neither. I would like to go to Scotland, if I may."

She had spent the time whilst she dressed quizzing her maid on the other landholdings owned by the duchy. There were options other than here and London.

"To the old castle?" he asked, his eyes widening in surprise.

"Yes. Do you think there will be enough servants if I take my two maids with me?" Sarah forced herself to keep her eyes locked with Oliver's, but inside she was screaming with rage.

How could he choose to return to London when I need him with me?

"I'm sure there would be," Oliver answered slowly, frowning in thought. "I will send a letter ahead of you, but I doubt they'll need to do more than air and prepare your rooms. All of the properties owned by the duchy are well-staffed and can be ready at a moment's notice."

Sarah nodded and bowed her head. Clearly, Oliver was more than happy to pack her off to a distant castle. Why was she surprised? All of her initial fears about their marriage were coming true. Oliver would not miss her presence, and yet her heart ached as though it were being slowly pulled apart at the seams. Tears slid down her cheeks before she could stop them and she tried to wipe them away, subtly.

"I'm truly sorry you have been so miserable, Sarah."

"Oh, Oliver..." Sarah opened her mouth, ready to tell him how much she would miss him, how much she loved him, how much she wanted her baby to bridge the chasm between them.

She was stopped by the look in his eyes. Sarah saw nothing but regret and loathing. She didn't know whether it was directed at himself or her, but she knew this wasn't the time for such declarations. Especially while she was feeling so fragile.

If she declared her love only to be rebuffed, she didn't think her heart could bear it. She would have to wait until she felt a little stronger.

Standing up with as much grace as she could gather, she said the only words she could. "I'll go and start packing."

<h1 style="text-align:center">Chapter Sixteen</h1>

Oliver travelled the eight miles to London on horseback. His mother said she was truly scandalised, but he preferred her ten-minute outburst of displeasure rather than having to listen to her obnoxious blabbering in the carriage for the whole trip.

They settled into the Lincoln townhouse. Oliver took the duke's bedroom, his mother the duchess's rooms. Oliver hated that his wife wasn't in the chamber adjoining his.

If someone saw his townhouse, they would assume nothing had changed in his life. While inside, Oliver saw the world with entirely new eyes.

~

AFTER A MONTH FROM HELL, Oliver gave in to his mother's blatant attempts at making him feel guilty about, as she put it, never coming out into society as his title demanded.

He attended a ball.

He stepped into the music-filled room and glanced around the richly dressed, assembled members of the London ton. Hopefully, he could dance once with Charlotte or his sister-in-law and then hide in the card room.

He spotted the effervescent Lady Charlotte and moved quickly into the safety of her company and joined the gentlemen standing in her circle.

"Lady Charlotte," he said, greeting her with his best courtly bow and a smile. He had few real joys nowadays, but seeing his true friends was one of them.

"John, Archie." He nodded to his best friends standing near her.

Charlotte curtsied, and the gentlemen inclined their heads with a smile.

"Oliver, I didn't realise you had come back to town." Charlotte held out her hand, and he bent over her fingers and touched his lips to her glove.

The gentlemen shook their heads in agreement, and Oliver clenched his teeth, forcing a smile to his lips. He hadn't been looking forward to this conversation with his friends.

"I've been back for a while." *A whole month, but who's counting?*

"Haven't seen you at the club," Archie admonished quietly, his elegant eyebrows rising in question.

Oliver lifted a shoulder in a half-shrug, glancing away for a moment.

"I've been busy with estate business and have been working with my fencing master quite a bit."

Every day actually. It was the only thing keeping his body in check. It stopped him from mounting his horse and galloping straight to Scotland. Damn his pride. He wanted his wife.

"Not to mention the fact that you are newly married," Charlotte teased with a cheeky grin and a sisterly nudge to his side. "Where is that beautiful wife of yours?" Charlotte turned her head, apparently looking for the blonde angel who belonged at his side.

Oliver steeled himself for what he had to tell Charlotte, and for the response he was sure to get.

"Sarah has gone to Scotland for the rest of the Season." He explained as nonchalantly as possible. He glanced away again, then returned his gaze to her frowning face.

"Pardon?" Charlotte leaned forward, as though she hadn't heard correctly.

"Sarah's in Scotland." His cheeks ached as he tried to maintain his smile and there was a heaviness on his chest that he couldn't seem to dislodge. He coughed.

"I'm sorry, Oliver, I must not have heard you correctly."

Oliver wasn't enjoying the play of emotions across Charlotte's face. They made him feel sick with guilt. She had never hidden her feelings well. It was the one thing she didn't seem able to do. He clenched his teeth together and tried once more.

"Sarah's in Scotland." He said it this time louder and with more feeling.

"What did you do?" Charlotte swung exasperated eyes heavenward and then fixed them back on his face.

"Charlotte, please." Oliver wasn't sure what else to say as he watched her boil dangerously close to exploding. Her face was turning red, and her eyes were practically spitting fire.

"What did you do?" Charlotte repeated the question, then lowered her voice when she noticed how many people turned to look at them. She removed the scowl from her face and plastered on a calm facade, although it was obvious the fire beneath was still burning.

"I came back to London without my wife." Oliver repeated the words he knew had to be said, but he was loath to say them. It still hurt that she had chosen Scotland over him.

"And you packed her off to a Scottish castle? Your new wife? Your *duchess*?"

"She wanted to go. She wasn't enjoying being at the estate and when I asked her whether she wanted to come back to London with me or stay there, she chose to travel to Scotland instead."

"That is impossible. You must have done something very wrong." Charlotte shook her head.

"I didn't do a thing. The servants and I welcomed her. It was only when my mother and sister-in-law arrived, that—"

"*No!*" Charlotte's voice lost the calmness and she glared at him.

Oliver groaned. This was too much, even for him. And he had plenty of practice managing difficult women.

"You let your mother and that *snake* of a sister-in-law visit, while you were on your honeymoon?"

"They didn't visit. They live there."

"Oh Sarah, you poor, poor thing," she murmured as if to herself, clasping her hands in front of her ample bosom.

"Charlotte, that is not fair. I didn't do anything—"

"*Exactly*. You didn't do anything to protect your beautiful, sweet, innocent wife from being set upon by the most scheming pair of women I have ever met."

Oliver had forgotten that Charlotte and Honoria had debuted in the same year. They were both duke's daughters and had moved in the same circles. It seemed that Charlotte's opinion of Honoria was similar to Sarah's.

"You stupid, ignorant..." As Charlotte blew air out her nostrils and started to wind herself up into a full-blown attack, help came from an unexpected corner.

"Lady Charlotte." Archie stepped in front of Oliver and bowed to her.

"May I have the pleasure of this dance?" The question was politely worded, but his stance and tone left little to decipher.

Charlotte shut her mouth and eyed Archie with disdain.

"Of course, my lord." Her eyes flashed daggers at Oliver even while Archie led her away.

"I wasn't quite expecting that response," Oliver muttered to John, the only one still standing near him.

"Charlotte is very fond of Sarah." John gave him a confused look. "You didn't allow your mother and sister-in-law to intrude upon your honeymoon, did you?"

"Not you, too." Oliver was ready to throw up his hands in defeat. If John wouldn't defend him, no one would.

"No, don't get me wrong. If Sarah wanted to go to Scotland, then that's fine. But why did your mother and Lady Sombury leave London in the middle of the Season to visit you?" John pointed out, his eyebrows rising in a question that Oliver had never thought to ask.

"They said they wanted to help, but, well, they didn't."

He didn't understand why his mother hadn't left Sarah and him alone. He knew that she didn't approve of Sarah as the new duchess, but he hadn't had the courage to ask his mother to back off, let alone to leave her home.

Her home... that just said it all.

❧

OLIVER BURIED himself for another month. When he finally resurfaced, he started attending his club, often spending the afternoons riding or talking with John, Archie or Rupert.

At his club, he placed a fake smile on his face when explaining that his wife had taken to the country for the remainder of the Season. Most of the gentlemen shrugged or gave him an understanding wink or nod. They probably thought he had discarded her, yet nothing could be further from the truth.

The one thing he couldn't force himself to do was indulge in an affair. He could hardly keep his food down when he thought of laying with another woman.

How could he ever touch another woman with the hands that had loved Sarah?

He was aware that everyone expected it. Rupert had gently suggested he look at finding a discreet mistress. He had been inches away from planting his fist on his friend's jaw.

One more month of the Season and he could return to his wife. He would find Sarah and demand they never separate again. Assuming that was, that she'd have him back at all.

~

AFTER AN AFTERNOON at his club listening to Archie complain about a ball his mother was forcing him to attend, Oliver decided he would make the effort to attend. Comrades in arms, and all that.

Oliver had been enjoying himself amongst his peers and friends in the card room, when a nasty voice broke through the cigars and sherry.

"Look who's here, and without his pretty wife." The snide comment came from behind John's back, and Oliver looked up to see a large man step out from his friend's shadow.

"Millington." Oliver inclined his head and turned back to Archie.

Patrick Millington moved around their group and took the seat opposite Oliver.

"So, how's married life?" he asked with a leer.

"Good."

"And where is the pretty new duchess?" Millington looked around the room as though he would see her there.

Oliver gripped his cards tightly in his hands, his palms beginning to sweat. He hadn't seen Millington since the night he had tried to make Sarah dance with him again, and Oliver had punched him in the stomach.

"She's in Scotland for the remainder of the Season."

For the first time, Oliver was glad Sarah wasn't in London. She would be horrified if she had to deal with this man again.

"What a pity." Millington sighed dramatically.

Oliver saw the interested looks they were getting from the gentlemen in the room, but did his best to maintain the illusion that he was in control of his temper.

He smiled and picked up his sherry, swallowing the sweet liquid with a harsh gulp.

John answered for him. "It is a pity. My sister especially wishes the duchess had returned."

"She's not the only one." Millington leered again and slapped John on the back. This time, Oliver smelled the liquor on Millington's breath and tried to unclench his fingers.

"Millington." John's tone was a warning as he moved restlessly in his seat.

Everyone in the card room was now watching their group. Oliver's face flushed with heat at being the centre of attention. The expression on Millington's face was satisfied, triumphant, and Oliver didn't know why.

He was the one who had won her; he had married her, taken her virginity and enjoyed months in her bed. Why was Millington looking so smug?

"Why do you care? She's nothing to you." Oliver shot back. Propriety be damned.

Millington laughed, the sound rough and too loud.

"But I was so hoping that she could be." His lustful eyes told Oliver more than his words could about what he wanted from Sarah.

"That is uncalled for." John surged to his feet in time with Oliver. Millington slowly followed. "Speak plainly, Millington."

Standing now, the bastard was within arm's reach.

"Oh, I just hoped now that she was married, Sarah would indulge herself like so many other married ladies."

Oliver lunged forward and wrapped his hands around the other man's throat, remembering the way Sarah had looked that first night.

"Over my dead body." He squeezed tight.

"Oliver, stop." John tugged at him.

Oliver forced his aching hands to relax and released Millington's throat reluctantly. He glared at the disgusting man, who was a mottled red, and turned to leave.

He heard Millington wheeze and cough, then speak. "You can't protect her night and day, do you realise that? When she's in London next Season, I will make sure she grants me an audience."

Oliver froze. As a married woman, Sarah wasn't as protected as virgins were. She was allowed to walk alone, ride in carriages alone and meet gentlemen in his home alone. Oliver had a vision of Sarah's lovely body held prostrate under Millington's, fighting him to no avail.

Oliver turned and swung, putting all his anger and pain behind his fist and hit Millington squarely on the side of the head. Pain splintered through his hand, and he roared. Millington went down and didn't get back up.

The rest of the night was a blur. A doctor was called, Oliver was rushed home, and a report was made to the authorities. No one blamed Oliver and as a duke, he was beyond reproach.

Millington regained consciousness the next day, with no lasting effects. Oliver only hoped he had the chance to plant the bastard properly the next time he saw him.

Chapter Seventeen

Many miles away in Scotland, Graves, Lincoln's butler, was indulging in a habit he rarely allowed himself. Gossip. His wife, the housekeeper, was worried about their new duchess.

"I don't like it, Isaac, I just don't like it," Mrs. Graves told her husband in bed that night. "She's clearly pregnant and miserable."

"Do you think the duke knows?" Graves asked.

How could the new duke he had known as a young man turn out to be so heartless? Her Grace was the most beautiful woman he had ever seen. She was also kind to the servants, clearly well-bred, elegant and thoughtful.

She was also definitely not born to be a duchess. She had been found making her bed, baking a cake in the kitchen and dusting the bookshelves in the library. Her actions would usually have sent the maids into a mad rush to stop her and do a better job themselves.

However, they had been warned of her need to do odd jobs like the dusting, through a carefully worded letter from the duke. Therefore, they had let her do whatever she wanted. In response, the duchess had seemed content.

"I don't know. But it would be horrible if he did. That would mean he got her pregnant, shipped her here, and then ran back to London to go back to bedding his whores," Mrs. Graves answered, with a shake of her head.

Graves clucked his tongue disapprovingly at his wife's language.

Mrs. Graves gave him that look which told him she knew exactly what young men did, and promptly turned over to go to sleep.

In another part of the ancient castle, Sarah sat awake with a book.

She found it very hard to sleep most nights. Her back hurt already, and she only had a small bump. She didn't know how she would cope when she was bigger. Sarah put her book of French poetry aside and blew out the candles next to her bed.

The fire in the grate cast a small amount of light in the room, and she lay down, pulling her gown up to her waist. She ran her hands over her belly. Lying on her back, her womb seemed to distend, and she could feel the protrusion of her developing babe. Sarah took so much pleasure from her growing child that she rarely thought of Oliver, only once an hour or so. The small flutter of movement deep in her belly made her heart lighten. Oliver had given this child to her in a moment of love and passion.

She still didn't know why Oliver had withdrawn from her, but she knew it had everything to do with his family. As her husband and as a man, Oliver had loved her. He had laughed with her, cared for her and brought her incredible pleasure in his bed.

But as a son and the new Duke of Lincoln, he seemed lost, angry, upset and frustrated. Somehow, their marriage had become that too. Over the past two months, Sarah had realised that she could have done more to hold their marriage together. She could have stayed by his side, talked to him, or stood up to his family more often, and she was resolved to do so when she went back to London after the babe was born.

She had decided to stay in Scotland and birth her babe in the ancient castle. She was happy here. The servants treated her with respect and warmth. They smiled at her and listened to her and didn't get upset when she did things that normal duchesses didn't do.

When Sarah had arrived in Scotland, she had spent her nights trying not to cry into her pillows and her days wandering aimlessly around the glorious castle. But after two months of good food, clean air and reflection, she was determined to get her husband back.

Sarah's mother had visited for two weeks the month before. Her mother had taken one look at her and known what was going on.

"Daughter, it appears that you need to weep, long and loudly," her mother had told her, running a loving hand down her cheek.

Sarah had said, "I shouldn't, Mother, it's not good for the baby."

"Oh, nonsense, I spent half my pregnancies in tears over nothing and all of you are beautiful children. Come here."

And thus, given permission to grieve, Sarah had cried and cried. So many tears fell that she felt severely dehydrated after she was done. Her mother had held her, rocked her, and had told her everything was going to be all right. To have faith in herself, her husband, and God.

The only thing that still bothered Sarah was the thought of Oliver going to another woman in London. It tormented her daily, but she clung to the memories of their passion, hoping he would not need to replace her. She was terribly afraid, as most husbands in his peerage would take a mistress. But then she would remember his promise to be faithful, lay her hand on her belly and try to be positive.

THE NEXT MONTH passed in a blur of alcohol-fuelled days and nights for the Duke of Lincoln. Oliver lost himself in the bottom of a port bottle, or several port bottles, to be precise.

He lay his head back against the head rest on his chair in his study and heard his butler announce a Mister Turner through a foggy brain.

Why was Archie here? He opened his eyes and groaned at the sight of his friend's gold embroidered waistcoat.

"Archie, I will go blind looking at a waistcoat like that."

"I think the alcohol will do more to your eyesight than my clothes ever could."

Oliver moaned. "Don't lecture me." He let his eyes close, and his head fell back against the head rest again.

"Join me at the Mossam ball tonight." Archie put as much command into his voice as Oliver had ever heard.

He grunted in reply. His sister-in-law had more bite in her than that.

"We have allowed you a month to get over that incident with Millington. It is time you attended another event."

Oliver groaned again at the use of the royal "we." He could only imagine that Rupert, John, and Archie had been discussing him.

"Would you sit down, for God's sake?" Oliver gestured with his hands, annoyed that his perfect friend would be here to witness him in such a state. Why could they all not just leave him alone to be miserable?

Archie chuckled. Oliver opened his eyes at the sound. It had been a long time since Archie had laughed like that.

Seeming to remember himself, Archie schooled his face into impassiveness.

"Let's get you some coffee and then get you into your evening clothes."

Oliver allowed Archie to order coffee and something to eat. An hour later, he was feeling better and made his way upstairs for a bath and to prepare for his first ball in months.

Two hours later, he wished he had never let his friend drag him out of the house. Two widows had propositioned him, as well as a bored married matron. He could not wait to leave. Why did they not understand that he didn't want anyone other than his angel, Sarah?

Oliver could finally admit it to himself and would out loud if necessary. He missed Sarah. He loved her and no one else came even close.

He was walking past a small alcove off the side of the ballroom, when he heard his name being spoken. Oliver would usually have ignored it, but something in the tone arrested his attention.

He sidled closer but kept out of sight so that the women could not see him.

"I cannot believe you and your mother-in-law managed to run off the new duchess so quickly. I thought it would take you months."

A snide little laugh that he recognised very well rang in response.

"It was very easy, really. We hardly did a thing."

Yes, Oliver thought bitterly. Other than everything you knew to make Sarah feel about as welcome as a flea.

And I did nothing to help her. Self-disgust bloomed in his chest.

"No, really, tell me. I thought the greatest love match of the year would prove almost unbreakable."

Oliver swallowed the lump that rose in his throat. Was that really how the ton saw his marriage? If only it had been true. He'd thought they could get through anything, but at the first hurdle they'd both fallen. Or rather, he had and he'd taken Sarah down with him.

Another horrible laugh sounded.

"Hardly. All we did was let her fall on her pretty face. She didn't know how to organise an informal dinner at home. She couldn't instruct servants, and she dressed like a peasant. She found out very quickly that she wasn't suitable to step into *my* shoes." Honoria's disdain was so obvious now that Oliver could not believe he had ever thought the woman would help Sarah.

Fool.

"But what will you do now?" asked her companion, apparently eager for the gossip.

"Now? Nothing. Oliver is exactly where his mother and I want him. By our side in London, a country separating him and his wife. He is so malleable. Nothing like my dear husband, the real duke."

Oliver's backbone stiffened at this evidence of how his sister-in-law really saw him. He could only imagine how miserable she would have made his life if he had married her. Being compared to his brother for every day of his life? The thought was enough to weaken his knees.

"Malleable, how?" asked her eager friend.

"Well, just last week his wife wrote to him asking him to visit her in Scotland. During the Season, can you imagine that? Intolerable." Honoria sounded disgusted at the prospect, despite the fact that she had left London for a month to join him and his new wife at their estate.

Oliver tried to recall the day Honoria was talking about, but could barely remember. His butler had read him a letter whilst he had been in his cups.

"And he chose not to go?" the other woman asked, apparently surprised.

"Of course, he wanted to go. But his mother made it clear that his wife was just having a fit of the vapours and that she could wait another few months."

Oliver gasped and then quickly covered his mouth. He did remember his mother raving about something that night, but he rarely listened to her anymore.

"Oh, that poor woman." The stranger sighed.

"I know, it is rather amusing, is not it?" The glee in Honoria's voice was sickening.

"What newlywed bride wants to know that her new husband would prefer to be gallivanting around London than spend time with her? It must have broken her heart."

The sadness in the stranger's voice hit Oliver the hardest.

Was that really how Sarah would have seen his staying in London rather than following her to Scotland? He would never have let her go if he thought she believed he was carousing.

Honoria's laugh was genuine now. She was truly amused.

"Serves her right, if it did. She had no right to marry so far above her station." Honoria's voice was so full of the victory, she sounded ecstatic.

"But what is it she wanted, do you think?" the stranger asked.

Oliver began to move away from the column, sick with guilt. His belly felt tight, as though someone had gut-punched him.

"To tell him she is *enceinte*, probably," Honoria replied bitterly.

"*Enceinte*? Already?"

"Probably. The lower classes never seem to have any trouble."

Pain, unlike anything Oliver had ever felt, smacked him in the chest. He doubled over, breathing hard. Honoria was poisonous. He'd honestly had no idea how deep her treachery lay.

"Do you really think she could be carrying his heir, though?"

Oliver was wondering that himself. Thinking back, he had spent every night for almost eight weeks in Sarah's bed without her flux. The reality of that hit him like a slap in the face. Why hadn't he counted the weeks? Was she really pregnant?

"My maid told me of her suspicions even before she left for Scotland. They had all noticed her lack of monthly linens."

Pardon me?

Oliver huffed, breathing hard from his nose. His hands clenched into fists as his throat ached with the need to scream.

Honoria had thought that his wife was pregnant. And yet, she had not only encouraged Sarah's departure to Scotland but had intentionally kept him in London so that he would continue to be unaware of her condition.

"That won't make it easy to separate them, if that is what you intend."

"Well, you never know. If Oliver stays on past the end of the Season, she may have died in her childbed before he can even reach Scotland."

Oliver hadn't been aware of making any sound. But from the way the two women in front of him gasped and jumped, he realised he must have.

Sarah had been right all along. This woman was worse than horrible. She was evil. Why hadn't he just paid her to leave?

He may not feel like the Duke of Lincoln, nor did he want the title or feel as though he deserved it, but he was.

Dammit, he was. With all the power and money that came with it.

And it was finally time he stood up and took control of his own life and destiny.

"You, my lady, will never enter one of my homes ever again," Oliver growled at his sister-in-law as he rounded the pillar, his shoulders flexing and straining as his arms shook with anger. "My brother may not have allowed a large enough annuity for you, but I will. You will live wherever you want, marry whomsoever you want, but you will not come near me, my estate, nor my wife ever again."

"Oliver..." Honoria began.

Oliver straightened to his full height and glared down on her.

"My name is Lord Oliver Lyre, Duke of Lincoln. You will address me as such."

"Your Grace," she squeaked.

Oliver turned and left without bowing, without even a word of farewell. He grabbed his coat, hailed his carriage and headed home as fast as his team of six could carry him.

Chapter Eighteen

O liver sent a note ahead to his Scottish estate, informing the servants that he would be joining his wife, but requesting them not to tell her, as it was a surprise.

He rounded the final bend in the road and looked out at the estate he had not visited in almost a decade. It was beautiful. Grand and ancient. He had always loved coming here as a child.

He was greeted by a young footman and the older, balding butler.

"Your Grace, it is splendid to see you here."

The old butler bowed and smiled.

Oliver searched his memory and came up with a name.

"Thank you, Graves, it's lovely to be here. Could you tell me where my wife is?"

The two footmen behind the butler shared worried looks and Oliver's stomach tightened with concern. Was she all right?

"Her Grace is walking the rose garden, Your Grace." Graves's eyes lit up at the use of Sarah's title.

Oliver could only assume his wife had found her place amongst his servants. Without the interference of Honoria or his mother, she was sure to have charmed them all.

Oliver followed a footman out to the gardens and stopped when he saw her. She was very clearly pregnant. Why she hadn't told him, he didn't understand, but it was clear that the condition agreed with her.

She glowed with good health. Her breasts had almost doubled in size and Oliver felt the stirrings of arousal for the first time in several months.

Sarah stopped along the path, bending backwards over her hand pressed into her lower back and looked toward the house.

She caught sight of Oliver and stared at him, blinking rapidly as though she expected him to disappear.

His heart pounded in his chest, and he inhaled slowly, forcing his heavy legs to walk over to his wife. He stopped and bowed to her.

"Sarah." His throat was tight with an unfamiliar emotion as she continued to stare at him.

Sarah gasped, "You're real."

Oliver laughed for the first time in months. "Of course, I'm real."

"But you wrote and said you couldn't leave London at the moment and wouldn't be coming to see me." The hurt he had caused her was evident now that he could see the black marks beneath her eyes.

"I know. Do you think we could go somewhere to talk?" he asked, conscious of the many servants now discreetly congregating around their duchess.

"Of course. My afternoon sitting room would be perfect."

She lifted her head and accepted his offered arm.

Oliver had spent the journey to Scotland rehearsing what he would say to his beautiful wife once he arrived. He knew he owed her many apologies, but where to start was the hardest question to answer. He had always found that being honest with Sarah worked best, but that would mean he would have to tell her everything. And the thought of exposing himself so totally was terrifying.

Sarah squeezed his arm as they entered her sitting room and let go of him. "I'm glad you decided to come, Oliver."

"I wasn't sure you'd want to speak to me after the way I treated you."

Her gazed dropped. "It wasn't you that treated me unfairly."

He waited, sure there was more to come.

She lifted her gaze and looked straight at him. "Why did you not protect me against them, Oliver?"

He swallowed hard. "I am so sorry, Sarah. I should have been your champion throughout the whole time my mother stayed with us, and I wasn't. I left you to defend yourself against the wolves, and that was terrible of me. I can only hope that you will forgive me."

Tears trembled on her lashes and she blinked them away.

"I forgive you, of course I forgive you Oliver. It just makes me so incredibly sad to think that you would let anyone treat me that way."

He grabbed for her hands.

"I promise you, Sarah, that I will never let anyone speak to you that way again. Nor will I dismiss your complaints and feelings as I did, which I know was my greatest mistake. How can I make it up to you?"

He'd do anything. Even live out here in Scotland if she wanted to. As long as he had Sarah, he was home. He could manage his family's estate through letters and short trips to London.

She squeezed his hands.

"I want you to work with me through our marriage. I don't want to ever feel so alone again."

He laughed. "Done. I will change your bedroom into a sitting room, or anything you want, and give away your bed to the poor. My Duchess of Lincoln will sleep in the duke's bedroom every night."

"Perhaps we could change my bedroom into a nursery instead," Sarah whispered.

Oliver cleared his throat.

"When you wrote to ask me to come to you here, was there something, in particular, you needed me for?" He smiled as she blushed and dropped her head.

"I did want to tell you something important, yes," she admitted softly.

Oliver's eyes lowered to her belly that was now barely visible beneath the material of her dress. "And that would be?"

Sarah looked up, and her eyes narrowed. "You really can't tell?"

Oliver laughed, stopped, then laughed again. "Oh God, it feels good to laugh again."

His cheeks ached from smiling, and his belly hurt in a strange way, too. He hadn't been happy in three months.

Oliver fought the urge to whisk her off to a bedroom and strip her clothes away. How desperate he was to get his hands on her again. But that would have to wait. They had things to discuss.

"I think I can see what you wanted to tell me, Sarah, but I believe it would be best if you said it instead."

Sarah smiled, her whole face lighting up as she seemed to realise his intention.

"I am bearing your child, my lord."

And there they were. The sweetest words he had ever heard.

Sarah stood up and moved toward him. Oliver stood as she reached for his hand and pulled it to her.

Oliver swallowed uncomfortably but allowed her to bring his hand to her belly. That first touch of his hand on the hard bump that concealed and protected his child brought a lump to Oliver's throat.

He brought his other hand up as well and held his child with both hands. The baby moved in response, and Oliver felt the tell-tale shift of flesh. Startled, he dropped both hands away.

Sarah laughed, pulling his hands back to her. "He's just happy you're here, Oliver."

"He?" Oliver drew Sarah onto the chaise lounge so they could sit together.

"I've decided it is a boy." Sarah shrugged and set her chin. She was obviously brooking no argument. He didn't mind, either way.

"All right. I have missed you so much." He brushed the hairs at the nape of her neck with his fingers and inhaled sharply as pleasure coiled deep in his gut.

~

"I HAVE MISSED YOU TOO."

Sarah moaned as his hot, soft lips captured her mouth in a kiss so sweet and gentle that it brought tears to her eyes.

"Let me show you my bedroom," she told her husband. Confident in his need for her, she decided it was the time that she showed him how much she wanted him. How much she needed him.

"We should talk first, about... everything."

"No, later," Sarah urged, tugging Oliver faster down the hall. There would be days, months, years, to talk about all the ways they needed to strengthen their marriage.

But for now, she needed to feel that incredible closeness that she had only shared with this one beautiful man that she loved.

The butler and several footmen stood near the entrance to the stairs. Oliver opened his mouth to dismiss them, but Sarah knew it was her time.

"Thank you so much, Graves. My husband and I will be dining in our room tonight. Can you send dinner up at seven?"

She lifted her skirts and began to ascend the stairs, her husband hot on her heels.

Her heart was beating heavily in her chest. She could not believe she had just invited her husband to bed her in the middle of the day. But it had to be done. She could not think straight.

All the tension of the past three months seemed to be focused on driving her insane with desire. She could feel the wetness between her thighs. Her nipples peaked beneath her dress and she could barely wait for Oliver to close the door behind him. What had pregnancy done to her?

"Sarah, I'm not sure if we should do this before we've had a proper talk." Despite what he was saying he was tugging at his cravat and unbuttoning his waistcoat.

Thank goodness for that!

Sarah tugged at her gown, loosely-laced in front to allow for her expanding tummy.

"I only want to know one thing, my lord, before you touch me."

If he lied about this, she was certain she would know.

Oliver's hands stilled on his shirt buttons as he awaited her question.

"Anything, Sarah."

"Have you touched another woman since we have been apart?" She didn't drop her eyes for a moment, watching Oliver for signs of discomfort.

He seemed to relax visibly, his shoulders dropping as a soft smile graced his now calm features.

"Oh, Sarah, I haven't touched another woman since that first night I met you," he confessed, his honesty evident in his eyes.

Sarah could have sobbed with relief, but instead, she pulled the gown off her body and dropped it to the floor, standing in only her chemise before her husband. Her nipples tightened further as they pressed against the silk, and the warmth of the room kept her from shivering.

He took the few steps that separated them, pulling her body against him. She reached up for him as he swooped down for a kiss so hungry it sent the already built fire in Sarah roaring to life.

Sarah pulled back and dropped down to her knees, the carpet soft against her skin.

She had spent the last month imagining what she would do to Oliver if she ever got him to herself again. She had planned a seduction based around his pleasure. She would make sure that he never left her again.

Her own body ached in anticipation of what was to come, but she'd happily wait for her own fulfilment if it meant giving him this.

"No, Sarah, you can't." Oliver gasped and pushed against her shoulder, trying to step back from her grasp.

Sarah smiled up at him, and with her eyes coaxed him closer again.

"I can. I want to. Please, Oliver." She was all but begging now, gesturing with her hands for him to come back to her.

"But you're my wife, and you're pregnant!" Oliver recoiled again with wide eyes and flailing hands.

Sarah laughed softly. "Exactly. My body hungers for you, Oliver. And I am your wife. I should be the only one to give you pleasure."

Oliver moved back within her grasp, looking encouraged by her words.

Sarah grabbed hold of his thighs and pulled him closer. She stared at his beautifully erect penis and was amazed again that this was what had given her a child. Smiling up at Oliver, she wrapped one hand around the base and pulled him closer with a hand around his thighs.

She stared down at the beautiful piece of flesh again and laughed as she watched it quiver with anticipation. At her laugh, a similar shiver swept through Oliver's whole body, and he groaned.

She ducked her head and sucked the beautiful, hot flesh into her mouth. It was hard but also soft, and slightly salty. She used her hands and moved up and down on him in a similar fashion that he had taught her to ride him.

He tried to pull away, but she held him tight to her. She wanted this.

"Sarah, stop, please, I'm going to..." Oliver groaned as she squeezed the base of him and moved faster. He threaded his hands into her hair and cried out as though his soul was being ripped from his body.

He jerked, spilling himself in spasms into her mouth. Sarah swallowed quickly and licked the tip once more. Oliver's knees began to shake, and she let him slip from her mouth.

Oliver tugged Sarah to her feet, and together they staggered the few feet to the bed and collapsed on top of the covers. He kissed her mouth and buried his face into her hair, seemingly embarrassed. She held him to her and heard him as he whispered into her ear.

"Thank you."

Sarah giggled, happiness filling her belly and making her feel a little lightheaded.

"You shouldn't have done that for me, though, it's not right." Oliver continued to speak to her, still hiding in her hair.

Sarah pulled back and made him look her in the eyes.

"So, you believe only whores can give their men pleasure like that?"

Her husband's eyes widened, and her cheeks heated as she used a word that she'd only said aloud once.

"I wouldn't know, my love. I've never had that done to me before. I just didn't think ladies did that sort of thing."

She grinned up at him, the weight of her anger lifting now that she knew how special she was to him. She wanted to be the one to bring him unknown pleasure.

"Oh, Oliver, you forget, I'm not just a lady, I'm your wife. My mother told me that everything you do to me I can do to you, and you had brought me pleasure that way before. So, I reasoned that it was possible to do it for you too."

Sarah laughed again and kissed his shoulder, tasting the sweet flavour of his skin against her tongue.

Chapter Nineteen

Oliver stared at his wife for a long moment. Was that really what her mother had told her? No wonder she had always been so eager and happy to do anything for him or let him do anything he wanted to her.

Remembering all the times he had brought her to climax with his mouth, he felt his already satisfied cock stir to life again. Sliding down the bed, he slowly pulled her chemise up over her burgeoning belly, exposing luscious breasts and golden curls.

"Perhaps I should return the favour, then." He smiled up at her, dipping his head to her nipples.

Sarah cried out when he licked first one hard, darkened nipple, then the other. She cried out again when he pulled one into his mouth and suckled greedily. She threaded her hands into his hair and held him there, urging him to suck harder.

Oliver continued to lick and sip at her nipples while he slid his hand between her silky thighs. She was so wet, he groaned. Unable to resist, he slid two long fingers into her, enjoying both her moan and the way her body bowed up in appreciation. He slid his fingers out and spread the moisture across that hidden bud and listened to her moan again.

Smiling to himself, Oliver pressed kisses to her belly, lingering over the stretched skin before moving down to paradise.

It didn't take long. Oliver flicked his tongue over her twice, inserted his fingers once more, and she shattered.

He didn't let her come down from her high but pushed at Sarah's shoulder so that she would roll over. She came up onto all fours so that she could roll how he wanted and accommodate their growing child.

Her beautiful, rounded arse came into view, and he knelt behind her to admire the curves of smooth skin. Oliver pushed gently down on her back and encouraged her to drop her head.

"Go down flat and open your legs for me," he whispered in her ear, the words arousing them both to even greater degrees.

Sarah parted her legs and put her elbows out for balance. Oliver saw her tilt her hips and watched the glistening slit come into view. The sight of her opening hit him right in the belly, and he gripped the warm flesh of her hips.

He inhaled slowly to calm himself, lined his cock up and buried himself to the hilt in one controlled thrust. Hot, wet flesh enclosed his entire shaft and a groan rumbled in his chest. She was tighter than he remembered and he had to clench his teeth against the need to explode immediately. He stroked her back softly, stilling his movements to give her time to adjust.

"Please, Oliver," Sarah moaned, moving her hips in the rhythm she wanted him to pursue.

"Have you missed me, Sarah?" Oliver asked her as he very slowly withdrew, the tip of his cock still embedded in her heat.

"You know I have."

"Have you missed me inside you, like this?" Oliver penetrated her as slowly and as deeply as he could. He gripped her hips tightly, stilling her gyrations.

"Please, Oliver."

"Please, what, Sarah? What do you need?"

He knew he was possessive and a little cruel, but since he had accepted who he was, he could not help letting these new and foreign emotions run free.

"You, please," she begged again, moaning as he penetrated deep, feeling her arse against his belly.

"Tell me." Oliver gripped her hips tighter.

"Harder, please. Deeper, more." Sarah moaned, rolling her hips and bucking against him.

Oliver's control snapped. She was wet and wanting him. He couldn't hold back any longer. He thrust ruthlessly into her, setting up a deep, pounding rhythm that reached her womb.

"You'll never leave me again." He rode her harder and faster.

"No, I won't." Sarah cried out, pushing her body flatter and raising her hips higher for him.

"You're mine, Sarah, do you understand? My wife, my love, mine."

Oliver couldn't believe the words that were leaving his mouth but knew he needed to say them, and she needed to hear them.

"Yes!" Sarah screamed as she flew apart and convulsed around him over and over again, coming harder and longer than she ever had before.

Oliver tried to resist, but her body milking his was just too erotic. A wave of pleasure hit him like a fist to the gut. Ecstasy overwhelmed him as he pumped his seed into her with a hoarse cry of pleasure.

His release seemed to trigger another smaller climax inside of her, and she cried out again and shuddered beneath him. They dropped forward and to the side to protect the babe, and fell into a deep and restful sleep.

Several hours later, Oliver awoke to a knock at the door that signalled their dinner had arrived. Not bothering to get up, he just looked down at his wife and sighed as happiness washed over him like a cleansing rain. She was back where she belonged, in his arms. And he was back where he belonged, by her side.

"My babe," Oliver whispered, gliding his hand over the hard, round belly in front of him. Sarah was still asleep, but Oliver could not rest a moment longer; he wanted her again.

He had assumed that a pregnant wife would dampen one's ardour. But soon after seeing Sarah, he realised that whether she was her usual svelte self or as big as a house, he would want her 'til the day he died. She was the most beautiful, sensual woman he had ever known.

Oliver didn't even wake her, he just rolled Sarah onto her side and stroked between her legs. Her folds were still slick, so Oliver moved his hand up until he could flick the extra sensitive nub. He fondled her for a moment or two, and when she, still half asleep, tilted her hips back invitingly, he lifted her leg up and forward, and slid into her from behind.

Oliver grunted his approval when Sarah came awake with a moan and tilted her pelvis to give him better access. He wrapped a hand around her breast, tweaking the sensitive nipple.

"I love you, Sarah." Oliver moved slowly into her scalding body, enjoying her depths, and then pulled almost completely out of her.

Sarah gasped and shuddered.

He had to tell her how he felt. "I love you for who you are, but I also love you for the person you make me want to be." Oliver moaned deep in his throat as she gripped him tightly inside her sheath. He shifted his hip angle and began pumping into her faster.

"Come for me, please, I need you." He was so hoarse he sounded ill.

Sarah shook her head and turned to look at him.

"I love you, please." He began moving slower so that she felt every inch as it slid inside of her. He moved the hand that was gripping her hip around to the flesh just above where they joined, and Sarah cried out in pleasure.

Sarah began moving her hips in time with his, and she closed her eyes.

Oliver felt her sheath tightening, and he hissed, "Yes," ruthlessly holding back his orgasm.

Just when Oliver's vision started to blur, he felt the change in her. Sarah cried out, and her body convulsed, Oliver held tight to her hips and with one more thrust, joined her.

~

SARAH LAY in the circle of Oliver's arms, completely happy for the first time in months. This was even better than it had been at the beginning of their marriage. He loved her now, and she finally felt secure in that knowledge.

"I love you, too." She looked up into the almost black eyes she knew better than her own.

"Never leave me again. I almost didn't survive it this time," Oliver said, kissing her quickly on the mouth, the move possessive and hard.

"I had to leave, Oliver. Your mother made me feel like the worst wife in the history of bad wives, and I couldn't keep pretending that I didn't miss you as you were, before they arrived."

Oliver pulled her tighter against his body, the heat and strength of him reassuring.

"You stopped coming to my bed," she whispered, the pain still very palpable.

"I know, I'm sorry. I drank too much port one night when my mother was being particularly nasty and could not make it to your bed. And then the next night I could not bring myself to do it either. I felt like I was failing you as a husband and failing my servants and tenants as the new duke—failing everyone, in fact—and I just could not, Sarah. Please, forgive me."

"I knew you were struggling with your new responsibility. I'm sorry I wasn't more sympathetic."

"You were. I just could not see past my own inadequacies. You did everything you could under the circumstances, more than any other lady would have."

"I knew I wasn't good enough to be a duchess, but I thought I could keep you happy in bed, at least." Salty tears stung her eyes. She didn't want to cry again, but she knew that they needed to talk about this and lay it to rest, once and for all.

"Sarah, I love you. I have loved you since you tried to comfort me at the opera only a week after we met. You make me feel like the most important person in the world, and after a lifetime of feeling superfluous, you are exactly what I need."

Sarah could hardly believe her husband meant those words, but as she looked into Oliver's eyes and saw that he was genuine, her heart began to sing.

"I need you to know something. You are more than I deserve. You are the best woman I could have chosen to be my duchess," Oliver told her confidently, earnestly.

"Then why did you let me believe that you agreed with your mother?" Sarah asked.

"The problem was that I believed I wasn't good enough to be the duke. I have been told since birth that I wasn't, and I always believed it. But I have finally realised that I am the duke, no matter what my mother says, and from now on I intend to act accordingly."

"How?" Sarah looked up at her beautiful duke. Proud, yet insecure and so beloved.

"Well, to start with, I need to start taking a more active interest in estate business. Talk to Archie about investments. Talk to my steward about the tenants. I also contacted the old Duke of Turret, a friend of my father who lives not far from here. We spent time at his estate when I was a child, and I always liked him. He and his wife never had any children. He would offer a wealth of knowledge I could learn from, and I think he would be an excellent mentor."

Oliver started listing off all the ways he could improve his holdings and the lives of his tenants, anxiously shifting his eyes to her face.

Sarah nodded encouragingly as Oliver began to smile.

"I know that you have never liked my sister-in-law, and given some of the things I heard her saying in London, I have informed her she is not welcome back in any of our homes. Ever again." Oliver's face took on a hardness that Sarah could not quite decipher, but his tone seemed furious.

"Really?" Sarah asked, amazed. She didn't like the woman, it was true, she almost hated her, but...

"Will she have to go back to living with her mother?" Sarah asked, biting her lip in concern.

"I have organised an annuity to be paid to her on top of what my brother left her, so that she can live wherever she wants. Just not with us."

Sarah frowned for a moment and then smiled cheekily.

"Like paying your mistress, you mean?"

Oliver sat up in bed, and her noble and beautiful duke stared down at her with a look of such horror that she burst out laughing, holding her belly as it rippled. It felt so good just to laugh.

Eventually she stopped, wiping the tears from her eyes.

"I'm sorry, Oliver, but your face..." She broke off into another round of giggles.

"I'm glad you aren't angry that we will be paying for her upkeep."

"Of course, I'm not, Oliver. She is your brother's widow. The estate should keep her, just not in our home. I wish you'd thought of it sooner," she teased with a knowing look.

"I wish I had, too. It would have saved us a lot of heartache and I would not have missed these months with you. And hurt you so much." Oliver looked down at her with sad brown eyes and swept his hand lovingly over her belly.

"I can't believe you got with child so quickly."

Sarah blushed. She wasn't sure if that was a good thing or not. She still wasn't sure if Oliver was happy about the baby or just glad that his heir was already organised.

"You're content with that, Oliver? I hope you're as happy as I am about the baby," she asked, trying not to sound as anxious as she felt.

Oliver sat up and leaned forward, pressed a kiss to her swollen belly and murmured, "I love you," against her skin.

Tears pricked Sarah's eyes, and she wiped them away before he could see.

"Now, tell me what you have been doing these past months. No more distracting me." Sarah flapped her hands at him, forcing him back up to eye level. "Please, Oliver," she all but begged, pressing a hand to his face, cupping his jaw in a loving way.

He sighed.

"I spent the first month fencing with my instructor and ignoring everyone. The second month was going to my clubs and the third month, drinking myself into oblivion every day."

Oliver exhaled sharply, his pain a tangible thing.

Sarah gasped. "I imagined you enjoying London's pleasures."

"I could not find pleasure in anything away from you." Oliver leaned forward to kiss her lips when they parted in surprise.

"Then why did you seem so relieved when I said I wanted to come to Scotland?" Sarah asked, determined to get all of her questions out of the way so that they needn't bring this subject up again.

"Because I knew you were miserable." His eyes welled up as he said the words and she rushed to reassure him.

"I was miserable, but never because of you. I blame myself..." Sarah started, silencing him when he was going to interrupt by pressing a hand to his soft lips. "I shouldn't have let your family upset me so much. I should have talked to you more. I let them come between us," Sarah said sadly, bowing her head in acknowledgment of her guilt.

"It was my fault, Sarah. I know it was. They hurt you because they knew it was the best way to hurt me. And I let it happen."

Sarah sighed heavily and leant across the bed to give her husband a soft kiss on the lips. She lingered and coaxed him with her lips until he rolled half onto her.

"Let's decide never again to let anyone else come between us. We'll always talk to each other first," Sarah suggested, pulling back to look into his eyes.

He nodded and swooped down for a kiss that turned into a loving and a worshiping of each other that lasted far into the night.

Epilogue

Three months later

Oliver paced the hallway, his shoulders aching and his arms stiff from the stress.

Another inhuman groan sounded from the door to his right, and he twisted around to pace down the hall runner once again.

"You really should stop that, Oliver. You'll wear out the rug, and your shoes." Archie's voice made him jump.

"I almost forgot you were here."

Archie lifted his head and gave him an incredulous look over the pages of his book. "Really?"

He gave his friend a smile, and Archie went back to his book. Archie had travelled up to see them a few weeks ago and had been excellent company for both he and Sarah.

The sun had risen while his wife had laboured all night. Her moans had turned to screams, and now they were grunting cries. He was tired and hungry, but nothing would move him from their bedroom door.

"It should be over soon, yes?" He shot an imploring look at Archie.

"How would I know?"

A loud bang sounded, and voices rose through the house, the cacophony of female voices and stomping feet getting closer and closer.

A loud wail broke through the sound, and his heart stopped for a moment.

A cry. A thin, small cry.

Oliver's heart began beating once again, filled with a bigger, brighter love for his wife than before. His child was here.

"Where is the woman?"

Oliver's heart sank. His mother was here!

The dowager duchess walked straight up to him, her nose high in the air.

The butler stood behind her with several footmen, all looking flushed and out of breath.

"It's fine, Graves. Please wait by the stairs. My mother will not stay long."

His mother's nostrils flared, her eyes sharpening like the lines in her face, making her seem hawk-like. Cruel.

"This is my home. I will stay as long as I like."

"You will not. You may say what you came to say, which is, of course, of great importance, or you would have put it in a letter."

A knock sounded, and the door to his bedroom opened. Oliver turned toward the midwife, her white apron smeared in blood.

"You have a son, Your Grace."

A tingle at the back of his throat signalled impending tears, so Oliver swallowed hard and walked forward, nodding at the midwife as he passed through into his bedroom.

It was hot, the moistness in the air and the heat from the blazing fire making perspiration bead on his upper lip.

Sarah sat in their bed wearing a white nightgown, her hair down around her shoulders as she lay propped up with pillows.

"Oliver. Look, isn't he the most beautiful thing in all the world?" Sarah's voice quivered as she stroked the still bloodied face of the baby in her arms. She looked pale and exhausted, her hair matted with perspiration.

"You are the most beautiful woman in the world." He sat upon the bed, stealing an arm around her and planting a kiss upon her head.

He hadn't been able to admit his fear, even to himself, but as the knowledge that they were both alive and well sunk in, relief washed over him like the waves of a storm. Cold, abrupt and with great relief.

"What should we call him?" he asked her.

The unwelcome voice came from the doorway. "Gerald, of course. After your grandfather."

Sarah froze, her shoulders becoming stiff beneath his arm.

His mother was inside his bedroom.

A place she was not welcome.

Oliver turned to her, cringing at the woman who stood at the base of their bed staring down at his son with a strange look of glee. She would be pleased he had an heir. Their line would continue. Her bloodline.

"You have no business here, Mother. Leave. Now."

She ignored him, walking around the bed to peer down at their son. "Where's the wet nurse? Call her this instant. Your wife is exhausted."

"I'm feeding him myself, Your Grace."

Sarah opened her white gown and exposed her creamy breast to their son, the squirming infant latching on quickly, contented sounds filling the air around them.

"Disgusting." His mother all but spat the word as she took a step back.

Sarah visibly cringed, and Oliver's control snapped.

"That is enough, Mother."

Oliver stood up and walked around the bed, grabbing the dowager by the arm.

"Remove your hands from my person this instant!"

She shrieked as he pulled her, bodily, from the room. His hands clenched her too tightly, but the anger in his belly grew worse as she screamed for help.

Hopefully, Sarah would forgive him for this.

He pulled her through the ante-room and out into the hallway and practically threw his other toward Graves.

"Graves, make sure my mother is packed off to London within the hour."

"You cannot do this, Oliver! I forbid it!"

"You forbid it! *You* forbid it? Mother, this is my home, not yours. I have told you that you may keep the London townhouse, but all the other property is now mine. You are forbidden from seeing my son, and my wife, and if you dare to intrude in our life once more, I will cut you off without a penny."

"You wouldn't dare."

Oliver took his time, glancing down his mother's expensive dress and up again, his gaze lingering on her jewelled necklace.

"Try me." His voice was deadly quiet and his mother cringed back. Yes, she had heard the truth in his words.

He stood straight, inclined his head and walked back into his bedroom, confident Graves would see to his wishes.

Back inside, the darkness enfolded him, relaxing Oliver once again.

"I am so sorry, my love. I promise that will never happen again."

Sarah glanced up at him, still feeding their son. "I heard what you said to her. You're sure that's the right thing to do?"

He bent down and placed another kiss on her head, smiling as she turned to get closer to him.

"Yes, my beautiful wife, it is. You, and our child, are the most important people in my life. Nothing will hurt you, ever again. For as long as I live."

Sarah nestled into his arms, and they sat there for many hours admiring every curve and wonder of their new son. Their world was only beginning, and Oliver would work as hard as he could, to make it a wonderful life, for all of them.

THE END

THE END

Lady Charlotte's Ruined Marquess

Prologue

Ten years earlier

"Your father wishes to see you, Archibald," the Marchioness of Hunting announced to the quiet room in which they sat, her red-rimmed eyes puffy and fragile looking.

Archie's once-happy heart dropped so low, he was surprised he couldn't see it lying on the carpet at his feet.

He dragged himself out of his chair and walked the few steps across the room to the heavy wooden door that marked the entrance to his father's domain.

His trepidation was almost crippling. His hands shook, and his desire to run away was so strong that Archie had to lock his knees in place so that he didn't obey what his instincts were screaming at him to do. He hung his head for a moment, squeezed his eyes shut, then released a long breath.

It was time to face his destiny.

He lifted his head and stared at the mahogany wood, raising his still shaking hand and knocking on his father's study door.

"Enter." His father's hoarse voice sounded through the solid barrier and Archie squared his shoulders.

Archie turned the silver knob, pushed open the door and saw another set of red-rimmed eyes, matching his mother's.

Archie gasped and bowed low to his father to disguise his surprise. His father couldn't have been crying, surely? There had to be another reason for his appearance. Perhaps it was the result of heavy drinking and fatigue? Archie could only hope.

"Sit down, Archibald," his father commanded, his strong voice croaking and rough.

Archie almost tripped over the rug in his haste. His father had never before asked him to be seated in his presence. He had certainly never used his Christian name before in such a way. Archie could only hope that his father might be about to comment on his upcoming birthday, although his detached and logical brain knew that this thought didn't fit in with the visible tears which he had seen his cold, aloof mother and his proud, drunken father shed.

"Archibald, we have received some bad news and it seems that your brother will no longer be inheriting the Marquisate."

This life-altering statement was delivered with all the excitement of a eulogy. Archie's father had always been proud of his eldest son. It had been obvious in both his actions and words. Archie's older brother was the charismatic, arrogant and handsome heir who had always looked and acted just like their father.

He cleared his throat and tugged on his cuff. "Pardon, sir? Do you mean that Arthur will not be inheriting?"

"Do not speak back to me!"

Shock ricocheted through his system, yet he schooled his features into an expression of proper regard with practiced ease. He had spent the last five years as part of a group of four youths referred to as 'The Spares.' The four members were all the second sons of rich, old and powerful families. None of these friends wanted their father's title, nor the responsibility that came with it. Archie felt the same way. To be told that he would have to forget all his plans for the future, of managing his money and breeding horses, was devastating. He felt sick to his stomach.

"My apologies, sir." Archie bobbed his head in a seated half-bow, his head spinning with questions. What was he going to do now?

He sat still and waited for his father to continue. He needed more information, but with the unbalanced mood his father was in, Archie knew better than to push.

The older man appeared to be mulling the words over in his head, twirling his empty liquor glass around in his hands.

"Arthur is dying. He has indulged in his taste for loose women far too freely and now he is going to die."

His father shook his head sadly.

Archie was completely shocked. If he had been standing, he doubted he would still have been upright. Was his brother dying? He knew Arthur had not been feeling well recently, but dying? And from the dreaded French disease? Archie was not close to his older brother, as there was more than six years between them, but he didn't want him to die.

Whilst Archie was trying to digest this new information, his father hit him with the next verbal sledgehammer.

"So, you keep yourself clean. Understand me? Stay away from the whores and make sure you marry a woman who will be able to handle the scandal when it comes. We will be sending your brother to Italy for an extended holiday, but if word ever gets out, the family's reputation will be ruined."

Archie felt his heart stop. Was his father asking him to stay away from women? For how long? His friends had already organised his eighteenth birthday. A night of drinking and his first time in a brothel, his first female.

Did his father mean that he couldn't bed a woman until he married?

As Archie's mind raced with the implications of what his father had told him, he felt his heart slowly disappear. It shriveled up, just like a grape left on the vine too long.

His father was telling him that he was to inherit everything. The estate, the servants, the title, the responsibility. Everything, including a name that would forever be remembered for his brother's grotesque death. The society in which Archie wanted to be accepted would soon scorn him. What woman would want him? As Archie thought about all the lost possibilities, he realised that his life would never be the same again.

Chapter One

Lord Archibald Turner, Archie to his friends, was the second son of the Marquess of Hunting. Archie had spent the last decade living an exemplary life. The epitome of gentlemanly behaviour, habits, and dress, without any of the excesses frowned upon but secretly tolerated.

He hardly drank, he didn't gamble, and he was a twenty-seven-year-old virgin. This, of course, meant he had never compromised anyone and had never taken advantage of the offers which were passed his way by the many unhappily married women of the *ton*. Archie spent more money on his clothes than all his friends combined, but that meant he always looked attractive and civilized.

Archie had spent the last six years fighting an intense attraction for one amazing woman. She was the only person who noticed him as more than the holy saint he pretended to be. She fought with him in public, teased him blatantly and laughed her full-bodied laugh at him. She was the only woman he had ever loved, and he wasn't sure how much longer he could bear standing close to her without declaring his intentions.

Lady Charlotte Dunford.

Archie groaned as his wayward member stiffened in response to said woman's laugh and the accompanying wobble of her generous breasts. He was wearing dark grey breeches that were so tight, they revealed everything. Archie had muscular thighs, unlike most of the men of the *ton* and his tailor often had trouble cutting his breeches just right. This wasn't usually a problem, but when the front of his breeches was quite visible due to a high-waisted, white waistcoat and cut away evening jacket, Archie began to panic. Desperate for something that would douse his ardour, he thought back to the last time he had seen Charlotte.

It had been almost nine months before.

Archie had been standing with his friend of over fifteen years, the former Lord Oliver Lyre, now the Duke of Lincoln. Oliver had shown up to a *ton* ball, without his new wife. Oliver had been explaining why his wife was in Scotland, rather than by his side in London, when Charlotte had become incensed and started scolding him in the middle of a crowded ballroom.

Lady Charlotte Dunford, his heart, his soul, the only woman Archie would ever want to marry. She was the only daughter of the Duke of Arrow, his friend, Lord John Dunford's younger sister, and the most beautiful woman Archie had ever seen. She was also a woman with a keen mind and a nasty temper when aroused, and unfortunately, Oliver had excited it that night.

"You've done what?" Lady Charlotte raised her voice at the Duke, casting angry eyes heavenward and then fixing them back on Oliver's face.

Archie wanted to put his hands over his ears to block the sound but gallantly squashed that ungentlemanly urge.

"Lady Charlotte, please," Oliver said.

Archie wasn't sure why Oliver, Duke of Lincoln, had let his duchess, Sarah, leave him to go to Scotland, but he felt perfectly sure that a public reprimand was not the way to go about finding out.

It was a pity that Lady Charlotte hadn't felt the same way.

"You've done what?" Lady Charlotte spat at him, quieter this time.

She removed the scowl from her face and plastered on her polite facade. Society did not approve of displays of excessive emotion and frowned upon public spectacles. Archie watched Lady Charlotte's attempt to conceal her feelings and could have told her not to bother. Lady Charlotte, having been a spoilt and indulged only daughter, had never been forced to school her features. She was, therefore, atrocious at pretending to feel calm when she felt otherwise.

"I returned to London without my wife." The duke repeated the words, obviously upset to be admitting the fact. His face flushed, his gaze darting around the room.

"And you packed her off to a Scottish castle? Your new wife? Your duchess?" Lady Charlotte enunciated each word calmly. Her expression was remote, but her words dripped venom. Archie held his breath. This was going to get very ugly, very quickly.

"She wanted to go. She wasn't enjoying living on the estate, and when I asked her whether she wanted to come back to London with me, or stay there, she chose to travel to Scotland instead."

Archie found this rather odd. He knew Oliver's wife, Sarah, and had seen the couple on their wedding day. Unlike most couples of the *ton*, who married for financial or social reasons, Oliver and Sarah's marriage had been a love match. Why had it gone wrong so quickly?

"What did you do?" Lady Charlotte asked again.

Archie could see the anger in Charlotte's eyes, he could feel the current of rage in her body, as though it was his own. He had always been able to do that. He could read her like no one else seemed able to do, not even her brother.

"I didn't do a thing. The servants welcomed her, and I took the utmost care to ensure her comfort. When my mother and sister-in-law arrived, they tried to—"

"No!" Lady Charlotte exploded.

Archie heard Oliver's groan and wished he could do the same thing. Must she always be so passionate about everything?

"You let your mother and that *snake* of a sister-in-law visit you while you were on your honeymoon?" Charlotte was incredulous.

"They didn't visit. They live there."

Charlotte seemed shocked by Oliver's reasoning, and Archie knew she didn't understand. She would never know what it was like to feel like you weren't wanted or needed by your parents. Once upon a time, he had felt the same way and it seemed that Oliver still did. Why else would he have allowed his relatives to invade what should have been his home?

"Oh, Sarah, you poor, poor thing." Lady Charlotte murmured to herself, clasping her hands to her breasts.

"Lady Charlotte, that is not fair. I didn't do anything." Oliver protested again. Archie could have told him it was pointless.

"Exactly. You didn't do anything to protect your beautiful, sweet, innocent wife from being set upon by the most cunning, jealous pair of women I have ever met."

Archie raised an eyebrow, wondering which woman other than the dowager duchess that Lady Charlotte meant. Probably Lady Honoria, Oliver's sister-in-law.

"You stupid, ignorant–" As Lady Charlotte started to wind herself up into a full-blown attack, Archie gathered his courage and quickly stepped into the line of fire.

"Lady Charlotte," he interrupted, moving in front of Oliver and bowing to her. "May I have the honour of this dance?"

Lady Charlotte shut her mouth and eyed Archie with disdain. Archie made sure his body language left her no room for argument, and he stood in a way that completely blocked Oliver from her line of vision.

"Of course, my lord," she managed, her eyes flashing daggers around him at Oliver even while Archie led her away.

Her hand on his arm felt like a burning flame to his coat. He had avoided dancing with her since her coming out ball and this was the reason why. He had always hoped that his reaction to her would diminish; hoped his body would learn not to be so sensitive to her, but it had never happened.

She had as much effect on him today, as every other day since he'd met her.

Archie pulled Lady Charlotte gently into a waltz position–it had to be a waltz, bloody bad luck—and started moving her expertly around the room. Neither of them had spoken yet, but her eyes spoke volumes. Lady Charlotte had now divided her anger and Archie wasn't sure if he would fare worse or better than Oliver.

"Go on. I know you want to," Archie encouraged, schooling his face into his usual mask of politeness. He had thought that after a decade of pulling this face, it would be second nature and no longer feel false. But when he was with Charlotte, every feeling was intensified, to the point of being almost painful.

"I have nothing to say."

Archie bit back a smile. Lady Charlotte never addressed him, never had. He found it quite funny. He had no title, so she couldn't refer to him like that. He had never given her leave to call him Archie, and yet having been around her brother for most of her life, she could call him anything she wanted. And yet Lady Charlotte didn't. She avoided referring to him at all, and if she was pressed, she occasionally called him 'my lord,' with a wry twist to her lips.

Charlotte's expressions were transparent. Archie could see every thought, every feeling as they crossed her face. At the moment, though, it didn't take a person familiar with Lady Charlotte to deduce her feelings. Her rage was there for the whole world to see. Her face flushed, her eyes narrowed and sparked with passion.

"Lady Charlotte," Archie began. She hissed at him through her clenched teeth.

He had always addressed her as Lady Charlotte, partly because it was her title, due her because of her fortunate birth, but also partly because it annoyed her. For the first time since Archie had met Charlotte, he didn't ignore her glare.

"Well, what would you like me to call you?" he snapped, letting some of his annoyance slip into his voice. Lady Charlotte's lips parted and her eyes widened, measurably. Archie didn't know if it was due to the tone of his voice or from his wording, but he couldn't take the words back now.

She opened her mouth to reply, then shut it again.

Archie waited. He danced them around the room, and he waited some more. Charlotte looked beautiful when she was angry. Her too-full lips parted slightly, and her bluer-than-blue eyes gave him a penetrating look, as if she was trying to read him. He knew she wouldn't see anything revealing on his face, but it never seemed to stop her from trying to understand him.

"Charlotte," she answered finally, her eyes wary as she awaited his response.

"Well, Charlotte, say what you are thinking, so you can feel better."

Archie tightened his hold on her reflexively, as he feared she would leave him on the dance floor if she got angry with him.

"May I call you Archie?" She burst out with this question, instead of answering him.

He almost laughed out loud and smiled, despite himself. He had meant that she should vent her anger at him, not ask for his permission to use his name.

"Of course." He inclined his head. Her spine stiffened again, her hand going rigid in his grasp.

He groaned internally. Why was it that everything he did seemed to annoy her?

"Archie, how dare you pull me away just because I was angry with Oliver? He deserves to know what an imbecile he is. Doesn't he realise that Sarah will be heartbroken that he has abandoned her for his pursuits in London?"

Archie frowned. How could Charlotte know this?

"Firstly, I did not pull you away. I asked you to dance." He tightened his hold on her hand, as though to illustrate the point.

"For the first time in five years," Charlotte muttered under her breath, looking down and away from him. "And right at that moment."

Archie inhaled against the sudden pain in his chest. She sounded upset that he hadn't danced with her regularly over the years. If only she'd known the torment he felt every time another man held her, she wouldn't have been so quick to chastise him about the time they had spent apart.

Chapter Two

Ignoring her jibe, Archie continued. "Secondly, how can you be so sure of Sarah's feelings?"

Was this something ladies discussed? Or was Charlotte making assumptions?

"Because that was always Sarah's biggest fear about marrying above her station. The day before they married, she told me that she would never survive if Oliver chose another woman over her, if he took a mistress, or decided to gallivant around London instead of being with her. He is not only doing that, but he made sure she was in a different country, where she can only assume the worst."

In typical Charlotte fashion, she was not only discussing a topic that any unmarried lady of breeding would avoid, but she also spoke with such passion that Archie wished he could kiss her, suck on her lips until they bruised.

Archie closed his eyes as the longing coursing through him made him want to drop to his knees and beg her to be his. He slowed their dancing as the orchestra stopped, his palms beginning to sweat. One day, he would do something very foolish when it came to Charlotte. He could only hope it didn't occur in a ballroom full of people.

"Charlotte, if you'd like, I could speak to Oliver. I don't believe he is happy to be away from his wife."

Archie led Charlotte away from the dance floor, dropping her hand as quickly as he could.

"It doesn't matter whether he's happy or not. She must be miserable."

And with that declaration, she stormed off.

Archie suddenly came back to the present with a jolt and smiled to himself at the memory he'd just been reliving. He recalled that had been the last time he had enjoyed a real conversation with Charlotte.

It was now nine months later; the beginning of another season, and she was miraculously still unattached. Archie watched her twirl around the room in the arms of a wealthy young lord and found himself wishing she would get married so he could also find someone suitable to marry. He could never commit himself to another until she was settled. It didn't make sense of course, but Archie couldn't bring himself to marry while Charlotte, the one and only woman he had ever really desired, was still available.

"Archie." Oliver approached with a genuine smile and shook his hand with vigour. Oliver was wearing a rose-coloured waistcoat, a black evening coat, and breeches. The ensemble sat very well on him.

Archie smiled warmly, his heart lifting at the sight of the Duke of Lincoln. His friend had never looked better, or happier.

"You look well, Oliver. How are things?" Archie asked the question more out of politeness than for any other reason, as he already knew that everything was well.

"Excellent. Thanks to your advice, my finances have never been better, and my new estate manager has everything running smoothly."

Oliver had been the second son of the late Duke of Lincoln, and he had once confided to Archie that his father had told him he would never inherit, so there was no reason to teach him anything about being a duke.

So, when at twenty-five years of age, Oliver had unexpectedly inherited the estate, he'd had no idea how to manage anything, let alone a dukedom. He had floundered considerably. Not only concerning the needs of his property and his many dependents including servants and tenants, but also concerning his position in society, where he was expected to fulfill the role of a duke to the manor born.

"And your family?" Archie asked, grinning widely at his friend.

"Sarah's extremely well, thank you, and my son is wonderful."

The pleasure that Oliver felt in those words was apparent. Sarah, his beautiful wife, glided up at that moment, her rose silk gown complementing her husband's attire. She slid her hand into the crook of her husband's elbow and Oliver seemed to glow like the stars.

"Archie," Sarah greeted him warmly, her smile mirroring her husband's.

"Your Grace." Archie couldn't resist addressing the lady before him with her new title, bowing deeply over Sarah's outstretched hand and placing a chaste kiss on her knuckles.

Sarah blushed crimson, the colour extremely becoming on her. She had been born a clergyman's daughter, and Archie knew that she was still a little overwhelmed about the title she had gained upon her marriage to Oliver.

She tapped at him playfully with her fan, reminding him that he should address her only by her first name. Archie laughed. His friend was very lucky.

~

ACROSS THE ROOM, Lady Charlotte Dunford watched the scene between Archie and their mutual friends, the Duke and Duchess of Lincoln, with a warmth heating her face. She averted her eyes.

Why did Archie never tease her like that? Why did he never smile at her like he was smiling at the duchess right now? Because he thinks you're a spoilt little girl, the cynical voice in her head reminded her.

Archie had been friends with her brother, Lord John Dunford, since Charlotte had been a child. Five years younger than John, she had been barely eight years old when she first met Archie. She had thought him polite, but nothing more. At eight years of age, she wasn't interested in boys and her brother's solemn friend had not commanded her attention. When she had reached sixteen and became a debutante, she had seen Archie as the man he was. Twenty-one years old, handsome as sin and as proud as a peacock.

He had danced with her once. As her brother's friend, he had been obliged to ease her way into society by offering to dance with her. Charlotte had felt safe with him, knowing he wasn't assessing her suitability as the perfect wife, as some of the more mature gentlemen had been. He had been polite but distant, and he had kept that distance for six years.

No, that was untrue. This dawned on Charlotte as she reflected on their association. They had also danced once, the previous year. Charlotte sighed at the memory.

She recalled how she had been furious at Oliver. Archie had whisked her away to prevent her from scolding his friend in public and thereby creating a spectacle. Archie was loyal to those he loved; he always had been. John always said that you could count on Archie to do the right thing, no matter the cost to himself.

During that waltz, Charlotte had finally seen a little of the real emotion Archie could express, which she had been looking for since she'd been a young girl. He had cracked open his mask for just a moment, and she had been shocked almost speechless. Lord Archibald Turner was not a heartless machine, it seemed. He had feelings; she just wasn't sure how many, or exactly what they meant. Either way, he had captured her attention that night.

Now, raising her social armour and breezing across the ballroom, she approached the young Duchess of Lincoln with her traitorous heart beating at a fast pace in her ears.

"Charlotte!" Sarah cried happily, her whole face lighting up.

She looks so well, was Charlotte's first thought. Sarah had always been slightly pale and a little thin, but now she glowed with happiness and was nicely plump after giving birth to her son just three months previously. She was also wearing a rose silk gown that beautifully complemented her creamy skin and blonde hair, not to mention the newly acquired curve of her bosom, which only added to her beauty.

Charlotte leaned forward and gave the Duchess of Lincoln a quick hug.

"Sarah, I have missed you," she told her friend honestly. She hadn't seen Sarah in almost a year, not since her wedding. Sarah had disappeared on her honeymoon and then hadn't returned to London. Until now.

Sarah's eyes glistened slightly and then she smiled brightly.

"I have missed you too, although I do remember a particular invitation from Scotland that you declined." She teased her friend, poking her lightly with her fan.

Charlotte suppressed a sigh. She would have loved to visit Scotland after Sarah's baby had been born, but the combination of envy for her happiness and respect for the young couple's need for privacy had kept Charlotte in London.

"I would have loved to visit you, my friend, but I know how much you enjoy having your husband to yourself," she replied, giving Oliver a sharp glance.

The duke looked at the floor in obvious embarrassment. He must have recalled that the last time he had seen Charlotte, she had railed at him for leaving Sarah in Scotland.

She smiled to herself. Good. He should feel bad about that. It had been a dreadful thing to do to his new wife.

"We all know that you never leave London, however odd that is, Lady Charlotte. Scotland would be far too uncivilized for you." Archie's cold voice broke into the conversation and Charlotte's gaze turned to him. Was he trying to make her look selfish in front of Sarah?

"Lord Archibald, good evening, sir," she replied haughtily, giving Archie a half-curtsey.

He bowed low in return. He was a marquess' son, but he was the second son, and she was the daughter of a duke. As they were both unmarried, she outranked him.

"I rarely leave London, it is true, but I would have loved to visit Sarah," she repeated, daring him to contradict her again.

Archie would usually have ignored any attempt to bait him, yet tonight, she seemed to succeed while barely trying.

"How can you say that you would have loved to have ventured to Scotland when you rarely even visit Hampshire in the off season?" he challenged, with a raised eyebrow.

"That's only because…" Charlotte began to explain, until her brother, Lord John Dunford cleared his throat, stopping her in mid-sentence.

She sighed loudly. John was correct. She could hardly divulge that by tacit understanding between her parents, her father took his long-time mistress to the country estate every year once the Season was over, while Charlotte and her mother stayed in London. It was common enough knowledge that her father had a mistress, but no one knew just how much time the duke spent with her.

How could she tell Archie why she couldn't leave London if John didn't want him to know?

"You are right, Lord Archibald, how remiss of me to forget how shallow I am."

Sarah gasped, but Charlotte ignored her, focusing instead on Archie. Although most of the time she hated him, part of her loved their exchanges. No one saw her as more than a wealthy duke's daughter, to be caught for marriage and used for her hostess skills, and to provide an heir. Those wanting to marry her included false flattery and flummery when they spoke to her. Archie never did any of that. Even if he only noticed her flaws, she liked how he treated her as a person, not as the daughter of a wealthy duke.

"Not shallow, Lady Charlotte, only too self-centred and focused on London," Archie replied, injecting humour into his voice.

Charlotte ignored the humour. She didn't want to smile and laugh with him. For some reason, she got a perverse pleasure out of sparring with Archie in public, and she wouldn't be backing down.

"Oh, *self-centred*? Really? Even better." She snorted inelegantly.

Archie just smiled at her, in a most agreeable manner. That annoyed her even more than a cutting reply would have done.

Charlotte had just opened her mouth for a blistering rejoinder when Sarah intervened.

"How is your brother, Archie?" Sarah asked, linking her arm with Charlotte's.

Charlotte looked down at Sarah's hand and realised she was being cautioned to be quiet. She noticed Archie's face pale slightly and wondered why.

"He is not so well. I thank you for asking, Duchess," he murmured. Sarah leaned forward and tapped him with her fan again.

He smiled reluctantly and fixed his mistake. "Sarah," he said.

Charlotte inhaled sharply at the exchange. How did Sarah know how to tease him, to make him smile? And to accept his teasing in return?

All Charlotte knew how to do was to annoy him—or get annoyed at him. Maybe she should try hitting him with her fan? Her fingers tightened reflexively on her new silk adornment, holding back the impulse. She knew she could never flirt so blatantly with Archie.

"What ails your brother?" Charlotte asked, wondering what everyone else knew that she didn't.

Archie's posture went rigid as he met her gaze. He had the most beautiful brown eyes.

"Arthur left for a grand European trip almost ten years ago. After a few years of travel, he came down with a lung illness which has kept him overseas. The doctors believe that the damp British climate will only worsen his condition."

Archie spoke so stiffly that it seemed a rehearsed speech.

How many times had he repeated that exact phrase? Was his brother so unwell? Still?

"So, is that where you disappear to every year once the season is over?" Charlotte didn't think about how much that question would reveal about her.

Archie gave her a quizzical look, but instead of answering, just inclined his head.

Charlotte flushed and tried her best to conceal her discomfort.

"I must go. Mother said she wanted to leave early tonight." Charlotte excused herself and moved away from the group, promising Sarah she would visit soon.

When she looked back, only one person was looking at her. Archie.

<h1 style="text-align:center">Chapter Three</h1>

The next day was a Saturday, and Charlotte needed to speak to her father about her birthday ball. Money was not among the acceptable subjects of discussion in her family, but she had decided to hire a second French chef to help with the catering and thought perhaps she should consult her father first.

Finding no sign of him in his usual place, the library, Charlotte located her mother in her sitting room, writing a letter.

"Is Father not at home, Mother?"

Her mother's shoulders stiffened and she knew what the answer was going to be. *Oh, dear!* Why hadn't she just asked the butler?

"He's gone to his whore." Her mother turned in her chair and beckoned Charlotte inside the room with a flick of her bony finger.

Her father had long ago established a mistress in a different part of town. As long as she could remember, she had been discreetly aware of the woman's existence. It had always seemed odd to her that her father had kept the same woman for so long. Charlotte thought that the idea of a gentleman having a mistress would be to change them regularly, for variety. But what did she know?

"Oh, I'm sorry, Mother." It was her automatic response and she steeled herself for the emotional onslaught that would surely follow.

"Why are you sorry, Charlotte? It is not your fault that your father is an ordinary man. No man ever stays faithful to his wife. You have been clever to remain unmarried for so long."

Charlotte's eyebrows rose. Inwardly, her belly squirmed in an uncomfortable way. Her mother thought that her not marrying was a good thing? Although she had never been pushed into marrying any of the men who had proposed to her, she had always felt that she was letting her mother down in some way. Obviously, she had been wrong.

"Oliver is faithful to Sarah," Charlotte murmured, dipping her head to avoid her mother's eyes.

Her mother made a very unladylike noise, close to a snort.

"That is only because she is little better than a whore herself."

Charlotte gasped. How could her mother say such a thing?

"Mother! Sarah is a beautiful person." It was true that most men of Oliver's standing would have made Sarah their mistress rather than marry her, but Sarah had been brought up as a lady.

"She is little better than a servant, Charlotte. I can only imagine that he married her because she tricked him into it. He may be faithful now, as they've only been married for a year, but give it time."

Her mother was smiling rather wickedly now, her lips turned up in a wider smile than Charlotte had seen in years.

Charlotte couldn't imagine Oliver ever wanting another woman whilst he had Sarah. But then again, didn't her mother have more experience in these things? What man stayed faithful his whole married life?

Which gentleman didn't have one mistress, or even more than one? She knew John did, and it was even whispered that her older brother, Cyril, had a wife and a mistress. Maybe her mother was right, and it was just a matter of time for Oliver and Sarah. The thought brought sadness to Charlotte's heart.

"You have done very well, Charlotte. A woman can enjoy being her own mistress. You need never know the humiliation of the marriage bed nor the pain of childbirth."

Charlotte stifled her sigh.

"So, you are happy for me never to marry, then, Mama?" Charlotte asked cautiously.

She couldn't believe she was having this conversation. Every mother she knew was practically throwing their daughters down the aisle, yet her mother didn't care one way or the other? Or even more extreme—preferred her daughter *not* to wed?

"Of course, I would like to see you marry, Charlotte. It is a woman's greatest achievement. But there are very few eligible, titled gentlemen available, and I refuse to allow you to marry below your rank."

Charlotte paled. If that was the case, then she'd probably never marry. There were few, if any, unmarried dukes in London nowadays.

Her mother continued. "You will never want for anything, as I'm sure your brother will continue to support you throughout your life. As your father does now."

Charlotte nodded, feeling her cheeks grow hot.

So, it was true, then. Her mother, apparently like all women before her, had only married so she could improve her station in life.

Charlotte had always believed she would marry for love, and had hoped to find a man with whom she could have a good, amicable relationship on which to build a steady love. A marriage based on mutual affection and not just the joining of two wealthy families.

Men like Oliver could marry almost anyone. They could choose a woman for her beauty, her bloodlines, or her dowry. Most women married the man who could make their lives comfortable.

But Charlotte had been born into a noble family, and few women of the *ton* had the comfort and resources she enjoyed. She had already been bestowed with some personal wealth by her father, and even had a small country estate of her own, which was currently leased.

As the daughter of a duke, she had high status in society. By the *ton's* standards, she would gain nothing of worth from marrying. However, the man who managed to win her hand in marriage would gain significantly.

An inner part of her knew that nothing short of unconditional love would tempt her into marriage. But unlike the case of Sarah, the young Duchess of Lincoln, most men would look at Lady Charlotte Dunford and see only what they could acquire.

Curtseying to her mother, she left the room with a new sense of inevitability and a heavy sinking feeling in the pit of her stomach.

A week later, it was the day of Charlotte's ball.

After Archie had pointedly sent her flowers on her real birthday, rather than on the actual day of her ball as everyone else had the year before, Charlotte had chosen to celebrate on her actual birthday. Archie would have nothing to complain about this time.

She had been secretly thrilled when his bouquet of flowers had arrived this morning. All her other friends and admirers chose expensive, well-known and therefore common flowers. Archie, as always, had chosen something memorable. A bouquet of yellow daffodils and a posy of pale pink rosebuds.

Charlotte wanted to take them up to her room and leave all of the everyday white and red roses in the foyer. Instinct told her that this would be too much cause for gossip. In the end, she told the footmen to take several bouquets to her room, including the daffodils.

As the day wore on, she found herself daydreaming about dancing with Archie at the ball that night. A fantasy indeed, as it would be a miracle for Archie to do such a thing.

That evening, she stood at the entrance to the ballroom to welcome her guests. Her parents stood beside her until most of the guests had arrived, and then excused themselves to retire to their respective domains. Her mother, to her group of friends, and her father disappeared in the opposite direction.

The room was comfortably full, and now that she had fulfilled some of her hostess duties, she walked through the ballroom speaking to people and accepting their congratulations. She was talking to Sarah, Oliver, their friend Rupert and her brother John when her skin prickled, and she turned to see *him*.

Archie had been making his way to Oliver's side without noticing her. The shock that registered on his face when he realised she was within speaking distance was almost comical. He bowed politely, wished her a happy birthday and then stood as far away from her as he could, while still within their circle.

"What about you, little sister? You're getting closer to being labelled as 'on the shelf'." John teased her with a smile.

"I don't believe I'll ever marry," Charlotte answered with an airy wave of her hand, making an announcement of the plan on which she had only recently decided.

"Pardon?" The almost uniform reply of the five people surrounding her, with their accompanying horrified faces and wide eyes, was enough to make her giggle.

"Why ever not?" Oliver asked, his eyebrows so high on his forehead they looked closer to being part of his hairline.

"What else would you do?" John shook his head, apparently baffled by the idea that a woman would choose to remain unmarried.

Charlotte laughed again, enjoying the attention and then the general silence surrounding her.

"I don't need the money or a home, and I don't necessarily think I want children. There isn't any other reason for a woman to marry."

Charlotte had spent several years thinking about marriage, and now that she listed the reasons out loud, she had the clear realisation that it was all true. Her conversation with her mother a few days earlier had merely solidified the idea. She had a yearly annuity on which she could live without her father's help, should the need arise. It was also true that she would have no objection to marrying a man if she cared for one, but she wouldn't be admitting to that. Not openly at least.

"What about love? Companionship?" Oliver wrapped his hand possessively around his wife's waist and pulled her into his side.

Envy ripped through Charlotte, and the feeling wasn't at all pleasant. If she remained a single lady, would this become a frequent occurrence?

"I am blessed with family and friends. Besides, from what I understand from most of my married friends, I'd be giving up a lot more than I would ever gain. If I do still feel a lack of something in my life, there are plenty of orphanages and charities on which I may expend my time and generosity."

Charlotte looked toward a group of young women standing together in the corner of the ballroom. It was well known that all three had husbands who rarely spent a night at home.

"Whatever do you mean that you would be giving up more than you gained?" Sarah asked, her voice rising to a squeak. Sarah was a vicar's daughter who had married a duke. She had gained a lot when she married Oliver, not just emotionally, but financially.

Charlotte laughed out loud and covered her mouth with her fan. Surely Sarah could see the humour in her question?

"I mean, legally, my husband would own me. I would no longer have any control over my money or assets and he, to make matters even worse, would have complete physical access to my person."

Charlotte shuddered and grimaced, then she heard her brother mutter under his breath.

"And you wonder why men keep mistresses?"

"What do you mean?" Charlotte glared at her brother, wanting to stamp her foot on the polished floorboards.

She didn't wonder why men kept mistresses; she already knew. Men were beasts, unable to contain their base urges, but she wasn't going to be the wife waiting at home for her husband to return.

"I mean, if a lady like you dreads going to her husband's bed, why would you assume a husband would want to bed you? He'd prefer the arms of a woman who would welcome him."

Although it was in no way appropriate for Lord John Dunford to be discussing such a thing with his unmarried sister, Charlotte smiled at her brother. She had never been an ordinary lady.

"I'm sure I have no idea what you mean, dear brother. What I intended to say was that he would even have the right to beat me," she replied.

~

ARCHIE CRINGED at the turn the conversation had taken. Why could his friends never stick to socially acceptable topics? The weather? The gossip? The fashion? He wanted to scream at them.

Pick one of those!

Staring at the birthday girl with an uncomfortable knot in his belly, Archie wondered why she was the only woman who ever made him feel like this. Out of control with his feelings. And a *woman* she was now, not a girl any longer. Tonight was her twenty-second birthday, and Archie had never seen her look lovelier. Dressed in an evening gown of golden silk, with her lovely shoulders bare and the upper swells of her breasts visible, she was the most beautiful woman in the ball room.

Although he didn't like it when her temper was directed at him, he had to admit that she did look amazing when she was flushed with indignation. He suppressed the uncharacteristic urge to chuckle, the ripples inside his belly almost uncomfortable. It had been so long since he'd felt like laughing.

"Well, dear brother, since you have raised the topic, from what my mother and my friends have said, I don't know how any lady could enjoy the bedding business." Charlotte's nose wrinkled in disfavour.

Archie knew that she was spouting a widely known belief that ladies hated the marriage bed, and even fallen women, or women of a lower class, found little pleasure in it. However, he didn't want to add to this inappropriate conversation in any way, so he kept his mouth firmly shut.

"What has Mother said?" John's eyes widened, and his mouth dropped open.

He was apparently shocked that "the conversation" had already come about, as Charlotte had never even been engaged. Archie was surprised himself.

"That I must lay still and try to think of something pleasant so that the time will go quickly. That it will hurt, but it is my wifely duty." Charlotte spat the words out as though they tasted foul. She shuddered, and Archie wanted to groan. He hoped that wasn't what was in store for him.

"Tell me about a lady who enjoys marital relations with her husband so much, she would willingly give up everything that I have?" Charlotte boldly asked their group.

They heard a stifled laugh, and everyone looked toward Rupert. Archie knew that some married ladies enjoyed Rupert's bed, but that was a different story.

Slowly, a small white hand was raised, and Archie's mouth fell open as his gaze met those of the hand's owner.

Charlotte stared at Sarah's raised hand. "You can't possibly be serious."

Her look of disbelief would have been funny, if Archie hadn't been so shocked himself.

Sarah blushed furiously but refused to be cowed by any of them.

"My mother told me that marital relations came down to the husband. If he loves his wife, then he will take the care and the time to make sure that she finds pleasure as well. Maybe that's why so many of your friends hate their marriage beds. They married for reasons other than affection and their husbands do not care for them," Sarah explained. She shot an apologetic look at her now-blushing husband.

Rupert and John looked at Oliver, both with surprised but envious expressions, and Oliver blushed even brighter.

Archie found himself again thinking that Oliver was one lucky sod.

"Well, although I am glad that some ladies enjoy their husband's bed, I am still convinced I will never marry." Charlotte looked sideways at her friend with lowered brows. She obviously wasn't convinced by what Sarah was saying.

"Please tell us, why now, sister dearest?" John persisted, his voice seeming harder, almost angry.

"Because I want things in a man that just don't exist," Charlotte announced to their group, a triumphant grin spreading across her face.

"Such as?" Oliver asked, before her brother could.

"I want everything in a husband, that a man of my class looks for in a wife," she announced, with a raised eyebrow and a flutter of her fan.

"Interesting, a touch backward, but please tell us how that is so impossible."

Oliver rubbed his chin thoughtfully.

Charlotte held up her hands and started ticking off the list on her fingers.

"He must, of course, be a gentleman. He must be of the right age, fair of face, intelligent and preferably someone who has at least as much financially to bring to the marriage as I have."

Archie knew that these criteria were difficult but not unachievable.

"A strong list, but not impossible. What age is the right age?" Oliver asked again, obviously going through the invisible list in his head, considering eligible gentlemen.

"Within fifteen years of my age," Charlotte answered.

"I don't see anything on that list that we can't overcome. What about a title? If you need that, then we might indeed have a problem..." John was speaking now. He had apparently been listening, as he wore a look of intense concentration. Perhaps he also had an internal list of eligible men.

"No, I don't care a whit about a title. I can continue with my own title if need be," Charlotte announced, with a flick of her dainty wrists.

As a duke's daughter, Charlotte was entitled to be addressed as Lady Charlotte for the rest of her life, even if she married someone below her rank or someone with no title.

Archie cleared his throat and leaned forward a little, joining the conversation for the first time.

"Then what is it that you find to be so insurmountable?" he asked her quietly. He could only think of two or three men that would suit her list, but indeed, it wasn't impossible.

"Because I want a husband to stay faithful, and I can think of only one way to ensure that. This particular attribute that I want is the one thing all gentlemen want in a wife, but the wife will never find in a man."

Everyone else in their small circle was so riveted by every word Charlotte spoke that they didn't see the danger. Archie, however, knew her too well, and he was aware that this particular glint in her eye indicated that she was about to drop an unexpected bombshell.

"I want a virgin."

# Chapter Four

"No!" Archie exclaimed. He almost exploded where he stood opposite Charlotte, his heart racing as fear set in.

He had been expecting something interesting to come out of her mouth, but not that.

Everyone else in their circle burst out laughing, including Sarah. The sound grated on Archie's nerves so intensely he had to bite down on the inside of his cheek to stop a scream erupting.

He glared at the men who were now looking at him expectantly, their eyebrows raised. Only Rupert wouldn't return his gaze.

Once the laughter died down, Charlotte smiled coolly, fluttering her fan in front of her beautiful face. She looked supremely confident that she had won her argument, and Archie's stomach sank.

"Now you know why I will never marry. My ideal husband just doesn't exist."

Archie knew what was coming and continued to glare at his friends, silently forbidding them from speaking. He saw Oliver open his mouth, but Archie's quelling look soon had him shutting it.

Archie ran through the rest of Charlotte's list, hoping there would be somewhere he was deficient. He was considered handsome, only five years older than her, a gentleman, and his finances were better than most. He couldn't be sure what Charlotte's exact monetary worth was, but her dowry alone would add considerably to any bank balance. Archie glared at his friends again as the realisation began to settle.

Oh God, he was the only man in London who had every trait she wanted in a husband. The idea sent rapid panic racing through his body, his palms sweating as he clasped his hands behind his back.

Rupert was pointedly ignoring Archie's pleading look, as he took Charlotte's elbow and shifted her slightly so she could look directly at him. Archie's breath caught; his heart pounded in his ears as he waited for her reaction. He was about to be unmasked.

"No, your impossible and perfect husband does exist. You're just going to have to marry Archie," Rupert announced with great aplomb and a flourish of his left hand.

The bottom of his world fell away. Without bowing, without a word, without even a thought other than the overwhelming urge to escape, he pivoted on his shining black heels and headed for the balcony.

Charlotte, who was a duke's daughter to her very bones, did the most unladylike thing he had ever seen her do. She ran after him and grabbed him by the elbow, pulling Archie to the side of the ballroom, away from all prying ears.

"What did Rupert mean by that?" She gripped his forearm tighter and stared up at him with intense blue eyes.

Archie stood straighter, trying to ignore the heat of her body pressed up against his.

"This is not an appropriate place to have this conversation." He side-stepped the question and tried to pull away from her grasp, but she sunk her hands deeper into the muscles of his arm.

"Well, where is appropriate then?"

Archie looked at her determined face and angry blue eyes and seriously debated telling her to go to hell. It was none of her business. His hot and hard body had other ideas.

"The garden."

Charlotte's eyes widened instantly.

"When?" she asked breathlessly, her throat working as she swallowed hard.

Archie's eyes narrowed. Lady Charlotte Dunford couldn't be seriously considering meeting him in the garden, unchaperoned. He may have been reckless enough to suggest a private meeting, but she wouldn't be silly enough to agree to it, surely?

"You want to know about my private life that much?" He had spent the last six years keeping his distance from her, and rightly so. Now that she seemed determined to know him better, he felt those long-held shackles falling rapidly away from his body.

"When?" She repeated the question, straightening and stepping back from him as was proper.

They were being watched, and Archie felt the disapproval of society raining down upon them.

"Ten minutes. In the arbour to the right of the garden." Archie dipped his eyes as though he were not interested in what he was saying. But the heat flaring in his cheeks was sure to give him away. At least to her.

Charlotte pasted on one of her society smiles that always made him wince and curtsied as though she was saying goodbye.

"See you soon, my lord." She came back up from her curtsey, and Archie had to strain his ears to hear her words.

He bowed to her automatically as she moved past him, back to his group of watching friends.

He strode off as though he was leaving, heading for the front door as if to ascertain the whereabouts of his coat.

He knew that this was going to change everything, but after being restricted and restrained for so long, he was suddenly filled with excitement. Would he finally be free to express his feelings to the woman he adored? If he did, who knew where that would lead them?

~

"WHAT DID HE SAY?" Rupert asked Charlotte as she returned to their group. He was obviously trying not to laugh, his mouth strangely twisted.

"He said that it was none of my business knowing anything about his personal life. What did you mean by what you said, Rupert?" Charlotte spoke sternly to the known rake of her brother's group.

If Archie did have that sort of secret, it hadn't been Rupert's place to announce it.

"I–" Rupert began, before being cut off by John.

"He shouldn't have said anything. Archie's going to be furious. And rightly so." John looked at Oliver, and they both shared a worried glance.

"But Rupert wasn't serious, was he? I know what you are like with women, John. I assumed all your friends were the same," Charlotte said, addressing her brother.

Again, Rupert started to open his mouth, and Oliver froze him out with his best ducal stare.

"Archie's a bit different than the average gentleman. But that's his business and certainly not a subject for ladies to be discussing. If you'll excuse us, I think we should be getting home to our son," Oliver announced, effectively cutting off Charlotte's questions and any further discussion.

"Yes, and Charlotte, please think about what I said," Sarah pleaded, reaching out to grip hands with Charlotte.

Charlotte smiled at her friend and squeezed her fingers back. Sarah lowered her voice when she came close and added, "And we can discuss this another time if you'd like more information." A lovely blush stained Sarah's cheeks, and she looked up at her husband with transparent adoration.

He flushed slightly and nodded to Charlotte.

"See you tomorrow night, most likely."

Charlotte excused herself as well, saying that she needed to find refreshment. But instead, she made her way slowly out the balcony doors and down the stairs that led to the garden.

Her breathing was irregular, and her heart was beating heavily, as though she had made a mad dash to the gardens, not walked out in as leisurely a manner as she could so as not to raise suspicion.

She had never before been alone with a man to whom she was not related. What had possessed her to agree to meet Archie in the dark, all alone?

She grimaced at herself. Yes, she knew exactly why she had decided. Because she was intrigued by him. A gentleman who was the very last man she would ever have assumed would ensnare her curiosity.

Charlotte caught a flash of movement within the bower and moved toward it. There was only one way to find out more about Archie, and that was to take a step that might lead to the ruination of her reputation.

ARCHIE HELD his breath when he saw Charlotte arrive through the dense screen of trees. She had come alone.

He had no intention of telling her the truth about his family and his brother's horrible secret, but he would tell her a little of what she wanted to know. If she thought him to be a pious saint, he might as well play on that trait.

Charlotte moved covertly over to him, took one last look around to make sure no one was watching her, then stepped into the alcove he occupied.

Their eyes met and he was breathless all over again. He dragged his eyes away but it was an effort.

Archie couldn't remember a time when another person had looked so directly at him. She was trying to find his soul just by looking, it seemed. The air had completely left his lungs. Struggling valiantly not to cough, he inhaled slowly.

"Well, what would you like to know?" he asked, his voice coming out much hoarser than he would have liked. But that's what happened when you had no breath to draw from.

Charlotte bit her lip, her apprehension, or fear, obvious.

Archie clenched his teeth against the bolt of lust that struck him at her innocently seductive gesture. Her eyes were huge pools of liquid blue, shimmering with uncertainty and something else that he couldn't quite identify. His groin was throbbing, his prick starting to swell. With difficulty, he forced his mind back to the topic at hand.

"Charlotte, we can't stay out here long. Ask your questions," he said, perhaps a little too forcefully.

She waited for a moment, then the words burst forth, too loud. "Is it true?"

"Sshh..." Archie reached out for her hand, and he pulled her closer to him, away from the balcony.

Her skin was so warm through her evening gloves, and she was so close, Archie felt his lungs closing up on him again. He took a step back from her, away from her heat.

"Is what true?"

Archie knew what she was asking, of course. He wasn't feeling very gentlemanly at the moment. He wanted to make her ask the question again, to see if she was as embarrassed as he. She looked beautiful when she blushed, and it was such a rare event, he wanted to see if he could make it happen.

She did blush, hotly. All the way from her provocative cleavage up to the roots of her dark hair.

"Is it true that you are a virgin?"

Archie clenched his jaw at the shock of Charlotte's straightforwardness. He considered lying to her, but that would be pointless. Since Rupert had let the truth slip so quickly, he couldn't very well lie his way out of it. Plus, he knew that John would tell her the truth if she nagged him enough. And if anyone could get to the truth by pure persistence, it was Charlotte.

"Yes," he said quietly, adding a slight shrug and consciously relaxing his stance.

He was excellent at expressing nonchalance in every situation. Here, with her, however, he found the posture uncomfortable and perhaps a little stupid.

"How is that possible?" Charlotte spluttered.

"What do you mean, how is that possible? You're unmarried and still a virgin, why shouldn't I be, too?" he asked more hotly than he should have. He knew it was unusual, but good God, she was looking at him as though he were the worst sort of lecher.

"I'm sorry, I didn't mean to insult you." Charlotte reached out her gloved hand and laid it on his arm.

She must have heard his swift intake of breath because she wisely took her hand back again.

"It's just unusual. But why? Really?" Charlotte asked again, looking him straight in the eye.

Archie's quick mind imagined what she was thinking, and he didn't want to draw out the pain. Could he take something away from this?

"What do I get if I tell you the truth, Charlotte?" Archie instantly wished the words back as soon as he had said them.

Why on earth was he voicing his true thoughts for the first time in his life?

He'd spent years lusting after his best friend's younger sister, knowing that he would never have her. But now, she was literally within reach.

Should he kiss her? Would she let him? What would be the ramifications? He couldn't marry her knowing what scandal awaited his family, even if she would have him. She'd refused wealthier, older, more titled men than him. The thought stiffened his resolve.

He reached out his hand and tugged her gently, deeper into the darkened alcove. Tingles of awareness danced up his arm.

"What do you want?"

Her voice sounded husky to his ears, and his body throbbed.

"A kiss," he answered softly. He was closer now, and Charlotte jumped back a little, her eyes huge as she stared at him.

He didn't want to scare her, but there was never going to be a better opportunity to kiss her than right now. Just one touch of those lips before he spent the rest of his life married to someone else.

"Considering your innocence, I wouldn't have thought you would want one." She tried to laugh, but it came out sounding strained.

Archie pulled her closer again. He didn't want her so far away anymore.

He gently pushed her up against the hedge and placed his mouth next to her ear, the hot contact of their bodies making his knees weak. "I won't kiss you unless you tell me I can."

Archie knew he should stop this insanity before it went too far, but he was so sick of his life. Almost ten years of fighting his every impulse. He had kept away from women who could be bought for pleasure, so he didn't contract a disease, and every marriageable lady, so he didn't drag them into his scandalous family.

He burned for Charlotte; he always had. He deserved one minute out of time, but he wouldn't force her.

"Tell me why, and you can kiss me," she said, so softly he would never have heard her if he hadn't been so close.

Archie moaned deep in his throat and raised his hands to encircle Charlotte's tiny waist. Without conscious thought, he leaned forward and told her what his heart had ached to do for years.

"Because, like you, I don't want to share with anyone else. I want a woman who has never known another man. I want a woman who is pure of heart, mind, and body and will only offer myself to her if I can gift her the same."

Charlotte gasped, and her body went rigid under his hands.

"And you've never found anyone who has measured up, apparently."

The petulance in her voice was obvious, and she was doing nothing to disguise it. Where had all Lady Charlotte's infamous natural flirtatious charm gone?

Archie laughed softly against her ear, enjoying the way she trembled when his breath caressed her skin.

Charlotte's knees buckled and Archie's hands gripped her tighter as he used his body to hold her up. She felt so good pressed against him that Archie growled low in his throat and told her the last thing he should have admitted.

"Only one. You."

Chapter Five

Charlotte gasped, and Archie took advantage. He turned his head and closed his lips over hers, taking control, ruthlessly. It had been years since he'd kissed a woman and he had never kissed a lady, but she melted into his arms like the most practiced courtesan.

Archie kissed her with every bit of longing and passion in his soul and felt the very tenuous hold on his control slip away. He ran his tongue along her lips, and when she opened her mouth, he eagerly slipped inside. He slid his tongue along her velvety one, and she shuddered in his arms. He stepped even closer to her, if that was possible, and ran his hands down to her deliciously rounded bottom. Charlotte had always been one step plumper than was fashionable. Archie had always seen it as Charlotte's way of standing out and had at the time dismissed it as another of her vanities. Now, he gloried in it. What a beautiful bottom she had, plump and firm. A real handful on either side for his hands.

Archie's heart was pumping so hard it was almost painful. He wanted her closer. He pulled her into the cradle of his hips, against the hardness of his arousal. That was when she pulled back.

"Archie, stop." Charlotte gasped, pressing her hands against his chest. "Please."

Her whispered "please" cut through the fog of passion surrounding him, sharper than any other tool might have done. He dropped his hands away from her glorious bottom and took two steps back.

His breathing was ragged, and his manhood was straining against his thigh. He used his considerable willpower to pull himself together and rearrange his hair and clothes. In less than a minute he was able to wipe all trace of their encounter from his person.

As long as anyone didn't look too closely at his evening breeches.

"My apologies." He bowed to her, frustrated and aching.

Charlotte took a step forward, closing the large gap between them and reached out a hand to touch his face.

"Please don't."

"*Please don't.* Don't what, Charlotte? Please stop kissing you? Please don't move away? What do you want from me?"

He turned away when he couldn't contain the flickering of emotion moving on his face.

It appeared that this night really could get worse. He had seen heaven, and now he was being dropped into hell. Why had he kissed her? Why did he have to torture himself with a taste of the one thing he could never have?

"Please don't hide from me. I just want to talk to you," Charlotte whispered.

Archie sighed heavily, letting his shoulders drop. Why did he suddenly wish for his dragon back? Why did he prefer the Charlotte he had always blatantly teased for her brashness and her fire? This meek Charlotte just would not do.

Archie spun around in disgust, at her and himself. Mostly at himself.

"Talk? About what, Charlotte? Have you got more embarrassing questions for me? I've revealed enough about myself for tonight, don't you think? Or do you want to see just how pious I truly am?" He raised a taunting eyebrow at her.

Charlotte's spine straightened as though tugged up by a marionette's string.

"I completely agree, Lord Archibald. Shall we retire to the ballroom?" Putting on her best social smile, she started to walk towards the entrance of the bower.

Archie heard voices enquiring as to her whereabouts, floating down from above on the balcony. He reached out for her, tugging her back into the safety of the bower.

"We can't leave together. If people see that we've been here alone, your reputation would be ruined."

"It would not be ruined. We are allowed to go for a walk in the gardens."

Archie gripped his courage and said what had to be said, a sentence he never thought he'd say. "I cannot marry you, Charlotte."

"I don't believe I asked you to do that," she all but hissed at him, as she spun around, eyes flaring with heat.

Archie took a step back at her anger. He hadn't meant to insult her. He had just intended to explain why it was important that they should not be caught alone together.

"It's not that I wouldn't want to, but–" he didn't even finish his sentence before she jumped in.

"I know, don't worry. You've always made it abundantly clear how unsuitable you think I am. How could I ever live up to the standards you have set for yourself and your future wife?" She was seething with anger now. Archie could sense it coming from her like steam from a boiling pot of water.

With a last scathing stare, she stalked right out into the light to join the women on the balcony.

"Here I am, Mama. I'm so sorry for leaving without telling you where

I was going. I had a terrible headache, but the night air seems to have cleared it right up."

"Were you talking to someone, Charlotte?" Archie heard the Duchess of Arrow ask her daughter; suspicion etched in her tone.

"No one," came Charlotte's reply. Then their voices receded as she shepherded her mother and the other dowagers of the *ton* inside.

Archie leaned his forehead into one of the high hedges. How had tonight gone from a typical *ton* engagement to his definition of hell?

Not only did Charlotte now know he was unlike other gentlemen of the *ton*, but he had managed to kiss her senseless and himself too, for that matter, and yes, insult her, all within the space of ten minutes. How could she honestly believe that he didn't think she was good enough for him? She was so far out of his reach as to be laughable.

He loved Charlotte. He had always loved her. She was the epitome of everything he wanted in a woman. Intelligent, outspoken, generous and full of passion. Not to mention, beautiful enough to make every man in England lust after her. But she could not be his, for the mere fact that he had to protect her.

How would she feel if she married him and he got her entangled in his family's scandal, should it ever become common knowledge? He would never do that to her.

So, he had to make sure he never kissed her again. Because the feel of her against him was like nothing he had ever experienced. And it wasn't simply the long-forgotten feeling of a woman pressed against him–it was *her*. It had always been her.

He felt her very presence down to the depths of his soul, and knew that if he ever had the good fortune to know her intimately, he would lose his heart fully and forever.

～

A FEW MORNINGS after her birthday ball, Charlotte paid a call on Sarah at her new townhouse. Oliver had bought the house for himself and his young wife, and he had given his mother the family's existing townhouse in which to live.

"Charlotte, it is so lovely to see you," Sarah greeted her friend with a genuine smile in the morning sitting room.

"Tea?" she asked, already pouring Charlotte a cup. "Milk?"

Charlotte took a moment to be amazed at how far Sarah had evolved, from the shy, socially inept young woman of a year before. She was now a supremely confident hostess, wife, and a perfect duchess. A credit to her husband's family.

"Yes, but no sugar," Charlotte answered, almost forgetting the question.

She would be happy if she could keep her tea down this morning. She had come to ask Sarah some more questions about her married life, and her stomach was alive with dancing butterflies.

"This house is beautiful, Sarah, but are you sure you would rather live here than in the Lincoln townhouse?" Charlotte took a sip of the fragrant tea, enjoying the heat as it flowed down into her tummy.

Sarah shuddered visibly.

"Yes, I'm very sure. I wanted a house that I could decorate and for which *I* could choose the furniture, without asking someone else's permission."

"You could have leased his mother a separate house."

That would have been the most obvious solution. No one expected Oliver to move to another house. In Charlotte's view, his mother, being the dowager, should have stayed either at their main estate out of town, or leased a small house for herself.

Sarah laughed musically, eating a biscuit whilst she spoke.

"No, Oliver had too many bad family memories there. I wanted somewhere where we could start fresh." Sarah smiled at the butler as he approached.

"Lady Wickersham and Miss Bartlett have called, Your Grace. Shall I tell them you are at home this morning?"

Sarah looked at Charlotte, and her eyes seemed to narrow. Dropping her voice to a whisper, she spoke.

"Are you here to take me up on my offer to tell you more about what my mother said to me?"

Heat flowed into Charlotte's cheeks. Was she that obvious? Before she could even answer, Sarah was sending the other ladies away.

"Please tell anyone else who calls this morning, Peters, that I am not at home."

The butler inclined his head respectfully and bowed, tactfully shutting the door behind him.

"You didn't have to do that, Sarah. I could have called on you at another time." Charlotte apologised profusely. She felt incredibly guilty now.

Sarah waved her hand like the veritable duchess she was.

"No, this is a perfect time. David is asleep, and you are here. There have to be some advantages to being a duchess, other than the prestige."

David. She still couldn't get used to the unusual name that Sarah and Oliver had chosen for their son. Charlotte laughed out loud and found herself wishing she and Sarah had grown up together. What a wonderful friend she would have been.

Charlotte had very few true friends.

"So, what would you like to know?" Sarah continued to sip from her teacup and eat another biscuit.

"I kissed someone the other night," Charlotte blurted out.

She hadn't meant to start the conversation so abruptly, but she had been dying to tell someone ever since it happened. Sarah was the most trustworthy person Charlotte knew. She had no intention, however, of telling her who she had kissed.

"At your birthday ball?" Sarah's eyes narrowed in suspicion.

"Yes, after you left." Charlotte bit into a biscuit before she could share more.

"I won't ask who, just tell me how it was. Was it your first kiss?" Sarah asked, leaning forward in her chair with an excited smile on her face.

"No, it wasn't my first kiss." Charlotte blushed so hotly she reached up and laid her hands against her cheeks to try and cool them down. She was never going to get through the conversation if she was this embarrassed at the start.

"But it was the first time that a man put his tongue in my mouth and the first time that I...ah...wanted to keep kissing." Charlotte stammered over the admission, but got the words out, all the same.

"Did you?" Sarah asked, not showing any revulsion at the idea. Instead, she looked intrigued.

"No. Well, he pulled my body into his, and he had, ah...he was...I got scared."

Now Charlotte truly did run out of words, so she stuffed a piece of cake into her mouth. At this rate, she was going to need to have the dressmaker let out all of her new ball gowns.

"So, he was aroused from the kiss, and you stopped him before he did anything else?" Sarah clarified, chewing her lip thoughtfully.

"Yes."

Charlotte bowed her head slightly, in gratitude. She wasn't sure she could have said it. Her mother and several married friends had explained the mechanics to her, and it sounded horrible.

"So why have you come here, Charlotte? I can tell you anything you want to know, but if you have some specific question, just ask me." Her eyes were bright, and Charlotte saw nothing to indicate that she wouldn't tell the truth.

She took a deep breath and exhaled slowly. If she never married, would that mean she never got to taste the passion that Sarah apparently enjoyed?

"First, I need to know if you were telling the truth, about, you and Oliver...and..." Oh, when had she become such a babbling idiot?

Charlotte had always prided herself on her ability to talk people into circles and out of them again. What was wrong with her?

Sarah laughed softly and leaned back in her chair, a dreamy look on her face.

"Charlotte, can I be completely honest—brutal even?"

"Please. That would be fine."

"If Oliver and I didn't have to leave the bedroom to eat, I'm not sure if I would ever leave."

Charlotte cocked her head to the side. What could she possibly mean by that?

Sarah apparently saw Charlotte's confusion and laughed musically again.

"Let me put that more simply. Oliver gives me so much pleasure in our bed that if we could make love all day and night, I would do it."

Charlotte's jaw dropped. She must have stayed that way too long because Sarah reached over and pushed her chin back up.

"You're serious? It's that good?"

Charlotte couldn't believe what her friend was telling her. It went against everything her mother and her friends had said about marital relations.

"Yes, it is," Sarah assured her, leaning back in her chair again and smiling a secret smile.

"But how? How could a man putting his, you know, inside you, how could that feel right?"

Charlotte was truly confused now. It sounded ridiculous.

It was the first time Sarah blushed, and Charlotte almost laughed.

"When I first heard my mother tell me it could be enjoyable if the man cared enough, I didn't believe her either. Then Oliver kissed me, and touched me, and I suddenly felt an emptiness inside me that needed to be filled. Oliver did that. I ached with hunger, and he knew what to do."

"What did he do?" Charlotte leaned forward in her chair as though she could absorb the necessary information via proximity.

"He kissed me and touched me until I almost died with pleasure."

Sarah blushed again but resolutely kept her head up.

Charlotte considered that. The concept of any pleasure, let alone such a cataclysmic event being possible, was surreal.

"Really?" she asked skeptically.

"You'll know when it happens." Sarah smiled a little smugly.

"Next, I need to know what I can do."

Now that she knew that it could be enjoyable, then maybe there were other things she could do that wouldn't ruin her.

"What do you mean, Charlotte?" Sarah asked, a confused expression passing over her face.

Charlotte blushed again at her audacity to ask such a forward question but didn't back down.

"What can I do to him to give him pleasure, too? If he tries again? Can I do anything that won't lead to me being ruined?"

Charlotte couldn't believe she was asking such things. But she had to know. If Archie wanted to touch her again, could she touch him without losing her virginity?

Sarah blinked once and picked up another biscuit.

Charlotte waited for her to finish and kept her mouth firmly shut, squeezing her hands tightly together in her lap.

Sarah sat chewing for a full minute, obviously deciding whether she would tell Charlotte what she wanted to know. Suddenly she smiled and leaned forward again.

"All right, I'll tell you, but you can't tell anyone that I told you any of this."

"I won't, Sarah, please," Charlotte assured her friend.

She leaned forward in a mirror image of Sarah's enthusiasm. She had the sudden urge to ask for a piece of paper and quill to write everything down but realised that that might seem a little too eager.

"First, my mother told me that anything your husband, or in this case, your lover, can do to you, you can do to him."

"Like what?"

Charlotte didn't understand what else there was to do other than the bedding, which a woman certainly couldn't do to a man.

"Like touching and kissing."

"Where?" Charlotte asked, her eyes widening. Archie had touched her waist and her bottom whilst he was kissing her. Maybe that what Sarah meant.

"Everywhere," Sarah announced confidently, then ruined the effect with a blush.

"Everywhere?"

She couldn't mean everywhere. Sarah nodded, a funny twitch happening at the corner of her mouth as though she were trying not to laugh. Charlotte filed that piece of information away and asked something more specific.

"Tell me what I can do without ruining myself."

"Charlotte, I'm not sure if I should give you information which could get you into trouble." Sarah bit down on her lip, looking hesitant now.

"Look, Sarah, I'm twenty-two years old. I'd never actually, properly, kissed anyone before but I...I have finally met someone I could love. But I need someone to help me. Please."

Even as she spoke the words, shock filled her. *Love?* Archie? Never! Or at least, she didn't think so...

She knew she'd said the right thing when Sarah's face warmed with understanding.

"Well, there are only two ways. You can touch each other with your hands or with your mouths." Sarah subconsciously touched her mouth as though illustrating her point.

"Where?" Charlotte asked, wide-eyed.

"He'll want to touch you here and here," Sarah said, running her hand from her breast to her lap discreetly.

Charlotte swallowed hard, thinking about the times she had touched herself in those places just to see what exactly men found so interesting. It hadn't felt like anything special.

"And I touch him there, too?" Charlotte asked thoughtfully, then Sarah's initial words registered.

"With my mouth?"

She gasped, lifting her hand to cover her mouth. Sarah couldn't be serious. Her friend pulled her lips tightly together and nodded.

"You can, although Oliver told me that most ladies don't," she confided, looking as though she was relieved to finally be able to tell someone that fact.

"But you...?" Charlotte couldn't finish the question. She couldn't even fathom the idea of Sarah, or anyone for that matter, kissing that part of a man.

"When you love someone, Charlotte, it makes you happy to make them happy. Whether that is buying them something they want, or making sure they eat the food they like. This is just part of that love. If you love them, you want to please them."

Sarah hesitated, then obviously decided she needed to say one more thing.

"Charlotte, the most important thing is to listen to your heart. If you're comfortable touching this man, do it. If you want to run, follow your instincts. I learned that early on, and it served me well." Something slightly painful flashed over Sarah's face, then it cleared. Her expression resumed its usual state of general serene happiness.

"Sarah, I don't know how to thank you. If I had listened to my other friends or my mother, I would always have assumed that pleasure was only for fallen women," Charlotte said unthinkingly.

She had been talking about her father's mistress. But then she saw Sarah blanch and realised how that must have sounded.

"Oh, please don't think I meant you. Please, forgive me," Charlotte begged. The woman had been so generous to share her knowledge.

Sarah laughed.

"No, it's fine. I believe you should have all the information. My mother thought that the reason most men of rank are unfaithful to their wives is that their wives don't enjoy bedding. If you want a faithful husband so much that you're willing never to marry, then maybe this information can help you."

"Now, tell me about your beautiful little boy," Charlotte encouraged her friend, happy now to change the subject.

Sarah laughed happily and swept into a lengthy discussion about the joys of being a mother.

Chapter Six

A week later, Archie was still chastising himself for kissing Charlotte. He hadn't been able to get a good night's sleep since, waking hot and erect, with visions of Charlotte naked beneath him.

He should have stayed away from the *ton* balls, where there was a possibility he'd see her again. It was a standard practice of his to attend one ball a fortnight and his club every other day. It was a system to which he had stuck for almost ten years. It made him feel reliable and stable.

For the first time in a decade, he wanted to break the rules. He had seen Dunford at his club during the day, and his friend had mentioned having to take Charlotte to Lady Marlow's ball that night.

Archie pulled the cord for his valet and took a deep breath. He couldn't wait any longer. He had to see her again.

He may be breaking all of his own rules, but if he didn't, he might never get another good night's sleep.

~

CHARLOTTE HAD BEEN deep in conversation about this season's hats when an awareness within her prickled and made her sit up straighter.

"Lord Archibald Turner," the butler announced.

Charlotte briefly closed her eyes. How could she be so attuned to him already?

She couldn't stop from turning to watch as Archie entered the room and looked immediately to his left. Her eyes met his. She was drawn to him with a strength that made her stomach tighten.

Archie turned on his heel and headed directly for the card room.

Charlotte clenched her hands into fists in her lap and glared at the back of Archie's retreating figure. She couldn't believe he'd looked directly at her, and turned away, going to one of the male hideaways at such events. Well, if he could ignore her after their kiss, she would do the same.

Charlotte glanced around the room and saw a new debutante surrounded by four gentlemen. She nodded. She could accomplish two things at once. Rescue the poor girl who looked like she was drowning in attention, and also engage her own interests. How else would she keep her mind occupied?

Charlotte sashayed across the room and greeted the beautiful young girl she had met the previous evening. "Miss Bartlett, so lovely to see you," Charlotte said.

"Ah...Lady Charlotte, lovely to see you too," the young lady stammered in reply, touching Charlotte's offered hand.

The young girl looked at her warily, but Charlotte ignored this, taking her by the arm and addressing the men in front of her.

"I hope you gentlemen aren't trying to overwhelm Miss Bartlett," she chided, with a coy smile.

Charlotte recognised all four of the young gentlemen in front of her. Two of them blushed brightly. They were both Charlotte's age and always acted as though they felt vastly inferior to her. The other two gentlemen, however, were Archie's age or a little older and could hold their own in any conversation.

"Lady Charlotte," the older two gentlemen greeted her as one. They bowed grandly, each taking turns to kiss her hand.

"How are you enjoying the evening, Lady Charlotte?" asked the gentleman standing closest to her.

Charlotte searched her memory and came up with a name, the Honourable James Withering, she remembered. He was the heir to Viscount Westleigh. Yes, he would do just fine.

"I'm having a wonderful time, Mr. Withering, although I am feeling a little disappointed." Charlotte sighed dramatically and pouted openly.

"And why is that, my lady?" her prey asked, looking genuinely concerned.

"There has been dancing going on for the last two hours at least and all I have done is watch from the sidelines." She sighed again for emphasis and gave her would-be champion a shy smile.

It was not ladylike to request a dance from a gentleman, but Charlotte knew how to get what she wanted. The simplest way was often just to convince the other person they wanted the same thing as her.

"Well, if you would grant me the honour of being my partner for the next two dances, my lady, I could rectify that problem for you," replied her gentlemen, with an air of benevolence.

He looked more pleased than could be easily described by this most public request.

Looking down at the beautiful young girl beside her, Charlotte shook her head regretfully.

"Thank you so much, sir, but I wouldn't want to abandon Miss Bartlett." Another obvious ploy for a dance, but one that also worked beautifully.

Within seconds, Miss Bartlett had been asked to dance by the other older gentleman and Charlotte was being whisked onto the dance floor. She had to give Mr. Withering credit—she rarely got asked for more than one dance, as that showed intent, but he seemed to have more courage than most gentlemen of the *ton*.

"You look lovely this evening, my lady," Mr. Withering told her, with a courtly twinkle in his eye.

Charlotte smiled warmly. She appreciated the comment whilst the man's eyes were still on her face. Too many times, a gentlemen's eyes hovered lower to her pushed up breasts, and then Charlotte did not dance with him again. Unfortunately, this happened more than half the time, and she would soon be running out of gentlemen with whom to dance. She knew her dress was beautiful and that her body was cleverly displayed, but a little courtesy went a long way.

"So, tell me about your new horse breeding program, Mr. Withering."

Withering looked genuinely surprised that she would know such a thing, let alone ask about it.

"I hadn't realised you had an interest in horses, my lady." Again, he spoke with the perfect combination of surprise and respect in his voice.

Charlotte smiled again, feeling guilty that she was using this kind gentleman just to forget another difficult one.

"I know it's not particularly ladylike, Mr. Withering, but growing up with my two brothers meant that I often had to listen to such talk. I found after some time that it became more interesting than talk of bonnets and ribbons."

Mr. Withering laughed loudly, and Charlotte joined him. She knew that she had a good knack for conversation, but she was still genuinely pleased when a gentleman appreciated what she had to say, rather than what she looked like.

They continued chatting through the next two dances, very easily.

ARCHIE TAPPED his fingers against the wooden table in the card room, wondering if he should leave through the side garden. He could barely restrain himself from going back into the ballroom to see Charlotte.

He had never felt like this before, so out of control. It was as though that one kiss had undone ten years of carefully constructed restraint.

"So, any tips on the latest investments, Archie?" John spoke to him from across the table.

Archie struggled to pull his mind back to the current topic. He noticed that many of the men around him had stopped their conversations to listen. He knew they looked to him because it was well known that he made real money in investing. He hoped that this regard would also hold him in good stead when the family scandal broke.

"At the moment, I'm looking into some shipping companies that have been travelling routes between India and England. But nothing is certain yet, I'll let you know, John," he said, not wanting the whole room to know his latest tip.

John smiled at him and looked back at his cards as Oliver walked in whistling; looking smug and satisfied as always.

"Oliver." Both John and Archie greeted him.

"Lincoln," chorused many of the other men.

Oliver tipped his head to the rest of the room and sat down with his friends. Although Oliver now bore the title of Duke of Lincoln, he wouldn't allow his closest friends to call him anything other than by his given name. It went against the grain for Archie to ignore protocol like that, but he cared about his friend's feelings more.

"Looking happier than normal, Oliver. Any news?"

Oliver leaned forward and pitched his voice low.

"Don't say anything to Sarah, because I'm not meant to say anything yet, but she's *enceinte* again."

"Already?" John asked, apparently surprised. None of them had any siblings within three years of each other, and Oliver's son was only just over four months old.

Oliver blushed and nodded.

Archie laid his cards down with a slow movement and gave Oliver an assessing look. Maybe he should ask Oliver about bedding when the time came. He seemed to keep his wife satisfied enough that she wanted to have his baby again within four months of her first birth.

Strange, but then again Oliver's wife had not been brought up within the *ton*. Perhaps Sarah had been telling the truth when she said that vicars' daughters had different ideas about their marriage bed.

Archie flushed at the thought, and Oliver gave him a quizzical look.

"What are you thinking about now, Archie?"

"Just thinking about how lucky you are, my friend," Archie answered honestly. How could he not?

Oliver chuckled, and John just shook his head.

"Not me. Wives are for men who want only one woman. Couldn't think of anything worse. I'll stay out of the parson's trap, thank you."

John always had a mistress. He never kept one around for more than six months, but he was never without one either. Again, Archie had to fight the strange urge to ask about John's latest bed partner, when Oliver said something that chilled Archie's blood.

"Well, it looks like your sister might have changed her mind, John."

"About?"

John shuffled his cards again. Archie knew he did that when he had a bad hand But the comment about Charlotte had unnerved him enough that he forgot about cards.

"About never getting married. I saw her dance the last two with Withering."

Archie grabbed his port glass and downed what was left in a single gulp, then called for more while the burn made him gasp and grimace. That bloody woman was going to turn him into a drunkard.

Oliver gave him a startled look but went on.

"Not a bad chap. Breeds horses, doesn't gamble much, decent fortune. Although I hear he keeps a long-time mistress in Essex Street."

Essex Street was in a nice part of town and Archie looked at Oliver in surprise and silent question. Reading his look correctly, Oliver explained.

"It usually means that he's in love with his mistress."

John grunted, "Or thinks he is."

"Well, then Charlotte won't marry him," Archie announced.

He was relieved that her strict list of rules would prevent Withering from marrying her. Although his heart was still thumping in his chest and he couldn't seem to calm it down.

"Maybe, although you never know what a man would do for a woman with whom he falls in love."

John grunted again, but Archie's heartbeat tripled in speed. He knew that Oliver was faithful to Sarah, but did that mean any gentleman could change his habits for a woman he loved?

Oliver stood up again, inclining his head.

"I think I'll go and see where Sarah is."

Archie chuckled, the feeling rippling through him and relieving some of the tension in his body.

"You know, you're not meant to care what she does, or to whom she speaks," said John, with a smile.

Oliver smiled back, obviously confident in the knowledge that such men would be unsuccessful. "I know, but I don't want my daughter listening to some rake trying to get my wife into bed."

Archie glanced away from his friend. He was so jealous of the emotion in Oliver's eyes that he felt sick to his stomach with it.

"Daughter?" John picked up on the point that Archie had missed in his green haze.

"Yes. Sarah's decided this one's a girl, and she was right the first time."

"Archie?"

"Yes?" Archie looked at his cards and tried not to let Oliver see the hope he knew would be flaring in his eyes.

"Want to join me?" Oliver asked lightly, but Archie saw the awareness in his friend's eyes. Oliver knew him better than anyone, and he wasn't doing a good job at hiding his eagerness to return to the ballroom.

Archie considered his options for less than two seconds before he stood and followed Oliver. Butterflies fluttered in his belly. Luck was on his side. Oliver's duchess wife, Sarah, was presently talking to both Charlotte and Withering.

Chapter Seven

Archie sidled up next to Sarah and tried not to let his face or body show the rather violent feelings he was experiencing. Desire and hatred were warring inside him like a pair of vicious mongrels, fighting for supremacy.

"Withering," Archie greeted the gentleman who had had the courage to partner for two dances with the spectacular Lady Charlotte Dunford.

"Turner."

"How are those fine horses of yours?" Archie knew the Viscount's heir through their mutual love of horseflesh. Withering liked racehorses especially, and Archie could see the passion was high.

Withering laughed and shared a glance with Charlotte. Archie raised an eyebrow and clenched his jaw. What had he missed?

"Lady Charlotte was just asking about the same topic. Perhaps you can tell Turner how my horses are, Lady Charlotte, as you listened so attentively."

Charlotte flushed, her full cheeks turning a bright shade of pink.

"Several of Lord Withering's well-known racehorses have been at stud recently and have produced two young fillies and a colt," she told Archie obligingly, neither smiling nor allowing any warmth into her tone.

Archie inclined his head in thanks but held his tongue. Charlotte turned her back to Archie and spoke directly to Withering.

"What are you planning on doing with the offspring, Mr. Withering? Are you planning to sell them, or keep them to race yourself?"

"I don't keep many horses to run, Lady Charlotte. I either sell them or keep them for breeding. The colt I will keep for breeding. His bloodlines are impeccable, but the two fillies, I will sell."

"Really?" Archie asked, interested now. "What are the horses' bloodlines? I'm looking to increase my breeding program next year."

Archie and Withering got into a discussion about bloodlines until Charlotte spoke into one of the rare silences.

"Are you enjoying the ball, my Lord Archibald?"

Archie glanced at Charlotte and noted the look in her eye. What was she up to?

"I am, thank you, Lady Charlotte," he bowed in acknowledgement, addressing her as formally as he had been addressed.

"Are you going away soon, my lord?" she enquired in a sweet tone. Again, that look was there in her eyes and Archie tensed up for the attack that was sure to come.

"No, my lady, I will not be leaving town until the end of the season." Or unless his brother got worse, he added silently to himself.

"But, my lord, why have you attended three balls in a sennight if you are not going away? I'm sure that in the six years since my coming out, you have never attended two balls in so short a succession."

When their whole group looked at Archie expectantly, Archie could have cursed aloud. How did she even know that?

"I didn't realise you knew so much about my habits, Lady Charlotte," he bit back.

Charlotte didn't even blush.

"Oh, I didn't even think about it until I heard one of the dowagers commenting on it. Then it made me wonder. I don't believe that you have ever been seen at more than one ball a sennight. Is there any reason you are here, especially tonight?" She fluttered her eyelashes and Archie clenched his jaw.

Before he could comment, Withering jumped in.

"We all need to marry at some stage, don't we, Turner?" He grinned, looking at Archie expectantly.

Archie nodded, although he wasn't planning on matrimony in the short-term.

"Oh, is that why you're here tonight, my lord? Are you looking for a wife?" Charlotte asked, and there was steel in her tone now.

Archie allowed himself a lazy smile.

"Well, there are some beautiful new debutantes this year," he agreed, watching Charlotte pale at this acknowledgement of his plans.

It was cruel to make a dig about wanting to marry a debutante, but how could he not, when she was purposefully annoying him?

Oliver cleared his throat as though he was trying not to laugh.

"You're planning on being the next to tie the knot, Archie? I hadn't realised you had met anyone you liked."

Archie smiled lazily again, enjoying the way Charlotte's eyes were sparkling. She would never be a good poker player. Her anger was too clearly written on her face.

"Well, Oliver, I must tell you that the only person I have met recently would be your lovely wife. It was such a shame you took her off the market before anyone else had a chance." He teased as charmingly as he could, giving Sarah his best smile. She leaned forward and hit him smartly with her fan.

Oliver laughed and Sarah *tsked* them both reprovingly.

"You are right, my lord. Who could compare with Sarah?" Charlotte's voice sounded hurt, defeated.

Archie's belly dropped with a painful lurch. He had told the truth, though he had cleverly disguised it. He hadn't met anyone recently he wanted to marry. Because he had met Charlotte many years ago.

Before he could think about what he was doing, he reached out and grabbed Charlotte's arm as she curtsied to leave.

"Charlotte," he pleaded, forgetting to be formal with her.

Her blue eyes flashed at him.

"Don't," she said haughtily. With a sharp move of her elbow, she dislodged his grip and moved to the other side of the room.

"What happened?" Withering asked, oblivious to both the tension and the reason behind it. He didn't even bother hiding his obvious disappointment that his hard-won companion had left so abruptly.

"You shouldn't have said that, Archie," Sarah murmured.

"It was the truth, Sarah."

Archie was unable to drag his eyes away from Charlotte's retreating form.

He heard a small moan of discomfort and turned to see Sarah getting paler by the second.

"Oliver, I know we just got here, but I'm afraid I'm not feeling very well," Sarah told her husband, putting an anxious hand to her stomach.

"Is it the baby?" Oliver asked, the pitch of his voice rising.

Withering took that as his cue to leave and bowed out. Archie knew it was the gentlemanly thing to do, but he couldn't leave his friends.

Lowering her voice to an almost inaudible level, Sarah whispered to her husband.

"Oliver, I think I'm bleeding."

At these words, Oliver immediately swung his wife up into his arms and looked worriedly at Archie.

He jumped to help his friend. "I'll grab the coats, call for your carriage and meet you out the front."

Archie ran off before Oliver could respond, his heart thundering in his ears.

～

ARCHIE DIDN'T KNOW what to do to help. He had never been so uncomfortable in his life. He was in Oliver and Sarah's carriage facing two people who didn't even seem to remember he was there. Archie had called for a doctor, retrieved their coats and met them in the carriage.

Now he was watching Oliver as he cradled his wife in his lap, wincing every time she moaned as a cramp hit her. Oliver met Archie's eyes in helpless entreaty, and Archie could do nothing. His stomach burned, making him feel sick and impotent.

"I've summoned your doctor, Sarah," Archie told her quietly, breaking the silence.

She lifted pain-drenched eyes up and gave him a brave smile.

"Thank you, Archie, but I don't think they can do anything now." She doubled over again with a moan, obviously in agony.

Archie stared out the window, wishing he had never broken his rule to come to tonight's ball. He shouldn't be here.

When they arrived home, however, Oliver wanted him to stay, and as uncomfortable as he was, Archie was happy to offer the moral support. He was halfheartedly reading a book in the duke's library when a very disheveled and haggard Oliver came in and dropped into a chair.

"She lost the baby." He moaned, dropping his head into his hands in apparent despair.

Archie was again at a complete loss. How did one comfort a friend at a time like this? He reached out and gripped Oliver's shoulder for a moment and then let go. That seemed to do the trick because Oliver sat back and asked for a port.

Archie handed him the glass that had already been prepared and watched his friend gulp down the contents, then reach for the decanter.

"Is she all right?" Archie asked, knowing it was a stupid question, but unable to prevent asking it.

Oliver laughed brokenly.

"She's in pain, but she's handling it well. She told me that her mother had a miscarriage between the births of herself and her sister. And it won't stop her from trying again as soon as we can."

Archie's mouth parted in shock at this obvious lack of common sense. What sort of woman had Oliver married?

"Why would she want to go through this again? We already have

David. I think I'll have to investigate some new methods of prevention."
Oliver seemed to be talking to himself, but Archie couldn't help listening.

Archie raised an eyebrow but said nothing. Obviously, abstinence
wasn't a choice for his friend.

Oliver saw the look on Archie's face and laughed sadly again.

"Don't think it's me, Archie. If I thought I could keep my door
locked, I would."

Before Archie had formulated a response to this startling and unbelievable statement, the doctor knocked on the library door.

"Your Grace, your wife is resting. I gave her some laudanum," the
doctor announced, with an air of importance.

"Thank you, doctor. Is there anything else we can do?" Oliver asked,
wringing his hands in a most undignified way.

"No, but I would suggest not trying again for at least six months," he
told Oliver sternly with a hard look in his eyes. Oliver paled but nodded
his head.

The doctor's face softened, and he spoke quietly.

"Although, Her Grace did tell me that she wouldn't be waiting that
long." With a small smile, he bowed himself out and left Oliver with
Archie.

"They all love her, you know," Oliver whispered, sinking into his chair
and reaching again for his port.

"Who?"

Archie found himself wondering again why Sarah would want
another baby so quickly.

"Sarah. Everyone loves her. The butler, the servants, the doctor, everyone." Oliver's voice trailed off as though he were fighting tears, and Archie
felt his own eyes fill.

"I know. We all do," Archie agreed, gripping Oliver's shoulder reassuringly again.

"Archie, I can't lose her...you don't understand...I can't." Oliver
moaned, unable to finish what he was trying to say.

Archie was horrified to see tears welling up in Oliver's eyes, and he
handed him his port glass again.

"She's not going anywhere, Oliver."

Archie was in completely unfamiliar waters dealing with real feelings.

He had dealt with some unusual emotions within his family before, but never this one.

Oliver cleared his throat and drank the port in one gulp.

"I'd better get to bed." Oliver's eyes strayed in the direction of the ceiling and Archie knew he wanted to get back to his wife.

"Of course, I'll see myself out." Archie bowed to his friend, relieved to be leaving, finally.

"Archie, thank you for tonight."

He nodded, shook hands with his friend and walked out the door.

THE NEXT DAY, Archie was standing outside Oliver and Sarah's townhouse again, his hand raised to knock on the door, when a red and flustered Charlotte ran out and almost knocked him over.

"Charlotte." Archie blinked, surprised to see her. He was even more surprised at her flustered appearance. Her face was all blotchy and tear-stained. He'd never seen a woman look as such in public.

Charlotte threw herself into his arms, sobbing.

"Oh, Archie."

Conscious that they could be seen by anyone passing by in the street, he ushered Charlotte back inside and into the front sitting room. The stoic butler looked sympathetic to both Charlotte and Archie's plights. He carefully left the door open and sent a maid for tea.

"It's all right. She's going to get better."

Archie was very conscious of the fact Charlotte was sitting on his lap with her arms wrapped around his neck. His skin tingled where she touched, and heat was pooling inappropriately in his groin. The only thing keeping him from ravishing her on the spot was the fact that she was heaving with sobs.

"It's not fair, it's just not fair," she wailed between tears.

"These things happen, Charlotte," he whispered, kissing the top of her head and letting his eyes close for a moment. He sighed and his body sank into the moment. It felt so good to hold her.

Charlotte hiccupped and shook, and slowly her tears dried up. The moment she realised where she was and who was holding her, her whole body stiffened, and she held her breath. She started to inch herself off his lap with as much dignity as was possible in the situation.

Archie didn't want to let her go but knew he had to.

"I am so sorry," she apologised with an even deeper blush, sliding as far away from him as she could on the chaise lounge.

"Don't be sorry. Just tell me what's wrong."

"What do you mean, what's wrong? You were here last night, weren't you?" She sounded shocked.

"Well, yes," Archie admitted.

"Then you know that she lost a baby. A child who would have been loved and cherished by two people who deeply love each other."

Charlotte seemed irrationally angry, but Archie preferred that over the sobbing.

"I know it's unfair, Charlotte, but Sarah said these things happen."

"You've seen her?" Charlotte gasped, her hand flying to her chest.

"No, but Oliver told me last night that Sarah's mother had also miscarried before."

"Oh." Charlotte sighed, her shoulders sagging.

Archie cocked his head. "What's wrong, Charlotte? You seem more upset about it than Sarah."

Charlotte stared at him for a moment, her blue eyes sad and searching before she finally admitted the truth to him. "I think I'm just jealous that you got to be perfect as always, and I missed out on helping my friend."

Archie chuckled and couldn't resist moving forward and handing Charlotte his handkerchief.

"I'm never perfect, Charlotte. I was just in the right place at the right time to help."

"Withering was there too, and he didn't help," she protested, then flushed.

"He hasn't been friends with Oliver for fifteen years," Archie said, before realising what Charlotte's response apparently said about her feelings toward Withering.

"So, does that mean that you're no longer considering Withering as a potential husband?"

Charlotte sniffed loudly and dabbed at her face.

"I thought I'd made it clear what I need in a gentleman, Archie, and Withering doesn't qualify."

Archie swallowed uncomfortably, a knot appearing in the pit of his stomach. Withering was perfect, except for his mistress. If Charlotte did want someone as untouched as she was, then she would have to marry someone barely over the legal age.

He laughed to cover his tension. "Then I'm afraid you're going to marry someone straight out of school, Charlotte."

She didn't say anything, just looked him directly in the eye with an expression that dared him to say such a foolish thing again.

The air between them crackled with tension and Charlotte leaned forward and pressed her lips to his.

Archie forced himself to stay still and let her kiss him. He refused to deepen the kiss for fear of losing control, but knew she needed some physical comfort from him.

Charlotte must have felt Archie's resistance and cupped his face in her hands to hold him close. She tasted his closed lips with her tongue and moaned in entreaty.

Archie pulled back abruptly, looking toward the door to make sure no one had seen.

Charlotte jumped to her feet in a rush, making an affronted gasping noise. Archie responded just as quickly, getting to his feet in no time.

"Thank you for keeping me company, Lord Archibald, but I think it is time I was getting home."

Archie grimaced inwardly at her use of his formal name. She always did that when she was angry with him.

"You're welcome, Lady Charlotte," Archie replied huskily, moved by the obvious emotion she felt for him.

She may not have known what she felt for him, but it was more than she seemed to feel for everyone else.

Charlotte grimaced and curtsied lower than was necessary, then all but ran from the room.

Archie heard the front door close and quickly readjusted his day breeches. They were not conducive to kissing Charlotte. Even when his mind didn't allow him to respond to her kisses as he wanted to, his body certainly still did. He calculated sums in his head until his body relaxed.

"His Grace is in his study," the butler informed Archie from his usual post, guarding the front door.

The elderly man was keeping his eyes low, and Archie wondered if he had heard or seen what had happened in the sitting room.

Archie struggled to maintain his aloof façade as he walked toward the study. He silently thanked Oliver for hiring discreet servants.

Chapter Eight

A few days later, Archie couldn't believe it, but he was doing it again. He was at a ball for the fourth consecutive week, and there was only one reason for it. Charlotte! He had to see her.

He stood at the side of the ballroom, watching her dance with a Scottish laird to whom someone had introduced him earlier. Nice enough fellow, but he wasn't good enough for Charlotte.

Tonight, she wore an evening gown of apricot silk. The neckline was more discreet than other gowns in which he had seen her, but that only made him want to know what was beneath her dress. He was aware that she would be more beautiful in reality than his imagination could ever hope to create.

As the dance began to slow to a close, Archie decided that it was time to make a move. She wanted him, he wanted her. He didn't know what they could share together, but the time had come to find out.

"Lady Charlotte, may I have the pleasure of this dance?" he requested, bowing to her before she could even leave the dance floor.

She placed her hand in his outstretched one and smiled up at him in an answer. As luck would have it, the band began to play a waltz. Archie swept her into his arms, holding her slightly closer than he should have, but not half as close as he wanted to.

"I've missed you," Archie told her quietly, the only thing he could think of to say. His face showed none of the emotion that sort of statement should have entailed, but he meant the words all the same.

Charlotte missed a step of the waltz and stumbled. If Archie hadn't been holding her quite so close, she would have pulled them both over.

"Really?" Charlotte asked, her eyebrows rising, shock colouring her voice and expression. "Your face doesn't say so."

Archie clenched his teeth and let a little, just a little, of his emotion show on his face.

"I've missed you," he repeated, his voice gravelly now. Some of the emotion he was feeling was obviously reaching his eyes.

Charlotte smiled, a small look of triumph on her face.

"That was slightly better, but you're going to have to work on your expressions."

"Why would I do that, my lady?" Archie asked, swinging her around a couple that was trying to get closer, perhaps to listen in on their conversation.

Archie knew they were attracting attention, but he just couldn't bring himself to care enough to do anything about it. He had known that dancing with a marriageable lady would garner scrutiny, but Charlotte was in a class of her own. Together, it was enough to have Archie wanting to run for the front door.

"So that I can know what you're thinking," Charlotte confided, looking up at him with a mischievous smile.

Archie laughed aloud at that comment and regretted it instantly when he saw even more people look at them with interest. Even though Charlotte was John's younger sister and he was not yet the heir of his family fortunes, the *ton* would still consider their marriage a relatively good match.

Damn.

He stared at his beautiful love for a moment, then slowly shook his head. She could never, ever learn what he was thinking.

"No, my lady, you will never know such a thing," Archie told her calmly, hoping it would always be the case.

"Why ever not, Archie?"

"Because if you knew what was going on inside my head, then you would be running away from me."

"I doubt that very much," she told him, while giving him a smouldering look through her eyelashes.

Archie felt that look as if he had been kicked in the vitals.

"Charlotte, you can't look at me like that, please."

Archie attempted to pull himself together, as though he were a shattered vase. His mask of indifference—where was it?

"Archie, I've missed you too," she whispered, looking up at him and tightening her hold on his shoulder.

Archie had to get her out of the ballroom. She couldn't hide a single thought or feeling, and at the moment, she was looking at him as though she could eat him up.

"Lady Charlotte, would you like to walk along the balcony?" he asked, pulling her to a stop and offering her his arm.

She looked surprised at the sudden change of pace, but took his arm and joined him as they stepped through the large door to the balcony. Cool night air surrounded them.

"Why did you stop us dancing?"

"Because you were looking at me as though I were a dessert you wanted to eat," Archie explained candidly, letting a little of his irritation show when his eyebrows pulled together in a frown.

Charlotte gasped, then a hysterical giggle erupted. She gently dislodged her hand and strolled slowly to the balustrade to look out over the gardens.

"It is a beautiful night, is it not?" she asked.

"Exquisite," Archie responded, not bothering to hide the longing in his voice.

Charlotte turned abruptly and stared at him, her blue eyes shining even in the dim light.

He walked up beside her and propped himself against the balustrade, without touching her. Her breathing sped up, and he watched her breasts rise and fall with such a kick of desire he knew he had to get her somewhere private.

"Charlotte..." Archie began, unsure of how to tell her what he was feeling.

"I spent a lot of time in this house when I was younger. Did you know that, Archie?" she asked airily, waving her hand at the mansion.

Archie turned to her, surprised at the sudden change in conversation.

"No, I didn't, Lady Charlotte." He answered automatically, politely.

"Indeed. Lady Moffat's daughter and I got along well, and we spent a lot of time together here before she married," Charlotte continued, her usually steady voice shaking.

"Indeed." Archie didn't understand where she was going with this but was simply enjoying the sound of her voice.

"And I know of a small room that is both out of the way and has a lock on the door," Charlotte said, conversationally.

Archie's jaw dropped. She couldn't mean what he thought she meant, surely?

"That would indeed be handy for two people if they wanted to be alone," he agreed, leading her to say more. Although he was half terrified of what that would mean for them.

"Indeed, it would, my lord, and I have an absolute yearning to see it."

"A yearning?" Archie repeated, swallowing the lump in his throat and trying to ignore the way his excited heart had picked up its pace.

"Indeed. I believe I will venture to the retiring room for a few minutes and then go visit that place."

Archie debated the intelligence of accepting Charlotte's offer. There was no wisdom in it, only foolhardy bliss.

"Would you tell me where this secret room is, Lady Charlotte?" he asked, tamping down his sensible side.

Charlotte smiled, her eyes sliding away demurely.

"It is through the front sitting room, my lord. You enter the sitting room, and there is a door to the left that enters into a letter writing room. In there."

She smiled brightly, bobbed a curtsey in farewell and headed off the balcony and through the open doors without a backward glance.

Archie stood still for several minutes, his mind a blur of conflicting thoughts. He couldn't do it, surely? If they were compromised, as Oliver and Sarah had been, they would have to marry.

Would that be such a bad thing? His inner self-asked longingly? Yes, it would be. He would be deliriously happy, for a while, and she would become miserable. She would hate him once she found out about his brother, and the scandal that was sure to befall his family. He couldn't abide it. He felt he could bear anything except Charlotte regretting her choice in marrying him.

Archie counted to one hundred slowly and then counted again. He had no choice; he had spent what felt like a lifetime keeping himself apart. Now a decade of yearning was assailing him.

He made his way through the house, watching for people following him and taking steady breaths to calm his racing heart.

He found the front sitting room and walked into it. It was lit by a few candles but was still quite dark. He blinked as his eyes began to adjust, then he saw the door to the left of the fireplace. As he walked over to it, his breathing rate increased and his palms became sweaty. Was Charlotte already in there, waiting for him? The idea made his stomach clench and had him almost running out of the room.

Instead, Archie locked his knees, took a deep breath and opened the door. The room would have been completely dark if it wasn't for a single candle on the writing desk.

"You came." Charlotte's soft voice drifted through the air like misty rain falling on the ground.

Archie groaned at the sound and stepped through the door. His eyes were still adjusting to the light, and he could barely make out her silhouette. He knew, however, that Charlotte could see him.

He turned and closed, then locked the door, before facing her again.

"Come here," he growled, barely able to restrain himself from reaching out to grab her.

She walked into his arms. Archie didn't hesitate. One moment he was standing alone and the next he felt her heat touch him, and he went mad. His lips swooped down, and he pressed hers open, possessively sweeping his tongue through her sweet mouth.

Charlotte moaned loudly at the invasion but instead of pulling away like she had last time, she shifted closer. Archie ran his hands from her waist up to her back, stroking the incredibly soft skin of her shoulders in long strokes.

Charlotte whimpered and ran her hands up under his coat, mimicking the way he was touching her. She tugged at the back of his shirt tails and freed them, running her hands up under his shirt as quickly as possible.

Archie gasped and arched backwards.

How had she done that, and why? He had never felt anything so amazing in his life. The heat of her hands and the softness of her skin against his back was as shocking as dunking his head in an icy pond. His cock was now throbbing painfully and digging into Charlotte's soft belly.

"Charlotte, don't," he urged her, pulling back so that her hands slid away. He moaned at the loss of contact but maintained control and moved to the chaise lounge, sitting down before his legs collapsed from underneath him.

"Why not, Archie?"

Charlotte followed him to the chaise and sat down next to him, reaching for him. Archie groaned when she grabbed both his hands in hers.

Didn't she know how much he wanted her? He had never sunk his cock into a woman's body before, but he could barely restrain himself from laying her down and lifting her skirts.

"Charlotte, you have to know how dangerous this is. I want you, badly. We can't do anything to jeopardise your reputation."

Charlotte smiled her secret smile, and Archie knew he was in trouble. She stood up, slid onto his lap and wrapped her arms around his neck.

Chapter Nine

Archie deeply inhaled her lavender scent and shuddered as she ran her hands over his chest, sending tingles up his spine.

"Charlotte, I don't know what you want from me. Why are you torturing me?" he asked, letting all the longing seep into his voice. He couldn't resist nuzzling the long column of Charlotte's neck as she bent toward him.

"I want you to touch me, and I want to be allowed to touch you," she whispered into his ear. Archie shuddered as she trailed small kisses across his smooth jawline.

Archie couldn't believe the array of images that now flickered across his passion-infused brain. Visions of breasts and endless inches of skin tortured him. His eyes had now adjusted to the faint light, and he could see her eyes and her face, both glowing brighter than the candle.

"What do you mean, Charlotte?"

She continued to whisper to him. "Sarah said there are ways of touching which wouldn't cause me to lose my virtue."

"There are, but..."

He knew there were other things he could share with her without taking her virginity. All of them would test his control to their limits, but it may be worth it to hold Charlotte this close and touch her intimately.

"I want to touch you, Charlotte, but do you want me to?" Archie asked, running his hand slowly up from her waist and caressing her right breast.

The nipple peaked and stuck out through the thin fabric of the dress. Charlotte gasped and arched into his hand.

Her breath hitched. "Do you know how?"

"Not really. I've heard what other people have said, but I think we're going to have to learn together. You tell me what feels good, and we'll go from there."

Archie chuckled wickedly. Her breasts were so plump and soft. She was so responsive he wasn't sure he was going to be able to touch her intimately and then to stop.

"I can't do that!" She buried her head deeper into the crook of his neck.

Archie grinned and looked down at her flushed face. Now who was being coy?

"Of course, you can. How else am I supposed to please you?" He flicked her tight little nipple with one hand whilst the other slowly reached up beneath her heavy skirts.

She moaned again, low in her throat, and wordlessly parted her thighs for him.

Archie swallowed down the lump in his own throat. She was so trusting, innocent, yet deliciously wanton. How she managed to be all three, he had no idea.

Charlotte clutched tighter onto his neck, the heat of her skin making his body burn. He dipped his head to Charlotte's lips, sealing off the sound of her squeal as he ran his fingertips along her thigh and then inward.

He found soft, damp curls and hot folds of skin. Charlotte clamped her legs together, trapping his hand there and went rigid in his lap.

"Are you well?" he asked, a little more concerned now that he was touching her. Concerned for her and himself.

His erection had just reached some previously unknown limit and was now throbbing in ecstasy and pain. She felt incredible, and he was far too close to spilling his seed.

Archie had heard his friends' jokes about how wet their bed partners became and the lips and petals that lay between a woman's legs. Now he could feel them. Slick with moisture, she was warm and aroused.

"Yes, I... just..." Charlotte tried to get the words out.

"Relax, I promise I won't hurt you." Archie soothed her. He caressed her breast again, stroking the nipple and cupping the fullness gently. *So beautiful.*

Charlotte opened further for him. This allowed him to start stroking over her most private place. He stroked down and found her moistness and upwards where she seemed to be most sensitive. Charlotte moaned and then gasped. He instantly stopped his movements.

"What's wrong?" His stomach leaped up in alarm.

Charlotte shook her head but Archie was frozen.

"Tell me, did I hurt you somehow?" He had no idea what he was doing. She was constructed so differently to anything he'd ever known. Where should he touch her?

"No," she whispered into his ear. "Keep doing that, please?" She arched up into his hand and sighed at the contact.

Archie moaned low in his throat, at her pleasure and her pleading tone. He swept his exploring fingers down and up again. Again, she cried out when he reached the top, but this time, he realised it was a moan of pleasure.

"There?" He found a tiny button within her folds and circled it with his fingers, again and again.

"Yes, there, please, don't stop," Charlotte cried into his ear, her body bowing up into his.

Archie knew that he was watching and feeling the tension of an almost-orgasm. He knew the tension from his past experiences with himself. He wasn't sure how she was experiencing so much pleasure without him being near the entrance to her body, but she was.

As she moaned and started moving her hips, Archie learned what real control was. He could feel the need for release rushing down upon him. Clamping a firm hand down on those desires, he tried to forget about his body and focus on hers.

He moved his fingers away and moved down in search of her opening.

Charlotte arched up to him, opening her legs wider. Archie knew he could put his fingers inside of her but wasn't exactly sure where and how to do that.

"Don't stop Archie, please." Charlotte's voice, husky with need, drove him mad.

"Where are you aching, Charlotte? Tell me, I need to know," Archie begged just as desperately. Where was the place he would put himself if they were engaging in the act?

"Back where you were before," she whispered again, her face burning against his neck, where she tucked it once again.

"Nowhere down here?" he asked, dipping his fingers between her thighs. Instinctively Charlotte opened her legs and pushed against his fingers.

Archie took the hint and pressed two fingers deep into the entrance to her body. His fingers slid in almost effortlessly. Her body was so wet and her muscles so ready, they greedily gripped his fingers and held on.

Charlotte gasped and arched her back but didn't protest as he thrust his fingers in and out of her. She reached for him and dragged his lips back to hers, opening her mouth and welcoming the plunging tongue that mimicked the movement of his fingers below.

Archie knew Charlotte was close to finding her ultimate pleasure, right there on his lap, but had no idea how to push her there. He kept up the rhythm inside of her body, enjoying the sounds she was making and the hot, wet feel of her around his fingers. His mind couldn't help imagining how good she'd feel around his cock and just like that he was horribly aware of his body straining to meet hers. He knew she must be able to feel him beneath her buttocks, even through all the layers of the fabric of her dress.

Charlotte moved on his lap, and he drew back to stare at her.

"Charlotte, you can't do that," he hissed through his teeth. He stopped moving his fingers inside her and could barely concentrate on anything other than her pelvis grinding down onto him and the pleasure throbbing in his balls.

She smiled at him knowingly and asked the obvious question.

"Why not? You like it." She purred like a practiced courtesan.

Archie groaned as he neared the precipice and quickly withdrew his fingers and pushed her away from his cock, further along his thighs.

"You stopped." Charlotte pouted openly. "I don't feel..." She stopped.

"You don't feel, what?" Archie asked.

"Nothing," Charlotte mumbled, ducking her head.

"Finished? Relieved?" Archie asked, knowing exactly how she was feeling, but unlike her, he knew what he needed.

Charlotte lifted her head and looked at him, her eyes wide and so uninhibited.

"Do you want me to keep going?" he asked. Even knowing that there was a possibility that he would finish in his evening breeches if she did.

"Do you know what I need?" she asked quietly.

"Not exactly, but I know where you want to go. I'll try my best to get you there."

Reaching between her thighs again he stopped as one of her hands slid down his chest and softly caressed him over the front of his breeches.

"What about you?" she asked, her voice sounding shy despite her brazen actions.

His cock jerked beneath her touch, all the blood in his body flowing to where her hand lay.

"Don't worry about me; I'll finish myself off later," Archie muttered, breathing rapidly. He attempted to push her hands away.

"I can't touch you, how you're touching me?" Charlotte asked, sliding closer so he couldn't dislodge her easily.

"Of course, you can...but it's probably better that you don't," Archie told her, trying his best to sound serious. It felt so good having her touch him there, he wasn't sure he could make her stop.

"I'd like to touch you, please." Charlotte sounded exactly like herself, and yet completely different. His brazen, fearless Charlotte mixed in with an excited, innocent but inquisitive Charlotte. The combination was lethal.

Archie moaned loudly when she continued to touch him, feather-light pressure over the crown of his aching cock.

"Harder, please." Archie pressed his fingers deeply within her, absorbing her moan as he set up an unforgiving rhythm.

Charlotte arched into his hand and groaned, pushing her hand along his length, matching the frantic pace he set with his fingers.

Archie knew he wasn't going to last much longer. In desperation, he used his thumb to press the small button she had liked him touching previously and was rewarded by a gasp from Charlotte and a tightening of the muscles within her already tight sheath.

They were both panting and kissing and straining against each other. Archie worked his fingers and rotated his thumb, praying for strength as her hands worked their magic on his starved body.

Just when he was sure he would finish before her, Charlotte screamed into his mouth and convulsed in his lap.

Archie sighed and let go himself, his orgasm crashing down on him in a hot, hard wave. He flooded his drawers and groaned loudly. They both convulsed several more times and then slumped together, lips still touching. They were barely kissing yet they breathed the same air. Slowly, they resurfaced.

"What happened?" Charlotte asked.

"We gave each other pleasure," he explained. His eyes were closed, his head still spinning like a top. "Women can experience pleasure, the same as men do, I believe. It's just that not everyone knows to achieve it."

Archie forced his eyes open and took in the beautiful view of her face still flushed from her orgasm. He carefully withdrew his hand from between her thighs and gently pulled the skirts down to cover her legs. She had beautiful legs. Maybe next time she'd let him kiss her in all the places he had just touched with his fingers.

Archie shook his head to dislodge the arousing image. Where had that thought come from? Next time? There couldn't be a next time for them. If he couldn't marry her, *not that she would have him,* he reminded himself, then there had to be no more of these encounters.

If she were compromised, he would have to offer to marry her and then she would hate him for deceiving her. That would be like hell on earth, having Charlotte as his wife, and yet having her despise him. He was literally between a rock and a hard place. He couldn't imagine either scenario working.

"We should go back to the ballroom." Archie gently pushed Charlotte from his lap and stood up next to her.

The wetness in his breeches was cold, and he cringed at the discomfort. He must go home to change instantly. He could not stay in soiled linen; Archie shuddered at the thought. He pulled his jacket together and fastened it at the front, glad the length covered the darkened material.

Charlotte sighed heavily, sounding content. "I can't believe you did that to me with no practice."

Archie struggled to keep the smug grin off his face as he took her hand and placed it on his elbow.

"Well, you had no practice and had no problem with the effect you had on me," he returned as calmly as possible.

Inside he was doing a little jig, but he didn't want her to know that. She had made him the happiest man on earth, but now he had to tell her that this would be the last time they could play with each other, and he was worried how she would take it after what they had just done.

Charlotte laughed musically.

"Perhaps we could meet again next week at Lady Dotherington's ball?" She squeezed his forearm suggestively.

Archie ached to say that he would love nothing more than to repeat tonight's experience, but he knew that getting any more involved with Charlotte would make it so much harder to walk away.

"Perhaps not, Charlotte." He gently patted her hand.

"Why ever not?"

He looked down into her bright blue eyes and knew he was going to have to be harsher than he wished.

"Because we can't be caught, and if we continue to meet like this then, eventually, we will be."

Charlotte sighed as they stepped through the door and moved over to a mirror in the sitting room. She surveyed herself critically in the brighter light. Her immaculate hair was slightly mussed but not completely undone, and her gown was slightly rumpled but not enough to be a problem. Her face, however, could not be shinier or more alive.

"Archie, I am not interested in trying to trap you into marriage. I know that you are probably the only man in London who fits my criteria," Charlotte began, holding up her hand to stall Archie when he opened his mouth to speak,

"However, I also want someone who *wants* to marry me. And clearly, you don't."

Archie swallowed uncomfortably, unable to lie out loud after his senses had been entirely obliterated. He just nodded. God strike him down; he was a fool.

"Good. I enjoyed what we just did, and I would be happy to enjoy something similar again. Please don't turn this into a drama, Archie." Charlotte gave an airy flick of her hand and his stomach dropped with a sickening lurch. Him? Turn this into a drama?

"Charlotte, I didn't mean to suggest that you would trick me into marriage."

"Good," Charlotte said, with an adjustment to her gown and a final critical glance at the mirror. She smiled then. "I believe pleasure agrees with me. My eyes are positively shining." Archie got an uncomfortable feeling in his stomach that he could only identify as fear. What had he started?

"However, you need to be getting home to change. I will see you next week."

Without waiting for a reply she swept out of the room, leaving Archie standing alone.

Why did he feel like he'd been used? He certainly shouldn't feel that way. He'd gotten exactly what he wanted. He'd found his release, and he had gotten his hands on and inside Charlotte. An amazing experience, but one he realised couldn't be repeated. Although he was glad she hadn't turned it into a hugely important thing, he hadn't liked it when she reduced what they'd just done to nothing at all.

TWO DAYS LATER, the question of whether or not to continue intimacies with Charlotte was answered for him. The day Archie had been dreading for ten years had finally arrived. His brother's doctor wrote from their country estate in Dorchester saying that his brother would not survive the week.

Archie had always told all of his acquaintances that his brother was overseas for health reasons. However, that had not been the case. His brother had been brought back to England soon after his illness had been diagnosed and Archie had spent every summer for a decade watching his brother slowly waste away. The physical symptoms were bad enough, but dealing with his brother's mood swings and occasionally vicious attacks were even harder.

Archie took his carriage straight to his parents' residence to join them. They were already waiting in the foyer, packed and impatient to get on the road.

They drove the fifteen miles in complete silence. Not a single tear was shed, and not a single word was spoken during the six hour trip.

There were three of them in the carriage and yet Archie had never felt so alone. His heart ached from sadness, and his muscles ached from the lack of movement.

All he could think about was the outcome of this night. How could they cover up how his brother had died? What would they do if the truth was discovered by others? Archie had always been surprised that his brother's actual illness had never been discovered by the *ton*, but now that death was imminent, people would start asking questions.

He missed Charlotte too, and that made his anguish so much worse. She would have comforted him if she had been aware of what was happening. She would hold him and kiss him and give him that succour he had never experienced, even as a child.

When he was young, about thirteen or fourteen, he had seen the local vicar's wife comfort her son. He had only been a few years younger than

Archie, too old for most mothers to bother caring for. He had fallen and scraped his knees whilst running in the village. His mother had come along, dusted him off and held him in her arms until he stopped crying. Then with a smile and a pat on the head, she had sent him off to play again.

Archie had never once had an experience like that. No comfort when he had been sick, no affection when he had been hurt. Now that his brother was dying and he would inherit a title he didn't want, that did not change. There would be no help offered from either of his parents.

They arrived at the estate and ascended the stone stairs. The butler was already there to greet them, bowing his head and opening the door. Archie followed his parents up the staircase. The smell of camphor and other burning herbs assailed Archie's nose, and he felt instantly sick to his stomach.

As they approached his brother's bedroom, Archie held his breath in hope, but the moment he heard his mother's agonized gasp, he knew they were too late. He halted for a mere moment, taking a deep breath to calm the thudding of his heart. Once stable, he moved silently into the room behind his parents and stood slightly to the side of his father so that he could see his brother's body.

No of his parents approached the bed, and Archie felt slightly ashamed of them. The parents who had brought him into this world made no move to touch the man who had been meant to be the next Marquess of Hunting. Their heir, and firstborn son.

Archie's mother choked on a sob and fled from the room, wailing as she moved down the hallway. His father stood a minute longer staring at his lost heir, but then also turned and left.

Archie remained. He sat in the chair next to his brother's bed and said a prayer for his soul. The body left behind was ravaged with the disease. The doctors had told them that he wouldn't last five years and yet he had stayed alive twice that long. He may have died a skeleton, but he had fought to live as long as he could.

Within the week, Archie had organised a small burial, monumentally small. A closed casket, of course, with the church vicar, the doctor, and only their three immediate family members in attendance.

He sent the death notice to the London paper and had the doctor cite chronic lung weakness as the cause. Archie did everything he could do to protect his family, but he still felt helpless.

He couldn't seem to shed a tear, despite his grief.

The next month passed excruciatingly slowly. Archie stayed on at the estate, sorting out tenant issues and paying the bills which his father had neglected. He received dozens of flowers and condolence cards but refused all offers of moral support or visits.

Then Charlotte sent him a note accompanied by a single red rose. It bore a simple message. "Thinking of you."

Finally, he cried.

Chapter Ten

Archie returned to London reluctantly, in full mourning. Knowing they would be unable to attend regular events, nonetheless, his parents wanted to be back in their townhouse.

The day after his return, his worst fears were realised.

"Will you be riding at all today, my lord?" his valet asked that morning.

"No, I believe I'll spend the day in my library," Archie replied, watching his valet adjust his neckcloth and arrange his hair.

It seemed a waste to put so much effort into his appearance when they weren't even receiving visitors, but a gentleman must always look his best.

As his valet was polishing Archie's shoes, Archie looked down and noticed his valet's posture. The normally starched appearance of the proud servant was slumped. What was wrong with the man?

"Jenkins, do you mind my asking you if something is the matter?"

Archie knew very little of his servant's personal life, but he was aware that Jenkins was married with three children and that he was a deeply religious person. Not to mention, amazingly skilled with clothing and fashion choices.

"Oh, nothing, my lord," Jenkins stammered, blushing a dark red.

Archie had known Jenkins for more than fifteen years, and he had never seen the man so ruffled.

"No, really, tell me. If I can help, you know I will," Archie reassured him.

"It's nothing about me, my lord..." Jenkins stuttered again, and Archie let discontent colour his tone.

"Tell me, Jenkins." Archie turned side-on in the mirror, checking for wrinkles in his coat. As usual, there were none.

"No, I beg your pardon sir, I will endeavor to be more cheerful this evening."

Archie wasn't sure that he should let the subject go, but good breeding demanded that he did.

He spent most of the day in the library, reading newspapers and doing research on different stocks. The odd thing today was the servants' behavior. He never usually noticed them, as a good servant should be almost invisible. They did their jobs expertly without ever bothering him. Archie had never felt he was being watched or that he lived in a house with thirty other people but today, he did.

Every maid who came to bring him tea or a meal glanced at him as though he were about to leap on them. They scampered out of the room so quickly he barely had time to say, "thank you." By the time it came around to dressing for dinner, Archie had had enough.

"Jenkins, tell me what is going on. The servants are acting most peculiarly."

"It is not my place, sir," Jenkins replied, helping Archie on with his waistcoat.

"It is, Jenkins. You are my eyes and ears below stairs. Tell me what is going on. Is it the new title? Is everyone worried I am going to close this house up, and they'll be without a job?"

That was the only plausible explanation. This was his bachelor residence, the one reserved for him as the younger son. As the new heir, it would now be possible for him to move into another, larger property.

Jenkins just shook his head, his eyes averted.

Archie turned around and gave Jenkins his best stare.

"Jenkins, you must tell me what is the matter."

"I don't know how to tell you, sir. You know I don't like to report on gossip."

Archie chuckled. His valet loved to gossip, but usually about the *ton*, never about actual domestic matters.

"Jenkins, if there is something I should know about, then please inform me."

"It's about your brother's death, sir." The man stopped work, looking down at the sparkling shoes he was polishing.

Archie swallowed painfully. It couldn't be out already, could it? They had only just arrived.

"Yes?" Archie asked, striving to keep his tone calm.

"I'm afraid that people have been talking about what he died of, my lord."

Archie could have shaken the man to get him to hurry up with his story but held his patience.

"What are they saying?" Archie asked quietly, feeling his stomach drop.

This was the defining moment of his life. Everything was going to fall apart, and all he could do was watch as it crashed around him. Like a vase, knocked over accidentally. You could only look on in horror as it broke into a thousand pieces, never to be the same again.

Jenkins was now bowing his head in obvious shame.

"They are saying he died of the French disease, my lord," he whispered, uttering the words so quietly that Archie thought he might have imagined them.

"And who has been saying this, Jenkins?" Archie asked, horrified to hear his voice so gravelly.

"Most of the servants, sir. I heard it from the kitchen maids, who heard it from the groom of that gentleman who visited your father yesterday."

That was it. Archie had to sit down. Swerving dangerously, Archie lurched toward his bed, landing on the ground beside it with a thump. Pain shot up his spine.

"My lord, are you all right?" Jenkins cried, coming to Archie's side in moments.

"I...we're ruined," Archie gasped out against the pain. His heart was thundering in his ears, and he couldn't slow it down. He had been terrified of this, and yet he was strangely relieved that the waiting was over.

He no longer had to wait for the axe to fall.

It had fallen.

❦

CHARLOTTE WAS WALKING down the hall toward the gardens when she overheard John and Oliver in the library, speaking in hushed tones.

She knocked once and then opened the door without waiting for them to ask her to enter.

"Oliver."

John and Oliver exchanged a worried glance, and then both rose to their feet. Oliver bowed to Charlotte and kissed her extended hand.

"How are you? And how's Sarah?"

"We're both very well, Charlotte. Sarah has missed you. You must come by to visit her again."

Charlotte flushed at the slight criticism in Oliver's words.

It was true that she hadn't been back to see Sarah since that first visit after her friend's miscarriage. It had been over six weeks now. Charlotte wasn't sure if she trusted herself not to confide everything in her friend the second she saw Sarah.

She still felt so raw about Archie's passionate display and then his obvious regret afterwards. It had been five weeks since that night, and she still couldn't come to terms with her vulnerable feelings. She missed

243

Archie so much, and the need to talk about him was a constant physical ache.

"I will, tomorrow. I'm sorry, I didn't like seeing her so unwell," Charlotte admitted, knowing that this was indeed part of the truth, if not the whole truth.

Oliver smiled kindly.

"I know it was difficult seeing her in pain, but she is much better now and is mending beautifully."

They all sat down in chairs around the desk, and Charlotte allowed a smile to cross her face. She knew that teasing Oliver was the easiest way to lighten the mood. However, there seemed to be a tense atmosphere in the study she didn't quite understand.

"It wasn't just that, Oliver. I had to visit her in the ducal bed chamber, and I found it most disconcerting." Charlotte raised her eyebrows briefly.

Oliver's eyes widened, and a deep blush appeared, extending up his neck and onto his handsome face.

"Well, Sarah doesn't believe in separate bedchambers, you see. Her parents only had one bedroom, and she believes it necessary for a good marriage to always be together."

He kept his face impassive, but Charlotte could imagine how much effort that took.

"What do you mean, Oliver?" John asked his friend, apparently confused. "You don't mean, every night, do you?" John's face showed a mixture of horror and jealousy.

Charlotte felt the same. What about monthly times? Sarah couldn't possibly want to share a bed with her husband then?

Oliver shrugged.

"I don't sleep well without her."

Charlotte stared straight at her brother; her shock mirrored in his brown eyes. As far as revealing words went, that sentence floored them both. Their parents had barely shared a bed to procreate. The idea of a duke and duchess sleeping together every night, in the same bed, was so foreign to them as to be laughable.

"What brings you here to see us today?" Charlotte asked Oliver, trying to fill the silence with words.

"Well, I was telling John how concerned I am about Archie. He won't receive me in his home, and he hasn't responded to any of my missives. I know he's in mourning, but he's surely allowed to meet a friend."

A strange, fluttery panic invaded her stomach at the sound of Archie's name. She was sure that everyone could read on her face exactly what had happened between them. It made her feel embarrassed and uncomfortable.

"Of course, he's allowed to accept visitors. He must know that," Charlotte said.

Archie was well known to be the most perfect of gentlemen. He always followed the rules down to the letter. Except, perhaps, with her.

John and Oliver shared another one of those glances and Charlotte felt her blood start to boil. What weren't they saying? If it had something to do with her Archie, then she wanted to know.

Oh, goodness. When had he become *her* Archie?

"Why are you two looking at each other like that? What is going on?"

Looking at their faces again she realised they were keeping something horrible from her.

"Oh my goodness, is Archie sick? Is he dying, too?" She whispered the last words, horror closing down her windpipe; she covered her mouth with her hand.

"Oh, no, no. Nothing like that." Oliver reassured her, reaching out to pat her other hand softly.

Charlotte's heart began beating again. She may have occasionally wished him bodily harm for ignoring her three letters and the flowers she sent over the past month, but she never actually meant it.

"It's just–" John began, then stopped, looking at Oliver for help.

"Oliver, she'll find out soon enough. She may as well hear it from us."

Oliver seemed to weigh these words up before deciding to act on them.

Charlotte felt each second as though it were an hour. Didn't they realise that they were torturing her? That every moment led her to believe something was wrong with Archie, and she bled a little more?

She clamped her hands together in her lap and squeezed her fingers tightly together, a numbness seeping into the muscles, then an ache.

"Charlotte, I'm afraid some new information has become common knowledge, and it is rather damaging to Archie's family name," Oliver explained, telling her the problem and yet frustratingly, not revealing anything.

"What sort of information? About Archie?" Charlotte's mind whirled.

What could people be saying about Archie? He did everything right, everything. He didn't even dabble in those socially acceptable vices that her brother did. Charlotte knew he liked women, so what could have happened?

"No, not about Archie. But now that his brother has died, Archie is his father's heir and will be the next Marquess of Hunting."

Charlotte hadn't thought about that. Would that mean he would be happier to marry her now that he had a title only slightly less prestigious than her father's? Would he take a mistress now? Charlotte clenched her teeth at that thought.

"So?" Charlotte gasped through the pain that her sudden jealousy caused.

"So, there are rumors about his brother's death that will cause problems for Archie." Oliver's jaw was clenched in obvious frustration, a muscle twitching in his cheek.

"What?" Charlotte asked. "People don't think Archie had anything to do with his death, do they?"

"Oh, for God's sake, Oliver, just tell her or she'll be imagining all sorts of crazy things," John almost shouted, obviously as impatient as Charlotte.

Charlotte clamped hard down on her bottom lip to stifle the flow of words.

"Archie's brother is rumoured to have died of syphilis, the French disease." Oliver whispered the words as though it was a great secret.

Charlotte blinked. What did that mean? She'd never heard of it.

Seeing her confusion, Oliver explained further.

"Syphilis is a horrible disease that causes great sickness and the body slowly wastes away."

"Yes..." Charlotte began slowly, trying to see the problem that would cause Archie's family. It was obviously a horrible way to die, but why would that affect him?

"Well, that's horrible for his brother, but what has that got to do with Archie?" Charlotte glanced at her brother and his friend again.

Oliver and John exchanged another one of those looks and Charlotte clenched her hands into fists in her lap to keep from jumping to her feet and hitting one, or both, of them.

"You only get the French disease from bedding whores," John told her quietly. "Dirty whores."

Charlotte was her mother's daughter and instantly saw the social ramifications this would cause. Archie would be tainted by association. Even if he were clean and healthy, the whole of society would now assume the entire family to be diseased and unclean.

Oh, my poor love.

"Archie won't agree to see you?" she asked, sitting up straighter in her chair. She was calm now, a plan forming in her head.

Archie needed her, and if that meant she went to his home unchaperoned and had to push past the butler to get in, she would do it. She wasn't the daughter of a Grande Dame for nothing.

Oliver eyed her warily. "No, he won't see us. He's probably worried that we'll either spurn him, or he's trying to protect us. Knowing Archie, it's probably the latter."

Oliver sighed and took a sip of the brandy in front of him.

"Is he still at his bachelor lodgings?" Charlotte asked.

John looked worried now, his eyebrows rising high on his forehead. "Yes, why?"

"I just wanted to send him some flowers and my condolences," Charlotte told them both coolly, standing up to flick her skirts into perfect folds with practiced ease.

"I will see you soon, Oliver. Give my love to Sarah." Charlotte nodded her head and swept out of the room.

Chapter Eleven

She calmly walked up the stairs and called for her maid. Changing into her darkest day dress in a navy blue, she readied herself for her confrontation with Archie. If her brother was right, then Archie would not want her anywhere near him or his house. He would be afraid to taint her with the brush with which he was being painted. Well, she just didn't care.

If people saw her enter his house alone, then she was ruined. Somehow, she couldn't dredge up the necessary horror at this idea. She never meant to marry if she couldn't have Archie, so what would it matter if she became "unmarriageable?" Even so, for Archie's sake, she would go at five o'clock in the evening. No one would be around. Everyone would be at home preparing for dinner or an event in the evening.

Dismissing her maid, she made her way down the stairs.

"I need the carriage, Stevens," Charlotte told their butler.

"Of course, Lady Charlotte. May I call for Lizzie?" He snapped his fingers, and a footman appeared next to him.

"No. I already have her doing something for me. I only require the small carriage, Stevens. I need to get out of the house and feel like seeing the park. I will be back within the hour. I won't be stopping anywhere."

She marvelled at how well she could lie when she had to.

The butler seemed slightly disturbed by this announcement but showed no other signs of disapproval.

Charlotte was within the confines of the small, unmarked carriage within ten minutes, her heart beating like a drum against her ribcage and her belly fluttering with nerves of every kind.

~

ARCHIE WAS SITTING in his library when he heard a knock at the door.

"Lady Charlotte Dunford, my lord," Archie's butler announced, his usually solemn voice even lower today.

"No," Archie almost shouted at Hill.

She couldn't be here; she shouldn't. Even as he thought up the words to negate his butler's decree, she glided into the room and stood to face him.

"Please ask Lady Charlotte to come back another time, would you, Hill?" Archie asked his butler, ignoring the angry look Charlotte shot him from over the butler's shoulder. His palms began to sweat, and a lump lodged itself in his throat.

"Thank you, Hill." Charlotte dismissed the man instead, giving Archie's old butler a reproving stare as she hustled him out the door and shut it firmly behind him.

Whirling around in a flurry of skirts, Charlotte looked like an avenging angel as she faced him.

"How dare you try to send me away!" she hissed, her hands clenched at her sides.

"Did anyone see you arrive?" Archie ignored her angry words and stood up, his legs shaking beneath him. "Maybe we can sneak you out through the servant's entrance, and no one will see you leave."

Charlotte ignored his words and sat down in the chair opposite his desk. She arranged herself appropriately, her face a mask of politeness as she gestured to his chair.

"Please sit down, my lord."

Charlotte's tone left no room for discussion and Archie had to quell the instant reaction of wanting to drop instantly into the chair opposite her.

Archie had no idea what she wanted but sitting down and discussing it would not be in his best interest. Or hers. She had a way of making him forget everything but her, and in his current state of melancholy, that was far too tempting a proposition.

"Lady Charlotte, I don't think you should be here. Perhaps I could call on you at your parents' residence?" He was imploring, still continuing to stand whilst she sat.

He had no intention of calling on her ever again of course, but he had to say something to get her out of his house. His bachelor household, for goodness' sake!

When she continued to gaze at him, he tried again. "You know very well that you shouldn't have called on me here. Unchaperoned, too." She knew every rule inside out and back to front. This meeting broke so many rules he was beginning to feel dizzy.

"Oh, pish posh," Charlotte said, as she waved her hand. "Are you expecting many visitors?" She quirked an eyebrow in an ironic question.

Archie sat down in his chair with a thump, the leather soft beneath his hands.

"You know, then."

It was no worse than he feared, but he had somehow hoped she wouldn't find out.

"About your brother? Of course, I know. My deepest condolences to you, Archie. Didn't you receive my notes?" Her eyes softened, and Archie wanted to kiss her.

No one had bothered to express their sorrow at the loss of his brother since his manner of death had become known. They were too busy talking about the scandal of his death. Why he had died. Archie had known it would be useless to try and hide the truth, and it had been. People always found out.

"Thank you, Charlotte," Archie whispered. "But you really must go."

"Why? I need to speak to you."

"If you are found in here with me, alone..." Archie began, but Charlotte cut him short.

"I know. I'd have to marry you. But since you have decreed, several times, that you don't want to marry me, I suppose I'd just be ruined."

Archie's mouth dropped open. She had believed him when he said he didn't want to marry her? Oh, God, if only that were the truth. He would give up his fortune, his new title, anything he could give up to marry Charlotte. But how could he? When his name was now ruined as he had always known it would be?

"I would never let you be ruined, Charlotte," he murmured.

"Better that, than be married for life to a man who didn't want me," Charlotte said spitefully, her eyes flashing at him.

"Of course, I bloody want you!" Archie shouted, without thought.

Charlotte gasped, her eyes wide.

"You know I want you, Charlotte, I have proved that time and time again, but as I have told you before, I cannot marry you." Archie knew he was being cruel, but the truth poured out of him along with his anger.

Charlotte stood up and walked to the back of the room.

"Cannot," she repeated then turned around to face him, her eyes shimmering with tears. "Or will not?"

"Charlotte, must you make me say it? My name, my family's name is now completely ruined. I could never drag you into what we have become. We will be lucky if polite society even accepts us after our mourning period has finished." He raked a hand through his already disheveled hair.

"You've known about your brother's illness for a long time, haven't you?" she asked quietly.

Archie didn't know what he had expected next from Charlotte, but that wasn't it. He was emotionally wrung out and had no strength to lie to her.

"Yes, my father told me the week before my eighteenth birthday," he admitted, dropping into his study chair without waiting for her to sit also.

"And that is the reason you have never visited a brothel before?" Charlotte prodded gently again.

Archie laughed a little bitterly. Everything Charlotte believed about him was about to be dragged through the mud.

"Yes, it is. My father told me to keep myself alive and out of the whorehouses. You've always told me I was self-righteous, but the truth is I was just too scared. Isn't it funny? I'm not any better than all of those men you despise for having mistresses, because if it weren't for my father, I would be the same."

"Why didn't you find a lowborn virgin and make her your mistress? You could have bedded her as much as you wanted and you wouldn't have risked a disease."

Archie stared at the woman opposite him. He was shocked by the fact that Charlotte had come up with this obvious solution because it had been one he had considered many times before.

"I couldn't afford a mistress," Archie countered.

Charlotte made an unladylike snorting noise.

"It's true. You have to pay for rent on a house, clothes, servants, jewels..." He realised too late his mistake and shut his mouth quickly.

"So, you had considered it?" she asked, still quiet.

"Yes, I had," he admitted, "I told you I was just as bad as any other gentleman."

Charlotte moved around him and placed her hands on either side of his face. He refused to look at her, obviously mortified. She moved again so that she was sitting on his desk in front of him and caressed his cheeks with her bare hands.

"It isn't what we wish we could do that makes us who we are. It's what we do that's important."

She exerted pressure on his jaw and after a moment, Archie let her have her way.

Raising his head, he looked into her eyes. Charlotte studied his face for long moments before she pressed her lips to Archie's and slid her arms around his neck.

Archie allowed the kiss because it felt so damn good to have her in his arms again, but he had every intention of stepping away from her once she'd finished. It wasn't until her tongue stole into his mouth and her body pressed against his as she slipped into his lap that his resolve disappeared.

He ravaged her mouth with all the pent-up longing in his soul. He loved this woman. He loved her heart, he loved her sense of humour, he loved the fact that she had come to his home to offer support despite the scandal. He ran his hands down her back, enjoying her small frame, grabbed her fleshy bottom with both hands and pulled her fiercely closer to his aroused body.

She moaned loudly and renewed her attack on his mouth.

Archie broke away, gasping, and pulled them both into a standing position so that he could get away from her. He turned his back, trying to control his body, which was shuddering with desire. He could lay her down right here in the study, and no one would know.

"Archie, please," Charlotte begged, pressing her body against his back and sliding her hands around his waist. Her persistence was confusing.

"Charlotte, what do you want?" Archie turned around, letting his anger get the better of him. "Tell me, please. I will give you anything you want, but do not make me wish I was a different person. Please, you are killing me."

This admission almost tore his heart out, but Archie couldn't bear her being so understanding, touching him, kissing him. If he couldn't marry her, then he couldn't have her at all.

"I..." Charlotte stammered.

"Charlotte, tell me what you want from me!" Archie was seconds away from walking out the door and not coming back.

"You," she whispered. Archie's heart skipped a beat. "I...want you." She repeated, a little louder.

"You're going to have to be more specific," Archie growled. She couldn't mean what he thought she meant.

"I want you to make love to me. Here. Now."

Archie was so stunned he could have been pushed over by a feather.

"But...you know I can't marry you." It hurt to say the words, but Archie made himself say them.

Charlotte blinked and set her jaw. Never a good sign.

"I want you," she repeated, and she pushed his jacket off his shoulders and roughly pulled his shirt out of his breeches.

Archie didn't know if he was dreaming, but for the first time in his life, heaven was being offered to him at the time when he most desperately needed it.

"Charlotte, we shouldn't..." He made one last attempt at a denial and Charlotte ran her hand lightly over the front of his breeches. Her touch burned through the material, igniting him in a way that he had never experienced before.

With a muttered curse that included a deity, Archie launched himself at her and began kissing her passionately, forcing her lips open with his own and stroking her tongue with his. Over and over again. His mind raced with every small bit of sexual information he had ever heard. He knew that sex for the first time hurt most women and with his lack of experience, he wasn't sure he could be as gentle as she needed him to be.

He broke away from her again, groaning with the effort it took to do so.

"Charlotte, you know I've never done this before. What if I hurt you? What if I don't give you enough pleasure?" His tone was anxious as he slid his hands up and down her back.

There would be nothing worse than that for him.

$\sim$

CHARLOTTE SMILED AT *HER* ARCHIE. She felt as if he was hers, all the way down to her soul. She knew she'd made the right decision today, because she loved this man with all of her heart.

Which other gentleman would still be trying to talk her out of this? And whom else would worry that he couldn't please the woman he was with? From what her married friends other than Sarah had told her, their husbands walked in, lay on top of them and then left.

Instead of dreading what was to come, Charlotte wanted to rip all of Archie's clothes off and beg him to take her.

"We'll learn together," she whispered, against his full lips.

She stroked down his chest and circled his nipples with her fingertips. They grew hard and stood out against his shirt and his breath hissed out between his teeth. Charlotte could hear Sarah's voice in her head telling her that there was more to lovemaking than just the bedding. You could touch and kiss every part of a man's body. Charlotte blushed at the thought, but that didn't stop her from untying the laces on his shirt with shaking fingers.

Archie stood there like a statue, breathing hard and clenching his fists on both sides. It gave Charlotte an incredible feeling of feminine power that she could reduce this controlled, virtuous man to a bundle of fire and nerves. She finished unlacing his shirt and pushed the garment off his shoulders.

Charlotte sucked in a breath and ran her hands lovingly over the muscles clenched in Archie's chest and arms. He was wiry and lean. Charlotte knew that he liked to work with horses and ride, but she hadn't realised that would make his body so beautiful.

"Touch me, please..." Archie begged her.

"I am," Charlotte half-giggled.

"Down here," he whispered, indicating the burgeoning flesh between his legs. "I need you to bring me to my release like you did that night at Lady Moffat's. I'll never last otherwise."

Charlotte smiled eagerly and ran her hands down the lean muscles of his chest.

Archie's lips spread open, giving her a wolf-like smile, all dangerous teeth as he opened his breeches. He guided her hand inside, and she wrapped her fingers around his already hard and hot staff. He groaned as she squeezed him and reached for the ties on her bodice with trembling hands.

Charlotte was in awe. What a scary and amazing thing for a man to possess. The skin was the softest she had ever felt, and yet it was solid and hard beneath the silky-smooth skin. She tentatively stroked him, around the bulbous head and up and down the shaft.

Archie moaned and pushed the material of her bodice down to expose both of her breasts. They popped out with a bounce, and she gasped as he curved his fingers around the flesh of one.

Charlotte bit her lip as heat unfurled in her belly. "I thought I was just touching you."

Archie laughed hoarsely. "Touching you arouses me."

He bent his head and sucked one of her aching nipples into his mouth.

Charlotte groaned and arched her back so that he would suck harder. She let go of his hard flesh and threaded both of her hands into his hair, holding his head to her breast.

Archie sucked both of her breasts one after the other, pulling back so that he could turn her around and finish undoing her laces.

"You are driving me crazy, Charlotte; I will never be able to pleasure you properly."

He yanked at the laces and Charlotte smiled at his need for her. This was exactly what she wanted.

"You have already given me more pleasure than you know."

"No, back to my original plan."

Charlotte frowned, her mind fuddled; what was that plan? He grabbed her hand and guided it back to his manhood. He wrapped her fingers around the thick shaft and made her stroke him tightly. Charlotte adjusted her grip to something mimicking his.

"Stroke me like this until I come," he choked out as she began to move her hand in the way he had just taught her.

"Come?" she asked, not understanding what he meant.

She was starting to breathe heavily. There was something very arousing about the pleasurable noises he was making and the flush in his face.

"Find my release."

"And you'll be able to find it again with me, later?" Charlotte asked, frowning. It suddenly occurred to her that he was trying to stop their love-making early.

"Trust me."

So, Charlotte pulled at his flesh the way he had taught her and within moments he was moaning and thrusting into her hand. He swooped down for one long kiss and groaned low in his throat. Charlotte kissed him back, then his body jerked in her arms and a warm fluid covered her hands and the shirt he held to his front.

Charlotte pulled back and watched with fascination as Archie's face filled with blood, his eyes closed in what appeared to be pain. Then he sighed and opened his eyes. The last time this had happened, Charlotte had been too caught up in her own orgasm to watch Archie's face. This time, she did, and it was a revelation.

"Your turn," Archie growled, wiping her sticky hand with the shirt and impatiently tossing it across the room.

Charlotte squealed when he picked her up into his arms and walked a couple of steps to the chaise lounge against the wall. He lay her down gently then stood back to stare down at her.

"Charlotte, if you want to stop, now is the time to say so."

Love blossomed through her like the wild ivy that grew around their house, thriving despite the gardener's attempts to control it. Charlotte swallowed the fear down, her stomach clenching almost painfully. She pushed her chemise and drawers down her hips and onto the floor, shivering despite the warmth of the room.

Chapter Twelve

Laying back again, she didn't move to cover herself like every instinct was screaming at her to do. There were a dozen candles lit in the room, and he could see every inch of her. What if he thought her ugly?

Archie swallowed, his eyes running the length of her body. Charlotte flushed at his perusal, embarrassed by the slick heat gathering between her thighs. She needed this man so much.

She held out her arms and Archie knelt down next to her and kissed her with his tender, soft lips. First, on the forehead and then on the eyelids, his hot breath moving over her skin. He made his way slowly down her trembling body, licking her with his wet, smooth tongue, her collarbones, her ribs, her navel.

Charlotte had never imagined that being kissed and fondled like this would feel so amazing. Everything he did made her want to cry out in pleasure and every once in a while, a lick of fire would find its way to that place between her thighs, and she would push her legs together to try and hide the evidence. She didn't know what to do with her hands, so she just pushed them down into the soft material of the chaise.

Archie ran his lips down to the curls at the apex of her thighs and flicked his tongue out to taste her there. Charlotte sat up and went to push Archie away. She couldn't believe he was about to kiss her there. He couldn't—anything else, but not there.

"Archie, you shouldn't..." she began and stopped.

He looked up and gave her one of those smouldering, "I want you" looks that she was starting to love.

"Trust me," he repeated, for the second time that night.

He moved to the end of the chaise so that he was kneeling directly between her legs and pulled her gently closer to the edge so that her legs hung over the side.

Charlotte covered her face in mortification. He was looking at her in a place Charlotte, herself, had never even seen.

"You are so beautiful, my Charlotte," he whispered, stroking the inside of her thighs and exploring her with his fingers.

She shuddered in response to his words, as well as his touches.

"You are mine, aren't you, Charlotte?" Archie asked as he slid his middle finger deep inside her already wet body.

"Yes," she moaned, mindless with need as she arched her back high.

Archie moved his finger inside her in a prelude to what was still to come. In and out, in and out, adding a second finger, stretching her body.

"Mine, tonight," he insisted.

Charlotte looked down at his fingers moving inside her, his head lowering to her flesh again.

It was time he knew the truth. "Not just tonight. Always."

Archie's eyes widened for a moment, and his fingers faltered in their movement. Then he fastened his mouth to her core, sucking and licking her over and over. And this time she didn't push him away. She couldn't. The heat built and consumed her, the flames licking her body as Archie's tongue drove her higher and higher, until she felt her orgasm roar down on her.

"Yes, Archie, yes!" she screamed as her belly tightened and the coiled spring released, sending shockwaves of pleasure along every nerve. She could feel Archie's fingers still moving as he pushed her over the hill and beyond.

Charlotte shuddered as Archie moaned against her flesh and gave her one more lick.

"Ahhh…" She cried out as he removed his fingers and got to his feet.

Her orgasm had been so powerful that tiny tingles of pleasure were still running along her limbs. She heard Archie divest himself of the remainder of his clothes, but couldn't bring herself to open her eyes.

"Charlotte, come join me." Archie's words broke through her haze as he pulled at her hand.

She forced her eyes open to see Archie lying on his side on the floor. There, between his legs was a huge pole, pointing toward her. Or so it seemed. He was enormous.

Oh, damn!

Having come this far, Charlotte decided that she would have to trust him not to kill her. She slid awkwardly off the lounge, landing beside him with a thump. Archie rolled instantly on top of her, and Charlotte clamped her legs together. The feel of his body completely naked against hers felt wonderful, but the fear of what he was about to do drove all other thoughts out of her head.

Archie smiled, but his expression was strained. Charlotte began to panic.

"Archie, I don't know if this is going to work. You're too big to fit inside me. I'm sure you'll kill me…"

"It'll be all right, Charlotte," he reassured her, with another tight smile.

"How do you know? You've never done this before. You could be much larger than most men."

"Just trust me," he whispered for the third time that night, dropping a kiss onto her nose. "You know, it could hurt you to start with."

Charlotte nodded. She had heard different accounts of the pain accompanied with penetration. She only hoped she experienced the lighter version of it.

"Kiss me again," she urged him, desperate to forget her worries and get back to the pleasure-drugged haze she had been in moments before.

Archie kissed her as though he wanted to devour her and she returned the kiss with equal fervour. He touched her breasts and belly, stroking the place between her legs until she thought she would go crazy with need once again.

Charlotte lifted her hips in silent invitation, and Archie took it.

Lifting himself up on his forearms Archie moved until the head of his staff was nudging her wet entrance. She gasped at the feel of it, and he caught her lips in another kiss and pressed forward.

Charlotte felt an overwhelming urge to push him off as he slid part of the way inside. This was just plain uncomfortable. He was fitting, some-how, inside of her, but it felt like the pressure would kill her. It was not painful exactly, but he was stretching tissues that had never stretched before, and the sensation was not pleasant.

"You know I have to..." Archie said, stilling within her.

"Just do it!" she cried, hoping this part would pass quickly.

Archie thrust hard, burying himself completely inside her. The sharp pain flashed, almost tearing Charlotte in two, or so she feared. Then just as quickly, it was gone. She lay still, listening to Archie tell her how beautiful she was, and feeling disappointed that her mother was right. This part she wished would be over as quickly as possible. She felt uncomfortable with her legs on either side of him, pushed apart, so she raised her knees and wrapped her legs around his hips, relieving some of the stiffness within her.

Charlotte bit back a moan as Archie arched his back and a delicious feeling sparked inside her. Different from the pleasure he had given her with his mouth. Deeper, more intense. Charlotte pushed up against him, and he pulled back and thrust into her again with more power. She gasped and wriggled. That was better.

He began moving with a rhythm, slowly at first, sliding in and out of her. It was quite odd really. Then he began to move faster, pounding into her harder and harder, and somehow she knew to squeeze her inner muscles, pushing them closer to their goal.

He pulled back onto his knees and brought her hips with him. This seemed to allow him to thrust easier, and Charlotte could look at his face better, which she loved. She could tell her own face was flushed and her breasts bounced in time with his thrusts which. all-in-all, was quite vulgar.

His eyes took all of this in while she watched his flat belly ripple and his eyes get ever darker with his arousal.

"Come with me, Charlotte. Now, please."

Charlotte saw the man she loved towering over her, begging with words and with his body for her to go with him, wherever he was going. It was happening again. Her body was tightening, the pleasure building to that crescendo.

With his final lunge and roar, Archie's flesh spasmed within her, and the warm pulse of his seed pushed her over that invisible edge, and she cried out, shuddering in his arms as he collapsed on top of her.

～

ARCHIE COULDN'T BELIEVE it had been so good. He had always known that once he felt a woman's body around him, he would never be able to go back. No, not just any woman. *Charlotte's* body. It was one of the reasons he had abstained for so long.

He knew what he had been missing now. He slowly disengaged and lay beside her, both of them still panting from their exertions. He had felt her convulse around him just as his world exploded and that had given him a satisfaction almost equal to the one she had earlier provided for him.

"Are you all right?" he asked, propping up his head on one hand.

Charlotte smiled one of her brilliant smiles as she turned her head to look at him.

"That was incredible," she answered. Then she reached for her chemise and pulled it over her head and down her body, covering her lush curves.

"Oh. I'm sorry. I think I've ruined your jacket."

Looking down to the spot Charlotte indicated, he saw the blood. Archie swallowed hard.

"I'm the one who should be sorry, Charlotte. I just took something from you which I had no right to take."

Regret and guilt were coming in hard, and Archie was drowning in it. His chest was tight, and he couldn't breathe properly.

"I wanted to give myself to you. I don't regret it," she said, and thrust her chin up, which forced him to look at her. "Do you?"

"Do I regret the most beautiful experience of my life? I can't," he answered honestly, some of the nerves settling in his belly on seeing her happiness.

"Good," she said, curling into his side.

Archie held her, wishing they were elsewhere. Alone in his bed, married, and somewhere that no one knew who his family were or what he was. He may have been the heir to the Marquess of Hunting, but it was now a title ruined with scandal.

"Charlotte, we have to get you home before anyone realises where you've been." Or what you've done, Archie finished in his head.

Charlotte stood up on wobbly legs and began dressing again.

"I don't care if people know I've been here. I'm not ashamed of loving you," Charlotte announced to the quiet room with all the fire she had always possessed.

Archie sighed. He should have expected this, and God, he loved her for her passion.

"Charlotte, I won't have your name ruined by your association with me."

"I'm already ruined, Archie. I've never wanted anyone but you, so what does it matter if the world knows it?"

"What? Do you think I'll allow people to call you a whore?" Archie jumped to his feet with a start, horrified that she would suggest such a thing. He pulled his breeches on, his sticky body uncomfortable and aching.

Charlotte faced him squarely, hands on her abundant hips.

"I didn't mean that," she shouted back. "And I wouldn't be a whore if you married me."

Archie took a step back from the powerful emotions brimming from every pore of his lover's body. He closed his eyes and reached deep inside himself for the mask he wore whilst in society.

"I'm sorry if you assumed I'd marry you, if you gave yourself to me."

Charlotte gasped and wrapped her arms around her body. Her eyes showed so much hurt and pain that Archie immediately wished the words back. Ruthlessly, he squashed the impulse to comfort her and instead started pulling on the rest of his soiled clothing, not caring that he could smell himself, and her, on his jacket.

Now that his brain wasn't fogged with the haze of passion, the voice of reason was reasserting itself. He had to keep her away from him. One more moment of intimacy and he would be down on bended knee begging for her hand in marriage and damn the scandal. But he could never do that to her, never.

"Charlotte, I know that one day you will find a man to marry who deserves you, but it's not me."

Charlotte just stared at him, then asked the one question he never thought she would ask.

"You don't love me?"

Archie jerked back as though she had struck him. Unable to lie to her face, he turned his back on her, so he faced the fireplace.

There was only one answer he could give. "No, I don't."

"Look at me when you break my heart, at least."

Archie closed his eyes in agony, yet turned at her request, hopeful his heart was now firmly locked away.

"I'm sorry if I have hurt you, Charlotte, but it is for your own good. Listen to me. Find someone to marry whose name isn't going to be scorned for the next century."

"So, you don't love me?" she repeated the question, apparently aware of the fact that he was avoiding lying to her face.

Archie steeled himself to lie again, but he wasn't sure if he had the strength. This was truly going to kill all and any feeling Charlotte had for him. He opened his mouth but was saved by a knock at the door.

"My lord, the solicitor is here to see you," his butler announced through the door.

"Thank you, Hill," Archie choked out, "Lady Charlotte requires her cloak, and I will need a few moments before attending to the solicitor. Put him in the morning room."

Archie heard the butler leave and sent a prayer of thanks for discreet and loyal servants.

"Go home, Charlotte. Thank you for your...condolences and support, but I think you must go."

Charlotte made an incoherent noise in her throat, and Archie turned away to open the door for the butler. He could barely breathe. Keeping a calm façade was taking every ounce of strength he had.

Archie was stunned by the pain he was in. Charlotte was acting like she was in love with him, and what had she said?

At least look at me when you break my heart. Oh God, she couldn't love him, she just couldn't. That would be too cruel.

"Lady Charlotte's cloak, my lord." Hill opened the door, bowed and handed Archie Charlotte's cloak. He took one look at Archie's ruffled and soiled appearance and nodded once, his face inscrutable.

"If you will permit me, sir, I will walk Lady Charlotte out, and you can see your valet in your room, before the solicitor."

The quiet suggestion brought home to Archie just what he must look like. Clothes that had clearly been removed and then hastily re-donned and the scent of male completion lingering in the air. Sick disgust twisted his gut.

He nodded once to Hill and held open the door for his heart to leave him once and for all.

Tears spilled down Charlotte's reddened cheeks, and she didn't even bother to wipe them away. She simply took her cloak, wrapped it around herself and followed Hill from the room.

Chapter Thirteen

Archie had thought the pain of losing his brother and his place in society would be hard, and for ten years, he had done everything in his power to prepare for the worst. He had realised very soon after Charlotte left his study that nothing he had ever experienced before came close to how he felt now.

It had been a month since he had made love to his one and only love, and he felt like she had walked away with his soul when she had left his home. He had nothing left inside of him. His heart beat so slowly that it was painful feeling its rhythm inside his chest every waking minute.

In full mourning and also in full disgrace, Archie did not venture out of doors. He did not go for rides, he did not go to his club, and he did not see his friends. He had always thought that when the time came, he would be content with his estate business. Meeting with the land manager, his broker, his banker, and the attorney. He would read his books at night, and he would be content. How wrong could one man be?

He missed his old life so much it choked him. He woke in the middle of the night struggling to breathe, sweat running off him. He had taken to bathing twice a day just to pass the time.

He missed the time with his horses. He missed wasting time talking to Oliver or pretending to drink with Rupert.

Archie had always assumed that once he became his father's heir and the worst was known, he could turn into an ordinary gentleman. He could drink all night, tup whores and gamble away his money. Instead of feeling free and rebellious, he was sad and empty. He would give anything to have his stoic, boring life back. To be able to marry the one woman he loved and by all impossible accounts, probably loved him too.

That was the real rub. The look on Charlotte's face when he had told her he still wouldn't marry her, even after they had shared the most amazing experience of his life. It had almost slain him. He would have preferred a public lashing over watching her face crumble, and her heart break at his feet. She had been so courageous, so brave, and he had been a coward.

How could he have turned his back on her when she knew the worst about his family, and yet she still wanted to marry him; be with him? He had spent the last ten years convincing himself that no woman would ever forgive him for tying her to a family with his reputation, and yet she had willingly come to him *after* she had found out. She had given herself to a man worth nothing in the eyes of so much of the *ton*.

Could she not care? Could she be willing to marry him—even love him? Despite everything?

It had taken a whole month of wallowing in his stupidity and pouring all of his efforts into rebuilding his father's neglected estate for him to realise that his friends hadn't turned their backs on him either, as he had expected. He had turned his back on them.

It was unbelievable, really. He had spent ten years fearing the worst, and now he was doing his best to make it come true.

All three of the original "spares" had been by numerous times, together and separately, trying to visit him and he had turned them all away. At the time, he had told himself that he was protecting them, but wasn't he just protecting himself? From the hurt he assumed they were about to bestow by cutting him off? Or could he just not face their condolences and pity?

That was more likely, he acknowledged. He didn't want men who had once respected his opinion and his self-control, pitying him. Or worse, realising that he had been faking his perfection under a tremendous amount of fear for most of his adult life.

Archie saw his life mapped out ahead of him. Decades of lonely days and even more desolate nights. He would be totally alone until he could convince some down-on-her-luck spinster to marry him, to continue the line. Knowing he could never love her the way he loved Charlotte.

Archie stood up suddenly and had to sit down again just as quickly. When was the last time he had eaten? He had no idea.

All at once he knew what he had to do. He had to get a special licence to marry Charlotte as soon as possible. They had an uncle on his mother's side who was a bishop. He would grant Archie what he needed. They were still in full mourning so a marriage would be looked down upon, regardless of his current situation. However, Archie knew that he would need more than just words to convince Charlotte that he desperately wanted to marry her. After all he'd put her through, he'd be lucky if she would have him now.

Feeling a spark inside of him stir to life, a purpose that he hadn't felt in a very long time, he ran to his rooms to change. He would organise a special licence today and call upon her tomorrow. He had a purpose now, and nothing and no one was going to stand in his way.

CHARLOTTE HAD SPENT the last month wishing she were dead and the last two days wishing she were buried so that no one could ever find her. How could she have been so stupid? Not only had she given Archie the most prized possession of any gently bred lady, but she had also given him her heart, and now she was lost without it.

Her energy was running out. She couldn't continue to pretend that everything was fine. She had tried to keep her routine so no one would know something was wrong. She went shopping with her maid for more dresses, gloves, and shoes that she had no intention of wearing. Attended afternoon teas with her mother, listening to people gossip about who was marrying whom, and whether anyone had seen Archie. If she had to speak to one more insipid lady, she would scream.

To make matters worse, she had been vomiting throughout the day. The smell of any meat turned her stomach. She could hardly get out of bed in the morning and was starting to worry that it was something more than a broken heart causing these things.

Charlotte sat in the afternoon sitting room, embroidering, when she heard the welcome sound of her friend's voice.

"The Duchess of Lincoln," their butler announced.

Sarah breezed through the door looking beautiful, her sky-blue dress perfectly offsetting her golden hair and cornflower blue eyes. Charlotte hadn't seen Sarah in three months, as her husband had whisked her off to their country estate after her bed rest had been completed.

"Sarah." Charlotte lay her embroidery aside and stood up to curtsey. She greeted her friend with the biggest smile she had conjured up in over a month.

"Charlotte." Sarah greeted her with a kiss on both cheeks, her warmth a balm to Charlotte's frayed nerves.

"What's happened?" Sarah asked with a worried tone, then drew Charlotte over onto the chaise.

Hot tears welled up in Charlotte's eyes, and she opened her mouth to spill something of her pain. The door swung open again, and her brother and Sarah's husband joined them.

"Are you crying again?" John asked rudely, his face set in a grimace.

"John Dunford!" Sarah scolded, as Charlotte's eyes filled to the point of overflowing.

John groaned and pointed at Charlotte. "I'm sorry, Sarah. But something is seriously wrong with her, and she won't talk to anyone."

"John, please..." Charlotte begged. She had thought she hid her melancholy well from her family.

"Tea and custard, your favorite, Lady Charlotte." A maid came in bearing a huge tray of saucers and desserts.

The smell of warm milky custard wafted up to Charlotte's nose, and before she could contain it, vomit erupted up her throat. She ran to the corner and deposited the tiny amount of food in her stomach into a potted plant there.

John groaned. "This is what I mean. She has been moping around the house for weeks and now she's sick all the time."

Charlotte thanked Oliver for his offered handkerchief and wiped her mouth. Despite the fact that she should have excused herself and gone upstairs, she moved slowly back over to Sarah's side while the maid removed the pot plant.

Charlotte sat down with a weary sigh, picked up a cup of tea Sarah had poured and sipped slowly. The taste of stomach acid lingered in her mouth, and she was pleased when the maid returned to collect the custard and the tray from the room.

Sarah's eyes seemed to be cataloguing all of her symptoms and with a little gasp, she hissed into Charlotte's ear.

"Charlotte, you're not!"

Charlotte paled at the horrified look Sarah was giving her, her stomach wrenching painfully. She was going to lose all of her friends and family when everyone ealized what she had done.

"She's not, what?" John asked, his tone one of bewilderment.

"I thought it was just a stomach complaint, but putting it all together, it makes sense," Charlotte admitted to her friend, collapsing further into her seat.

She hadn't had her monthly flux, and she was so tired and sick all the time it could only mean one thing.

Instead of shying away from her as Charlotte had expected, Sarah moved closer and was holding Charlotte within her arms in seconds. Heat surrounded her, and Charlotte gave in and sobbed against her friend.

"What are you going to do?" Sarah whispered into Charlotte's ear, rocking her as though she were an infant.

"I believe I'll retire to our country estate this year and stay for a while," Charlotte said calmly, pushing herself up to a seated position again.

She finally accepted that her night with Archie had created consequences beyond what they had both imagined.

The light of comprehension was dawning in Oliver's eyes, but John was still at a loss regarding what was going on.

"The Earl of Totherham," their butler announced. This was Archie's new title.

Charlotte put her head on Sarah's shoulder and clung to her hand. This day could not get any worse. She had wanted Archie to come to her for over a month, and today was the day he chose?

Sarah gave her a suspicious look and held her harder. Charlotte let another tear escape and allowed her friend, who was once a vicar's daughter, to give her the comfort she so desperately needed.

ARCHIE'S HEART was thumping so loudly he was surprised he could hear the butler as he was announced over the roaring in his ears. He was shocked to find such a large group assembled in the parlour as he entered, but he bowed politely.

He moved toward Charlotte. He had spent an hour with his valet, preparing for this moment, and he didn't want to pretend indifference. He was shaved and oiled, pressed and perfectly dressed.

"Charlotte, may I have a private word?" he asked, skipping the formalities. His throat was raw and sore from too much drinking and the silent screaming of the past month.

Charlotte shook her head in answer, and a silvery tear slipped down her cheek. Archie's heart clenched hard in his chest. *Why was she crying?*

"Tell me what the hell is going on!" John fairly yelled, and Archie took a step back, shocked. What had he walked into?

"My apologies, John. I didn't realise I interrupted something."
John waved his hand dismissively.

"You didn't, Archie. All I know is that Charlotte has been ill for weeks and now she's talking about retiring to the country until next season. Why would you do that, Charlotte? You know we don't go out there." John addressed his sister with a stern tone of voice. He was apparently baffled, but there was a wealth of meaning in his words that Charlotte was obviously ignoring.

It hit Archie like a lead weight. He took in her face, the faint smell of vomit in the room and his actions of a month ago.

"You're pregnant," he breathed, unable to believe it and yet speaking the words as soon as they entered his mind.

"She's what?" John and Oliver both yelled.

"Impossible, tell them it's impossible," John urged Charlotte, taking a step closer to his weeping sister.

Charlotte closed her eyes and seemed to sway against Sarah, the two women locking together like limpets to rock.

Opening her eyes, she took a deep breath and Archie held his breath, waiting for the words that would determine his future.

"It's true."

Archie gasped, and John wheeled back and collapsed into a chair.

"Who, for God's sake?"

Archie opened his mouth to interrupt, but Charlotte was refusing to look at him. She sat up straighter, moving away from Sarah to address the room.

"The father has refused to marry me so I will be having the baby in the country and will stay there. I have no wish to burden my family with the stain that this will cause, but I will not give it up either."

Guilt hit Archie hard, with burning hot intensity. Did she believe such a thing?

"He won't marry you? What sort of bounder seduced you?" Oliver cried.

"Was it rape?" Sarah asked from next to Charlotte, the only one brave enough to ask the question.

Oh, God, no!

"No," Charlotte cried, sitting back down next to Sarah and squeezing her hands.

"Well, we'll find someone else to marry you. You are not giving birth to a bastard, Charlotte. Maybe someone who needs an heir but hasn't any children..." John was mumbling now, thinking about possibilities and options for his beloved sister.

Archie hadn't moved since Charlotte had announced that she was, indeed, with child. He felt as though he had been hit with a mallet, unmoving and pained. He had finally decided that enough was enough, he would beg Charlotte to forgive him and to marry him, and now she had to. He should have felt relieved, but he didn't. He wanted her to choose him because he loved her, not because there was a child.

He then heard the words John was raving, and his control snapped.

"Stop!" he roared, pushing his hands out to the room as though he could halt the insanity around him.

Archie staggered over to Charlotte and went down on his knees in front of her. He reached for her hands and clasped both of hers in his. She looked up at him with tear-stained eyes, and his heart did a little misstep.

"Marry me," he urged, squeezing her hands for emphasis.

"No." Charlotte shook her head and bit her lip, two more tears slipping down her pale cheeks.

"Yes," he insisted, holding onto her hands when she tried to pull them away.

Archie heard a growl behind him, knowing it was John and shivering at the prospect. He also knew he had only seconds left before a fist would land somewhere on his body.

"I love you. I have loved you since you were sixteen-years old and debuted in the most horrible white dress I have ever seen. Marry me, please."

Archie had so much more to say, but hands were pulling at him, and he had to let go of Charlotte's hands so that he could confront his friend.

John and Oliver pulled him to his feet and spun him around.

"Why are you offering to marry her, Archie?" John asked, his face a mixture of fear, anger, and trepidation.

"Because I love her, I have always loved her. I just didn't want to offer for her when my family's name was so badly ruined. But now, I have no choice. I must."

"You're proposing to marry her, despite the baby? Or because of the baby?" John asked, his face showing signs of hope and fear, warring.

Archie took a deep breath and told the truth, knowing full well what was going to happen, and he deserved it.

"Both...it's my baby," he announced quietly. The stillness in the room meant the words echoed as though he had shouted.

Chapter Fourteen

John's fist ploughed directly into his jaw, causing Archie to spin backwards, pain splintering across his face and through his brain.

John was on him in a second, pummeling his stomach until he was hauled away by Rupert and Oliver.

"You bastard," John hissed, breathing like he'd finished ten rounds in a boxing ring.

Archie fell into a chair, breathless, his lip bleeding and beginning to swell already. He coughed, his ribs screaming at him.

Charlotte pulled the cord for the butler and ran to him, throwing herself into his lap and covering his face in kisses and touches.

"Oh, my love, are you hurt? Show me, show me." She ran her hands, soothing but frantic, all over him.

Archie winced as his bruised body screamed out in pain but gathered her close despite it. He wanted to press his head to her breasts and let her comfort him, but he heard another low growl and knew he needed to have it out with John first.

"Darling, would you and Sarah go upstairs for a little while? I need to talk to your brother." Archie choked out the words as soothingly as he could, considering he had been punched in the stomach only a moment before, and his breath was still missing.

"But..." Charlotte half-protested, her gaze flicking between Archie and her angry brother.

"It will be all right," he reassured her, and despite their audience, he pressed a quick kiss to her lips.

"Charlotte, please." He stood up slowly and pushed her gently towards Sarah.

For the first time, Archie looked at Charlotte. She did look pale and extremely tired, and yet she'd never looked more beautiful to him. A child, *their* child. He could barely believe it.

"You'll be married next week," John declared from where he was forcibly held down.

Charlotte stamped her foot. "John, you cannot tell us what to do!"

Archie pulled out the piece of paper he had in his breast pocket.

"I organised a special licence yesterday," he told Charlotte, with eyes only for her.

"Even before you knew?" She trailed off, her hand sliding down to cover her belly, her womb, containing his child.

He followed the path of her hand and then looked back up to her face.

"Yes. I love you," he repeated, this time quietly, only for her benefit.

Charlotte's smile was brilliant, warming him from the inside out. She then left the room with Sarah. As he had requested.

One down, one to go.

"You better have a good explanation for this, Tother."

Archie flinched at John's use of his new title. It was not a good start to the conversation, but Archie reined in his wild emotions and sat in the chair opposite John. Rupert and Oliver had a firm grip on John's shoulders and Archie trusted them not to let their friend have his head, and pound Archie into the dust. Although technically he deserved it, he didn't want to get married looking like a bloody mess.

"The only explanation, John, is that I lost my mind."

John growled. "If I hear one insult about my sister, I am going to wring your neck."

"No, John, you misunderstand me," Archie quickly corrected, holding up his hands in a peaceful entreaty. "I love your sister, I always have. But there is no excuse for the fact that I made love to her before we were married. None."

John's shoulders sagged when Archie openly admitted he was wrong.

"Then why? For God's sake, Archie! Why?"

"I have known about my brother's illness since the week before I turned eighteen." Archie had decided it was best to explain everything.

They all went silent, looking at each other with surprised expressions, but it was Rupert who put it all together.

"So that's why you wouldn't come to the brothel, then or ever," Rupert said.

"Yes. My father informed me that I would be his heir and that I was to keep myself out of the whorehouses." Archie kept his chin high but had to break his composure to wipe the blood off his chin as it began to drip toward his clothes.

"So where does Charlotte come into this?" John growled again, his eyes narrowed, his jaw clenched.

Archie counted himself lucky that they were sitting in a reception room and not John's study where his dueling pistols were kept.

"I would have courted Charlotte and proposed years ago, but I was always terrified of what would happen when everyone found out how my brother died. I feared that even if I kept my reputation spotless, people would still paint me with the same brush," Archie confessed, feeling the load that he had carried on his shoulders for so long lift from him. It felt good to confess his fears and secrets. He had been so stupid to keep it to himself for so long.

"So? What happened?" Rupert asked. Releasing his hand from John's shoulder, he kept one eye on John and the other eye on Archie.

"A few months ago, Charlotte and I started to talk and get to know each other better. I had spent so many years keeping her at arm's length that I just couldn't do it anymore."

"I always did wonder why you two had such an intense dislike for each other," Oliver murmured.

"Self-preservation, I'm afraid. Well, at least on my behalf," Archie told them quietly with a wry smile.

He wasn't sure if Charlotte had wanted him for all the years he had desired her, but he would find out soon enough.

"So...?" John prompted, sitting forward in his chair and apparently wanting more specific information.

Archie took a breath and guarded himself for the next attack.

"So, almost five weeks ago Charlotte visited me at my house to express her condolences..."

"By herself?" John asked, his face incredulous.

Archie nodded, trying not to put any of the blame on Charlotte, but not wanting John to think he set out to seduce her either.

"And I was so totally out of my mind. I just couldn't fight her any longer."

"So, you ruined her," John said flatly, obviously still angry but looking quite defeated at the same time.

A wry smile touched Archie's lips.

"We ruined each other, I'm afraid. I could never have anyone else but her."

Archie looked around the room, and only Oliver smiled at that. He was the only one who knew what it felt like to make love, rather than the rutting variation in which his friends indulged.

"Then why did she say the father of her baby wouldn't marry her?" John asked now, that hard glitter reappearing in his eye.

Archie swallowed down his guilt and gave them the honest truth.

"Because, initially I told her I couldn't."

"You what?" John yelled, surging to his feet. Rupert and Oliver stayed close but didn't try to restrain him.

Archie dragged himself to his feet, not sure if he even had the strength to raise his arms if it came to a real fight. But John didn't seem interested in fighting, physically. He started pacing like a restless animal.

"You ruined her and then refused to marry her! What sort of gentleman are you?" John cried, obviously frustrated beyond bearing.

"John, I know I was wrong, so very wrong. But I preferred Charlotte to be able to marry someone with a good name. Someone who would be accepted by society, rather than be mine. How could I draw Charlotte into that scandal?" Archie knew that the argument had merit, but also knew that ruining her and not marrying her was an even greater offence.

John growled again, low in his throat.

"And yet, you did."

Archie only nodded. If he had known Charlotte was pregnant, he would have come to his senses weeks ago. That result had never even occurred to him, which showed how off his game he was.

"My father is expected home in an hour. You can have your meeting with him to discuss the settlement, and then you can be married."

Archie just nodded, his arms and legs feeling weaker by the second.

"Archie, are you all right?" John asked, concerned now.

His head was spinning. The blackness came in to claim him and after weeks of not eating or sleeping, he gave into it.

HE CAME BACK to consciousness with his head in Charlotte's lap and her refusing to let him go.

"If what you say is true and we will be married, possibly even tomorrow, then I have every right to hold him until he awakens. He's unconscious, for heaven's sake!" She sat on the floor with him, stroking his hair soothingly. Archie was loathe to open his eyes in case she stopped.

Charlotte must have felt his breathing change because she was soon asking, "Archie, are you awake? Open your eyes, my love."

He reluctantly blinked open his eyes and found himself still in the sitting room. He was surrounded by Charlotte, John, Oliver, Sarah, Rupert and four or five servants.

"I'm all right," he said, attempting to sit up. His head spun so fast that he lay back down again with a moan.

Charlotte wrapped her arms around him protectively and held him tight. The heat of her made him instantly relax, his eyes closing on a sigh.

"Archie, rest, please."

Someone growled at this.

Archie summoned the energy to open his eyes again. He asked, "May my fiancée and I have a few moments alone, please?"

He knew he must look ridiculous lying on the Aubusson rug with his head in Charlotte's lap, but he stayed where he was, nonetheless.

"I think you've had enough moments alone, don't you?" John asked, his tone dripping with sarcasm.

"John!" This admonition came from Sarah, and it was Oliver who finally stepped in to help them.

"I think they can have a moment alone to discuss their wedding."

He gathered the assembly like the duke he now was and swept out of the room.

"Are you sure you are fine?" Charlotte asked, her voice trembling.

Archie sat up slowly, swallowing the bile that rose in his throat and turned around to face her, his palms sweating.

"Me? How are you?" he asked, sliding his hand to her still flat stomach, feeling the softness there.

A strange happiness settled over him, something that had been missing from his life for a very long time.

Charlotte blushed crimson at his touch but did not move away. Instead, she moved into his touch, warming his heart all the more.

Chapter Fifteen

Charlotte had never known real terror until she had heard John calling for help because Archie was ill. She had spent half an hour pacing her room, answering all of Sarah's questions and reassuring her friend that it wasn't her fault. The poor woman had got it into her mind that it was what she had advised that day in her sitting room that had led Charlotte to sleep with Archie.

Charlotte was happily relating how wonderful it had been when she had heard the yell. Not mindful of anything but getting to Archie as quickly as she could, she flew down the stairs and had dropped to her knees before him. Seeing him lying there, so still and pale, had made her feel like her insides had been scooped out. She'd thought he had broken her heart irretrievably, but she had been wrong. It seemed that the silly thing still beat only for him.

"I'm a little apprehensive about the immediate future, but otherwise, I feel fine," she told him honestly.

"You'll be all right. *We'll* be all right, Charlotte. You and the baby are going to be healthy and well. We'll travel to my father's estate for our honeymoon, and just decide not to come back until next season."

Charlotte's smile faltered. She wasn't worried about the scandal or the baby. She was worried that Archie was only marrying her because she had trapped him. It was the oldest trick in the book on how to land a good husband, and she hated herself for it. She was sure he despised her for it, too.

Charlotte dropped her head and refused to look at him.

"What's wrong?" Archie asked, pulling them both up and onto the chaise lounge, placing her on his lap and wrapping his arms around her.

"Everything," she cried, letting her tears fall.

Archie crooned and stroked her hair, telling her that everything was going to be all right.

John chose that moment to stick his head in and just as quickly stuck it back out again.

"Charlotte, I'm sorry you're going to have to marry me. If I could have saved you from this pain, I would have."

Charlotte laughed, the sound somewhere between a sob and a gulp. Pulling her head up so that she could look at him, she put all her strength into her glare. "I want to marry you. I've always wanted to marry you."

Archie pulled out his handkerchief and blotted her face, the move so endearing as to make her sob again. He truly was a gentleman.

"Then why are you crying?" he asked gently.

"Because you don't want to marry me." She whispered the feared words, biting her lip as the tears began to fall down her face again in unending hot waves.

Archie cradled her face in both of his hands and forced her gaze up to his.

"Charlotte, listen to me and listen carefully. The only, and I mean the only, reason I have not asked you to marry me before now, was that I couldn't bear the idea of you being cut directly or embarrassed by my family's reputation being ruined. I couldn't bring you into that."

"So that stopped you from asking me? For how long?" she whispered, fear and hope flaring alive in her heart.

His eyes told her that he was speaking the truth, and it would be in Archie's character to protect her in such a way.

"Years. Almost since the moment I met you again at your coming out. I fell in love with your wit and your fire, your passion for life and your wicked sense of humour. You are also the most beautiful woman I have ever seen in my life."

Charlotte blushed at his words and wrapped her arms around his neck.

"So, you do love me," she whispered again, tendrils of hope heating a path of light through her heart and body.

"I do," he repeated and pressed his soft lips to hers.

It had been forever since they had kissed, or that was how it felt to Charlotte. Her lips clung to his, and she moaned loudly when he encouraged her lips to open. He swept his tongue into her mouth.

A loud noise, a throat being cleared, brought them both back to reality.

A smiling Oliver and a red-faced John stood in the doorway.

Charlotte blushed again and stood up. Archie followed more slowly. Oliver turned away with a smile, and John started turning purple.

"I think it's time for you to wait in the library," John told Archie with a look that brooked no argument.

Archie turned to Charlotte and bowed over her outstretched hand.

"Get some rest, my dear." He gave her a wink that was at odds with his formal words and left the room.

Charlotte straightened from her curtsey to see John staring at her.

His analytical gaze roamed over her face and he sighed loudly.

"You're looking better already."

～

IT TOOK VERY little time to work out Charlotte's wedding settlement. Once her father had been informed about Charlotte's condition, it was pretty much settled. He called Archie a few choice names, which Archie agreed with, and then they went on to discuss the financials.

Archie was pleased to realise he could easily afford the pin money her father was currently giving her, and he even signed a document to make sure she kept the property she owned in her name. He had no wish to take anything away from her. From what she had originally said about her not wanting to marry because of her future husband's power over her, he was determined to give her as much freedom as possible.

Her dowry was also very generous. It had been increased from ten to fifteen thousand pounds as she had remained unmarried, and although Archie would have liked to refuse it outright, he was soon told that it was not negotiable. He found it amusing that they thought he might back out of the wedding if he didn't get everything to which he was entitled. Maybe Charlotte would like to invest it for the baby, or go for a European trip? He'd ask her in a few days' time.

Later that evening, Archie found himself inside the library of Rupert's bachelor townhouse. He was still contemplating the wisdom of his visit when the devil himself walked in.

"Archie, my man. Come to enjoy your last night as a single man?" His friend asked the question jovially, a bottle of port in his left hand and a bottle of brandy in his right.

"I've come for some advice, Rupert," Archie told his friend. He tried not to sound as horrified as he actually was, to be asking such things.

"Will you have a drink?" Rupert asked, the resigned look in his eye telling Archie that he didn't expect a "yes."

Archie hardly ever drank spirits. He had always avoided anything that eroded his self-control.

"Yes," he said with a definite nod. "Port, fill it up."

He was going to need courage tonight, and if that courage came in a bottle, then so be it.

Rupert's eyebrows shot up, but he didn't say anything, just filled up a glass of expensive port and gestured to a chair.

Archie reached for his drink and swallowed half of the glass in one gulp, almost choked, and then sat down slowly in the chair.

Again, Rupert's eyebrows shot up, but he didn't say anything about Archie's uncharacteristic display.

"So, I should congratulate you on your upcoming marriage. Charlotte's probably the only sane woman in the *ton*. And a duke's daughter, too. You've done well."

Archie smiled at Rupert's attempt at light conversation. The man was as subtle as a cow in a sitting room.

"Yes, I have. Despite everything." Archie still couldn't believe he was marrying one of the few ladies of the *ton* who any man would give his eye teeth to have.

"Archie, you know that none of us think any less of you because your brother was...unlucky." Rupert looked down at his port, and Archie felt the usual anger swelling in his gut.

"Unlucky," Archie repeated, finding the word grossly inadequate.

"I'm sorry, Archie, I don't know what else to say," Rupert said gruffly, obviously uncomfortable with the topic. He gave a shrug and Archie felt a little sorry for his whore-mongering friend.

"Look, Rupert, my brother's death was horrible and gruesome. If the details help put you off bedding every whore in London, then I will be happy to share."

Rupert opened his mouth, but Archie held up his hand.

"I came here for advice about bedding, so I shouldn't disparage you for having the experience I need. Forgive me."

Rupert nodded stiffly, but the burning anger in his eyes remained.

"What do you want to know?" he asked through slightly clenched teeth.

"I want to know what else I can do, other than what I already know," Archie said quickly, swallowing the rest of his port and gesturing for more.

"Tell me what you know and we'll go from there." Rupert smiled, and Archie knew his friend thought this a great joke. To have the prude come to the rake for advice was quite the back flip for Archie.

"Charlotte—" He stopped. How could he share what he and Charlotte had experienced?

Rupert cleared his throat loudly.

"I think it might be better if we just talk about bedding and women in general. I don't think I can stand thinking about Charlotte that way."

Archie looked at Rupert, a little puzzled about the slight flush staining his friend's handsome face. Then he remembered that Oliver and Rupert thought of Charlotte very much like a younger sister, a feeling he had never shared.

"Well, I touched and kissed her breasts."

"Ah... the woman's breasts, please." Rupert brought up his hands to cover his ears in an age-old gesture of not wanting to hear what was being said.

"Sorry, the woman I bedded a month ago. I touched and kissed her breasts." Archie grinned at his friend. It was vastly amusing that Rupert should be so flustered.

"Sucked too?" Rupert asked.

"Yes, but not much," Archie said with a slight frown. He wasn't quite sure if he had done that correctly.

"Most women enjoy sucking, harder than you think they want, but less than you want to."

"All right. Then I touched her between her legs until she came and then I climbed on top." Archie flushed at the memory and buried his face in his glass once again.

"She came just from touching?" Rupert asked, skeptically.

"And licking," Archie admitted, blushing completely for the first time since he'd arrived.

Rupert cleared his throat again, obviously as uncomfortable with this conversation as Archie. "And you know that she *came*?"

"Yes," Archie nodded. He tried to pretend he was answering questions about something less personal, like the weather.

"How?" Rupert asked.

Archie clenched his teeth. He had asked for Rupert's advice, and now he had to be as honest as possible.

"Well, she cried out, shuddered and inside she...ah, clenched. Over and over again."

Now he was blushing again, the heat in his face rather uncomfortable. Inside his trousers, his prick would usually be swelling at the memory of his time with Charlotte, but one look at Rupert's face and his prick stayed calm.

"You have my felicitations, my friend. Most men don't care anything about a woman's pleasure. They don't even realise it is possible for a woman to orgasm."

"I have listened to you, drunk, over the years and picked up on a few things you know," Archie told Rupert honestly, giving credit where credit was due.

One of the only reasons he knew anything about what to touch or to expect with Charlotte, was due to the boasting Rupert did whilst in his cups.

Rupert choked on his port and then started to laugh, really laugh, like they had back in school.

Archie smiled at the sound, wondering why he couldn't remember the last time he'd heard such a deep happiness in his friend's voice.

"So, what sort of advice do you need? It sounds like you could give lessons, Archie."

"I want to know the best way of positioning her. Can you do it other ways than just on top?" Archie was shocked at his forthrightness, but as he watched Rupert fill up his glass for at least the third time, he knew why. "And any other pointers?"

God, he was slurring now.

"Well, there's three main ways and a hundred versions within them. You on top, her on top, or from behind." Rupert was starting to get into this instructor role now, his eyes glittering excitedly.

"Her on top? Are you jesting?" Archie just couldn't imagine it. How would that work? How could he move if she was sitting on top?

Rupert chuckled, then smothered it with a cough.

"It's true. Not many ladies of the *ton* would try it as they don't even like going to bed with their husbands. But that's the three."

"From behind?" Archie asked skeptically now. How? As horses mated? That was a rather unsettling thought.

"Yes, most women I know love that one. You can lie down, kneel or stand, and you can position her legs any way you want."

Archie's body stirred as he imagined the possibilities. If she was on her knees leaning forward, yes, he could see how that could work. Then another consideration surged to the front of his alcohol-hazed brain.

"But what if your bed partner is...ah...pregnant?"

Rupert looked shocked at the question but then the penny dropped, and he looked uncomfortable again.

"Honestly, I've never bedded a pregnant woman, Archie. You might want to ask Oliver." He was avoiding Archie's eyes now.

"Can you guess, though?" Archie asked.

This was imperative. He knew that his mother had taken to her bed as soon as she was pregnant with both his brother and himself, never to stir until after the birth. Was it safe for pregnant women to be as active as he hoped to be with his new wife?

"Well, I can imagine it comes down to comfort for you both. Although as she gets bigger, I would suggest on your knees from behind." Rupert was again avoiding looking directly at Archie. Archie had to assume it was due to the questions being more personal, as Rupert didn't want to think of Charlotte in that way.

"No...other tips?" Archie asked, barely able to get the words out as his tongue grew fuzzier and the heat from his belly spread down his arms and into his legs.

"Just enjoy the experience, my friend; you've waited long enough."

Archie grinned and knocked back the rest of his port. That was exactly what he intended to do.

Chapter Sixteen

The wedding was a small and private affair. There hadn't been time for Charlotte to have a custom-made wedding dress, so she'd had a team of seamstresses brought in, who had worked through the night to alter her mother's dress to fit her. It looked beautiful. A high neck with white lace embroidery, a tight-fitting bodice, and flowing white chiffon for the skirt.

Due to Archie's family still being in full mourning, the wedding had to be small, and most of the guests were wearing black or another sombre colour. Charlotte didn't see any of that. All she saw as she walked down the aisle on her father's arm was the man she loved. And by his admission, Archie loved her too.

The ceremony was short, but no one in the church doubted the way the bridegroom and bride felt about each other. Charlotte and Archie glowed with love for each other, their eyes telling the world just how happy they were.

Later that same day, they journeyed to Archie's family estate twelve miles from London. During the ride Charlotte's stomach churned, and they had to stop every hour for her to be sick or get some fresh air. Archie tried to make her stop at an inn in a nearby town, but she was determined to be in their marital bed that night. She had missed Archie with every beat of her heart, and although the pregnancy had made her very strange in the stomach, it had also made other parts of her body newly sensitive.

Charlotte had lain awake in her bed the night before her wedding, taking an inventory of her new body. Her breasts were slightly larger, and her nipples were even more sensitive. She had shyly run her hand down between her legs just to see if that too had changed and had been shocked at the level of feeling even her own hand could elicit. She couldn't wait to be taken to bed, a proper bed this time, and make love to her husband.

"We're here, Charlotte." Archie's voice floated through her dream, and she came awake slowly.

Charlotte's eyes fluttered open. "Archie, it's lovely." She sighed as she took in the well-cared for gardens and a new extension.

Archie helped her down from the carriage, her legs wobbling slightly when they touched the ground. Archie dove to catch her and there, in front of almost every servant of the estate, her new husband kissed her. Lovingly, slowly and thoroughly.

Charlotte was enjoying the feel of Archie's warm, thick lips on hers when he seemed to stiffen and lift away from her. Frowning at the loss of contact, she raised her hands up to his hair to pull him back down, when she noticed fifty pairs of eyes looking at them. Or trying not to look at them, was perhaps a better description. Blushing furiously, she allowed Archie to pull her up and to his side.

Clearing his throat, he introduced her to the principal staff members and then she was shown straight to her room to freshen up.

Charlotte put on her most daring evening gown, cut in a French design that barely covered her breasts. She had never actually worn it, buying it in a rebellious mood and then never having the courage to wear it in company. However, as a newly-married woman, she had packed it knowing it would come in handy, especially if she wanted Archie to carry her off to bed as soon as it was feasible.

She was shown into the dining room by the butler. The footman who opened the door could barely keep his eyes away from her bosom.

Archie approached her with a look of calm on his face but it seemed schooled rather than genuine.

"My dear, you look lovely."

Charlotte was instantly disappointed. Was that all she got? Her nipples were about to pop out in front of ten footmen, and Archie thought she looked "lovely?"

Pasting a fake smile on her face, she sat down to their dinner.

They chatted amiably about their day and the house, over five courses.

During dessert, Archie couldn't seem to keep his eyes on her face any longer, and kept dropping to her cleavage. "Is that a new dress, Charlotte?" he asked casually.

"Not at all, my lord, I've had it for three years."

She swallowed a sip of her wine and watched for the tiny signs of distress upon his face. If she hadn't known Archie well, she wouldn't have seen the slight downward tilt of his mouth and the stillness of his body.

She stilled too, and waited for the next question.

Archie spooned a piece of apple pie into his mouth. Then he asked with a smooth and gentle tone, "You've worn it often, then?"

Charlotte feigned shock and ignored the question.

"You don't like it, my lord? I am so sorry. I had forgotten how much you enjoy fashion. Should I change into something more suitable for the rest of the evening?"

With a completely straight face Archie told her, "Oh, yes, my dear, it pays to stay in fashion. I believe that we shall have to stay here at the estate. We can't have you wearing such an outdated dress in company."

Charlotte was so disappointed she could barely prevent tears from rolling down her cheeks. She truly couldn't tell if he was teasing her or not. Maybe he was disgusted with the weight she'd put on? Maybe he didn't like her showing off flesh that should be kept on the inside of her dress?

She wiped away a single tear that escaped down her cheek. Then Archie pushed back his chair with a squeal as the chair leg scraped the floor.

He rushed straight over to her and bowed.

"Charlotte, would you join me for a drink in the music room?"

Charlotte nodded and stood up, her dessert all but forgotten. Her stomach churned and her eyes filled with more salty tears.

Walking her into the music room, Archie shut the door behind them and with a small twist he pushed her up against the wall.

"Archie," she cried, shocked but thrilled as her husband finally showed signs of wanting her.

He swooped down for a hot, passionate, and wet kiss. He demanded and she gave. He pressed his erection into her, and she moaned as she ran her hands through his hair.

Thank God, he's not angry!

Archie pulled back to look at her and smiled down at her. She knew her face was flushed, but she was too excited about her husband's hands on her to worry about how she looked.

"I can't stand the idea of anyone else seeing you in this dress, Charlotte. I'm sorry that you thought I was serious. I was just feeling very jealous that other people had seen these amazing breasts and I was trying to make a joke to defuse my jealousy. I'm not sure that it worked."

Whilst he spoke, Archie reached up and scooped her breasts out of the tiny piece of silk that held them in.

Charlotte gasped and then moaned as he softly pinched each nipple with his fingers, while he simultaneously bit down on the side of her neck.

His possessiveness was affecting her differently than she thought it would. Charlotte had always thought a jealous and possessive husband would be a hindrance, but she was finding it so exciting her heart was tripping over itself. Her body was ready for him this very minute.

"No one has ever seen me in this dress, Archie," she whispered, arching her back so that he would repeat his caresses.

"But you said..." he began, lifting his head and giving her a confused look.

"I said the dress was three years old, which it is. But I never wanted to wear it before tonight. I wanted you to want me," she whispered.

"Oh, I want you, Charlotte." Archie groaned, licking across her collarbones.

"You haven't touched me all day," she sulked, pouting. But she was unable to stop herself from running her hands up his chest and clinging to his muscled shoulders.

"Not because I didn't want to. I was just so scared, with the pregnancy and the stress…I wasn't sure if you'd want me to ravish you in the daylight or wait 'til we could be in your bed, in the dark."

Charlotte laughed, so relieved she couldn't describe the sensation. They still had so much to learn about each other, but this was a good start.

"You mean, like our first time? So proper. On the floor, in the middle of the day? In your library?"

Archie blushed at this reminder.

"Shall we go to bed now, my wife?" Archie asked politely, stepping back and offering her his arm.

Charlotte pulled her dress back up over her breasts and nodded.

Without another word, Archie towed her along the hallway, past three footmen who all looked at the ground, up the carpeted staircase, and into the main bedroom. His bedroom.

"This is where you will sleep for the next seven months, and this is where you will give birth to our child," Archie whispered into Charlotte's ear as he applied himself to unlacing her gown.

Charlotte couldn't believe the overwhelming emotions threatening to engulf her. Archie had married her, he loved her, and now he was going to consummate their marriage in the ducal bedchamber. Charlotte wasn't sure if Archie had deliberately brought her to his room rather than hers, or if it had been unconscious. Either way, she was secretly thrilled. Did he want to sleep with her every night just like Sarah and Oliver did? A tear slid unheeded down her cheek.

Archie turned her around to kiss her and saw the tear.

"Or we can sleep in your room, if you prefer," he offered hastily.

Charlotte smiled up at her new husband and put every bit of happiness she was feeling into it. She noticed he hadn't offered to sleep separately.

"Archie, I'll sleep anywhere you are, my love. Anywhere."

A small smile crept onto Archie's face.

"The stables?" he asked, grinning so that it was obvious this time he was joking.

Charlotte pushed her tiny chemise off her shoulders and let it slither to the floor, leaving her naked.

"Anywhere," she repeated with quiet conviction as Archie looked his fill.

Charlotte was beginning to think she should have kept herself covered up, her husband took so long to react. Then Archie dropped to his knees in front of her. Looking up at her, he whispered, "You are so beautiful you make my heart ache."

He bent forward and kissed her belly with a reverence usually reserved for something holy. Resisting the urge to cry again, Charlotte brought her hands up and threaded her fingers through his thick, brown hair.

Rising from his kneeling position, he lifted Charlotte up and into his arms. She giggled and smiled at him as she clung to his shoulders. She loved how strong he was. Slowly, he lay her down in the large bed, the soft mattress cushioning her weight. The blankets had been turned down, and the room was warm from the fire that had been going all day.

Charlotte watched from the bed with hungry eyes as Archie stripped off his clothes.

To her, Archie was the perfect man. Taut and lean with a face so handsome it could have belonged to an angel.

He stripped off the last of his clothes and went to join her on the bed.

"No," Charlotte cried, sitting up to reach for him.

Archie paused, his eyebrows rising and his mouth tightening around the edges.

"I want to look at you. I didn't get to last time." She rushed to reassure him, her eyes greedily taking in every inch of her perfect man. The whipcord, strong muscles, his flat stomach, the large and thick appendage already thrusting forth from its bed of dark brown curls.

"Do I pass, ma'am?" Archie asked with a mock bow and a smile.

Charlotte couldn't help the answering tug deep between her legs as he smiled at her. *Pass?* He was not only utterly beautiful, but the fact that no other woman besides herself had ever seen this sight, gave her satisfaction deep inside her heart.

"I love knowing that no one else has ever seen you like this," she whispered, tearing up again.

Bloody pregnant nerves.

Archie's face sobered.

"And you will be the only one ever to see me like this, Charlotte. I promise," he vowed, moving over to lie down next to her on the bed.

Charlotte blinked rapidly, trying not to cry again. Archie knew her so well now. His gift of faithfulness was the only one she wanted.

"You'll never leave me now," Archie growled at her as he rolled over her, moaning at the contact as he lay down on top of her.

The feel of his bare flesh upon hers was startling, and they simultaneously moaned. His naked body came into full contact with hers, and his erection thrust impatiently between her legs. Charlotte instinctively opened her thighs and wrapped her legs around his narrow hips.

Chapter Seventeen

Archie gasped as his aching cock pressed into her wet entrance, naturally, easily, due to her position. He hadn't meant for that to happen so quickly. He had wanted to savour their connection, to build her up slowly to that amazing crescendo of pleasure. He reared back on his arms and tried to pull back. Charlotte moaned.

"No, Archie, come to me." She locked her legs in place and pulled him deeper into her willing body.

Archie was lost in her welcoming heat. How was she so ready for him from one kiss? He hadn't even licked her breasts or done any of the things he had been planning, and yet she was open and wet for him. He sank deeper, her muscles tugging him in further until he was sunk to the balls in her tight heat.

Charlotte moaned and pulled Archie's head down for a kiss.

He began moving, slowly at first and then with harder and longer strokes. Charlotte began thrashing against the bed, her hard nipples brushing the hairs of his chest in a way that was driving them both mad.

Archie made a split-second decision, needing this to be more than a quick tumble for both of them. He held on to her tightly and rolled them so that she lay on top of him. Moving her legs out from under him he kissed her and filled both his palms with her breasts.

When Rupert had suggested this position, Archie hadn't been quite sure how it would work. But now he knew why it would become one of his favourites. He had so much better access to her body from this position. He kneaded her left breast with his right hand and moved his other hand down to that spot between her legs where she loved to be touched.

Charlotte sat up straight and looked down at him. Lifting herself up by her thighs, she rose off him slightly and then moved down again, experimentally. Archie moaned at his wife's natural wantonness, and she smiled with triumph. She rose up again a little higher and came down hard.

Archie moaned louder this time, pleasure splintering through his body. Both his hands gripped her fleshy hips, urging her to move faster. He began lifting her on him and then bringing her down.

Charlotte grabbed both of his hands to stop him from controlling their movements and put them both on her breasts. He took a deep breath and let her take the lead. She began moving on him, up and down in a beautiful rhythm that pushed Archie closer and closer to the edge. He was surprised when she slowed down and began frowning.

"Archie, I need you to help please, I need..."

Archie felt himself careening toward a climax but knew she was not. He carefully lifted her off him and pushed her back down onto her back. Ignoring the need in his loins, he moved down her body so that he could suckle at her breasts. They were a darker red now, no longer pale pink. What had Rupert said? He should suck harder than he assumed she would want, but not as hard as he would want to.

Smiling to himself, Archie dipped his head and pulled one long nipple into his mouth and sucked. Softly at first, waiting for a response. Charlotte moaned and pulled his head harder into her. Archie complied, sucking harder until she gasped. Pulling back, he looked up and smiled.

"Too hard?" he asked.

Charlotte shook her head. "No, keep doing that please."

Archie grinned at her and attacked the other breast, enjoying the plump flesh and the sweet taste of her skin. He moved his hand down between her thighs and rubbed the little nub, the spot she so loved to be touched.

"Archie, please, I need you," Charlotte begged, tugging on Archie's head to try bringing him up to her.

Archie ignored her and kept up his dual assault. Tugging at her nipples with both his lips and his teeth, he suckled until she was pushing him closer again. He flicked that sweet bit of flesh until he heard it.

Charlotte cried out, clenched her legs together, trapping his hand whilst her body spasmed and shook. He loved watching her find bliss in his arms. There was nothing better.

When she stopped shuddering and opened her eyes, she held her arms out to him. Instead of immediately going to her as his cock begged him to do, he reared back onto his haunches and smiled.

"Could we try one more thing?" he asked, both nervous and excited to be asking for such a thing.

"Of course."

"Can you roll over onto your hands and knees?" he asked, making flipping signs with his hands.

Archie could tell he had shocked her, as Charlotte's eyes widened, but she did what he asked. She turned slowly; her face still flushed.

She rolled over onto her hands and knees, tucking her bottom under.

Archie enjoyed the sight of her beautiful, plump behind for one moment before laying a hand on her. She jumped as though stung, then relaxed as he stroked up her back and down.

Archie was a little worried. How was this going to work? Better if he could see what to do, he supposed.

"Open your legs for me," he murmured, surprised at how deep his voice had gone.

Charlotte gasped and arched her back a little as though she'd get up, but settled and opened her legs an inch. Archie chuckled softly and moved his hands down to her thighs, gently pushing them further apart.

He could tell she was trying to hide her flesh from his view and spoke soothingly to her, trying to ease her fears.

"Charlotte, you are the most beautiful thing I have ever seen. Show me how much you want me, show me where you need me." He stroked between her legs and she gasped again, moving unconsciously toward his hands.

She tilted her pelvis back for him and lowered her breasts to the bed. Archie groaned as her plump pink flesh came into view and his gut clenched with need. Now he understood. Charlotte was aroused and pink, wet and waiting for him. He knelt behind her, felt for her entrance with one hand and guided the thick head of his cock there. Pressing in once again, he was surrounded by newly tightened tissues and gasped at the pleasure.

His head swam, and he had to grip her hips to stop himself from falling away from her. She moaned softly, and he thrust in fully, sheathing himself to the hilt. Oh God, he had never been in her so deep. She was glorious.

Archie was too far gone to wait for her again, he thrust one last time and let go of his control. The hot wave consumed him, flowing down from his chest, spreading into his belly and settling into his balls as his cock pulsed, his seed spreading inside her.

Exhausted, and with his head spinning in the clouds, Archie waited a moment, gently stroking Charlotte's back. When his thighs began to shake, he pulled out of her body and they rolled together onto the bed.

Charlotte settled naturally against him, and Archie closed his eyes, smiling as they fell together into sleep.

When Charlotte woke, the sun was streaming in through the open curtains and Archie was stroking her back in gentle, repetitive motions. She came to herself slowly, the warmth of Archie's chest beneath her cheek and the salty smell of his skin in her nostrils.

The scent of their lovemaking lingered in the air and on the sheets. Charlotte blushed lightly at the memory of all they'd done on their wedding night. How could she have known that such pleasure could be found within her body?

"Good morning, wife," Archie greeted her, chuckling as he spoke.

"Good morning, husband," she answered, kissing his chest and then lifting herself up to look at him.

The dark circles under his eyes had faded, and he looked so heart-breakingly beautiful that her own heart skipped a beat.

"How are you feeling?" he asked, frowning as his eyes searched her face.

Charlotte closed her eyes as nausea crept in.

"Nauseous, and sore," she murmured, feeling tender in spots she hadn't felt since the first time they had made love. She lay back against the pillows, trying valiantly not to be sick.

Archie leaned away from her and brought back a dry piece of toast.

"The kitchen brought this up not so long ago. The housekeeper assured me it would settle your stomach."

Charlotte stared at Archie for a moment and then at the toast. Had he asked his housekeeper about her pregnancy already? When? Hot tingles in her eyes told her that tears threatened her composure as the full impact of his thoughtful gesture hit her.

"Don't cry, Charlotte. I'm sorry. Are you that sore? Do you want me to order a bath, or..."

Charlotte laughed through her tears and launched herself at her husband, kissing him soundly on the lips before snatching the toast from him. Laying back against the pillows again she took a tentative bite and waited for her body's reaction. Her stomach gurgled a little, but nausea stayed the same, no worse. She ate the whole piece slowly, and the sick feeling subsided.

"May I have my tea?"

Her considerate husband choked out a laugh and handed her a sweetened cup that she sipped gratefully. Incredible. She'd been so afraid to tell anyone about her condition that no one had helped her through it.

"Are you sure you're fine?" he asked again.

"I feel much better, thank you," she answered, sighing happily as her whole body relaxed.

"And your...uhh..." Archie made a vague motion to the lower half of her body and arched an eyebrow.

Charlotte hid a smile in her teacup.

"My..." she repeated, looking at him with an expression conveying as much innocence as possible.

Archie cleared his throat. "You said you were sore."

Charlotte laughed again.

"So, you can touch it and kiss it, but you can't say the word?"

Archie's mouth kicked up in amusement.

"I apologise, madam wife. How is your honey pot this morning?"

Charlotte choked on her tea and sprayed half of it across the bed.

Archie laughed out loud.

Charlotte shot him a murderous glare and dabbed at the wet spots on the quilt.

"My *honey pot* felt sore and bruised this morning, thanks to my lusty husband," Charlotte retorted.

"I could kiss it better..." Archie offered, trailing his hand under the sheet.

Charlotte flinched back, and his happy face sobered. "I'm sorry."

"No, don't apologise. I just need to have a long soak in the tub." Well, she hoped that's all she needed.

"And how's our baby this morning?" Archie asked quietly, running his palm gently over her lower belly.

Charlotte felt a shiver run through her whole body at his touch.

"Fine, I think," she answered just as quietly. She really should see a doctor and find out what the recommendations were for her condition.

"I hope it was all right to do everything we did last night."

Charlotte watched Archie's face and could see many different emotions flickering across his eyes. It was going to take years to learn how to read him properly, and she didn't feel like waiting that long.

"What are you thinking?"

Archie's face instantly cleared into a polite mask.

"No," Charlotte wailed. She pushed him onto his back and swung up over him.

"Charlotte, we can't..."

"Archie, I can't tell what you're thinking most of the time, so I need you to tell me. Tell me if you're worried about something. Tell me if you need something. The only way our marriage is going to survive is if we talk to each other."

Charlotte had her hands on his chest and her eyes bore into his. She was determined they would have a good marriage. If that meant physically restraining him on occasion, then she would.

Archie lifted his hands to caress her soft nipples, smoothing the sides of her flesh.

Charlotte noticed where his eyes were lingering and felt his arousal jutting up against her buttocks. Making a noise of frustration, she pulled the covers up around her upper body and glared at him.

"Tell me what was worrying you a moment ago."

"I can't remember," Archie murmured, pulling at the quilt she had firmly wrapped around her body.

"You said, you hoped we didn't hurt the baby," Charlotte reminded him, keeping a tight hold on her covers.

Archie opened his mouth, then closed it again.

"Oh, that. Yes, well, I thought that maybe I should have left you to sleep. Perhaps I should have gone to another room last night, so I wouldn't be tempted to make love to you again."

Charlotte smiled as she remembered the way Archie had woken her during the night and made love to her, slowly and very thoroughly. She moved down so that she could lay down on his chest but could still look at him. It took some maneuvering around his erection, but she managed it.

"Never apologise for making love to me. I loved every second of it."

"But, you're sore..."

"Of course, I am, it was only my second and third time. I'm sure it will get easier from now on."

Archie's smile showed a hint of relief. "So, the baby's fine?"

"The baby's fine," Charlotte confirmed, laying her head down onto Archie's chest again.

She let herself drift slowly back to sleep.

Chapter Eighteen

Archie left Charlotte sleeping peacefully and went to his study. He tried to attend to his ledgers and books, but they would not capture his attention. His beautiful wife had done far too good a job of that this morning.

Why would she want to know his thoughts and desires? Would she strive to give them to him, or would she use them against him?

He physically shook his head to dispel the thought. Charlotte would not use his desires against him.

Last night, she had not only allowed him every intimacy as her new husband, but she had been willing to try anything that he asked of her, seeming to enjoy everything as much as he had. And, God had he enjoyed it. He wasn't sure how long he could wait to bed her again.

No, she needed rest. He didn't want her shying away from him because he wanted her too much. He remembered his mother doing that. Shying away from his father if he ever tried to touch her. Around the waist, on the hand, any physical affection was forbidden, for her sons as well.

Was Charlotte right, though, that the only way they would have a successful marriage would be if they shared their feelings? What a foreign concept.

A knock sounded on his study door, and he called "Enter," expecting the butler.

Instead, his beautiful wife breezed into the room wearing a lovely walking dress of pale green.

"Charlotte!" He stood and greeted her with a bow.

Charlotte smiled that gorgeous, cheeky smile, moved around the desk, pushed him down into his chair and climbed onto his lap. Before Archie had time even to react, she planted a quick kiss on his lips and twined her arms around his neck.

"Good morning again, Archie."

He swallowed painfully and the lump in his throat threatened his composure. This couldn't last, could it? She looked so happy to see him, and she couldn't seem to keep her hands off him. Could he have found what Oliver had? Instead of thinking about it, he pulled Charlotte closer and kissed her thoroughly, teasing her tongue with his until she giggled.

"I was hoping to go for a picnic luncheon. Would you show me your home?" She shot him an impish smile.

Archie looked out his window for the first time that morning and noticed the sunshine.

"Of course, what time?" he asked, not sure how close they were to lunchtime and not wanting to let her go so that he could look at his pocket watch.

"Now, if you're not too busy?" Charlotte arched an eyebrow in challenge.

Archie smiled and nodded in acceptance. Of course, he had things to do, but this was his honeymoon, wasn't it?

They made their way on foot along one of the many paths around the lake, until they found a tree with sufficient shade from the sun. Ever afraid of sunspots, Charlotte had brought her parasol, but didn't wish to hold it over herself whilst she ate.

Archie happily laid out the picnic rug and arranged the food on it. The cook had put together pieces of cold chicken, sandwiches, fruit and even some cold apple cakes.

Archie waited for her to sit and then lay down opposite her. He told her about the history of his home and the number of tenants and responsibilities that came with the estate. He didn't think he had ever talked so much or been so at ease with another person before. And to have that with Charlotte was beyond his wildest dreams.

"So, tell me why you changed your mind about us marrying?" Charlotte asked once he'd stopped talking.

Archie's good mood shattered. He didn't want to have that conversation right now, nor think about that time of his life ever again. But he knew she deserved to hear the truth.

"I just couldn't lie to myself anymore."

"What do you mean?" Charlotte asked, stretching out her hand and drawing his into her own.

Archie felt the reassuring touch of her fingers and drew in a steadying breath. He had been waiting for this question for the last few days. Because of her pregnancy, he'd never had the chance to explain just why he had been so stubborn about not marrying her. Now that he had to tell her, he didn't want to. He wanted to forget the last twenty-seven years of his life and focus on the next forty.

"I thought I could live without you, but I was wrong. I was miserable, and I just couldn't bear it any longer."

"So, you did lie to me..." Charlotte's voice trailed off, but he knew exactly what she was asking.

"Yes, I lied. I told you I didn't love you, but I did. Will you forgive me?" He asked the most important question of his life and held his breath, his pulse beating hard in his ears.

Charlotte bent her head and softly kissed Archie's lips. "Of course," she whispered. Straightening up again, she added, "Although I still don't understand why you didn't marry me five years ago."

Archie laughed; he couldn't help it. He had been wondering the same thing.

"Would you have married me if I had asked you five years ago?"

Charlotte tilted her head to the side and stared at him. "Maybe. If you'd shown me the true you."

Archie thought about that. He probably wouldn't have. She'd been so young, and he had been so scared of breaking even one rule. She would have likely concluded that he was a boring individual and would not have bothered.

"Maybe it's better that we are together now, rather than then," Archie murmured, looking down at the delicate white hand in his.

"Yes, but you had to go through that horrible time alone. Thinking you had lost everyone. I could have helped you." Charlotte dropped her gaze to her lap, where she picked at her apple cake.

"Charlotte, you did help me. If you hadn't come to my study that day, I could still be in my self-made hell." Archie told her, his heart sick at the thought.

It was almost impossible to remember that this same day last week he was barely eating, trying to simply survive from one minute to the next. Now, he was sitting in the sunshine with his new wife, the only woman he had ever wanted, or loved.

Charlotte looked up and gave him one of her best smiles.

"But why were you so worried then?"

Archie sighed. Charlotte was so optimistic. She always had been.

"Because I still think that you are going to suffer because you have married me. I'm sure you heard people talking about my family and me when you were in London. How are you going to feel when people start whispering about you, or me? What if you heard that I had the same illness as my brother?"

Archie was voicing his worst fears, and his stomach was getting tighter with every word. "I could never live with you hating me."

Charlotte took a deep breath and her blue eyes darkened.

"Archie, you are my husband, and you are now my priority. You and our child. I will never listen to any idle gossip about you and not defend you. Your brother has died of a horrible disease but that has nothing, and I mean nothing, to do with you."

Archie looked at her angry expression and felt a slightly hysterical laugh bubbling up. "But what if society refuses me, us?"

"Oh, who cares about society?" She waved her hand dismissively.

"You do," he answered. She had spent her whole life in the ballrooms of the haute *ton*, wouldn't she miss it?

"I've never cared what they thought about me. I only spent so much time there because it staved off the boredom."

Archie gave her a confused look, and she sighed.

"Archie, you don't realise that as women we are educated only to the point where we can entertain a room full of people and run a home once we are married. I couldn't go to my club, I couldn't run an estate, I wasn't married, and I did not have a child. What else was I supposed to do?"

Archie thought about this and realised he had never really considered what life would be like for a lady of his class. Their choices were very limited.

"So, if we are cut off, you won't hate me?"

Charlotte laughed; the sound slightly shocking to Archie when they were discussing something so serious.

"Archie, I love you. Even if we are completely shunned, which I don't think will happen, I would be happy to stay here forever. I will have you, our baby, and a beautiful home where our friends and family can visit any time."

Archie sat up now, unable to believe his ears. Why hadn't he trusted her? Why hadn't he simply asked her what she wanted? He could have saved them both so much pain.

He went up onto his knees and moved over to kiss her.

"I LOVE YOU," he whispered against her lips. Archie kissed her so sweetly, tears slipped unheralded down her cheeks.

The familiar stirrings of desire swirled within her belly, but she was still very sore. She wasn't sure if it was the pregnancy or the amount of penetration from the night before, but she was much sorer than after their first time together.

Pulling away from their kiss, she encouraged Archie to lay with his head in her lap. Stroking his brow and silky-smooth hair, he closed his eyes, obviously at peace. They stayed that way for most of the afternoon.

After another beautiful dinner, they retired separately. Charlotte wanted another bath, and Archie needed to write a letter of business.

After her bath, Charlotte dressed in her sheerest nightgown and walked next door to Archie's rooms. Slipping into his bed, she sat up and against the many pillows and waited for him.

He arrived ten minutes later, his surprise at her presence obvious.

"I thought you might not want to share a bed tonight," he crooned, shedding his clothes, one item at a time.

Charlotte just smiled, pleased she had read her husband correctly. He would not have come to her if she had stayed in her room, and that would just not do. She was still quite sore but knew there were other ways to please her husband than with her "honey pot," as he called it. She blushed just thinking the phrase, and Archie noticed.

"What are you thinking about?" he asked her, a beautiful smile spreading over his handsome face.

"I was wondering what you usually wore to bed," Charlotte answered, which wasn't a total lie. She wanted to know what she would have to strip off him.

"I don't usually wear anything to bed. Would you like me to wear a nightshirt?" he asked respectfully and reached into a drawer.

She laughed. There was no way she was being denied the feel of his hot, smooth skin against hers.

"No, I want you to sleep as you always do."

"But..." Archie trailed off, his eyebrows drawing together in thought.

She continued to stare at him, so he nodded and slowly stripped himself of all of his clothes and stepped toward her.

Charlotte slid out of bed and stood in front of the fire in her white nightgown that cleverly hinted at the body beneath. She beckoned him with her eyes.

He quirked an eyebrow in question and took a deep breath. Charlotte was enthralled. Archie had the most magnificent body. Lean and muscular with beautiful thick legs and a flat belly. His member was already thickening and rising even as she looked at it.

"Let's get into bed," Archie suggested, taking her hand to lead her there.

Charlotte let him guide her back to bed, but only so she could watch him walk. His vitals swung, and he seemed to be getting control of his body. That just wouldn't do, either.

Archie crawled beneath the covers, pulling the blankets up to his chin. Charlotte grabbed the sheer layers of her nightdress and pulled it over her head. Archie made a choking noise and sat up. Charlotte watched her husband carefully for indications of how he felt. She was completely naked, with her back to the warm fire.

"Charlotte, I thought we should have a night off from lovemaking. You're still too sore." His voice sounded strange, as though he were choking.

"I am still sore. I wasn't going to make love to you."

She whipped the blankets back down his legs and saw his fully extended member. She chuckled happily. At least she knew he still liked her appearance.

"Charlotte, please stop torturing me." Archie groaned as his hands clenched spasmodically, forming fists at his sides.

Charlotte crawled onto the bed and kissed her husband. She slid her tongue into his mouth, and he moaned again, letting her tongue play with his, sliding together, giving each other pleasure.

Charlotte exerted pressure on Archie's chest and pushed him flat.

"Stay there. It's my turn to show you how much I love you," she commanded.

Archie smiled hesitantly and lay back.

Chapter Nineteen

Charlotte surveyed the beautiful body spread out before her and wondered if she could put her mouth straight down onto him. Looking back at his face, she thought he might not be amenable to that. Better to work up to it.

She knelt beside him and ran her hands over his little pink nipples and his broad, lightly hairy chest. Archie moaned and closed his eyes, his face showing signs of pleasure and happiness. She lay down next to him and began kissing his body. She first touched her lips to each nipple and then down the middle of his chest.

Slowly, inch by inch, she moved closer and closer to her target. She could hear Sarah's voice in her head. "When you love someone, you want to please them," so Charlotte kept kissing. Around his navel, down to the curly, rough hairs that guarded his sex.

"Charlotte, I don't think you should kiss down there." Archie's voice was strained.

She stopped and looked up. Archie had his eyes closed and was talking through clenched teeth.

What had Sarah said? *"Oliver said that most ladies don't."* So, that was the problem. Archie was still worried about doing the right thing by society.

"Why not?" she asked, wrapping her palm around him and giving his flesh a long, slow tug with her hand.

Archie groaned, and his hips flexed up.

"Because you're not meant to," Archie hissed out, still speaking through his clenched teeth.

Charlotte giggled and kissed his lips. Archie groaned and opened his eyes.

She tilted her head and set her lips to his hard flesh. He watched with wide open eyes as she kissed up and down the shaft.

"Charlotte, ladies aren't supposed to..." He trailed off as she licked the large smooth head of his member.

Charlotte laughed again and waited for him to look at her. This was a lot more pleasant than she had expected.

"Archie, I am your wife, and I want to. You do this to me, so I should do it to you."

"But..."

"Archie, have you ever put this inside another woman?" she asked sharply, gripping the base of his thick shaft as firmly as she dared.

"No, you know I haven't!"

"And do you intend to?" Charlotte asked, stroking him slowly, trying to confuse him as much as possible.

"No, of course not," he answered, closing his eyes.

"Then since I am your one and only lover, I should fulfill your every need, as you do for me."

Charlotte saw the worry still evident in her husband's eyes and did the only other thing she could think of. She twirled around so that she could still kiss him but so that he could touch her, too.

"I am still sore, so be careful, but I want you to feel how much I like doing this. My body can't lie. Neither can yours."

And with that, she spread her legs slightly, and opened her lips and sucked the pink head fully into her mouth.

Archie groaned as he stroked his fingertip over the small nub of her pleasure and she moaned low in her throat. Seeking confirmation that she was enjoying herself, he slipped his fingers slowly between her legs and found her so wet that he gasped.

Charlotte turned to look at him and smiled. "See?"

Then she began in earnest. She gripped the base of his penis in one hand and started sucking at the other end.

"Charlotte, please stop, I'm going to come if you keep doing that."

Perfect. Charlotte sucked harder and started pulling at his flesh with her hand.

She sensed the tightening of Archie's body and felt one of his hands hold her head closer. So she moved at a pace, as though she was making love to him.

He groaned like his soul was being ripped from him. His pleasure exploded into her mouth and Charlotte swallowed the salty taste of him on reflex, licking the tip and sucking him one more time.

Archie made loud gasping noises and threw an arm over his sweaty brow.

Charlotte smiled to herself and maneuvered around him. She curled into her sleeping position on the side, waiting for Archie to "spoon" her.

He moved sluggishly, but managed to pull up the quilt, covering them both. He curled his hot, strong body around hers. He sighed and kissed her hair.

"Thank you," he whispered into her ear.

"You're very welcome." Charlotte sighed, pulling his arm around to rest on their child.

She fell instantly asleep with the knowledge that she had just fully satisfied her husband.

THEY CONTINUED this way for the next three months. Talking during the day and spending their nights learning the secrets of each other's bodies.

Charlotte had taken to writing letters to friends and family most days and having frequent naps in the afternoons. This gave Archie plenty of time for estate business and his horses. He promised her he would teach her to ride, once she was no longer pregnant.

Charlotte's pregnancy was going beautifully. Almost five months along, her belly was a hard, rounded swelling, jutting out between her hips. Archie loved the changes in her body and told her so frequently that Charlotte could never feel upset or disconcerted about the vastly different curves.

The nausea was gone, and Charlotte's healthy appetite was back. For food as well as her husband. He was insatiable. Archie would make love to her morning, noon and night if she allowed him, and occasionally she did.

The first test of their marriage came in the form of an invitation.

Archie knocked on the door of what was now Charlotte's morning sitting room. She sat at her embroidery. He entered to find her singing softly to their baby.

She raised her head. "Yes, my love?" Charlotte frowned slightly at his expression. "Are you all right?" she asked, moving to stand.

"No, don't get up." He stopped her, sitting in the chair opposite hers.

He unfolded the invitation in his hand and offered it to her.

"We've been invited to the christening of Oliver and Sarah's son," Archie explained unnecessarily, as Charlotte read the invitation herself.

"Oh, that's wonderful. Two weeks. Well, that gives us plenty of time to pack and travel to London. I need to order a few new dresses, too," she explained, rubbing her belly with a satisfied smile.

Archie stopped short. He wasn't sure if he wanted to go and he didn't know how to explain that to his wife. He had worked out that he could drop to half mourning the same weekend as the christening, but it would be the first public event he would attend since his brother's death.

"You want to go?" Archie croaked, his nerves getting the best of him.

He had lost the easy ability to disguise how he was feeling around his wife. Charlotte had worn down all resistance with her constant questions and attention. He liked to think he had helped her, too. She glowed with love, and he enjoyed the idea that he put that light there.

"Of course. Don't you?" Charlotte's eyes were wide with surprise.

"I'd like to go, but it will be the first event since my brother's death." Archie hoped she wouldn't need a better explanation than that.

Charlotte studied his face for a moment, before speaking.

"Archie, we don't have to go, not if you don't want to."

He let out a breath he didn't know he had been holding.

"But it would be very rude of us to decline without a proper reason. After all, the Duke and Duchess of Lincoln have specially invited us," Charlotte reminded him with a smile.

Archie clenched his teeth. He knew he was being herded the way Charlotte wanted to go, but didn't know how to fight her. Yes, it would be rude to decline an invitation from not only his best friend, but also one of the most powerful families in London.

"Charlotte, what if you are treated badly because of your marriage to me?" Archie voiced his most profound fear.

Charlotte laughed. "Archie, I love you. If anyone wants to cut me from society because I married you, then I am happy never to speak to them again. Our friends want to see us, and that is what's important."

Archie considered her words and watched her eyes and face for evidence that she was lying. He saw none and exhaled slowly. If Charlotte was willing to brave the *ton*'s censure, then who was he to be scared? He was the one who had been preparing for it for the past ten years. What was he really worried about? He swallowed audibly and asked the one question that terrified him.

"And no matter what, you won't stop loving me?"

He dropped his eyes to the floor, unable to hold her gaze. Despite the desperate need to see her face when she answered, his fear of seeing something he didn't like was greater.

Standing up, Charlotte moved over to Archie and forced her way onto his lap. She put one hand on Archie's chin to pull his eyes up to hers, and she used the other hand to guide his to her burgeoning belly.

"Archie, I have said this before, and I will say it every day if you need to hear it. I love you. Nothing will make me turn away from you, ever."

Pushing his hand harder into her bump, she continued. "You and this baby are my whole world, and I will happily give you as many children as you want. So that we can have a loving family like neither of us had."

Archie blinked several times, forcing hot tears away. Was it possible?

"Archie, you have made me happier than I ever imagined possible. If you keep it up, I promise I will stand by you through anything."

He felt himself beginning to hope. Just like the sun coming through the cracks in the clouds on a winter's day, her words filtered through the fog of his uncertainty. He smiled softly and felt a tear slip down his cheek.

Their baby chose that moment to give its first big kick, right under Archie's hand.

"Oh, did you feel that?" Charlotte grabbed his hand and pushed down even harder.

Archie felt the armour around his heart shatter, as his heart swelled with love for this woman. For Charlotte, who had dragged him, kicking and screaming, into the sunshine.

"I love you," he whispered pulling her face to his for a kiss that had his body aching for her.

"Come to bed," Charlotte whispered against Archie's lips, standing up and pulling him with her.

Archie fought the urge to throw his wife over his shoulder and run up the stairs. Only her belly stopped him.

"Lead the way, my lady." He bowed with a cheeky smile.

They travelled to London the following week.

～

LONDON HAD NEVER LOOKED BRIGHTER to Charlotte. She was married, with child, and loved beyond comparison. What else could make her life better? Well, perhaps, not being shunned by people who had known her, her whole life. That would be a good start. She had never been so disgusted with the *ton*'s behaviour before.

They had arrived in London a few days before, and Charlotte had instantly set out to order new gowns to accommodate her expanding figure. She had been asked to come back at a later time when the shop was closed, so that people wouldn't know that she frequented that modiste. Charlotte had stormed out and instead found a small but beautiful shop with an English modiste.

"I am the new Countess of Tother," she announced to the modiste. "Would you like my business?"

The young lady had blinked and curtseyed.

"Indeed, I would like that, your ladyship. Can I get you a cup of tea?"

Charlotte had a little cry, to be perfectly honest, and then proceeded to order more gowns than she could wear in a season. She had money, and Archie thought she was beautiful. She would have the best of everything.

Driving home in her carriage, she started to realise that Archie had been right to worry about society's reaction to them. She had known, of course, what might happen, but to be affronted by a shop lady was just too much.

She pasted a bright smile on her face and swept into her new townhouse.

"Good day, my lady," their ancient butler said, and bowed deeply.

Charlotte blushed brightly. She still hadn't become accustomed to seeing the man who knew exactly when and where she had first made love to Archie. The poor man looked just as uncomfortable every time he saw her, but Charlotte wouldn't have changed him for the world. He ran a tight ship, and he had saved her several times from embarrassing or insulting visitors.

"Is his lordship in the study?" Charlotte asked, pulling off her cloak and gloves. She handed them to a waiting footman.

"Yes. Mister Rupert is with him."

The old butler's mouth turned down slightly, and Charlotte suppressed a smile. The butler was a stickler for tradition and disapproved of Rupert's flagrant disrespect for drinking hours and his disrespect toward married women.

Rupert had visited on their first day in London and had given Charlotte a loud, smacking kiss on the mouth in congratulations. The poor butler had almost expired on the spot. Truth be told, Archie hadn't been too impressed either. But Charlotte knew Rupert's weakness now, and she would stop the rake in his tracks.

"Thank you, Hill," she said, gliding up to the door of the study.

She heard two male voices within, and a laugh she recognised as her husband's. It was wonderful to hear him so happy.

She knocked once and pushed open the heavy door.

Both gentlemen jumped to their feet on her entry. Rupert gave her a sly smile and looked at Archie.

"Countess," Rupert greeted her, stepping forward to touch her, in goodness knows what way.

Instead of moving toward him, Charlotte flattened her palms on her belly and pulled the dress taut around the prominent bump.

"Hello Rupert," she greeted him with a serene, Madonna-like smile.

Rupert stopped in his tracks, his eyes falling to her belly. He flushed noticeably and straightened to his full, imposing height.

"You are looking very well, my dear," Archie said, as he walked forward and greeted her with a bow and a kiss to her outstretched fingers. For good measure, he ran his hand possessively over his growing child.

She heard Rupert's throat gurgle, though she was unsure whether it was with amusement, or embarrassment.

"I've been shopping," Charlotte announced, with the air of someone very important.

"Oh, no," Archie groaned dramatically. "Please tell me there is enough money left to pay the servants."

Charlotte just laughed and sat down.

Archie looked at Rupert with alarm, but Rupert only laughed.

"You're lucky you don't have any sisters," he said.

Rupert had three sisters and more than ten nieces. He was surrounded by women.

"I found a new dressmaker who is making everything I need for the Season. She also recommended a baby shop I'm going to visit tomorrow."

"That sounds great, love," Archie said absently, moving back to his chair. "New dressmaker? I thought you only wanted to go to that French modiste on Bond Street. You've been waiting for three days to see her."

Charlotte flushed but refused to look away from her husband's keen stare.

"That shopkeeper decided I wasn't important enough to serve on priority, so I found one who wants my business."

Archie gave her a startled look, and even Rupert looked uncomfortable as he, too, took his chair.

"Do you mean to tell me you were denied service because of your new status?"

"Not at all. She was still happy to make my clothes, but she didn't want me seen in her presence. So, I refused to go back, and found someone more than happy to have me patronise her shop." Charlotte told them both the honest truth.

"You were denied access because of me," Archie choked out.

Rupert stood up and bowed.

"I think I'll be going, Archie. I'll see you at the christening on Sunday." Rupert gave Charlotte an apologetic smile. She didn't blame him for wanting to leave such a conversation.

"Yes, indeed," Archie recovered enough to say, the look in his eyes showing his mind was far away.

Rupert headed for the door, but as he opened it, he turned back to say something. "We still love you both," he said. With that rather shocking statement, he fled.

Charlotte smiled fondly as the rogue ran for cover.

"He has a heart of gold somewhere under all that swagger. I'm sure of it," Charlotte declared, laughing despite herself.

Archie dropped to his knees in front of her and kissed her tenderly for a moment, before pulling away once again. He sat in the chair closest to her.

"Tell me what happened today. Did they upset you?" Archie asked, holding her hands in a time-old gesture of support.

"I am the daughter of a duchess and a future marchioness, Archibald. No one upsets me," she declared as haughtily as possible.

Her husband knew her too well to believe it. "They did," he said, sitting down in his chair and pulling her down onto his lap.

"Archie, please don't be upset. It's true, I was a little shocked, but it doesn't matter."

"It does!"

Charlotte gave up and just kissed him. Kissed him until they were both panting and desperate.

He made love to her right there, in the study, where it had begun, all those months ago.

Chapter Twenty

After Charlotte's traumatic experience of buying a new gown, Archie decided to find out just how bad the situation was.

He went to his club the next day, dressed in full mourning, but very fashionable clothes. He was lucky enough to find John instantly and sat down with him. The club was quiet, owing to this time being the end of the Season and Archie was grateful. His jumping belly and sweating palms were great indications that he was suddenly feeling not so courageous.

"Archie." John greeted him with an enthusiastic handshake and cleared his throat.

"I saw Charlotte this morning. She is looking wonderful."

Archie blinked. He hadn't realised Charlotte had visited her parents alone. He had been too busy with his bank manager this morning to even ask her about her plans.

"She is," Archie agreed quietly, his eyes darting to a man in the corner of the room who was giving them black looks.

"I'm not sure if I should be sitting with you, John," Archie apologised, beginning to rise.

John grabbed him by the sleeve and unceremoniously hauled him back down.

"Archie, you're not only my best friend, but my brother-in-law as well. If you should be sitting anywhere, it is here." John called for port, and a footman scurried over with two glasses.

Archie picked his up and drank it in one gulp, the burn making him gasp and hiss.

John chuckled and called for more.

"Don't tell me, married life isn't as good as Oliver makes it out to be," John joked, watching Archie as he gulped down more port.

Archie almost choked and put his glass back down with a hurry.

"No, Charlotte's wonderful," Archie answered quietly, twirling his glass between his palms. He did not look up, until the liquid warmth began to help his cold belly.

John cleared his throat meaningfully, and Archie dragged his eyes up to see an old friend of his father's standing in front of them.

"You shouldn't be here, Turner," the man said to Archie, his head held high, a walking stick gripped in one hand.

"I have every right to be here, sir," Archie replied respectfully. He stood and bowed to the older man. He wasn't being shown any manners, but he hadn't forgotten his.

"Your brother was a disgrace." The old man glared at him, obviously eager to get to the crux of the matter.

Archie nodded his head once in agreement. He couldn't help feeling the hypocrisy of the situation. The men in this room were the very worst whore-mongering rogues and yet his brother was a disgrace?

"I'm going to ask the club to bar your admittance." The older man snarled now, his lip quivering in his anger.

Several of the other older men exchanged looks amongst themselves. Some were resolute, ready to back him up, others seemed embarrassed and worried.

"You must do what you must do," Archie declared, comfortable in his ostracism.

John stood up next to him.

"Then you can ask for my membership to be rescinded too. Because the day the future Marquess of Hunting is barred from this club, is the day I have no wish to be a part of this club."

The reminder of who Archie would be in the future, seemed to deflate some of the older man's anger. John's presence took care of the rest.

John threw some money down onto the table and gave Archie a look that said that it was time to leave.

They gathered their coats and left without speaking.

They decided to walk back to their townhouses rather than taking a carriage. Along the way, Archie gathered his courage and spoke to his friend. "Thank you, John, but you don't need to lose your position for me."

John harrumphed and kept walking. He was mumbling under his breath, and Archie couldn't help the slightly hysterical laugh that escaped his throat.

"What's so funny?" John asked, scowling at him as they made their way along the street.

"Nothing, nothing at all. It's just that, after ten years of waiting for the worst to happen, it has. And you have stood by me."

John flushed, his handsome face becoming pink in a way Archie had never seen it.

"Archie, you're not your brother. You have proven that a hundred times over the last ten years."

"But the *ton* doesn't recognise that," Archie pointed out.

"Blast the *ton*," John muttered, walking even faster and kicking at the cobblestones with his polished black boots.

Archie walked along the road next to his brother-in-law and wondered why he wasn't angrier. He should be, after all. He'd lost everything he once valued. The respect of his peers and his place in society.

But the warmth of the sunshine on his face, and John beside him, gave him a greater sense of self-worth than he'd ever had. Something he must ponder for a while.

~

ARCHIE GOT HOME to the message that his wife was feeling ill. He rushed straight to their room to find her not there. On enquiry, he found the countess asleep in her bed. *Her* bed! They hadn't slept apart in almost four months and tonight she had decided they would?

Archie stood at the door that linked their rooms and paused with his hand on the knob. How could he go to her when he had been asked not to do so? Their marriage was strange, in that she had always come to his bed, not he to hers. He knew that all husbands across the English aristocracy had separate bedrooms and only visited their wives when required. It had never been that way for them, and it felt horrible now.

Archie moved back to his lonely bed and climbed, naked, into it. He had slept in this bed alone for more than ten years, and yet tonight it felt as cold and as empty as a Scottish loch. Archie pulled the blankets around him tighter and shivered.

What could he do? Perhaps Charlotte truly wasn't well? And if so, why didn't she tell him so herself, or at least allow him to hold her.

It was true, they had never spent a night in each other's arms without making love, or some variation of intimacy. But that didn't mean he couldn't control himself. Perhaps that was it? Perhaps she was sore, or tired, and was scared to rebuff him in bed? If that were so, he would strive to be a more considerate husband. Perhaps he had worn her out the previous night? He cringed at the memory. Or this morning when he had made love to her again?

He had known that the honeymoon would not last; he had just foolishly believed that she had been as happy as he.

The next morning, Archie arose early and set out for a ride. He rarely rode in London, but he needed to get out into the fresh air today. He rode around the parks and over as many hills as he could find. When the horse was tired, Archie headed home and went straight to his study. He attacked all the estate business he had put off and tried very hard not to think about what he would say to his wife later that day.

~

THAT EVENING, dinner was a stilted affair. Neither of them seemed to know what to say. Charlotte was dumbfounded. The only conversation went along distant, polite lines.

"Are you feeling better today, Charlotte?"

"I am, thank you, Archie," she said and then silence fell again.

Charlotte retired to her bed but sat up waiting for her husband. She was testing him again. She had never slept in her new bed before yesterday and yet Archie didn't seem annoyed by the sudden change.

Snuffing out her candle finally, she burrowed down into her bed with a small sob. Why wouldn't he come to her? She buried her head into her pillow and started crying.

Minutes later, Archie thrust open the door and walked straight into her room. He was carrying a candle and wearing a nightshirt. Charlotte looked up at his entrance and blinked. Archie put the candle down on his side of the bed and put his hand on the covers. He didn't make any move to slide into the bed, just quirked an eyebrow.

Relief and love overflowed within her. "Oh, Archie," she sobbed, holding out her arms for him.

Archie pulled back the covers and climbed in next to her. He sat up against the pillows and pulled Charlotte into his strong arms. She burst into a fresh round of tears and sobbed on his chest. Archie held her whilst she cried and cried, crooning and stroking her hair.

"I'm sorry I didn't come sooner."

"I just want you to love me, nothing else matters." Charlotte burst out into hysterical sobs. All she wanted was her husband's love. Why had she felt the need to test him?

Archie lay back against the pillows and pulled Charlotte to him. She was no longer sobbing, but she still clung to him in desperation.

"I love you, Charlotte. I'm sorry I haven't been here for you."

She shook her head against him, wiping at her dripping nose and eyes. "No, no, please don't be sorry. That's what I didn't want."

Archie sighed and held her tighter. "Just sleep, my love."

Charlotte fell asleep almost instantly, the exhaustion of the previous day's emotional upheaval too much for her. Archie loved her, and that was all that mattered.

THE FOLLOWING Sunday was David's christening. Archie wore half-mourning, and Charlotte chose a beautiful pale blue dress from her new dressmaker. Archie was relieved that their marriage appeared to be back to normal. They had made love all morning and were both in high spirits.

"I cannot believe you are showing your face here."

Charlotte and Archie both turned to find a richly dressed older lady glaring at them.

"We were invited," Archie calmly replied. He didn't even know the woman in front of him. How could he have offended her?

"Then you should have refused. You shouldn't be allowed to enter society after what your brother did."

Archie felt his stomach drop but took strength in the solid warmth of his wife next to him.

"My brother has paid for his crimes, my lady, unlike most men of the *ton*. Don't you agree that death was payment enough?"

"Yes, I do actually, but what about you?" the old woman snapped again.

"Me?" Archie let his eyebrows rise comically high on his forehead.

"Yes, how dare you marry Lady Charlotte? She could have married anyone she wanted, and you chose to drag her into a family that is diseased. You could give it to her, or her child."

The lady eyed Charlotte's waistline critically and smiled smugly.

"And that is not a three-month belly. So, either you married her when she was with child by someone else, or you are as bad as your brother." The old woman, who in her day would have been very handsome, was smiling nastily now.

Archie felt anger, hurt, and embarrassment in equal quantities, and was finding it hard to work out which emotion was strongest. Heat flooded his face and chest making it hard to breathe.

But before he could open his mouth to answer the old battleaxe, he felt Charlotte's hand on his arm, squeezing tightly.

"I married Archie because I love him," she declared hotly, her sincerity ringing out clearly. "His poor brother was unlucky but was not unusual in his habits, as I'm sure you know. Also, I wouldn't be casting stones regarding the size of my belly. Your daughter had a six-month babe, if my memory serves, and I can guarantee you, at least I know who the father of my child is."

Archie choked on a laugh, and he had the unseemly urge to clap. His wife was incredible. Absolutely wonderful.

The old battleaxe began choking on her bitterness, her face turning an ugly shade of purple as she screwed up her face.

Charlotte pulled herself up to her full height and looked down at the old dragon.

"If you will excuse us, we need to find a good place to sit so that we can watch the christening of our friend's child."

Archie would be told many years later that no one there that day remembered anything else that was said. Except for the fact that Lady Charlotte was indeed in love with her husband and would happily fight off anyone who dared speak ill of him. No one else tried.

Archie looked up proudly from his seat as his dearest friend spoke out from the front of the church.

"Thank you for attending the christening of our son, David. The duchess' family have a tradition that they only inform the chosen godparents of their child on the day of the christening."

There was a general murmur of agreement from Sarah's extended family and silence from the rest of the *ton*. It was most unusual.

"We decided to stick with tradition and have not told our friends that we have chosen them."

Oliver smiled hugely, and the collective group held their breaths. It would be a great honour to be named godparent to the heir to the Duke of Lincoln. The *ton* knew Oliver and Sarah had a highly unorthodox marriage, and Archie understood that no one would be entirely surprised they had chosen to adhere to some alternative tradition.

"We would like to invite the godparents to the front of the church. The Earl and Countess of Tother."

Oliver and Sarah both beamed and looked expectantly at their chosen champions for their son.

Archie's heart leapt, and his wife's hand tightened in his. How could they do this? They had just been shunned by the better half of the *ton* and now were given the greatest honour that could be bestowed on two people.

Archie looked down at his beautiful, loyal and loving wife. He smiled. If Charlotte believed in him, and Oliver and Sarah believed in them as a couple, who was he to try to refute that? He stood up, gently pulling his wife up next to him, and together they walked up the aisle.

They moved to the front of the church and thanked the Duke and Duchess of Lincoln, their beautiful friends, Oliver and Sarah. Archie calmly took their firstborn child and heir in his arms and proceeded to renounce Satan and promise to raise David as a loyal Christian.

Archie spent the entire service outside his body looking down. How could he have ever thought he could live a life without his friends and family by his side? How could he have ever imagined that Charlotte couldn't overcome anything that life could throw at her?

He would one day be the Marquess of Hunting. He was wealthy, handsome and healthy. He had a wife who was surpassed by none, and she loved him as much as he loved her. Life couldn't be any sweeter.

Epilogue

"Archie, if you don't get this book off my table..." Charlotte began yelling at him.

She was cranky as she always was when she was almost nine months heavy with child. Her third child in five years, to be precise.

"I'm sorry, Charlotte. I shouldn't have left it there," Archie said quickly, picking up his book on stud farms and tucking it under his arm.

He had only put it down for a moment so that he could pick up William, their four-year-old son, and then he had become distracted.

They already had two sons, William, who was four, and George, who was two. They were both wonderful children, boisterous and full of life. William looked just like him, with intense brown eyes and a beautiful smile. He was quieter than his brother and liked to have his parents read to him.

George was more like his mother in both looks and personality. He had a temper that could bring the house down, and blue eyes that could melt your heart.

Archie knew that Charlotte was hoping for a girl this time, and he couldn't help hoping for the same. He wanted a little girl with Charlotte's face and maybe a little of his personality. Another George in temperament and they were in trouble. Each child already had a nursemaid, but if they got a baby girl with Charlotte's personality, they would be hiring another one.

Charlotte was a wonderful mother, attentive and kind. She loved spending time with the boys and could usually be found reading them stories in the nursery or running around with them outside. However, as she was due to give birth to their third child any day, she was as large as a house, and as cranky as Archie had ever seen her.

"Perhaps I could coax you into having a lie-down?" Archie asked with a suggestive smile. They hadn't made love in weeks, and he knew it would be months until he could touch her again.

Charlotte gave him a startled expression that soon changed into something more serene.

"Yes," she declared, putting out her hand so that he could help her to her feet.

Archie pulled up his wife as gently as he could and then saw a very unusual look on Charlotte's face.

"What's wrong, my love?"

"I need the midwife, Archie," she explained, putting her hand to her belly as the first cramp hit.

"Oh, oh!" Archie exclaimed, towing his wife gently up the stairs before sending for the midwife who was stationed in the village.

Six hours later, Archie was holding his new baby daughter, Lady Sarah

Claire Turner. She had brilliant blue eyes and a mop of black curls. Archie's heart had melted a little when he had met his sons, but the moment he met his daughter, he knew he could never love anyone more.

"She's perfect, Charlotte," he whispered, two tears slipping down his cheeks.

Charlotte sighed and lay back against her pillows.

"As perfect as you are, my love," she whispered before she drifted off to sleep for a hard-earned rest.

THE END

Lizzie's Recalcitrant Earl

Prologue

1805

The week he turned twenty-one years old, the Honourable Rupert Willoughby packed his bags and bade goodbye to his family. Which also meant farewell to the servants and all the trappings of wealth to which he was accustomed.

The festivities thrown for him had been magnificent and the night with his friends, truly excellent. But now that he had finally reached manhood, there was one more thing for Rupert to do and that was to finally move out of his family home and into bachelor lodgings. His time for drinking the heady wine of freedom and sowing his wild oats had finally arrived.

On his way out the door, he was called into the study by his brother, Henry, who had married the wife chosen for him, and who had inherited the Earldom of Sweeting when their father had passed away a few years earlier.

Rupert knocked on the door and waited, impatiently tapping his feet.

"Please enter," Henry called through the thick, wooden door.

He grinned and took a deep breath. He had no idea what this was going to be about, but hoped it wouldn't take long. His life was calling him, and he didn't want to be late.

He pushed open the door and walked into the opulent, yet tastefully decorated room.

"Good evening, my lord," Rupert said, bowing to his brother before sitting down in the chair opposite.

Rupert had always viewed his brother more like a father than a sibling, Henry being fifteen years his senior. They were brothers and yet they hardly knew each other.

"Firstly, I'd like to congratulate you belatedly on your birthday yesterday. I'm sorry I wasn't there for it," Henry apologised, with what appeared to be honest regret.

"No need, Henry. I know it was essential to be with your wife." Rupert waved his hand dismissively. His brother had been at their country estate whilst his wife was in her confinement. Rupert had known that their fifth child was due any day. They already had four daughters.

"I did, but I am back to speak to you because of what has happened," Henry said, in a rather pompous tone. By Rupert's estimation, there was obviously something serious to report.

"I'm sorry, I don't quite understand. Is everything all right? Mary is not unwell?" Rupert asked, hoping nothing untoward had happened to his sister-in-law. The woman had never been particularly warm toward him, but he didn't wish any ill upon her.

"She gave birth to another girl." Henry groaned, his mouth turning down and his nose wrinkling.

Rupert grimaced internally. He knew that his brother needed an heir, but how many more children could they have?

"Oh...well, congratulations," Rupert said, unable to think of anything else to say.

His brother gave him a rather dry look and placed his hands on the desk in front of him.

"I have no wish to continue to produce daughters. The doctors have told me that more than likely, Mary can only bear female children." His brother hesitated for a moment, then spoke again. "I have a son, after all," he announced, with a victorious smile.

Rupert frowned. He'd known his brother had a long-term mistress, but he hadn't realised that she had borne him a son. Apparently, his brother took this to mean that the continual arrival of daughters couldn't be his fault, as he had sired a son with another woman. Rupert saw the holes in this logic but kept his mouth tightly shut.

"I didn't realise you'd had a child with someone else," Rupert said instead, temporarily blinded to the primary issue his brother was trying to raise.

Again, that smile, a sickening grimace of teeth and lips.

"Yes, with another on the way."

Rupert was struck with a rather frightening realisation. His brother was in love with his mistress.

"But, surely, you will keep trying for an heir with your wife?" he asked quietly, the reality of what his brother was trying to convey slowly sinking into his brain and his heart beginning to pound against his ribs.

"No, I won't be. *You* are my heir."

Rupert's heart sank and his breath caught in his throat. *No, I don't want this.*

"But Henry..." he protested, almost gasping for air as panic began to set in.

"It is settled," Henry announced with finality, holding his hand up to ward off any further rebuttal from Rupert.

"I will increase your allowance as befits your new station," his brother added. "You will have a suitable wife chosen for you in the near future, and she will be the one to produce our heir. It is quite simple. I had thought you would be happy about this."

Rupert could see his life slipping away before it had even begun. He had never wanted this responsibility. He hadn't even decided if he wanted to marry at all.

"But..." Rupert vainly tried to protest once more, a cold sweat breaking out on his brow.

"It is decided." Henry stared him down, his almost black eyes boring into Rupert's.

A familiar stirring in his blood alerted Rupert to a change in his body that he often ignored. He knew he had a temper. By physically abusing his body on a daily basis, he kept it in check with lots of riding, boxing, and rowing. But it was always there, simmering away underneath. His grandfather had the same disposition. He had heard the older servants speak of it. No one except his friends had ever seen the fire unleashed, though. They'd told him bluntly that it wasn't an occurrence they ever wished to see repeated.

Rupert stood up and used what size he had to try and intimidate his brother. He was six feet four inches tall, well over his brother's five feet, eleven inches. He was still lean, but he was developing strength and his shoulders were already considerably wider than Henry's.

"No!" Rupert ground out through clenched teeth, his fingers flexing and extending in shaking movements. "I will not have you choose me a wife to act as your broodmare."

"You will do as you're ordered," his brother shouted, his round face turning a mottled red.

"I will not. If you choose a wife for me who cannot bear sons or any children at all, what will happen to our name?" Rupert argued.

They both knew that a female could inherit the title, in rare circumstances, but a male heir was preferred by all involved.

"You must marry, and soon," his brother said, insistently.

"I will not. I haven't even moved out yet." Rupert almost shouted, clearing his throat in embarrassment as his voice almost broke.

"Then I will cut you off," Henry announced, with a flick of his hand. This was his one and only advantage. He held the power to either make Rupert's life easy and pleasant, or tough indeed.

Rupert frowned at his brother, feeling flames of anger licking their way along his spine.

He held his fists by his side, taking a long, deep breath before he spoke. "Do that, and I'll join the army and disappear. You will never have control over me again, and your precious title can go to the butler for all I care."

He turned toward the door, ready to do exactly what he'd said he would and damn the consequences. He would not be controlled like this.

"Wait," Henry called out, a note of desperation in his voice.

Rupert stopped just before he reached the door, but refused to go back to his brother's desk. Instead, he simply turned and stared at Henry, pouring every ounce of anger into his glare.

"Thirty. Marry by thirty, and I'll make sure you never want for anything," his brother bargained, evidently unwilling to lose his only blood-linked male heir.

Rupert clenched his teeth and used all of his willpower to push back his anger. Slowly, it retreated, like a black cloud into the distance. At last, he could see clearly again.

His brother leaned forward on his desk, no longer in a position of power. He was begging.

Rupert forced his brain to think. Thirty seemed a very long way off. He was barely one and twenty. Nine years he had. Nine years to sow his wild oats. Nine years to drink enough liquor to kill a sailor. He had nine years of sweet freedom before he finally sold his soul to his brother for the sake of money.

After a few moments, he nodded. "Done."

The decision was final.

Chapter One

London 1813

Rupert Willoughby was strikingly handsome. Or so he'd been told, for as long as he could remember. The combination of truly blue eyes and black hair had enticed many a beauty into his bed.

Thanks to his brother's wealth and generosity, he had an excellent allowance. Rupert's best friend, the former Lord Archibald Turner, now the Earl of Tother, an original member of their group, "the spares," was a dab hand at the Stock Exchange. Archie often advised Rupert about how to invest his money and thus, he was set for the future. Rupert would never have to seek employment as so many second sons had to do.

He secretly wanted a wife such as his friends Archie, and Oliver, Duke of Lincoln, had found. Sarah, Duchess of Lincoln, and Charlotte, Countess of Tother, were both ladies who could hold an intelligent conversation and also manage a household. Both were beautiful, and much more than merely decorative. Rupert wasn't sure if he would ever find such a woman for himself and certainly not one who could hold his interest in the bedchamber. It would probably be better to find a 'suitable" wife and continue to live as he already did. As long as he produced the required heir, his responsibilities to his brother and the family would be met.

At the Duke and Duchess of Lincoln's annual ball, Rupert eyed the beauty talking to the Countess of Tother. The former Lady Charlotte Dunford looked very well, beautiful, in fact. She was still quite blissfully happy with her marriage to Archie, and if Rupert wasn't mistaken, could very well have been *enceinte* again. Unlike many of the women of the *ton* who all but hid throughout their pregnancies, Charlotte glowed with good health and happily stood in the centre of a crowded ballroom. She had no qualms showing everyone how happy she was to be bearing another child for her husband. Rupert shook his head against the unfamiliar notion. It was confounding.

Next to her, however, was a young lady whom Rupert had never seen before. She had hair as blonde as Sarah's. She had tan skin in comparison to Charlotte's paleness, but the colour suited her hair. He couldn't see her eyes very well from where he was standing, but it appeared to him that they looked quite dark. She was striking. She had high cheekbones, classic features, and an amazing smile that affected him even from where he was standing, right across the room. Rarely had Rupert seen a more beautiful woman.

She was short in stature and had high, firm breasts, swelling above her low neckline. The blue of her dress and her wedding ring proclaimed her married. Or widowed, perhaps. Either way, she was the perfect rendezvous he needed. He was a little bored with his latest mistress.

Rupert adjusted his coat with a quick tug and straightened to his full height. Feeling confident, he walked over to the two ladies.

"May I beg you for an introduction to your friend, my dear Charlotte?"

Charlotte smiled tightly, knowing his habits well. She turned to include him in their circle, which surprised him a little, but his friend's sister did have perfect manners.

"Of course, Rupert. Mrs. Elizabeth Symmons, may I introduce a friend of ours, the Honourable Rupert Willoughby, the younger brother of the Earl of Sweeting."

Rupert heard the warning in the introduction and smirked inwardly. Charlotte was fiercely protectively of those she loved. It was one of the things he liked most about her.

The beautiful blonde curtseyed prettily and gave him a sunny, open smile. Rupert bowed in return, surprised by the artlessness of her expression.

"May I have the pleasure of the next dance, my lady?" he asked, giving her his most charming smile.

Elizabeth smiled back, glancing quickly at Charlotte for permission to leave her alone, which Rupert respected. When Charlotte smiled back in return, the beautiful woman turned to him.

"Of course. Thank you, sir," she replied confidently, placing her small hand in his.

She was petite, yet Rupert felt the firmness of her grip and observed the way she held herself. This would not be a woman over whom one could easily walk, he realised.

"You are looking charming this evening, Mrs. Symmons," Rupert told her, as they swept onto the dance floor.

Elizabeth laughed, her bright eyes sparkling with gaiety.

"Why, thank you, sir. And indeed, you are looking very handsome."

Rupert grinned, surprised by her words. He didn't believe he had ever had a compliment returned before. Most women only fluttered their fans and gave him the eyes. The eyes told him how flattered they were that he had given them his attention. The eyes also indicated to him just how quickly they would fall into his bed. Mrs. Elizabeth Symmons wasn't giving him the eyes, nor was she flirting with him. How strange. She was difficult to read.

"How are you enjoying the evening?" Rupert asked politely, maneuvering her expertly around the many couples on the dance floor. He didn't dance often, but he considered it part of his seduction routine and therefore made sure that he was rather good at it.

"Oh, I am enjoying it very much. I have recently come out of mourning and have never felt so decadent for wearing a colour before." Elizabeth looked down for a moment on her beautiful blue evening gown.

Rupert smiled inwardly. A widow, was she? That was perfect. Affairs were much less stressful when there wasn't a spouse to take into consideration all the time. Would Elizabeth Symmons like just a night or two in his arms? Or would she perhaps want something more permanent? A longer time frame would work out quite nicely, Rupert thought, his mind jumping ahead with plans for her seduction.

"You must be lonely," Rupert murmured, giving her a look that was meant to be both respectful, yet meaningful to those who knew how to interpret it.

He swept his eyes subtly down to her neckline, where there was a swelling of flesh. He shifted his stance slightly, as his cock thickened in his breeches. He was surprised, but also delighted. He hadn't experienced such a strong attraction to a woman in a very long time. His body was alive, all but screaming out to lay her down on the nearest flat surface and have his wicked way with her.

His body and mind declared war. It was his primitive self, versus the cultured *ton* gentleman. If he were truly honest with himself, he had been bored for quite some time. Nothing was ever new or exciting anymore, but he had a feeling that this woman would be different.

"Indeed I am, my lord."

~

LIZZIE LOOKED up at Rupert's handsome face, seeing him with fresh eyes. Was this gentleman in the market for a wife? He looked a few years older than her, but that was never a good indication of the intention to settle down. A man could be five and twenty, or five and forty and still be an eligible match. Unlike a woman, who had certain limitations, this handsome man in front of her did not. Lizzie inhaled discreetly and noted that he didn't smell of too much alcohol. His clothes were tailored rather beautifully. He either had independent means, or he was searching for an heiress and had spent every penny on looking delicious. Lizzie couldn't tell which. She would have to ask Charlotte for more information about this gentleman. But Lizzie could tell that the man in front of her was confident, almost arrogant, in his countenance.

She looked up again and caught her breath when Rupert met her gaze. Something new and unusual stirred in her belly whenever she looked into his rather remarkable black eyes. The feeling wasn't altogether pleasant, but at the same time, it was exciting. He was the first gentleman to spark any interest in her since the death of her husband.

"Perhaps you would permit me to escort you home tonight?" Rupert suggested, his eyes now taking on a strange sort of leer. He couldn't mean what she thought, surely?

"I don't think so." She frowned. He couldn't be serious, could he? Her mind was racing. Was he suggesting that she take him home and... bed him?

Something in his gaze hinted that was exactly what he wanted.

Any ideas she had of him as a potential husband ended right there. She mentally catalogued him as a rake and by definition, not interested in marriage. She wiped the smile from her face and straightened. She was almost a foot shorter than he was, but anger began to build in her belly, lending her an extra inch or so of height in her straightened spine.

"I can be very persuasive, ma'am," Rupert whispered, his voice laced with honey and giving her a grin which, she was sure, had won many a woman before her.

She snorted, glaring up at the man she had momentarily considered as a prospective husband and now viewed as a big oaf.

"You can be as persuasive as you like, sir, but I am not in the least interested in a dalliance."

"I can assure you, I will make it a pleasurable interlude." Rupert drew Lizzie away from the main body of dancers so that they were on the edge of the dance floor. At least he had pitched his voice low.

Again, he flashed that dazzling smile and Lizzie frowned. Rupert Willoughby hadn't been denied before, that was plain to see. His thumb gently stroked her hand and that strange flutter moved low in her belly, again. It was time to nip this in the bud.

"I want a husband, sir, and children, not an interlude, however pleasurable. Can you give me what I want?" Lizzie batted her eyelashes and injected honey into her own tone. She knew the last thing this charming rakehell of a gentleman would want was to be shackled forever to one woman. The best way of making him stay away from her was to be honest about what she wanted from this year's London season.

Rupert's eyes widened, and as they continued their dance, he tripped and stumbled a little. Lizzie gripped his hand and waited for him to regain his composure, trying not to laugh.

"Uh, no," Rupert answered, his calm facade wavering completely now.

Lizzie watched the play of strange emotions run across Rupert's face and wanted to smooth his furrowed brow with her fingers. This thought was shocking enough to pull her out of her daze, and she snapped out the first thing that came into her mind.

"Then, you will never get me into your bed. I suggest that you take home the woman in green who has been eyeing you for the past hour, and leave me alone."

Damn! She hadn't meant to be so obvious in her jealousy. She dropped her hands from Rupert's, turned and stormed away.

∼

RUPERT WATCHED HER GO, feeling something akin to complete shock. He had never been denied before and had never had to fight for something he wanted, as friends of his had had to do. Ladies clamoured for his company in bed. He had never had to try too hard before. Rupert wanted them, and they gave him everything they had. It had always been very simple.

Rupert discreetly looked in the direction Lizzie had indicated. There was, indeed, a beautiful woman in a green gown giving him looks that could only be described as desirous. That was the norm.

He would get an introduction to her, take her for a walk or a dance, and within a few moments, she would be in a carriage on her way home to meet him. If, of course, she hadn't decided that the study would be easier.

He took another look.

The woman in green seemed like a "can't wait until we get home, let's go to the study" type lady. Rupert felt no urge to go up and speak to her, no call to tup her, nothing. It was like his libido had departed when the woman with whom he had been dancing did. Most unusual.

He turned and noticed Mrs. Elizabeth Symmons chatting again with Charlotte. Rupert watched as Charlotte threw back her head and even heard her laugh from where he was standing. He couldn't stop the flush that spread across his cheeks. Were they laughing at him?

Turning on his heel, he headed straight to the card room to drown his disappointment in a brandy.

Chapter Two

Lizzie watched Rupert walk toward the card room and couldn't suppress her triumphant grin. Charlotte, Countess of Tother, had laughed loud enough to be heard clear across the ballroom. That would teach him not to be such a cad. Despicable!

"I can't believe he had the gall to proposition me so," Lizzie exclaimed to her friend, huffing in exasperation. Why would he have propositioned her? Did she appear to be a lady who would be easily enticed by a handsome face?

Charlotte giggled again, a milder version of her previous laugh, but still, a show of genuine amusement.

"What I can't believe is that someone has turned him down. That would have to be a first for Rupert." Charlotte chuckled again, loudly, fluttering her fan to try and cover some of the noise.

"What do you mean? Why would a woman indulge in that sort of activity outside of marriage? It's not as though it's even pleasant." Lizzie shook her head.

She looked up and noticed Charlotte blushing crimson. The unshakeable countess never blushed, so Lizzie was quite confident she must have said something terribly wrong and obviously inappropriate. Oh, she could be so common sometimes!

"Oh, dearest Lady Charlotte, please forgive me for saying such a thing in your company. You are obviously not accustomed to such a common expression." Lizzie apologised profusely. Having spent a year as an army wife, such speech was now commonplace to her. How could she have forgotten where and with whom she was conversing?

The countess burst out laughing afresh, even louder than she had when Lizzie told her what Rupert had wanted from her. Now it was Lizzie's turn to heat with embarrassment and confusion. Charlotte suddenly seemed to notice the curious looks they were receiving, thanks to her rather unladylike outbursts.

"Shall we stroll along the patio?" Charlotte suggested invitingly, linking her arm with the other woman's and turning them both toward the doors before Lizzie could even reply.

"Of course," Lizzie murmured, happy for an opportunity to go out into the fresh air. She had forgotten just how stuffy London ballrooms could be. She missed the countryside immensely. As they stepped onto the balcony, Charlotte led Lizzie to an unoccupied corner and turned her around, so they were face to face.

"I'm sorry Lizzie, I shouldn't have laughed. You didn't shock me at all with your words," Charlotte explained, whispering in a conspiratorial sort of way.

"Really? Then why did you blush so brightly?" Lizzie asked, confused now.

Charlotte flushed rather prettily again, and Lizzie wanted to bite her tongue. Why was she saying everything that came into her head? When would she learn to control her words?

"Because you said that there was no pleasure in the bedchamber," Charlotte explained, with a rather guilty smile.

Lizzie eyed her friend critically. Surely Charlotte wasn't suggesting what Lizzie thought she was? "Well, there wasn't for me...not that it was unpleasant all of the time," she hastened to add, feeling that she was being disrespectful toward her late husband with her words. He had tried to be gentle with her and had never deliberately hurt her, unlike some of the husbands in the stories she had heard. The marriage bed had never been something to which she'd looked forward, but, in fairness, she'd never dreaded it either.

Charlotte seemed to be battling with what to say next. She wasn't speaking, and yet her eyes were telling Lizzie just how much she disagreed with Lizzie's opinion on matters of the bedchamber.

"You enjoy it?" Lizzie squeaked, not sure if she could believe what she was reading in Charlotte's face. How was it possible?

"Yes, I do," Charlotte admitted, apparently battling another urge to laugh. The corners of her mouth kept lifting up, as though they had a mind of their own.

"Oh." Lizzie sighed. She had heard that some women did. Thinking back, there had been moments with her husband that had been pleasant. He had kissed her occasionally, or touched her in ways that had given her pleasure. It was just the bedding that had been uncomfortable. Perhaps there were men who could make that part pleasurable too? It seemed unlikely, but she supposed it was possible.

"Really?" Lizzie asked again, her eyes opening wide. She searched Charlotte's face for any sign that she wasn't serious.

This time Charlotte lost the control over her laughter and giggled openly.

"Archie is a little different from most men and my marriage is a love match. I think that helps," Charlotte explained, with a smile that showed how much she was hiding in that statement.

Lizzie pondered this. Her marriage had been a love match too. Well, perhaps not exactly, but it hadn't been about dowries and connections. Perhaps if there were more affection in her next marriage, there would be more pleasure?

Either way, she wasn't risking becoming pregnant or ruining her reputation for the sake of finding out from the Honourable Rupert Willoughby.

"Perhaps my next husband will make it more pleasurable. But all I want is a home and children," Lizzie announced, unfazed by this turn of events.

In her experience, her husband would come to her bed three or four times a month, and leave after about ten minutes. It would be a small price to pay for a child if she managed to conceive in her next marriage.

Charlotte simply nodded, but Lizzie could tell she wanted to say more.

"Well, if you ever find that you need to talk to someone about it, let me know," she offered with a kind smile.

Lizzie thought that very unlikely but thanked her all the same.

She was twenty-five years old and had been born late in life to her parents, who had loved each other very much. Both parents came from good families. Her father was the son of an earl, and her mother was the daughter of the younger brother of a duke. Her father had been an academic and her mother, after marriage, had discovered that she had a talent for languages.

Lizzie had never wanted for anything. She had made a good match at twenty-three with the second son of a viscount who had a commission in the army. He had been a kind husband, but he drank a little too often and had sometimes gambled too much. Lizzie had some income from her parents, and she had often had to resort to using her money to pay for essentials when her husband had been too frivolous. Lizzie didn't mind too much about that. She didn't need fancy gowns and trips away. But after less than twelve months, her husband had died from a fever. Lizzie had been left a childless widow at the age of twenty-four.

Now, she was back in London. She had been given a small townhouse by her mother, who believed that a lady should always be independent, if possible. Lizzie also had a small income from both her husband's family as well as her own. She had no need to marry a man with deep pockets, yet she didn't want a fortune hunter who would marry her for her money, either. Lizzie hadn't told anyone of her situation, and she hoped it wouldn't become necessary to do so. She wanted a good husband who wanted to look after her, not one whom she would have to look after instead.

Lizzie knew exactly what she wanted in a husband. She wanted a man who preferred the country to town and didn't gamble or drink to excess. A man who wanted children and didn't wish to have them banished to the nursery the moment they were born. She wanted a large family after growing up as an only child, and she wanted a father for her children such as she had once had. A man who was interested in her and their children the way her father had been interested in her and her mother.

Thanks to her loving and attentive parents, Lizzie had been brought up in good society and had never been submitted to the neglect and abuse that many other children had been–or suffered. She also wanted a man who would be faithful, however unusual that seemed to be in a *ton* marriage. She was hopeful she would manage to find such a match if she tried.

Being a widow meant that she had fewer rules to contend with than the virgins flitting around the ballrooms. That didn't mean, in any way, that she wanted to sample the men before choosing one, but it just meant that she could go for walks and have private talks without being forced to marry, as she would have, had she been an unmarried lady.

She had spoken the truth to Charlotte. Lizzie didn't enjoy the bedding part of marriage, but she understood that it was necessary for procreation. And it wasn't horrible, just a little uncomfortable. She had to admit that part of her had enjoyed the comfort and pleasure her husband had taken in her body. Regardless, no matter how she felt about it, she was determined to marry again. Lizzie wanted nothing except to have a comfortable life with a husband and children by her side. No rake, no matter how handsome, was going to tempt her to change her mind.

Chapter Three

Rupert visited Archie and Charlotte, the Earl and Countess of Tother, the next day. As Archie was with his solicitor, so the butler informed, Rupert was shown into the sitting room where Charlotte sat embroidering as he entered. She placed her needlework aside as soon as she saw him and smiled from her comfortable place on the chaise.

Rupert had often found it amusing to tease Charlotte, once she was married to his friend. She knew him well enough to know that he mostly bedded bored, married ladies. So, he played on that with her, touching her arm or shoulder, just to see her reaction. He would never betray Archie in such a way, of course, but Rupert still liked to tease. Charlotte always blushed furiously and swatted him away. She never looked scared or he wouldn't have continued, she just looked wholly uninterested in what he was suggesting.

He admired her loyalty.

However, Charlotte was pregnant again and that meant no teasing. Rupert had never bedded a woman who was *enceinte* and never intended to do so. Once his future wife had conceived, he could see himself staying out of her chamber for the foreseeable future. There were always plenty of available women for him. He needn't bother his wife.

Looking at the healthy glow of Charlotte's cheeks, though, Rupert knew that Archie didn't feel the same way.

"How does it feel to find a woman who doesn't want you?" Charlotte asked with a cheeky grin and a hand straying to her softly rounded belly.

Rupert's eyes locked onto her hand. He couldn't drag his gaze away from the picture of Charlotte gently caressing herself. The thought made him blush, despite his conscious effort not to respond in any obvious way. Rupert knew he should be listening to the words Charlotte was saying, but he couldn't ignore what she was doing.

Archie was lucky to have such a sensual wife.

Charlotte stood up with a smug grin plastered on her face and advanced on Rupert.

"Would you like to feel the baby, Rupert?" Charlotte asked, moving closer to where he was sitting and reaching out to grab hold of one of his hands.

"No, thank you." Rupert almost shouted, moving away from her as fast as he could. He was shocked and terrified that she would suggest such a thing. A lady was meant to disguise herself when she was with child, not call attention to it. How dare she ask him to *touch* it?

"The baby has just started to move. It is really quite amazing," she smiled as she backed him into a corner of the sitting room. Charlotte's dress swished softly as she moved and Rupert realised he had never heard such a scary noise before. His heart was pounding wildly behind his black vest. She was getting closer and he was trapped.

"No, Charlotte, please." Rupert was all but yelling now, panic setting in as his shoulders hit a wall. How had he backed himself into a corner?

Charlotte reached out to him and grabbed both of his hands. Her own hands were soft and warm to the touch and Rupert instinctively relaxed. Her touch was oddly reassuring and he forgot to fight her.

Charlotte brought his resisting hands up, and because he wouldn't allow her to bring them closer to her belly, she brought her belly to him. It was shocking to Rupert that he almost had her stomach and breasts touching his jacket, because she was only scant inches from that feat. He had never been so close to a woman he wasn't in the act of seducing.

Rupert was trapped, by both his curiosity and by this woman whom he had known for fifteen years. It wasn't proper. She was married to one of his friends and yet there was some sort of perverse desire to know what it felt like to hold a child still growing in its mother's womb.

Without any further preparation, his hands were on either side of her round, hard abdomen. Rupert sucked in a lungful of air and tried to drag his eyes away from the incredible image of his hands cupping Charlotte's growing babe. His hands instinctively moulded to the shape and he felt the warmth of her through her dress. There was a small flutter of movement and then a strong push against Rupert's right hand. At that exact moment, something inside Rupert shifted irrevocably and his heart melted a little.

That strange pull that he had been feeling ever since his friends had married women they loved seemed to increase in strength. Fear made Rupert's breath whistle through his throat. How was he going to survive such a situation?

"I see you finally got your hands on my wife," Archie's drawl came from the direction of the door.

Rupert pulled his hands away so quickly he couldn't have looked more guilty. He tried to take a step back and away from the beautiful woman who he had been touching and realised he was already pressed up against the wall.

"I'm sorry, Archie, I didn't mean to..." Rupert hurried to apologise, his cheeks flushing with an intense heat.

Archie put out his hand and beckoned his cheeky wife, who promptly returned to his side with a satisfied smile on her face.

"Have you been harassing my friend, Charlotte?" Archie asked his wife with a teasing grin as he wrapped an arm around her swollen waistline.

Charlotte rubbed her belly again as she leaned into his embrace.

"Not at all, my lord. I thought I would introduce Rupert to the next member of our family. After all, he would make an excellent godparent."

Rupert exhaled sharply. Had he been kicked in the chest?

He had never been asked to be a godparent to any of his sister's children, nor even one of his brother's five daughters. They had always expressed their belief that he was too irresponsible. It had hurt every time they had chosen others, although he never said so.

Rupert swallowed against the rather embarrassing urge to shed tears of emotion and noticed Archie watching him with those keen, hawk eyes that never missed anything.

"You're supposed to ask Rupert if he would like to be our next child's godfather, not just announce your intent, Charlotte." Archie chided good-naturedly, directing his wife back to a chair.

Charlotte dropped into the armchair with more grace than a woman of her size should be able to muster. Raised by a formidable duchess, Charlotte was a lady in every sense of the word—her liking of her husband's marriage bed notwithstanding.

"Why? We weren't asked to be David's godparents. It was just announced at the christening," she answered, giving her husband a playful swat with her hand.

They both turned and looked at Rupert expectantly. Was he meant to act as though it had been a request?

"I would be honoured," Rupert answered gruffly. Unable to say anything else, he bowed in thanks. How could he be getting so emotional over such a thing? He really was changing. It was a sobering thought and he cringed.

"See?" Charlotte smiled happily at her husband and thanked the maid who had brought in tea, cakes and whiskey.

Rupert saw the alcohol and knew it had been brought in on a tea tray for him. Archie hardly ever drank hard spirits, and never this early in the day. Obviously, the butler knew him well. The thought saddened him a little. When had he become predictable? Boring, even?

"Whiskey or tea?" Charlotte asked him politely, already reaching for the whiskey bottle.

"Tea please," Rupert responded before he could stop himself.

After Charlotte's earlier assault on his person he really needed a whiskey, but was sick of being the man everyone expected him to be.

Charlotte's eyebrows shot up, but she didn't say anything except to ask, "How do you take it?" . She poured the tea into three cups.

"Milk and two sugars please," he told her with confidence. When was the last time he had actually drunk tea? He couldn't remember, but decided to brazen it out and sat down gratefully into a chair opposite her. Archie sat also, in the chair closest to his wife. He reached for a cake and absently touched Charlotte on the back of the neck.

Rupert watched Charlotte lean into the caress like a flower facing the sun. It only took that one small gesture and Rupert had to look away from his friends. He had never wanted Charlotte; never thought of her that way. But sometimes Rupert wished he could find what his friends had found. A woman who had the qualities of both a wife and a mistress. Someone who would keep his home running, make him laugh, attend to his children, join him in social outings *and* happily join him in his bed. Charlotte was pregnant for the second time in twelve months and Sarah had just given birth to her second son in less than two years. There was much bedding going on and his friend's wives obviously enjoyed it. Sarah had even said as much the year before. Rupert coughed at the memory.

"Have you seen Sarah and Oliver's new son yet?" Charlotte asked him as she bit into one of the cakes on the tray.

Rupert looked up from his beverage. Sometimes he wondered if Charlotte was a mind reader. How could she have known he had been thinking about such things?

"Yes, last week. He looks just like Oliver," Rupert said, to no one in particular. He had been surprised when he had received a summons to meet the new Lincoln baby. He had never seen a baby who was only a few weeks old before.

Sarah, however, being a vicar's daughter, had been anxious to have the baby christened at the earliest opportunity, and this time it had been a small, family affair.

Even his nieces had been kept away from everyone until they were several months old. It had been amazing. The infant had been rather cross looking, red and wrinkled, but miraculous in its perfection as a tiny human being. Rupert would never say this out loud, but the experience had actually made him yearn for a son himself.

Charlotte chuckled loudly.

"Well, who else would he look like?" she asked, smiling as though it would be unusual for a cuckoo to be born into a nest of the *ton*. Hah!

Rupert stared at Charlotte a moment longer and could barely believe this was the same woman who had once proclaimed she would never marry because a husband would have access to her body. Rupert marvelled at how incredible it was that things could change when someone met the right person.

"True. His wife is Sarah, after all," said Rupert. His implication was that any other lady of the *ton* might have been having an affair, having provided her husband with an heir, but certainly not Sarah, with her impeccable reputation for loyalty. Rupert knew it in his bones.

Charlotte and Archie gave each other a puzzled look.

"No witty rejoinder about the average married lady of the *ton*?" Archie asked, giving him a quizzical look.

Rupert shook his head. What could he say? How could he joke about arranged marriages and faithless women when Sarah and Charlotte were now his examples and the wives of his closest friends? It would dishonour all of them, not to mention the fact that he didn't lie well.

"That's only because of Lizzie," Charlotte scoffed, giving her husband a knowing look. "Rupert finally found a widow who didn't jump directly into bed with him at the first opportunity."

Rupert gripped the tiny teacup tightly, setting it down after a moment lest he break it. It was Charlotte's intention to get a rise out of him of course, but he still fought the anger, unwilling to let her win.

"I haven't given up on that widow. She just needs to get to know me better," Rupert declared, with all the arrogance he possessed. And considering his appearance and breeding, that conceit was considerable. So, it was quite a blow to his pride when Archie and Charlotte both laughed.

"Well, you have charmed more women that I can count, Rupert. I'm sure it won't be that difficult," Archie said quietly, taking a sip of his tea.

Rupert smiled indulgently, Archie had heard about his conquests so frequently that when it came to his wedding night, the virginal Archie had come to him for advice. Rupert had never admitted it, but he had taken that fact as a huge compliment.

"You both are so wrong. If you think Lizzie is just like every other bored matron, then you are in for a surprise." Charlotte smiled smugly and bit into a sugary shortbread.

"How is she so different?" Rupert asked, succumbing to the delicious looking sweets in front of him. Biting into an apple cake, he almost groaned in pleasure. He really needed to invest in a better chef at his own home.

Elizabeth Symmons may have said no to him once, but how long could that last? For how long could she hold off? He had never really pursued a woman before, but it couldn't be very different from a normal conquest. He would just savour it more when he finally won her.

"You mean, apart from the fact that she is present during the Season this year for the sole purpose of remarriage?"

"Well, that doesn't mean she can't dally with me," Rupert argued, setting his jaw.

What would be the problem with that? It had happened to Rupert before. He would bed a widow who would try to trap him into marriage, only to find him immovable on the subject. The widow would then move on and marry the next suitable gentleman soon after and he, too, would be onto the next available lady. That was the best thing about bedding widows and married women. He couldn't be forced to marry any of them.

"Why would she waste her time?" Charlotte asked him with a straight face. Well, as straight a face as Charlotte could pull, considering that her eyes were laughing. She never could hide her feelings very well and Rupert frowned at what she wasn't saying.

"Charlotte, coming from you, isn't that a bit hypocritical?" He was fed up with being fodder for this couple's amusement. If there was one thing he deplored, it was hypocrisy and here was a woman who had married because she was pregnant!

"What do you mean by that?" Charlotte asked, flushing with discomfort at the obvious implication.

Rupert, seeing the danger, ignored Archie's angry glare and answered regardless.

"I mean that if a lady like you can indulge before marriage, why wouldn't your Lizzie?"

Charlotte jumped to her feet and Archie followed just as quickly, placing his hand in the small of her back to steady her. Rupert followed suit, his anger still rising. Archie put his other hand out to calm her, but she shook it off.

"The difference is love, Rupert, which you wouldn't understand. I have loved Archie for a long time and our actions were because of that fact. Not for any other reason. Until you learn about love, you will never have the privilege of knowing a woman like Elizabeth Symmons!"

Charlotte turned on her heel and walked straight out of the room.

A moment of silence went by and then he heard his friend's heavy sigh.

"You shouldn't have said that, Rupert."

Archie hadn't moved since Charlotte had left the room, but Rupert could see how hard he was fighting to remain still.

"I should go," Rupert announced, feeling foolish. Why did he let his temper get the better of him? Charlotte had only been joking. Did it really bother him *that* much that he had missed out on a frolic with her friend? *Surely not?*

"You will not. You just insulted my wife, who is in a delicate condition, and for whom I know you care a great deal. Now you and I will have a talk and I want you to tell me what the hell is going on."

Rupert regarded his stoic and gentle friend in astonishment. He had never heard Archie use such language before.

"Please accept my apologies. I am very sorry indeed for speaking indiscreetly to Lady Charlotte ...um...the countess." Rupert spoke stiffly. Unaccustomed as he was to apologising, this pricked his pride considerably.

"So, you should be," Archie retorted, his arms now calmly tucked behind his back. Rupert wasn't fooled for a moment. There was a fire still blazing in Archie's eyes.

His friend continued to look at him expectantly and Rupert sighed. What could he say? That he was jealous of his friend's marriage? Never! He would rather be thrown out of a carriage at high speed than admit that.

"I simply let my temper get the better of me, Archie. The truth is, I find her teasing goes slightly too far at times. But I accept that I shouldn't have said anything."

"You're not telling me the truth, Rupert."

He sighed loudly. Damned if he'd tell Archie the truth. A thought came to him and his mood lightened.

"I'm bored with my latest mistress and I'm a bit frustrated. I'm not accustomed to abstinence, old friend." Rupert grinned devilishly at Archie, who up until a couple of years ago, had been a virgin.

Archie just stared at him with his cold, assessing, brown eyes and said nothing. Rupert swallowed uncomfortably, wondering what his friend could see. Was his loneliness so obvious?

"Did you get my letter about the latest investment that I think you should place money in?" Archie asked, changing the subject for reasons unknown.

Rupert sighed inwardly, grateful that his friend had obviously chosen to show mercy.

Rupert stayed for another half hour, talking to Archie about his latest tips and trading advice, before making his excuses and leaving. Archie had even recommended a new horse breeder with foals for sale from a bloodline that Rupert had been wanting to buy into for years. However, none of this mundane talk distracted Rupert completely from his confusion. That night, a bottle of whiskey did. At least for a few hours.

Chapter Four

Lizzie missed the countryside. It was her home, the place she was happiest and most comfortable. London suffocated her. She had an urgent need to get out into the fresh air, so she put on her prettiest walking dress, picked up her matching parasol and strode down the front steps of her house, thanking the lord that, as a widow, she did not need to wait for an escort.

It was a short walk to the nearby park and she desperately needed to see something other than cobblestone roads, the inside of a carriage or yet another ballroom.

Ten minutes later she was strolling beneath beautiful oak trees, lost in her own little world. She vaguely sensed someone behind her and moved to the left of the path, so the other party could pass if they wanted to do so. Lizzie was feeling peaceful and didn't bother to look and see who was following so closely behind.

"Mrs. Symmons?" Lizzie was astonished to hear Rupert's voice. She whirled and there he was in front of her. He greeted her with a bow.

Lizzie stared around, unable to decide exactly what to do. Random thoughts whirled through her head.

Where did he come from?

He's alone. I am alone.

Has he planned this, somehow?

He can't really be here for me, can he?

"The Honourable Mr. Willoughby. Good day," she returned, finally curtseying.

"Please, call me Rupert." he invited her, seemingly out of breath. Had he rushed to catch her up? "I really don't like my last name," he added with a charming smile.

"Oh, I couldn't possibly," Lizzie exclaimed, surprised by his forwardness.

She had never had a gentleman pursue her with such dishonourable intentions before. It was quite disconcerting how effective he was at the task. Lizzie's heart beat twice as quickly as it should have and her body tightened in all sorts of unusual places.

She began to walk along the path again, faster than before. Rupert trailed at her heels.

"Why ever not? Charlotte does," he pointed out amiably, pulling up beside her and easily matching her fast pace with his long legs.

Lizzie slowed and let him walk beside her. Charlotte did call him by his first name, but she had known the man for most of her life. Also, Rupert wasn't trying to get Charlotte into bed.

"The countess has known you for many years. But I have not. No, I don't think so," Lizzie said gently, twirling her parasol and watching as two children raced across the park ahead of their governess. Such a beautiful scene, one for which she wished so desperately.

"For how long were you married, Mrs. Symmons, before your husband's untimely demise?" Rupert asked, his question taking her by surprise.

"Eleven months," Lizzie replied, still watching the children. The scene before her was such a wonderful sight, but for her, it was like a double-edged sword. She loved to see children, happy and healthy, running about, but doing that left a hollow feeling in her belly. Would she ever have children of her own?

"And you were happy?"

"Yes and no," Lizzie answered honestly. She had decided that being herself as much as possible was the best way to handle this rather intimidating gentleman. He would soon back off from his pursuit of her when he realised what sort of lady she was. Surely, he would soon turn his quest to a more willing female. The thought saddened her a little and Lizzie focused her mind back on the question he had asked.

"We had a good marriage as far as most modern marriages are measured. But he was a little too wild. He was always gambling and drinking with his army friends," Lizzie explained, looking directly into Rupert's eyes for the first time since he had happened upon her.

My goodness, but he was handsome.

"Ah," Rupert nodded, and then made a hand gesture that encouraged her to continue talking.

"When I marry the next time, I really need a gentleman who will be happy to spend more nights at home with me. I want a man who likes children, and who wants an active role in their lives," she explained, not sure why she was revealing such information to a man who had so casually propositioned her.

Perhaps that was why. So that he would know for sure that she wasn't the right one for him to pursue.

Lizzie began walking again, then stopped, wanting to look at Rupert one more time. It was completely unfair that he was so incredibly handsome.

Rupert gave her a charismatic smile and then laughed. The sound was musical, with the headiness of sweet sherry about it.

"There aren't a lot of men who actively want to play a part in their children's upbringing, Mrs. Symmons. My father certainly didn't in our case, and my brother doesn't with his children."

He grimaced and she wondered what had caused such displeasure. Squashing the urge to contain her curiosity, as any well-bred lady should, she asked him straight out.

"What were you thinking about, just then?" She pointed her finger at his face in one of the most unladylike gestures she had ever dared make.

As quick as a flash, his look disappeared and a haughtiness reserved for the *ton*'s elite appeared in its place. Lizzie wanted to pound the man on his oversized chest.

"Nothing of consequence," Rupert said, in an obvious lie. She stared at him a moment longer before calling him on the untruth.

"Liar," she pronounced, and with a flip of her hand to dismiss him, continued walking.

~

RUPERT STOOD STILL for a full ten seconds, frozen in shock. No one had ever had the gall to say such a thing to him and no woman had ever walked away from him before. *Ridiculous situation!*

It took him several moments to catch up with her even with his considerably longer legs. He knew he should be furious that she had said such a thing to him, but the problem was that it was true and, therefore, he had no grounds to be angry with her.

They ambled along at a slower pace, until Lizzie stopped at a park bench and sat down. Staring around at the view, she sighed with what appeared to be happiness.

Rupert watched her uneasily. He was being ignored and he did not like the feeling. He had never been ignored by a woman, not once in his life. Lizzie seemed as happy and relaxed as though he weren't standing over her, all six feet, four inches of him.

He cleared his throat audibly, but she didn't respond.

Rupert set his jaw against the anger settling in. He considered walking off and leaving her alone, but that wouldn't suit his purpose.

"Elizabeth," he growled, unable to bear being ignored a moment longer. How humiliating, and him the *ton's* most popular rake.

Lizzie's eyes snapped to him at last.

"I did not give you leave to use my Christian name," she said, fire flickering in her usually warm brown eyes.

Rupert grinned, ecstatic to have elicited a reaction. He felt like a five-year-old but at least he finally had her attention.

"You were ignoring me," he said, giving her his most charming smile and crossing his arms across his chest. He hoped the action would high-light his manly chest and muscled arms.

She glared at him.

"Of course, I was. If you don't want to have a proper conversation with me, you may as well leave," she snapped again, waving her hand toward the edge of the park.

Rupert's smile fell off his face as quickly as it had appeared. What was she talking about?

"Of course, I want to have a proper conversation with you," he argued, confused now. When had he given her the impression he *didn't* want to talk to her?

"Then why did you lie to me?"

Rupert opened his mouth to deny her claim, then shut it again with a snap. She wasn't the usual *ton* lady. He couldn't charm his way out of this. Fear prickled on his skin as he chose to do something he rarely did with anyone, even his friends. His senses told him to run, but instead he moved to the other end of the park bench and sat, turning to face her.

"I have never shared my thoughts with anyone," he admitted, guarded despite his best intentions to remain charming. It had been a long time since he'd been completely honest with anyone and it was difficult.

Lizzie's shoulders seemed to sag as if with relief.

"Then say that, but don't lie to me. You asked me a question and I told you the truth. I expect the same in return. I am not someone who tolerates lying and I'm not someone you are going to charm into your bed. Stop trying so hard. I like you much better this way," she stated, then flushed as Rupert's eyebrows shot up.

One of the most genuine smiles of Rupert's life spread across his face. *She likes me now, does she?*

Lizzie held up her hand. "Don't start feeling pompous about that. I'm not sure you can manage to be honest for more than one sentence."

The barb hit somewhere near Rupert's heart and he shifted uncom-fortably. Why did he have a sudden and rather intense urge to pull her into him for a kiss?

What insanity is this? They were in the middle of a very public area. She would be ruined. Hell, *he* would be ruined. Forever!

"I was thinking about my brother," Rupert explained gruffly, before he lost the nerve. The words stuck in his throat. He coughed loudly and swallowed.

Lizzie smiled encouragingly.

"He has five daughters and doesn't intend to have any more children with his wife. Therefore, I am his only male heir."

"Does he have other children?" she asked softly, seeming to realise what he had left out.

"Yes, he has two sons by his mistress," Rupert admitted, flushing despite himself.

He had once had a French mistress who said the most shocking things to him in bed and yet she had never made him even the slightest bit embarrassed. In this moment, however, his cheeks heated.

"That must be difficult for his wife. Does she know?" Lizzie asked politely, her tone not one of condemnation or disregard, but of calmness.

Rupert's face darkened again. Yes, she knew. He had heard their rather nasty conversation a couple of months ago. His sister-in-law had been begging her husband to return to her bed and his brother had stated that he was sick of bedding a woman who couldn't conceive a son or give him any pleasure in the bedchamber. Then the countess had started screaming about her husband's whore and Rupert had left the house.

He nodded tightly, unable to talk about the private conversation he had accidentally overheard.

"Well, I sincerely hope my next husband doesn't keep a mistress. I'm not sure I could handle the betrayal."

Rupert quickly got on the defensive, thinking of what his brother must have endured, going to an unwilling wife's bed. He had never bedded a woman who didn't want him, and he wasn't sure he could if he had to do so. Another reason why marrying a *suitable lady* for him was a most disturbing idea.

"Well, it really depends on the man. Most men consider mistresses to be vital for their sanity," Rupert announced, in as casual a manner as he could.

"What is that supposed to mean?" Lizzie asked, looking horrified.

"I mean that a lot of wives hate going to bed with their husbands. Would you blame your husband for seeking out another woman in that case?" Rupert asked, leaning back against the park bench, one arm outstretched. He couldn't believe he was having this conversation with Lizzie.

"I would never deny my husband," Lizzie burst out, blushing furiously when Rupert gave her a rather meaningful look.

"Yes, dear lady, but would you *enjoy* it? There's a big difference between duty and enjoyment." He smiled knowingly. His point had been made.

Lizzie looked as though she were ready to jump to her feet in outrage. Just as he thought she would do so, she stilled instead and looked at him in thoughtful silence for a moment.

"That is something my next husband can discover for himself," she declared, sticking her nose in the air in the ultimate gesture of obstinacy.

Rupert burst out laughing, stopped, looked at her face and then exploded with laughter again.

"You make me laugh so much. However do you do that?" Rupert wiped a tear away from his eye. He hadn't laughed properly in such a long time. It felt wonderful. His belly fluttered with happiness and an unaccustomed lightness filtered through his body.

"Well, I am glad I provide you with something to laugh at." Her tone was dry, but a tiny smile hovered about her lips. "Perhaps you would walk me to my carriage, Rupert?" Lizzie tentatively used his name for the first time. Warmth spread through him at her use of his Christian name. Were they friends now?

She waited for him to offer his hand and help her to stand up.

Rupert jumped to his feet, and took her hand with what he hoped was courtly grace. They walked slowly back to where their carriages were waiting, companionable silence between them.

"It was lovely talking to you, ma'am," Rupert said, bowing and chastely kissing her knuckles before he handed her up to her carriage door.

"It's Lizzie," she said quietly, smiling at him with true kindness. She really was an amazing sight to behold.

"Lizzie," he repeated, and as he watched the retreating vehicle, his heart thumped fast. Even faster than the beat of the horses' feet as they carried his new friend away.

Chapter Five

"The Spares" still met on a regular basis. Despite Oliver now being the Duke of Lincoln and Archie being the Earl of Tother—his honorary title until he inherited the Marquessate from his father—Rupert still thought of their group as "The Spares," the name they had acquired when it had consisted solely of younger sons of aristocrats.

They met at their club for drinks often and tonight was one of those occasions.

"How is my sister?" John asked Archie, throwing a card down in front of him. They were playing poker, not for money but simply for fun. Rupert was competitive by nature, but the other three weren't and they never wagered any money.

"She is well, John." Archie quirked a brow at his childhood friend who was now his brother-in-law. "She misses you. Why don't you join us for dinner tomorrow?"

John shifted in his chair and dropped his gaze to his cards again.

"I'm not sure of my arrangements tomorrow but thank you for the invitation," John replied, giving no indication of whether he would accept or not.

Rupert shared a confused look with Oliver, both of them feeling the cutting knife of unease settle in the silence.

"Sarah misses Charlotte even when they don't meet for a day. It's amazing how close they have become." The Duke of Lincoln spoke thoughtfully of his wife.

Archie's brown eyes softened again as they did every time his wife was mentioned.

"I know. I am very happy that they get along so well. This means our sons will grow up together, just as we did." Archie smiled fondly, looking at John again who still refused to look up from his cards.

"Another drink?" Rupert asked gruffly, oddly moved by what Archie had said. He had never thought about it like that. Oliver and Archie had sons only a year apart. They would grow up together. Go on holidays together. Begin school together. As the youngest son, he had never been able to play with anyone. He had been extremely lonely.

"Definitely," John replied, lifting his hand to call a footman, who brought over the whiskey decanter.

"More?" Rupert asked the other two, who were still nursing their second drinks. John and he were at least into their fourth, with many more to come, Rupert was sure.

"No, no," Oliver and Archie both chimed in, moving their glasses out of Rupert's reach.

"Why, you old fuddy-duddies," Rupert scolded good-naturedly, pouring himself a drink.

"Can't have another in case the wife finds out?"

Archie smiled his secret smile and Oliver sighed.

"Unlike you gentlemen, I wish to be sober enough to please my wife in bed tonight." Oliver joked, his smile showing how much he was looking forward to the task.

Rupert laughed but John choked on his whiskey. Gone were the days that they joked about their mistresses; now they were joking about their wives. How times had changed.

"But hasn't Sarah given birth recently?" John got the words out before coughing roughly to dispel the whiskey that had found its way into his lungs.

"It's been two months," Oliver reminded him, smiling whilst he sipped his own whiskey.

John stared at Rupert in obvious horror. Rupert stared back and shrugged. He had no idea how long you had to wait before the bedding process could continue. He had always assumed one had to wait at least a year, but then again, what did he know about love matches? Or the birthing process and its aftermath. Perhaps it wasn't necessary to wait that long. Looking at the shared glance between Oliver and Archie, Rupert guessed he had been mistaken about having to wait a year.

John poured himself another huge whiskey and downed half of it. Rupert blinked. What was wrong with John tonight? He was obviously bent on forgetting the world. Rupert recognised the signs well.

"Are you serious?" John asked again, obviously unable to believe what he was hearing.

Oliver laughed at the look on John's face and even Archie smiled again.

"The doctor said six weeks." Oliver shrugged casually but couldn't wipe the smile off his face.

John took another long drink and looked at Archie. "You t...t...t...oo?" he asked, slurring the question.

"Do I need to be sober enough to please my pregnant wife, or did I only wait six weeks, too?" Archie asked, in a rare show of sly humour.

John turned beet red but resolutely held Archie's stare. "The six weeks bit."

Archie shared another glance with Oliver. "Six weeks was more than long enough," he drawled, in another rare show of his masculine side.

Archie had been a virgin for so long, he had never joined in on any of their conversations when they had discussed women in the past. Rupert had always secretly wondered if Archie enjoyed it as much as they did once he finally started. Now it seemed that he did.

John gurgled in his throat before saying, "I am truly shocked."

Rupert burst out laughing with Archie and Oliver. John did look shocked. His eyes were glassy and his hair was unkempt. When had that happened?

"Just wait until you are married too, John. You'll know all these things firsthand."

"Hardly. *If* I ever marry, my wife won't be the only woman I will bed."

Rupert chuckled at John's arrogance. He had also thought similarly. He wasn't so sure he wanted that anymore. Looking at Oliver and Archie, they both appeared to be the happiest of men. There wasn't a gentleman at the club who looked happier or healthier than those two.

Archie and Oliver both frowned at John's words but said nothing.

"I think it's time to go home," Oliver announced, drinking the last of his whiskey. "My entertainment will be wanting to go to sleep soon."

Rupert grinned at his friend. That was one way of talking about the blonde-haired angel whom Oliver had married.

Archie rose too. "I also need to be getting home."

Rupert sighed. Gone were the days that the three of them would be trying to drag Archie by the scruff of the neck into a brothel. They'd never achieved it and now that he had Charlotte, they never would.

"Looks like it's just you and me," John said to Rupert, dragging his coat on.

Rupert watched John stagger around with some envy. Rupert was considerably bigger than all of his friends, so he needed a much larger amount of alcohol to become intoxicated.

John led the way out of their club and they hired a carriage to take them to a local up-market brothel. The building had heavy curtains drawn across every window facing the street. Light shone out dimly from the glass, the brightest being the window to the right of the front door. Rupert knew that one was the sitting room where most of the girls sat, waiting to be chosen.

Rupert was as randy as he had ever been, but he stopped at the front step. How was he going to do this? He had spent the past week thinking about nothing other than Lizzie. Was he really going to assuage that lust in another woman's body?

John called out, "Come on!" from the front door and Rupert walked up after him.

The madam greeted them with familiarity, giving them a generous smile and a warm greeting. They were good customers.

John quickly picked a young brunette with large breasts and staggered out of the sitting room with her.

Rupert sat on the chair he was offered and looked about the room. It was the first time he had looked at anything other than the girls. The room needed a good cleaning and some work done on the plaster. There was also a nasty smell coming from one side of the room where someone must have vomited recently.

Rupert crinkled his nose in displeasure. He suddenly felt like leaving.

"Who would you like, Mr. Willoughby?" the madam asked, sitting on the armrest of his seat and stroking his arm. She saw his hesitation and changed her approach.

"I have a new girl I have been offering only to special customers."

She clicked her fingers and a young girl appeared. She would have been just older than sixteen and had hair the colour of Lizzie's. She smiled shyly at him and dropped her shawl so that he could get a better look at her half-clad form. She was in little more than a chemise. Her skin was beautiful and her breasts pert and well-shaped. Rupert perused her happily and waited for his body's reaction.

Nothing.

He chuckled to himself. He was in a room with more than ten women, all with their charms displayed for his pleasure and he felt absolutely nothing. His cock didn't stir. He sighed.

He wanted Lizzie. His body twitched at the mere thought of her and he laughed, out loud this time. If he pictured Lizzie, he could take this new girl. He could do that. He wasn't letting himself be emasculated by a woman he barely knew.

"I'll take her," Rupert announced, throwing back the last of the cheap whiskey the madam had poured for him.

The young girl's eyes widened when she saw how big Rupert was, but she resolutely turned and led him out of the room.

Rupert stumbled behind her down the hallway, glad she didn't have a room upstairs. He wasn't sure he could manage stairs in his current state.

The young prostitute moved into a dimly-lit room that was clean by a brothel's standards. Rupert took a moment to enjoy the silence, then he began to undress. Jacket, cravat and shirt were dumped on the floor.

The young girl's eyes widened again, but this time Rupert saw less fear and more excitement her gaze. He knew his body was pleasing to most women. They often told him he was strong and muscular.

She lifted her skirts and lay back on the bed, displaying a beautiful pair of young, smooth thighs and pubic hair the same colour as that on her head.

She smiled gamely and held out her arms to him.

Rupert stifled the need to roll his eyes. He wasn't ready, nowhere near ready.

"I need you naked," Rupert told her gruffly, clearing his throat loudly.

The girl blushed pink. *Heavens, she really is new!*

She stood up and began unlacing her chemise. She had very little on except the chemise and a bulky skirt. Both were pooled around her ankles within moments, her need to please both reassuring and disconcerting.

She shivered visibly and Rupert's heart sank, as did any level of arousal he had acquired. He couldn't do this. She was barely old enough to be here, but she did have a gorgeous young body. Pert little breasts topped off by red nipples, a flat stomach and long legs. She was lovely. But he couldn't get his body to respond.

Get a grip, you pansy. Rupert dropped his pants, displaying his flaccid penis.

"Lie on your stomach," he told her, moving over to the bed so he could stand behind her.

The girl did as he asked and spread her legs a little for him. Rupert closed his eyes and pictured Lizzie. His blonde-haired, brown-eyed girl. Her face swam into view and Rupert imagined her smile, her lips parting as though she wanted a kiss from him. His body stirred to life.

Rupert opened his eyes and ran his hands over the beautiful derriere of the girl in front of him, enjoying the satin-smooth skin and soft flesh beneath his fingertips. She turned her face slightly so that he could see her profile and the momentary stirring dissipated instantly.

His senses came alive as though he had been sobered with a bucket of cold water. He could smell the other men who had been in this room. The girl in front of him wasn't Lizzie, and she didn't want him for anything more than the money she would be paid. He was absolutely disgusted with the whole situation—but most of all, with himself—to the very depths of his stomach.

He hauled up his pants and grabbed his jacket and shirt.

"Thank you," he yelled and, still half-undressed, he broke out the door. He couldn't stay in that room a moment longer. He'd truly embarrass himself if he did.

The madam walked into the foyer to see who was making such a racket, her eyebrows high in surprise when she saw him. Rupert tucked his flaccid penis back into his breeches and hastily dressed.

"Mr. Willoughby, if she isn't what you want—" The madam began, with an angry glint in her eye.

"She was lovely, beautiful. It wasn't her at all. I just can't tonight…" Rupert did not the poor girl to be punished for his lack of focus. He threw too much money at the woman, flung open the heavy door and rushed out into the clean air.

Dishevelled, embarrassed, but relieved to be out of there, Rupert took a big breath and shook his head. With a heavy sigh, he gestured to a passing hackney carriage and made his way home.

Chapter Six

Lizzie had been almost yawning through a casual evening of socializing, until she heard a woman over her shoulder sigh and say in a gushing tone, "Oh, he came. I hoped he would."

Lizzie somehow knew who the woman was talking about. She could sense Rupert's presence as he entered the room.

She closed her eyes, fighting the urge to drop her head into her hands. She knew Rupert was a rake. Every woman in London seemed to know him intimately, but did that fact really have to be thrown around like the latest fashion? Lizzie had assumed that such knowledge about a gentleman would make him distasteful. Unfortunately, nothing about Rupert seemed to be off-putting. Instead, the knowledge of how desirable everyone found him made her nervous and the fact that he seemed to still be pursuing her despite all her refusals to play his game, made her excited. To admit anything less would be a lie.

She enjoyed the interest in his eyes and the feminine satisfaction of having such a masterful male want *her*.

Lizzie turned to the elderly lady beside whom she'd been sitting and asked her a question about how she had enjoyed her dinner. It took every ounce of effort she possessed to focus on the woman, but for the life of her, Lizzie didn't hear the words.

Lizzie refused to look as he walked over to her, but her skin goosebumped in uncomfortable awareness nonetheless. It was infuriating that a man could have such an effect on her. Infuriating, and intriguing.

"Mrs. Symmons," drawled the amused voice from behind her.

She quelled the instant smile that sprang to her lips and instead rose to her feet and turned. There he stood, all six feet, four inches of male, muscle, and strength. She tilted her head to look up at him and offered a tiny smile.

"Good evening, Mr. Willoughby," she greeted, aware of others watching and making sure she curtseyed appropriately.

"Would you care for a turn around the grounds, Mrs. Symmons? The gardens are very fine in the evening air."

"Thank you, sir, but I would much prefer to visit the music room. Do you know where it is?" she asked.

It was quite obvious to her that Rupert never had to pursue a woman before. He had none of the normal subtleties. He was playing a very straightforward game. Like a bull at a gate, he had her in his sights and he was charging.

Lizzie had known that the first thing Rupert would try to do when he saw her again, would be to lure her somewhere private. Although Lizzie had a feeling that she would enjoy being alone with Rupert, perhaps staying inside the house with others around them would be safer for her sanity and her reputation.

"I do, indeed, Mrs. Symmons," Rupert said, offering Lizzie his arm and drawing her close as they walked in search of the music room. His size and warmth made her knees shake a little, the need to lean on his strength deep within her.

"Are you enjoying yourself tonight, Lizzie?" he asked, as they walked along the hall and entered the music room.

Her heart thumped when she realized the room was vacant.

"I *am* enjoying myself, thank you, Rupert," Lizzie answered, allowing her hand to fall from his arm and walking to a wall where several string instruments were mounted. She needed distance to think more clearly. Her need for a husband and indeed, a well-built man, was beginning to make itself far too clear to her.

"Do you play, Lizzie?" Rupert asked, running his hand lovingly over the keys of the pianoforte.

Her laugh rang clear in the air, too loud as always. She closed her mouth and put her hand on her belly to stifle the trembling deep within her.

"I wish I did. My mother didn't believe it worth the time to practice music, but languages? Yes, she would abide me practising those."

She smiled at the memory of her many language lessons. Her late mother had been an unusual woman and Lizzie still missed her so much, it hurt.

Rupert's brows rose. "How many languages do you speak?"

"Not many," she lied, then laughed again as though he had told a good joke. She was certain he really didn't want to know. Most men found her intelligence intimidating and some insulted her, calling her a bluestocking.

Rupert growled, coming up to grab her and tickle her in the ribs as though she were a child. Lizzie twisted away, giggling despite herself. She had rarely been tickled, even as a child. What a strange thing for him to do.

"You told me you cannot abide lying. Now, tell me how many languages you speak," he demanded, scowling with what looked like mock outrage. Lizzie took a few steps back and found the wall pressed into her back. Rupert had stalked her right to edge of the room, but despite her earlier reservations about his dishonourable intentions, she didn't feel at all scared.

Instead, his closeness called to her; pulled her in.

They were alone now, but what would happen if someone walked in? She put her hands up to rest upon his chest, making no move to push him away. His chest was warm and rock-solid, and her imagination ran wild. What did he look like, beneath these clothes? Her thoughts created heat in her cheeks. But still she did not withdraw from touching him.

He leaned closer, bringing his hands up to her face and tipping her so their lips met. Her eyes widened as his mouth brushed against hers, softly, almost reverently.

Lizzie held herself very still as the warmth of his full lips caressed hers. A wonderful stirring of pleasure rose in her belly. Determined to get full measure from this kiss, which must surely be a once-off, she rose up onto her toes and threw her arms around his neck as she had seen her maid do once to one of the footmen. She pressed her mouth more firmly against his and clung, hoping he would know what to do next. She had rarely been kissed by her husband and didn't quite know what else to do beyond this moment.

He dropped his hands to her hips and pulled her into him. She could feel his hard flesh and that instantly caused a spark of arousal to course through her. Rupert dipped his tongue into her mouth and she moaned at the pleasure. The sound seemed to encourage him. He plundered further; deeper.

Lizzie was swept into the most amazing kiss of her life. Rupert was holding her as though he desired her desperately and kissing her as though she were the only one he'd ever wanted. She kissed him back as enthusiastically as she knew how, wanting to share the pleasure with which he had filled her. Stroking his tongue with her own, she gripped his black, shoulder-length hair in her hands, threading her fingers through it.

"The music room is this way, I believe." A female voice came from outside the room and down the hallway.

Rupert and Lizzie both heard it at the same time. Quickly breaking apart, Rupert rushed across to a bookcase, presenting his back to the doorway to make it look as though he were searching for a book.

Lizzie took a moment to realise she needed an occupation and saw a pack of cards on a small table. She quickly hurried over to pick them up and began shuffling as she dropped into one of the chairs surrounding the table. She was breathing faster than normal and hoped her flushed cheeks and rapid heartbeat wouldn't give her away.

A gentleman and two ladies walked into the room without knocking. They were all elegantly dressed. The younger lady, a pretty blonde, seemed to know that she was attractive. There was a confidence in her manner that spoke of self-assurance.

"Rupert," she cooed when she saw him, then sauntered over to the bookcase and wrapped a proprietary hand around his elbow.

~

RUPERT'S STOMACH PLUMMETED. Of all the rotten luck! Well, at least thanks to Elise's presence, his erection, the one to beat all other hard cocks, was instant history. He should remember that trick if ever he needed it again.

"Elise," he sighed, trying subtly to disengage her hand from his elbow.

She finally removed it with a pout, but grazed her nails over his arm whilst she did. Rupert suppressed a shudder.

"Elise, we'll meet you in the parlour?" The older, darker-haired lady enquired, moving toward the door with a sly smile.

Elise nodded and smiled her thanks, then turned stony eyes on Lizzie.

Despite her obvious unease, Lizzie started laying out the cards on the table in front of her to start a game of Patience.

Rupert saw the look in Elise's eye and knew he was in trouble. He had barely spent a week in her bed before moving on. She was vain and selfish, and he had been turned off her soon after their first night together.

"Rupert, I have missed you. Would you escort me home tonight?" she purred softly. Not so softly that Lizzie wouldn't hear, but enough for it to appear that she was attempting to be discreet.

Rupert didn't dare look directly at Lizzie, but he could see her out of the corner of his eye. She hadn't stopped in the dealing of her cards, but he knew she had heard Elise's offer from the obvious stiffening of her spine.

For one second, he considered taking Elise up on the offer. It was true that she was a rather nasty woman, but she would let him sate his desire in her body all night if he wanted. He would finally be rid of some of this tension. It had been weeks since he'd lain with any woman and Lizzie was driving him half out of his mind.

Lizzie, the woman who wanted marriage—a breed of woman that Rupert had sworn not to pursue. Why was he even bothering with her? Rupert knew that if he left with Elise, then he would never get the opportunity to be intimate with Lizzie. That's all it would take to ruin his chances with her completely.

Looking down into Elise's eager face he realised he wasn't ready to give up on Lizzie. He may not want marriage, but this overly-willing woman would not fill the need inside him. It went so much deeper than the needs of his body. He didn't know how to articulate what he wanted, but somehow, he knew that Lizzie held the key.

"Thank you, Elise, but I'm afraid I already have plans for this evening," he lied smoothly.

Elise's eyes flickered a warning. She glanced at Lizzie again.

"I can wait. Shall we meet later in the week, then?" she asked, her mouth setting into an angry line.

At that moment Rupert realised he would never bed Elise again, and that it be best for everyone if he let her know it.

"I'm afraid I'm no longer available, Elise," he answered, giving her a direct look that would have had most men running from the room.

"You cannot be serious, Rupert!" Elise replied plaintively, looking back over at where Lizzie sat, playing Patience. She placed both hands on her hips and her face began turning red.

"Tell me that little mouse is not the reason for denying me," she demanded, pointing at Lizzie.

Rupert clenched his jaw and inhaled sharply through his nose.

"Mrs. Symmons has nothing to do with the situation, Elise. Leave her out of this. I am not interested in you anymore. Find someone else to escort you home," he added, before walking over to Lizzie and sitting in a chair opposite her.

"May I join you at cards, ma'am?" he asked calmly, pleased that he had managed to rein in his temper.

Lizzie merely nodded and gathered up the cards on the table before handing him the pack.

Rupert eyed her and knew he was in trouble. Elise had been easy to deal with, although he knew she hadn't given up on him. She was like a dog with a bone, that one.

Lizzie was a completely different type of lady. She seemed deep in thought, no longer lost in feeling or as carefree and happy as she had been before Elise walked in. He was in deep, deep trouble.

"I'm sorry you had to witness that," Rupert apologised. He had always relished his rakehell reputation, as it gave him free rein to do what he wanted, whenever he wanted. No one ever expected anything from him, except a good time while it lasted. For the first time in his life, he actually wished his reputation wasn't quite so obvious. How was he going to gain the trust of this beautiful and sincere person when women were practically seducing him in front of her?

"I'm sure it happens often enough." Lizzie shrugged as if uncaring, but her sad face drove home the truth. She wasn't unmoved by what had just happened.

Rupert smiled politely, not quite sure how to handle this situation. Frequently, he'd had jealous ladies competing for his attention and even several ex-mistresses in one room at once. It had been rather entertaining. This was very different. For the first time ever, he actually cared about what the lady in front of him was thinking and feeling.

He wanted to make her happy, not sad.

"Shall we play poker? I assume you know how to play," he said. As an army widow, he assumed she'd likely know a number of card games.

Lizzie stilled. "Of course, I know how to play poker."

Rupert grinned at the acerbic edge in her tone, and dealt the cards, relief coursing through him in calming waves. Were they back on an even keel once again? He hoped so.

"Do you have a current mistress, Rupert?"

His head lifted in shock, staring at the lady who had just asked one of the most forthright questions any woman had ever asked him. He swallowed awkwardly, not knowing how to answer honestly and still retain Lizzie's company.

She sighed, the sound tugging at his heartstrings in a painful way. "And I suppose you gamble and drink often as well?" She continued with her questioning as though he had already answered the first.

He opened his mouth, but nothing came out. Should he just ignore the mistress question and answer the second one? He swallowed the lump in his throat once again and smiled gamely at her.

"Not as much as in my salad days," he admitted. There was no gentleman who didn't gamble and drink. It was the excesses that would be a problem.

"Thank you for being so honest," Lizzie said, with a slight tremble in her tone. She stood up, dropping her hand to the table.

Panic fluttered in his chest, like a caged bird.

"Lizzie, please don't leave," he urged, reaching out to grab her by the wrist. She couldn't leave now, surely? Did she find his past so abhorrent?

"It has been lovely getting to know you," she said politely, pulling out of his grasp before doing something extremely odd. She leaned over and cupped his cheek, in a brief caress of tenderness.

Rupert leaned into her touch without thinking, his eyes closing of their own volition as warmth spread through his heart. When her hand dropped away, he jumped to his feet in a panic. This couldn't be over. It just couldn't.

"I haven't visited my mistress since I met you. I swear it," Rupert told her, uncaring that he was now begging.

Lizzie smiled sadly, shaking her head as she backed away toward the door.

"But for how long can you wait? I may never be ready and you'll go and visit her and I'll be devastated."

A vise-like clamping around his heart caused Rupert to press his hand to his chest. She cared; she really did. He had succeeded in affecting her as deeply as he himself was affected by her, but now he didn't know what to do. He had hurt her.

"I don't want any other woman, Lizzie. No one but you arouses me anymore."

Lizzie simply raised a questioning eyebrow, and then walked to the door.

Rupert stood transfixed, a victim of his own machinations.

"You didn't answer the question," he forced out of his almost-frozen lips, before she disappeared.

Lizzie turned and frowned at him.

"The languages. How many?" he prompted, and her frown cleared.

A glint appeared in her eyes as she smiled softly.

"Five," she answered.

Impossible.

"English, French, Gaelic, Italian and Latin."

He gaped at her. What woman spoke so many languages? She really was a rare gem indeed. He strove for a nonchalant smile, though his heart was aching at the thought she would soon be gone.

"Latin?" he said, raising his eyebrows.

"My parents were scholars," she whispered, before leaving the room. She pulled the door shut behind her with a gut-wrenching finality.

Rupert fell back into his chair with a loud sigh, staring up at the ornate ceiling as if it could provide much-needed assistance.

Yes, he had a mistress, a woman whom he had visited often, initially. However, those visits had recently dropped back to almost fortnightly. Rupert had been thinking of giving her up when Lizzie had dropped into his life and now, he wished he had paid the woman off weeks ago.

He did gamble and drink occasionally, but that didn't mean he was like Lizzie's husband. He would never ignore Lizzie so that he could go out enjoying himself.

He was getting ahead of himself again. What was it about this woman that had him almost ready to jump down the church aisle? Maybe it was her unrelenting determination to accept nothing less than marriage. Either way, Lizzie was different. But could he marry her? He hadn't planned on marrying for several years more and then he had planned on a traditional marriage of convenience, not the love match his friends had found.

Love match?

Where had that thought come from? He desperately needed another drink.

Chapter Seven

Rupert requested his butler obtain Lizzie's address, before he went to bed and fell asleep with a heavy heart. He wasn't sure what he was going to do if he found her, but he couldn't sit idly by and allow her to walk out of his life forever.

The next morning, he was woken at a most unlikely hour, his head pounding from lack of sleep.

"I'm sorry to disturb you, sir." Rupert's butler apologised, laying a letter next to his head.

Rupert groaned and stretched, disoriented. What time was it? It could barely be dawn.

"What is it?" He grumbled, rubbing his hands down his face and groaning again as he blinked slowly awake.

"I have news about Mrs. Symmons and thought you may want to know as soon as possible."

Rupert shot up straight in bed and snatched for the letter on his pillow. Sleep forgotten, his body began to hum with happiness. Had the butler found her already?

"Tell me now," Rupert demanded, ripping open the letter in impatience.

"Mrs. Symmons received a missive yesterday requesting her presence at a country estate in Kent. Her estate, I believe."

His heart sank at the news.

"She's gone." His shoulders dropped and the letter fell to the sheets. How had his butler found out this news in such a short space of time?

"I believe it is only for a few days, sir." The butler nodded impassively, but remained standing beside him as if he hadn't finished imparting his information.

Lizzie owned a country estate? Why did he not know this? Perhaps herlate husband had left it to her. Or her parents.

"Is there anything else, Grimmit?" Rupert asked impatiently, glaring up at the starched man.

"The estate is several hours' drive away, sir. If you wanted to surprise the lady, perhaps, you could arrive for lunch?"

Rupert's nervous belly did a little lurch and a skip. He nodded and smiled up at the man standing above him.

"Order a bath, if you would, Grimmit."

The older man's lips kicked up in a rare smile and he bowed out of the room.

Rupert leapt out of bed and pulled on some drawers. Stretching out his back, he began pacing restlessly within his room. The servants brought in his bathtub, then left to retrieve hot water.

He walked over to the window and opened the curtains, letting daylight into his usually dark bedroom.

He couldn't leave things as they were between him and Lizzie. He needed to tell her why he was the way he was, and perhaps explain why it would be advantageous for both of them to indulge in a brief affair for their mutual pleasure. She had responded well to his kiss and he knew he could give her so much more pleasure in the bedchamber if she allowed him the time.

"Today is the day," he vowed, watching the sun rise over the far hills for the first time since he was a child.

~

UPSTAIRS IN HER BEDROOM, Lizzie was having her hair arranged by her ladies' maid when the housekeeper burst in, all-a-flutter.

"Ma'am, you have a visitor!" The elderly woman before her practically bounced as she spoke, unable to contain her obvious excitement. The overly plump lady was flapping her hands like a bird.

"A visitor?" Lizzie repeated, handing her maid a pin from the dresser and trying to hide her smile as she envisioned her housekeeper as a goose at Christmas luncheon.

Who would be visiting me? She had only arrived late the day before. Surely gossip in this part of the country couldn't be quite so speedy?

"Yes. The Honourable Mr. Rupert Willoughby has called on you."

Lizzie's heart flip-flopped and she gasped as panic descended. He couldn't really be here, surely? She swallowed the lump in her throat and turned away from the mirror.

"Did you say... The Honourable Mr. Rupert Willoughby?" Lizzie repeated slowly.

The housekeeper nodded, her face flushed like a teenage girl's.

"Tall, well built, wavy hair..." Lizzie began.

"And bright black eyes," the housekeeper finished for her. "Pardon me, ma'am."

Lizzie sighed, and let the hand that held another pin, drop into her lap. It had to be him. No one would know of their association enough to say it as a joke and no one else looked like Rupert in any way. He was certainly striking, especially with those eyes.

Lizzie stood up on legs that were suddenly a little shaky. She'd had a great deal of time to think on her carriage ride to the estate and during the previous night, when she'd barely gotten any sleep. Something strange was happening to her. All she could think about was that kiss and how it had made her feel.

She wanted Rupert. She finally admitted that to herself as the sun rose this morning. She desired him on a physical level that she had never experienced before. She had never believed she could feel such things.

Perhaps it wouldn't be *such* a bad thing if she had a short affair with this gentleman before she remarried. She had no one else in mind as yet, as no one had caught her attention in any way.

Maybe he could teach her about passion and about the pleasure that was to be found in the bedchamber, if such a thing was to be pleasurable at all. Lizzie was sure that Rupert would know. It may also help her in keeping her future husband happy and secure. Perhaps it wouldn't, but Lizzie knew she didn't want to miss out on this very rare opportunity.

Rupert had made it crystal clear he was not the marrying type and she wasn't sure that she would even want a man like him as her husband. He was wild and irresponsible. He probably couldn't support himself, let alone a wife. There was evidence to the contrary, of course, but she didn't want to think too much on the virtues of the Honourable Rupert Willoughby. She already liked him a little too much. If she happened to fall in love with a rake, then she would indeed turn out to be the fool.

She looked once in the mirror to check her hair and dress, to see that her appearance was respectable. There was nothing opulent about her attire, but she looked neat and tidy. She smoothed the material at her waist and descended the stairs.

"The gentleman is waiting to see you in the sitting room, ma'am," the butler told her with genuine warmth. His old, wrinkled face lit up with a rare smile.

Lizzie suppressed the need to groan. Why was everyone so happy to see her getting attention from a male? It wasn't like he was a suitor.

"Thank you, Leaves. Mr. Willoughby is a friend from London who has travelled up with some news, I believe. Would you be so good as to show him to the dining room and make sure there is an extra place for him at luncheon?" She barely succeeded in keeping a straight face as she told the white lie. This butler had known her since she was in the nursery and it was a little embarrassing to have to explain to him who Rupert was, despite the innocence of their association thus far.

"Of course, my lady." The man bowed, looking a little disappointed at her explanation.

She tried not to sigh and headed into the dining room. The cook had prepared for an army as usual, and for once, Lizzie was excessively grateful.

She sat at the head of the table and folded her hands in her lap, her breath shuddering as she struggled to maintain her calm. He was here and they were essentially alone.

The door opened and her suitor strolled in, his morning clothes pristine despite the travel.

"Mrs. Symmons, please forgive my intrusion." Rupert bowed to her, then walked around to her end of the table.

Lizzie let the smile spread across her lips, unable to keep the happiness that his mere presence elicited inside her. It was amazing how different she felt here, in her home. It was almost as though London had been stifling her desire for this man. Here, where she was warm and safe and happy, her feelings were blossoming like a rose in spring. And he had only been in her presence a few seconds at most.

"Not at all, Mr. Willoughby, you are very welcome. Please join me." Lizzie gestured to the chair opposite hers.

"It looks as though your cook anticipated more than one person for lunch," Rupert commented, glancing down the table as though he expected more guests to arrive.

Lizzie laughed as Rupert's eyes swung back to her.

"Not at all, my lord. My cook enjoys her employment, and I am here so infrequently nowadays that she spoils me when I am."

"Ah," Rupert sighed, obviously relaxing as his shoulders dropped and a soft smile replaced the stilted grimace that had been there before.

"How was your journey?" Lizzie enquired, helping herself to warm chicken and roast potatoes. She had long ago told her staff she could serve her own food at the table, at least when she dined alone. Or almost alone, in today's case.

"Oh, it was very pleasant, thank you," Rupert answered conversationally.

They chatted about the different methods of travel over lunch, happily eating and relaxing in each other's company. It was the worst possible thing for Lizzie's desire to have a simple affair with this man, as she could see herself doing such a thing every single day.

"Would you care to go for a ride, Rupert? I have a horse in my stables that you may like." She had to stop herself from imagining him as a husband. He was an acquaintance who found her desirable. Nothing more than that.

Rupert's eyebrows shot up rather charmingly. Lizzie chuckled at his surprised expression and waved him toward the door so that she could go upstairs and change.

"Please see the butler for whatever you need, and I will meet you at the stables in ten minutes."

∼

RUPERT FOUGHT the urge to swing Lizzie up into his arms and charge up the stairs with her. Did she understand the innuendo behind what she had said? Was she offering a ride of the sort he would like? Or did she seriously own a horse that could handle his weight?

It seemed the latter was the truth.

The rather stern-looking butler directed him to where he could borrow some riding pants and a shirt. Both articles of clothing were an uneven fit, but Rupert couldn't bring himself to care about his appearance. He would usually be dressed beautifully to ride. He had the latest style of riding clothes in his residences, styles that sculpted his large frame perfectly. None of that mattered with the adrenaline pumping through his system today. He was so excited to see what Lizzie had in store for him. She had been noticeably warmer at lunch and he could barely suppress the manic grin that wanted to spread across his face as he headed out to the stables.

They were very well maintained, with several staff on hand. Lizzie lived very comfortably indeed.

"I see you found our stables, Rupert." Lizzie greeted him with a smile as she walked into the building that housed her horses.

Rupert's breath caught in his throat and all he could do was nod at her. Her riding jacket was slightly too tight and curved around her ample breasts like a lover's caress. She looked so delicious he wanted to drop to his knees and eat her up right there in the hay. She was so tiny he could have picked her up and carried her home, but again, there was a strength in her that he was determined not to ignore.

"What horse do you have that you think can handle me, Lizzie?" Rupert asked lightly, trying his best not to put too much innuendo into his question. She was, after all, a true lady and he had no desire to offend her if she didn't mean anything by her offer.

"This one," Lizzie announced in a similar light tone, opening the door to a stable further down the row.

Rupert stepped forward. Inside the stall was a huge bay stallion. He was restless and pacing, in obvious need of exercise.

"He's beautiful." Rupert marched close, unable to keep the awe from his voice as he reached out a hand and stroked the stallion's neck.

Lizzie smiled and entered the stall with him.

"You couldn't have surprised me at a better time. This fellow is on loan for breeding purposes, but he almost injured one of the mares yesterday. The grooms have been saying that he needs a good, solid ride to settle him down and yet none of them are game."

Lizzie smiled up at him and again Rupert wondered at her words. Did she know what she was inviting when she talked of such things? He could give her a ride that would ruin her for every other man she would ever meet in future.

"Luckily I decided to call on you, then," Rupert agreed, treading carefully.

"Yes, it is." Lizzie walked over to a stall opposite and signalled to one of the grooms.

"Please saddle up Thunder for Mr. Willoughby and have Rose readied for me." She pulled on her gloves with practiced ease.

Rupert smiled at her use of the horses' names.

"Rose?" he enquired, envisioning a sweet little mare for his sweet little lady.

A moment later the two horses were presented to them and Rupert gaped up at them. The mare Lizzie was to ride was almost as big as the stallion they had for Rupert.

"Lizzie, you can't possibly ride a horse that large," Rupert exclaimed, looking down on her dainty head and wondering how on earth she was going to handle such a creature.

Lizzie thanked the groom and allowed him to hoist her up into the saddle. She swung her leg over so that she could ride astride like a man, and gave him a smile that could only be called flirty.

"I can handle a large animal, sir," she said. And with that, she turned the huge mare around and broke into a trot.

Rupert laughed out loud at her feisty word play and swung up onto the massive stallion. He hadn't ridden in the country for months and was looking forward to a punishing gallop. London had so many rules, he had barely been allowed to canter in town.

He trotted up next to Lizzie and called out, "If this stallion is in a rut, is it safe to have your mare so close to him?"

Lizzie laughed again, her lovely long hair blowing in the breeze behind her. Rupert shifted in his saddle as his body throbbed and his skin heated. There was no other woman he would rather be with. Her laugh was the most magical sound in the world and gave his very soul pleasure to be around.

"Rose is his mother. She won't put up with any nonsense."

As though to prove Lizzie's point, Rose snapped her teeth at her offspring and he slowed down to match her gait.

Rupert laughed out loud, surprised to be having such a good time. In fact, he couldn't remember the last time he had felt this happy.

"Ready?" Lizzie asked, turning Rose's head so that they faced an open and empty field.

Rupert turned Thunder in the same direction, nodding in agreement, despite not knowing exactly what she had in mind. He was ready for anything.

Lizzie squeezed with her thighs and dug in her heels. Rose surged forward with a grunt and broke into a gallop.

Rupert gripped the reins and his heart picked up the animal's bruising pace. If she wanted this horse ridden hard, then so be it.

He flicked the reins, dug in his heels and the powerful body between his legs surged forward.

Lizzie leaned over Rose urging her to go faster.

Rupert's body stirred at the sight of Lizzie's thighs spread and her bottom in the air. He kicked his stallion harder. The powerful body surged and raced ahead. Rupert let the horse have its way. He ran through a thicket of trees and clear across another field. Sweat trickled down his brow and he wiped it away, eventually pulling the horse back to a trot. The horse, too, was breathing hard, but seemed fit and ready for more. Rupert turned the horse and noticed Lizzie standing, leaning against a tree watching him from half a field away.

He flicked the reins onto the horse's flank and charged over. He loved the feel of a horse's body. The warmth, the power and the thrill of the speed. *What an animal!*

He crossed the same field again and made his way back to where Lizzie stood. He circled around her a couple of times until she laughed and twirled to keep up with him. That was when he jumped down. Unable to resist, he picked her up, kissed her hard on the lips and set her down again.

Lizzie's eyes widened and then she smiled hesitantly.

"It seems you enjoyed that," she said.

"I did, thank you. It has been a long time since I got to ride such a magnificent animal." Rupert ran his hand over the horse's neck and lovingly patted its rump.

The stallion flicked his head once, as though in approval and walked off to join his mother in a feed of grass.

"Is this your husband's estate?" Rupert asked, not wanting to be rude but curious all the same. Had she married money?

"No, it is my father's estate."

Her answer had no bearing whatsoever on their relationship, although it could make her prey to a fortune hunter if it became known in London that she was a widow with means of her own.

That thought made him frown and he shook it off. He didn't want to think about what would happen tomorrow to his widow who was searching for a husband.

"You seem happier here than in a ballroom in London," he remarked, taking in her flushed cheeks and the easy way she stood. She looked healthy and happy and unfortunately for him, even more beautiful than he had ever seen her before.

Lizzie laughed, her eyes shining at him as the melodic music of her laughter surrounded him.

"I love it here. If I had a choice, I would rarely visit London."

"Really?" Rupert asked, surprised. Most ladies he knew would never leave London if they didn't have to do so. They would always spend the first weeks of the season complaining about how bored they had been in the off-season, and how much shopping they needed to do.

"Do you really love London so much?" Lizzie asked, averting her eyes.

"Oh, no, not me." Rupert said. He enjoyed the diversions of town, but he was always relieved to return to his family's country estate post-season. Six months in London was quite enough.

"I haven't met many ladies who prefer the country to town."

Lizzie looked up, cocking her head to one side.

"Well, sir, perhaps you have not been associating with the right sorts of ladies."

She shied away and Rupert berated himself for accidentally bringing forward the topic of his experiences with other ladies.

He walked over to where she had trounced off, and pulled up her chin so that she had to look at him.

"Perhaps I haven't," he agreed, using his other hand to pull her into him.

Lizzie's hands came up to his chest and she tiptoed up to meet his lips. Rupert captured her sweet mouth, sighing in bliss. It was so good to have his hands on her again. It was not just good; it felt *right*.

A rumble of thunder sounded in the distance and Lizzie pulled away from Rupert's embrace.

"We'd better get back before it starts pouring." She sighed and walked over to the horses, rearranging her clothing on the way.

"Race you back to the house," she said, laughing as she ran over to Rose.

Rupert followed and effortlessly hoisted her up onto her saddle. Striding back to his own horse, he quickly mounted. He could smell the rain now; it wasn't far away.

"Let's go!" He flicked his head at the house and grinned like the devil himself. She'd better ride fast. He couldn't wait much longer to get his hands on her.

They rode back at a punishing pace, the drop in temperature and slight sweetness to the air forcing them to move quickly. The heavens opened up just as they arrived back at the stables.

There was only one groom on duty and he took both horses inside to care for them.

"We'll wait in the adjoining stable for the rain to stop if you need us," Lizzie called out to the groom, ducking out into the rain to run across to another outbuilding.

"Make sure you don't need us," Rupert said in a forceful tone, making it clear to the young groom that they wanted to be alone. The man nodding in understanding as he led the horses back for a much-needed rest.

Rupert stalked after Lizzie through the heavy rain, stepping into the clean, spare stables and shaking his hair. Lizzie had removed her wet coat, hat and gloves and was inspecting her riding habit for damage.

Rupert ripped off his own jacket and stepped purposefully toward the woman who had been tormenting him with desire for weeks.

Chapter Eight

"No, I want to talk," Lizzie cried, bringing her hands up to the large chest in front of her and pushing him back. If he started to kiss her, she would never be able to say what she needed to say.

Rupert's full mouth compressed into a thin line, but he nodded and stepped back.

Lizzie sat down upon one of the hay bales and gestured for Rupert to sit also. He was far too tall for to remain standing if she was seated. Lizzie felt like a pixie next to him. He was as big as an oak, and just as dense if he thought she would allow him to treat her the way he had treated his other ladies.

"Tell me how you found out where I was and why you left London to come here and see me," Lizzie demanded, looking directly into his brilliant blue-black eyes. She was learning to read his face and didn't want to miss any subtle changes in expression.

Rupert blinked.

"I didn't like how we ended our conversation the other day and I hoped to change your mind."

"But you still don't wish to marry," Lizzie reiterated, making sure that they understood exactly where the other stood on this topic. Her needs hadn't changed in that department, though she may be ready to rethink her strategy.

"No," Rupert whispered, almost regretfully.

"Tell me why," she said quietly, knowing that Rupert pretended to be a classic, thoughtless, unfeeling rake, but she could sense that he really wasn't so. She was convinced that she couldn't desire someone with no heart, no soul, and no feelings for others. There had to be more to him than what seemed obvious to others.

"Marriage is for men who want to stop living the life they have," Rupert spouted, throwing in a charming smile. That was an attempt to escape her interrogation, she was sure.

"Do you still see your mistress?" Lizzie asked, watching his face carefully, ready to pounce on any sign of lying.

"No," Rupert told her, looking her directly in the eyes.

"Why not?"

She knew that Rupert had convinced himself that he wasn't ready to marry, but if he had given up his mistress just so he could be with her, didn't that indicate a stronger than normal desire?

"We had tired of each other." Rupert smiled charmingly and Lizzie saw the truth in that statement. However, he wasn't telling her the whole truth. She could see his eyes were shadowed. There was something he didn't want her knowing, she was sure.

"Do you have a new mistress?" Lizzie asked, as lightly as possible. Could he have found someone else in the past few days?

"No, not yet," Rupert said quietly, his eyes beginning to burn.

"Why not?" Lizzie asked, pushing for more information. It seemed that he was willing to change his life for her, travelling out of London and giving up his mistress, but for how long would this last?

"Because I want *you*!" Rupert declared, with soul-burning intensity.

"Only me?" Lizzie asked, standing up on shaking legs.

Rupert twitched uncomfortably, obviously not liking where the conversation was heading.

"Lizzie..."

"Only me?" she repeated, this time more demand than question.

Rupert nodded sharply and Lizzie mimicked the move, happy in part.

"Tell me why you don't wish to marry," she asked again. If she was going to throw away her morals and indulge in a purely physical affair with Rupert, then she needed to know more about him.

"I told you–" he began, his eyes flashing.

"No, you lied to me. Tell me the real reason," Lizzie demanded, all five feet, four inches of her body rigid and determined to ascertain the truth.

RUPERT LOOKED AWAY and tapped his fingers against his knees for a moment, then finally spoke.

"Because, unless I can have a marriage like Archie's and Oliver's, I don't wish to marry."

"You think it's impossible to have a union like those of your friends?" Lizzie asked, surprised he felt that way. Surely Rupert could see that if his friends could find happiness, he could do so also.

"Not impossible, but a love match is rare in our society. The norm is to be trapped into a marriage as are most of the *ton* gentlemen, or even into a forced marriage owing to circumstance. I don't want a union... like my brother's." Rupert all but whispered the last words.

Lizzie let a breath out slowly, her heart aching at the pain she heard in Rupert's words, but she pushed forward regardless. She needed to know why he was so terrified of the one thing she craved so much.

"Tell me, why is the thought of a love match and subsequent marriage so horrible?"

His lips twisted and his brow furrowed. "My brother's marriage started out with mutual affection, but as the desire for a male heir brought more and more daughters, any real feelings that were once there between them turned to hatred," Rupert explained, almost choking on the words.

"Is that why you are so adamant you don't want to marry yet? You don't want to be your brother's heir, so you're letting it turn you off marriage entirely?" Lizzie's mouth fell open.

That was not rational, although she understood his abhorrence to the weight placed upon him. Since his brother had failed to provide a legitimate male heir, Rupert would now be responsible for siring the next Earl of Sweeting. He would hate to have that forced upon him, especially if it meant marrying for a reason other than love, as his friends had.

"But your brother has five daughters. Can't daughters also inherit their father's estate in the absence of a male heir?" asked Lizzie. "Why shouldn't the next incumbent of the Sweeting estate be a countess instead of an earl?"

Rupert shook his head. "Tradition," he replied. "The title of our house has always been carried by a male heir. Anything else is unthinkable."

"This bias against female heirs is ridiculous," said Lizzie, with passion. "Traditions have to change."

"They won't change so easily," replied Rupert. "Not in our time, at least. Can you imagine how ridiculous it would be to have the title holder of the Sweeting estate unable to attend to her duties because she is confined due to pregnancy?"

"I would love it if you could have the courage to say that to our friend Charlotte, the Countess of Tother," said Lizzie drily. "She hasn't allowed pregnancy to confine her one little bit. She'll be the next de facto Marquess of Hunting, mark my words. Besides, have you forgotten? England has already had several queens. Queen Elizabeth was one of the greatest sovereigns England has ever produced. So how can your brother allow this bias against females to destroy his marriage and pressure you? I think it's ridiculous." She sniffed to show her disgust.

"Ah, Lizzie, good Queen Bess was a rare exception. She was uncommon. The truth is, a male heir is always better for the family, the estate and the entire country. Female heirs in general just de-stabilise the natural order."

Lizzie's anger rose at Rupert's words, but she decided to keep it in check for the present time at least.

"Marriage is so final. Even if you don't suit with someone, you're stuck with them for life," Rupert muttered, standing up and staring out the window, brushing dirt from his palms.

"That is very true." Lizzie sighed. She knew that only too well. Even in the few months she'd been married, she had often wished she hadn't been tied indefinitely to a man who would rather bet on a horse race than spend an evening with her.

Rupert turned to face her suddenly, his eyes blazing with passion. He wet his lips with his tongue. She could feel her gaze drawn to the fullness of his bottom lip.

"We'd have something so much better, Lizzie. We could spend time together, talk, and enjoy each other's company. And then part if we tire of each other." He urged her to consider what he said, opening his hands with his palms up in a gesture of hope.

"And if we didn't tire of each other?" she asked, voicing her most worrying concern. Lizzie knew Rupert would most likely get tired of her once he had enjoyed her body a few times, but she wasn't so sure she would feel the same way. The man in front of her was changing, and his beauty was now shining brighter than it ever had. He was as honest as a child, as passionate as a rogue. He was a man she could love with all her heart and if he couldn't love her in return, she would surely be crushed.

Her question still hung in the air.

"Then, we marry." Rupert choked out these words, his discomfort evident as he shuffled his feet.

"That simple, is it?" Lizzie asked, placing her hands on her hips as anger continued to stir in her belly. What if she, after spending time with him, decided she didn't want to marry him? Had he thought about that? Big rake that he was, could she trust him not to break her heart every night he didn't come home?

"Would you not marry me if asked?" Rupert cocked his head to the side as he stepped closer to her.

"I don't know, and you won't either unless you ask in earnest," Lizzie shot back, annoyed that he couldn't see how much more she wanted from him. She may have been content with lukewarm affection from other gentlemen, but from Rupert, she would require his whole heart.

"I am the heir to an earl," Rupert explained, with a smooth voice and a smile, oozing *tonnish* charm and creeping closer still.

Lizzie wanted to laugh at his attempts to charm her, but stuck her nose in the air instead.

"I don't care about any of that. I have money and an estate. I want a man who loves me, Rupert. Who desires me..."

"I desire you!" Rupert growled, now within touching distance.

"My body you desire, not me as a person," Lizzie reminded him, annoyed despite her resolution not to be. She was so much more than a lump of flesh to be fondled, didn't he see that?

"No! I desire a woman who can speak five languages, is honest as the day is long and wants children beside her, not just in the nursery!" Rupert growled again, unknowingly spouting off the words that would draw her in completely. Did he understand her? Could he want her for who she really was?

Lizzie swallowed the uncomfortable lump in her throat. She couldn't take it anymore. He was so close now; she could feel the heat of his breath and her body ached with need for him.

"Kiss me, please." She couldn't take any more of this banter. There was no one around to hear them or see them and she wanted nothing more than to feel his arms around her.

Rupert moved forward and swooped, his lips diving to capture hers. He wrapped his strong hands around her waist and lifted her high. She instinctively wrapped her legs around his middle and opened her mouth to his searching tongue.

Finally, something inside her cried, and they each moaned in unison.

Rupert kissed her deeply as he walked the few feet to one of the stable walls and pressed her up against it. The wall was dirty and hard, but Lizzie didn't care. She needed him closer. He held her there with one hand under her bottom and using his other hand, tugged down her bodice to give him access to one breast.

Lizzie cried out as he exposed her nipple, arching her back to encourage his touches. He dipped his head and licked the tip, suckling her gently.

"Oh, Lizzie, I want you so," Rupert groaned against her skin, thrusting his pelvis into Lizzie's open thighs and pressing her higher on the wall.

Lizzie moaned in response and tugged on Rupert's hair so that he would bring his lips back to hers. She needed him everywhere. Her mouth wanted his kisses, her breast wanted his touches and between her legs, she was beginning to feel wet and hot and very uncomfortable.

Rupert thrust his tongue into her open mouth, and she sucked on the hard muscle, drawing it deeper into her. She broke away, panting as she ground against him.

"Yes, Rupert, please." Lizzie panted, unable to breathe. She was on fire. Rupert's hardness was pressing against the sensitive spot between her legs. She had never realised that area could be so sensitive, but he was giving her pleasure already. Liquid fire raced in her belly. She needed him there. She had never felt like this before. Lizzie finally understood why people coupled for more than procreation.

Rupert continued kissing her, pulling away only to dip his head and draw her breast back into his mouth. Lizzie arched her spine to give him unrivalled access and rotated her hips to entice him further.

Rupert groaned, but did not move to touch between her legs, where she was aching for him. Lizzie began to thrash. She was ready to bed. What else could she do to encourage him to hurry up? She needed him, and he didn't seem to feel the same way. Why wasn't he laying her down to join with her?

"Please, Rupert," she begged again, pulling his face back up to her so that he could look into her eyes. Frantic brown met smouldering blue. Then something strange came over Rupert's face, something desperate.

"Tell me you want me," he demanded, rucking up her skirts in hard, measured tugs until he was pressing against the slit in her thin drawers.

Lizzie moaned and tilted her pelvis in an invitation as old as time.

Rupert gasped as his fingers came into contact with her skin, his gaze snapping up to meet with hers.

"Where do you want me?" he asked almost incoherently. Lizzie understood him.

"Here," she panted, pressing one of her hands between her legs and in return caressing him. She ran her hand over him and marvelled at the hardness there, feeling an intense kick of female satisfaction when Rupert closed his eyes and moaned in obvious pleasure.

"What do you need, Lizzie? Tell me," Rupert urged again. Lizzie heard the words, but could barely understand him. She knew the tone, though.

"This, please," Lizzie panted again, caressing him boldly over his breeches once more. This time, she concentrated on the hard, rather considerable length of flesh beneath her palm. She flattened her hand against him and realised she didn't cover most of him. Was she going to be able to do this?

An inhuman noise rumbled out of Rupert's chest, and Lizzie practically heard his control snap. Holding her effortlessly against the wall with his body, her legs wrapped tightly around his hips, Rupert tore open his breeches. Lizzie cried out as the coiled tightness in her belly built up.

His fingers probed the slit in her drawers and then he ripped open the material, cold air drifting over her hot, wet nether regions.

Lizzie could feel the violence in him, in the tremble of his shoulders, the rock-hard strength of his body. Instead of being afraid of his strength, of what he could do to her, she revelled in it. She encouraged him to an even greater need. She wanted him to want her as much as she wanted him, to the exclusion of all others. She moaned when his warm and gigantic hands cupped her bare buttocks and positioned her. Apprehension made her still. She wanted him desperately, but would it be as uncomfortable with Rupert as it had been with her husband?

No, this would be different. She was sure of it!

The worry flew out of her head as quickly as it had arrived when Rupert ran his fingers between her legs, rubbing her over and over again. She jumped and gasped as heated sparks tingled in her legs, in her belly, making her nipples ache and her insides throb with wanting. Lizzie couldn't help the moans that bubbled out of her throat, a pleasure that was unknown to her until now, coursing through her veins, her body clenching in anticipation of what was to come.

Rupert gripped her hips and positioned her body so that the head of his engorged penis lay at her entrance. He pressed in slowly. Lizzie grabbed tight to his shoulders as he slid in effortlessly, her tight, wet core gripping him. The ache inside her body sighed in relief, but there was more to come, she was sure of that. Rupert grunted and plunged to the hilt, burying himself completely within her tiny body.

Lizzie gasped in surprise and clung tighter to the man in her arms. He was so much larger than her husband had been. The breadth and length of him was almost overwhelming. Her greedy body welcomed him. There was no pain, only pressure and an incredible feeling of fullness where she had been empty and aching.

Rupert stilled, thankfully, holding himself there, deep inside her body. The feeling of fullness relaxed and the need in her belly still tugged at her.

Rupert seemed to be shaking from the strain and gasping for breath.

"Are you feeling all right?" he asked, gruffly.

Lizzie saw the concern and something odd fluttered near her heart. He cared. Despite the fact that he was buried deep inside her, he had stopped to ask about how she was feeling. He hadn't continued what he'd been doing. He was waiting for her to say it was all right. She had expected pleasure from a man as experienced as Rupert, but she had not expected so much care. Tears of surprise and joy came to her eyes and silently slipped down her cheeks.

Lizzie watched Rupert's face crumple. He shifted as though he was trying to dislodge her. That wonderful feeling of fulfilment and fullness was about to be taken away from her. She cried out in distress, and her body clamped down on him. Internally, she was pulling him back inside and externally, she was wrapping her arms and legs around him like a limpet on a rock.

"No," she cried, grabbing his jaw with both hands and pulling his face back to hers. She kissed his surprised mouth and pulled back only a tiny bit so that she could whisper against his lips, "I need you, please don't stop."

Rupert stared into her eyes as though determining her honesty, his gaze wide and searching. Then his mouth tightened, and he grabbed her arse, thrusting back into her, hard.

Lizzie didn't dare look away. His blue gaze watched her with such intensity she was afraid he'd stop if she dared to close her eyes.

A moan fell from her lips. He thrust in again harder. He was moving slowly, controlling each thrust, angling her hips to rouse her body.

Lizzie was dying, she had to be. Nothing had ever felt so right. She could feel the pleasure in every part of her body. Her hands burned, her toes were curling and that place between her thighs he was pleasuring, was alight.

Lizzie started screaming. It was too intense. She wouldn't survive this. She tilted her pelvis to meet his, to try to take him in deeper.

Rupert groaned against her, pounding harder.

The tension within her belly wound as tight as a spring. Rupert was pushing her higher and higher up an unknown hill. Then he thrust once more, and she fell. Off that hidden cliff edge, into an abyss that caused her body to spasm and convulse, and the greatest pleasure she had ever known washed over her.

Rupert gripped her hard and bellowed in pleasure as he pulled out of her body and shook in her arms. He turned so that his back was against the stall door and slid to the floor.

They landed with a light thump and Lizzie couldn't help the giggle that escaped her. Rupert normally looked Herculean-strong, yet at this precise moment, he looked as happy and vulnerable as a child.

Chapter Nine

Rupert forced his eyes to open and took in Lizzie's happy, flushed, and shining face.

Unable to resist, he kissed her long and deep, feeling himself stir beneath her bottom. Lizzie pulled back and her expression changed. Her previously ecstatic eyes widened and a new smile replaced the old.

Could he want her again? So soon after being sated? Impossible! She wiggled her bottom, and his flesh twitched and began to stiffen. A deep groan escaped his throat as blood began to pulse through him yet again.

Lizzie unwound her beautiful legs from around his waist and placed her knees on either side of his thighs. The heat of her skin and the intense look in her eyes made him grab her hips tightly. She rocked her pelvis back and forth, her still moist body caressing him in slow, agonising strokes.

Her moan was soft, ending in a gasp that hit him right in the gut. He was rising to meet her and when Lizzie angled herself so that he was rubbing over her lips, Rupert threw his head back against the wall. Lizzie closed her eyes and began to raise herself up, until his cock was cold and needy, then slowly she impaled herself on him.

It was agony. A beautiful, sweet, torturous agony. The longer he watched her face twisting in bliss, the more he couldn't believe what was happening. He had only just experienced the most mind-numbing sex of his life and now, only moments later, it was happening again.

Lizzie's eyes flew open as she moved up and down on him, riding him as one would a horse. He'd never experienced anything like it. She threw her arms around his shoulders and pulled his head toward hers for a kiss.

The kiss ignited between them like port thrown on a fire. Tongues mating, parrying and thrusting as their bodies moved in unison. Rupert couldn't sit there without moving one second longer. He gripped her hips and started moving her on him. Up and down, faster and faster, bucking beneath her in a matching rhythm. Her breath hitched and soft moans of pleasure erupted from her throat. Keeping the rhythm going with one hand, he reached between them with the other and pulled up her skirts. Crisp curls and slick flesh met his searching fingers, and he rubbed the area above their joining. Lizzie cried out and arched her back, pushing herself down onto his hand as she rode him harder and harder.

The amazing rush to orgasm began to tingle in the back of his thighs, the heat rushing up his back. Determined not to finish without her, Rupert flicked his thumb over her, faster, even as he pumped his hips to make her move along with him. It was an awkward rhythm to maintain, but he refused to leave her wanting.

Lizzie's gasps got louder and louder until she stopped with a strangled groan and her channel began convulsing all around him, begging him to join her. He moved faster and let the orgasm steal over him, his head exploding in a shower of light as heat poured through him.

Damn! Quick!

He pulled out from the slick heat of her body, his seed pulsing between them, over her skin and turning his legs to jelly.

Even as his orgasm was still rippling through his body, he marvelled at the fact he had barely removed himself from her body before it had been too late. He had always controlled his orgasms.

When he had begun, he'd asked one of the women at the whorehouse about preventing bastards. She had laughed at him but had taught him to pull out before he released his seed. He was usually excellent at getting a full measure of pleasure whilst still having control over where he spilled himself. He had never pulled out so late before.

Thanks to the position they'd chosen, she'd surely be covered in his essence. Cringing, he wrapped his arms around her and planted a kiss on top of her head where she'd collapsed against his chest.

She didn't stir.

"Lizzie?" he whispered, but he was only answered by her soft, even breathing.

Rupert let his head fall back against the stall door and held her tighter in his arms. It was so good to hold her like this. He had never spent the night with a woman before, even with his permanent mistress. He always preferred to go home to sleep in his own bed. The intimacy of sleeping together was always a step further than what he wanted to share with any of his women.

With Lizzie, though, he had the sinking feeling that if they were anywhere near his home, he would carry her to his bed, curl around her and fall fast asleep.

The thought had him moving. Old habits die hard and his fear never really died.

Rupert lifted Lizzie gently off him and lay her down on the straw. He stood up on shaky legs and fastened his breeches with fumbling fingers. Some of the fastenings were ripped, so he pulled his waistcoat down to cover the damage.

Lizzie's beautiful, sleeping face made his chest ache. Could he really have a good marriage like his friends had? Is this how it had begun for them, too? Strange feelings of tenderness with a person you had just met? Of everything being right with the world, despite it all being new?

He righted Lizzie's bodice again, regretfully tucking her perfect breast away. Lifting Lizzie up into his arms, he was amazed again at how light she was. She stirred briefly whil he carried her toward the house and lifted questioning eyes to his.

"Ssh, I'm going to tell them you have a headache and need to lie down. Just close your eyes," Rupert crooned to her, grateful in a somewhat cowardly way that he didn't have to deal with the aftermath at this moment.

She nodded gently, tucked her head into his neck and fell into a deep sleep.

~

THE NEXT DAY, Lizzie relived every moment of her time with Rupert in the stables. She even found herself running her hand between her legs during her bath, just to see why and how she had felt those moments of pleasure. She found she could, in fact, elicit some feelings using her own fingers, but it was nothing as intense as when Rupert had touched her.

The difference between the moments with Rupert and the bedding she had experienced with her late husband was immense. Her husband would lie between her legs, thrust into her despite her discomfort and leave soon after. It wasn't degrading or embarrassing as her friends had described it. He had found pleasure in her body and that had been enough.

Now, she knew what her husband must have felt at the end when he would flood her with his seed. That was also different. Rupert had pulled out of her body at the end and spilled himself on her skirts rather than inside of her. She assumed it was to prevent conception, although after being married for a year without any pregnancies, Lizzie feared that she was barren. Either way, his actions were thoughtful and showed his caring nature.

He was gone by the time she had awoken from her nap and in some ways, she'd been glad. She wanted time alone to sort out her feelings and she had to complete the few matters that had called her to her country estate in the first place.

She would be back in London for a ball the following night and she couldn't wait until she saw him again.

~

RUPERT SAT in his study the following afternoon, drinking his port very slowly. He had been over and over each moment of his encounter with Lizzie in his head and he still couldn't work out why it had been so different with her, so soul-shattering.

He had slept with every type of woman imaginable. Some were sensual and active in their attentions. Other women preferred a more passive role. Some of the more experienced women had even pleasured him with their mouths and whispered erotic words into his ears.

Nothing in his past had ever caused an orgasm that compared to the two he had experienced the previous day. He had barely touched her, and had been completely dressed, yet the urgency, the pleasure and the passion had been unsurpassed by any other encounter.

Why? He wanted to know. Was it the lack of bedding in the previous month? And if that was so, why was the second orgasm with Lizzie, moments after the first, just as good? Was it her? It had to be. She was beautiful and had a perfectly shaped body, but it was something more than that. Something in her aroused a passion in him, a response from him that had never been called on before.

Rupert couldn't wait for their next encounter. He would be in control this time. It would be in Lizzie's bed where he could kiss and touch her until she screamed. He smiled to himself, seeing in his mind's eye the tears of joy Lizzie had cried at their initial joining. Which is what they were, he had realised later. At the time, he'd been so horrified that he might have hurt her. Rupert could still feel the ache where his heart had cracked a little.

He sighed and rubbed that part of his chest where he still felt it. Something about this whole tryst was different. He wasn't sure if he was going to come out on the other side as the same man. He'd never been so obsessed with a woman. Even during those times when he had regular mistresses. He would dally with married women who offered themselves to him, but he had never been possessive. With Lizzie in his life, he desired no one else. And the idea of her being with another? He couldn't even entertain the thought!

Tomorrow he would meet her again and his fate, it seemed, was in the hands of the gods.

~

"WHAT ARE YOU DOING HERE, RUPERT?" John asked, as he walked into the Somerville ball. Dressed in his best evening clothes, he could barely contain the excitement simmering in his blood. Lizzie would be here. He was going to see her again.

Wiping his face of any signs of emotion, Rupert raised an eyebrow at John.

"Why wouldn't I be here? There are ladies aplenty."

John huffed next to him.

"Come, get a drink with me. I think Oliver and Archie are in the card room."

Rupert looked around the crowded room and found Lizzie in a heartbeat, his gaze going toward her like a homing pigeon.

"I'm sorry, no. If you'll excuse me, John." Rupert didn't wait for an answer from his friend, but headed straight into the thick of the crowd. His heart was pounding in his chest as he stepped up to the small group of ladies surrounding Lizzie.

"Mrs. Symmons, may I have the pleasure of this dance?" Rupert bowed to where Lizzie stood, along with Charlotte, Countess of Tother and Sarah, Duchess of Lincoln, the wives of Archie and Oliver.

Lizzie gave him a coy smile and held out her hand.

"Of course, sir," she answered, not even bothering to look at Sarah and Charlotte. Rupert, on the other hand, could see their amazed expressions.

He swung Lizzie into his arms and started waltzing her around the room. It felt so good to have her in his arms, he had to quell the urge to whisk her straight off to a place where he could have her all to himself.

"Are you wearing your drawers?" Rupert asked Lizzie, mostly to shock her. He certainly succeeded. Her eyes grew round and an involuntary gasp left her open mouth. Then she smiled.

"Are you?" she asked, with a flirty flutter of her eyelashes.

Rupert burst out laughing and several gentlemen turned around to look.

Sobering quickly, embarrassed by the attention, Rupert danced her away from anyone close to them.

"You didn't answer my question, ma'am," Rupert scolded.

"Neither did you answer mine, sir," Lizzie reminded him with a grin.

Rupert's cheeks flushed with heat.

"Of course, I am," he answered.

"Well, so am I," Lizzie returned, giving him an enchanting smile.

"Could you leave them at home next time?" Rupert asked, pushing his luck with her good mood.

"Would you like that?" Lizzie asked, frowning.

"Yes, I would like to know that you are naked beneath your dress, waiting for me and no one else knowing about it," Rupert confided, smiling as though he was joking. Inside, though, he was shocked at himself for asking. She wouldn't do such a thing for him. Would she?

"Is that a common request of yours to your mistress?" Lizzie asked, as if striving for sophisticated nonchalance. "I've never requested it, no," Rupert answered slowly. Why would she ask such a thing?

"What's wrong?" she asked, eyebrows drawing together.

"You aren't my mistress," he declared, feeling like he should tell her the difference if she didn't already know. The word mistress for a woman such as Lizzie didn't suit. It would be degrading.

"Then, what am I?" Lizzie asked, cocking her head

"You're my lover," Rupert corrected her.

"What's the difference?"

"Money, mainly," Rupert admitted, ruefully. Most of his other mistresses had lived in a house he permanently rented in a cheap part of town. Otherwise, they were married or widowed and still received gifts of jewellery and the like.

"I don't want your money, my lord."

"What do you want then, Lizzie?" Rupert asked, his mood serious for once.

"You," she answered quietly.

His heart did a dance in his chest and his throat constricted. He'd never heard any words so sweet. Did she want only him? That had to be a first in his life. No expectations, no needs or requirements?

Rupert finished the waltz with a courtly bow to his beautiful partner and began walking her back to her friends.

"May I escort you home tonight?" he asked politely, pitching his voice not to be heard by other guests nearby.

"No," Lizzie answered with a smile.

Rupert's smile faltered and he opened his mouth to utter a sentence that would indeed sound like a whine.

"You can meet me there later," she explained, giving his hand a squeeze and slipping a calling card into his palm. She curtseyed and made her way back to the other ladies.

Rupert watched her go and discreetly slipped the card into his jacket pocket. He made his way to the card room and barely felt his feet touching the floor. He had gotten everything he had ever wanted. At that moment, he couldn't have been happier.

Chapter Ten

Lizzie fiddled and bounced in her seat the whole carriage ride. She was glad she had asked Rupert to meet her at home as she couldn't possibly have allowed people see them leave together. But she knew that he would have kept her entertained on the carriage ride.

She hurried up the steps to her front door and it opened even before she knocked.

"Ma'am," her butler greeted, taking her pelisse, hat, and gloves.

He stepped closer and lowered his voice.

"There is a Mr. Willoughby in the study, ma'am. Would you like me to show him to the sitting room?" The old butler seemed unsure about what to do. Lizzie faltered for a moment. This was the same man her father had hired to look after his home years before. Her throat tightened and her

412

cheeks warmed. She was embarrassed to admit she had a man visiting her. Well, that had to change and her butler would have to get used to the idea. As did Lizzie herself.

"No. My chamber. In about fifteen minutes please, Saunders." Lizzie spoke breathlessly.

To his credit, the old butler's expression remained reserved.

"Of course, ma'am."

Fifteen minutes later, Lizzie was dressed in her sheerest nightgown with her hair unpinned and falling down her back.

Rupert knocked but didn't wait for a response. Instead, he quickly entered the room. He seemed as restless as a caged animal.

He stopped in his tracks when he saw her seated at her dressing table, his eyes widening, then he began undressing.

First his jacket, waistcoat, and cravat, then he pulled off his boots and stockings. He left on his shirt and breeches and started toward her.

Her belly tightened, and her hands trembled as she moved them restlessly in her lap.

He was here. Finally.

"Are you feeling... well?" Rupert asked, his brow furrowing.

Well? Lizzie smiled and stood up, closing the short distance that separated them with a few quick steps. Her arrogant big man wanted reassurance that they were making the right decision. She could see it in his eyes.

"I am very well. I am looking forward to this, Rupert," she whispered, reaching out for him. She finished unlacing his shirt and pushed the material from his shoulders. It was like unwrapping the best gift she had ever received. She'd never been more excited, not even on her wedding day. Her heart raced and a squeal caught in her throat.

Tonight was going to be spectacular and there was no downside, no risk. She knew Rupert would take care of her.

As the shirt fell away, Lizzie gasped, taking a few moments to catch her breath. Rupert had a body that rivalled the ones she had once seen in a pugilist match. Huge shoulders and massive, muscular arms. Did he box to maintain his physique?

Lizzie could stand still no longer, running her hands up his arms and over his chest in absolute enthrallment. He had a light covering of almost black hair over his golden skin and she had the sudden urge to kiss every inch of his chest. Still too shy to do so, Lizzie contented herself with exploring the warm skin beneath her fingertips and smiled coyly up at the man who was allowing her to caress him in such a brazen style.

Rupert held perfectly still and Lizzie stepped so close there was no gap between their bodies. She rose up onto her tiptoes and pressed her lips to the hollow between his collarbones, savouring how warm and soft his skin was. Lizzie flicked her tongue out very gently to taste the skin there and was rewarded with a groan from Rupert as his hands came around and roughly grasped her bottom. Only two layers of silk kept his hands from her skin.

"Ssh," she whispered, stroking his chest with her hands. "I won't hurt you." She didn't know where the words came from, but she felt like she had captured a wild beast, unused to the touch of a human. She didn't believe he was afraid of the physical side of things, but she sensed that he was skittish about any tenderness she might want to show him.

Rupert closed his eyes and shuddered under her caress.

She moved her hands to his breeches, unfastening them quickly and pushing them down his hips in one swift move. She had to slide down his front to accomplish this and found herself eye to eye with his impressive manhood. She was amazed that his huge organ had fit inside her so well, but fit it had. Twice already. She looked up to his face, but Rupert's eyes were still closed.

Unable to resist, she pressed a single, soft kiss to the large head of his organ, thanking it for all the pleasure it had given her two days before. Rupert's breath hissed between his teeth and Lizzie loved the fact that she was affecting him so much.

She stood up again and ran her hands over his chest, amazed that he was allowing her to take such liberties with his body. Her husband hadn't even removed his nightshirt when he had come to share her bed. Now she had this amazingly virile, naked male in her bedroom and willing to let her explore with him.

Lizzie stepped around Rupert's massive frame, running her hands lightly over his back and down to his sculpted behind. He was truly magnificent; like a warm, live sculpture of marble come to life.

Rupert raised his hands and pushed her nightgown off her shoulders. She let it slide all the way down to her feet and stood in front of him, unashamedly naked. There was no need to be silly or embarrassed. She had, after all, been married and there was no need to feign modesty now.

A feral growl rolled out of him as he picked her up and placed her gently in the centre of the bed.

Lizzie lay back against the pillows, not lifting her hands to cover herself. She had never been completely naked in front of a man before and certainly not with the candles still lit. Rupert had shared himself with many beautiful women. Would he desire her still? Or would she come up short in the comparison?

Rupert shook his head.

"Am I all right?" Lizzie asked nervously. Perhaps she was too small? Or her breasts not full enough?

"All *right*?" Rupert croaked. "You are the most beautiful woman I have ever seen." He dropped a kiss on her lips and she frowned. Lying wasn't necessary. She was already in bed with him. He didn't have to seduce her now.

"You don't have to lie, Rupert. I'm not going to turn back now," Lizzie assured him, a little disappointed.

Rupert laughed. A true, deep chuckle.

"Lie? About what? Look at my face, Lizzie."

Lizzie dragged her eyes up to meet Rupert's, his lie still hurting her inside.

"You are the most beautiful woman I have ever seen," he repeated with emphasis, speaking slowly and clearly.

She stared into his brilliant blue eyes and watched for any tightening of his mouth or ghosts in his eyes that would indicate an untruth. All she saw was fire.

"Kiss me," Lizzie whispered, sliding her fingers into his shoulder length hair and gripping the back of his skull.

Rupert slid on top of her and captured her mouth in a profound and possessive kiss.

Her head spun. As if he sensed her overwhelm, he moved back, then down her body, urging her legs apart. He took one of her nipples into his mouth and she arched up, wanting him closer. Rupert sucked and gently bit one of her nipples. When Lizzie moaned, he lifted his head and gave her a devastating smile.

Lizzie smiled back and turned her body so that he could do the same to her other breast. He laughed and bent his head to her eager flesh again. He made his way down her body, gently kissing and licking every inch of skin that he found along the way. When Rupert hit upon the centre of her, he planted a kiss on top of the dark blonde hair there.

"Rupert, are you sure you should be doing that?" Lizzie asked, faintly mortified that his face would be so close to that part of her. She tried to close her legs, but he wouldn't allow it. She began to cover herself with her hands, but he held them to the side. Lizzie felt panic rise. This could not be correct behaviour.

Rupert laughed at her modesty and ran his tongue around the bit of flesh just beneath the parting of her lips. Lizzie screamed in acute pleasure, grabbing handfuls of the quilt on either side of her, but no longer trying to stop him.

She couldn't believe how amazing what he was doing to her felt. His tongue was playing havoc with her flesh and she was tightening on the inside as she had done during their time in the barn. She started panting, feeling herself pushed toward that amazing plateau of pleasure.

Rupert stilled and pulled himself up so that he was face to face with her.

"Not this time," he murmured, licking her lips and giving her a taste of what he had loved.

"I want us to come together," he announced, moving his hips into position.

"Come?" Lizzie repeated not quite understanding what he meant. She had been so close to that ultimate pleasure; why had he stopped?

Rupert clenched his fists on either side of Lizzie's head and plunged into her. He buried his head into her hair and groaned.

Lizzie yelped in surprise at the deep and sudden penetration. She became accustomed to him very quickly and wrapped her legs around his hips and slid her hands around his back.

Rupert began moving, slowly at first and she moaned in time with his thrusts. She had never experienced such feelings before. How could this man turn her into such a wanton creature, who revelled in every move and thrust of his body?

"Rupert, I'm going to..." she groaned into his ear, her back arching so that her pebbled nipples brushed his chest. She didn't know what was happening to her, but she was about to fall into that sea of rippling flesh and pleasure.

Rupert thrust harder.

"Come for me, Lizzie, now," he groaned.

Her body quivered and shook and then she cried out, convulsing around him. He pulled out of her once again and hot seed spurted onto her belly as he groaned loudly, warmth sliding between them.

Lizzie gripped his sweaty back, holding him down, keeping him with her, terrified he would leave.

Rupert collapsed onto his side, breathing heavily. He reached across to the wash stand, pulled close to the bed. He wrung out a wet cloth and carefully cleaned Lizzie's soft belly. She watched him from beneath half-closed eyes and waited for him to finish.

Sleep pulled Lizzie under its dark cloak, and she wrestled to stay awake a moment longer. She curled onto her side in her sleeping position and bumped her bottom against Rupert's side. He stilled for a few moments, neither moving away from her nor getting any closer.

Then the heat emanating from his huge body wrapped around her and dreams from Heaven came down to greet her.

Chapter Eleven

Still half asleep, Rupert was warm and comfortable, dreaming about a minx wriggling on his lap. As the last of the darkness wore off, and he blinked his eyes fully awake, he realised the minx in his lap was real. The soft weight of her breast filled his palm, her delicious bottom pressed against his morning erection.

How was he still in Lizzie's bed? He never stayed the night. His valet would wonder where he was. Shaking his head to dislodge that strange thought, he kissed Lizzie's shoulder in greeting and started to roll away from her.

Lizzie gripped his hand tighter around her and whispered, "Stay," deliberately pressing her bottom up against his aroused member.

The urge to flip her over and crawl back on top of her was strong, but there was an even more overwhelming urge to run. Panic set its spurs in hardest as a hollow darkness created a pit in his stomach.

"I have to go," he said, louder than he should have.

Lizzie released his hand quickly this time and allowed him to slide out of bed uninterrupted. He dressed quickly, tucking his annoyingly aroused member back into his breeches.

"What's wrong, Rupert?" Lizzie asked quietly, sitting up in bed and pulling the sheet up to cover her breasts.

"Nothing at all," Rupert lied, unable to look at her.

He moved over to the mirror and quickly tied his cravat and waistcoat. He had done this a hundred times before. Why were his hands shaking so much?

"Why don't you climb back into bed? It's still early." Lizzie tried once more, her voice soft and non-threatening.

Rupert had the strangest urge to laugh. If he was honest with himself, he wanted nothing more than to turn around and climb back into her bed. And stay there, wrapped in her embrace. Perhaps forever.

Why did she have to do this to him? He had been perfectly happy living his rakehell life. Well maybe he had been getting a little bored with it, but even so. Why did she have to come along and confuse him when he wasn't ready? He wasn't thirty yet! He had more time.

So, as he always did when he was pushed past his limits into uncomfortable territory, he lost his temper and lashed out.

"Lizzie, please stop nagging at me. You are not my wife. We had a splendid time last night, but I need to get back to my house. We'll meet again soon." As soon as the words were out of his mouth he regretted them, but it was too late.

Lizzie gasped and then nodded, her brows coming together in a scowl.

"I'm sure you know the way out," she said stiffly, her pain-drenched brown eyes flashing before she turned away and presented him with her back.

Rupert felt her hurt and shame as though it were his own. It choked him, especially knowing he was the cause. He spent one more moment looking at her, just to torture himself, before he silently grabbed his coat and walked out.

. . .

Two weeks later, Rupert found John exercising at their boxing club. The two friends enjoyed the physicality of the sport; the sweat. It was very ungentlemanly, but that didn't stop them. The physical benefits were evident also, another thing they both enjoyed.

Rupert stood for a moment, watching John with an opponent. John was very graceful and controlled. He reminded Rupert of Archie sometimes, despite their other differences. The bell rang, and John stopped, shook hands with his opponent and walked out of the boxing area.

"Rupert," he huffed, pleased to see his friend.

"John," Rupert greeted his only unmarried friend. Sometimes he felt that Oliver and Archie had an affinity because of their wives and that he and John had been left in open space. But they had each other, which was comforting.

"Come have a whiskey with me?" John suggested, pulling his jacket on. The boxing club had a small drinking area for its members to unwind and to get to know each other.

Rupert hesitated for one moment. He needed to hit something. Then again, whiskey was like water to him. He could box after they had a drink.

"I haven't seen you for a few weeks," John said casually, taking a long swig of the best whiskey the club offered, which wasn't anywhere near the standard Rupert and John usually drank.

Grimacing at the burn, Rupert answered with a shrug.

"Just been busy."

"New mistress?" John asked with a lopsided smile.

Rupert frowned. He only wished that was the reason he had been off the circuit.

"I have been visiting a new lady recently, but I don't think it'll be a permanent thing." Rupert breathed unevenly, hoping he was lying. He couldn't talk to John about Lizzie. He simply couldn't.

"No loss, I'm sure. There's always another one waiting to fill the position, isn't there?" John laughed out loud at his joke.

Rupert tried to smile but didn't quite manage it. John was correct about one thing—there were always other women waiting. He was always inundated with calling cards and letters.

The problem was, Rupert wasn't sure anymore if he wanted anyone other than Lizzie.

"You?" Rupert asked, trying to deflect the attention away from himself.

John smiled, although it did not reach his eyes.

"I'm currently moving my latest out, and the new one goes in next week." He spoke as though he was exchanging horses. It was a conversation that had never bothered him before, but for some reason today, it made him uncomfortable.

"Six months up?" He tried to joke, knowing that John had a rule that no mistress lasted longer than six months. It must have cost him a fortune to pay them off, but then again, John had money. They all did.

"Not even. Four." John laughed, shaking his head.

"What was wrong with her? Or do I not want to know?"

"The stupid wench started talking about the long term, babies and such." John huffed in disgust and smacked his palm down onto the table.

Uh-oh, Rupert thought. The poor woman had broken John's ultimate rule.

"Oliver and Archie seem happy, don't they?" Rupert muttered, once John had finished making noises.

John looked up in obvious alarm.

"We're not going to talk about them, are we?" he gasped.

"Why ever not?" Rupert asked, honestly surprised by the horrified look on his friend's face. The four of them had been friends since they were thirteen-years-old.

"Because they're married now. They've changed."

Rupert blinked, not sure how to answer that. They had changed, it was true, but Rupert thought it was for the better.

"So, if I got married you wouldn't want to see me anymore?" Rupert asked John lightly, smiling as though it were all a joke.

"It's not that, they are just so goddamn happy, I'm sick of it. If you got married, you wouldn't turn into them." John raised his glass of whiskey. The implication made Rupert feel sick.

Was that really how John saw him? As a man incapable of loving his wife, or of being faithful to her? "Did you see the new figures on the exchange this morning?" Rupert asked, changing the subject abruptly. He couldn't talk about the subject of women, relationships or marriage anymore.

All he could think about was how he had left things with Lizzie, and how his inadequacies had made themselves known.

He was utterly exhausted.

Chapter Twelve

Three weeks later, Lizzie was at her wit's end.

Two weeks ago, she had met Viscount Courtney at a small private ball. He had quickly shown interest in Lizzie, and she had encouraged him. Not knowing where she stood with Rupert since he had stormed out of her bedchamber in a huff, she had decided to encourage the attentions of this new and eligible suitor.

Viscount Courtney was a rather nice-looking gentleman. He had cropped brown hair and brown eyes. He was taller than Lizzie but was no imposing figure. He liked to read and manage his profitable estate. He had come to town specifically to find a wife. A wife who wanted to move to the country and who wanted to continue his family's tradition of having at least six children.

Lizzie went for two private walks and a ride with the viscount. He had also called on her at home several times and had danced with her at several balls. He was pleasant and quiet. He was everything she had originally set out to find. He didn't need a dowry and was happy to court her, an older widow, rather than go straight for an eighteen-year-old debutante.

Whilst on a walk the day before he had proposed marriage between them—a marriage based on mutual interests and respect. However, instead of accepting with alacrity as she had fully expected to should he ask, she had wanted to bring up her breakfast on his shoes. She had prevaricated and not given him an answer yet, although she had promised one in the next few days.

Lizzie was so confused about her own feelings that she had finally decided to do something about it. She really couldn't stay in this limbo state any longer and knew she had to either convince Rupert to marry her or put him aside forever.

Since she hadn't seen Rupert in a while, she needed to know where they stood. Rupert hadn't contacted her, but he also hadn't been at any of the balls, luncheons or dinners she had attended. He had simply disappeared, and Lizzie was too proud to ask Charlotte or any of her other connections where he might be.

Lizzie missed him dreadfully, and if she was going to make her life with someone else, then she needed to close the door on Rupert first. Everything still felt so unfinished, and as though her heart had a great big, gaping hole in it. It was a horrible feeling and not one she had ever expected to experience.

She had accidentally learned from Charlotte this morning that Rupert was attending the soirée Lizzie was also attending tonight. She couldn't wait. She was determined to find out what was happening with Mr. Rupert Willoughby once and for all.

When she arrived at Lady Melbourne's house party, Lizzie's body was humming with anticipation. After taking off her drawers at the very last minute before leaving the house, she felt positively naked. She was so aware of that part of herself that wanted Rupert so much that she kept clenching those internal muscles. It was horribly uncomfortable to be so aroused with no relief in sight.

Lizzie stood in a small circle of people, trying to discreetly look around the room. She couldn't see Rupert. Was he in the card room with some of the other men? Or was he off with one of his many women? The thought made her frown and her heart ache in a rather painful sort of way.

"He's in the music room I believe, Lizzie," Charlotte murmured into her ear so that no one else could hear.

Lizzie flushed guiltily but gave Charlotte a grateful smile.

"Excuse me." She curtseyed to their group and made her way along the hallway to the music room. She hadn't seen Rupert since the morning he had left her room.

"Would you please get off me, Elise?" Rupert's voice came through the open music room door, loud and annoyed.

Lizzie stalled outside the door, not sure whether she should retreat or burst in on them. She had no right to interrupt, as she wasn't his wife. So, she stayed still and listened.

"I heard your latest mistress has gone. Why don't you take me home instead?" The woman purred.

"Because I am not interested in you or what you are offering. I told you I am not available." Rupert's syllables were clipped, and Lizzie could hear the restrained anger in his tone.

"But I know what you like. I could..." the woman purred again.

Lizzie almost gagged.

"I don't care what you think you know, I'm not the same person I was a month ago. I don't want a mistress any longer." Rupert spoke slowly and succinctly as though he were talking to a child.

Dead silence.

"You plan on *marrying*?" The incredulous voice sounded almost wounded.

"At some stage, yes, Of course, I do," Rupert said, quieter now.

"Then you can play until then," the woman said, her voice oozing honey.

Lizzie tried not to smile; obviously, the woman was married, or she'd be trying to talk him into marrying her instead.

"Elise, listen to me. It is over between us. Stop."

The command in the words was unmistakable, and Lizzie decided this was the time to enter. She may not get another opening.

She walked through the door, trying to look as though she hadn't been listening.

"Oh, good evening," she greeted them both with a polite and falsely surprised smile.

"My lord," she then greeted Rupert directly, curtseying lower than was necessary.

Rupert gave Elise a look that clearly told her to leave.

The blonde looked ready to commit murder. She stared between Rupert and Lizzie and her eyes narrowed.

"Are you telling me that this little mouse has you under her spell? You couldn't possibly want *her*." Elise pointed at Lizzie and all but spat the words.

Rupert gave Lizzie all his attention, and didn't even glance back at the blonde.

"Please leave us," he said, rudely flicking his wrist toward the entrance of the room. The woman stormed out and Lizzie couldn't help the smile that lifted her lips. Rupert followed Elise quickly, closing the door and sliding the lock into place.

Her pulse quickened as he turned back to her. Just seeing him after all this time was a powerful aphrodisiac. He seemed to feel the same way, if the greedy look in his eyes was any indication.

"God, you're beautiful, Lizzie. I've missed you."

"I've been here. Where have you been?" she demanded. Lizzie had originally assumed that Rupert had moved on from her. But after hearing his conversation with Elise, she was almost certain he hadn't.

"At home, at my club, nowhere special." Rupert shrugged, moving back to stand by the fireplace.

"Really? Haven't been interviewing new mistresses?" Lizzie couldn't resist asking.

"No, I told you I don't want anyone but you," Rupert said, the aloof mask falling from his face and showing her how much he meant what he said.

She gasped at the raw emotion on his face, but clenched her teeth against her growing need. First, she wanted answers.

"You still feel that way? I thought after you left my bed so abruptly three weeks ago and never came back that you had decided I didn't quite fill the position." Lizzie allowed her hurt to show. Her eyes shimmered with tears at the remembered pain but she blinked them back before they could fall.

"I'm sorry if I made you feel that way. I had no plans to be with anyone else." he admitted

"Then why did you leave like that?" Lizzie asked the question she had waited three weeks to know.

"Because I wasn't sure if I was ready for a commitment that included waking up next to you," Rupert admitted gruffly. "Why was it so horrible?" Lizzie asked, choking on the words. She'd never woken up in the arms of a man. Her husband had always slept in his own bed following intercourse. "No, that was the problem. It felt good and reasonable.., and like something I could do every day of my life." Rupert admitted. "When I woke with you in my arms, everything felt so right that it scared me. It scared me so much I ran. I'm not proud of how I handled things that morning. But that's the truth, Lizzie."

"Why were you so scared? What was the problem?" Lizzie asked, exasperated now. He truly was like a five-year-old in a twenty-eight-year-old body.

"The problem is that I have never spent the night with anyone before!" Rupert barked.

"Never?" Lizzie repeated, shocked. Hadn't he slept next to all of his mistresses?

"Never. Waking up with you in my arms and your soft body curved against mine..." Rupert's hands curled as though still holding her.

"Tell me," Lizzie whispered, desperate for some clarity.

"I can't explain it to you. I had to leave, but I didn't mean to hurt you." Rupert answered gruffly. Lizzie sighed heavily, disappointed with his response. It was clear that he felt something for her beyond physical, but why could he not admit that? She was half in love with the big oaf, and he was running scared from his feelings for her. How was she ever going to truly know how he felt? How was she going to tell him that she was considering marrying someone who was the Anti-Rupert?

Easily, she realised. Just open your mouth and tell him.

"Viscount Courtney proposed to me yesterday," she announced, biting the metaphorical bullet. She strolled, pretending casualness, over to the piano and sat down on the stool.

If she wanted a test of Rupert's feelings, then this would certainly be it.

"Has he indeed?" Rupert said, stilling suddenly. "And what answer did you give him?" When she glanced up at him, Rupert's face was studiously blank.

"I haven't yet given him an answer. He is offering me everything I thought I wanted. He is a gentleman who spends most of his time on his country estate. He comes from a large family and intends to continue the tradition," Lizzie explained, blushing. It felt very strange discussing marrying, and therefore procreating with another man, when you were talking to your lover.

"You can't marry him," Rupert exploded.

"Why not?" Lizzie asked quietly. She looked up at him with eyes that begged him to give her a reason, any reason.

She was so confused. She had finally achieved exactly what she had thought she wanted. A polite, quiet gentleman had offered her marriage and family.

And yet she was no longer sure if she still wanted that calm, average existence she had once believed to be the pinnacle of achievement.

"Because...because..." Rupert floundered, throwing his arms around. He looked like the epitome of a ruffled gentleman.

Why not indeed. Lizzie studied him with a frown. A respectable, rather dull, but nice gentleman was offering her exactly what she wanted, but what Rupert himself refused to offer. Obviously, he wasn't sure he could offer her marriage, but he didn't want her marrying someone else?

Annoyance rose in Lizzie's breast.

"Because *why*, Rupert? You need to give me a proper reason," she persisted. She knew Rupert cared for her, but how *much* did he care? As much as he had for every other lover he had taken? More? Enough to offer for her? Or just enough to not want to stop bedding her quite yet?

"Because I still want you," he said. "I thought you were enjoying our... this." He gestured between them. "I've never spent the night with a woman sleeping in his arms before you, Lizzie," he said again, as if that explained everything.

She smiled sadly.

"I *am* enjoying this," she gestured in the replica of his hand movement. "Although I wasn't sure after what happened three weeks ago that we were still..." she trailed off and did the gesture again. "I haven't seen or heard from you since then."

"Of course, we are. I'm so sorry I hurt you." Rupert apologised again. "I shouldn't have left it so long to contact you again."

"Please keep enjoying it—enjoying us," Rupert whispered, pulling her into his arms and bending to kiss her lips.

Lizzie pushed at his chest and kept him from kissing her.

"Are you suggesting I continue bedding you *and* my new husband?" she asked, shocked to the core. Did she mean so little to him? Did he think her that disloyal that she would treat either him or the viscount in such a disrespectful manner? Did he not mind the idea of sharing her? She had wanted to kill that piece of trash that had accosted Rupert here a few minutes earlier.

Rupert's eyes darkened, and his hold on her arms became almost painful.

"Never," he growled, barely speaking the syllables. His hold tightened further, and Lizzie gasped.

She saw the clouds of a storm rolling in across his features. It was clear now that Rupert had a temper, and the very idea of Lizzie bedding another man seemed to be causing it to rear up. She felt both dismayed and excited by the knowledge that she could create such passion in the man in front of her.

"You are mine," he growled again, sweeping his hands beneath her skirts and lifting her up on to the pianoforte. He pushed her body down to make her lay flat and flipped her skirts up to her waist.

He let out a gasp when he discovered she was naked beneath her skirts.

RUPERT MOANED his pleasure at seeing her sex laid out before him, so ready for his touch. He remembered once asking her if she would come to a ball naked beneath her skirts for him. He had never even considered the idea that she might do as he asked. The idea that she had only him in her mind, and not this new man, drove his need higher than it had ever been.

He forced her thighs wide and opened her to his gaze. She was beautiful even here. Light pink and soft, and Lord help him, already wet for him. Unable to resist, he pressed his thumb deep into her passage without warning, to prove to them both how ready she was. She arched her back, and opened her mouth on a moan.

"Rupert," she begged, trembling hard. "I need you. I want you to *possess* me."

He wanted more than that. He wanted to mark her, to show her and everyone else that she was taken. That she was his.

He wanted her so much..

"Take me, please," she moaned, gripping his thumb with her inner muscles.

Rupert groaned and watched her writhe in pleasure. Her fingers clenched his hand where it lay on her belly, holding her down. He removed his thumb and took both of her hands in his, interlinking their fingers. Lizzie looked up at him then, and Rupert could see her need. His heart jolted in realisation.

I love this woman.

DESPERATE FOR RUPERT TO possess her, Lizzie writhed beneath his touch. He held her thighs open wide, still gripping her hands with his. He looked down at her beautiful flesh, knelt on the ground and buried his face between her legs.

That first press of lips on her most sensitive flesh made her scream. She didn't care anymore whether someone might hear. She could only focus on the pleasure that Rupert delivered between her legs. Rupert didn't stop at her scream. He ran his tongue around her swelling flesh and down the crevice, before thrusting his tongue into her over and over again. She cried out her pleasure in time with his tongue thrusts. She tried desperately to sit up and reach him, but Rupert held her ruthlessly down. He returned to the flesh of her swollen bud and suckled, stronger and stronger, and her pleasure grew and grew until she could contain herself no longer. She cried out her orgasm, her body convulsing over and over again beneath his mouth.

Spent from the most intense moment of her life, she lay limp and helpless, but Rupert wasn't done with her. He got to his feet with a surge and ripped open his breeches. His erection sprang proudly forth, huge and purple.

"You're mine," he growled, guiding his manhood to her dripping entrance and setting the head at the opening.

"Say it, Lizzie," he demanded, not giving her body what it craved most. "Say you're mine."

Lizzie wrapped her legs around his buttocks and tried to pull him inside her. He held perfectly still and stared down at her.

Lizzie looked up and saw the blue eyes she knew so well. Tonight, they were almost black. He was on the verge of something quite life-altering, she could feel it.

"Make me," she whispered, wriggling her hips so that she got some pleasure from the position, despite his statue-like stance.

A growl filled the air around her as he seemed to lose all control; all gentlemanly concern for her as a delicate lady. He grasped her hips tightly in both hands and thrust hard, so deep he knocked on her womb in one push. Then he pulled back and thrust as deeply again. And again. This was no slow burn of mutual pleasure, no gentle persuasion. This was possession, and it called her to respond despite the violence.

Rupert didn't hold back, pounding into her small body with a force that threatened to break her. She didn't care. She was lost. She could feel nothing but a continuous pressure, filling her, changing her, demanding that she tell him that she was his and his alone.

"Yes," she answered the silent question his body was asking.

"Say it. Say you're mine," Rupert demanded, unrelenting in his hammering.

Lizzie felt it building faster than it ever had. She was going to scream again.

As if Rupert felt her tighten he slowed to almost no movement. He pulled out and pushed back in, slowly, gradually.

Lizzie groaned. How could he do that to her? She didn't want care, she wanted him as he had been a moment ago. No finesse, just pure need.

She looked up and saw the set face, the tightened jaw and the blue eyes that were glittering mutiny. Lizzie would declare herself or he wouldn't release her from this sensual torment.

"I'm yours," she whispered. "Yours, Rupert.".

RUPERT SHOUTED in triumph and picked up the pace.

"Only mine," he demanded.

"Yes, only yours," she agreed, moaning and arching her back as he started to move as fast and hard as he had before.

She screamed out loud and arched her back as she came, and Rupert kept thrusting through her orgasm and beyond. She quivered in every muscle before collapsing heavily, her eyes closing.

Rupert wouldn't have that. He bent down and captured her mouth, devouring her essence; her taste. He thrust his tongue into her as possessively from above as he was below. His release was imminent. He had barely managed to survive her declaration and her unbelievable orgasm. Now that she was face to face with him, looking into his eyes and holding him tightly, he knew he was gone.

He swelled within her, an answering groan pulled from her lips. He started to withdraw and something strange happened. "No," she demanded, beneath him, tightening her sheath around him.

Rupert felt his release descend, and he tried to push back from Lizzie to spill himself upon his handkerchief, but he couldn't pull away. Lizzie had dug her heels into his buttocks, and her arms pulled him closer. He looked into her face, desperate. It was going to be too late.

"You're mine too," she declared, her sheath caressing his organ.

And his release started. He buried his head in her neck and cried out. His cock thrust up to the hilt and his seed spilled into her body while he enjoyed the full caress of her slick walls. Nothing had ever felt so good—he thought he might faint from the pleasure. He slumped against her, completely drained, and she held him tighter. Stroking his hair, she murmured again, "You're mine too."

He sobbed and pulled abruptly out of her body and away from her. Fumbling with his open breeches, he stumbled to the door.

Lizzie's skirts fell back into place as she gingerly slid off the pianoforte. "Are you okay?" she asked with genuine concern in her voice. Rupert felt as though he was being tortured. He was terrified at what was happening. He had never felt this way, ever, in his life.

"I have to go, I'm sorry," he apologised, unable to see any other way of dealing with the overwhelming emotions that flowed through his body and mind.

"Okay, if you must," Lizzie murmured.

Rupert looked over his shoulder once as he opened the door. Regret filled him at the confused look in her expression.

"I didn't hurt you, did I?" He asked gruffly, running a hand through his dishevelled hair.

Lizzie shook her head emphatically. "Physically? No."

But her feelings were once again hurt. He could tell by the sadness in her beautiful eyes.

I love you, he wanted to shout. But he was too afraid.

Instead, he simply stared at the woman he loved and then ran from the room.

What was he going to do? He had experienced the most incredible joining of his life that went far beyond the physical realm. Could he marry a woman like Lizzie? A woman who would expect fidelity? A woman who would expect children? Hell, he may have just given her a child. He heard her declaration ringing in his ears as he pounded out the front door and called for his carriage.

You're mine too!

Chapter Thirteen

"Lizzie, it is so good to see you!" Charlotte exclaimed, seated on her chaise in the middle of the formal sitting room. "Forgive me for not getting up, my back has been ever so sore." She smiled serenely and rubbed her large belly.

Lizzie curtseyed and sat down opposite her friend. Her envy of Charlotte's condition made her heart ache, and she had to swallow against the unwanted tears.

"Don't be silly. You're splendid for seeing me at all. If you were like our mothers, you would stay reclined on the chaise for the next three months," Lizzie joked, attempting to ease her own discomfort with humour.

Charlotte chuckled, and Lizzie smiled. When was the last time that had happened?

"What brings you to visit, Lizzie? Would you like a cup of tea? Do you have something on your mind?" Charlotte asked, cocking her head to one side.

Lizzie grimaced. How did this person know her so well? Was her broken heart status so clearly written on her forehead?

Charlotte and Lizzie's mothers had been childhood friends, and she'd seen Charlotte throughout their lives. She was a kind, fiery, beautiful lady, who Lizzie admired greatly.

"I've come to say goodbye, dear Charlotte. I've decided to go home," Lizzie explained, trying her best to sound cheerful.

She was running away, and that didn't sit well with her. But she could see no other way. She'd refused Viscount Courtney on principle, and now that she'd lost Rupert, her heart was broken.

"But the Season isn't even half finished, Lizzie. I thought you were hoping to remarry this year?" Charlotte asked, her tone puzzled.

"I...ah..." Lizzie's prepared speech stuck in her throat, and she looked down at her hands clasped in her lap.

Lizzie heard the swish of silk skirts as Charlotte made her way over to her side.

"Tell me what's happened," Charlotte probed, sitting down next to Lizzie and sliding her hand into hers.

Heat tingled in the back of her throat and moved up into her eyes.

"It's Rupert," Lizzie sobbed, unable to hold back her tears anymore. She hadn't been able to discuss this with anyone and the weight of it was hurting her.

Charlotte inhaled sharply and opened her mouth wide. "Archie," she screamed.

Lizzie covered her ears. She'd never heard a lady scream before.

At least, other than her own screams when Rupert pleasured her so intensely.

"No, no, you can't tell him anything." Lizzie grabbed her friend's hands, shocked that Charlotte would betray a confidence. Why would she be calling for her husband?

Charlotte frowned. "I'm sorry, Lizzie, but if you want to know why Rupert has done something, or how he feels, then you have to ask someone who knows him. My husband has been friends with that scoundrel for almost twenty years, and if anyone can give you an insight into Rupert Willoughby, it's Archie." Charlotte nodded once and finished her speech with a smug smile.

"He's not a scoundrel," Lizzie whispered, a tear sliding down her cheek.

"You called, my dear?" came an amused voice from the door.

Lizzie looked up and gave Archie a thin smile. His smile was cordial and not the least bit angry that he had been summoned in such a way. Lizzie didn't think any gentleman should be subject to this sort of questioning. But Charlotte was right. Lizzie wanted answers, not just a shoulder to cry on.

Archibald Turner, the future Marquis of Hunting and the current Earl of Tother, inclined his head. Instead of running away as Lizzie expected him to do, he instructed the butler that they weren't to be disturbed, stepped into the room and shut the door.

Charlotte's husband was very handsome, but quite serious. He was much leaner in build compared to Rupert. His eyes were gentle and his attire that Lizzie so often found overwhelming, was quite dull today. For some reason, Lizzie found that comforting.

"How can I help?" Archie asked, sitting down opposite them. He showed little emotion on his face, but Lizzie saw kindness in his eyes.

"Tell him," Charlotte urged Lizzie. The command in her voice was unmistakable.

Lizzie glared at her friend. What did Charlotte expect her to say? That Rupert had given her the most incredible pleasure of her life and then ran away when things became too serious between them?

Never. She wasn't even sure she could articulate the words. She shook her head and refused to open her mouth.

"Rupert seduced her, and now he's ignoring her," Charlotte announced.

Lizzie gasped. "He didn't seduce me."

"But he did take you to his bed?" Charlotte prodded.

"Yes," Lizzie whispered although it had never been in his bed. She looked down again, hanging her head.

"How often? If you don't mind me asking." Archie's voice came quietly through the silence.

Lizzie sighed. If she ran away to her country estate, she would never know why the man she loved had run from her. Archie was the best person to ask. But how did one guess what was in another's heart?

How could she divulge what had happened between them the last time they were together? It would be too embarrassing.

"Three different days, several times," Lizzie answered, heat racing up her neck and flourishing over her face like the fire crackling in the grate.

Archie cleared his throat. "I'm sorry to say, that isn't unusual. Rupert has always shared a woman's bed for as long as they were both agreeable and then moved on. I'm sorry," Archie apologised, clearing his throat yet again.

He was clearly uncomfortable, shuffling on the chaise and glancing to the ground when she looked at him. However, at the behest of his wife he was doing his best to help. For this, she would love Archie and Charlotte forever.

"You don't have to apologise. I know he's a rake." Lizzie picked at the white lace on her waistband.

"Then how can I help you?" Archie asked, looking between them with his eyes wide, clearly baffled as to why he had been dragged into this awkward conversation.

Lizzie received a sharp jab in the thigh from Charlotte and looked at her, startled.

"Ask him. If you want to know something, ask."

Her bright smile gave Lizzie confidence, and she blushed again as she readied herself for the conversation to come. This went against every rule that she had ever been taught about polite society. Then again, Archie and Charlotte were aristocracy. If they sanctioned such talk, could it be so bad?

"I was wondering why I scared him so much," Lizzie explained, clenching her skirts in her hands.

"I don't understand what you mean," Archie asked, gently again.

"Well, the first time was relatively normal. The second time he stayed overnight at my house and said he got scared because it felt good to wake up with me and..."

Archie's swift intake of breath stopped her mid-sentence.

"He stayed the night with you? Slept...with you?" he asked, his eyes wide.

"Yes," Lizzie admitted, blushing again at Archie's direct look. Why was that so unbelievable?

"Why is that so shocking?" Charlotte asked, echoing Lizzie's thoughts. She was apparently confused as to why Archie had stopped Lizzie at that point in her story.

Archie shifted in his seat and cleared his throat again.

"Rupert never sleeps the night with anyone. He doesn't like to establish any intimacy."

Charlotte made an unladylike scoffing sound and Archie hushed her.

"Charlotte, there's a big difference for a man between the physical bedding activity and real intimacy. That's why most men go to brothels, because they can leave immediately afterwards. It's what separates the whores from wives or true lovers," Archie explained, more emotion in his voice than Lizzie had ever heard before.

"Not that you'd know," Charlotte reminded him with a smug smile.

"Not that I'd know," Archie returned, giving Charlotte a smile of such sweetness that Lizzie had to look away for fear of crying again. Why couldn't Rupert love her like that?

"So, the fact that he spent the night with you means something, Mrs. Symmons," Archie explained quietly, speaking the words slowly as though they were a foreign language.

"Oh, it's Lizzie," she exclaimed, amazed that she had never given Archie leave to use her first name.

"Thank you, and please call me Archie." He smiled warmly, and Lizzie smiled back.

"So, explain to me why he got so upset that morning and ran out," Lizzie asked again, shuffling to the edge of her seat. It still didn't make sense to her.

Archie smiled sadly. "I can't tell you exactly why, but I know that Rupert has spent the last ten years making sure that no woman has meant anything to him. Every woman he has been with has been disposable."

"He told me he wants no one else except me," Lizzie whispered, a tear escaping her eye at the memory. She dashed it away with the back of her hand.

Archie stilled as both ladies turned to look at his shocked expression. He cleared his throat and then coughed loudly.

"Then that would be a first," he said, obviously trying not to say too much.

"And there's one more thing, but I'm not sure I can say it," Lizzie announced quietly, jiggling in the excitement of revelation. What she was about to say was beyond inexcusable.

But she was bursting with it, and the news would erupt soon enough.

"You can tell us anything," Charlotte encouraged, patting Lizzie's knee again.

Lizzie took a deep breath, amazed she was even considering this.

"Well, last week when we were together, he made me say I was his and only his, so that I wouldn't marry Viscount Courtney," Lizzie confided. This was something that she knew she shouldn't share, but it seemed important somehow.

"Holy God," Archie breathed, looking more shocked by the minute. He was blinking rapidly, and his eyebrows had risen on his forehead.

"And there's one more thing, but I'm very embarrassed to admit it," Lizzie murmured. She was totally committed now; there was no holding back. She took a deep breath and told them. "The real reason I want to leave is that I'm afraid he won't forgive me for what I did to him. I can't handle seeing him with other women. It would break my heart."

"What could you have done to him?" Charlotte asked, looking between Lizzie and Archie as though the answer could be found there.

"Well, he has always, well, not finished inside..." Lizzie trailed off, mortified, but determined to finish. She looked down at her lap, then snuck a peek at Archie.

Archie blushed but nodded in understanding.

"But last week, well, he'd said I was his and I only wanted to prove he was mine too and I wouldn't let him pull away," Lizzie blurted out in a rush.

Lizzie looked at her friend and found that Charlotte had her mouth hanging open. Lizzie had an overwhelming urge to laugh. To confound

Lady Charlotte, future marchioness and daughter of a dragon dowager duchess, was a remarkable thing.

Archie stood and paced, growing more agitated and more restless with each step. He murmured to himself, flinging his hands behind him and then forward again.

Lizzie opened her mouth to speak, but he held up his hand to stop her.

"Could you let me think, please?" And without waiting for a response, he continued pacing.

He continued for a full minute, the longest of Lizzie's life. Then he sat down again with exuberance.

"This is incredible," he breathed, his eyes bright.

Lizzie looked over at Charlotte to see a rather warm expression building in her friend's face. She obviously enjoyed seeing her husband look so excited. Even Lizzie had to admit that Archie was rather handsome when he was smiling. He should do it more often.

"Why?" Lizzie exclaimed, dragging her wandering mind back to the conversation. "Why is it incredible, and why would it cause him to run out on me?" she asked, frustrated to the extreme.

Archie laughed hysterically, then sobered quickly.

"I apologise." He bobbed his head in a half-bow.

Lizzie waited with drawn breath.

"Rupert never does that. Ever!" he stated, letting out the breath he had been holding.

"Okay, so he doesn't do that. Why is it such a big issue?" Lizzie asked, still not understanding the problem.

Archie laughed again, a beautiful, rich sound.

"Rupert has a severe issue with producing illegitimate children. His brother has two and favours them over his legitimate daughters. Rupert has always done everything he can not to produce children with his mistresses," Archie explained, still excited at this discovery.

"I don't think it's going to be a problem. I didn't conceive after eleven months of marriage," Lizzie murmured unthinkingly, then swallowed hard.

"It only takes once," Charlotte said, a laugh hidden in her voice.

Archie smiled again, this time giving his wife an indulgent smile and Lizzie found herself wondering how Charlotte's marriage had started.

"So, he's upset with me because he might have sired a child?" Lizzie asked. Her brows were knitting together in confusion. If that was the problem, then she was hugely disappointed in Rupert.

"No. That he even did it at all, is the problem. Rupert has always had control of his affairs and his body. He told me once that he had never even been tempted to stay inside a woman past a certain point. And you have to realise that you didn't make him, he's twice as strong as you. If he wanted to leave you, you wouldn't have been able to stop him," Archie explained, giving Lizzie a kind smile.

"So, he wanted to stay with me?" Lizzie asked, bewildered. She had been berating herself for the past week for holding on to him. It had never occurred to her until this moment that a man like Rupert could pull away if he wanted to.

"Yes, I think he did, and that for Rupert would be a problem," Archie explained again, giving Charlotte a pointed look.

"I still don't understand." Lizzie sighed, twirling her wedding ring around her right ring finger where she had moved it when she'd come to London to re-marry.

"Rupert hates that he will one day have to marry to secure his brother's heir. He never wanted that responsibility and has avoided love at all costs. You have surprised him, and he is terrified that you are making him want things he has avoided for so long," Archie murmured.

It was probably the most words she had ever heard the earl say.

"So, he cares about me," Lizzie concluded quietly, speaking more to herself than anyone else.

"Yes, I believe so," Archie agreed just as softly.

"I thought he did. I don't know why that was so wrong," Lizzie said, voicing the sadness she had been feeling since that day in the music room. Why was it so terrible for them to care for one another? Rupert had to marry at some stage, and she wanted to marry him. Why was he running away from a relationship that would be filled with passion and mutual affection?

"It isn't wrong. Rupert is readjusting his whole outlook on life and that is apparently causing him problems." Archie shrugged, accompanying it with a wry smile that conveyed an understanding of where Rupert was at presently.

"Thank you." Lizzie smiled, despite the fresh tears she could feel tingling in her eyes. She felt better. She didn't understand fully, but her problem was shared and therefore it had been halved.

"Now, my dear, may I go back to my study?" Archie faced Charlotte, giving her a mock scowl and a bow.

"Yes, and thank you, my love." Charlotte smiled up at her husband.

Archie stepped closer to his wife and dropped his voice to a whisper.

"Are you feeling well?" he asked.

Lizzie had the feeling that if she weren't there, Archie would have touched Charlotte. He was obviously restraining himself.

Charlotte nodded, rubbing her belly happily again.

Archie's eyes lingered on Charlotte for a moment longer and then he bowed to them both and left the room.

"So, what exactly does all of that mean?" Lizzie asked, turning expectant eyes on Charlotte. She wanted to understand better. Perhaps Charlotte could interpret everything that Archie had said.

Charlotte chewed her lip a moment, puzzled.

"I think that means that Rupert cares for you," she announced slowly.

"I thought so, but why is that such a big deal?" Lizzie asked, still no closer to understanding why Rupert had such an issue caring about her.

Charlotte began laughing and kept laughing, holding her belly on either side to contain the ripples of movement.

They both heard the front door close and turned toward it.

"Who do you think that is?" Lizzie asked.

"Doesn't matter, the butler will turn them away," Charlotte reassured Lizzie with a flick of her hand. Like most people of her class, Charlotte had servants milling around her since the day she was born. She trusted them to do as she asked, no questions asked.

"So why did you laugh?" Lizzie asked quietly, wondering why something that was so devastating to her could be so humorous to somebody else.

"You have to understand how I see Rupert, Lizzie. He has always been the *ton's* foremost rake. Handsome, charming and ruthless in his relationships. He has a permanent mistress and dallies with any woman who wants him."

Lizzie frowned at the reminder of who Rupert was, but Charlotte continued regardless.

"And now the rake is no more. He wants you and only you, and I just love it."

"But he doesn't want me, or he wouldn't be hiding."

Charlotte laughed again. "Of course, he does; that's *why* he is hiding. I will give him one month to come to his senses and ask you to marry him. Otherwise, I will find you a husband myself."

Charlotte grinned, and Lizzie couldn't help the small flutters of hope coming to life beneath her breast. She could only hope that he did want her, because now that she knew for sure it was he that she wanted, no one else would do.

Chapter Fourteen

A s though a judge was in his ear, Rupert could hear the man speaking, adjudicating his life. *Here sits Lord Rupert Willoughby, heir to the Earl of Sweeting, drinking alone.*

How miserable.

"Rupert." Archie's voice greeted him moments before his friend sat down opposite him.

Rupert grabbed his port glass and squeezed the crystal, staring into the depths of the red liqueur. He did not want to see his perpetually happy friend. Archie may be reserved, but his happiness radiated like a lone star at night.

He was not in the mood for any luminescent good moods.

"Archie, you know I love you and Charlotte, but you do not want to be around me today."

"Why ever not?" Archie asked, calling for more port.

Rupert groaned and shifted irritably in his seat. Why couldn't he just be left alone to be miserable? He should never have left his house.

"Don't you have a pregnant wife to watch over?" Rupert asked, unable to get the image of his hands around Charlotte's swollen belly out of his mind. That moment had rocked the foundations of his world. A condition that he had always considered a necessary evil now took on the guise of something beautiful, sensual even.

"She has company today," Archie said lightly, taking a sip of the golden liquor.

"Who?" Rupert looked up at his friend's strangely smug expression, suspicion burning in his gut. Archie had not found him by accident.

"Lizzie," Archie announced with a knowing smile, taking another small sip of his drink.

Rupert groaned and put his head down on the table with a large thud.

"Are you going to stay there?" Archie asked, amusement obvious in his jovial tones.

Yes, forever.

"Did you know that out of the four spares, John's the only one to be still considered as such," Archie said calmly.

"The Spares" was what the group of their four friends had been referred to. They were all born the spare sons of wealthy, titled, old aristocratic families. Oliver had inherited after his brother and father had died. Archie was his father's heir now that his older brother had passed and Rupert was his brother's heir after the latter had failed to produce a son.

Rupert groaned at the reminder but lifted his head and thrust a lock of black hair off his forehead.

"And if John's sister-in-law fails to have a son, then he'll inherit too," Rupert laughed humourlessly. Amazing. How the mighty had fallen.

Archie nodded silently and took another sip of his port. "That is true."

Rupert stared at his friend. Archie had obviously come to tell him something, so why didn't he get on with it?

When his solemn friend said nothing more, Rupert clenched his fists and brought them both down onto the table in front of him, hard. There was no one else in the room, and he glared openly at Archie.

"Are you going to tell me how Lizzie is, or did you mention her to torture me?" Rupert asked angrily.

Archie's eyes narrowed, but Rupert could still see the humour in them, and it made his belly tighten.

"Well?" he repeated through clenched teeth.

"She's well," Archie answered with a smile.

"Well? She's bloody *well*?" Rupert repeated. How could she be well when he was confused and lost, and so many other horrible emotions he had never experienced before that made him lose his appetite and lay awake in bed at night.

"How else should she be?" Archie asked, cocking his head at Rupert as though he were puzzled. Rupert shook his head, trying to clear the anger and the port-fog, since he'd been drinking for many hours already today. He had to focus on this conversation.

"We had a slight misunderstanding last week, and I thought she might be upset with me," Rupert admitted reluctantly. Was he ready to talk about what had happened between him and Lizzie? Seeing the knowing look on Archie's face, it seemed his hand was being forced.

"I didn't realise she was your latest mistress," Archie said casually, flicking a piece of invisible lint off his jacket.

Rupert clenched his teeth against the overwhelming feeling to smash his fist into something.

"She isn't." Lizzie had never been his mistress. His lover maybe, but never his mistress. The word was too common. She wasn't common, and what Rupert felt for her wasn't common.

"So, you aren't bedding her?" Archie asked lightly.

"I was," Rupert admitted darkly. He hated the admission being phrased as though it was past tense. She wasn't in the past for him, and after he had all but forced her to refuse Viscount Courtney's proposal, he hoped he wasn't in her past either.

"So, you've found someone to replace her?" Archie asked, a small amount of interest entering his voice.

Rupert shook his head.

"Rupert, I owe you, more than I can say, for standing by me after my brother's death, so I have brought news for you. Lizzie was planning on going back to her estate for the rest of the Season, but I believe Charlotte has talked her out of it."

Rupert was still lost. He clenched his massive fists and loosened them gradually, taking in a deep breath. How could that be?

"Why would she leave?" he asked quietly, staring at the table on which now stood an empty bottle of port. Had he drunk all of that?

"I believe she is worried that you will flaunt your latest conquest in front of her," Archie answered, waving his hand as though it were obvious.

"I wouldn't do that," Rupert said quickly. "And why would she think such a thing?" he said quietly, mostly to himself. Had he hurt her that much by breaking off contact between them? He hadn't meant to damage their relationship. He just needed time to think.

"She believes that she did something to upset you, not the other way around."

Rupert swallowed painfully, speechless for the first time in his life. He had to know more.

"Did she tell you why?" he whispered.

Archie nodded and Rupert, who had never backed down from a fight before, dropped his head and refused to make eye contact with his friend.

How horrific. Could Lizzie have revealed what had passed between them?

"What did she tell you?" he croaked, and then roughly cleared his throat. He couldn't seem to raise his head. How was he ever going to look at Archie again?

Archie set his glass down on the table with a clunk.

"She told us that she cares about you and doesn't want anyone else."

Rupert swallowed another lump that had lodged in his throat and tried to speak. Nothing came out. He placed his hand on his stomach to try to calm the unsettled feeling there. He tried again. "I think I've messed everything up, Archie," he admitted, the weight of his guilt terrifyingly massive.

"I thought I had too, and look where I am now," Archie reminded him.

Rupert couldn't help smiling at the memory of Archie lying unconscious, his head in Charlotte's lap. No one had known what had been going on between them until Charlotte had announced her pregnancy. At that moment Archie's future had seemed very precarious.

"So, what do I do?" Rupert asked, lifting his heavy gaze to his friend.

"Do you want to marry her?"

"I don't know," Rupert answered honestly. The idea was foreign. When he was younger, he had believed he would never marry. Then when he found out he had to, he had thought he would have a modern *ton* marriage. A marriage in which he would continue his discreet affairs and she could have hers. He had never assumed he would find a woman he *wanted* to marry.

Archie made an impatient noise and pushed himself back in his chair. "Bollocks."

"Pardon?" Rupert asked, blinking at the cuss word coming out of his perfect friend's mouth.

"You heard me. It's quite simple. She loves you, and you care about her. You must marry for your brother's sake at some point, and she wants a family. What's stopping you? It appears to be a simple solution."

Rupert blinked at how easy Archie made everything seem.

"I never really thought to marry," he admitted honestly. His parents had a horrible marriage where they had different lives, and his brother's marriage, which had started out so different, was now worse than that of his parents.

"Look, Rupert, if all of us took our parents or siblings' marriages as examples, none of us would marry. But look at Oliver and me. We're making a success of ours," Archie crooned.

Rupert thought that was a slight understatement and grinned wryly. He released a huge sigh and let the words come that he had been locking in a box for weeks.

"And if I can't be faithful? Or she can't have children?" Rupert voiced his greatest fears. He did love Lizzie. But what would happen if he couldn't be faithful, or God forbid, she cuckolded him when he was still faithful to her?

Archie made another disgusted noise. "Do you want anyone else now?"

"No," Rupert admitted, embarrassed. He'd always had several interests at once. No one woman had ever held his attention for long. The fact that he admitted that Lizzie did spoke volumes.

"Then why do you assume that's going to change?" Archie demanded again.

He obviously wasn't going to let Rupert out of this dilemma easily.

"And as for having children, that is a gamble you take with any wife. You never wanted the title, so if it passes to a distant cousin, do you care?"

Rupert heard the words, but they took a while to sink in. Was that the problem? Was he so worried about failing as his brother had, that he would sacrifice being with the woman he loved?

A weight Rupert hadn't been aware he had been carrying, shifted. As though shackles had been unlocked, Rupert's entire body became lighter, happier. Why did his life have to end because of a promise he had made seven years ago? If he married a woman he loved, his life would only get better, not worse.

"You're right," Rupert said slowly, as though the idea hadn't quite cemented in his mind yet. What was he waiting for? An archangel to come down from heaven and hit him on the head? Lizzie wanted him, and Rupert loved her, so why was he sitting here wasting time?

He stood up abruptly, swaying from fatigue and port.

Archie laughed, grabbed Rupert's forearm and tugged him back into his seat.

"I think you need a coffee, then you can see her."

Archie smiled openly at Rupert, and for the first time, Rupert was struck by how truly happy Archie was. They, as a group, hadn't realised the weight and responsibility Archie had always hidden behind his polish and social armour. With the weight lifted, he looked younger and indeed more handsome.

Rupert obligingly drank the coffee that was put in front of him, and even ate the steak they served him. He was impatient to get to Lizzie, but talking to a woman you had grievously injured required one's full attention. There was a possibility that there would be some grovelling involved.

Chapter Fifteen

Half an hour later they were on Archie's front step.

"Just remember to tell her the truth," Archie advised before they reached the front knocker.

"Pardon?" Rupert almost shouted in panic, pulling Archie back a step.

"I know you would prefer just to propose and get on with it, but she won't want that. She'll want a full explanation, and she may not forgive you straight away."

Rupert stood dumbstruck. Was Archie serious? He had thought just to apologise, propose and get her into bed as quickly as possible. Wasn't that how it was going to happen?

"Did you have to explain everything?" he asked, suspicious.

Archie flushed lightly, his usually pale complexion pinkening.

"Yes, but after the wedding. I was lucky," he said with a rather wolf-like smile. "She had to marry me."

And with those words ringing in his ears, Rupert followed Archie into his townhouse.

"Does my wife still have her guest with her?" Archie asked the butler.

"Yes, my lord. They are in the dining room, sitting down to a light luncheon. Shall I tell the housekeeper to set two more places?"

"That would be wonderful," Archie replied without even glancing at Rupert, and again Rupert found himself being dragged along behind his friend.

A waiting footman opened the dining room door, and Rupert was thankful that, being Archie's home, they wouldn't need to be introduced.

"Hello again, Lizzie," Archie greeted Lizzie as he walked up to the end of the table where the ladies sat.

"Just set two more places here," Archie motioned to the footman who had moved to the opposite end of the table.

Charlotte smiled at her husband and held out her hand.

"I didn't realise you had gone out, my dear." Her eyes twinkled.

Archie bowed and kissed her hand. "I went to the club and was lucky enough to find Rupert there."

Rupert couldn't pull his eyes away from where Lizzie sat opposite Charlotte, looking pale and so beautiful. He had known how much he loved her, but he had forgotten how the very sight of her stopped the air in his lungs and made his body quicken.

LIZZIE LOOKED DOWN into her soup and clenched her jaw tightly, tingles crawling up her spine. She had no wish to see him. Why had she not run away without telling anyone?

Archie indicated which seat Rupert should take, which was opposite Lizzie and next to Charlotte.

He bowed to his hostess. "Charlotte," he greeted her, kissing her hand.

"How is my future godchild this day?" He reached out rather slowly and gently lay his hand on Charlotte's large belly.

Lizzie choked on her tears as she watched Rupert reverently caress Charlotte's still-growing child. How often had she dreamed of carrying a baby? She had never thought Rupert would be a man to touch another man's pregnant wife in such a way.

Lizzie could feel a sob rising in her pained throat and then the words registered as though they were being spelled out for her slowly.

"Godchild?" she questioned, noting the tears in Charlotte's eyes as well. Perhaps it wasn't a standard gesture for Rupert to make?

"Good afternoon, my lady," Rupert greeted her politely, bowing, but not making his way around the table to touch her.

"About two months ago Charlotte informed me that I was going to be the godfather to their next child. I was honoured to be told I was their choice."

He gave her a smile that told her how happy he had been that day, but there was something else in his face. He looked calm, more so than she had ever seen him.

"Sit down, Rupert, and dine with us," Charlotte invited cheerily.

"Thank you," he returned, sitting down.

"How is little John?" Rupert asked politely, enquiring about Charlotte and Archie's son. He was just over a year old and quite a little devil.

Charlotte laughed happily and began regaling him with tails of her offspring's first words and the like. Lizzie's head was spinning, and anger as well as guilt swirled in her like a stormy sea.

Why was everyone acting like this was an everyday occasion? Didn't they know how uncomfortable she was? How much did she not want to be here?

"Should I ask for some lunch for you, Rupert? Have you eaten?" Charlotte asked, apparently concerned.

"Archie and I ate at our club, thank you," he murmured.

Lizzie looked at him and noticed dark smudges under his eyes. Perhaps he hadn't been eating properly? When he caught her eye, he smiled at her, and she dropped her gaze to her plate, stabbing at the apple tart with her fork.

Rupert reached for a glass of water, and Lizzie stared, sharing a concerned look with Charlotte. What was wrong with him?

"Yes?" he asked.

Charlotte just smiled, but Lizzie couldn't hold in the words.

"Why are you drinking water? Are you ill?" she asked, genuinely concerned. Did he have a fever? She began to stand up to check, but his chuckle made her sit down again.

"I just thought it was a good time to start looking after myself, is all." He laughed again and asked for more water.

"Any particular reason?" Charlotte asked, her eyes falsely innocent.

"Yes. It's time to marry, I believe, and no lady wants to marry a drunkard, does she?" Rupert asked rather rhetorically. He took another sip of his water.

"Have you chosen the lucky lady?" Charlotte asked, grinning despite her best efforts.

Rupert nodded. "I have. I just have to ask."

"You're getting married?" Lizzie asked, dumbstruck. Could Rupert be so cruel as to come here and rub her nose in the fact that he had found the person he wanted to share his life with? He couldn't seem to spend a moment with her without losing his sanity, yet not even a week later he had found the woman to whom he would be tied eternally.

"Hopefully, I..."

Lizzie ran. She picked up her skirts and fled from the dining room. Her heart was pounding, and her hands were shaking, but she needed to get away from these terrible people, now. How could they not care at all for her feelings?

She made it to the front door and reached to collect her coat and bonnet, ready to make a mad dash into the street.

Rupert came charging down the hallway like a bull, and she squealed. He hefted her up onto his shoulder, and she beat her fists on his back and shrieked as loudly as she could.

How dare he handle her like some errant child?

He ignored her feeble attempts to free herself and turned to address the butler who had rushed into the entrance area at the ruckus.

"Mrs. Symmons and I need to talk privately about a misunderstanding. Is there somewhere we can have that conversation?"

Lizzie hit Rupert's massive back again and attempted to get away. But he was too big, too strong, and her body was simply in too awkward a position.

Rupert started moving, walked into a room, shut the door, locked it and put the key in his pocket. Only then did he place Lizzie carefully down into a chair.

Lizzie put a hand to her pounding, spinning head. How dare he announce he was getting married and then prevent her from leaving? What did he want? One last tumble before he was tied for life to another woman?

"What the hell do you think you are doing?" Lizzie exploded, her need to scream again gathering in her overheated body. She pushed herself to her feet, needing to kick, punch, yell.

Rupert fell to his knees in the middle of the sitting room.

Lizzie froze. The heat leached from her face, but she remained standing. Her angry words stuck in her throat. Rupert was on his knees, in the middle of the day, looking at her like she was the sun and the moon combined.

"What are you doing?" she asked, rather obtusely.

"I'm proposing marriage to the woman I love," he announced, all the love that Lizzie had hoped to see in his eyes, shining back at her.

Her knees sagged, and she fell back into the chair behind her. Was he serious? When had he changed his mind? When had he realised this?

"When did you figure out that you loved me?" Lizzie asked, dazed.

Rupert swallowed visibly. "I realised it when we made love on the piano," he told her, refusing to get up from his knees until she gave him an answer.

"But...you left me!" she all but screamed at him. Why was the man so confusing?

"I know. I was terrified of what it meant. But I've come to apologise and tell you the truth. I didn't think falling in love would happen to me. But it has, and I'm hoping that you will make me the happiest of men by consenting to sleep next to me for the rest of my life."

Lizzie blinked like an owl. Did The Honourable Rupert Willoughby just declare love and an intention of fidelity? Impossible!

"You won't have any other women?" Lizzie asked doubtfully.

"No, I won't. If you promise not to consort with anyone else, either."

Lizzie choked on a laugh. Her? Cuckold him? "Why would I go to anyone else when you're all I want?" She sighed.

Rupert's face lit up like a yule log. "So, you'll marry me?"

Lizzie chewed on her lip. Of course, she was going to marry him, but she needed to establish a few things first.

"Where would we live?" she asked, cocking her head.

She had never disclosed to him how much money she had. Few people knew, even if he had bothered to ask around.

"Wherever you like. I currently live in my bachelor townhouse, but I also have a small country estate if that is where you would prefer to be. I also have a rather good income due to Archie's advice on investing. I am my brother's heir, so although I couldn't afford to buy us a townhouse initially, we won't lack any other comforts."

Lizzie smiled at Rupert's attempts to reassure her. He wasn't used to talking about his assets, that was quite evident.

"Children?" Lizzie asked, crossing her arms. She had been overwhelmed when she had seen him touch Charlotte's pregnant belly, but it gave her hope that he would someday look at her like that.

Rupert swallowed.

"I want children," he whispered. "With you."

"Girl children?" Lizzie couldn't help asking. He would be under a lot of pressure to produce an heir. Would their marriage go the same way that his brother's had if they couldn't beget a son?

"Any sort that comes our way. I never really cared about the title, so if it passes to my cousin, then that is the way it is supposed to be," he declared.

"Oh, what if I can't," Lizzie cried helplessly, letting her hands fall into her lap. Here she was, making Rupert earn her trust and respect, and yet she was the one with the fear of being found unsatisfactory.

Rupert dragged himself up onto the chair next to her and gently pulled her into his lap. Lizzie went into his arms gladly, settling into his lap with a sigh and burrowing into his shoulder.

"Whatever happens, happens, Lizzie. I just want *you*."

Lizzie sobbed against his shirt, the stress from the past few weeks welling up inside her and breaking forth, like the pressure of water breaking free.

"I just want you too," she sobbed happily, tilting her head up for a kiss.

His big hand came around her chin and pulled her face up to his.

"Then you'll marry me?" he said, uncertainty still swirling around those amazing blue eyes.

Lizzie laughed and wrapped her arms around his neck.

"Of course, I'll marry you, I love you too." And with that declaration, Rupert kissed her and kept kissing her, and would continue all the days of their lives.

Epilogue

Lizzie had been wrong about one thing. The happiest day of her life arrived two years after their wedding day. It had taken her more than a year to conceive, and when she finally did, she had been so worried for her baby she had hardly moved from her bed. It was only the assurances of both Charlotte and Sarah that had gotten her up and moving again.

She had been afraid to let her rather large husband into her body too, and he had been remarkably understanding about her fears. Both Sarah and Charlotte had been pregnant with their third babies around the same time, and they both professed not to be able to get enough of their husbands.

Lizzie had decided to try and found that her body was the same. Her touch also gave Rupert the intimacy he needed, for she had found that since their wedding day he did not sleep without her. Even through those weeks of her flux and choice of abstinence, he would hold her all night.

And now, almost two years to the day since she had married her handsome, blue-eyed man, she had given birth to his son. A replica of Rupert, he had black hair, blue eyes and the most gorgeous face Lizzie had ever seen.

Rupert had been there for the actual delivery, which had been most unorthodox. As was customary, he had been sent from the bedroom when the pains had started. But after more than twenty-four hours in labour and when the pains had gotten so fast and so intense that Lizzie couldn't help screaming out, Rupert had burst in to support her. He had voiced concerns early in her pregnancy that she would not beear a baby with his height well and he had been terrified that she would die and leave him. He had held her hand, mopped her brow and promptly burst into tears when his son had been laid upon Lizzie's breast.

The birth had been difficult, but the doctor assured them that it had all been perfectly normal for a first baby.

"He is perfect," Rupert cooed at his son.

Lizzie lay against the pillows. The maids had come and helped her while Rupert had held their baby. She was now clean, bathed and exhausted. While she'd been attended to, Rupert had taken the baby's swaddling off and laid him out on a blanket, naked. He was perfect. Long and thin, Lizzie was sure he would fill out like his father in no time.

"You're happy we had a boy?" Lizzie asked, elated despite her determination not to care about the sex.

Rupert looked at her and gave her a smile so sweet that her heart melted all over again.

"I am, but when he was laid on your chest, I didn't even know what he was. I just knew that we had a baby and you were still here with me. Nothing else mattered."

The tears welled up, and she let them, happier than she ever had been.

"Thank you so much for loving me," Lizzie whispered through her tears.

"No, thank you for never giving up on me," Rupert said fiercely, cupping her face and bringing her lips up to his for a perfect kiss.

"So, six weeks 'til I get you to myself again?" Rupert asked, not sounding entirely disappointed by this.

Lizzie nodded, weary and sublimely happy. Slowly, with her husband and child by her side, she drifted into sleep.

~

RUPERT STAYED WATCHING his wife for a long time after she fell asleep. He sat in the chair next to her bed with his newborn son in his arms and gave thanks for all of his blessings.

He had finally found the woman who was his other half, his equal, his *better*. She loved him unreservedly and had total faith in their marriage. That, in turn, left him feeling confident and loved. He had been jealous, initially, of any men who danced with her or tried to get her alone. But she had proven to be unstintingly loyal, and he had been the same.

He often laughed with Archie about the fact that he had once been worried that he couldn't stay faithful to one woman. Lizzie fulfilled every fantasy he ever had in the bedchamber. And when she hadn't been able to give him that during part of her confinement, the comfort of her warmth and presence in his bed was enough to keep him satisfied.

And he now had a son. The next heir to the Earl of Sweeting. Rupert's mouth curled into a wry smile. His father would have been proud. His brother would be elated. It was bittersweet. He wanted a son for his sake, not just as the heir to a fortune and title.

He looked down at his son and smiled again.

"We'll just have to make sure we take after Archie and Oliver, my boy. Lots of brothers and sisters for you."

He looked down on Lizzie's sleeping form, taking in her larger breasts and beautiful skin. His cock stirred, and he sighed. He would always want this woman, no matter what she looked like or what they had gone through.

She was his, and he was hers, through and through.

Rupert rocked his son to sleep, still chuckling gently. He would give Lizzie the large family she wanted, and he knew in doing so, he had found his purpose in life.

. . .

THE END

Hannah's Rakehell Duke

Chapter One

"Who is the young lady visiting you at present, Charlotte?" asked Lord John Dunford, swallowing back the bile that rose in his throat. His sister and her husband were truly nauseating. They stroked each other constantly and made eyes across the table at every meal. He'd never seen such a besotted pair! And to think that Archie had, once upon a time, been John's best friend!

Charlotte and Archie, the present Earl and Countess of Totherham and future Marquess and Marchioness of Hunting, finally looked away from each other. In the end it was Archie who addressed his query, not Charlotte.

"She's my cousin, Hannah Turner. She arrived yesterday evening,"

Archie murmured idly, stroking Charlotte on the back of the neck with his fingers.

John glared at the man whom he'd once considered a friend. There was a time and a place for such affection, he thought, and it was certainly not at the dining table, during mealtimes, when other people were present.

Archie cleared his throat under John's glare and dropped his hand away.

"Really, John," Charlotte snapped, her eyes flashing dangerously. "If you don't like how we are with each other, you can go back to off-season London and enjoy the resulting boredom that comes with it."

John ignored his sister's snide comment, shifting in his chair. He had nowhere else to go and they all knew it.

"Tell me about your cousin, Archie."

Surely there must be something here to amuse me while visiting my sister...

"Hannah," Archie said again, a winsome smile stretching across his usually solemn face.

John's gaze darted across to Charlotte to find the same look on her face.

How odd...

"Hannah is, well..." Archie twisted his wrist in the air as though searching for the right word to describe his cousin.

"American," Charlotte finished for her husband.

"Really? Well, then, I am intrigued." John had never met an American woman before and he had heard they were indeed an unusual breed.

"Is she a widow?" he asked hopefully. Perhaps Hannah was the perfect someone to take his mind off the fact that his life was in a veritable shambles.

His three best friends had all married themselves off and he had been left standing alone. Not only had they been bound into wedlock, which would have been tolerable, but they had all made love matches. They had stopped drinking and carousing and were generally so smitten with their beloved wives it was sickening to be around any of them.

Even the Honorable Rupert Willoughby, heir apparent to the Earl of

Sweeting, a man who'd drunk his way through every brothel in London, was now up to his neck in love.

John now had nowhere to go before the London season commenced —unless he wanted to witness all the canoodling by his former drinking buddies and their wives. He'd spent his adult years visiting his friends' homes, because his family estate in Hampshire was too awkward and uncomfortable to stay for longer than a few days. His mother became more and more resentful every year owing to the long-term presence of her husband's mistress, who was firmly esconced in the Dower House. Because of this discord, his father spent more and more time with the other woman. It was not a pleasant situation.

Archie had his family's magnificent home in Kent and John had always been welcome there, for which he was grateful. But John could barely tolerate Archie and Charlotte's company nowadays. It was bad luck for him, because he was out of choices. Oliver and Sarah, the Duke and Duchess of Lincoln, were at their own grand country estate with their two sons and Rupert had taken his beautiful new wife to France.

"Hannah is yet unmarried, but looking for a match this coming season. Her father, a distant cousin of mine, contacted me last year and I offered to sponsor her," Archie said, giving John a meaningful stare.

A virgin? *Damn!* He wasn't going near her, then.

John laughed, trying to ignore the meaning behind Archie's stare and release some of his built-up tension. If Archie thought that John would be married off any time soon, let alone to a virginal American, he was setting himself up to be sorely disappointed.

"I'm glad I can meet her first, then, Archie," he joked. "I can warn her to keep away from the dangerous rakehells who haunt London."

John chuckled again as unease flickered over his friend's face. Archie needn't worry. What the hell was John going to do with a virgin? What *could* he do, other than flirt with her to annoy Archie?

"I think that would be an excellent idea," Charlotte said, surprising him with her compliance. She and Archie shared an unreadable look, before Charlotte placed her hands on the table and leaned toward John. "Hannah should be back in the stable by now. Go and introduce yourself, brother."

"Are you certain..." Archie murmured to his wife.

"Think about it, dear husband. Just think…"

Slowly, a smile erupted on Archie's face. "Indeed." The sudden light in his eyes was a little too mischievous for John's liking.

"Why would she be in the stables?" John asked, confused.

None of the ladies he knew were ever found in a stable.

"She'll be attending to her horse, I'm sure," Charlotte said.

"She rides?" John asked, unable to quell the slight interest that pricked his voice. Although it wasn't totally unheard of, a lady who rode was rare, although Lizzie, Rupert's wife, certainly did. Perhaps Hannah was also a country girl and they could share their passion for good horseflesh. Maybe spending a little time with her wouldn't be such a loss after all.

"Mmm." Archie nodded and put his arm back around his wife's chair.

That decided it for him. He wasn't staying here a moment longer to watch any more of the wonderful show titled, *My Sister and her Sap of a Husband.*

"Then I shall go introduce myself." John stood and bowed to his relatives. Although he was using the woman as an excuse in a way, he was interested in meeting a new female. She sounded fascinating. An American lady who rode horses? He thought he had bedded every sort of woman available, but this was something new.

John trotted off toward the stables, fresh air filling his lungs. His heart felt lighter just by being outdoors. He tilted his head up to enjoy the sun and glanced across at the large green field behind the house. Once upon a time, he and Archie used to talk about nothing but horses. Now all of Archie's conversation revolved around his sons, his wife and his estate. John was bored with all of that.

He rounded the stable doors and stopped dead in his tracks at the sight of the person before him. Was that… a woman? The person looked like a well-dressed stable hand.

Could this really be the American cousin, Hannah?

He watched a moment longer, noting the graceful arm movements, the hint of lush skin and shapely thigh. His body stirred. Yes, definitely a woman.

She was rubbing down a magnificent horse with the exuberance of a seasoned horseman. She had a thick, bristled brush and she worked her way expertly across the animal's hide, making gentle chattering noises to the horse.

He held his breath as he moved closer. Hannah had long, red-gold hair that fell down her back, unbound, and she wore male riding pants and a shirt. Looking closely, John realized that the riding habit must have been especially tailored as no pair of breeches designed for a man would ever fit a behind like hers. It was so delightfully well shaped, he wanted to reach out and squeeze it.

Reminding himself that he was staring at a virgin who wanted to marry soon and that she was off-limits for many reasons, John closed the gap between them.

He cleared his throat loudly, to get her attention, but she just kept on brushing.

John bowed deeply and spoke in a loud voice.

"Miss Turner? John Dunford, your servant."

The lady in front of him jumped and whirled around with a laugh. Sunshine illuminated the air around her as if she were an angel in disguise.

"You're Charlotte's rapscallion of a brother? Good to meet you! I'm Hannah. That's what you may call me. I'd like that."

Rapscallion? John was still processing that when the woman, with bright blue eyes and a brilliant smile, stuck out her hand for him to shake.

John stared at her in stunned silence for a moment before good manners forced him to shake the proffered hand. He still had gloves on and she did not, and he found himself wishing he hadn't dressed so formally today. He was flabbergasted. Dumbstruck might even be an appropriate word.

Hannah was the most beautiful creature he had ever seen. More beautiful than Sarah, Lizzie and Charlotte combined. And that was a significant observation, because he admired all of his friend's wives.

It didn't seem to matter to his eyes that she was covered in dirt, her hair was windblown and she was wearing a man's clothing. She simply glowed with good health and a sensual promise that he'd have been a fool not to recognise. Her fine bone structure and prominent cheekbones spoke of aristocratic breeding and her full lips would make any woman envious. And any man ache to kiss them.

An uncomfortable sensation twisted deep in his gut. He was confused as to how to act; what to do. He had barely laid eyes on her and yet the effect she had on him was vastly different from any other woman he'd ever met.

Questions came shooting through John's head.

Why did she shake my hand like a man would?

Why is she here in the stable grooming her horse herself?

Why is she looking at me with her clear blue eyes, without a hint of fear, arousal or even disdain?

What was wrong with him, that the sight of her seemed to stop the breath in his chest?

"Hannah," he repeated slowly.

"Can I help you, John?" the beautiful, disheveled woman asked, moving to the other side of the horse.

John watched her sure, strong hands working the brush and realised that this was not a new occupation for her. She had obviously spent much of her life doing that same task. She was a lady, was she not? Ladies simply didn't groom their own horses.

Pull yourself together, man.

"I was ordered by my sister and Archie to find you and introduce myself." John smiled as he spoke, finally able to call on the easy charm that he usually possessed.

"Charlotte and Archie are a bit of a stickler for the rules, aren't they?" Hannah chortled and John put out his hand as if to steady himself. *Good God.* Had his knees just weakened at the sound of her laugh?

"They are," John agreed, wondering for a moment if he had just insulted his sister and friend. A smile quirked one side of his mouth. This was delicious.

"Are you staying for long, Hannah?"

John reached up to loosen his cravat, throwing caution to the wind. If she could dress in riding breeches, he could at least loosen the necktie threatening to choke him.

Why was there suddenly not a breath of fresh air around?

"Oh, most likely. My parents have sent me over here to marry an Englishman. Quite given up on me, they have." Hannah continued to speak to John without looking up from her work.

"Why would they give up on you?" John asked incredulously. She was spectacular to look at and seemed to have an easy, happy disposition. Why would anyone despair of her not finding a husband?

"I'm five and twenty." Hannah shrugged with seeming indifference.

"No." John breathed the word out slowly, unable to believe she was any older than one and twenty. Her skin had a glow of youth most *ton* ladies seemed to lose at sixteen.

Hannah looked up, saw his shocked expression and burst out laughing.

He flushed with heat. Why was she laughing at him? He clenched his jaw and crossed his arms across his chest.

He was six foot two inches tall and by no means thin. He worked hard to keep the muscle he had and yet in this moment, Hannah made him feel small and inadequate. Not a feeling he liked, nor one to which he was accustomed.

As if she sensed his displeasure, Hannah straightened up from her hunched posture and cocked her head to the side while she gazed at him. She was much taller than most of the women John knew, easily five foot ten inches. It was a rare opportunity, to be able to look into a woman's eyes so easily and he found himself enjoying her unusual height.

"Are you stuck up, too?" Hannah asked, as she put the brush down. She came around the horse and stood in front of him, placing her hands on her hips like a queen.

John couldn't stop his gaze travelling down her body.

Archie's cousin had wide hips and strong, nicely curved thighs. *Those thighs could ride him for hours.*

John's traitorous body rose at that thought. Or at least, a certain part of him did. He willed his suddenly hard flesh back down. To no avail.

"Are you quite finished looking me over?" Hannah asked, flicking her long hair back over her shoulders.

John exhaled at the flush of her cheeks and the dangerous glitter in her oceanic eyes. She was spectacular when angry.

"Well, you do make a fetching picture, my lady," he drawled, stepping closer to pick up her hand.

She shook him off and placed her other hand square in the centre of his chest.

"Back off," she hissed through clenched teeth.

"Pardon me?" John asked, his eyebrows shooting up his forehead.

Hannah didn't repeat what she had said. Instead, she shoved him backwards with one strong push of her hand.

John stumbled two steps back, a strange gargled laugh rolling out of his throat as he did so. He would never have assumed a woman would do such a thing.

"I don't appreciate false compliments and I don't like charming dandies. So, I suggest you get used to a woman in breeches. I suppose I will see you at dinner."

John rubbed his chest where she had touched him, and watched slightly bemused as Hannah stormed off in the direction of the house, her arms swinging angrily and her beautiful thick hair moving around her like a cloud.

His eyes drifted lower and once again lust kicked him in the gut like a solid horse's hoof.

She really must get a coat that covers that derriere of hers, he thought idly, as he followed her more slowly back toward the house.

What sort of lady was immune to his charms, still unmarried at twenty-five and yet somehow was so spectacular looking?

He grinned as a burst of happiness rushed through him. Perhaps this year's season wasn't going to be so dull after all? At the very least, he didn't feel sorry for himself anymore.

At dinner, Hannah was even more beautiful than John had imagined she would be. He had thought that once she was clean and tidy, her quality of disheveled loveliness might diminish a little. Instead, it was as if a penny that he had found in the dirt had been washed and polished and had turned out to be a golden sovereign.

Once again, her hair was mostly loose, defying every tradition for ladies to have their hair arranged up everywhere except in bed. He could barely take his eyes off its red-gold lustre.

"Your hair really is spectacular, Hannah," Charlotte said with awe, echoing John's thoughts.

Hannah chuckled good-naturedly and John's stomach tightened in a feeling he was beginning to identify as being solely related to the American. "That silly maid of mine tried to put it all up. It hurt my head. I will never understand how you do your hair like that every day."

Charlotte put her hand up to her beautifully coiffed hair and sighed.

"I had headaches for years when I was younger, but one becomes accustomed to it."

Her words surprised him. He'd never thought about the discomfort of such hairstyles for women in society.

"At least corsets are no longer in fashion." Charlotte giggled, her full breasts heaving over her dress. John looked away from his sister.

"One of the many reasons I am grateful to be alive today and not thirty years ago." Hannah smiled at Charlotte and took a long sip of her red wine. "I do like this wine, although I really prefer a good whiskey."

John spat wine out all over his thankfully-empty plate.

He coughed, then pounded himself on the chest to clear the airways. She drank *whiskey*? What *lady* drank whiskey?

"Are you all right, John?" Archie asked mildly, not commenting on the mess that now splattered his dining table.

"I apologize," John said hurriedly, leaning back so that the servants could clear away everything in front of him and lay out fresh cutlery, plates and glasses.

Charlotte had lifted her napkin to her mouth and Hannah was glaring at him with fire in her eyes.

John shrugged and tried to collect his dignity, which seemed a little lacking whenever he was in Hannah's company.

"And what's wrong with my drinking whiskey?" Hannah asked, placing her glass of wine down on the table with a thud.

John picked up his own glass of wine, that had been refilled. He swallowed it without tasting the liquid, and smiled at the beautiful enigma before him.

"There is nothing wrong with it, Hannah. I have never known a *lady* who drank whiskey, that's all."

Except someone like the madam of a brothel, maybe...

Hannah frowned and looked across at her cousin with a quizzical look on her face.

Archie inclined his head. "It is not common for ladies to drink liquor here, Hannah, that is true."

"Well, I shall not be changing myself for anyone." Hannah shrugged, calling to one of the footmen.

"Excuse me, what is your name?"

"Robbie, my lady." The young footman flushed and bowed.

"I would like the whiskey tray now, please. If that's all right with you, Charlotte?"

Hannah glanced across the table at her new friend, anxiety showing in her expression for the first time.

Charlotte smiled brightly. "Hannah, you may have anything in this house that you wish. You are our guest and I want you to be happy here."

John watched the play of emotions cross the other three people's faces and for the first time in a long time, he was highly entertained. Charlotte was clearly having a great time. Archie was amused, but wary. Hannah's jaw was set with determination.

The whiskey tray arrived and John held up his hand.

"One for me, also, please."

Hannah looked at him in surprise. "Can you recommend one?" she asked.

There were three bottles on the silver tray.

John recognised each one by the colour and shape of the bottle and pointed to his favourite. "That one is very good," he said.

He thought himself quite the connoisseur of whiskey and was pleased to have someone to share it with. Archie did not drink much himself, but thankfully, he kept a stock here for guests.

Hannah dismissed the servant and poured two measures of whiskey. John pushed back his chair to stand up but instead of allowing him to retrieve it himself, Hannah stood with his glass and walked around the table to hand it to him.

"Here you are," she murmured.

John jumped to his feet, by reflex. He didn't think he had ever remained sitting whilst a lady was standing.

Hannah stepped back and laughed. "Oh, do sit down," she said, swatting at his arm in an attempt to encourage him to sit.

She moved back to her chair and John sat down gratefully.

What sort of woman was this? It was the second time in the same day that she had hit him like an errant schoolboy! And he found himself grinning widely as he lifted the whiskey to his lips.

Chapter Two

John couldn't sleep. His mind galloped like a stallion at the races. He ached for the release of a woman's body and his current mistress lived far away in London. They had already agreed that she would be moving out of his townhouse the following week. He'd tired of her, as he tired of all his mistresses, and she'd reached his six month limit. Every mistress he'd ever had knew that it would only be temporary. He made that clear from the beginning, and only chose to be with them if they agreed to his terms.

Six months was not long enough to form a permanent attachment, which meant he could uphold his lifelong decision to never allow his heart to be given to a woman.

And therefore, he would never be in a position to hurt anyone the way his father had hurt his mother. And their family.

He shifted again, almost groaning at the level his body was in need. He stroked his half-erection for a moment. He had not masturbated for years and did not wish to do so now. He'd always had women available for that purpose, yet now his flesh pulsed with need and no relief was in sight.

Getting out of bed, John pulled on his robe and slippers. Perhaps one more whiskey would put him to sleep?

Though he suspected it would take a lot more than one to forget a certain curved derriere, and that flaming red-gold hair...

John took his lit candle, left his room and walked along the hallway in the guest quarters of the manor house.

Where would Hannah be sleeping? *Would* she be asleep right now, or as wide awake as he was?

He had never corrupted a virgin before. In fact, he had deliberately steered clear of any such lady. But Hannah was a mystery that he couldn't get out of his head. At twenty-five, was she really still a virgin?

A light flickered beneath the door of the library. Like the proverbial moth to the flame, John walked toward it. Who would be awake at this late hour? Was Archie having trouble sleeping, too?

He pushed on the heavy door and entered the room. Not Archie. It was Hannah.

She sat on one of the chaise lounges, reading a book. She was in her nightwear and her feet were tucked up underneath her, like a child.

John's heart pounded against his chest as he tiptoed over, stopping just before he reached her.

She blinked when she finally realized he was there. "Oh! Hello John." Her voice was quiet as she greeted him, before she looked back down at her book.

She looked so innocent and yet somehow sensual. He had a decision to make. He could excuse himself, get the whiskey he sought, and pass out within an hour. Or he could sit down and talk to this strange woman and find out if there was any chance she could quench the ache in his groin.

He stepped forward and bowed, before taking a seat opposite her.

"What are you reading?"

He crossed his legs, trying to hide his fairly obvious erection.

She bent the corner of one of the pages and closed the book. "Oh, just an old novel. I've read it before, but couldn't resist picking it up again."

She moved her legs out from under her and stretched them out in front.

He couldn't stop himself from looking down at her beautifully formed feet. *My God. Even her feet are arousing! Where are her slippers?*

"Are you unable to sleep?" he managed to croak out. "Why are you still awake?"

Hannah cocked her head to one side. He had noticed that she tended to do that when he said anything for which she was unprepared. It was as if she needed time to consider a response.

"I *was* having trouble sleeping, so I thought I'd get up and try to tire my brain with a little reading. And you?"

John grinned. How could he frame his answer in a delicate manner?

I kept thinking about you and my body went into overdrive with this damn erection.

"I rarely sleep before two in the morning," he said. "They retire so early here."

Hannah blinked, then frowned. "Why would you stay awake so late on purpose?"

John stared at her for a moment and waited for the smile that would indicate she was joking. When it didn't come, he realised that she really had no idea what he was talking about. He tried to explain. "London balls, parties and such generally go on quite late into the night. However, life in the country is very different. The London season has quite spoiled me for country life, I fear."

"Oh, in America we never stay out so late. If that is the case, I am going to struggle here in the London season, indeed." Hannah sighed, getting to her feet.

John jumped up, his body far too aware of how nicely her nightgown clung to her lush curves. Heat was coiling up inside him once again, his hunger growing by the minute.

"I think I'll be going to bed now."

"Shall I escort you to your door?" he asked, interested to see her response. They were alone, dressed for bed and it was the middle of the night. Would she be interested in him staying in her bed tonight?

Hannah nodded. "Yes, if you wish." She left the book on the table and walked toward the door.

John grinned devilishly as he enjoyed the view of her rear. If she didn't want her book, perhaps *he* could put her to sleep?

"Did you court much in America?"

Hannah looked back at him over her shoulder, and then laughed. "I was engaged once, but no. Not many men have courted me." Her eyes moved over him in what he considered an assessing way.

His erection lengthened and pushed against his nightclothes. Surely, she could see it?

It seemed not. She slipped out of the library and he quickly followed.

When they reached Hannah's door, she opened it and turned to face him. "Thank you," she said.

She looked ethereal, bathed in candlelight, her night gown almost transparent in the shining firelight. She was too beautiful to resist.

John didn't think, he simply leaned closer and pressed his lips against hers, pushing her into the door frame.

Hannah went still as if in shock, then she began to respond, moving her lips against his. The sensation was divine. Then she pushed at him with her hands as though she wanted to stop. John pulled back, confused.

"Let me put this down," Hannah said, a husky tone purring through her voice. He stepped back and she placed the candle she was holding down on the floor at a safe distance, then righted herself again.

Satisfaction shot through him. He *had* been right about her. She obviously wasn't a virgin. How could she be at her age?

He stroked a hand down her beautiful face and gripped the back of her head, loving the feel of her unbound hair flowing between his fingers.

He forced her lips open this time with his own, absorbing her surprise and licking the inside of her mouth.

She gasped, but gripped both of John's upper arms, holding him close. Heat rose in his body, making him ache for her.

John broke off from her intoxicating lips, gasping for air. All the blood in his body was rushing to his groin, making his cock throb and harden. He was going to finish in no time at all tonight.

He stepped away from Hannah and walked into her bedroom. He was far too attracted to this woman, he realised, as he panted for air. His response to just a simple kiss was making him slightly dizzy.

John threw off his robe and stepped out of his slippers. He was naked now in the warmth of her bedroom.

He turned to find Hannah still leaning back against the door jamb, the door still wide open. She was staring at him with something akin to shock. Her mouth was hanging open.

"Shut the door and come join me," he coaxed.

Hannah's eyes travelled greedily across his chest, then discreetly dipped to where his erection was standing to attention.

She crossed her arms over her chest.

"Just because I let you kiss me does not mean I want you to spend the night."

It was John's turn for shock. His mouth fell open. Impossible! She'd been sending out all the right signals. What did she want? Had he missed something?

"If you are looking for something more permanent than just one night, I do need a new mistress," he offered, knowing that he would love to have six months with the delicious body in front of him.

Hannah's eyes widened and she seemed to draw herself up, her chest filling up with air. She walked toward him slowly, as though she was savouring the moment.

John smiled at her again. Was this an invitation to stay? But she didn't look happy. Instead, her mouth turned down and she looked him square in the eye.

Whack. John's head flung sideways as Hannah's open hand connected with his cheek and sharp pain exploded in his face.

"What the deuce was that for?" he roared, holding his hand to his cheek and stumbling backward.

"Get out of my room," Hannah said, her eyes narrowing to slits.

"But... I don't understand..." John stepped forward. What had happened to change the mood so quickly?

Hannah ran across to her bedside table and picked up a silver candlestick.

What was she going to do with that?

"Get out of my room!" She screamed at the top of her lungs and heaved the candle stick at his head.

John ducked, narrowly avoiding a disaster, and scooped up his robe and slippers from the floor.

He heard footsteps and knew that others were on their way. He would be caught here if he didn't escape quickly and Hannah would accomplish what no other woman ever had.

Trap him in a compromising position.

A virgin had managed to trap him? Would they think John was attacking her? Or worse, would they try to make him marry her?

Fear made him run, his legs pumping hard as the echoes of the steps of whoever had run to Hannah's aid chased him.

He was back in his room much sooner than should have been possible.

His erection was gone and he was suddenly exhausted. How on earth had that gone so exceptionally wrong?

Chapter Three

"Thank you again, Archie, I'm sorry I woke you up." Hannah ushered her cousin toward the door, needing some time alone after a far-too-emotional night.

"I thought you were being attacked," Archie exclaimed, obviously keen to know what had caused the uproar that had woken him from a sound sleep.

Poor innocent cousin...

"I have bad dreams sometimes, Archie. I am terribly sorry. I hope it won't happen again." Hannah bit her lip and tried to look bashful. Hopefully, Archie believed her tale. She didn't want to get John into trouble, for despite his faulty behaviour, he hadn't hurt her. She also didn't want Archie thinking badly of her, either.

"Well, goodnight then." Archie sighed, walking back along the hallway to his bedroom and his waiting wife.

Hannah closed her door, laying her back against it. What exactly had happened here less than a half hour before?

She had thought John wanted a kiss, and she had desired that, too. She had only been kissed a handful of times and never by a man as handsome as John. Not that she had ever seen a man as handsome as John, but that was rather beside the point now.

How dare he believe her to be a whore? Someone who simply wanted to be a mistress for a time. Because that was what he had implied, offering her the opportunity to be *his* mistress. As if she should be grateful for that little tidbit of interest thrown her way.

Never! If she'd wanted that, she could have stayed in America.

Hannah picked up the candlestick and weighed the heavy silver object in her hand. Oh, how she wanted to throw it again, just thinking of the insult John had flung at her. But it would attract unwanted attention yet again and she didn't dare upset her cousin more than she had already done.

How dare John think her mistress material? She was an untouched virgin, looking for a husband. What had she done to make him think that he could get away with saying such a thing to her?

Shame washed over Hannah like heated rain as she climbed into her bed. Perhaps she should have slapped him from the moment he had tried to get close to her. She hadn't realized it would be such a bad thing to allow him a kiss.

Just one kiss was all she had wanted.

Hannah closed her eyes and sighed deeply. She would find out why he had thought that of her first thing in the morning.

~

JOHN SLEPT UNTIL NOON. He had awoken when the sun first rose and forced himself back to sleep. He didn't want to face the day and what might happen. Had Hannah told them what had happened? Who had come to her aid in the middle of the night?

Her behaviour still baffled him. Why had she kissed him so passionately, and then banished him from her room in such a way? Did she believe he would hurt her?

No! He had seen anger flashing in her eyes before she had thrown that candlestick, not fear. A reluctant smile played on John's lips. She was truly magnificent when angry; strong too. Those silver candlesticks weighed a fair amount and she had hurled hers with real force. It was no wonder someone had awoken after she'd thrown it.

Being almost knocked out by a candlestick was a first for him.

No woman had ever been that angry with him before. His mistresses were always told from the beginning what his expectations were. They had a maximum of six months under his protection. He would allow them a generous allowance, clothes and the use of his town house. They were not to expect to stay longer, nor to get clingy or possessive and they weren't to ask a lot of personal questions. John visited them two or three times a week and he was content with the arrangement, as were they. No one had ever complained before. He had no need of a woman outside of the bedroom.

He pulled himself to his feet and rang the bell pull for his valet. May as well face the music and see what story the red-haired American had spun them all.

An hour later he was walking downstairs to the dining room when he was pulled up short by a seductive voice.

"John, wait."

He stopped, fear clutching at his stomach before he bowed stiffly. "Miss Turner."

He eyed Hannah warily, looking for signs of hostility. She looked beautiful and bright-eyed. No sign of their late-night dispute showed on her face.

"I told you to call me Hannah. I would like to speak to you privately, John. Would you join me in the library for a moment?"

She didn't wait for his response. Instead, she simply turned and walked into the library.

John hesitated. His stomach dropped and nausea swam in his gut. He hadn't felt like this since he had been called to the headmaster's office at Eton.

But he was no longer a young boy of fifteen and he could now handle anything thrown his way. John girded his proverbial loins and walked into the library after her.

Hannah was standing down near the Latin books, so John stayed where he was. Better not to be within throwing distance.

A small smile lit her face. "I could hit you from here, you know."

John laughed out loud, a real laugh that made his chest ache. Sobering, he smiled at Hannah. "You didn't hit me last night."

"You're quick," she admitted, shrugging, before moving to sit down in a chair closer to where John stood.

He refused to sit. He didn't want to discuss anything with her. This was why he avoided any sort of relationship with a woman. Because everything beyond sex was awkward and caused unnecessary pain and hurt for everyone.

Women were for gratifying his sexual needs and that was all. His sister Charlotte was probably the only woman to whom John enjoyed talking. Though, he had to concede that Lizzie and Sarah weren't too bad, either. His two friends' wives were intelligent, interesting women.

John shook his head in frustration and began pacing. Even his own thoughts were betraying him now.

"What do you want, Hannah?"

She straightened and her cheeks coloured at his tone. She didn't dip her head or look away, and it was surprising to John how much he liked that about her.

"I want to know why you thought it was okay to proposition me last night."

John stopped walking. Was she serious? "Because I thought you wanted me."

John most certainly still wanted her. Even in a simple, conservative day dress she looked delectable. Her hair was pinned up at the sides today, but was otherwise flowing over her shoulders in red-gold waves.

Hannah flushed so prettily that John groaned. He was instantly hard again and these breeches would not disguise that fact.

"If that's all, then kindly allow me to take my leave." John bowed and began edging toward the door.

"No, it's not all," Hannah cried, surging toward him with a hand outstretched.

"Shh." John put a finger to his lips.

"I want to know why you thought I was available. Do you usually corrupt virgins? Charlotte said you were a rake as far as women are concerned, but an otherwise honourable man. Was she wrong? About the honourable part?"

John's eyebrows lifted. She *was* a virgin? He had stripped to nothing in her presence.

He was damned for sure.

He collapsed into the nearest chair and Hannah sat down opposite him.

"Well?" she demanded again.

He was speechless.

"I... didn't realize." How was he going to get out of this one? He was as good as married if anyone found out what he'd done to her last night.

He waited for the discomfort that would usually come with that thought. He looked at the beautiful woman opposite him and imagined running his hands through that hair every night. The thought gave him a strange warmth and comfort and an arrow of madness shot through his centre.

"No," John said out loud, forcing some anger into his mid-section.

This was all her fault.

"You wear your hair undone like a dock trollop and traipse around the house in your nightwear. You wear men's breeches, for goodness' sakes, that show off every curve of your hips and arse and you expect me not to think you're available?" John jumped to his feet and glared down at her.

Hurt, shame and anger washed over Hannah's face in alternating, striking waves. John couldn't bear it. This was why he never spoke to 'the fairer sex.' He couldn't bear their tears, their feelings or their thoughts. He wanted to leave.

"Good day." John bowed and began to turn.

"Thank you for being honest," Hannah whispered, wrapping her arms around herself.

John swallowed guiltily as he left her alone. What was he going to do with her now?

～

HANNAH COULD BARELY SMILE at lunchtime. The sadness consuming her heart made every cell in her body weep. How could John so easily rip away every defense she had?

She knew that the men in America thought her to be too boyish and rough. Most of them wanted her as a friend, not as a wife, and she hadn't minded. However, she hadn't thought about how her nature would be interpreted in London. Until now.

As they sat around the huge table in her cousin's country house, she had an idea.

"Charlotte, is there any way we could go to London next week?" Hannah asked, as a plan formed in her head. It was still a few weeks before the London season would begin, but surely that wouldn't be a problem?

Charlotte blinked in obvious surprise.

"Of course, we can, Hannah. I asked you if you wanted to do that when you first arrived. Any particular reason you've changed your mind?"

Hannah smiled with as much confidence as she could muster.

"It was brought to my attention that I don't exactly look like a typical English lady and if I want to attract a husband, then I must alter my appearance. I thought I should order some new gowns; perhaps get my hair cut and styled."

It cut her to the quick that she was thinking of changing any part of herself, but she simply couldn't have the gentlemen in London treating her as John had.

Charlotte's gaze darted across to John and then back to Hannah with an angry expression tightening her lips. "Who would say such a thing to you?"

"John, of course. Who else?" Hannah answered, without missing a beat.

Changing her dresses, she'd do. Change her forthright nature? That wasn't going to happen.

"John? He doesn't know anything about London ladies. He certainly doesn't associate with them." Charlotte scoffed and glared at her brother again.

John cleared his throat loudly and Hannah twisted in her chair so that she could look directly at him when he spoke.

"I never said you had to change, Hannah."

She blinked. *Was he joking?* "You called me a dock trollop."

There was a gasp from Charlotte and a loud scraping noise as Archie pushed back his chair and shot to his feet, clenching his hands into tightened fists. "You did *what*?" He bellowed at John.

Hannah sat back in her chair. She was shocked for the second time in an hour. Her cousin, Archibald, had quite a temper. Who would have believed that?

John stood up too, leaning onto the table so that he could glare back at the seated females.

"I... did... not."

She blinked. "You most certainly did."

John's mouth tightened. "Well, I didn't mean it exactly like that."

"One would hope not." Charlotte's voice was tight and her eyes flashed anger at her brother.

Hannah considered telling her cousin and his wife about John's indecent proposal, but realized it would not suit her purpose. It was even possible that telling the whole truth may land them both in a marriage that neither of them wanted and she couldn't have that.

"Sit down please, cousin," she said to Archie, waving her hands at him and looking at Charlotte for support.

Charlotte reached out for her husband's hand and whispered to him. Archie gradually relaxed enough to sit, but his breathing was still rapid. John sat also, throwing back his entire glass of whiskey in one shot.

"Let me put it more delicately. John pointed out to me today that the way I wear my hair and the fact that I wear breeches is not very ladylike."

John opened his mouth to object, but Hannah stopped him with a stare. Didn't he realize that she was giving them the nice, edited version?

Charlotte glanced at her husband, then back at Hannah.

Hannah sighed. *Oh, damn it.* "You agree with him?"

"Not exactly, but I do suggest that we revise your wardrobe to fit local requirements." Charlotte said gently.

Hannah sighed. Her cousin's wife was right. They had tried to point her in the right direction when she had first arrived and she had been too unaware to realize it.

"If money is required, you know that I will..." Archie began, before Hannah stopped him with a raised hand.

"Archie, I have plenty of money, too much, if the truth be known. I just didn't want to waste it on clothes that I may never wear again."

"But if you marry a peer, you will spend a lot of time in London."

Hannah ignored that suggestion. She didn't want to spend a lot of time in town, no matter who she married.

"So, shall we go shopping in London, next week?" Hannah asked, knowing that this was Charlotte's earlier intention anyway, so she was likely to fall into the plan with gusto.

Charlotte glanced toward her husband, who nodded after a moment's calculation.

"It's settled, then." Charlotte clapped with delight.

Hannah ignored John for most of the day and retired early to bed after spending some time with Charlotte, planning the proposed shopping trip. She had almost reached her room when she saw John staggering down the hallway toward her.

John stopped when he was level with Hannah, leaning against the opposite wall.

"Looks like you can't handle your brandy, sir," Hannah joked, clutching her candlestick close to her body.

Her father drank a lot of spirits, so John's level of consumption wasn't a new thing for her. However, there was something about the way John chased oblivion that made her think he was running away from something.

"I didn't call you a trollop." John slurred, stepping closer.

Hannah put out her hand and pushed him back a little.

"You did, John, and then you offered me the opportunity to be your mistress. That would make me a whore. I am not a whore and you are not welcome in my bedchambers."

"Not welcome, not welcome..." John slurred repeatedly and staggered off down the hallway.

Hannah stared after him with a heavy heart. Such a lost soul. A beautiful man on the outside, it was true, but Hannah couldn't be certain he had a heart to match. Something was terribly wrong with Lord John Dunford.

Chapter Four

John left to visit another of his friends the next day and Hannah and Charlotte packed to depart.

She said goodbye to the beautiful country estate that she enjoyed so much and set out toward London. Also travelling were Archie and Charlotte, their son William and their beautiful baby boy, George.

Although Hannah was sure that the weeks leading up to the season would be sluggish, they actually flew by.

She was fitted and refitted, measured and re-measured for dozens of dresses, bonnets, pelisses and boots. She would never know what and when to wear which outfit when there were so many changes of clothes in a day. Thank goodness Charlotte had assigned a ladies' maid to Hannah, or it was possible she'd have worn her new riding habit to a ball!

"Do you like this colour on me?" Charlotte asked, holding up a lavender cloth that looked too simple for Charlotte's usual taste, when they were browsing in a cloth emporium.

"I love the colour, but I'm not sure that this is your usual style."

Charlotte blushed and Hannah gasped. Had she just insulted her only friend in London?

"I didn't mean anything by that, Charlotte. I simply meant that you tend to favour bolder colours."

Hannah stopped apologizing when she heard Charlotte's laugh.

"I'm soon going to need clothes which are light, comfortable and loose fitting around the belly area," Charlotte confided, walking over to where Hannah stood in front of the mirror.

Why would her cousin's wife need that type of dress? The reality of the statement hit Hannah slowly. Then the light dawned. Charlotte was pregnant! Again.

"Oh, how lovely!" She jumped forward and hugged Charlotte tightly. When she pulled back, Charlotte was grinning from ear to ear.

"I'm hoping for a girl this time," she whispered, stroking her belly in a loving manner.

"That would be three babies in four years, God willing." Hannah sighed. She longed for a family like Charlotte's. She truly wanted children causing havoc and a husband with whom to share her life.

"Is Archie pleased?" Hannah asked, reaching out and discreetly caressing Charlotte's growing belly. She was shocked to find a small, firm swelling already.

"Archie puts a lot of effort into these babies. He has no option but to be happy."

Hannah cocked her head to the side, unsure of Charlotte's meaning.

Charlotte smiled. "Oh, I'm sorry. I shouldn't make jokes like that. I keep forgetting you aren't married."

"And a virgin too, despite…" Hannah stopped herself too late.

"Despite what?" Charlotte asked, her eyes narrowing dangerously.

What John thinks of me…

"Despite my five-and-twenty years," Hannah finished.

Charlotte looked unconvinced. "If you ever want some advice or have any questions, Hannah, please feel free to ask me."

Hannah returned the smile. Her mother had never been very forthcoming with information about procreation, but she understood the mechanics well enough. She had seen horses and other animals breed.

Also, thanks to John, she had an idea of what happened to a human male body when aroused. Heat bloomed in her cheeks at the memory and she turned away to hide her blush.

"Thank you, Charlotte. I appreciate everything you have done for me."

Charlotte walked to another area in the shop where the cloth for children's clothes was displayed.

"I'm surrounded by males, Hannah. Your company is very soothing to me. You are welcome to stay with us as long as you wish."

Hannah joined her cousin's wife, now her friend, in admiring the beautiful fabrics. She'd forgotten that Charlotte had only Archie and her sons for company. It must be nice for a woman surrounded by male family members to have a woman to talk to for a change, Hannah mused.

THE NIGHT of her first ball had arrived and Hannah had almost bitten her nails clean off.

She had a divine dress of mint green silk. It had a modest neckline and longer sleeves than those to which she was accustomed. However, despite its apparent modesty, it clung to her bosom in a way that was slightly embarrassing.

Hannah walked hand in hand into the room with Charlotte, unable to give her cousin his wife for a moment. She needed Charlotte more, on this occasion.

Charlotte guided her charge over to the drinks table and bent close to whisper in Hannah's ear.

"You look beautiful and you are charming. We all love you. Now, enjoy your evening."

Hannah took a slow, careful breath and turned to meet a blonde angel who was greeting Charlotte.

"Sarah," Charlotte cried, kissing the beautiful woman on the cheek.

"Hannah, this is my friend Sarah. She's the Duchess of Lincoln."

Hannah blinked. Was she meant to curtsey? Charlotte and Archie hadn't instructed her much on the etiquette of addressing the aristocracy. Having grown up around it, she assumed they didn't even think about it.

"My lady," she said uncertainly, and dipped low. A duchess was at the top of the social tree, if Hannah remembered correctly. That required a low curtsey.

Sarah smiled beautifully and held out her hand. "It's Sarah, please. We've heard so much about you."

Sarah turned to greet the man coming to her side. He was young and handsome, with blond hair and light blue eyes. He slid a possessive hand around his wife's waist. Hannah couldn't help but immediately like him. He reminded her of Archie.

"Hannah, this is my husband, Oliver. Oliver, this is Archie's cousin, Hannah."

Oliver didn't blink about the fact that his title wasn't mentioned and Hannah, once again, wasn't sure if she was meant to curtsey.

Oliver took her hand and chastely kissed the knuckles.

"It's lovely to meet you."

"Oliver is a good friend of Archie's," Charlotte explained, gesturing to where her husband stood, speaking to an elderly gentleman.

"Oh, I was just thinking that you reminded me of Archie," Hannah said without thinking, then covered her wayward mouth with her hand.

All three people laughed and Hannah blushed.

"Why?" Sarah asked with interest. "They look nothing alike."

Hannah smiled. "It was the way he held you close like that." Hannah pointed at Oliver's hand and watched as Oliver, not Sarah, blushed.

Hannah turned to Charlotte, giving Oliver a moment to calm down.

"It's so hot in here. Is that normal?" Hannah asked, fanning herself vigorously.

"One has to adjust to these discomforts. I was quite overwhelmed at my first ball. I'm from the country," Sarah confided.

A dim memory of Charlotte's chatter about her friends popped into Hannah's head and she realized who Oliver was.

Hannah was unable to imagine the beautiful and elegant woman in front of her, ever feeling overwhelmed by anything.

"Well, being from America puts me at an even greater disadvantage,"

Hannah began to explain, then stopped abruptly as she saw John approaching.

Her mouth went dry and her already warm body flushed with heat. He looked absolutely scrumptious in evening wear.

"And why is that, Hannah?" John asked, as he bowed in greeting.

It took Hannah a moment to realize what he was asking.

"Because I can't remember any of your aristocracy rules. I can never remember when to bow, to whom to address as what, not to mention your silly fashions." She indicated how her hair had been piled on top of her head and grimaced expressively.

John studied her hair for a moment. "You look beautiful, no matter what you are wearing, Hannah." he said, without a hint of irony.

Charlotte, Oliver and Sarah all turned to look at John in a puzzled manner.

Hannah laughed without humour as her gaze wandered around the room. She couldn't really believe anything John said to her. It was all she could do not to roll her eyes every time he opened his mouth.

"What are those people doing?" Hannah asked, pointing to a couple discreetly slipping out of the room.

"Are they married? Or courting? Don't you have rules about supervision?" Hannah asked the group.

Charlotte covered her mouth with her hand as she coughed and Sarah blushed. John cleared his throat.

Wasn't anyone going to answer her question?

"The lady is married, but not to that gentleman," John explained, dropping his voice and stepping closer so that Hannah could hear.

"So, they're going to..." Hannah's voice trailed off.

She couldn't believe it. What sort of place had she been sent to by her family?

"This inconsistency between the behaviour of men and women is disgusting." Hannah spat, indicating where another married woman was walking out of the room discreetly, with a young rake.

"It's just the way it is," John murmured.

That was the most ridiculous excuse ever, and of course John would agree with it.

"Well, I think it's hypocritical nonsense. Why can a woman do what she likes only after she is married, but a man can always do exactly as he pleases?" Hannah huffed, taking a long sip of her sherry.

"Well, if you're looking for a virgin husband, Hannah, Charlotte married the last one in England," John muttered.

"John!" cried Sarah and Charlotte in unison.

"Is it really so?" Hannah turned toward Archie, utterly intrigued by this idea that a man would wait for marriage, as a woman did.

Archie gazed at his wife with a rather winsome expression and then looked back at Hannah. He didn't have to say anything, yet Hannah chuckled at the obvious answer to her question. "Well that just improves my opinion of you, cousin."

"Thank you," said Archie in a dry tone.

~

JOHN WAS STRUGGLING with this conversation, a biting pain pulling at his stomach.

"Not that I need a virgin," Hannah went on. "But someone who hasn't been with half the women in London would be good." She squinted and peered around the room as though she could tell by looking at a man how many women he had experienced in his lifetime.

"That begs the question of how many is too many?" John asked her, deciding to jump into the fire.

Charlotte gasped at his question, but Hannah, true to form, bit her lip as though she were thinking about a clever response.

"Well, let's be generous. Let's say he's thirty and has been sowing his wild oats for ten years. Let's give him five women a year. That makes fifty women in total."

"That sounds horrible when you add them up like that," John muttered. It *was* horrible when he thought about it that way. He had bedded at least twice that many women. Over the last few years, the average would be about five a year but in his younger days, when his blood had been hot, there had been many more than that.

He'd never considered how many that would mean over time.

"Yes, it does sound horrible. How would you, as an eligible gentleman, feel if I'd had fifty lovers?" Hannah asked, turning to look directly at him.

John saw red. His hands clenched spasmodically at his sides. A ripping jealousy gripped his stomach and he wanted to hurl something.

Never! She will never know any other man.....

John blinked as the possessive comment passed through his mind.

"I would be disgusted," John told her honestly, swallowing. He shifted from foot to foot. Perhaps he should take Archie and head for the card room?

"And yet I am expected to marry a man like that?" Hannah asked, looking at the Duke of Lincoln as well. Oliver, the big traitor, smiled and gripped his wife in a possessive way. It was quite obvious he didn't care either way. He had his beautiful wife and that was all that mattered to him.

"It isn't the same," John argued, getting Hannah's attention again. It wasn't. Men and woman were different.

"Of course, it's the same," Hannah argued, tsking in impatience, the sound low in her throat.

She obviously didn't understand how things were and why they were set up that way.

"But don't you want a husband who can please you? Who knows what he's doing in the bedroom?" John asked, sure this was a clear winning point.

"Oh, is that why men consort with the ladies of the night? In order to practice pleasing their wives?" Hannah asked, with a flutter of her eyelashes.

There was a sudden stillness within their group that could only be deciphered as shock. Oliver and John knew well what it was like to bed a whore and they knew that their partner's pleasure was the last thing on a man's mind in those moments.

Hannah had obliterated his argument in one clean stroke and John wasn't sure if he should be angry or impressed at her ingenuity.

"That's just what I thought. Very well then, if I get the opportunity to take a lover, I'll make sure I choose a rake. But I'm going to marry a gentleman," Hannah announced with a smile. "Oh, there's Mrs. Haversham, our neighbour in London, over there. I must say hello, she's been so helpful since I arrived here." Then she was gone, making her way across the room to the side of an older lady.

John stood dumbstruck. Had Hannah said that he had too much experience for her? Who would have thought that women like this existed? His father had always encouraged him and his brother to sleep with as many women as possible. That had most certainly meant both before and after they were married. The thinking had been told that few ladies of quality enjoyed bedding, so it was best not to bother them too often. He looked at Charlotte and Sarah and realized with a shock that his father, the all-powerful Duke of Arrow, had been quite wrong.

Chapter Five

H annah awoke to see the sun streaming through her open curtains. She never slept past sunrise. What time was it?

She stretched and climbed out of bed. Seeing the clock on the mantle-piece read almost eleven o'clock, Hannah gasped. What a lazy way to start the day! She called for her maid and quickly dressed, then made her way down for breakfast, hoping she would finally be able to ride a horse today. Archie had promised her that she would still be able to do so during her stay in London.

"Good morning, Hannah," Charlotte called from the sitting room. "There's breakfast still on the table in the dining room, if you want toast."

Hannah walked into the sitting room to find that Charlotte had company and was entertaining her guest with tea and muffins. A much better alternative to toast, in Hannah's opinion.

"I would love a muffin and a cup of tea if you two don't mind me joining you?"

Hannah looked at Sarah, Duchess of Lincoln, who was sitting on the chaise longue opposite Charlotte. "Your Grace," she added respectfully, curtsying with a smile.

Sarah frowned at her. "Sit down and join us, Hannah. I told you at the ball last night to call me Sarah."

Hannah picked up a muffin and sat down. As an only child, she'd never had the chance to enjoy this sort of atmosphere, with many girls around the same age at home. It was lovely. She finally felt like she had a sister in Charlotte.

"How did you sleep?" Charlotte asked.

"Very well, thank you. I rarely sleep well, but that late night made such a difference."

Sarah chuckled. "It took me so long to get accustomed to town hours. People here sleep until noon, begin their day after lunch and then are up half the night. It's not natural." Sarah shook her head and took a sip of her tea.

"John seems to like those hours," Hannah murmured absently.

Charlotte and Sarah's heads turned toward her so quickly she jumped.

"Did I say something wrong?"

Sarah looked at Charlotte and Charlotte placed her cup of tea down. "No, Hannah, not at all. I just didn't think you liked John very much."

Hannah swallowed. She was going to have to be careful here. She knew how women liked to gossip in America and guessed that women in England were probably no different.

"I don't particularly, but he is one of the few gentlemen to whom I have spoken. I was referencing one of the only opinions I know."

She looked down to her plate and picked up her muffin, biting into the sweet cake before lifting her gaze and smiling at the ladies.

Charlotte stared at her with a meaningful look. "John isn't the best example of a gentleman, Hannah."

"Obviously!" Her tone was more scoffing than she meant it to be, and both ladies stared at her again. She picked up her teacup to hide her face. She realized she needed to learn to curb her reactions a little.

"Did John do or say something he shouldn't have?" Charlotte probed gently. Hannah knew she had to be very careful what she said.

"Well, he has said a few inappropriate things, but nothing damaging. Why? Does he have a reputation for corrupting virginal young ladies?" Even as she said the words, she frowned. She couldn't see John in that way, despite everything that had happened between them.

Charlotte shook her head. "No, not at all. He rarely speaks to any ladies. John tends to keep most women in a certain category." She grimaced as she spoke, and Sarah sighed.

"A certain category?" Hannah ate the last bite of her muffin and dusted her hands off.

Charlotte and Sarah exchanged a worried look.

"Oh, speak freely, please." Hannah waved her hand, giving the two ladies permission to disclose any information they thought was necessary.

Charlotte cleared her throat. "John has a rule."

"He has a rule?" Hannah asked, her imagination running rampant. *Like, a bedroom rule?*

"Yes. He keeps a mistress for six months, then replaces her." Charlotte took another sip of tea as though she were talking about the weather.

"Why would he do that?" Hannah asked, genuinely curious. *Why would a man replace his mistresses so often? Why did he tire of them that quickly?*

Charlotte sighed. "I believe it's because of my parents. My father has had the same mistress for more than fifteen years. She lives at our country estate in the Dower House. My mother hates the situation, but there's nothing she can do about it. It has turned my mother into a very bitter person, and we don't tend to visit the estate as much as we would like to because of the awkward atmosphere."

Sarah laid a comforting hand on Charlotte's arm.

Hannah frowned. "I don't understand." *What did that have to do with John?*

"Our whole family has suffered from my father's behaviour. I have never asked John, but I think he does everything he can to try not to be like our father."

Hannah could see Charlotte's point, but it still wasn't making sense. She knew first-hand how a parent's behaviour could affect their children. But what did John's father's obviously being in love with his mistress have to do with John's need to replace his mistresses so often?

"He's always nice to me." Sarah smiled.

"You are an exception." Charlotte laughed.

"Lizzie likes him too," Sarah argued.

Hannah liked the fact that Oliver's beautiful wife was defending John. It meant that he wasn't *all* bad.

"Who's Lizzie?" Hannah asked, wanting to create a family tree in her head for John's friends.

"Oh, Lizzie is Rupert's new wife. John's the only unmarried 'spare'," Charlotte answered.

Hannah was beginning to feel a little stupid. "What's a 'spare'?"

Sarah and Charlotte both giggled.

"Oh, that's a nickname the men have for their group. Aristocratic families tend to aim for an heir plus a spare son in case something happens to the first, so that their inheritance goes to a blood relative. John, Oliver, Archie and Rupert are all the spare sons of titled, rich families. Their group was called 'The Spares' even when they were at school," Charlotte explained with another winsome smile.

"But isn't Oliver a duke?" Hannah asked, feeling slightly stupid. She hated asking so many questions. She wasn't used to being so ignorant about everything.

"Yes, that's the strange thing. Of the spares, Oliver inherited, Archie will inherit when his father dies, and Rupert is his brother's heir. John, well..." Sarah looked at Charlotte uncertainly.

"John will inherit too if he's alive when my elder brother dies, provided my sister-in-law doesn't have a son," Charlotte explained, looking a little sad.

"Do they have daughters?" Hannah asked, knowing that there was some difference between English American inheritance laws.

"No. They've been married for five years and have no children at all."

Hannah cocked her head to the side and put all the pieces together. "So, John could inherit too?"

"Yes, John could inherit too," came a dry male voice from the doorway.

Hannah turned toward the familiar tones, her mouth turning up in a smile.

"Hello, John," she called, waving at him despite being caught gossiping about him. "Charlotte and Sarah were just filling me in on the history of the 'spares'. Amazing that you all may become heirs, isn't it?"

John prowled into the room. "Yes, amazing."

His eyes blazed and Hannah caught her breath at the passion that clearly lay beneath the cool façade.

"Charlotte, Sarah." John bowed to his sister and her friend.

Hannah stood up and watched him carefully. His eyes were shadowed. Was he worried about what had been said?

"Found out anything interesting, Hannah?" John asked with seeming interest. But his smile was forced.

Hannah swallowed down the need to tell him the truth. She found it very interesting that he changed mistresses like people changed their wardrobes. One season, one look and the next, a completely different one.

"Not really. I would love to meet Lizzie, though."

John's face softened and she wondered if that was due to his affection for Lizzie or for Rupert.

"I believe you would get along with Lizzie and Rupert very well."

A real smile spread across John's face, his famous aloofness forgotten for a moment. He had just paid her a real compliment and she wasn't sure how to handle it.

"So, you're the only one left unmarried, John?"

John's eyes and mouth went flat and the smile disappeared. "Yes."

She was shocked to find the need to tease this strange man was so strong. But she supposed he deserved it after everything they'd been through in such a short time.

"So, you'll be next to get married?"

She could only imagine what sort of woman John would choose to marry. Would she need to put up with his mistresses as well?

"If I decide to marry, then of course I'll be next. The other three are shackled for life."

A smile crept across Hannah's face. He had taken the bait like a fish.

"Of course, you'll marry. If you are next to inherit, you'll need an heir too." Hannah flashed John a huge smile, then watched as his jaw clenched and a muscle in his cheek throbbed.

"I don't have to do anything I don't want to do. Why? Are you offering, Hannah? Would you like to be a future Duchess of Arrow?"

Hannah heard the gasp from either Sarah or Charlotte, but didn't look away from John's handsome face. His brown eyes were blazing and she was enjoying the conversation far too much.

"Oh no, not me. I told you just last night I couldn't marry a man who has been with half the women in London."

Hannah couldn't resist a glance to her side. The two other women had their mouths open in obvious shock.

"You did. It's just a pity you don't know what you would be missing." John ran his eyes slowly down her body and Hannah's nipples hardened beneath her dress. How could such a man make her body respond like this?

"Don't worry, you're on my list if I want an affair, though," Hannah added, her temper getting the better of her. "A six-month affair."

Again, horrified gasps came from the other side of the room, but John's mouth kicked up in amusement.

Hannah couldn't help her answering smile.

"I am honored, my lady." John bowed.

Hannah laughed to diffuse the tension in her own body.

"Don't be. I'm not sure yet if you're at the top of that list."

She revelled in the shock in his eyes, and smiled serenely. "I'm going for a ride, unless you need me for anything?" Hannah looked at Charlotte.

"No, not at all," Charlotte recovered enough to say.

"I'll see you later, then. So lovely to see you again, Sarah," Hannah addressed her new friend.

"You too, Hannah." Sarah said, with a warm smile that contained more than a hint of amusement.

Hannah curtseyed to the room and then turned to leave, excited to be able to undo her hair and let go.

John's voice sounded behind her. "I will come with you, if that's all right?"

Her heart sank. If John came along, she would have to behave at least a little bit like a lady.

"I was looking forward to letting my hair down, so to speak." she replied, her mouth grimacing out a polite smile for John. "I don't think you can stop yourself from insulting me and I can't do that dance again."

JOHN FELT a growl growing in his chest. He wanted to dance with her. A dance that would require her hair out and her naked up against a wall, on the floor, on a bloody horse. He didn't care where.

"I promise to be a perfect gentleman."

Hannah looked indecisive, so he threw in a sweetener.

"You can wear whatever you wish, Hannah, and if I accompany you, I can take you to private grounds where your horse can stretch his legs without you being seen by the *ton*."

When Hannah's eyes lit up, he knew he had said the right thing.

"I'll meet you in the stables in fifteen minutes, then." She curtseyed and left.

John waited until she'd gone and then turned to his sister,

"That's very nice of you John, but please make sure you keep your promise that she isn't seen. She'll never make a good match in London society if people see her in breeches and a shirt."

John couldn't help the indignation that spilled out of him. "Hannah should be accepted for the person she is. Damn the *ton*."

Charlotte's eyes widened. John left before she could comment again.

He had a date with a wild woman and a horse and his valet would need every second of the next fifteen minutes to get him dressed.

TWENTY MINUTES LATER, John found himself running down the stairs. His valet had assured him that no lady could get out of her dress and into a riding habit in fifteen minutes. John wasn't so confident when the lady in question was Hannah.

John was proven correct when he saw that the beautiful American virgin stood waiting for him, riding crop in hand.

"You're late!" she called out, and cracked the riding crop across her hand. John's loins tightened at the action. Gods, this woman was unusual. "Let's go," she added impatiently.

Hannah gripped the reins on her large stallion, stepped into the stirrup and swung herself up into the saddle. John watched in awe. What lady had strength and dexterity like that?

John shook his head and swung up onto his own stallion. Hannah was in a class entirely of her own.

"Follow me," he called over his shoulder as he directed his horse out of the stables.

He didn't stop to see if she kept up with him. He had every confidence she would. Instead, he just steered his horse through a few short streets until they reached an open field.

Hannah pulled her own horse up next to his, moments later.

"If we cross over that fence, then we should be safe to do anything you like, without judgemental eyes on you," John said, grinning devilishly.

Hannah's laugh rang out like a church bell and she flicked her riding crop out at him. It artfully connected with his horse's flank, just below John's thigh.

John's horse lunged forward and he leaned into the saddle. He was always partially aroused when Hannah was around, but he was harder than a rock now. The erection was uncomfortable against the pommel of the horse, but he pressed into it, happy for the distraction of pain.

"Come on," Hannah yelled over her shoulder as she passed him at an outright gallop.

Her horse jumped the fence, with feet to spare. The large body of his horse went up and over the obstacle and John felt the awe in him grow. He loved the power of his stallion, the muscle, the strength. Each step, each jump, emphasized the power of the beast between his legs.

As they slowed, Hannah pulled off her long coat that hid her costume and revealed her riding breeches and a shirt tucked beneath a jacket. The coat dropped to the grass and she sped up again. Next, she pulled off her hat which contained her unbound hair and the beautiful locks uncoiled down her back. Long, flame colored, sunshine tresses flowed behind her.

John gasped at the sight of her as pre-cum wet his riding breeches. She was incredible. A virtual goddess on horseback.

He could barely think, unable to do anything but imagine bending Hannah over and taking her from behind like an animal. What had happened to him?

They slowed as they reached an incline, finally stopping at the top of the hill.

Hannah turned to him. "Brutus loves to run, so if you can keep up, we'll gallop as far as he'll go, then stop, turn around and gallop back here again."

John smiled at the challenge in Hannah's eyes. He was a keen horseman and he knew his bloodlines. Hannah's horse wasn't a pure breed, but he *had* been bred for size and speed. He had long lean muscles and was taller than even John's stallion.

"Ladies first," John indicated the direction they should ride.

Hannah made a loud whooping noise and dug her heels into the side of her horse. He broke into an instant gallop and fell into an easy rhythm. It was obvious to John that the horse enjoyed having Hannah as his rider.

John groaned as his body responded to her once more. Images of Hannah, naked except for her riding boots and crop, made him harder still.

He dug his heels into his stallion's side and set off after this devil of a woman who had bewitched him with her flame hair and her unusual manner.

They rode across one field and cleared another fence. John concentrated on his horse's rhythm and gave the animal his head. His horse enjoyed the chase. It had been too long since the last time, for both of them.

Riding so fast meant John began to perspire. Sweat trickled down his back and on his brow. He wiped it with his sleeve, grinning. He felt alive. He was sweating, with the wind blowing his perfectly combed locks out of their carefully constructed shape. His heart was thudding against his chest, in both excitement and arousal.

For the first time in a very long time, he was exactly where he wanted to be and wouldn't have changed a single thing.

~

HANNAH PULLED her beautiful Brutus back down to a trot. He was breathing hard and covered in sweat. He had almost reached his endpoint. She spotted a cluster of trees and steered Brutus that way. When they reached the shelter of the trees, Hannah jumped down and turned around to see where John was. Was he lost somewhere along the way?

Just as she began to wonder, he appeared, and when he reached her he trotted past. He stopped his horse two trees away from her and Brutus and dismounted. He rode a magnificent stallion, an animal it was hard not to admire. John handled him with a master's touch, the perfect balance of respect and power. He didn't even carry a crop.

He walked toward her, his skin glistening with perspiration.

"How long will your horse need to rest?" John asked, as he pulled off his gloves.

Hannah met him halfway, pulling off her own jacket and gloves. She wiped the sweat from her brow and looked up into the sky. "Oh, half an hour should be enough."

She looked around. There wasn't a person to be seen for miles. What a relief! She turned to speak to John and couldn't miss the hunger in John's expression as he swooped in for a kiss. His hands wrapped around her face and Hannah grabbed at John's waist for balance. She moaned as John stroked the sensitive flesh of her face, cheeks and neck.

"Oh, God, do I want you," John groaned against her neck, as he ground his erection into her belly.

Hannah's anger swelled along with her arousal. She wanted him too, but that didn't mean they could just give in to their baser instincts like wild beasts!

She swung the riding crop with painful accuracy and connected with John's backside.

He released her and arched back, howling in shock and pain.

"Why the hell did you do that?" he yelled, furiously rubbing his behind.

Hannah couldn't help the hysterical laugh that bubbled out of her mouth. He just looked so ridiculous, buttoned up and perfect in his riding costume, yet rubbing his sore behind and swearing like a sailor.

"The last time you kissed me, you asked me to be your mistress. I don't intend to give you another opportunity to do so!"

John snorted like her horse and Hannah laughed again. She hadn't laughed this much in a long time. Perhaps John was actually good for her.

"I won't repeat the offer."

Hannah snorted inelegantly back. "You wouldn't dare."

John steadied himself and stepped back over to her.

Hannah raised her crop hand, but John grabbed her arm and twisted it behind her back. She hissed. He wasn't hurting her, but she couldn't get out of his grip. He held her, not increasing the pressure but not letting her go.

"I don't want you as my mistress," he said in a low voice. "I wish I didn't want you at all."

With her arms pinioned behind her back, Hannah felt completely helpless. The position left her breasts jutting forward. She should have been scared. She *knew* she should have been petrified. John was a large, powerful man. If he wanted to hurt her, he could have done so.

And yet there was nothing but excitement threading through her body, a pulsing dance of nerves that made her breath hitch and her nipples tighten.

John's hold on her slackened and Hannah dropped the riding crop. Suddenly, she didn't want to fight him.

His words had finally registered. He didn't *want* to want her? "Why, what's wrong with me?" she choked out, insecurities swamping her.

What was so wrong with her that John couldn't bear the thought of wanting her? Why did he find it so wrong?

"Are you jesting?" John gasped, moving both of his hands to grab her buttocks and hauling her against him. His arousal was thick and hard. Hannah gasped in shock as she reached out and grabbed a hold of his arms to steady herself.

"Nothing is wrong with you and that's the problem. You are a beautiful, clever, outspoken, bloody, painful woman who is driving me insane!"

John bent his head and began kissing and sucking at the skin of her neck. Hannah arched her head back to give him better access and gripped John's arms to anchor her.

"You can't have me, you know." Somehow, she managed to gasp out the words, though her voice was a trifle hoarse.

"I know I can't. You are a marriageable virgin who should be running like mad from me."

John punctuated his words with kisses on her skin and a roll of his hips that caused an answering pull of desire deep in her belly.

"Why? Because you change women as often as you change your clothes?"

John pulled back. "What have you heard?"

"That you never hold a mistress longer than six months."

John let Hannah go and walked away from her so abruptly, it was like he'd thrown a bucket of cold water on all the hot places that he'd just ignited.

She watched him with a frown prickling her brow. She needed to know how he really felt about women in general, and why he changed his mistresses so frequently.

"That is true, I like variety." John chuckled as though he had told a great joke and yet the smile didn't reach his eyes and sound rang false. In fact, he looked as cold as a fish.

"So, you believe all women are the same?" Hannah asked. "Interchangeable, almost?"

John studied her, then nodded. "Yes. In my life, women *are* interchangeable, easily replaceable. They offer physical relief, that is all." John's face had paled as he spoke, and it was as though the moments of heat and need between them only a minute or two earlier had never happened.

"We're all the same, are we?" Hannah asked, placing her hands on her hips.

John swallowed and his eyes seemed troubled.

"There are exceptions to the rule, but generally, I have no use for a female outside of the bedroom."

"And love? Where does that fit in with your rules?" Hannah fired at him.

"Love is for fools."

Hannah couldn't stop the groan that surfaced from her throat. From what she had heard then, John surrounded himself with people he would label as fools.

"Do your friends know what you think about them?"

John's face dropped. "What do you mean?"

"Do they know you think them fools?"

"I don't—"

"Ah, but John, you do. According to your own rules. All three of your best friends have made love matches. Does that make them all fools?"

John swallowed and looked down. He kicked at a clump of dirt and looked over to where the horses were happily eating grass.

"My friends are exceptions."

Hannah sighed. He was so full of contradictions. "And you? Do you not think that one day you could also be an exception?"

John's head snapped up. "I will not fall in love. I'm not capable of it."

"You mean you don't want to, because of your father?"

"You don't know anything about my father."

"I know that he has a long-term mistress that he obviously loves. It's a pity really. I feel sorry for him. He has spent most of his adult life in love with a woman who isn't his wife."

John laughed, the sound dark rather than joyful. "A *pity*? Is that what you call it? A pity that he has made my mother's life miserable? A pity that we have spent half our lives cooped up in London during the off-season because we didn't want to go to the country estate and experience the awkward atmosphere? Is it..." John stopped abruptly.

Hannah saw anger and regret running over John's face.

"Go on."

John shook his head. "No."

"You've never really spoken about this, have you?"

John glared at her and Hannah glared back. It was clear to her that no woman or man ever challenged John. Perhaps he needed it. Just as her stallion needed to run, John needed to be pushed.

"No, I haven't. It is not suitable conversation for polite company."

And here came John's classic defence. He would hide behind his social armor and avoid difficult topics about love and feelings for as long as he could.

"Oh yes, you are the epitome of gentlemanly conduct. Don't think you can fool anyone but yourself, John. You are no gentleman and you should realize that."

Hannah walked back over to her horse and pulled herself up into the saddle.

They rode back to the house in complete silence, a strange rift between them where before, there had been a connection.

Hannah walked her horse into his stable and stayed inside with the animal for some time, watching as a stable hand removed the saddle and bridle and taking over the brushing when it was time. She was far more comfortable staying there with her horse, than facing the man who couldn't even be honest with himself, let alone with anyone else.

Chapter Six

John watched her walk away and handed his horse's reins to the stable hand. He listened to Hannah for a moment, as she crooned to her horse in the next stable along, before he left. It would not pay to remember just how special and unusual she was.

He needed to think of Hannah in the same way he did all women. Except for his sister and her friends, of course. They were exceptions to the rule. But for his own protection, he couldn't think of Hannah as an exception. He needed her not to be special. Not to engage his thoughts and his feelings. Not to ensnare his heart when he knew he could not return the favor.

He had no heart. At least, not where love was concerned. It had withered and died the day his father placed his mistress in their family home.

John headed straight to his room and had his valet draw him a long hot bath. He needed to find a new mistress, quickly. He was frustrated and he needed the release that only a certain type of woman could give.

He recalled the letter he had received the previous week. His most recent mistress had been having difficulty finding new accommodation and since he hadn't yet replaced her, he'd allowed her to stay until she found somewhere suitable.

He decided he would visit her one last time. Then he was sure that this stupid infatuation with the American would disappear for good.

THE NEXT MORNING, John awoke from a restless sleep filled with erotic dreams featuring a certain flame-haired American, and got ready early. He had plans for the day and none of them included seeing Hannah. She had made his night-time hours almost unbearable.

He was hurrying down the stairs, desperate not to be seen, when he tripped and fell. Pain seared up the inside of his leg as he twisted and landed badly, several steps down.

He tried not to call out beyond a shocked groan as fire shot up from his calf, but the loud crash alone was enough to make people come running.

So much for sneaking out of the house undetected.

The footmen crowded around as John pulled himself into a seated position, sweat breaking out on his forehead at the pain in his leg.

"Out of the way, please."

It was Hannah's voice. Of course, it was. John closed his eyes and groaned more loudly than before. She was the last person he wanted to see. And the very last person he wanted to see him in such a helpless state.

"Jennings, call for some ice, and could you two please help John up, so that he can sit on the chaise longue in the sitting room? He can rest his leg up that way."

John opened his eyes and stared at Hannah. That was the most sensible course of action, by far. Who would have known a lady could think of such a thing?

"Wouldn't it be better to get him back to his bedroom, Miss Turner?" The old butler was a little perturbed.

John shook his head at the idea of being hoisted back up two flights of stairs. Before he could tell the butler that he couldn't bear that, Hannah came to his rescue again.

"Certainly not! Imagine carrying him up all those stairs and the pain he'd have to endure. Please see to the ice, Jennings, and you two footmen, please help Lord Dunford into the sitting room."

Hannah stalked off ahead of them and John was left with the footmen. They pulled him up from his sitting position onto his feet. He bit his lip when he tried to put weight on his ankle, but the two men soon supported his weight enough so that he could hobble into the sitting room.

Hannah had just finished piling all the cushions up at one end of the chaise. She pointed to the opposite end.

"Sit there and place your leg on these cushions," she told him. "Where is the ice?" she enquired of the footmen who had assisted John. They assured her that Jennings, the butler, was attending to that and then went straight off to find out if he needed any help.

John moaned when he sat and swung his leg up, more sweat covering his face as nausea rolled through him.

Hannah did everything she could to make sure he was comfortable. She placed another cushion behind his back and went to the sideboard and pulled out the whiskey decanter. John looked on in silence as Hannah poured out two glasses of the liquid. One small measure and another, overly large. Unsurprisingly, she walked back over and handed him the larger one.

"I know its barely past breakfast, but drink up. It will help."

Slightly dazed at her capable manner, John lifted the glass and took a gulp.

She sat down in the chair opposite him and sipped hers more delicately. "Are you feeling any better?" she enquired.

John was surprised at the signs of concern in Hannah's demeanour. She sounded calm, but sipped again at her whiskey and he noticed her hands were shaking.

"Yes, sore and no doubt will be a little bruised. But yes. Feeling comparatively well, thank you. Are *you* all right?"

John found it a little strange that he was reassuring her, when he was the one who was hurt. "Thank you for stopping the servants from carrying me upstairs."

Hannah dropped her gaze away from his. "I'm fine," she said quietly. "I just saw you begin to tumble and got a bit of a fright. You might need to ask your physician or maybe a surgeon to look at that ankle, just to be certain. But from what I know, it appears to me you'll only have a sprain. Certainly a few bruises, too."

"Yes, to add to the ones I already have from your riding crop." John was merely teasing, but his words got a reaction. Her head shot up and her eyes narrowed. Her fear for his safety diminished as she gripped her glass.

"If you didn't try to kiss me all the time, I wouldn't have to resort to violence."

John laughed and opened his mouth without a thought. "Oh, sweetheart, you've been using violence on me since the day we met."

Hannah gasped and John keeled over laughing at her horror-filled expression. He laughed and laughed until his sides ached. Despite the pain in his leg, he hadn't felt that good in years. In fact, he couldn't remember laughing so much. Ever.

When he finally looked back at her, Hannah was smiling with her head cocked to one side.

"What's wrong?" he asked her, still grinning.

"Nothing, you just..." Hannah stopped and blushed.

"Don't tell me you're speechless, Hannah. I can't believe that you won't say what you are thinking."

Hannah's blush deepened. "You will take it the wrong way."

"I sincerely doubt it." John smiled, knowing that no matter what she said to insult him, it wouldn't change the fact that she had obviously cared enough to help him when he fell.

"I was wondering if you are in pain?" Hannah said, and John grimaced at the blatant lie.

He shifted his leg on the pillow, trying to find a comfortable position. He did in fact feel as if his whole foot was burning.

"I am, to be honest," he admitted, and Hannah stood up and moved over to him. She reached out and began to slowly undo his boot.

"If I take this off, we can apply the ice directly to your ankle."

John swallowed as the pain dulled. Her mere presence was soothing to him.

"I'm not sure about putting ice on my ankle. Maybe a warm bath would be better?"

Hannah shook her head. Her fingers brushed aside the laces of his boot and touched the skin of his leg.

Fire raced into his groin.

"I can do that," he began, leaning forward to brush Hannah's hands away.

She smacked him like a five-year-old child and John automatically laughed. Would this woman ever stop surprising him? She took the ice from the shocked butler who had just arrived and John flicked his head to dismiss the old man, who quickly bowed and disappeared.

Hannah knelt beside the chaise and wrapped the ice in her handkerchief. Then she gently arranged it over the sorest part of his ankle Cold relief swamped his foot and John could only moan in gratitude.

"It will hurt more soon, but keep it on for several minutes. It will help."

"And how do you know all of this, Hannah?"

"I was a clumsy child. I often twisted my ankle when thrown from my horse or whilst running," Hannah explained softly, her eyes entirely focused on her task.

John couldn't help the frown that appeared across his brow. *Thrown from her horse? How often? Had she been badly hurt?*

"Our family physician always insisted that ice reduces the swelling. Heat can feel good but sometimes make things worse."

John nodded, knowing that there was swelling happening in his breeches as well as his ankle. Thank goodness he didn't need to stand up immediately.

"You never told me what you almost said, earlier," John reminded her, hoping she would insult him again. The fact that she was providing more succor than he had ever experienced from a woman before was not helping him to lose his obsession with her.

Hannah smiled and continued to stare down at his foot and ankle.

"Just that you look very handsome you when you laugh. And I haven't seen you laugh often. Not genuinely."

John was glad he was sitting down, because otherwise, that comment would have knocked him on his backside. Of all the things he had expected her to say, that wasn't one of them. He swallowed, uncomfortable. This woman touched him so deeply, that every word she spoke caused him to ache.

"Hannah, I..."

He started to reach for her but people bustling into the room interrupted them.

"Oh John, what happened to you?" Charlotte came rushing over to his side. Behind her stood Archie, equally concerned, but also looking a little amused.

John groaned inwardly. His sister really had the worst possible timing.

"What happened? The butler said you fell down the stairs? Has the surgeon been called?" Charlotte's voice got higher as she spoke.

Hannah stood up and put a reassuring hand on Charlotte's arm.

"A twisted ankle, Charlotte. No cause for alarm, I would say. A day or two and he'll be running up and down the stairs again. Ready to fall all over again if he so wishes."

Hannah looked at John for the first time in minutes, grinning, and John's ribs constricted around his heart.

Oh my God! I am falling in love with this woman!

He registered the thought with speechless shock. He opened his mouth, but nothing came out. He just nodded, not even sure what she'd said. *I am in love with Hannah Turner..*

"Oh good," said Charlotte, obviously relieved. "Because we have all been invited to an important dinner on Saturday night. What an inconvenience, had John been confined to bed."

Charlotte beamed and John groaned.

"Another ball, Charlotte?" Hannah sighed and John looked over toward her. He could sense she was slowly deflating. Perhaps Hannah hated the circuit as much as he did? He had never asked her about it.

"No, not this time, Hannah. We're going to a dinner party."

"Oh? Whose?" Hannah asked absently, sitting down again in the chair opposite John. Now that she knew John was all right and he appeared to be doing better, her energy seemed to have fizzled out.

"Rupert and Lizzie's."

"Really?" Hannah obviously perked up at that news, sitting up straighter and looking happy. "I can't wait to meet the last 'spare' and his lovely wife," she said gaily, with a glance at John and away.

"Lizzie has been informed of your situation, Hannah, so you should have a dinner partner arranged for the evening."

"Oh." She rolled her eyes and Charlotte sat next to her with a pointed stare.

"You know that's why you're here, Hannah. It's what the London season is really all about. Not just the business of Parliament. Parties and balls abound, so that everyone who is anyone can admire you and see how beautiful you are."

Hannah huffed and looked up as Archie came to sit down and join them.

"But I haven't met anyone suitable yet."

She wouldn't meet John's eyes when she said this. He knew he wasn't suitable, but it pained him that she blatantly thought so, too.

"You will on Saturday. I will make sure of it," Charlotte said, smiling smugly.

The thought of Hannah charming any other man unaccountably annoyed John. He huffed out a little breath and Archie shot him a look.

"I think we should get John upstairs," Archie announced, obviously having decided he needed to help.

Hannah opened her mouth as if to refuse, but John held up his hand. "I think that would be a good idea. I would like to lie down properly, now. In my own suite."

Hannah opened her mouth again and John looked directly at her.

"I feel much better, now," he said. "Thank you so much for your assistance."

Hannah blushed and inclined her head.

An extra footman was called and between him and Archie, John was led from the room.

HANNAH HELD her pelisse tightly around her shoulders. Charlotte had talked her into wearing her most risqué gown for Rupert and Lizzie's dinner party. The sleeves barely stayed on her shoulders and the neckline was cut very low. The colour was pale as was appropriate for a virgin according to her *modiste,* but the cut of the dress left little to the imagination.

"Hannah, this is the Honorable Rupert Willoughby and his wife, Mrs. Willoughby. Mr. and Mrs. Willoughby, meet Miss Hannah Turner, Archie's cousin from America."

Hannah curtseyed awkwardly and raised her head to look at the newly-married couple. The first thing she noticed was how striking the man was. Rupert Willoughby was not only tall and broad, he also had the most piercing blue eyes Hannah had ever seen. Her cheeks heated a little when she looked over at his diminutive wife.

Hopefully she hadn't been ogling the poor man.

"It's lovely to meet you both," Hannah murmured with an apologetic smile at Lizzie.

Lizzie just chuckled as if used to people admiring her husband, and extended her hand.

Hannah took it in her own and held it a moment.

"Any relative of Archie's is as good as a relative of Rupert's as far as we are concerned, so please feel quite at home with us. And call me Lizzie, dear Hannah."

Hannah's face lit up with the warmest smile she had given in days. What a lovely, gracious woman Lizzie was.

"Thank you," she said, squeezing Lizzie's hand and moving over to the area where the footmen were taking coats.

Taking a deep breath, Hannah turned and allowed Archie to remove her pelisse.

The air around her went still and quiet as almost every person in the room turned to look at her.

Hannah's knees went weak with the need to run away from this gathering. She hated getting so much attention and with this dress, she had known that all eyes would be on her.

Help came from an unexpected source.

"Hannah, may I escort you into the sitting room?"

John appeared out of thin air, blocking most of the people from her view. He held his arm out and Hannah grabbed at it, feeling in need of support.

"Thank you for that, John," she whispered as she clung to him.

She looked up and noticed his cheeks were rosier than normal and his eyes were intense.

"Have you been drinking already?" she asked.

John laughed, but didn't answer the question.

Several people turned to look at them and John guided her toward the fireplace. From there, he left her to walk over to the whiskey decanter on a side table, and poured two glasses.

Hannah hesitated when he handed her one of the glasses. She would be damned if she changed for anyone, but surely there were rules he was breaking.

"I haven't had a drop today but thanks to you looking like that, I think I'll start now."

John clinked his glass with hers and downed his glass in one gulp.

Hannah clenched her empty hand into a fist. What was wrong with how she looked? Did he hate her dress as much as she did?

She opened her mouth to ask him when John gave her cleavage such a hot look that she didn't speak. Instead, she lifted the glass to her mouth and drank. It was going to be a long night.

Lizzie approached at that point, calling out as she walked toward them.

"Hannah, I would like to introduce you to your dinner partner for the evening."

Somehow, Lizzie had very cleverly inserted herself and a rather handsome gentleman between Hannah and John.

"This is Algernon, the Baron Osborne. Lord Osborne, meet Miss Hannah Turner all the way from Virginia."

Hannah smiled at the man in front of her and curtseyed. She was pleased to realise it was her best attempt yet.

"Charmed to make your acquaintance, Miss Turner," Lord Osborne replied, bowing appropriately.

Hannah could have sworn that John actually growled, but she chose to ignore the strange sound.

"Please call me Hannah," she said. "We Americans don't really stand on tradition."

The baron's eyes widened and a smile spread across his face.

"Of course, Hannah. If it pleases you, you may address me as Algernon."

"What an unusual and lovely name. Algernon." Hannah let the name roll off her tongue, wondering if it was something she could say every day for the rest of her life. There was an awkwardness to it, she realised. Unlike John, which was easy to say. And felt far more right coming from her lips. She frowned at her nefarious thought, shooting another smile at the baron in front of her.

"You drink liquor, Hannah?" Algernon asked politely.

Hannah flushed with heat, despite her determination to remain calm.

"I do, though I have been told it is not considered very ladylike over here."

Algernon chuckled. "That's only because we men like to separate from the ladies after dinner and we do enjoy our liquor. I think it would be quite a novelty to have a wife who could enjoy such a comfort with me. Do you not agree, John?" Algernon turned to include John in the conversation. The latter took an automatic sip of his aleady-refilled glass.

"I don't think so, Algy. Why would any man want to spend more time than necessary with his wife?"

Hannah gasped and narrowed her eyes at the rake of a man standing before her.

"Lucky you aren't married, then, John. I pity your future wife, whoever she may be."

Lord Osborne opened his mouth and laughed so loudly that Hannah took a step backwards.

"Did you hear what she said?" Algernon continued to laugh and slapped John on the shoulder.

She cocked her head at the two men, wondering why her remark was considered so hilarious.

⁓

JOHN CLENCHED his teeth together so tightly, he was afraid he would crack one of them. Who was this chump of a baron to slap him on the back, as though they liked one another's company?

John forced himself to laugh along with Algernon, not really believing that what Hannah said was funny at all.

He was glad he wasn't married. He didn't have a wife to answer to and he felt *bloody* lucky for that fact.

"What is so funny?" Hannah asked, cocking her head to the side, in that fashion that John secretly loved.

He almost groaned out loud. Not love. He hadn't meant to think that. He couldn't afford to love anything about the woman standing in front of him. Except for her body, maybe. That may just be worth loving.

But it would need to be temporary. Just like one of his mistresses.

"The way you said that, Hannah, believe me, was pure poetry. I have never seen anyone talk to Lord Dunford with such disdain, and I don't believe I ever will again."

The idiot went off into another round of laughter and Hannah smiled, obviously pleased with Algernon's enjoyment.

When Algernon offered his arm to take Hannah in to dinner, John swallowed, his stomach twisting into a horrible knot. Why did it feel like someone had just punched him?

He watched as Hannah walked off with her partner and then reluctantly turned to Lizzie, who was standing beside him, having escorted a woman over to meet him.

"Lord John Dunford, this is the Honourable Mrs. Mary Presley. Mary is recently out of mourning for her late husband and it took me ages to coax her into joining us tonight. You will make her welcome, won't you. John?"

Lizzie studied him carefully, and John thanked her with a relieved smile. At least there would be someone who might take his mind off Hannah.

He surveyed the widow and found her to be young, very young. She would be at most, twenty and one. She was pretty and petite, but unfortunately, John felt no stirrings of desire when he looked at her.

His heart sank. "It is a delight to make your acquaintance, Mrs. Presley," he lied, bowing to the woman.

The young woman smiled and curtseyed. When she rose, she scanned him in an appraising manner. Yes, this widow was definitely up for a good time. What a pity she did nothing for him.

"It is a pleasure to meet you, Lord Dunford. I have heard a lot about you."

John smiled with all the etiquette that had been drilled into him since childhood.

"Indeed," he said, inanely. "Shall we?" John held out his arm and, when she eagerly jumped forward and took it, escorted the young woman in to dinner.

Chapter Seven

For the first time in his life, John wished he had a second set of eyes. He could barely concentrate on the delicious courses that Lizzie's servants had served up to him because all of his attention was engaged by the woman seated at the opposite end of the table to him. Hannah was involved in such titillating conversation, her laughter and that of her companions could be heard all around the table.

Unlike Hannah, Mrs. Presley barely seemed able to string a sentence together.

When the sumptuous dinner was finally finished, John's neck was sweaty and his fingers itched for the huge glass of brandy he knew would be waiting for him when the gentlemen retired.

Rupert called for port and cigars for the gentlemen and John happily escorted the widow back to the company of the other ladies in the sitting room and walked out into the hallway.

As he stepped closer toward the men's den, he heard Hannah's sweet voice excusing herself and then she made her way out of the room. She was probably heading off to apply powder to her nose, John thought.

He looked toward the men's sanctuary, the curling smoke of cigars calling out to him, even as he heard Rupert's chuckle and Archie's smooth voice.

He turned on his heel and charged straight at Hannah, grabbing hold of her elbow and dragging her along the hallway.

"John! What are you doing?"

He didn't answer, he just pulled her into the library and shut the door firmly behind them and turning the key in the lock.

"John!" Her indignant tone just made him want to lay her down and cover her with his body, so that she couldn't speak any more.

"What are you doing, flirting with Baron Brainless like that?" John hissed at her.

Hannah gasped, her nostrils flaring.

"I can flirt with whomsoever I wish. I'm here to find a husband."

"Well, look for a proper man. He is not the one for you."

She needs someone with balls. And a brain.

"Well, who is, then?" she asked him. "The proper man? The one for me? Do tell!"

He scanned his memory for anyone who might be a good fit for this gutsy, amazing American lady. Unfortunately, not a single fellow he knew, past or present, came to mind.

"No one I know."

She rolled her eyes in an exaggerated movement.

"So, I'm supposed to go back to America, unwed and alone? A failure in my family's eyes?"

"No, of course not!" John snapped, running a hand through his hair in frustration. Why was she asking him these questions, which he couldn't answer?

"How dare you say such a thing to me, John. I need a man to marry and you are chiding me for some harmless flirting with a respectable candidate."

A candidate? And... chiding? Now, that was low. He was not chiding. And flirting was never harmless when the lady in question was a virgin. A widow, sure, but society had different rules for widows.

"It's not harmless when that same man wants to get you into bed before your wedding night! And if he does, he may not go through with the wedding. You never know with men."

Hannah's nostrils flared and she threw her hands up in the air.

"You can't talk! You have offered me the position as your mistress, kissed me several times and tonight, you flaunted that little floozy right under my nose! Did you bed her in the broom closet whilst I was *flirting*, John? I did see you both go missing for a little while."

The heat in John's face surged from merely uncomfortably warm to flaming heat. "I did no such thing!"

Hannah's eyes narrowed as she put her hands on her hips and glared at him.

"You were touching her all through dinner and then afterward, she came into the sitting room looking very disappointed. What's wrong, John? Not up to the task tonight?"

John saw red and his heart went into overdrive. He grabbed the woman in front of him and pushed his body against hers, taking several steps forward until her back was pressed against a wall.

"Listen to me," he growled when Hannah fought against him. "Does this feel like I would struggle to take a woman tonight?"

He pressed his erection against Hannah.

She gasped and her face flushed. In anger or in arousal? Perhaps both. John couldn't tell.

"I don't know what you're capable of doing, do I?"

John pinned Hannah tighter as she continued to struggle. He bent close, so that he could whisper into her ear.

"You drive me insane. I want no one but you. If I thought I could rut on that woman and forget you, I would. But when she offered herself to me after dinner, I couldn't think of anything but you. And I refused her advance. Because of *you*!" John growled as his now completely aroused body dug into her belly, searching for access to her beautiful skin. "I cannot get you out of my head, Hannah. You're all I can think of!"

Hannah gasped and struggled again, causing pleasure to zing along his veins.

"Let me go. You don't really want me." Her voice became higher-pitched, almost a squeak, and her chest rose and fell with exertion.

"Oh Lord, I want you so badly, Hannah."

John lifted a hand to caress Hannah's face. Her eyes widened, but she finally stopped struggling against his hold.

"Do you really want me to let you go? I will if you say so," he murmured.

There was silence while he waited, and then her answer whispered over him. "No, I don't want you to let me go."

Groaning, he leaned in and captured her lips in a fierce kiss that was all about need. There was no finesse in his technique tonight.

He swept his tongue against Hannah's lips and she opened her mouth to him. He groaned again and took full advantage of her invitation. Sliding both of his hands down to her bottom, he pulled her in to him and devoured her mouth.

Hannah ran her hands through his hair and gripped his head. She continued to kiss him back as her hands began to move down his back. She cupped his buttocks the way he cupped hers and a shiver of anticipation shot through him.

He broke off their kiss to whisper. "You are so beautiful." His lips traced a line down Hannah's sweet, soft neck. Her scent rose around him. He didn't want to beg, but the words seemed to form on their own volition. "Touch me, Hannah. Please."

IT WAS THE 'PLEASE' that did it for Hannah. She believed him when he said that no other woman aroused him at that moment because she felt the same way. She had met, spoken to and walked with countless gentlemen since her arrival in London.

And the only one who filled her thoughts and her dreams, was John.

She wanted only John.

Feeling bold in their mutual desire, Hannah slipped her hands around to John's maleness, eager to find out what pulsed beneath her hands.

She slid one palm over the length, unable to hold the whole amount in one hand. Hannah gasped at the size and hardness of him. Could a piece of flesh really feel like that? Everywhere on her own body was so soft.

"Hannah..." John's voice sounded strained.

Then the next thing she knew, he had pulled her down and around and she was suddenly sitting in John's lap on the chaise.

"I just want to touch you. Please trust me," John whispered into her ear as he lifted her skirts up with his free hand.

Hannah glanced toward the locked door. The strange thing was, she didn't really care what would happen to both of them if they were caught in here together. She had to know what all the fuss was about.

And her body was burning for John's touch.

She lost her nerve the moment John's hand reached her inner thighs. Clamping her legs together, she stilled his hand where it was.

"Are you sure you should do that?" she asked, a moan escaping her throat when John lightly bit her ear and caused a shiver of sensation to course down her spine.

"I shouldn't, but I want to."

"Can I touch you too?" she asked, itching to reach back down where her hands had been only moments before. The differences between their bodies interested her a lot and now that she finally had access to a man she desired, she was unable to leave him alone.

"Yes," John groaned, as he shuffled her further along his thighs, allowing a gap between their bodies now and pushed her hand back to his groin.

Now what did she do with it?

"What do I do?"

John chuckled, sounding pleased by her question. "Press your palm along the length."

When Hannah rubbed her hand up and down the length, John moaned out loud and the sound made her insides tighten and clench in a pleasurable way.

"Yes, like that. Now open your legs and let me give you pleasure."

Hannah ducked her head into John's neck, so that he couldn't see how embarrassed she was and opened her legs for him.

He moved his fingertips and gently grazed the crinkly hair at the apex of her thighs.

"No undergarments?" John asked, sounding shocked.

"I don't like them," she admitted, pressing her hand along John's length again. Was he disgusted by her unladylike habit?

"Never wear them. I love that you are naked beneath all of these skirts."

He pressed his thumb onto an extra sensitive piece of flesh and Hannah shot up in his lap.

"John! That feels..." Exquisite. She couldn't get the word out. She was suddenly breathless.

"I know. Kiss me again."

Deciding to trust the one with the experience, Hannah tipped up her head and offered her lips to him.

John used his thumb to circle her flesh again and again. It was simply amazing, the sensations of pleasure that wove through her body with each touch. She would never have believed anything could feel so good. John then slipped his fingers back between her legs and spread the moisture that had accumulated there.

"God, you're wet."

Heat spread across her cheeks as John nipped at her ear and throat in that beautifully passionate way he had.

"Is that bad?" she asked, unsure if her body was doing what it was meant to be doing.

John laughed again, the sound throaty and deep. "No. It means you want me to do this. I love it."

John pressed one long finger deep into the entrance of her body and Hannah only just contained a scream as pleasure speared her insides.

"Shh," John murmured, capturing her mouth in another kiss.

He added a second finger to the first one and Hannah moaned as the sensation of thickness inside her doubled. How could such a thing feel so incredible?

Then she realized that she had both hands around John's neck again and she wasn't giving him any of the pleasure that he was sharing with her.

Another moan escaped her lips when he used both his fingers and his thumb on her, the combination both overwhelming and incredible in its pleasure. Tingles pulsed down her legs and added to the overall feelings building in her belly.

She dropped her hand to where John was bulging against his evening breeches. She pressed her fingers against him and rubbed up and down. She attempted to use the same rhythm John used on her, getting faster in her strokes as his fingers worked faster on her.

"Stop Hannah, please. I can't finish in my breeches."

Hannah didn't understand that sentence. "I don't want to stop, and where else can you finish?"

John groaned and pulled out his handkerchief. "Unfasten my breeches and touch me properly."

Hannah swallowed as fear took over. She looked into the sweetest brown eyes she had ever seen and noticed that he wasn't pushing her, or trying to take anything from her. He was pleasing her without taking her virtue.

With shaking hands, she unfastened his breeches as quickly as she could, and John's member sprang out. It was long and thick and came from a bed of hair darker than his head.

Hannah looked up and fresh desire filled her when she saw the hunger clearly written on his face.

She leaned into him for a kiss as she reached in and grabbed him with her hand. He was warm and soft, yet hard all at once. His flesh leapt when she touched him, which made her grab him tighter.

"Like this," John whispered, wrapping his hand around hers and guiding her in the movement that he liked.

She did as he told her and moments later, John was thrusting into her hand. Hannah felt a glow of pleasure at being able to please him, just before her own pleasure began to cloud her brain.

John flicked his thumb over her sensitive flesh again, over and over, until she was arching her back and urging his fingers deeper into her canal. She wanted to scream at the delicious pressure that felt like she was about to explode.

Hannah did cry out when John sped up his movements and her whole body peaked in pleasure. She was suddenly shaking and burning as wave upon wave of pleasure washed over her.

"Oh God, yes, Hannah, yes," John groaned as her shaking began to subside and he wrapped his handkerchief around her hand and his staff. Hannah continued to stroke him as her growled, and a hot wetness spurted all over her hand and the handkerchief.

John as he threw back his head and closed his eyes, his body shaking just as much as hers had.

John looked up into her eyes and Hannah couldn't resist leaning forward and giving him one more lingering kiss before she drew her hand away.

John withdrew his hand from her, too, and thoughtfully pulled her skirts back down before attending to himself.

Hannah slid off John's lap to give him more room to clean himself and lay her head against the chaise back. How could she never have known that such pleasure existed? No wonder John was chased from pillar to post by married and widowed women. If you'd had a taste of such a thing, why would you ever want to stop?

The thought was sobering and Hannah stood to inspect herself in the mirror. She looked flushed and her lips were swollen but overall, she still looked like herself. If only she *felt* like herself.

John finally finished and stood up, fixing his clothes and checking his appearance in the reflective glass of a cabinet.

"That was truly wonderful, Hannah. Thank you."

He sounded sincere, but something had changed in his tone and she lamented the loss of the heat and passion they'd just shared.

"Thank *you*, John. I had no idea such pleasure existed."

John smiled and stepped closer.

"We will be missed, so I think I need to get back to the gentlemen. Do you think you can head back to join the ladies without raising too much suspicion?"

She bit her lip. How long had they been in here? She supposed she could tell her cousin's wife that she had experienced unexpected monthly cramps or bleeding.

"Yes, I'm sure I can."

"Very good. Let's go, then."

John held the door open for her and checked the hallway. No one was in sight.

"All right, well. Goodbye, John."

"Goodbye Hannah."

John's beautiful lips quirked up in a smile and Hannah gathered her skirts, took a deep breath and walked out of the warm room where a man had shown her the greatest pleasure she'd ever known.

And as she stepped back into the sitting room to apologise for being so tardy, she didn't need to fake her tiredness or fatigue. Her head was spinning and her belly was still cramping with the pleasure that had been given to her.

After hearing that she wasn't well, dear Charlotte excused both herself and Hannah and they headed straight home. As she lay in bed alone that night, her head was full of everything she'd experienced. Now that she'd tasted the sweetness of John's passion, she knew she wanted more.

Chapter Eight

John stared at the carved wooden door in front of him. He'd seen this same townhouse a thousand times in the past ten years and yet tonight, it seemed unfamiliar. Foreign.

A scream somewhere in the street behind him startled him and he tugged at his jacket, pulling it closer. Suddenly, he hated this part of town.

He lifted his hand and knocked, the front door swinging open with a suddenness that spoke of Kate's enthusiasm for his visit.

"John." Kate's painted mouth curved up in invitation as she held open the door for him. She was clad only in her sheer nightgown. One of the many things he'd bought for her, in the six months she'd been his mistress.

"Kate. Good evening." He stepped inside and let her kiss him in greeting, turning his head so that her tacky lips only brushed his cheek. He drew away and she frowned, before closing the door behind him.

He waited for the normal feelings of lust to flood over him. This woman was available, ready and willing. And technically, still in his life.

He felt nothing.

"Come this way," she said, in a tone dripping with honey.

She took his hand and led him to a bedroom they'd used often in the past six months. Despite the fact that she was meant to be moving out as soon as she found a new protector, when he'd asked for a visit this evening when he'd contacted her a week before, she'd accepted with alacrity. The girl was probably hoping he'd change his mind, keep her on longer. But that was not going to be the case.

The way he was feeling, with lead in his gut and a sour taste in his mouth, he knew there would be no rise out of him tonight.

"Do you have brandy, Kate?"

Her brow furrowed. "Yes, in the other room. Shall I get it?"

"Yes. Please."

Her hair was lackluster and her skin did not shine. Not like Hannah's did. Why was he suddenly noticing these things? He'd never even been aware of them before.

She left and he tugged on his cravat, loosening the restrictive material a touch.

A week ago he had thought to come here and slake his lust with Kate one last time, but now, the thought turned his stomach. It wasn't Kate. She hadn't changed.

It was him. He didn't even recognise himself when he stared at his reflection in the mirror.

Hannah had given him a taste of her passion and she now slept many streets away, in the safety of Archie's townhouse, while he could not stop thinking about her.

Surely, he should be slaking his lust with his mistress rather than fantasizing about a marriageable virgin? He'd been stupid to do such a thing with Hannah. If they'd been caught, her reputation would have been destroyed, and both their lives would certainly have changed irrevocably. But he hadn't been able to stop himself. Not when she'd looked at him with such need in her beautiful eyes.

But Hannah was not his to claim.

He was a rake. Not marriageable material, and Hannah deserved so much better than him.

This was where he belonged. This was *who* he was.

Kate re-entered the room and handed him a large glass of brandy.

"Thank you."

He took it and drank half of the contents in one swallow, relishing the burn as it slid down his throat.

He fell into a nearby chair and stared at the slight woman before him. She'd always been too thin for his particular taste, but he'd never given it much thought before tonight. Now he compared her to the perfection of Hannah's strong, feminine body and found his mistress severely lacking.

"Do you want me, John?" Kate began to sway in a dancing movement, her hips tilting and rolling, and her fingers lowering the material of her nightgown down from her shoulders until her small breasts were visible.

He felt nothing. No reaction at all.

"Beautiful," He lied, quickly throwing back the rest of the brandy, his already inebriated brain loving the new level of alcohol.

What was wrong with him?

Kate toyed with her nipples, drawing them to tight peaks in a pretty display and yet all he wanted to do was grab a cloak and hand it to her, telling her to cover up.

What had Hannah done to him? Where was his fire? Where was his legendary lust for women that could never be quenched? Only a few weeks earlier, he'd been drowning in the heat of his hormones. Tonight, he sat staring at a half-naked woman and he may as well have been playing cards with his friends.

"Please stop, Kate."

She frowned at him and pouted. "What do you mean?"

"I'm sorry. I can't do this."

He pulled himself to his feet, swaying as the alcohol coursed through his veins, making his head light.

She pulled up her nightgown and slid it back into place, then reached for a heavier gown that lay over the back of one of the chairs. When she was fully covered, he relaxed, relieved now that she was not expecting anything from him. He didn't have to perform. He couldn't, even if he had wanted to do so.

"I came to ask if you need another week to collect your things and move out?"

Her mouth dropped open as she stared at him, then she glared with a heat he had rarely seen before. "You still want me to leave? I thought this visit meant you wanted me to stay?"

"No." He shook his head, sadly.

She scowled at him. "So, it really is true that no woman ever lasts longer than six months with you, John? I thought that to be a myth."

"Sorry, but that is correct. Six months is my maximum. I did tell you that at the start of our time together and I have said it all the way through our liaison."

"Well yes, but I didn't believe you."

"Let me know where you are staying, and I will send a final payment. That should help you get set up in a new situation."

"You're a bastard, John."

He staggered to the door and half-bowed to her.

"It's been a pleasure knowing you too, Kate."

He let himself out of his house and inhaled breaths of fresh air.

He was staying with his older brother during this year's season, having committed to spending more time at *ton* events.

His elder brother, Edward, had yet to produce a male heir by his wife, Margaret. The pressure was slowly and carefully being applied to John's neck.

Perhaps that was another reason why he was not feeling quite well in himself right now.

He wandered along the road, heading back toward his brother's house and feeling lost within himself.

Who was he, now? What was the right path for him to take, moving forward?

He needed to get home and reassess what he was going to do with his life. He'd be thirty the following year and he knew that his family's pressure to marry and produce children would increase. He had absolutely no need for a wife, nor for a title and yet, as he continued down the cold, dark street, he could feel the walls of a cage closing in on him.

∼

JOHN'S WORLD had tilted on its axis and it was all Hannah's fault. Those few precious moments in the library had changed everything for him. She'd been passionate and beautiful and everything he had never imagined a woman could be. He also knew her to be intelligent and feisty, as at home on the back of a horse as she was in a sitting room.

The opposite of every thought he'd ever had about what a woman was usually like.

But the thing that was confusing him the most was her passion and what it could mean for his future. If an actual lady like Hannah could enjoy his bed and give him the physical comfort and companionship he craved, was a monogamous marriage truly possible?

Looking at his parents' union, he'd grown to loathe the very idea of marriage. However, since watching his friends fall under the spell of their women, he'd begun to realise that an alternative to misery was indeed a possibility.

Even when he'd watched Rupert fall in love with Lizzie, John had never really believed it was possible to feel that way about a woman. To be so smitten and so content together. And yet, here he sat, unable to think about anything other than how incredibly amazing Hannah was, and he began to imagine what it might be like if they were wed.

Feeling a hand rest on his shoulder, John looked up to see Oliver's kind gaze studying him. He had been visiting Oliver and Sarah for an evening and had been lost in thought for most of the time he'd been there.

"Join us in the card room for a brandy?" Oliver invited, giving John's shoulder a squeeze.

He took a deep breath and nodded, dragging himself up by the metaphorical bootstraps. His soul felt heavy today and with that heaviness came a bone-deep tiredness. However, when he walked into the card room, he saw a pair of familiar, dark blue eyes and his spirits lifted a touch.

"Rupert," he greeted his friend with a smile. "I'm sorry I didn't get much of a chance to talk to you the other night. I disappeared into the library for a while."

And spent half of the evening finding out how beautifully passionate Hannah is.

Rupert grabbed him into a bear hug, squeezing him tightly. John laughed and stepped out of his friend's embrace. When had Rupert ever hugged him? In fifteen years, he couldn't remember a single moment when this had happened. His friend had changed, with marriage to the woman he loved.

"You never can chat properly at those dinners," Rupert said, shrugging offhandedly. They'd had a small amount of time together after the dinner, but Rupert, being the host, had been mostly engaged in conversation with other gentlemen whom John didn't know very well.

They all sat down together around the card table.

"The new house is to your liking?" Oliver asked Rupert.

"Yes, though it needs refurbishing. We're happy there. I've ordered us a new bed, too." Rupert winked, his message clear.

John couldn't help smiling. Rupert may have recently married, but he seemed to be the same man as before, which was strangely comforting.

"Married life as boring as they say?" he asked Rupert, leaning forward in his chair and attempting to re-connect with the man who, once upon a time, had been as cynical as he was.

Rupert, Oliver and Archie all burst out laughing and it was at him, not at his question. John couldn't stop the heat rushing across his face. He lifted his hand and called for more brandy.

"I was serious with the question," John muttered, staring down into his empty glass.

"Definitely not for me," Rupert answered with another laugh.

John poured all four of them large glasses of brandy and held his up.

"Then I'm happy for you, all of you," he choked out, before guzzling the contents down in one long gulp.

Archie, who rarely drank, did the same thing, disguising his gasp with a cough. Oliver was next. Rupert waited for a moment, looking at John. Weighing up the situation correctly, he downed his drink and filled their glasses again.

John looked at the three men who had once been his universe, his family and his saving grace. They had been there for him for more than half his life.

"What's wrong, John?" Archie asked gently, reaching out and laying a hand on John's sleeve. He removed it after a moment, but the heat of his hand remained, giving John strength.

"All my life, I didn't want to be like my father, loving the wrong woman and making my family suffer for it." John reached for his brandy glass again, but Rupert pushed a glass of water at him.

John was startled by his friend's gesture and stared into Rupert's eyes. They were startling blue, but they were clear.

"Just alternate," Rupert said. "It reduces the headache." John took a sip of water and grimaced. Not quite the same kick.

He took a deep breath and forced himself to keep going with his declaration.

"I look at you three and I can't imagine any of you doing what my father did, to your wives. So, I want to know more. Tell me how and why you ended up, like... you know..." *Happily married. In love.* John couldn't say it. Instead, he stumbled to a stop. Surely his friends would know what he needed. to ask and more importantly, what he needed answered.

"You go first, you were the first to fall." Rupert indicated to Oliver and took a long drink from his glass of water.

"Well..." Oliver laughed. "I don't know what to say."

John just stared at his friend. He didn't know how to ask for the advice he needed. He wasn't even sure exactly what he wanted to hear.

Oliver tapped his fingers on the rim of his brandy glass and stared at the empty crystal with unfocused eyes.

"Sarah was a surprise for me. When I inherited the title, I assumed I would have to marry someone like my sister-in-law." Oliver shuddered.

The hairs on John's own neck prickled at the thought. What a horrible woman Oliver's sister-in-law was. Ugly and domineering, a veritable horse of a female.

"But I just... I fell in love with Sarah. She was kind and beautiful. She made me think that I could be happy with her. And I am. That's it..." Oliver finished with a sheepish shrug.

John swallowed. Was it really that simple?

He turned to Archie, his brother-in-law. Archie had seduced his sister right under his nose. That fact still rankled.

Archie smiled in a similar manner to Oliver.

"For myself, I had always thought that I would never marry because of how my late brother's lifestyle brought about his unfortunate illness. Or I thought that if I did marry, I would have to marry a woman who would be happy to be in an outcast family." Archie shrugged and Rupert reached over and squeezed his shoulder.

John swallowed uncomfortably and reached out to take another sip of his water. It went down much easier the second time and he didn't wince.

"But Charlotte was exactly what I needed."

"No details please." John held up his hand with a grin, lightening the mood considerably.

The other men chuckled and Archie smiled.

"She was my opposite, my balance. She was fire and determination when I was cold and polite. She made me feel all the things I didn't want to feel. She made me believe I had a right to love someone like her." Archie seemed to want to say more, but his words appeared to stick in his throat.

He motioned to Rupert and John realized that Archie was finished disclosing his personal details. That was a pity. He should have liked to learn more about his sister's married life. Not the physical details, of course, but more about their love for one another.

Rupert grinned. "I married the best lover I ever had."

The four of them laughed at that, Typical Rupert, always the joker.

"Seriously John. I was very similar to these two. I thought that because I was to inherit, I had to marry an appropriate lady. Which meant a marriage like my parents had, with duty, coldness, conflict and separate beds and..."

"Hold on," John stated, holding a hand up to stop his friend.

A memory of Oliver saying that he and Sarah shared the same bed every night swam up in his memory.

"Do you share the same bed? Every night?" he asked with incredulity. Rupert couldn't possibly be doing that!

Rupert shrugged and grinned slyly. "It has its advantages."

John blinked.

"But what about that time during the month when you can't..." He trailed off. This topic was not discussed within gentlemen's circles.

Rupert flushed. *Good God,* his friend was blushing!

"I sleep better with her," Rupert replied gruffly.

John turned surprised eyes to his other friends.

"Always," Archie nodded.

"Always," Oliver declared. "I would be sent to Scotland if I denied her that."

Oliver chuckled as though he was joking, but John could tell that he was being serious. He knew that Sarah had left Oliver for Scotland early on in their marriage. There was obviously a story there.

John turned back to his most rakish friend. He didn't want to be distracted again.

"Finish what you were saying, Rupert."

Rupert took a long sip of his brandy and gasped. "John, I married the woman whom I wanted above all others. The one with whom I fell in love. It really was that easy. And I have never for one second regretted the decision."

John compiled the thoughts in his head much quicker than usual. Drinking water helped with all sorts of things, it seemed.

In summary, his friends had married women who were ladies, but not the typical *ton* lady. The women were all different to their men but complimented them. They were ladies with good hearts and minds as well as beauty. If Rupert was to be believed, they were also wonderful in bed. It sounded to John that what his friends felt about their wives, was exactly how he felt about Hannah.

"Thank you," John said to all of them. He downed the rest of his water.

"I have some information about a new investment, the East India Shipping Company, that you all may find interesting," Archie began, and John forgot his problems for a little while. He could think about them later. They were never far away.

~

WHEN JOHN RETURNED to his brother's townhouse, he heard the command.

"Please come into the library, John."

He cringed, hearing the tone in his older brother's voice.

He followed Edward into his darkened study and sat down at the mahogany desk. A bottle of port sat on the surface, two crystal glasses accompanying the full decanter.

"Port?"

For a moment he considered saying, I'll have water, but then he gave in.

"Yes. Thank you."

He accepted the glass and sat down in the chair. His skin was prickling in awareness and he was trying not to fidget.

"How have you been, John? How was your time in the country this year?"

John gulped down some of his port. In thirty years of life, he didn't think he'd ever been asked about his welfare by his brother.

Edward must be worried.

"It was a touch tiresome, if I may be honest. Watching our sister and her husband fawning all over each other for several weeks was somewhat annoying. But at least I had somewhere pleasant to stay and enjoy country society."

His brother stared at him for a moment as they both recalled the tension their father had brought into their lives by the presence of his mistress in close proximity to their country home.

"I enjoy going to the Scottish estate, once the season is over, John. The estate affords several fine houses and if you want to spend time in one of those at any point throughout the year, you only need ask."

John nodded his thanks. At the same time, he wondered where his brother stashed his mistress through those long months with his wife.

But he didn't dare ask.

He finished his port and reached for the bottle. He had the feeling he was going to need fortification for the next part of this conversation.

"We need to discuss the matter of the dukedom's inheritance."

"Why? Is Father unwell?"

They both knew that their father was in excellent health. He was barely around their mother at all, spending most of his time with his mistress. He attended *ton* events of course, when obliged to do so, but did little else to stress himself.

"No. This is about the succession. As of now, I am the heir and you are listed as my heir, should I die without legitimate male issue. The doctor does not believe Margaret will ever provide me with a legitimate heir and I have no wish to try to divorce her and bring such a scandal down upon our family."

"Agreed," John replied. "But there is still hope, I am sure."

Margaret, having been married off to Edward when barely out of the schoolroom, was only four and twenty.

"The doctor does not seem to think so. I have sired four children by now, so it is not me. Margaret must be barren. Moreover, there seems to be a history of barrenness in her family. Several of her aunts, although married, have remained childless. I have long since stopped going to her bedroom."

John grimaced at the evidence that their father's choices had impressed on them both in an obviously harmful way. John couldn't love anyone and Edward was happy to love anyone who wasn't his wife.

"I hadn't realised I had any nephews or nieces, albeit born on the wrong side of the blanket, if you'll forgive me..."

"I have two of each. They are beautiful children," Edward said, pride colouring his tone.

Edward didn't address the fact that John would have liked to know his brother's children. He seemed to be following in his father's footsteps.

"Do you know if we have any brothers or sisters from our father?" John had never thought about it before and hadn't even cared, if the truth be known. But seeing the scenario unfolding as it was now, he wondered if he had missed out on something.

"I believe he has had several with his mistress. They all live out on the country estate, with her."

"Have you ever met them?"

"No." Edward didn't seem in the least interested in doing so, either.

John wanted to howl at his brother's lack of emotion. For gentlemen who had enjoyed spreading their seed and their love around, the Dunford males certainly didn't appear to have any real emotions.

"Is that all, Edward? Because if not, I am away to bed."

He needed to be alone and dream about Hannah's beautiful body and think about the now-empty house on the cheap side of London town.

"No. That is not all. Now that you are my heir, it is your duty to provide the dukedom with an heir. Preferably an heir and a spare, as Father did. So, I am going to ask you to marry as soon as possible. I have someone in mind, if you have no particular preference."

Damn you to hell! Never!

He was not being auctioned off to the highest bidder as had all the eligible men of his family before him.

"I do have a preference. And that is not to marry."

"You must marry. You have no choice. It is your duty."

Duty! A wave of nausea flowed over John and he closed his eyes so as not to shout right into his brother's face.

When he opened his eyes, he had clamped down a little on his anger. But only a little.

"Edward, I do have a choice. Who is next in line in inheritance after me?"

Edward's face tightened and screwed up in an ugly grimace. "Cousin Harold."

It was John's turn to cringe. Cousin Harold was a simpleton and a gambler. He would run the estate into the ground within a matter of months.

"You only have to provide an heir, John, along with a spare. Not a difficult job for you, with a fertile woman. I will rent you a handsome home in town and you can keep as many mistresses on the side as you want. Just marry a *ton* lady and you can have anything your heart desires."

John's memory flashed back to that horrible night when he'd seen what sort of marriage his parents had and he never wanted to experience anything like that. A dutiful marriage of convenience was the last thing to which he'd willingly agree.

He stood and began to pace the room. He would not be like his father and his brother. He had sworn an oath to himself that he never would, but did that mean he was damned a lonely fate? Could he, perhaps, be like Oliver? Like Rupert and Archie?

Was a good, solid marriage possible for a man like him?

"I will not marry someone of your choosing."

He'd be lumped with a cold young thing that he'd toss aside in a year, just as his brother had done to Margaret.

"You have one year, John."

That should have been ample time, but he wanted more than that. If he was going to offer a home to a woman who could compete with Lizzie, Sarah and Charlotte, he needed to be worthy of it.

"Rent me a town house in St. James's. I want to be in within the month."

His brother's eyes widened at the demand.

"Do this, Edward, and I will marry a woman worthy of being the mother of a future Duke of Arrow."

His brother stood up and extended his hand.

John stepped forward and shook his brother's hand in agreement. "Done."

Chapter Ten

Hannah tapped her foot against the furniture, bored out of her mind. She wanted to do something other than take tea with ladies who could do nothing but gossip about the latest fashions.

Luckily, Charlotte regularly visited Sarah and Lizzie and they visited in return. They had interesting conversation, most of the time.

"Lord John Dunford is here," the butler announced, stepping into the room.

"Oh, good God." Hannah jumped to her feet. What was she going to do now?

"What's the matter?" Charlotte asked, putting down her needlework.

Charlotte's needlework was exquisite, but Hannah would rather make a dress for herself than embroider a cushion cover, if she had to sew. At least that would be useful.

"Ah. I..." How could she explain to Charlotte how she currently felt about John?

Charlotte, noticing Hannah's agitation, turned toward the butler.

"Jennings, kindly direct Lord John to the study to meet the earl and chat for a while. We ladies need half an hour to finish what we are doing."

"Yes, my lady."

The butler bowed out of the room and Charlotte turned to Hannah.

"What has happened? Why have you suddenly developed a strong reaction to John?"

Something in Hannah's face must have clued her in. Charlotte's eyes grew wide and then her mouth made a large 'O' as though shocked. "Please don't tell me you're falling in love with my brother? He's my own flesh and blood, so I mustn't speak ill of him, but I fear to say he is a total rake. Not at all a desirable suitor for an innocent young lady like you."

Hannah collapsed onto the chaise, her belly tightening with need as she heard John's deep voice ricochet down the hallway.

"Tell me, Hannah and quickly. I need to know what has transpired between you and my brother."

Charlotte's brow had tightened into a frown.

"Oh, no, Charlotte. Please don't worry about me in that regard. I know what sort of man John is."

Hannah had met many of John's type back home in Virginia. Rakes and dandies were not exclusive to London.

She had to admit to herself that she respected the fact that John hadn't tried to get her into his bed. Not since he'd learnt that she was a virgin, anyway.

But he was also the first man to tempt her and if ever there was a man with whom she would want to dally, it was Lord John Dunford.

"Good." Charlotte's relief was obvious. "Because although I do not believe my brother to be a debaucher of innocents, he is still a man. And, let us be honest, a man of highly carnal appetites at that."

"Yes. I know. I am not intimidated by him."

Charlotte's eyebrows flew up and a strange look passed over her face. Perhaps Hannah shouldn't have agreed so readily?

"Then, what troubles you still, Hannah?"

Should she tell Charlotte what tortured her? She didn't have a sister, nor did she have any other trusted friends in England, so perhaps Charlotte was the best person to whom to speak? Although, perhaps Charlotte would be biased, as John was her brother?

"I... I had a moment with John at Lizzie and Rupert's dinner party, and I... I would like to enjoy some more time with him, if you think it would be possible?"

Charlotte's eyes widened and she shuffled to the edge of her chair, her small, round tummy protruding from her dress.

"Did my brother do something inappropriate? If he did, I will reprimand him severely. You are in our care!"

The poor woman's face was turning red with obvious shame and horror.

"Oh no, Charlotte! Please never worry about me in that way. I am well capable of taking care of myself."

Charlotte seemed to relax a little, but she chewed on her lip in a worried way.

Hannah tilted her head, pondering the wisdom of her decision here. "Maybe it's best that I speak to someone else about this?"

Lizzie might be better. She was a lot more relaxed than Charlotte and newly married, albeit for the second time.

Charlotte shook her head emphatically. "No, I'm sorry. I struggle to see my brother in any light other than how I've always seen him. How the other ladies in the ton see him is likely a different matter altogether."

That was interesting. "How *do* you see him, Charlotte?"

Charlotte softened, her whole body relaxing and a genuine smile appearing on her face.

"John's wonderful. No doubt, he's a rascal and has been with half the available women in London, but he's always been a wonderful brother to me, kind, loving and patient." She giggled. "He punched Archie, one of his best friends, in the face when he found out I was pregnant."

"Pregnant? *Before marriage?*"

Charlotte nodded sheepishly, her pretty face staining red. "Yes, we were rather more passionate than we should have been."

Seriously? Hannah couldn't imagine this quiet, reserved lady being passionate, or anything near it.

"I didn't know."

Charlotte shrugged. "I was deeply in love with him and full of the impetuousness of youth, so making love to Archie was very natural for me."

Hannah had never thought of it that way.

"I can't imagine such a thing being natural, or, well, I couldn't, until the other night," she said.

Being with John had awoken a devil inside her. Need clawed at her belly through the night and she finally understood the hunger that people spoke about men having.

Her mother had always said she should have been born a boy, the way she rode horses and rough-housed with her cousins. So perhaps this was another one of those traits she had inherited from her father.

"The other night, John... kissed you?"

Hannah nodded, her belly jumping with nervous energy as she waded into this much needed conversation. "Yes, and touched me until we both found satisfaction. I don't know what the word is for it."

Charlotte swallowed visibly. "Well, then, I can see why you *would* want to see him again," replied Charlotte slowly.

"I do, Charlotte. And I know your brother is not the marrying kind. So, what do I do while I wait for the right suitor to come along?"

"What about Baron Osborne whom you met at Lizzie's that night? Was he not a good match for you?"

Hannah sighed, her heart at odds with her head in this way. "Yes, he is a good match, but I did not feel anything for him. I have waited this long to be married, Charlotte. I don't want to choose the wrong person now."

She didn't want to say it, but she didn't want a boring life, nor a husband to whom she would soon grow indifferent. She wanted fire, and passion, just like Charlotte seemed to have.

"I agree with you, Hannah. Marriage is for life and you want to pick a man who loves you, or at least respects you. If I have learnt anything from my marriage, and the marriages of Sarah and Lizzie, it is that those two qualities are essential for contentment in marriage."

Hannah took a deep breath, unsure how of how the things she was thinking would sound, once spoken aloud.

"But in the meantime, do you think it would be all right to perhaps, dally with your brother a little?"

Charlotte bit her lip again, obviously conflicted, and Hannah's heart squeezed tight.

She tried not to panic as the time stretched on, but instead, waited for her cousin's wife to respond. This was something she very much wanted to know. She hadn't met anyone in London so far who made her feel the way John did. He made her angry. So angry she wanted to throw things at his head. But then, she wanted to kiss away his pain and find out why he seemed so broken.

All very worrying signs that she, perhaps, was more enamoured of him than she should be.

And yet, she did not wish to stay away from him. She hadn't waited this long to finally feel that spark of attraction, to just walk away from it. She wanted to see where these overwhelming feelings would take her. Where they would take both of them, provided Lord John Dunford felt for her as she did for him.

"I believe it wouldn't be bad for you to spend some time with John, as long as you are both discreet. If you are compromised, he will have to marry you. And I would not wish that sort of marriage upon you."

That sounded ominous. "What sort of marriage do you mean, Charlotte?"

"The sort of dutiful marriage that my parents have, that my elder brother, Edward, has. John's marriage would be the same, I am sure of it."

Hannah still did not know what sort of marriage that was, but before she could ask, the door swung open and Archie stepped in.

"Are you ladies ready to receive visitors now?"

Charlotte stood up, extending her hand so that her husband would walk forward and kiss it. As he did so, Hannah watched her cousin and his wife and saw the hints of romance of which Charlotte had spoken.

Then, Lord John Dunford walked into the room and liquid heat poured into Hannah's belly. The man was so handsome! Her eyes ached from staring at his perfectly sculpted lips and cheekbones.

When he looked her way and their eyes met, her body quivered in that place where John had so cleverly stroked with his fingers that last, magical night.

"Good day, Miss Turner. I mean, Hannah."

"John." She curtseyed and gave him a smile, unable to prevent from expressing how happy she was to see him.

If Charlotte thought it wasn't a bad idea for the two of them to spend some discreet moments together, why shouldn't they? Hannah's excitement grew.

"I have invited John to stay a few nights with us, my dear," Archie was saying, when Hannah's senses had finally relaxed enough to hear what was being said in the room. "He is quite stifled at your brother's home and until he moves into his new townhouse, I thought here would be a good place for him to stay."

Charlotte shot Hannah a worried look and Hannah smiled back at her cousin's wife, trying to convey that this was a good thing. It was more than good. This was perfect!

Charlotte turned back to her brother. "Of course, dear brother. You know you are always welcome in our home," she said.

The men bade their goodbyes as they departed to spend some time at their club and the rest of the afternoon passed quickly.

Hannah was soon being dressed for dinner and a bold plan began to form in her mind. *She would ask John to teach her the ways of the bedroom!*

She wanted to know more about this, she decided, before she got into a marriage with someone where she would be expected to perform a duty she did not understand. And if there was one man who could teach her such things and then happily walk away, it was Lord John Dunford. Of that, she was certain.

Chapter Eleven

John went down to dinner with a happy heart. He observed inwardly that just being around Hannah made him happier than anything else. His club had bored him, made him sullen. Even the boxing ring, that great outlet for frustration, lacked lustre. But here, in this house, surrounded by his most beloved relatives and friends, not to mention a certain red-haired, American woman who tested every limitation set on her sex, he was truly at home.

"Do you have any plans for tomorrow, Hannah? I thought perhaps we could go for a ride, if you wish. Or perhaps I could show you some more of London's delights?"

Hannah smiled and opened her mouth to reply, but Charlotte cut her off before she could answer.

"Hannah has a walk planned with Lord Doveton, tomorrow afternoon."

"Damn," Hannah muttered and John's eyebrows rose. He had never heard a lady swear before. What would the American woman do next? Did she have any more surprises hidden up her exquisitely designed sleeve?

"Hannah? You said you liked Lord Doveton. Didn't you?" Charlotte sounded faintly vexed.

"I did, but walking in a park cannot compare to riding Brutus." *Especially in the company of Lord John Dunford....*

John flashed his sister a smile. He knew the way to Hannah's heart.

"Honour your engagements, Hannah. You are here to seek a suitable husband and John is not a candidate for that. Are you, dear brother?"

John lifted his wine glass up and gave his sister a silent salute, not answering the question as he drank some of the peppery wine. It was too early to show his cards and Charlotte was the last one he wanted messing in his affairs.

"True," Hannah answered, sounding glum. "Thank you, Charlotte, you are correct as usual. Can we go riding the day after, John?"

"Yes of course, Hannah. Please enjoy your walk tomorrow and do give my regards to the lovely Dovey." He smirked as he continued to drink.

Doveton was about as interesting as a glass of water, John thought, but let Hannah show the *ton* what a respectable lady she was. It would make an even better story when he, Lord John Dunford, married the American and stole her out from under all their noses. A plan was forming in John's mind and he revelled in the secrecy.

"Are you ready for the port and cigars, John?" Archie asked him.

He nodded and stood up, walking around the table to clasp Hannah's hand. "Perhaps we will run into each other later?" he murmured.

Hannah smiled up at him and leaned forward to whisper, in a discreet manner. "I may read a book if I am unable to sleep."

So, she would be in the library again? Oh, good! So, his talents in the library had not been forgotten.

"Good evening, Hannah."

She gave him a blinding smile and he walked away, his loins aching with thoughts of her wrapping her delicious body around his.

He spent the next few hours playing cards with Archie and relaxing by the fire, seeing images of Hannah's glorious hair dancing in the fireplace, to tease and taunt him.

She would be red-hot in the bedroom, he was sure of that, with her need to throw herself completely into everything she did. Her body, strong from all the horse riding, the fiery temper that he'd seen, would roll into passion between the sheets.

His cock ached and he inadvertently groaned as he pulled his gaze away from her.

"John, I've been meaning to ask you something. Since when did the plan evolve for you to get an additional house in town?" Archie cocked an eyebrow and John grinned.

Not much got past his friend. Indeed, practically nothing did.

"Edward has made it clear that, since his wife has been unable to produce his heir apparent and probably never shall, the responsibility to perpetuate the Dunford line and its hold on the Dukedom of Arrow is my responsibility, officially or unofficially, as the case may be. He has therefore asked me to get on with doing my duty and to marry this year."

"He what?" Archie sat up straighter in his chair, still nursing the same port he'd poured hours ago.

"He all but demanded that I marry as soon as possible and produce an heir, so I requested my own residence in town. In St James's, of course."

Archie's mouth dropped open and John laughed at his friend's reaction. "Oh, come on, Archie. You're a family member, for heaven's sake. Surely, you knew this day was coming?"

Archie nodded, his eyes still wide and staring straight ahead. "I did, of course, but only if our sister-in-law did not produce an heir for your brother."

"Well, she has not and according to Edward, it doesn't look as if she ever will. So, the pressure has fallen upon me to do the right thing by the family." And amazingly, the more John thought about it and said it aloud, the more comfortable he felt with this new direction his life would take.

"Did you tell him you wanted more time? What about the next in line? Couldn't you just pass the dukedom on to your cousin?"

John frowned at his brother-in-law. "No. I will not allow our title and estate to pass to some dim-witted cousin. What's wrong, Archie? Do you think I'll be such a terrible husband that you can't imagine my ever being married?"

He continued to glare at his brother-in-law and Archie raised his hands in a sign of surrender. "I didn't mean that, John. It's just that, as long as I can remember, you never wanted to marry. I don't want you being forced into something that you abhor."

John let go of his anger as quickly as he could and blew out his breath in a long sigh.

"I'm not sure what you know about my parents' marriage, but it is an ugly state of affairs."

Archie inclined his head. "As is the arrangement that my own parents endure."

"Yes, but your parents, unlike mine, have some dignity, some discretion. My father, on the other hand, has always openly flaunted his mistress in my mother's face, causing much misery and I... did not want that for my own family."

"There is a choice, John. You don't have to be like your father. I think I would take a gun to my temple if I found I was anything like *my* own father."

John shuddered at the idea. "Don't even joke about it, Archie. You are my sister's whole world. She would die without you."

Archie lifted his port glass as though to say, 'thank you', and John felt an unusual swell of love for his long-time friend. "You are a good husband, Archie, and a devoted father. Charlotte is very fortunate indeed to have you."

Archie looked at him with searching eyes. "Thank you, brother. I am very fortunate, also. She is my very life."

John began to shuffle in his chair and stood up, moving to the door. This much emotion made him vastly uncomfortable, his chest becoming hot and heavy.

"Goodnight, Archie. Thank you for your hospitality."

He opened the door and as he turned to leave, he twisted back around.

"Please don't tell anyone, even Charlotte, about my intention to marry this year. I don't want my sister to try to influence my choice."

Archie nodded, a quirk at the edge of his mouth indicating that he understood John's request. After all, he knew Charlotte better than anybody else did. "I will do no such thing, my friend. Be assured of it."

"Thank you."

John walked toward his room, passing the library on the way and finding it empty.

Perhaps Hannah found that she could fall asleep and was already in bed?

No, he hadn't been wrong about the invitation he'd heard in her voice earlier in the evening. He would get dressed for bed, then come back and check for her again.

He went back to his room, got into his night shirt and wrapped a dressing gown around himself. His heart was beginning to pound in his chest, the excitement building before he'd even left his room.

He marveled at the effect Hannah had on his body. He'd never experienced anything like it.

He picked up the candlestick, which looked remarkably similar to the one she'd thrown at him in the country house, and grinned with good humour as he moved down the hallway to the library.

He stepped up to the door and pushed it open, his breath catching when he saw the candelabra containing five glowing candles lighting up Hannah's beautiful face.

"You came."

He stepped into the room and clicked the lock into place.

"Of course, I did."

He placed his candlestick down on a side table and stepped closer. Hannah jumped to her feet and wrapped her arms around his neck, lifting her mouth for his kiss.

He wasted no time in accepting her invitation and swooped down to devour her. He pulled her tightly against his hungry body as his tongue plundered her mouth. She tasted divine, like everything sweet and sensual. Wine, chocolate dessert and brandy all in one.

Her night gown was thin and as his hands roamed over her lush behind, he reveled in the feeling of her firmness and strength.

Ladies of the ton were soft, fragile, and somewhat like a pillow, if they weren't painfully thin. Hannah was tight and felt completely different beneath his hands. He'd never confuse her for anyone else, that was for damn sure.

He pulled away, breaking the kiss so that he could stare down at her. "I want you so much, Hannah. Will you come back to my room with me?"

He knew he shouldn't seduce her tonight, or indeed, any night. But he wanted her more than he'd ever wanted any other woman and if they were as wonderful together in the bedroom as he expected they would be, then he planned to get a special license and marry her as soon as he could.

"Yes. I feel the same way, John. Will you show me what it feels like to be with a man?"

He nodded, his chest tightening with too many emotions. He had a strong desire to be her first and only man. That was a very special bond that he'd never before thought of sharing with a woman.

"Come with me."

He took her hand and drew her out of the library, checking the hallways to ensure no one was watching. He stopped only to pick up the candles and moved swiftly back toward his room.

His heart was pounding, his skin tingling with nervous energy. They both quickly walked into his room and he shut the door behind them, taking a moment to turn the key.

He would show Hannah how much he cared and give her many reasons to choose him. The pleasure he planned to bring her in the bedroom would be only one of those reasons.

"Come here, my beautiful one." He placed the candelabra on a sideboard and pulled her into his arms, kissing her soft brow, feeling the silky skin of her arms as they wrapped around his body.

"If I take you for a lover, will anyone else marry me?" Hannah whispered.

John leaned back so that he could look into her beautiful eyes.

"Why would you marry anyone else?" he asked, baffled by her question. What sort of virgin thought of marrying another while she was with her lover?

Hannah laughed, looking at him as though he should know what she was talking about. "Well, I won't be marrying you, so I'm just asking if this will ruin me or not? I know you assumed, owing to my age, that I wasn't chaste, so perhaps others will, too?"

John stilled. She didn't want to marry him? Was that what she had just said? Well, he would fix that. He *would* ruin her for any other man. He'd give her such pleasure, such passion, she'd never want another.

"No, it'll be all right. I'll teach you what to do. How to enjoy pleasure," he soothed, undoing the laces at the back of her nightgown and pulling the material down.

Hannah gasped, but remained still as he slowly exposed her body, like a flower opening up its petals to reveal the perfect centre.

John turned her around and kissed the base of her neck, running his hands around her slim waist.

"I want your hair down," he whispered, tasting the skin beneath her beautiful hair. She smelled of sunshine and rain.

"I thought you didn't like my hair down," Hannah whispered, her voice strained.

Damn it, she sounded hurt. Had his previous comments made her think ill of herself?

He squeezed her tightly. "I love your hair when it's down, that's the problem. You looked far too beautiful that day for everyone to see you like that."

"So, you want to keep me all to yourself, do you?" Hannah joked, reaching up and pulling the pins that restricted her glorious, burnt-sunshine coloured hair.

John turned Hannah back around, staring down into her eyes.

"Always," he vowed with truth, capturing her mouth with his, before she could say another word.

Chapter Twelve

Part of him felt guilty for seducing Hannah under his sister's roof. She *was* under his sister's protection, after all. But he couldn't seem to stay away from her. She had bewitched him; caught his attention and not let go. And underneath all the lust, something pure drove his intentions.

He had no intention of loving and leaving this woman. Not Hannah. She was unlike any other woman he had ever met, and had somehow changed his outlook on love and marriage so thoroughly that he barely recognized himself these days.

John plunged his hands through the hair that he loved and moaned loudly as the silky strands slipped between his fingers. Hannah reciprocated his passion, sparring with his tongue as it tangled with hers.

Desperate to see the body that had so bewitched him, John loosened Hannah's shiftand let it fall from her shoulders down toward the floor. It pooled at her feet, revealing her perfection. He stared at her, wanting to revel in the moment he first saw Hannah like this. Naked and utterly beautiful. Her nipples were small and pale pink, peaked and pointing at him as if begging for his attention.

John reached out and weighed a breast in his hand. The weight and the warmth of her skin against his palm created an answering call of desire in his body.

He had to swallow down the need to push her up against the wall and take her quickly. His body was hard and ready, but she was an innocent. She needed care and coaxing from him, not rough play.

Instead of rushing ahead as his own body screamed at him to do, he focused on his breathing. In, out, in, out. If he just kept it going, he would be fine.

"Are my breasts all right?" Hannah asked, peering down at them.

John smiled. She really was taking this like a lesson, with a teacher who would critique her.

"They are perfect. A good size, soft and…" He pinched the semi-erect nipple softly between his thumb and forefinger, her moan delighting him.

"Responsive," he finished.

John swept Hannah up into his arms and laid her on the bed. She scooted back and ducked beneath the covers, pulling them up to her chin.

Did she think that was going to stop him from finishing what they had begun?

John laughed, tingling happiness filling up his chest like a glass filling with wine as he pulled off his shirt, boots, stockings and breeches. When was the last time he had laughed when making love to someone? Never!

Hannah's eyes were bulging, with a hint of fear showing in their blue depths, so he stopped at his drawers. She had seen him completely naked before and had thrown a candlestick at him. But tonight was going to be very different.

His erection was rather plain to see, but that extra layer between them would stop him taking her too soon.

His goal, now, was marriage. And not just any sort of union. He wanted a good marriage, a happy marriage. Which meant that she had to remember this night as the best night of her life. He wanted this to be the first of many nights together.

John shifted back the covers and climbed into bed with her, rolling onto his side and pulling her close, against him.

"I will make this as painless as possible, Hannah. And you can ask questions or tell me to stop at any time. Is that all right?"

Hannah nodded, but she was shaking in his arms, despite the heat in the room. His fearsome, strong American girl was terrified and there was nothing of which to be scared. At least, he didn't think so. Bu there was one new thing about this night for John. He'd never taken a virgin before.

But if Oliver and Archie could achieve such a thing, he was certain he could also do it.

"I'm a little afraid," she admitted softly. "But I know you know what you're doing. That's why I chose you," she said.

He stared at her quivering lips. It would be hard to go slow, but he had to, for her sake. "I need you to know how important this is for me too, Hannah. I've never met a woman like you. You're very special."

She smiled a little and he wasn't sure she believed him. But when she tilted her head up in an invitation to kiss her, nothing else mattered.

He bent his head and captured her mouth, coaxing her lips gently apart. Slowly, she relaxed in his arms. He increased the pressure of his lips and tongue until she moaned, pressing her naked breasts against his bare chest and running her hands through his hair.

John growled with need and rolled on top of her, enjoying the soft heat of her skin against his. Hannah opened her legs wide and he settled between them as though he'd done it a thousand times before.

As though they were made for each other.

"Is it all right if I touch you like this?" Hannah asked, gripping his skull with one hand and running her other hand down his back.

John shuddered with desire? *Was it all right?* She was going to unman him! How could a virgin be so wantonly affectionate?

"Definitely all right," he growled, moving down her body. "Touch me anywhere and everywhere you wish."

When he reached her breasts he started to take one hungry nipple into his mouth. Until she squealed and stopped him, covering her breasts with her hands. "What are you doing?"

John laughed again, wanting to please her more than anything.

"I intend to kiss every inch of your beautiful body," he declared, drawing her hands away from her breasts. Such beauty should not be covered.

"Aren't you just going to, you know?" Hannah bumped her pelvis up into his belly and John shifted position so that she could grind her mound against his erection.

They both moaned at the same time, as sensations of pleasure rushed through him. "Oh my, yes, *that*," he said.

Hannah breathed raggedly, her eyelids dropping to half-mast.

He kept thrusting gently, imitating the action of love making with only one thin layer of material separating them.

Hannah moaned again and raised her knees to fit him better.

John's need grew as his body found the area it wanted. He partially penetrated her, over and over. Careful not to squash her, he held himself up on his elbows and looked down into her beautiful face.

Hannah bent forward, biting his shoulder and running her nails down his back.

John half fell on her, both hands going beneath her bottom so that he could control their movements better. She bucked and squealed beneath him, making it so much more enjoyable than he was used to. It was a delight to ride *with* her.

Feeling himself getting closer and closer to that final glory, John made a split-second decision. He would come now so that he could get some relief and therefore focus on her. He would never be able to give her any sort of pleasure if he got inside her now.

John sped up his movements and put out an arm so he could take some of his weight. He dropped his head so that he could kiss her neck, then put his lips to her ear.

"I could take you now, but I want you to feel pleasure."

"I am. This feels wonderful," Hannah whispered, digging her nails into his shoulders, harder, deeper.

"I'm going to come now, so that I can love you better," he told her, shocking himself as his words filled the gap between them.

"I don't know what you mean," Hannah said, wriggling beneath him again.

"Just wrap your legs around me and rub those delicious nipples on me," John panted. He was almost there; he could see stars forming behind his vision.

Hannah did as he asked. She wrapped her legs around him and arched her back.

John's head exploded. He came in his drawers like a mere boy, groaning and shuddering in Hannah's arms. Heat rolled over his back as that perfect release flooded through him.

Careful not to collapse on top of her, John rolled to the side and turned her with him. She kept her legs wrapped around him and the closeness felt so right.

Instead of pushing him off like every mistress or whore he had bedded would have done now that he had finished, Hannah stayed pressed up against him, stroking his hair and holding him tight with her arms, as well as those long and sexy legs, wrapped around him.

"Are we stopping now?" Hannah asked, the disappointment clear in her voice. There was no condemnation, but he could tell she knew there was so much more that he had not shared with her.

John stared into her clear, blue eyes, still panting and trying to get his breath back.

"Not at all. Just give me a moment." He grinned and rolled out of bed away from her, quickly stripping off his drawers and wiping himself clean. Then he turned back to Hannah and feasted his eyes on her long, lithe body.

Hannah pulled the covers back over herself.

John chuckled at her coy behaviour and slipped beneath the covers to rejoin her. It would take him a while to recover, but they had all the time in the world.

"Your turn," he smiled, and pulled Hannah against him.

"I need to know what you are going to do to me," Hannah breathed, her body shifting restlessly.

"I'm going to kiss and touch you here," John ran his hand over her lovely breasts, "and here," he allowed his hand to drift slowly over her soft belly and down between her legs.

Hannah jumped with a squeak and clamped her legs closed over his hand.

It didn't stop him exploring her slickness with his fingertips. "You're so ready," he sighed happily, sliding his fingers between her slippery folds.

She stilled his hand with another squeeze of her thighs. "I'm getting a little nervous now. Can we slow down?"

He didn't know what to do with that request. He'd said he would stop if she asked, but he hadn't thought she'd take him up on the offer.

Every woman he had ever taken to bed had either been paid to be there or was an experienced widow or mistress. He had never had to cajole or tread lightly.

The other confusing thing was that John knew she was aroused but she was asking him to stop. How could he make her trust him like she had that night at Rupert's house?

He slid out of the bed, wanting to put some distance between them so he could more easily do as she asked. A look of shock and disappointment crossed Hannah's face. So, she did want to be with him, he was certain of that. Perhaps all virgins were like this? Their virgin nerves kicked in.

How could he change this, so he could help her overcome them and lead her to the pleasure and enjoyment that he hoped to bring her?

He stood before her, completely naked, the fire warm on his back while he considered.

"Would you like to touch me, then?" he asked, opening his arms, palms up.

Hannah looked at his body with a greedy gaze. He knew his form was well shaped. He was a young man who did a lot of physical exercise. He had no softness, no fat. Hopefully Hannah liked what she could see.She nodded slowly. "I would like that," she said, slightly hesitant.

"Then come on over here, and touch me," he invited, not moving from his place in front of the fire. "If you want to."

Hannah pulled the blanket up over her head and John wanted to dive back under the covers and stroke her back to ease her nerves. Beg her forgiveness for pushing too hard.

But he stayed where he was. He knew her to be a strong woman, capable of fighting for what she wanted if necessary. Hopefully, this would be one of those things?

Finally, Hannah lowered the blankets and rolled out of bed on her side.

She walked, completely naked, to him. John's heart beat hard against his sternum, for what felt like the very first time. Each thud was heard and acknowledged. This was his woman, and she was coming to him voluntarily.

He'd been right. Hannah was meant to be his.

She reached up and ran both hands down his chest, following the lines of his stomach and then up again. Her hands were soft and tender, causing a *frisson* of pleasure to skitter along his skin.

When she ran her nails lightly over his nipples, he moaned, unable to keep his pleasure to himself. His cock stirred to life again, quicker than he'd expected.

Hannah stepped back when his erection reached out and touched her belly.

She eyed that part of his body with a mix of curiosity, fear and desire. What he wouldn't give to feel her hands on his aching shaft.

"You can touch everything," he invited softly, clasping Hannah's hand and wrapping it around his shaft. "Just like the other night at Rupert's house. Do you remember?"

Hannah's eyes widened and her lips parted, but she didn't step back. Or loose her hold. Instead, she stroked him gently as she had learnt. Up and down.

It was exquisite torture.

John stood still for as long as he could, heat curling in his balls as she stroked along his length. She was so close, her body so arousing. She alternated between stroking his chest and his stomach with tentative touches, then switching her attention back to the swollen head and shaft of his manhood.

His fingers flexed at his sides as the need grew.

"May I touch you now, Hannah? I want to bring you pleasure too."

Hannah hesitated, then reached up and pinched both of his nipples at once.

His breath whistled through his teeth and his arousal bobbed against her belly.

"Yes. You can touch me, John." Hannah swallowed visibly.

John was determined to return her to the state of arousal she had been in when she had finished with him the other night. He placed both hands gently on her breasts and caressed them, circling the nipples and stroking the soft undersides of her flesh.

Hannah smiled and leaned into his caress.

He ran one hand down her soft belly and slid his fingertips into the crinkly hair at the junction of Hannah's thighs. The hair there was just as he had imagined, a soft red that blended against her cream-like skin.

He didn't plunge his hand deep. Not yet. Instead, he sought out the small bud that would give Hannah the most pleasure and began to stroke it.

Hannah moaned and grabbed hold of his arm for support.

"Lie back down on the bed and I'll show you more," he promised.

He had never spent so long with a woman before. It was much more pleasant than he had expected it to be.

Hannah climbed back onto the bed and this time only pulled the blankets up to her waist.

"Well, come and show me then," she invited in a sultry tone, waving her hands at him, her strength and hunger clearly on the rise.

Her impatience pleased John immeasurably and he all but jumped into the bed. This time she came willingly into his arms. He pulled her against him and ran his hands down Hannah's back so that he could feel her skin and enjoy her gentle curves. It was incredible, the heat and softness of her delectable body. John had never lain like this with a woman before, both people naked, facing each other. It was so much more personal and special than what he had experienced in the past, but with Hannah, everything was different.

He *wanted* everything to be new and special with her. And for her.

"This feels incredible." He moaned into her hair.

Hannah pulled back and looked up into his eyes. He wanted to look away. It was too much. But he didn't dare. She seemed pleased with what she saw and pulled his head down for a kiss.

Hannah bumped her pelvis up against John's and he laughed against her lips.

"Something amusing?" Hannah pouted, running her hands lovingly through his chest hair.

John sighed and allowed his thoughts to flow freely to his mouth. "I have never had such a good time with a woman before."

"But we haven't even..."

"Even if we stopped now, tonight would still be the most amazing night of my life," he admitted, swallowing the fear that gripped his chest. How could he be so honest and emotional with her? It went against everything he'd believed in all his life.

She smiled, the most blinding smile John had ever seen. She tugged at his back so that he would lie on top of her.

He swooped down to kiss her again and lay between Hannah's legs, his erect cock resting against her belly.

He knew he could take her now, but she wasn't ready. Not ready enough to experience the ultimate pleasure, anyway.

John smiled down at his beautiful lady and kissed her hard on the lips. He worked his way down to her breasts and gently sucked one of her tight nipples into his mouth. Hannah gasped, but threaded her fingers into his hair, encouraging him to stay where he was.

He smiled against her soft skin and moved over to the other breast.

Inch by inch, he kissed his way down to the place between Hannah's legs.

"You're not going to kiss me there, are you?" Hannah started to object.

"You'll really like it," John promised, flicking his tongue out to graze the most sensitive part of her.

Hannah jolted and opened her legs wider. She seemed to come back to herself and looked down at him again.

"And I can do this to you?" She sounded as though she didn't really believe him.

John's mouth went dry. He wasn't sure he was comfortable with that idea.

"You can..." he said slowly, licking her again to distract her.

Hannah wiggled and gasped. "Why do you say it like that?"

"Because ladies don't usually." He nuzzled her inside thigh.

"But you're doing it to me." Hannah inhaled sharply, arching her back slightly.

"True, but I don't do this often either."

He lifted his head to see something intense burn in Hannah's eyes. She lifted her pelvis up to him and he grinned as he dipped his head again, drawing her swollen nub into his mouth. He sucked gently and inserted his middle finger deep inside her.

She moaned and grabbed at the mattress either side of her. John inserted a second finger, enjoying the tight clasp of her body around him.

"You are so wet, beautiful woman." He spoke against her flesh. "You want me."

Hannah giggled and thrashed. "Of course, I want you, stupid man," she muttered, her back arching up again as John found a sweet spot inside of her. "Oh... goodness..."

He flicked his tongue over her clitoris until he could feel her tightening inside, her body squeezing his fingers. If she was still able to talk, then she was nowhere near close enough.

He lapped up her juices while his fingers stretched and filled her. Just as he felt her muscles tighten again, he stopped.

"John, no, please," she begged as he withdrew his fingers and moved up her body.

He hovered over her, looking down into her eyes, seeing the very soul of this kind, beautiful woman and hoping this would be only the first of many times he saw it.

He positioned himself at her entrance. "We come together this time," he breathed, and pushed slowly into her.

John had never taken a virgin before and had never thought he would do so. Hannah's body welcomed him with its warm, wet clasp, but she was so tight. It felt like heaven to him, but he knew she likely didn't feel the same way. Not this first time. He looked down into her blue eyes and kissed her deeply, wanting to distract her from any pain she might be feeling.

She wrapped her arms about his neck and moved her tongue between his lips. John thrust hard, breaking through her barrier and planting himself deep within her.

Hannah cried out and stiffened beneath him.

Some part of him marveled at the fact that such a beautiful woman of Hannah's age had been a virgin, but he had never doubted her integrity. She wouldn't have lied. It didn't suit her truthful personality.

He remained still, wanting to give her body time to adjust to the intrusion. The sweat began to bead on his forehead at the effort, but he still didn't move.

After what felt like an eternity, Hannah began to relax. Her legs, which had locked him in place, began to shift restlessly and she began stroking his back again.

John could have shouted in joy.

He began to move, withdrawing slowly and then thrusting back a little harder. His spitfire from America began to respond. She lifted her legs and wrapped them about his waist and John said a little prayer for strength.

He picked up the pace and began to thrust harder and harder, her moans spurring him on. She began to thrash, her nails digging into his shoulders so harshly, she could be drawing blood. He didn't care.

"John, I'm going to..." Hannah gasped into his ear, her head coming off the pillow.

John's own pleasure multiplied as her body contracted around him.

"Give it to me, come for me. Only me." John moaned in time with Hannah as she shouted and spasmed around him, over and over again.

Then John's own orgasm began, hot fire racing down his legs as his balls tightened and pulsed between his thighs. At the very last moment, he realized what was happening and jerked back, pulling out just in time to spill himself on the sheets between Hannah's legs.

He fell onto her breasts, overwhelmed by the most intense orgasm of his life.

After a minute or two he pushed away, not wanting to crush her beneath his weight. But she wouldn't let him up. She grabbed him and tried to pull him back down. Then she fixed him with a gimlet stare.

"Lie down. I like holding you."

John immediately relaxed into her, though he rolled slightly to one side so he wouldn't squash her. He liked holding Hannah, too. He moved his head so that he was resting on her breasts. Her breastbone cushioned his cheek and her arms went about his shoulders.

He breathed deeply, inhaling the scent that was uniquely Hannah.

"That was amazing. Thank you." Hannah sighed, running her hands through his hair again and again.

The move was comforting, as was her closeness. He'd never experienced anything like it before and although he was the more experienced of the two of them, he was no longer feeling like it.

"We can enjoy it as much as we want. Forever." He sighed, comfortable and happy, knowing they would have a good future together. He couldn't guarantee anything, of course, but she rocked his world in the bed chamber. That had to count for something toward a good future.

Rupert had said it would.

He nuzzled in closer and suddenly noticed a difference in Hannah. She was no longer stroking his hair. Instead, she had become unnaturally still.

"What do you mean, John?"

He pulled up to face Hannah.

"I want to marry you as soon as possible."

There, he had said it. He hadn't thought it would be so easy. But the words had tumbled out, naturally.

"I don't think so," Hannah murmured, sliding out of John's reach and twisting away to climb out of bed.

Her beautiful body disappeared from his view beneath her night dress and gown. What had happened? They'd just shared what he believed to be an incredible moment and he'd done what he thought she wanted. He'd proposed marriage. A proper proposal. Wasn't that the reason she was in London?

"Hannah, I don't understand. I thought that was what you wanted. You came to bed with me."

She turned to face him and tied her dressing gown beneath her breasts. "I know I did, and it was wonderful. But I came to learn about lovemaking. To indulge myself with an experienced man—one with a rake's reputation. I never expected you to offer marriage." Hannah's face flushed scarlet as she spoke, and sudden anger stirred in John's belly.

"So, you are refusing me?" His words came out colder than he'd intended but he was in shock. She wanted marriage... but not with him?

Hannah sat on edge of the bed and looked at him with soulful eyes.

"John, you are a renowned rake. You told me yourself that love is for fools and that any woman is replaceable and interchangeable. How can I marry a man who feels that way? *I'm* a woman. That means you feel that way about me, too."

John swallowed, tears forming in the corners of his eyes. He blinked them away and turned his head so she wouldn't see them.

He *had* said that, and he had been a fool. His pride was balking at her rejection and his teeth set in anger. Holding on to the last of his dignity, he turned back to face her.

"Thank you for a wonderful night, and for your virginity."

Hannah frowned and John bit his tongue, the devil in his mind rising up to stop him saying more.

She stood and straightened her spine, flicking her long hair over her shoulders so that it flowed around her like a sunset ocean.

"Thank *you* for your experience. I'm sure no one else could have done as good a job." Hannah spoke in clipped tones, before she headed to door, turned the key and slipped out quietly.

John sat in his empty bed looking at the door for a long time after she'd left. How had it come to this? How had he been reduced to this sad, empty shell of his former self?

Where was the fire and rage that had once fueled him?

He had just offered marriage, when he thought that would never happen, and the woman he wanted—the woman he had come to love— had just rejected him because of his own infernal reputation!

He rolled back onto the pillows and lay awake for many hours, unsure of what tomorrow would bring.

Chapter Thirteen

Hannah tugged on her lace-covered walking dress and sighed as the lady's maid applied another flower to her upswept hair.

"Don't you think that's enough, Anne-Marie?"

"Yes, *madame*. If you think so." The girl grabbed her things and hurried from the room. Hannah was struck with guilt.

It wasn't Anne-Marie's fault that Hannah was in such a foul temper. She'd slept terribly, tossing and turning most of the night, her heart pounding and her mind in turmoil.

John had proposed to her! Proposed marriage! Why had he done that?

She had achieved her goal. She had enjoyed one night in John's bed. She now knew what to expect in her marriage and she had appeased that terrible need that had been clawing at her since John had entered her life.

But what to make of the terrible fuss after their lovemaking had finished?

Had he proposed marriage out of guilt or a need to do the right thing? He couldn't possibly love her. He was a rake, and he thought little of women.

What had been his motivation? "Stop it." She pushed to her feet and glared at her reflection. She would not be brought down by a rake like John Dunford.

She had a gentleman to walk with today and more gentlemen to meet tonight. One of them would surely be respectable and still arouse her body the way John did.

Her shoulders sagged. *Damn it.* Even her thoughts betrayed her. But her recalcitrant mind did have a point. She did want to feel the passion and those tendrils of love for her husband that she had experienced with John.

However, she needed to feel those things with a man who was right for her.

She nodded her head and strode out through the door, bouncing down the stairs and into the foyer.

"Miss Turner. I am to accompany you to the park today."

Mrs. Mabbs, the housekeeper, stepped up to her, a parasol in her hand.

"Oh, Mrs. Mabbs, what has happened? Is the Countess feeling unwell?"

She'd assumed her cousin's wife would be the one to chaperone her. Charlotte seemed to have more interest in Hannah making a good match than Hannah did.

"The Countess is abed. The doctor advised her to rest."

That didn't sound good. "Oh, perhaps I should stay, then?"

"No miss. We must go. Lady Totherham demanded it."

Of course, she had.

Hannah released a sigh. "Thank you, Mrs. Mabbs."

She moved toward the front door and heard a creak behind her. She turned, her heart leaping into her chest as John walked slowly and deliberately down the stairs, staring at her all the while.

"Enjoy your walk, Miss Turner. I'm sure Dovey will put on a good show for you."

The cruel twist of his lips made her fists clench on the handle of her parasol.

Just because they had been intimate, did not give Lord John Dunford the excuse to be rude to her. Nor should he expect to have any control over her.

"I'm sure he will, my lord. Good day."

She turned and strode out through the front door, hurrying to the waiting carriage. Her chaperone followed her and together, they made their way to the park.

Lord Doveton was there waiting for her. As soon as the carriage stopped Hannah climbed out and extended her hand toward him.

"Good day, sir."

"Good day, Lady Hannah."

"Miss Turner, actually. But you may call me Hannah, please."

The smile on his face dropped and he tried to hide it by kissing her hand and then turning to walk beside her.

"Shall we?"

They began ambling along the narrow road that wound through a rather odd-looking park to her. So manicured. So unnatural. Nothing like the natural beauty and wildness of the open spaces near her father's tobacco plantation at home in Virginia.

The housekeeper trailed a discreet distance behind them.

"Tell me more about yourself, Lord Doveton."

"Well, my father is an earl and my mother is the daughter of a marquess. They live in Kent most of the year and I spend as much time in London as I can."

She frowned and looked up at the blue sky, trying not to judge the man beside her too harshly. What sort of person defined themselves in that way?

"Do you ride horses, my lord?"

"Oh no, not at all. Unclean beasts." Doveton shuddered and Hannah stifled the loud sigh she felt building up. He was making this a little too hard.

Why did she automatically think of John? He would never answer in such a way. She didn't want someone fixated on social status, who preferred town to the country and defined himself by his parentage.

John seemed to hate his responsibilities and loved horses. She wasn't sure about his preference for town as they'd never discussed it.

She shook her head to clear her muddled thoughts. She had to stop thinking about John.

"Are you looking to marry soon, Lord Doveton?"

That question made him smile and he indicated a park bench where they could sit and discuss this new development in the conversation.

She sat down, despite the fact that it meant she had to look straight at the gentleman to whom she had been recommended as a future spouse. At close range, she could see the unhealthy pallor of his skin and the slight yellow tinge that she knew indicated excessive alcohol consumption.

How John did not have that same colour, she did not know. Probably the boxing and riding that Charlotte had mentioned he did often as exercise kept him fit and healthy.

Her eyes fell to Lord Doveton's waist and a shudder shivered up her spine. What sort of soft, paunch belly would he have? How would she be able to be with a man who did not compare favourably with John?

"I am very much in favour of marrying this year... Hannah."

He reached over to take her hand and there was a twist in her gut that was not at all pleasant.

"Are you financially independent, my lord?" she asked sweetly, deciding to weed out just what sort of man he was.

"I... ah, rely on an income of sorts, like most men of my rank."

So, in other words, he was looking for a dowry to fund his lifestyle.

She waited for his response and finally he asked. "I believe, being American, you would have something to contribute to the marriage as well?"

She did. A considerable amount, but she didn't want to buy herself a husband, and certainly not one who did not live up to her standards of what a person should be. Honest. Strong. Healthy.

"I am a hard worker and a pious, generous soul. I was told that was what gentlemen in London would value," Hannah forced out, her tongue turning to ash as she baited the man before her. She was no longer chaste, but he did not need to know that. And technically, she hadn't lied. She hadn't actually said virginal.

"Oh, well. I did not expect... I mean, you being American, I..." He stammered over his words and now, she wasn't sure what he was trying to say.

Her temper began to boil as her brain drew all sorts of conclusions, one of which was that being with John for a night had been a good idea. They didn't expect her to come to them intact anyway. "What do you mean, sir? You assumed that, being American, I would have plenty of money? Or was it that you thought I might not be virtuous? Which of those traits made you more inclined to marry me?"

His eyes widened and his mouth opened and shut like a simpleton.

She glared at him and huffed. "Well?"

She certainly could not marry a man who couldn't keep up with her in conversation. That was the very least of her criteria. He could be old, balding and pudgy, but at least he should be honest, and have a clever and quick mind.

Like John.

When Doveton still did not answer, she lost her temper.

"Grrr." She stood up, turned around and marched back to the carriage, her shadow trailing behind her.

The footman scampered down off the carriage, but she was too impatient to wait, throwing open the door and climbing up herself. The housekeeper wasn't far behind her.

She crossed her arms over her chest and huffed the whole way home. Was that really the crème de la crème of London society? She had been sadly misled if that was the case.

When she got back to the Earl of Totherham's townhouse, she jumped out of the carriage and went straight inside, heading for her cousin's study. Hopefully, John wasn't in there too.

She knocked on Archie's door and pushed it open, finding him reading a document at his desk.

"May I have a moment, cousin?"

Archie nodded, giving her a soft smile. "Of course, you may, Hannah. How may I assist you?"

She marched in and sat down on the soft leather chair, feeling very much like a woman on a mission. Her life had just become a sorry state of affairs.

"I would like to marry. I have reached an age where I want a family and a home of my own."

She loved her parents, but it was time to move on with her own life. She had begrudged their interference initially in sending her here, but now she saw the wisdom of it.

Archie blinked at her and leaned back in his chair. "Yes. I thought that was why you came to London?"

Archie's calmness had a settling effect on Hannah and she relaxed into her chair, finally seeing how Charlotte and Archie's opposite personalities meshed together so well.

"I did. However, I wasn't altogether on board with the idea. I believe I haven't been focusing correctly."

No, I've been too busy shopping, socializing and falling for a handsome rake who is just not suitable.

She may have had money, but certainly not enough to be able to stay in London forever, living on a whim and the good grace of her cousin.

"You have done everything right so far, cousin. Please don't be harsh with yourself. You settled in with us over the break, bought new clothes, socialized. That is all anyone ever does."

"Well, I am not attracting the right suitors."

Archie's solemn face changed to one of amusement, his lips perking up. "I take it Doveton did not suit you?"

She rolled her eyes and glared at her cousin. "You know he doesn't. The man can barely string a sentence together."

"And he needs a fortune."

She continued to glare at him. "Why did you not stop me from meeting him if you knew that?"

Archie shrugged. "Fortune hunters are not all bad. Everyone needs to live. And I assumed you would work it all out on your own, Hannah. You are a clever young lady."

The compliment stopped any anger that had accumulated and she relaxed once more into her chair. "Archie, I need your help. Can you introduce me to any gentlemen that you think *may* be suitable?"

Archie sat forward in his chair. "I could, if you gave me some idea of the qualities you would like in a gentleman."

She had just opened her mouth to answer when the door swung open and John stepped in.

"Oh. Hannah. I didn't know you were in here."

To avoid looking at him, she turned back to her cousin. "We were having a private conversation."

"No, wait. I think John could be helpful here, Hannah. Include him, if you will." Archie turned to John, who was now leaning against a bookcase like the handsome devil he was. "John, Hannah was just about to give me a list of the attributes she needs in a husband. You know the *ton* better than I do, nowadays. Perhaps you can suggest someone for my fair cousin?"

JOHN IMMEDIATELY WANTED to scream at both of them.

Me! I'm the best choice for her.

But instead, he continued to play his expected nonchalant role.

"Of course, Archie. However, I do remember a conversation very similar to this one that was the start of your undoing." He pointedly looked at his friend and Archie smiled back, his memory as perfect as John's. Charlotte had acquired Archie's interest not long after declaring she would only marry a virgin. It had shocked everyone when she actually got what she wanted.

He turned his attention back to the woman who'd refused his proposal only the previous night. "Tell me, Hannah. What do you desire in a husband?"

It was a struggle to look at her and ask such a question, and when she finally turned to him, anger clear in her gaze, he smiled brightly. He loved that he affected her so much. Perhaps the battle was not yet completely lost.

"I need a gentleman who *wants* to be married."

"Of course! No man will marry—or even offer for it—unless he wishes to do so."

She glared at him and twisted in her seat to face Archie, who threw them both a strange look.

John didn't respond. He was quite enjoying the fact that she could not hide her strong reaction to him.

"I want someone who doesn't need my money, but of course, I'm not afraid of hard work, so if he owns a property that needs me, I'm ready to work. Anyone who is decent, honest and kind will be perfect for me."

John went to ask a question and she jumped in again. "Oh, and he has to like horses and he must not be too old nor overly rotund, if possible."

Her gaze slid unerringly to his flat stomach, and he puffed out his chest at her obvious need to find someone fit and healthy. If he'd set the bar last night, she was going to have trouble finding another gentleman who competed with his physique.

"Well..." Archie began. "I will have to think about it. If you are happy to marry a man well beneath you in rank, it will open up the pool considerably. Don't you think so, John?"

He nodded, wondering how Hannah would manage being married to a farmer.

He thought back to the first day he'd met her and, unfortunately, he could see her doing very well as a farmer's wife. She was so genuine. He could see her doing well married to anyone. Except him, apparently.

"I'm sure her family didn't send her all this way to marry a nobody, Archie."

"True. We will find someone suitable for you, Hannah."

She stood up. "Thank you, cousin, but please know that the most important attribute to me is a good heart. Everything else, I can compromise on."

SHE TURNED and left the room in a cloud of skirts and John fell into the chair she had just vacated, her final arrow slung right between his ribs, hitting its target.

Archie stared at him, his narrowed gaze one of knowing accusation. "John?"

"Yes, Archie?" came the reply.

"What have you done?"

John lifted his nose and called on his best polite face. Archie was the king of polite regard, but John had also been tutored from the cradle to mask his emotions. "I don't know what you mean, Archie."

His friend stood up and walked over to his bookshelf, pushing aside a book or two and coming back with a decanter and some glasses.

He poured the drinks in silence and handed one to John.

He chose to alter the subject, the memory of some news from his valet floating into his mind. "Is my sister well? I heard she was abed today."

Which John thought was very unusual for his outgoing sister. Nothing usually kept Lady Totherham down.

"She is. The doctor suggested bed rest when she had some abdominal pains and because of the baby, she obeyed. But she'll be up again tomorrow, I'm sure of it."

"Baby? Pregnant again? Damn it, Archie. You don't waste time, do you?" He lifted his full glass of port and toasted his brother-in-law.

"I squandered my life for far too long, John. Never again!" Archie sat down into his chair, a satisfied smile on his face.

That was far too heavy a statement for this time of the day. John swallowed some of his port and nursed the glass in his hand.

"I want to learn more about my current investments, Archie. Will you help?"

"Of course, John." His brother-in-law and oldest friend nodded.

"It's about time I learned where my money is and what it is doing."

Archie had always been a dab hand at the Exchange and John had followed all his advice to the letter. Thanks to Archie, he had a very healthy sum of money on which to live comfortably, but until today, he hadn't understood where any of it came from. The time had come to change that.

Or had it? Did he really want all of these new changes in his life? Or was he just fooling himself?

He drank a little more, then gestured to Archie, who re-filled both of their glasses.

"Shall we go out tonight, Archie? We could go to the club or somewhere more colourful perhaps?"

Archie levelled him with an intense gaze. "Like a brothel, John? Certainly, I'll come with you. I'll just leave my pregnant wife at home to go have sex with some random woman half the *ton* has been inside. What a great evening that will be."

Archie's characteristically dry tone made the horrible suggestion even worse.

John leaned back in his chair and crossed his ankle over his knee, a strange uncomfortable sensation pushing him further than he'd ever gone with Archie.

Was he really ready for a life of respectability?

"Why not, Archie? You must be sick of your wife."

He didn't mean the stupid words spewing out of this mouth, but there was a part of him that was spoiling for a fight.

"Oh, I am. Shall we go then?" Archie's tone was sarcastic as he stood up and walked to the door and the moment gave John time to think.

Acid hit his gut like a bucket of hot water.

What was he doing? Or saying? He didn't want to go and find another woman. He wanted Hannah. And he certainly didn't want to see his sister's marriage go the same way as his brother's had. A dutiful union of cold indifference if one was lucky, or a dutiful union of hostility if one wasn't.

He didn't move, and Archie opened the door for them both. "Come on then, John. Get up. Show me how wonderful *your* world is. You want to be like your father now, I assume? And shall I aim for the same end as my brother?"

If there was any chance of him standing up to see how far Archie would take this bluff, those words silenced that devil. Archie's brother had died of syphilis and it had almost ruined the lives of Archie and other family members, too.

He sighed loudly. "Sit down, Archie."

Archie glowered at him, then finally shut the door and sat down in his chair, downing his drink until the port was all gone.

Then he poured himself another one.

"What are you doing, Archie?"

"I don't know, John. Perhaps I'm trying to shock you into considering where your life is going. What are you doing with yourself? We both know how you feel about Hannah."

"I beg your pardon?"

"Oh, come on, man. Do I really need to go out and find my cousin a decent husband when you're obviously in love with her? Should I parade in front of you all of her potential suitors and hope you come to your senses before she marries another?"

What could he say to *that*? How did his friend read him so well?

"You heard me, John," Archie said, when he didn't respond. "My cousin is a good woman and I'm guessing you've seduced her."

"I..." He couldn't lie quickly enough and Archie obviously saw through him.

"I knew it!" Archie slammed down his glass, sloshing port all over his desk. "How could you? I never thought you would take a virgin. I thought she'd be safe from you. Have you really changed that much?"

Safe from him? Is that how his friend really saw him?

Archie's fury was painful and hurt the edges of John's already frayed soul.

"I asked her to marry me, Archie."

He lifted his gaze to his friend, so he didn't miss the shock that passed over Archie's usually impassive face. The redness in his friend's cheeks drained away and Archie's mouth thinned. "Well. That's... unexpected. And what did she say?"

John didn't answer, just dropped his gaze and took another gulp of his port.

"She said no?"

"She did." And he still wasn't over the shock of that rejection.

"Good God."

"That's about right."

"Well, what are you going to do about it?" Archie asked.

John shrugged, not looking up. What could he do?

"John, you can't give up."

He lifted his gaze once again to his friend, frowning at the man he trusted and loved. "What *can* I do, Archie? She said no, after we'd shared a bed. She thinks I'm an unconscionable rake."

"And Charlotte thought I was a pious saint who didn't even like her and look where we are today. You cannot give up if you've finally found the one woman who made you think that marriage is possible. Or… is this all just because of your brother's proposal? Because if I was wrong about you being in love with her…"

John held up a hand to stop his friend's impending rant.

"No. You're not wrong."

Was it true love that he felt for Hannah? The feelings of care that he felt for her, and the changes he was willing to make to his life for her sake made him think it could well be.

"Then you need to make her see you in the right light."

"What right light, Archie? I *am* a known rake. I have a mistress—or at least, I did up until I met Hannah. I've slept with half of the *ton*. She isn't wrong about what sort of person I am."

Archie huffed and tapped his fingers against the desk. "John, you are my best friend and my brother-in-law, but that does not make me blind to your faults. You are a drinker, a reprobate and a scoundrel."

"Thanks very much." *Talk about kicking a man when he's down.*

"But you are fiercely protective of those you love. Your sister, us, the Spares. You are a good man, honest and true. Yes, you are, and I believe you will be an excellent husband to the woman who captures your heart. And I believe that Hannah could be the only woman strong enough, and *unique* enough, to do that."

John stared at Archie, unable to believe what he'd just heard.

"I *want* to be all that, but… How do you know I can be?"

He didn't even believe it of himself! How could Archie?

"You already are that man, John. And honestly, look at Rupert! If a good woman can change him, you'll be an easy conversion."

That comment made John grin. None of them had ever thought Rupert would be happy with one woman, but today, he was the very picture of domestic happiness.

"That was a bit of a shock," he agreed, remembering Rupert's wedding day. That big oaf was twice the size of his lovely wife and had cried double the amount of tears she had, which had been very surprising indeed.

"And you are more loving than Rupert to begin with. Look at how protective you were of Charlotte, when we married. Your father and brother didn't care one whit about her. But you did."

A flash of heat flowed up John's neck and into his face. He narrowed his eyes at Archie. "I'm nothing like either my brother or my father."

A long moment ticked by, as the fire crackled in the grate.

Archie stared at him and said a word that would change John's life forever.

"Exactly."

Chapter Fourteen

"Stop fidgeting, Hannah."

Hannah pulled her gaze back to Charlotte, who was glowering at her for the second time that evening. "I'm sorry. I didn't mean to do that."

"Are you looking for someone in particular? Has someone caught your eye?"

Hannah sighed. They were at yet another ball and the same group of men were circling, as they did every other night.

"No one has caught my eye. Not yet."

"Archie said he'd introduce you to a few appropriate gentlemen tonight, so we must sit back and relax. We will find you a good husband Hannah, I am sure of it."

Hannah took her cousin's hand and squeezed it, hoping the affectionate gesture would relay to Charlotte how grateful she was for all the care and trouble she and Archie had taken. "Thank you, Charlotte. I really appreciate everything you've done to help me."

Archie stepped up at that point, greeting his wife with his customary kiss to her gloved hand and a soft look that only they shared.

Next to him was a passably handsome man and Hannah smiled politely at him.

"Hannah, may I introduce, Lord William Hanley. We were at Eton together."

"It's very nice to meet you, my lord."

The man's eyebrows shot up in a way to which she was becoming accustomed. Her accent definitely raised eyebrows, but it was yet to be seen whether the gentleman's curiosity was piqued, or whether he was put off.

"American?" He turned to Archie. "I'm sorry, my good man."

And he turned and walked away. Well, that settled the curiosity debate, she thought, twisting her fingers together until they hurt, hoping to distract herself from the ridiculous tears that threatened to fall.

This was hopeless.

"What was that, Archie?" Charlotte hissed at her husband.

"I am so sorry, Hannah. I did not realize that William was averse to marrying an American. Such an odd response, indeed. I simply told him that you were my cousin, who had arrived in London for the season..."

Hannah's shoulders sagged as she fought off an intense feeling of defeat. Perhaps it was time to go home? Maybe England was not for her. If she went back to America, she could perhaps find and marry a plantation owner. Then at least she could look after horses every day.

Charlotte grabbed her hands and squeezed them tightly. "Do not give up, my friend. Everything will be fine."

"I am fine, but I need a little air. I'll be back soon."

She broke away from her cousin's wife. Charlotte's breasts were spilling over the top of her dress and the waist was becoming tight. Soon, the Countess would be unable to accompany her husband or his cousin to social events. Her pregnancy was becoming more obvious by the day. It was bound to draw comment if she didn't start to hide from public view soon.

Hannah wandered around the ballroom, wondering if there was access onto the patio outside, watching the dancing and feeling so very alone.

"Good evening, Hannah."

She jumped as John stepped in front of her, bowing politely. "May I have this dance?"

Her tummy clenched at the sight of his handsome face and suit, cut to the shape of his lithe physique.

Memories from their night together surfaced, filling her body with heated wantonness.

"Yes, I'd like that."

He took her hand and together they moved on to the dance floor.

He guided her around the dance floor, and when she stumbled on one of the steps, his arms tightened, correcting her without anyone else noticing.

"Thank you for guiding me once again, John."

She flushed with heat as she realized too late she'd just inferred that their lovemaking was something else with which he'd guided her.

"My pleasure, as always, Hannah." He gave her another one of those smiles that made her belly jump and she couldn't help but chuckle.

She'd missed him. She missed their banter; his touch. Everything, in fact. Such a shame that he was a rake and so unsuitable for marriage.

A thought occurred to her and she decided to test a theory. She'd never really looked at any part of him other that his rakish ways.

"Tell me more about yourself, John."

He grinned, albeit looking slightly startled. "I am... me. What would you like to know?"

"Do you really love horses as much as you purport to do?"

He laughed. "Yes. If I could ride my horse every day, I would. These *ton* events bore me senseless, but since all my best friends are happily married, I seem to spend more and more time here at these events."

"Why don't you spend more time in the country then? I mean, don't most ducal households have country estates?"

He swallowed in an obvious manner, his throat working overtime as he seemed to think carefully before he spoke.

"Because..." he paused before continuing. "I don't talk about this. No one knows except our family."

The music stopped then, and Hannah allowed him to escort her off the dance floor and out onto the patio, where a few other couples stood, enjoying the fresh air.

"Thank you," she said. "I was feeling rather stifled in there. Please, do go on. If you feel comfortable enough to do so?"

"With you, yes. I think I do feel comfortable enough to share." John took a deep breath and exhaled loudly. "My father has a mistress who lives permanently in our main country estate. In the Dower House, actually, masquerading as a widowed relative of the family... I believe she has children who live with her, too. Half-siblings of mine. Her presence there creates tension in our family and my mother has become quite bitter over the situation."

"Oh goodness! How difficult for you all. That's unusual, isn't it, to keep a mistress at the actual family home?"

She knew that many men of rank, even those who didn't have the money to do so, kept a mistress. But the idea was for the whole thing to remain discreet. Why would a duke disrespect his wife—his family—in such a manner?

"Yes, it is unusual, and a source of embarrassment for us all. We stopped going there long ago. My mother could not cope with the situation and even now, we find it difficult to tolerate her dreadful anguish and depression which has resulted from this situation."

The pain in his voice was obvious and Hannah reached across and lay her hand on John's jacket, squeezing his arm through the thick fabric.

"I'm so sorry. It must have been hard growing up around a situation like that. Seeing the way it affected your mother, and your whole family."

Her own parents had a good marriage. Her father may have had his dalliances—she wouldn't have known if he had—but he was always at home with her mother when she needed him. Every day, in fact. Always. And they showed affection to one another, too, which had impacted positively on Hannah herself.

"My father's behaviour is the main reason I have kept my own affairs unemotional. Casual. I didn't want to end up like him. Or my brother for that matter, who has followed closely in my father's footsteps. His wife... their marriage..." He shuddered. "The coldness is hard to tolerate."

"Oh, I'm so sorry." John's rakish behaviour suddenly made more sense to Hannah. In a way, she respected him for not wanting to marry, out of fear he would hurt his wife as his mother had been hurt. There must be some good in this man. "Thank you for sharing that with me, John."

"So, I suppose that's who I am, Hannah. A man who has tried hard not to become what his father was. I don't want to hurt my future wife with my affairs. I want to be honourable. A good man."

"I believe you can be, John."

At that moment, she truly did believe it. She could check with Charlotte as to the integrity of the story he told her, but she already knew she didn't need to do that. Despite all of John's faults, he was honest to a fault. "Are you financially independent, John?"

A question she'd asked Doveton and one she knew John would answer quite differently than Doveton had.

His eyebrows rose high on his forehead. "I am, mostly thanks to good investment advice from Archie and his almost encyclopaedic knowledge of commerce. Are you also independent, Hannah?"

The return question surprised her and she smiled back. "As my parents' only child, yes, I am the sole heir of the family's tobacco plantation. My parents have already invested a sizeable amount of money into a trust for me, so I have personal income and am quite independent already. Thank you for asking."

"So, Miss Hannah Turner. You're a tobacco heiress," he said, smiling.

"I am indeed."

They both turned toward the gardens, and Hannah lookedup at the starlit sky, considering what John had told her. Perhaps she had been too hasty in her decision regarding him.

"John," she began. "I—"

"John Dunford... I was wondering if you'd be here tonight." A woman in a red dress and with beautiful raven black hair sashayed up to them. Hannah recognized her from several of the balls she'd already attended, but she didn't know the woman's name. Her full breasts were pushed up and together to make a huge indent that Hannah could have fallen into and probably gotten lost in. She was certain many men's gazes would land there and be stuck.

"Lady Grisham. May I introduce Miss Hannah Turner, the Earl of Totherham's cousin from America."

The woman's gaze flicked up and down as she noted Hannah's dress, grimacing when she moved back up to Hannah's red hair. One delicate eyebrow rose, as if she were disgusted by what she was looking at.

Despite the coldness Hannah was clearly receiving from this woman, she was determined to be civil.

"Lovely to meet you, my lady. Are you enjoying the ball?"

The woman sneered. "I wasn't. My tiresome husband is already rolling drunk and had to be taken home. But I am now. Will you accompany me home tonight, John?"

She slid her hand along John's arm in a seductive move.

Hannah snorted as if she had been the one who had been propositioned. "Perhaps he would, if he wasn't already coming home with me. Sorry, dear lady, but you're a touch late."

The woman in red shot her a murderous look. "I'm sure I can persuade him otherwise. John and I have a long-standing history which you, a stupid American, cannot possibly understand."

John was standing in the middle of them and hadn't said anything yet, but as he gently removed the other lady's hand from his arm, Hannah was filled with an angry confidence.

"Perhaps John is tired of your used wares. I suggest you go find someone else to attend to you, my lady. This man is no longer available to service you!"

She huffed at the woman and tugged John closer to her.

She didn't dare drop eye contact from her nemesis and watched as the woman tossed her head in the air like a filly in heat. She didn't let go of John's arm until the woman stomped off.

Hannah growled in her throat, the adrenaline coursing through her veins making her heart pound.

"What a horrible person," she hissed, finally turning around to see John staring at her, his eyes wide, a bemused smile on his face.

"I can't believe you said that, Hannah. I thought we weren't spending time together anymore?"

"Well, I didn't really mean it, I just wanted her to go away. The air around her was poison. Why would you be with a woman like that?"

He shrugged, his face rippling with what looked like disappointment.

"Honestly? Because she was available and willing," he said. "I would never force anyone to be with me and she was always enthusiastic. Her being married meant there was no way of being trapped into a union I did not want."

A question jumped off her tongue. "So, being with me was different?"

Goodness, why couldn't she leave the other night where it was meant to stay? In the past.

"In more ways than one, Hannah. Being with you has changed the way I see women and I thank you for coming to my aid there, even if you were indeed fibbing when you said I was coming home with you."

She grinned at him. "You are coming home with me. Are we not staying under the same roof?"

He bowed so that she couldn't see his face. "Yes, indeed."

There was a touch of regret in his tone now and she felt herself wanting to reach out to him, kiss him and reassure him that she did not want to hurt him.

"I would like to spend another night with you, John. Would you consider teaching me more?"

Chapter Fifteen

"You see me as a teacher of sorts, Hannah?"

She nodded, meeting his gaze. "Yes, I do."

A man who knew more about lovemaking than she ever would.

When he hesitated, she realized how disappointed she'd be if he said no.

"I trust you, John. Please come home with me."

There was a fire in his eyes now, that she had missed. She wanted him to desire her.

"Of course. Shall we leave now?"

She nodded. "Yes. Let's tell Charlotte we are leaving."

"Very well."

They went inside and found that Charlotte and Archie, too, wanted to leave. They all travelled home together in the carriage in happy silence, the occasional word being spoken about the evening they'd just enjoyed.

When they arrived back at Archie's townhouse, her cousin and his wife excused themselves to go to bed and Hannah rushed to her room to change out of her ball gown and put on her night attire.

Her lady's maid took too long and Hannah rushed her, pulling at the material in her haste to get naked quickly.

"But my lady, you will spoil the dress."

"I'm fine. Please go. I will see you in the morning."

Anne-Marie's face dropped and she slouched away.

Hannah felt a moment's regret at being a little short with her maid, but she was impatient to feel the pleasure that John had shown her the other night.

She waited impatiently, until finally, there was a light knock on the door. She hurried to open it, grabbing John and pulling him inside the moment she saw him standing there.

His deep chuckle rolled around the room as he put down his candlestick and pulled her into his arms.

"Excited tonight, are we?"

"Yes."

She began pulling at his clothes, desperate to see the body of which she'd been almost afraid the other night.

Why she thought she'd be content with just one night, she didn't know. Because now that she had the chance to experience more, she was burning with need once again.

John stepped back and, with a few knowing tugs, his clothing dropped to the floor. Soon he stood before her, naked and glorious.

She stared her fill, sighing at the knowledge she may not see this sight again. She still wasn't sure if this was the man meant for her, or if she could handle his rakish ways. But for tonight, she decided to ignore any thoughts of permanence that rose to tease her mind.

Tonight, she wanted to experience pleasure and learn more about the ways of physical enjoyment between a man and a woman. It was nothing more than that.

At least, that's what she told herself, though deep down she knew she was lying.

Being with John was far more than that. It was everything.

"Now it's your turn, Hannah." John nodded at her and she began to loosen her nightgown and allow it to fall down. A tremor of nervous tension passed through her belly, but she supposed it was only fair that if she wanted to see him, then he would want to see her as well.

She opened her night dress, untied her chemise and let the material whisper to the floor.

He stared at her openly and she tried not to cover herself, instead taking the time to look back at him. His muscles were so large, so smooth and shapely. She loved the breadth of his shoulders. They reminded her of the hardworking plantation workers back home in Virginia.

Such masculinity, all wrapped up in an educated gentleman with a cheeky devil inside him. A heady combination.

"You are so beautiful, John."

He made a strangled noise as he charged forward and wrapped his arms around her, kissing her hard on the lips before picking her up and carrying her to the bed.

He lay her down and she reached for him, running her hands over his smooth skin, loving the tougher hair, the hardness of his body, so very different from hers.

He set his lips to one of her nipples and she arched her back, desperate for the deeper contact. He suckled her, causing a tug and a pull between her legs that was simply divine.

This time there was no fear. She was certain there would be no pain and no blood, if her mother's advice in Virginia, before her departure for London, could be believed.

She reached for his hair, threading her fingers through the luxurious strands as he made his way down her body, kissing her belly and thighs and settling between her legs.

She opened for him, knowing the pleasure that was waiting for her.

He licked at her female parts and she closed her eyes, allowing the hot waterfall of sensation to cascade over her. Every flick of his tongue, every moan of his that vibrated against her, had her groaning and writhing on the bed.

The tension in her lower tummy was tightening, hot sparks of sensation tingling down her legs.

John slid up her body and took her mouth, kissing her deeply and sharing her taste with her.

He lined up his body with hers, but she wanted to try something first. She pushed him back and he quickly rolled away, the fear on his face a palpable thing.

Goodness, he wasn't kidding when he said he'd only take a willing woman.

She glanced down at his staff, now thick and red and pressing into her thigh. She so wanted to explore his body as he had hers.

"Can I kiss your body too, before we, finish?"

He nodded. "Of course, but I'm not sure what you mean."

"Lay back."

He moved up and lay back onto the pillows, his eyes wide and his expression unsure.

She moved to kneel between his spread legs, staring down at his incredibly strong body. His manhood was long and erect, in this position now laying almost flat up his belly.

"I want to touch you."

She moved forward and kissed his chest, flicking out her tongue to taste his skin before moving over to his nipple and giving it a little suck as he had done to hers. He smelt faintly of cigars and a sweet alcohol that she wished she could also taste.

A moan rolled through his chest and she smiled against his skin, loving that she could elicit that response from him.

She tasted the other nipple and then shuffled down. His skin tasted slightly salty, the grooves of his muscles amazingly sexy against her lips.

She moved further down and stayed on her knees, pushing her hair back and out of the way so that she could bob her head and take the head of his manhood into her mouth.

"What are you... No... Hannah..."

She looked up at him and John's mouth was wide open, his arm muscles tightly clenched and bulging.

Oh, that's right. He said ladies didn't do this.

She grinned as she bobbed her head once again, sliding her lips over and down to taste him as he had done to her.

She licked and tickled his flesh, listening for his groans so she could work out what he wanted the most.

She took as much of him into her mouth as she could, tasting a saltiness that made her swallow. That was different.

As was all of this. His flesh was so different to what she'd expected. Silky smooth, so soft and yet it was thick and hard, red, the veins bulging.

Suddenly John grabbed her under the arms and pulled her up, so she was straddling him, his rod stiff and hard beneath her bottom.

"If you want to be in control, Hannah, jump on and ride me." His tone was hoarse and his eyes were dark with passion.

She didn't want to seem naive, but she had no idea what he meant.

"Like this. Come up a bit."

He lifted her up and she shuffled her legs to where he indicated. He grabbed his shaft and positioned it beneath her wet and aching cleft.

"Now slide down and ride me, as you would your horse."

That sounded ridiculous, but who was she to disagree with him?

"All right."

She rocked her hips and slid down, gasping as his flesh forged a path inside her, filling her right up.

"Oh my..."

She gasped as she moved down until she sat on his belly, his long shaft fully seated within her.

He grabbed her hips and lifted her, pulling her back down again quickly, showing her what to do. Tingles of pleasure ricocheted through her belly.

"Oh, I understand now."

She put her hands down to rest on his shoulders and began to imitate his motions. Lifting up and then sliding down, using her strong thighs to keep up the rhythm.

He stared up at her. Fire blazed in the warm brown depths of his eyes.

"Oh damn. Oh, God."

"What's wrong?"

She stopped and he groaned, squeezing the flesh of her hips tight. "Nothing's wrong," he panted. "You are so amazing. I can barely control myself."

She liked the sound of that.

She kept moving, along his length and down. Loving the tight feeling of his body connected to hers, filling her. As if he was truly a part of her.

He was heaving beneath her, his face red, his eyes squeezed shut, but she was not quite feeling the same things she had that previous time.

As if he was aware of her need, his eyes popped open and he grabbed her, flipping them both over so she was flat on her back and he was on top of her. He thrust hard, right up to the hilt inside her.

She screamed out and wrapped her legs around his waist, fire exploding in her belly as exquisite sensation burned.

He bent his head to whisper into her ear. "I'm going to go fast; tell me if it's too much. Is that all right?"

She nodded and grabbed onto his upper arms.

He pulled almost out and thrust back again, hard, tendrils of pleasure weaving through her belly and down her legs as he did so.

He did it again, moving harder and faster. She couldn't keep her eyes open, her throat burning with her cries. She could feel nothing but where they joined, an all-consuming blast of passion.

The bed was shuddering and John's back was covered in sweat. This was what she had always wondered about. What inspired a man to act like a wild animal. It was *this*, and it called to that wild side of her just as hard and deep. She matched his thrusts wither own, and screamed for more.

The coiled spring inside her tightened to breaking point and she began to mewl, thrusting her hips to meet him, chasing those feelings he'd already shown her so many times.

John cried out, slamming into her, hard and fast, until she exploded. A kaleidoscope of light flashed inside her head and John released his heat inside her, pulses of her own release doubling in intensity. She bit down on his shoulder, her body squeezing and milking John's organ which was still jerking inside her.

He collapsed onto her, panting and groaning, pulling her with him as he rolled to the side.

His heart was thundering against her ear and she sighed as she squeezed him tighter. This was the part she loved so much. After their pleasure had exploded, when there were a few minutes of peace. Where everything else in the world seemed to go away and she could believe that there were only the two of them and everything would be okay.

"I didn't pull out, Hannah. Oh, God. I'm so sorry."

She lifted her head, still feeling the blissful effects of their lovemaking like a cloud wrapped around her head. Her vision was blurred, and it felt like all the strength in her muscles had been stripped away.

John, however, looked shocked. The determined set of his jaw worried her.

"It's all right, John."

"No, you don't understand. You could get pregnant. We'll *have* to marry now."

She jerked back and sat up, pulling the blankets with her.

"Pardon me?" She knew that children were conceived in the marriage bed, but she'd never known the biological mechanics.

"I left my seed inside you. We must marry."

"Are you saying you did this on purpose? Were you trying to make me marry you?"

Why would John do that?

Despite the fact that she was beginning to think John might be the only man in London able to handle her, she couldn't stand the thought of choice being taken away from her.

Yes, she was beginning to think of John differently and perhaps she would reconsider his offer. But in this moment, he wasn't asking her. He was telling.

"Hannah, do not be stupid. Of course, I didn't do that on purpose. I was carried away in the moment, in the glorious..." He shook his head. "You will have no chance of marrying anyone else now."

She slid from the bed, picked up her dressing gown and wrapped it around her. She would not let him do this to her. What sort of marriage would they have if it started this way?

When she spun back around, her breathing was ragged as she struggled to stay calm. "I will wait until my next monthly cycle and, if it comes, we do not need to worry about this." She knew that was what indicated a pregnancy and hers was only a few days away. "My bleeding should begin in a few days, so I don't believe it will be a problem."

John scowled at her, getting out of bed himself and pulling his own clothes back on in a haphazard manner.

When he was dressed, he stared at her. "Why are you being so stubborn, Hannah?"

"I'm not. I simply want to make a choice about whom I marry, John, just like you do. I have no wish to be forced into anything."

"You? Forced? I'm not forcing anything! You are the one who will be left destitute and alone if I do not marry you. Come on, Hannah, I am a duke's son. I will inherit a lot of money and comfort. We are a good match."

Anger drilled into her, going right for her core. She glared at him and crossed her arms over her chest. He thought that was what would get her to marry him?

Obviously, he knew nothing about her at all. How ridiculously disappointing!

"I will never be destitute. I have means of my own."

"But Hannah, I will have a home in town to offer you. My brother is arranging a house for me, as I am an heir to the ducal estate. My brother has no son, nor any chance of having one as his wife is barren. When I marry and produce an heir, which I have agreed to do this year, we will inherit more than you can imagine."

He may as well have thrown a bucket of icy water at her head.

"You've promised to do *what*?"

He went to say more and then stopped. She could see him trying to consider his options, so she asked again. "Did you just say that you, a man who swore he'd never marry, promised his family that he would marry *this year*?"

"Yes," he muttered, as if suddenly realising her reaction was not one of joy. "I told you," he added. "My brother has no heir. I need to marry and produce offspring for the sake of our ducal family's prestige."

His calm façade was back and Hannah could no longer see the man she loved.

Hot tears sprang to her eyes. She was in love with John. Could he not see that? Damn it all to hell!

"Well, please give my felicitations to the dutiful bride, whenever you find her."

She marched to her bedroom door and opened it. "Get out."

"But if there's a babe..."

"There won't be." She pointed to the hallway. John looked at her with big soulful eyes, then finally grabbed his candlestick and walked out the door.

She slammed it behind him and threw the lock into place.

Who did he think he was? Had he intended to trap her with the same situation that women had used on men for years?

Her cousin's wife included, if Charlotte's tale was to be believed.

Well, that was not Hannah. She would not be forced into marriage for anything other than love, nor would she trap another into a commitment that would bind them for the rest of their lives, unless the man loved her in return.

She stomped over to her bed and pulled the sheets off the mattress. She started tearing off anything that smelled of the passion they'd just shared.

Then she wrapped herself in a blanket and lay down on the bare mattress, hot tears now streaming unchecked down her cheeks.

"Damned man."

Chapter Sixteen

Lord John Dunford woke early after a fitful night sleep, and called for his valet. The sun was barely poking its head above the horizon and his poor valet looked bleary-eyed and not ready to work.

"I must see my banker, first thing this morning."

He changed into his best day suit and had finished breakfast before most of the household was awake. He had changes to make in his life, big changes. Hannah's continued rejection made it very obvious that, to win the hand of the woman he loved, he had to become a new man; a better person.

Perhaps the man he was always meant to be.

He had floated through his life for far too long, with no direction and with no real goals.

Now he had one.

He wanted a good marriage, a beautiful home in the country and a wife he loved. He had found the woman, but he had yet to convince her to become his wife.

John walked up the steps of his bank, knowing he was finally on the right path for his future.

"My lord," said the manager, greeting him with obvious surprise at seeing John this early in the morning.

He was ushered to the manager's office, where he sat down and got straight to business. "I want to buy a house."

"Of course, sir. You may have to sell some shares and move some money around, but you should be able to buy almost any townhouse in London."

John was glad to hear that. Archie's tips were obviously paying off, but a London townhouse was not the reason he was here.

"I don't want a house in town."

The manager looked shocked. "Where else would you want to live, my lord?"

"I want a house outside of London, close to my sister's house in Kent and one that has plenty of land for horses and riding."

Hannah would enjoy being out in the country and having his sister and her cousin close by would be a blessing for all of them.

"An estate? But sir... Those properties are expensive. You may need a loan. A large one."

John doubted that, with his brother willing to buy him off to ensure he produced an heir. Either way, he would make this happen.

"I don't care. Just find me a suitable property. Please get in touch with my brother. I'm sure he will be willing to offer some security if that is needed."

The banker reddened and began to shuffle papers. John did not care what it took, but he would buy a house for Hannah, no matter what.

"I am sure it will not be necessary to consult with your brother, my lord. You have a property in Covent Grove. We could use that as collateral." The banker was avoiding his gaze, aware of why John would own a townhouse in that part of London.

Of course! That would be key to convincing Hannah that he was a changed man.

"I wish to sell that house immediately. Will that make a difference?"

"You don't need to sell,my lord, we can simply use it as collateral."

John held up his hand to stop the man. There was no one living in that house anyway now, and he had no intention of ever straying from Hannah. "I want it sold. It's empty and has been for some time," John lied smoothly. A week was 'some time', technically.

"I have my own townhouse in which I will continue to live, for now. I intend to marry and my wife-to-be needs open spaces and clean air. Find me a property that suits my purpose and sell the other house as soon as possible."

"You will need to contact your solicitor for some of those things to be put into play, my lord."

"Thank you. I will."

They talked some more, nutting out some of the finer details, and then John walked out of his bank with a clear head and an obvious path laid out in front of him.

~

HANNAH MISSED JOHN. He'd moved out of Archie's home without so much as a farewell and a week later, she ached for him.

At night she dreamed of the passion they'd shared and during the day she missed his playful banter. She had been angry the night he'd proposed marriage again, but now, it all seemed so silly, the way she'd misunderstood him. He had been trying to be honourable.

And what had she done in return? She'd thrown his attempt at honour right back in his face.

Archie was making it all worse. He had been presenting her with appropriate suitors again and again each night. She wanted to cringe every time a new man appeared. Tonight, they were at yet another ton event and everyone who was anyone was there. Rupert and Lizzie, Charlotte and Archie. She'd even seen Sarah and Oliver dancing earlier in the night.

It seemed there was a Spares reunion this evening, which made John's absence even more accentuated.

"Hannah. I need to introduce you to someone." She heard Archie's voice and turned to face him, a sigh sitting heavily on her chest.

"Archie, please. I'm really not capable of any more tonight."

Her cousin simply smiled, ignoring her. He stepped to the side, exposing the person behind her.

Hannah's heart leapt in her chest.

"Miss Hannah Turner, may I have the pleasure of officially introducing you to Lord John Dunford, my brother-in-law and one of my oldest and dearest friends. John is looking to marry this year and I think you two would make a great match."

Hannah heard Charlotte's gasp from beside her, but she only had eyes for John.

"Would you like to dance, American tobacco heiress?"

Pleasure flooded her belly and a smile lifted her lips. "I would, English rake. Thank you kindly, sir." She curtseyed and took his proffered hand.

They began to circle the dance floor and Hannah stared up at him, unable to drag her eyes away from the man who'd brought her body to life and was perhaps the only man in London who could handle her loose tongue.

"You left without saying goodbye." She was unable to stop herself uttering the accusation.

"Yes, I needed to put some things into place before I could come back to see you."

She stumbled and John's hands gripped her strongly, saving her from embarrassment in front of the many eyes that were watching them.

"Oh, what do you mean?"

"I can't bear another rejection from you, Hannah, and I wanted to make sure I had all of my affairs in order."

Hot tears stung her eyes and an overwhelming need to cry rushed through her.

She stalled their dancing and tried to pull away.

"Please let me go, John. I know I hurt you, and I'm so sorry for that, but you don't need to do this."

She was going to cry, right there in the middle of the dance floor. She was ashamed of her behaviour and wished she could run and hide before she lost control in front of everyone in the room. Which was, she realized with horror as she glanced around, practically every member of the ton.

Her botton lip trembled and again, she began to pull to get out of his grip.

~

HORROR SLAMMED into John as Hannah began to crumple before him. She had it all wrong.

There was no more time for teasing games. He knew what he had to do.

"Hannah, look at me. Please."

She blinked her big blue eyes rapidly and looked up at him, unshed tears shimmering in the dark depths as her bottom lip continued to tremble.

"I am not teasing. I want you to marry me."

Hannah blushed, her whole face turning pink as she averted her eyes.

"John, if this is about that night, you don't need to worry. Nothing eventuated from that night after all. You do not need to feel obliged in any way."

It wasn't about that night. He needed her to know that.

He dropped to one knee in the middle of the ballroom. To hell with his pride, to hell with everyone. He would show Hannah and all of them that she meant the world to him or ruin himself forever in the attempt.

The band stopped playing, and all eyes turned toward them. The room became eerily silent.

He tried not to think about anyone else and instead, focused on the woman standing before him with her hands hovering over her mouth.

"Hannah Turner, I *love* you. So much more than I ever thought to love anyone. I know I have said some silly things in the past, but I've changed. I want you and only you. And if I stray from our marriage, you have my permission to publicly horsewhip me in the middle of town."

Hannah gasped and tried to tug him up from the floor. "John, get up, please. People are looking."

John just smiled. "I know, and I don't care. Marry me. This is officially the third and fourth time I've asked. I love you! Surely, you can't keep saying no?"

"Can we not talk about this later?" Hannah insisted.

John saw how much Hannah wanted to leave, but she hadn't run away from him yet. She wasn't going to leave him alone on his knees, vulnerable in front of the whole *ton*, and that gave him hope.

"No, we cannot. Now is the time. I have sold my old townhouse and bought you a house in the country. Room for your horses—as many as you want. I have renounced my old ways. What else can I do to show you how much I love you? Unless... you don't love me?"

John swallowed. Was that it? Perhaps all of his efforts had been in vain.

"Of course, I love you, you bloody... man!" Hannah huffed, throwing her hands in the air.

Relief flooded him. "Then you'll marry me."

Hannah got down on her knees in front of him and gripped both of his hands in hers.

The room was completely quiet. John knew all the people present were hanging on every word that was said. The last of the Spares had fallen, to his knees, to be exact.

"If you promise to always love me, always talk to me, and always work with me on what we need to work on. And don't hurt me. Please don't hurt me, John. Or I will take you up on that offer to flog you in the middle of town." A soft smile shimmered on her lips and his heart rejoiced.

"I promise," John said without hesitation.

"Then of course I'll marry you."

A tear slipped down Hannah's cheek and John rubbed it away with his thumb.

"My Hannah," he whispered, before leaning in and kissing her lightly on the mouth.

The room exploded into applause, the loudest coming from right beside them as people crowded the dance floor.

John stood up and pulled Hannah to her feet with him. Rupert and Archie stood next to them, their faces beaming with huge smiles.

"A celebration is in order!" Rupert shouted, corralling them all off the dance floor.

John and Hannah were swamped by well wishers and John didn't let go of Hannah at all. He knew if they were separated it might take hours to get her back and he didn't want to be separated from her for one second more than they had to be.

"Perhaps we could go home?" John suggested, squeezing Hannah lightly around the waist.

"Our house, I think," Oliver suggested.

Within the hour they were all back at Oliver's townhouse, drinking sherry and making toasts. The ladies sat in a circle, their men standing at their sides.

"To the newly engaged couple. May you be always be as happy as you are today," Oliver said, lifting his glass and clinking it with every person in their group of eight.

John couldn't wipe the smile off his face. He had never been so happy in his life.

"May you have many sons, but also many daughters," Archie added, rubbing his wife's pregnant belly for good measure.

They all laughed at that one and clinked their glasses again.

"To only one bedchamber for the rest of your days." Rupert grinned, Lizzie pinching him playfully on the leg.

John returned his friend's grin, knowing that he too wished for that same thing.

Seven pairs of eyes suddenly turned to look at him and John cleared his throat.

"To 'the Spares, the most blessed of men." John smiled and looked around at his three friends. They had been through hell and back together but here they all stood. Better men for it and their women at their sides. "And their beautiful, amazing ladies."

All four ladies stood as one and raised their glasses.

"To the Spares and their ladies," they all recited and, as one, drank.

Epilogue

Many years later

"John Dunford. I saw you flirting with her. I did. After everything we've been through together. How could you!" Hannah wrapped her arms around herself and looked out the window of their carriage.

It was so hard pretending to be upset, when inside she was bubbling with excitement for what was to come.

"Hannah. My beautiful one. I don't know what you're talking about. I never did anything. The only woman I ever flirt with, is you." John sounded confused, and rightly so, but Hannah persisted, trying to sound sincere.

"You did. I saw you. Did you disappear with her when you went to the card room tonight?"

Hannah tried again to sound teary and affronted, but she knew where he'd been all night. She'd checked the card room several times herself. He'd been there the whole time.

She trusted her husband, but it always served to know what was going on. He was still a very handsome man and she'd had to fight off many a widow and bored married lady in the past decade of marriage.

"Hannah. I would never stray. I promised you I wouldn't. Please believe me!"

"No. I think I'm going to march straight to the stables and grab my riding crop, John. I think you need to remember to whom you belong."

She turned to glare at him and saw the heat in those depths, that had never stopped making her insides turn to liquid need.

"I wouldn't mind something like that, Hannah… If you need to treat me like your stallion, as long as you ride me, too."

"Grr…" She lashed out and hit him in the shoulder, not needing to fake her anger this time. He was such a tease.

"Stop it! Aren't you satisfied enough with all those women fawning all over you? It's because I've grown fat, isn't it? They all see what I've become and they think they can get you now."

Her voice broke and John slid over to sit beside her.

Despite her façade, she could feel the truth creeping in.

"You are not fat, my beautiful one. You're feeding our babes, and you couldn't be lovelier."

She'd had four sons over the past ten years. Twins in the past year. She was bigger than she liked, but with breastfeeding her sons, she ate a lot more than she normally did and her body it was showing the excess pounds.

"I have never desired you more." John told her, his tone thick with need and the love she'd grown to desire more than air itself.

The carriage slowed and then stopped. They were home. On their own country estate. A place she loved more every single day.

"I don't believe you, but I do believe that whipping is just what you need, John. Let's go."

She pushed open the door and he grabbed her elbow.

"Dearest, please believe me, I didn't do anything wrong tonight."

They'd gone to a small dinner party with local gentry and she had encouraged one of the women to flirt with her husband. She knew he'd enjoyed it but she also knew it had been harmless fun.

She hurried out of the carriage, unable to continue this charade much longer. She'd thought it would be easy, but the woman she'd arranged to flirt with her husband had reported how quickly he'd shut down any advances.

John hadn't given her a moment's insecurity in ten years and she adored him for that.

She hurried up the stairs, the front door opening as the butler anticipated their approach.

She gave her cloak to the footman and John hurried to do the same.

"Hannah, please. How can I convince you how much I love you?"

"Come with me."

She inclined her head and headed toward the ballroom, where lights flickered and a room full of people awaited John's appearance.

He grabbed her in the hallway, dragging her against his tightened body.

"I still desire you, Hannah. So much. Can't you feel it?"

Yes, she could, and she desired him all the more for it.

"I can. And I still love you, John. I love you more with each passing day."

He stepped back, worry flickering across his face.

"I feel like this is a trap, Hannah."

"Hardly, my love. This is me showing you how proud I am of you. All of us."

She took his hand and pushed open the door.

The room exploded with raucous clapping and cheering and John fell back against the door.

"Happy birthday!"

Hannah held tight to his hand and pulled him closer. "Surprise, my perfect husband. I know you didn't want to celebrate your fortieth birthday, but I couldn't let it pass by. Forgive my complaints in the carriage. They were all... untrue."

A strange grin spread across his face and he looked at her with new eyes. "You did all this for me?"

"Of course. You deserve it. Go. Enjoy the evening."

She went to push him forward, but he leaned in to whisper in her ear. "You owe me a stallion ride, my beautiful wife."

He grinned at her startled look and then Rupert rushed over with a glass of whiskey for them both. Hannah took hers and winked at the big man who she'd grown to love and trust with everything in her. "We can ride later, my love."

John staggered off, into the fray.

His whoops of joy were soothing on her heart as she watched from afar.

She'd gone to a lot of trouble to find many of John's friends from school—men who had moved away or gone abroad. It had taken her months of planning, but here, tonight, in their home, were dozens of people who truly loved John.

Their children were all sleeping upstairs and tomorrow a picnic would ensue and the chaos of their huge household would be in full swing.

John had conquered every fear she'd ever had.

Every day had been loving and thoughtful. Still cheeky as ever and a true devil in the bedroom, but he had basked her in love, and she had tried to do the same for him. Theirs truly was a love match.

Their lives and those of their friends were happy and full.

'The Spares' had twelve children between them and Hannah made sure they spent time together regularly.

Life was wonderful and full of love and laughter. Everything she'd ever wanted and so much more.

THE END

~

I hope you've enjoyed the *Heir and the Spare* series. These four men were my first of many imagined heroes.

My next Regency romance series is the *Seymour Siblings*. It is slightly more traditional than the Spares, but I hope you like it.

Download book 1- The Duke's Marriage of Convenience is ready to download: https://books2read.com/u/47YE9L

Or read on for a sneak peek into book 1:
The Duke's Marriage of Convenience – Chapter One

~

Chapter One

A gentle breeze swept across the lush green pastures of the sought-after estate in the county of Somerset. The staff at Woodlock Manor had been busy preparing for a very important visit by two young people, who were arranged to be wed. The betrothed couple were to finally meet, after many months of negotiations between their respective families.

The atmosphere at Woodlock Manor was bustling as the help prepared every last detail. The maidservants served a delicious breakfast on the terrace, while the manservants ensured the grounds were in pristine condition. Merriment and excitement were in the air.

However, in the east wing of the manor, submerged nearly entirely in a bath of warm water, Lady Kitty Dunne did not share in the excitement of those around her.

Of course, she would not openly admit her misgivings in front of the two young maids, who were busy washing her long, black hair. The sweet aroma of flowers allowed her to drift into a surreal wonderland where there was no need for her to jeopardise her beliefs for anyone, let alone a man she had never met.

Arranged marriages were simply archaic, to Kitty's way of thinking, and she could not believe that she was being forced into such a dire situation.

But her temporary wonderland dreams were very far from the real world, as she was fully aware. Her mother, Lady Dunne, the Countess of Dunne, had prepared her only daughter for this exclusive gala, as she ceremoniously referred to it, and proceeded to compliment her daughter's suitor as a man of integrity and outstanding reputation.

He was considered one of the most eligible bachelors in the county—if not the country—and his wealth far exceeded most of the other eligible men. This was the sole reason Lady Dunne and her husband, the Earl of Dunne, had desired that James of Somerset wed their daughter.

Despite the earl's formidable reputation, their family was on the verge of bankruptcy. The earl's business partner had embezzled a great deal of money from their joint business venture, leaving Lord Dunne to stand among the ruins of his fortune as the ashes rained down around him.

Arranging a marriage between his daughter and James of Somerset would ensure their family's financial survival and rescue them all from a life of poverty.

Of course, Kitty was well aware of the situation, but it most certainly did not stop her from expressing her distaste for the arrangement itself. Despite not having ever met Lord James, and the fact that she was in no position to judge him or despise him, she was, however, not impressed with the depths to which her parents had stooped.

Her annoyance at her parents had somewhat coloured her view of her new suitor, even before their first meeting.

Unfortunately, there was not much she could do regarding the situation. Plans had been made, and her family had travelled to Woodlock Manor to meet with Lord James.

The bedchambers were far more luxurious than she had ever seen, with light rose inlaid wallpaper and gold trim. The furniture was constructed of solid cherry wood, and three large windows provided a panoramic view of the meadows outside. It was certainly a comfortable and luxurious lifestyle in which she was likely to find herself in future, but no amount of extravagance in the entire world would make her wish this of her own accord.

"There you are, my lady," the maidservant said in a soft voice, and

Kitty transferred her glance to the serving girl rather than continue focusing on the sunlight that danced through the drapes.

"Oh, do make haste, child." Lady Dunne, who had been sitting quietly on a chaise near the window throughout the duration of Kitty's bath, spoke in an impatient tone. "There is still much to do."

Kitty rose to her feet and allowed the maidservants to wrap her in soft muslin as she stepped out of the bath. The warm air inside the bedchamber allowed a comfortable transition from the heat of the bath water to where she would now be dressed for her meeting with Lord James.

The young maids worked gently and diligently as they first dried Kitty's tresses with a cloth, and afterward dressed her in her inner-wear, the soft fabric skimming her skin. The sensation caused her to shiver, but it was more a reaction born of anticipation and nerves, rather than excitement.

The weight of responsibility sat heavily on Kitty's shoulders. She was aware this was the only way in which her family's financial survival could be ensured, and she most certainly did not wish for her mother and father to be punished for something that was entirely out of their hands.

The servants slipped a lovely, pale blue day dress over her head and assisted her in straightening it out, then tying it at the back. She caught sight of her reflection in the mirror and a small smile brightened her visage.

She had not expected to enjoy any part of this ridiculous preparation, but she had to admit, the dress was perfection. The colour suited her skin perfectly and the style accentuated the curves of her body. She was not as petite as most young women her age, but her curvy body apparently made her even more sought-after by Lord James, if the gossip she'd overhead among the maidservants was anything to go by.

Her mother, of course, disagreed.

"It is a good thing you have been blessed with a striking face, my dear child," Lady Dunne pointed out nonchalantly. Every time she did this, the action annoyed Kitty immensely. She was convinced her mother did not approve of her daughter's body because Kitty enjoyed being out of doors. Even more appalling, at least according to her mother, was Kitty's love of horses.

Kitty had been interested in the amazing creatures since she was a young child, and had ridden her first mare when she was only five years of age. Her father had taught her to ride, which annoyed the countess no end.

In the countess' opinion, it was not proper behaviour for a lady of Kitty's stature and lineage to be undertaking such unladylike pursuits. Of course, Kitty paid her mother little heed, and spent much of her free time riding her father's horses. She adored them and hoped that her future husband would at least share her love for the majestic beasts. If not, their dinners as a married couple would be rather quiet.

One of the maidservants gently brushed her dark locks, while the other intricately wove the hair with her fingers, placing white blossoms between the layers.

Kitty studied her reflection as she was transformed from a young woman who spent too much time out of doors, into a refined lady who would soon be the Duchess of Somerset.

Lady Dunne moved across the room, catching Kitty's eye in the mirror. Her mother's expression was even more pleased than her previous one.

"My dear girl, may I be so bold as to say you have not looked more beautiful in your entire lifetime."

"That certainly does not seem complimentary toward my usual ungainly features, Mother," Kitty retorted with a grimace.

"I wish not to insult you. You look beautiful, was all I was trying to say."

"Then why not simply say it? There is no need for such theatrics," Kitty said.

Lady Dunne pursed her lips, apparently stopping herself from uttering a word that was not suitable to be heard, especially by their host's young staff.

Kitty was not entirely convinced her mother was right about her current state of beauty, but she knew better than to argue.

"Where is Father?" she inquired instead.

"I left him to his own devices, although I do suspect he is in Lord James's grand library. You are as aware as I am about how your father can immerse himself in a world that does not exist," Lady Dunne answered.

This time it was Kitty who pursed her lips to stifle the words that nearly escaped. It was no secret that the marriage of her parents was also arranged, and despite enduring a union that had lasted more than twenty years, Kitty was well aware of how miserable both her parents were to this day.

It was one of the reasons she was so set against arranged marriages. Sometimes, love did not grow with time.

Her father was a quiet man, passive at the best of times. A well-read gentleman of fine lineage and intelligence, he was not boastful, nor did he treat his servants and staff as if they were beneath him. He was humble and would often be found in the kitchen late at night, playing cards with some of the manservants. Or even in the stable, wandering among his beloved horses.

Her mother, on the other hand, had been raised with a silver spoon of privilege in her mouth, and would not even dream of speaking directly to a maidservant. It was simply a product of her family experience, but her mother's haughty attitude often infuriated Kitty.

Kitty had inherited her father's kind heart, and adored the maidservants at their own estate. She would miss them all dearly when she no longer resided there.

Soon she would become the Duchess of Somerset, and settle in Woodlock Manor with her new husband, and staff she didn't know. It would most certainly be a strange and difficult adjustment, especially since she did not wish for this marriage to take place at all.

It was not that Kitty did not believe in love. She simply didn't believe in forced love. One cannot be compelled to fall in love with a particular person, and as her father had philosophized many times, sometimes the heart desired what it desired, no matter how inconvenient.

Kitty pressed her lips together as she gazed at her reflection and cocked her head. Nervous bubbles rose up inside her, despite her best attempts to not allow this meeting to affect her too much.

She was to meet the man she would soon marry, whether it was what she wanted or not. There was no need to be nervous. She had only heard great and noble things about Lord James, but unfortunately that knowledge did not make the coming situation any less stressful.

Other people's words were not credible. Most of them did not know the man personally.

"Utter perfection." Her mother beamed beside her, distracting Kitty from the imminent tragedy that lay before her. "There will be no doubt that His Grace will fall madly in love with you the moment he sets his gaze upon you, my dear."

Kitty glanced at her mother over her shoulder and tried very hard not to roll her eyes. Perhaps her mother was under the impression Lord James may fall at her feet in a love-filled swoon, but she was not convinced. Not in the least.

In fact, she was not certain that she would even meet with her betrothed. Through the window, she eyed the thick foliage of trees on the other side of the meadow. It was abundant enough to get lost in, if one wished it.

"Are you ready, my dear?" Her mother smiled and held out her hand, sheer excitement radiating on her face, her green eyes twinkling with hope.

Despite Kitty's initial instincts to show defiance, or perhaps give a witty retort that her mother would certainly not appreciate or find amusing, she reined in her rebellious feelings and nodded quietly. She stood up from the stool, ready to face her future.

The skirt of her dress slid to the floor and Lady Dunne's eyes sparkled even more. Her mother clutched a hand against her chest and sighed.

"Utter perfection," she repeated.

Unfortunately, Kitty didn't feel anything like perfection.

~

Read on here:
https://books2read.com/u/47YE9L